FREEDOM!

FREEDOM!

edited by
Mark Tier
and
Martin H. Greenberg

FREEDOM!

Copyright © 2006 by Mark Tier & Tekno Books. *Give Me Liberty* copyright © 2003; *Visions of Liberty* copyright © 2004.

A Baen Book

Baen Publishing Enterprises
P.O. Box 1403
Riverdale, NY 10471
www.baen.com

ISBN 10: 1-4165-2072-4
ISBN 13: 978-1-4165-2072-6

Cover art by Carole Heyer

First Baen printing, July 2006

Library of Congress Cataloging-in-Publication Data

Freedom! / edited by Martin H. Greenberg and Mark Tier.
     p. cm.
   ISBN-13: 978-1-4165-2072-6
   ISBN-10: 1-4165-2072-4
   1. Science fiction, American. 2. Science fiction, English.
   3. Freedom--Fiction. 4. Anarchism--Fiction. I. Greenberg,
   Martin Harry. II. Tier, Mark.

PS648.S3F74 2006
813'.0876208--dc22
                    2006010801

Distributed by Simon & Schuster
1230 Avenue of the Americas
New York, NY 10020

Printed in the United States of America

10 9 8 7 6 5 4 3 2 1

Acknowledgments

GIVE ME LIBERTY first published by Baen Books January 2003: "Introduction," Mark Tier copyright © 2003 by Mark Tier; "Monument", Lloyd Biggle, Jr. copyright © by Street & Smith Publications, first published in *Astounding Science Fiction* June 1961. Reprinted by permission of the author and his agent, The Owlswick Literary Agency; "Gadget vs. Trend," Christopher Anvil copyright © 1962 by Conde Nast Publications Inc. First published in *Analog*, October 1962. Reprinted by permission of the author's agents, the Scott Meredith Literary Agnecy; "The Ungoverned," Vernor Vinge copyright © 1985 by Vernor Vinge. First published in *Far Frontiers* vol. 3, 1985,reprinted by permission of the author; "Historical Note," Murray Leinster copyright © 1951 by Street & Smith Publications Inc., copyright renewed © 1979 by Conde Nast Publications, Inc. First published in *Astounding Science Fiction*, February 1951. Reprinted by permission of the agent for the author's estate, the Scott Meredith Literary Agency; "The Weapon Shop," A.E. van Vogt copyright © 1942 by Street & Smith Publications. First published in *Astounding Science Fiction*, December 1942. Reprinted by permission of the author and his agents, the Ashley Grayson Literary Agency; "Second Game," Kathleen MacLean & Charles de Vet copyright © 1958, 1986 by the authors. First published in *Astounding Science Fiction*, 1958. Reprinted by permission of the author and their agents, the Virginia Kidd Agency, Inc.; "Committee of the Whole," Frank Herbert copyright © 1965 by the author. First published in *Galaxy*, April 1965. Reprinted by permission of the William Morris Agency, Inc. on behalf of the author; "And Then There Were None," Eric Frank Russell copyright © 1951 by Street & Smith Publications. First published in *Astounding Science Fiction*, June 1951. Reprinted by permission of the author and the author's agents, JABberwocky Literary Agency.

VISIONS OF LIBERTY first published by Baen Books July 2004: "Introduction," Mark Tier copyright © 2004 by Mark Tier; "The Unnullified World", Lloyd Biggle Jr. copyright © 2004 by Lloyd Biggle, Jr.; "The Right's Tough," Robert J. Sawyer copyright © 2004 by Robert J. Sawyer; "The Shackles of Freedom," Mike Resnick & Tobias S. Buckell copyright © 2004 by Mike Resnick & Tobias S. Buckell; "A Reception at the Anarchist Embassy," Brad Linaweaver copyright © 2004 by Brad Linaweaver; "According to Their Need," Michael A. Stackpole copyright © 2004 by Michael A. Stackpole; "Pakeha," Jane Lindskold copyright © 2004 by Jane Lindskold; "Devil's Star," Jack Williamson copyright © 2004 by Jack Williamson; "Renegade," Mark Tier copyright © 2004 by Mark Tier; "The Colonizing of Tharle," James P. Hogan copyright © 2004 by James P. Hogan.

CONTENTS

PART I

GIVE ME LIBERTY

Introduction

Mark Tier

When Patrick Henry spoke his immortal words, "Give me liberty or give me death," on the eve of the American revolution, the last thing he expected was for the British to *give him* liberty. Indeed, in the history of mankind, you could count the number of benevolent rulers who have *given* people their liberty on the fingers of one hand—and still have plenty of fingers left over.

History shows there's only one way you can be sure of gaining your liberty: *take* it.

Which is exactly what Patrick Henry proposed to do. His stirring 1775 speech concluded:

> Is life so dear, or peace so sweet, as to be purchased at the price of chains and slavery? Forbid it, Almighty God! I know not what course others may take; but as for me, give me liberty or give me death!

This is a collection of stories about people who, like Patrick Henry, *take* their liberty.

Just as liberty is a powerful urge in the human heart, so liberty is a recurring theme in science fiction. Yet the majority of the stories in this book are unique even within the imaginative realm of science fiction. They propose taking the ultimate in liberty: doing away with government entirely.

They show the ultimate truth of the saying that Thomas Jefferson made part of our history: "Eternal vigilance is the price of liberty."

When Jefferson used the phrase at the signing of the American Declaration of Independence was he talking about the British? Absolutely not. He was naming the *American* government a far greater danger to the liberties of Americans than the British (or much later, Soviets) could ever be, a sentiment widely shared by the American revolutionaries.

Jefferson's declaration was co-opted and corrupted by cold war politicians. Eternal vigilance, they told us, was required to protect our liberties from *external* enemies like the Soviet Union. In the name of freedom they erected the powerful welfare-warfare state that continues to invade our liberties to this day.

Stories like Lloyd Biggle's "Monument" and Frank Herbert's "Committee of the Whole" demonstrate the ultimate truth of Jefferson's statement: that eternal vigilance against our *own* government—not external enemies—is the price of liberty. A lesson that has, to our detriment, been forgotten.

I first read most of these stories as a teenager, beginning with A.E. van Vogt's "The Weapon Shop." I can still recall the excitement that gripped me then—what teenager could resist the idea of a gun that would fire only in self-defense? Sold by shops that government officials (and criminals) simply couldn't enter?

You might argue that such a teenage fantasy should remain where it belongs—as a teenage memory. I can only respond that yes, when I first read it, the idea of liberty that gripped me then through van Vogt's story was merely an abstract ideal. As an adult, my teenage ideal has taken on whole flesh, so to speak. This, of course, is not the place for a discourse on liberty (or anything else). All I can say is that, as an adult, I can think of numerous times when van Vogt's gun would have come in real handy. And when I see the injustice and oppression around the world, if van Vogt's weapons shops were to suddenly appear as they did in his story, I'd say the demand for his guns would far outstrip even his wild imaginings.

Ah, but you might respond, if there's no government wouldn't society collapse into barbarism?

I suggest you read Eric Frank Russell's classic "And Then There Were None"—my favorite story in a book full of favorites. If you've never read this story before (and quite likely you haven't, as it's been out of print for far too long) I envy you. I've re-read this story many times, but there's no time like the first time.

The possibilities that Russell offers in just a few thousand words is mind-boggling.

Then there's Vernor Vinge's neglected gem, "The Ungoverned." As the "Republic" of New Mexico invades the peaceful anarchy of Kansas where can your heart lie but with the truly free people—the *ungoverned*?

Do you sometimes think that bureaucrats should be strangled with their own red tape? Then you'll love Russell's "And Then There Were None." Do you feel like dancing with joy when a ruthless dictatorship collapses? Then you'll cheer along with Murray Leinster in "Historical Note." And shouldn't petty tyrants get their just deserts? They have no choice but to surrender in "Gadget vs. Trend" by Christopher Anvil—and are delightfully defenseless in van Vogt's "The Weapon Shop."

I feel sure you can't fail to be inspired by these wonderful stories about the ultimate freedom. Whether I'm right about that, I know you're in for a lot of fun in the following pages.

Monument

Lloyd Biggle, Jr.

It came to O'Brien quite suddenly that he was dying.

He was lying in a sturdy woven-vine hammock, almost within reach of the flying spray where the waves broke in on the point. The caressing warmth of the sun filtered through the ragged *sao* trees. The shouts of the boys spearing fish off the point reached him fitfully on playful gusts of fragrant wind. A full gourd hung at his elbow. He had been half-dozing in a drowsy state of peaceful contentment when the realization snapped coldly across his idle thoughts and roused him to icy wakefulness.

He was dying.

The fact of death disturbed him less than the realization that he should have thought of it sooner. Death was inevitable from the instant of birth, and O'Brien was a long lifetime from babyhood. He wondered, sometimes, just how old he might be. Certainly a hundred, perhaps even a hundred and fifty. In this dreamy land, where there were no seasons, where the nights were moist and the days warm and sunny, where men measured age by wisdom, it was difficult to keep an alert finger on the elusive pulse of time. It was impossible.

But O'Brien did not need a calendar to tell him he was an old man.

The flaming-red hair of his youth had faded to a rusty gray. His limbs were stiff each morning from the night's dampness. The solitary hut he had built on the lovely rise of ground above the point had grown to a sprawling village, as his sons, and grandsons and great grand-sons, and now great-great grandsons, brought home their wives. It was the village of *langru*, the village of fire-topped men, already famous, already a legend. Maidens were eager to mate with the young men of fire, whether their hair was red or the native blond. The sturdiest youths came to court the daughters of fire, and many of them defied tradition and settled in the village of their wives.

O'Brien had enjoyed a good life. He knew he had lived far beyond the years that would have been his in the crazed rush of a civilized land. But he was dying, and the great dream that had grown until it shaped his life among these people was beyond his reach.

He jerked erect, shook his fist at the sky, and shouted hoarsely in a long-unused language. "What are you waiting for? What are you waiting for?"

As soon as O'Brien appeared on the beach, a dozen boys came splashing towards him. "Langri!" they shouted. "Langri!"

They leaped about him excitedly, holding up fish for his approval, waving their spears, laughing and shouting. O'Brien pointed up the beach, where a large dugout canoe was drawn up on the sand.

"To the Elder," he said.

"Ho! To the Elder! Ho! To the Elder!"

They raced ahead of him, scrambling furiously for places because the canoe would not hold them all. O'Brien waded into the melee, restored order, and told off the six he wanted for paddlers. The oth-ers raced into the surf after the canoe, swimming around and under it until the paddlers got up speed.

The boys shouted a song as they dipped their paddles—a serious song, for this was serious business. The Langri wished to see the Elder, and it was their solemn duty to make haste.

O'Brien leaned back wearily and watched the foam dancing under the outriggers. He had little taste for traveling, now that his years were relentlessly overtaking him. It was pleasant to lounge in his hammock with a gourd of fermented fruit juice, acting the part of a venerable oracle, respected, even worshipped. When he was younger he had roamed the length and breadth of this world. He had even built a small sailing boat and sailed completely around it, with the only tangible result being the discovery of a few unlikely islands. He had trekked tirelessly about the lone continent, mapping it and speculating on its resources.

He knew that he was a simple man, a man of action. The natives' awe of his supposedly profound wisdom alarmed and embarrassed him. He found himself called upon to settle complex sociological and economic problems, and because he had seen many civilizations and remembered something of what he had seen, he achieved a commendable success and enjoyed it not at all.

But O'Brien knew that the sure finger of doom was pointing directly at this planet and its people, and he had pondered, and debated with himself on long walks along the sea, and paced his hut through the hours of misty night while he devised stratagems, and finally he was satisfied. He was the one man in the far-flung cosmos who could possibly save this world that he loved, and these people he loved, and he was ready to do it. He could do it, if he lived.

And he was dying.

The afternoon waned and evening came on. Fatigue touched the boys' faces and the singing became strained, but they worked on tirelessly, keeping their rhythm. Miles of coast drifted by, and scores of villages, where people recognized the Langri and crowded the shore to wave.

Dusk was hazing the distant sea and purpling the land when they made the turn into a shallow bay and rode the surf up onto a wide, sloping beach studded with canoes. The boys leaped up and heaved the canoe far up onto the beach. They slumped to the sand in exhaustion, and bounced up a moment later, beaming with pride. They would be guests of honor, tonight, at any hut in the village they chose to visit. Had they not brought the Langri?

They moved through the village in a procession that gained in numbers with each hut they passed. Respectful adults and awed children stepped forth and solemnly followed after O'Brien. The Elder's hut was apart from the others, at the top of the hill, and the Elder stood waiting there, a smile on his wrinkled face, his arms upraised. Ten paces away O'Brien stopped and raised his own arms. The villagers watched silently.

"I greet you," O'Brien said.

"Your greetings are as welcome as yourself."

O'Brien stepped forward, and they clasped hands. This was not a native form of greeting, but O'Brien used it with the older men who were almost life-long friends.

"I ordered a feast in the hope that you would come," the Elder said.

"I came in the hope there would be a feast," O'Brien returned.

With the formalities thus satisfied, the villagers began to drift away, murmuring approval. The Elder took O'Brien's arm and led him past the hut, to a small grove of trees where the hammocks hung. They stood facing each other.

"Many days have passed," the Elder said.

"Many," O'Brien agreed.

He looked at his friend closely. The Elder's tall, gaunt frame seemed as sturdy as ever, but his hair was silvery white. The years had traced lines in his face, and more years had deepened them, and dimmed the brightness in his eyes. Like O'Brien, he was old. He was dying.

They settled themselves in the hammocks, and lay facing each other. A young girl brought gourds to them, and they sipped the drink and rested in silence as the darkness closed in.

"The Langri is no longer a traveler," the Elder said.

"The Langri travels when the need arises," O'Brien said.

"Let us then talk of that need."

"Later. After we have eaten. Or tomorrow—tomorrow would be better."

"Tomorrow, then," the Elder said.

The girl returned with pipes and a glowing coal, and they smoked in silence while fires leaped high in the darkness and the rippling night breeze brought the savory odors of the coming feast blended with the crisp sea air. They finished their pipes and solemnly took their places of honor.

In the morning they walked together along the shore, and seated themselves on a knoll overlooking the sea. Sweet-scented blossoms crowded up around them, nodding in the wind. The morning light sparkled brightly on the leaping water. Brightly-colored sails of the fishing fleet were pinned flower-like to the horizon. To their left, the village rested sleepily on the side of the hill, with only three thin plumes of smoke drifting upwards. Small boys romped in the surf, or walked timidly along the beach to stare up at the Elder and the Langri.

"I am an old man," O'Brien said.

"The oldest of old men," the Elder agreed promptly.

O'Brien smiled wanly. To a native, *old* meant *wise*. The Elder had paid him the highest of compliments, and he felt only frustrated—weary.

"I am an old man," he said again, "and I am dying."

The Elder turned quickly.

"No man lives forever," O'Brien said.

"True. And the man who fears death dies of fear."

"My fear is not for myself."

"The Langri has no need to fear for himself. But you spoke of a need."

"Your need. The need of all your people, and of my people."

The Elder nodded slowly. "As always, we listen well when the Langri speaks."

"You remember," O'Brien said, "that I came from afar, and stayed because the ship that brought me could fly no more. I came to this land by chance, because I had lost my way, and because my ship had a serious sickness."

"I remember."

"Others will come. And then others, and then more others. There will be good men and bad, but all will have strange weapons."

"I remember," the Elder said. "I was there when you slew the birds."

"Strange weapons," O'Brien repeated. "Our people will be helpless. The men from the sky will take this land—whatever they want of it. They will take the beaches and even the sea, the mother of life itself. They will push our people back to the hills, where they will not know how to live. They will bring strange sickness to our people, so that entire villages lie in the fire of death. Strangers will fish the waters and swim. There will be huts taller than the tallest trees and the strangers that crowd the beaches will be thicker than the fish that run off the point. Our own people will be no more."

"You know this to be true?"

O'Brien inclined his head. "It will not happen this day, or the next, but it will happen."

"It is a terrible need," the Elder said quietly.

O'Brien inclined his head again. He thought, *This lovely, unspoiled land, this wonderful, generous, beautiful people . . .* A man was so helpless when he was dying.

They sat in silence for a time, two old men in the bright sunshine, waiting for the darkness. O'Brien reached out and plucked the blossoms near him, one at a time, and crushed their fragile whiteness in his hands.

The Elder turned a grave face on O'Brien. "Cannot the Langri prevent this thing?"

"The Langri can prevent it," O'Brien said, "if the men from the sky come this day or the next. If they delay longer, the Langri cannot prevent it, because the Langri is dying."

"Now I understand. The Langri must show us the way."

"The way is strange and difficult."

"We shall do what we must do."

O'Brien shook his head. "The way is difficult. Our people may not be able to follow, or the path the Langri chooses may be the wrong one."

"What does the Langri require?"

O'Brien stood up. "Send the young men to me, four hands at a time. I will choose the ones I need."

"The first will come to you this day."

O'Brien gripped his hand, and moved quickly away. His six great-great grandsons were waiting for him on the beach. They hoisted the sail, for the wind was at their back on the return trip. O'Brien looked back as they moved swiftly out of the bay. The Elder stood motionless on the knoll, hands upraised, as long as O'Brien could see him.

❖　❖　❖

O'Brien did not know the official names of the planet, or even if it had an official name. He was only a dumb mechanic, but a good one, and he had been knocking around in space since he was twelve. He had gotten tired being the bottom rung of everyone's ladder, so he had gotten himself a battered government surplus survey ship, and scraped together some supplies, and given a dispatcher five hundred credits to be looking the other way when he took off.

He had no right to be piloting a spaceship or any other kind of ship, but he'd seen it done enough to think he knew the fundamentals. The ship had a perverse streak that matched his own. He had to exhaust his profanity and kick the control panel a few times before it would settle down and behave itself. Pointing it in the right direction was another matter. Probably any bright high school kid knew more about navigation than he did, and his only support came from an out-of-date "Simplified Astrogation for the Layman." He was lost ninety per cent of the time and only vaguely aware of his whereabouts the other ten per cent, but it didn't matter.

He wanted to see some places that were off the usual space lines, and maybe do a little prospecting, and enjoy being his own boss as long as his supplies lasted. He couldn't stop at any of the regular ports, because the authorities would take one look at his nonexistent license and ground him permanently. But some of the smaller, privately owned ports were always in need of a good mechanic, and he could slip in for a night landing, work a couple of weeks until he'd earned enough to get his ship restocked, and slip back into space without exciting anyone.

He did his prospecting, too, nosing about on dozens of asteroids and moons and small planets that were either undiscovered or forgotten. Quite inexplicably he struck it rich. He stuffed his little ship with platinum ore and started back to civilization to realize his fortune.

As usual he was lost, and he wandered aimlessly through space for a month, conserving his fuel and nursing his worn engines. This planet had seemed his best chance, and it was almost his last chance because a faulty fuel gauge misled him, and he ran out of fuel and crashed on landing.

The natives made him welcome. He became a hero by turning his flaming pistol on a large species of bird that sometimes preyed on children. He used up all of his magazines, but he rendered the bird extinct. He explored the lone continent, and found deposits of coal and some metals—insignificant, but enough to lead the natives immediately into a bronze age. Then he turned to the sea, gave the canoes outriggers and sails, and continued his exploring.

By that time he had lost interest in being rescued. He was the Langri. He had his wives and his children. His village was growing. He could have been the Elder at a relatively young age, but the idea of him, an alien, ruling these people seemed repugnant to him. His refusal enhanced the natives' respect for him. He was happy.

He also began to worry. The planet had such scanty natural resources that no one would be attracted to it by prospective plunder. It had another resource that rendered it priceless.

It was a beautiful world. Its beaches were smooth and sandy, its waters were warm, its climate admirable. To the people of the myriads of harsh worlds whose natural riches attracted large populations, dry worlds, barren worlds, airless worlds, it would be a paradise. Those who could leave their bleak atmosphere domes, or underground caverns, or sand-blown villages for a few days in this sweet-smelling, oxygen rich atmosphere could face their lives with renewed courage.

Luxury hotels would line the beaches. Lesser hotels, boarding houses, cottages would press back into the forest. Millionaires would indulge in spirited bidding for choice stretches of beach on which to locate their mansions. The beaches would be choked with vacationers. Ships would offer relaxing sea cruises. Undersea craft would introduce the vacationers to the fantastically rich marine life. Crowded wharves would harbor fishing boats for hire. Industries would grow up to supply the tourists. It would be a year-round business because the climate was delightful the year around—a multibillion credit business.

The natives, of course, would be crowded out. Exterminated. There were laws to protect the natives, and an impressive colonial bureau to enforce them, but O'Brien knew too well how such laws worked. The little freebooter who tried to pick up a few quick credits received a stiff fine and a prison term. The big-money operators incorporated, applied for charters, and indulged in a little good-natured bribery. Then they went after their spoils under the protection of the very laws that were supposed to protect the natives.

And a century or two later scholars would be bemoaning the loss of the indigenous population. "They had a splendid civilization. It's a pity. It really is."

The young men came from all the villages. They swung lightly down the coast with flashing paddles and rollicking songs. Twenty at a time they came, tall, bronze, their blond hair bleached white by their days in the sun. They beached their canoes along the point, and moved with awed reverence into the presence of the Langri.

His questions startled them. They grappled awkwardly with strange ideas. They struggled to repeat unutterable sounds. They underwent tests of strength and endurance. They came and went, and others took their places, and finally O'Brien had chosen a hundred.

Back in the forest O'Brien built a new village. He moved in with his hundred students, and began his teaching. The days were too few and too short, but they worked from dawn until darkness, and often far into the night, while the other natives loyally brought food, and the villages in turn sent women to prepare it, and the entire people watched and wondered and waited.

O'Brien taught what he knew, and improvised when he had to. He taught language and law and science. He taught economics and sociology and military discipline. He taught guerrilla warfare and colonial procedure. He taught the history of the people of the galaxy, and the young natives sat under the stars at night and stared open-mouthed at the heavens while O'Brien told of flaming space wars and fantastic creatures and worlds beyond worlds.

The days passed, and became a year, and two years, and three. The young men brought wives to the village. The young couples called O'Brien father, and brought their first born for his blessing. And the teaching went on, and on.

O'Brien's strength waned. The damp nights left him feverish, and his swollen limbs tormented him. But he labored on, and he began to teach the Plan. He ordered practice invasion alerts, and his grim

seriousness startled the natives of other villages out of their gay
indolence. The Plan slowly took on form and understanding.

When finally O'Brien was too weak to leave his hammock he gathered the most brilliant youths about him and the lessons continued.

One bright afternoon O'Brien lost consciousness. He was carried
back to his village, to his favorite grove near the sea. Word went out
along the shore: the Langri is dying. The Elder came, and the head
men of all the villages. They placed a woven canopy over his hammock, and he lived on through the night, unconscious and breathing
laboriously, while the natives waited humbly with heads bowed.

It was morning when he opened his eyes. The sea was lovely in the
soft sunlight, but he missed the shouts of the boys rollicking in the
surf. *They know I'm dying,* he thought.

He looked at the saddened faces of the men about him. "Friends . . ."
he said. And then, in a tongue that was strange to them, he whispered,
"before God—before my God and theirs—I have done my best."

The fire of death leaped high on the beach that night, and the
choked silence of mourning gripped the villages. The next day the
hundred young men moved back to their village in the forest to
grapple doubtfully with the heritage the Langri had left to them.

II

The *Rirga* was outbound on a routine patrol mission, and
Commander Ernst Dillinger was relaxing quietly in his quarters
with his robot chess player. He had neatly trapped the robot's
queen, and was moving in for the kill when his communications
officer interrupted.

He saluted, and handed Dillinger a message. "Confidential," he
said.

Dillinger knew from his apologetic manner and the speed with
which he made his departure that the news was not good. The man
was already closing the door when Dillinger glanced at the message
and uncoiled himself in an anguished bellow. The bellow brought
him scurrying back.

Dillinger tapped the paper. "This is an order from the sector governor."

"Yes, sir." The communications officer made it sound as if that information was somehow news to him.

"Ships of the fleet do not take orders from bureaucrats and fly-by-night politicians. You will kindly inform his highness that I received my orders from Fleet Headquarters, that I am currently on a third-priority assignment, and that the fact that I am passing through one corner of his alleged territory does not give him automatic control over my movements."

The communications officer fumbled, and produced a notebook. "If you will dictate the message, sir—"

"I just gave you the message. You're a communications officer. Haven't you got enough command of language to tell him to go to hell in a flattering way?"

"I suppose so, sir."

"Do so. And send Lieutenant Protz in here."

The communications officer made a panicky exit.

Lieutenant Protz sauntered in a moment later, met Dillinger's foreboding scowl with a grin, and calmly seated himself.

"What sector are we in, Protz?' Dillinger asked.

"2397," Protz said promptly.

"And how long are we going to be in Sector 2397?"

"Forty-eight hours."

Dillinger slammed down the message. "Too long."

"Some colony in trouble?"

"Worse than that. The sector governor has lost four scratchers."

Protz straightened up and swallowed his grin. "By all that's space-worthy! Four of them? Look—I have a leave coming up next year. I'm sorry I won't be able to see you through this, but I wouldn't give up that leave if it were a dozen scratchers. You'll just have to find them without me."

"Shut up!" Dillinger snarled. "Not only does this oaf of a governor lose four survey ships at one crack, but he has the insufferable nerve to order me to start looking for them. *Order*, mind you. I'm letting him know that we have a chain-of-command procedure in the space navy, but he'll have time to get through to headquarters and have the order issued there. They'll be happy to oblige, of course, as long as the *Rirga* is in the general area."

Protz reached over and took the paper. "So they send a battle cruiser to look for four survey ships." He read, and chuckled. "It could be worse. We might find them all in the same place. The 719 turned up missing, so they sent the 1123 to look for it. And then they sent the 572 after the 719 and the 1123, and the 1486 after the 719 and the 1123 and the 572. Lucky thing for them we happened to be here. That nonsense could have gone on indefinitely."

Dillinger nodded. "Seems curious, doesn't it?"

"We can rule out mechanical failure. Those scratchers are dependable, and four of them wouldn't bubble out at the same time. Do you suppose maybe one of these worlds is civilized to the point of primitive space travel, and is picking them off?"

"Possibly," Dillinger said. "But not very likely. Not more than a tenth of the planets in this sector have been surveyed, but the entire sector has been charted, and the fleet used it for training maneuvers a couple of times. If one of these worlds has developed space travel, someone would have noticed it. No—I figure we'll find all four scratchers on one planet. The same trouble that caught the first caught the others. Whether we can do any good remains to be seen. An unsurveyed world can offer some queer kinds of trouble. Go down to the chart room, and see if you can narrow down the search area. We might even be lucky."

Twenty-four hours later Fleet Headquarters made it official, and the *Rirga* altered course. Protz paced the chart room, whistling cheerfully and making deft calculations on a three-dimensional slide rule. A technician was verifying them on a battery of computers, and having trouble keeping up.

Dillinger scowled at the co-ordinates Protz handed to him. "You figure this system is as good a bet as any?"

"Better than any." Protz stepped to the chart. "The 719 last reported in from here, on course—so. There are three possibilities, but only this one is directly on its course. I'd say it's ten to one that this is it. There shouldn't be more than one habitable planet. We can wind this up in a couple of days."

Dillinger snorted. "Only one planet to search for four scratchers!

You've been in space too long. Have you forgotten how big a planet is?"

"Like you said, we might be lucky."

They were lucky. There was one habitable planet, with a single, narrow, sub-tropical continent. On their first observation they sighted the four glistening survey ships, parked neatly in a row, on a low rise overlooking the sea.

Dillinger studied the observation data, squinted at the film strips, and exploded. "Damn! This will cost us a week, anyway, and those fools have just taken some time off to go fishing."

"We'll have to land," Protz said. "We can't be certain."

Dillinger looked up from the film strips, a faint smile on his face. "Sure we'll land. Take a good look at these. We'll land, and after I kick those scratcher crews in the pants, *I'm* going fishing."

The *Rirga* came ponderously to rest a thousand yards down the shore. There were the inevitable scientific tests. A security unit made a meticulous search of the landing area, and dispatched a squad to investigate the survey ships under cover of the alert *Rirga* gunners. Dillinger strode down the ramp, sniffed the sea breeze hungrily, and headed towards the beach.

Protz came up a moment later. "The scratchers are deserted. Looks as if they just walked off and left them."

"We'll have to root them out," Dillinger said. "Notify headquarters."

Protz hurried away.

Dillinger walked slowly back to the Rirga. The landing area was being consolidated. Patrols were pushing inland and along the shore. One signaled the discovery of a deserted native village. Dillinger shrugged indifferently, and went to his quarters. He poured himself a drink and stretched out on his bunk, wondering if there was anything on board that would pass for fishing equipment.

Protz's voice snapped out of the intercom. "Commander?"

"I'm relaxing," Dillinger said.

"We've found a native."

"The *Rirga* should be able to cope with one native without harassing its commanding officer."

"Maybe I should say the native found us. He wants to speak to the commanding officer."

Dillinger's reflexes were slow. It was a full ten seconds before he sat up abruptly, spilling his drink.

"He speaks Galactic," Protz said. "They're bringing him in now. What shall we do with him?"

"Set up a tent. I'll receive him with due ceremony."

A short time later, resplendent in a ribbon-decked dress uniform, he hurried down the ramp. The tent had been set up, and an honor guard posted around it. The men were, it seemed to Dillinger, struggling to keep their faces straight. A moment later he understood why. The native was a model of bodily perfection, young, intelligent-looking. He wore only a loin cloth of doubtful manufacture. His red hair was dazzling in the bright sunlight.

Standing before him in full dress uniform, Dillinger saw the humor of the occasion, and smiled. The native stepped forward, his face serious, his manner confident. He extended his hand. "How do you do. I am Fornri."

"I am Commander Dillinger," Dillinger responded, almost automatically. He stepped ceremoniously aside, and allowed the native to precede him into the tent. Dillinger, and a number of his officers, filed after him.

The native ignored the chairs, and faced Dillinger. "It is my sad duty to inform you that you and the personnel of your ship are under arrest."

Dillinger sat down heavily. He turned to Protz, who grinned and winked. Behind him an officer failed to suppress a chuckle. Because the native had spoken in a firm tone of voice, his words carried beyond the tent. Much whispering and some ill-concealed laughter drifted in to them.

A red-headed native who possessed not so much as a dull spear had calmly walked in and placed the *Rirga* under arrest. It was a gag worth retelling—if anyone would believe it.

Dillinger ignored Protz's wink. "What are the charges?"

The native recited tonelessly, "Landing in a restricted area, willful avoidance of customs and quarantine, failure to land at a proper immigration point with official clearance, suspicion of smuggling, and bearing arms without proper authority. Follow me, please, and I will lead you to your detention area."

Protz was suddenly solemn. "He didn't learn to speak Galactic like that from the scratcher crews," he whispered. "It's only been a month since the first ship was reported missing."

Dillinger whirled on the officers that surrounded him. "You will kindly stop grinning. This is a serious matter."

The grinning stopped.

"You see, you idiots, this man represents civil authority. Unless there are special arrangements to the contrary, military personnel are subject to the laws of any planet which has a central government. If there are several autonomous governments . . ." He turned to the native. "Does this planet have a central government?"

"It does," the native said.

"Do you have the personnel of the survey ships under detention?"

"We do."

"Order all personnel back to the ship," Dillinger said to Protz. He said to the native, "You understand—I'll have to communicate with my superiors about this."

"On two conditions. All weapons which have been brought from the ship are considered confiscated. And no one except yourself will be permitted to return to the ship."

Dillinger turned to Protz. "Have the men stack their arms at a place he designates."

Eight days passed before Dillinger was able to get down to final negotiations. Before the conference started he asked to speak with one of the survey men. Natives brought him into the tent, tanned, robust-looking, wearing a native loin cloth. He grinned sheepishly at Dillinger.

"I'm almost sorry to see you, commander."

"How have you been treated?"

"Perfect. Couldn't ask for better treatment. The food is wonderful. They have a drink that I'll swear is the best thing in the galaxy. They built us some huts on the seashore, and told us where we could go and what we could do, and left us alone. Except for the ones that bring our food, and some fishing boats, we hardly see any natives."

"Three native women apiece, I suppose," Dillinger said dryly.

"Well, no. The women haven't come near us. Otherwise, if you're thinking of naming this planet you can call it Paradise. We've been mostly swimming and spearing fish. You should see the fish in that ocean!"

"You weren't harmed?"

"No. They took us by surprise, and disarmed us, and that was it. Same went for the other ships."

"That's all I want to know," Dillinger said.

The natives led him away, and Dillinger opened the negotiations. He sat on one side of a table, flanked by two of his officers. Fornri and two other young natives faced him across the table.

"I am authorized," Dillinger said, "to accept unconditionally your listing of fines and penalties. Four hundred thousand credits have been transferred to the credit of your government in the Bank of the Galaxy." He passed a credit memo across the table. Fornri accepted it indifferently.

"This planet's status as an independent world will be recognized," Dillinger went on. "Its laws will be respected by the Galactic Federation and enforceable in Federation courts where Federation citizens are involved. We shall furnish your government with a communications center, so that contact with the Federation can be maintained, and ships wishing to land may obtain official permission.

"In return, we shall expect immediate release of personnel, return of equipment, and departure clearance for Federation ships."

"That is satisfactory," Fornri said. "Providing, of course, that the terms of the agreement are in writing."

"It will be taken care of immediately," Dillinger said. He hesitated, feeling a bit uneasy. "You understand—this means that you must return all weapons which you have confiscated, both from the *Rirga* and the survey ships."

"I understand," Fornri said. He smiled. "We are a peaceful people. We do not need weapons."

Dillinger took a deep breath. For some reason he had expected the negotiations to collapse at that point. "Lieutenant Protz," he said, "will you see that the terms are drawn up for signature?"

Protz nodded, and got to his feet.

"One moment," Dillinger said. "There is one thing more. We must have an official name for your planet. What do you call it?"

Fornri seemed puzzled. "Sir?"

"Up to now, you have only been co-ordinates and a number to us. You must have a name. It is probably best that you name your own planet. If you don't, someone else will, and you might not like it. It can be your native name for the planet, or a descriptive term—anything you like."

Fornri hesitated. "Perhaps we should discuss the matter."

"By all means," Dillinger said. "But one word of caution. Once the planet has been named, it will be infernally difficult to change it."

"I understand," Fornri said.

The native withdrew, and Dillinger settled back with a smile, and sipped from a tumbler of the native drink. The drink was everything the survey man had claimed.

Perhaps Paradise would be a good name for the place, he thought. *But then—better to let the natives decide. Paradise might mean something very different to them. All sorts of complications resulted when planets were named by outsiders.* He remembered the famous story of the survey ship calling for help from a swamp on a strange planet. "Where are you?" Base had demanded. The survey ship gave its coordinates, and added, quite needlessly, "It's a helluvaplace." The people of that planet had been trying for two centuries to have its name changed, but on all the official charts it was still Helluvaplace.

"Your sun, too," he called after Fornri. "We'll have to name that."

Three hours later they were in space, on their way to Fron, the sector capital. Protz looked back at the dwindling planet, and shook his head. "*Langri*. What do you suppose it means?"

On Fron, Dillinger reported to the sector governor. "So they call it Langri," the governor said. "And—you say they speak Galactic?"

"Speak it rather well, with a kind of provincial accent."

"Easily accounted for, of course. A ship touched down there some time in the past. People liked the place and stayed, maybe. Did you see any traces of such a ship, or ships?"

"No. We didn't see anything except what they wanted us to see."

"Yes. Awkward position you stumbled into. Not your fault, of course. But those survey men . . ." He shook his head. "What beats me is that they learned Galactic. Normally the aliens would learn the native language, unless there was a crowd of them. There is a native language, isn't there?"

"I can't say. I never heard any of them speak anything but Galactic. Of course I didn't hear them talking among themselves. They withdrew well out of hearing whenever they had to confer about something. But now that I think about it, I did overhear some kids speaking Galactic."

"Interesting," the governor said. "Langri—that must be a native word. I'd better attach a philologist to the staff we'll place there. I'd like to know how they happened to learn Galactic and keep on speaking it, and I'd like to know how long it's been since there were aliens in their midst. Very interesting."

"They're an intelligent people," Dillinger said. "They drove a good bargain, but they were very civilized about it. My orders say I'm to pick up an ambassador for Langri, and the personnel to form a permanent station there. Know anything about that?"

"I'll furnish the personnel for the station. The ambassador has been appointed, and he should be along in a few days. In the meantime, give your men some leave and enjoy yourselves."

A week later H. Harlow Wembling, Ambassador to Langri, waddled up the ramp to the *Rirga*, carrying his ample paunch like a ceremonial badge of honor. He bullied the duty officer, snarled at the crew, and, when Dillinger called at his quarters to pay his respects, demanded a member of the space navy to serve as his valet for the duration of his time on board.

Dillinger emerged wiping his brow, and gave Protz his precise opinion of the new ambassador in words that made the executive officer wince and rub his ears thoughtfully.

"Are you going to give him what he wants?" Protz asked.

"I told him," Dillinger said, still savoring his remarks, "I told him that the only person on board likely to have that much free time would be myself, and I lack the proper qualifications. It's too bad. It's really a shame."

"Oh, we'll be rid of him in no time."

"I was thinking of the natives on Langri. It's politics, of course.

Wembling will be a party stalwart, getting paid off for years of loyal service and campaign donations. It happens all the time, and most of the appointees are decent enough. Some of them are even competent, but there's always the exceptional case where a man thinks the word *Ambassador* in front of his name elevates him forty degrees towards divinity. So why does our planet have to draw this one?"

"It's probably nothing to worry about. These political appointees never keep their jobs long. Anyway, it's no concern of ours."

"It's my concern," Dillinger said. "I negotiated the Langri treaty and I feel some responsibility for the place."

They delivered Ambassador Wembling to Langri, along with the personnel to set up a permanent Federation station. There was one last-minute altercation with Wembling when he suddenly insisted that half of the Rirga's crew be left to guard the station. Then they were back in space, ready, as Dillinger said, to forget Langri and get back to work.

But he did not forget Langri and there were many times in the months and years that followed that he found himself reminiscing dreamily of perfect beaches and water swarming with fish and sea air blended with the perfume of myriads of flowers. *Now there would be the place for a vacation,* he would think. *Or for retirement—what a place that would be for a retired naval officer!*

III

An obsolete freighter, bound from Quiron to Yorlan on a little-used space route, disappeared. Light-years away a bureaucrat with a vivid imagination immediately thought of piracy. Orders went out, and Lieutenant Commander James Vorish, of the battle cruiser *Hiln*, changed course and resigned himself to a monotonous six months of patrolling.

A week later his orders were canceled. He changed course again, and mulled over the development with Lieutenant Robert Smith.

"Someone's been stirring up an indigenous population," Vorish said. "We're to take over, and protect Federation citizens and property."

"Some people never learn," Smith said. "But—Langri? Where the devil is *Langri*? I've never heard of it."

Vorish thought it was the most beautiful place he had ever seen. To the west, that is. Trees stretched glistening pale-green foliage over the narrow beach. Flowers were closing delicately beautiful petals as the evening sun abandoned them. Waves rippled in lazily from an awesomely blue sea.

Behind him, the hideous skeleton of an enormous building under construction stood out sharply in the dusk. The afternoon shift was busily and loudly at work. Clanging sounds and thuds echoed along the shore. Motors chugged and gurgled. Mercifully, the uncertain light disguised the havoc the construction work had wrought in the unspoiled forest.

The man Wembling was still talking. "It is your duty to protect the lives and property of citizens of the Federation."

"Certainly," Vorish said. "Within reason. The installation you want would take a division of troops and a million credits worth of equipment. And even then it wouldn't be foolproof. You say part of the time the natives come in from the sea. We'd have to ring the entire peninsula."

"They're unprincipled scoundrels," Wembling said. "We have a right to demand protection. I can't keep men on the job if they're in terror of their lives."

"How many men have you lost?"

"Why, none. But that isn't the natives' fault."

"You haven't lost anybody? What about property? Have they been damaging your equipment or supplies?"

"No," Wembling said. "But only because we've been alert. I've had to turn half my crew into a police force."

"We'll see what we can do," Vorish said. "Give me some time to get the feel of the situation, and then I'll talk with you again."

Wembling summoned two burly bodyguards, and hurried away. Vorish strode on along the beach, returned a sentry's salute, and stood looking out to sea.

"There's nobody out in front of us, sir," the sentry said. "The natives—"

He halted abruptly, challenged, and then saluted. Smith came down the slope, nodded at Vorish, and faced west.

"What'd you get?" Vorish asked.

"There's something mighty queer about this situation. These 'raids' Wembling talked about—the natives usually come one at a time, and they don't come armed. They simply sneak in here and get in the way—lie down in front of a machine, or something like that—and the work has to stop until someone carries them away and dumps them back in the forest."

"Have any natives been hurt?"

"No. The men say Wembling is pretty strict about that. It's gotten on the men's nerves because they never know when a native is going to pop up in front of them. They're afraid if one did get hurt the others would come with knives or poison arrows, or some such thing."

"From what I've seen of Wembling, my sympathy is with the natives. But I have my orders. We'll put a line of sentry posts across the peninsula, and distribute some more about the work area. It's the best we can do, and even that will be a strain on our personnel. Some of the specialized ratings are going to howl when we assign them to guard duty."

"No," Smith said. "No, they won't. A couple of hours on this beach are worth eight hours of guard duty. I'll start spotting the sentry posts."

Vorish went back to the *Hiln*, and became the target of an avalanche of messengers. Mr. Wembling would like to know . . . Mr. Wembling suggests . . . If it would not be too much trouble . . . Compliments of Mr. Wembling . . . Mr. Wembling says. . . At your earliest convenience . . . Mr. Wembling's apologies, but . . .

Damn Mr. Wembling! Vorish had been on the point of telling his communications officer to put in a special line to Wembling's office. He breathed a sigh of relief over his narrow escape, and gave a junior officer the full-time assignment of dealing with Wembling's messengers.

Smith strode in out of the darkness from his job of posting the sentries. "Native wants to see you," he said. "I have him outside."

Vorish threw up his hands. "Well, I heard Wembling's side of it. I might as well hear theirs. I hate to ask, but I suppose Wembling will let us have an interpreter."

"He might if he had any, but he hasn't. These natives speak Galactic."

"Now look here." He paused, shook his head. "No, I see you aren't joking. I guess this planet is just different. Bring him in."

The native introduced himself as Fornri, and confidently clasped Vorish's hand. His hair blazed vividly red in the cold glow of the overhead light. He accepted a chair, and sat down calmly. "I understand," he said, "that you are members of the Space Navy of the Galactic Federation of Independent Worlds. Is that correct?"

Vorish stopped staring long enough to acknowledge that it was correct.

"In behalf of my government," Fornri said, "I ask your assistance in repelling invaders of our world."

"The devil!" Smith muttered.

Vorish studied the native's earnest young face before venturing a reply. "These invaders," he said finally. "Are you referring to the construction project?"

"I am," Fornri said.

"Your planet has been classified 3C by the Federation, which places it under the jurisdiction of the Colonial Bureau. Wembling & Company have a charter from the Bureau for their project here. They are hardly to be considered invaders."

Fornri spoke slowly and distinctly. "My government has a treaty with the Galactic Federation of Independent Worlds. The treaty guarantees the independence of Langri, and also guarantees the assistance of the Federation in the event that Langri is invaded from outer space. I am calling upon the Galactic Federation of Independent Worlds to fulfill its guarantee."

"Let's have the Index," Vorish said to Smith. He took the heavy volume, checked the contents, and found a page headed *Langri*. "Initial survey contact in '84," he said. "Four years ago. Classified 3C in September of '85. No mention of any kind of treaty."

Fornri took a polished tube of wood from his belt, and slipped out a rolled paper. He passed it to Vorish, who unrolled it and smoothed it flat. It was a carefully written copy of an obviously official document. Vorish looked at the date, and turned to the Index. "Dated in

June of '84," he said to Smith. "A month and a half after the initial survey contact. It classifies Langri as 5X."

"Genuine?" Smith asked.

"It looks genuine. I don't suppose these people could have made it up. Do you have the original of this document?"

"Yes," Fornri said.

"Of course he wouldn't carry it around with him. Probably doesn't trust us, and I can't blame him."

He passed the paper over to Smith, who scrutinized it carefully and returned it. "It would be a little odd for classification of a new planet to be delayed for a year and a half after the initial survey contact. If this thing is genuine, then Langri was reclassified in '85."

"The Index doesn't say anything about reclassification," Vorish said. He turned to Fornri. "Until we were ordered to this planet, we had never heard of Langri, so of course we know nothing about its classification. Tell us how it happened."

Fornri nodded. He spoke Galactic well, with an accent that Vorish could not quite place. Occasionally he had to pause and grope for a word, but his narrative was clear and concise. He described the coming of survey men, their capture, and the negotiations with the officers of the *Rirga*. What followed brought scowls to their faces.

"Wembling? Wembling was the first ambassador?"

"Yes, sir," Fornri said. "He mocked the authority of our government, insulted our people, and bothered our women. We asked your government to take him away, and it did."

"Probably he has plenty of political pull," Smith said. "He got the planet reclassified, and got himself a charter. Pretty effective revenge for a supposed insult."

"Or maybe he just saw an opportunity to make money here," Vorish said. "Was your government given formal notification of the termination of the treaty and Langri's reclassification?"

"No," Fornri said. "After Wembling there came another ambassador, a Mr. Gorman. He was a good friend of my people. Then a ship came and took him and all of the others away. We were told nothing. Next came Mr. Wembling with many ships and many men. We told him to leave, and he laughed at us and began to build the hotel."

"He's been building for nearly three years," Vorish said. "He isn't getting along very fast."

"We have hired an attorney many worlds away," Fornri said. "Many times he has obtained the conjunction, and made the work stop. But then each time the judge has stopped the conjunction."

"Injunction?" Smith exclaimed. "You mean you've made a lawsuit out of this?"

"Bring Lieutenant Charles in here," Vorish said. Smith routed the *Hiln's* young legal officer out of bed. With the help of Charles they quizzed Fornri at length on the futile legal action taken by the government of Langri against H. Harlow Wembling.

The story was both amazing and pathetic. The Federation station had taken its communication equipment when it was withdrawn. The natives were helpless when Wembling arrived, and they knew better than to attempt a show of force. Fortunately they had found a friend on Wembling's staff—Fornri wouldn't say whom—and he had managed to put them in touch with an attorney and the attorney had gone to court for them enthusiastically, many times.

He could not intervene in the matter of the violated treaty, because the government had sole jurisdiction there. But he had attacked Wembling's activities on a number of counts, some of which Fornri did not understand. In one instance Wembling had been accused of violating his charter, which gave him exclusive rights to develop Langri's natural resources. Wembling's work on his hotel was halted for months, until a judge ruled that a planet's vacation and resort potential was a natural resource. The natives had just won the most recent round, when a court held Wembling liable for damages because he'd torn down an entire village in clearing ground for the hotel. His charter, the court said, did not permit him to usurp private property. But the damages had been mild, and now Wembling was back at work, and the attorney was trying to think of something else. He was also lobbying to get something done about the broken treaty, but there had been no promise of success there.

"Lawsuits cost money," Vorish observed.

Fornri shrugged. Langri had money. It had four hundred thousand credits which the Federation had paid to it, and it had the proceeds of a good weight of platinum ore which the friend on Wembling's staff had managed to smuggle out for them.

"There's platinum on Langri?" Vorish asked.

"It didn't come from Langri," Fornri said.

Vorish drummed impatiently on his desk. The Langri situation involved several noteworthy mysteries, but just for a start he'd like to know how the natives had happened to be speaking Galactic when the first survey men arrived. And then—platinum ore that didn't come from Langri. He shook his head. "I don't think you'll ever defeat Wembling in court. You may give him a few temporary setbacks, but in the long run he'll win out. And he'll ruin you. Men like him have too much influence, and all the financial backing they need."

"The conjunctions give us time," Fornri said. "Time is what we need—time for the Plan."

Vorish looked doubtfully at Smith. "What do you think?"

"I think we're obligated to make a full report on this. The treaty was negotiated by naval officers. Naval Headquarters should be filled in on what's happened."

"Yes. We should send them a copy of this—but a copy of a copy may not swing much weight. And the natives probably won't want to turn loose the original." He turned to Fornri. "I'm going to send Lieutenant Smith with you. He will bring a couple of men along. None of them will be armed. Take them wherever you like, and guard them any way you like, but they must make their own photographs of the treaty before we can help you."

Fornri considered the matter briefly, and agreed. Vorish sent Smith off with two technicians and their equipment, and settled down to compose a report. He was interrupted by a young ensign who gulped, flushed crimson, and stammered, "Excuse me, sir. But Mr. Wembling—"

"What now?" Vorish said resignedly.

"Mr. Wembling wants sentry post number thirty-two moved. The lights are interfering with his sleep."

In the morning Vorish strolled around the project to take a good look at Wembling's embryo hotel. Wembling joined him, wearing a revoltingly-patterned short-sleeved shirt and shorts. His arms and legs were crisply tanned, his face pale under an outlandish sun helmet.

"A thousand accommodations," Wembling said. "Most of them will be suites. There'll be a big pool on the terrace overlooking the beach. Some people can't stand salt water, you know. I have the men laying out a golf course. There'll be two main dining rooms and half a dozen small ones that will specialize in food from famous places. I'll have a whole fleet of boats to take people fishing. I might even have a submarine or two—those jobs with rows of observation ports. You might not believe it, but there are hundreds of worlds where people have never seen an ocean. Why, there are worlds where people don't even have water to bathe in. They have to use chemicals. If some of those people can come to Langri, and live a little, now and then, a lot of head doctors are going to be out of work. This project of mine is nothing but a service to humanity."

"Is that so?" Vorish murmured. "I wasn't aware that yours was a nonprofit organization."

"Huh? Of course I'll make a profit. A darned good profit. What's wrong with that?"

"From what I've seen of your hotel, the only minds you'll be saving will be those of the poor, broken-down millionaires."

Wembling indulged in a grandiose gesture. "Just a beginning. Have to put the thing on a sound financial basis right from the start, you know. But there'll be plenty of room for the little fellows. Not in water-front hotels, but there'll be community beaches, and hotels with rights of access, and all that sort of thing. My staff has it all worked out."

"It's just that I'm trained to look at things differently," Vorish said. "We in the Space Navy devote our lives to the protection of humanity, but if you'll look at the current pay scale you'll see that there's no profit motive."

"There's nothing wrong with taking a profit. Where would the human race be today if nobody wanted a profit? We'd be living in grass huts back on old Terra, just like these Langri natives. There's a good example of a nonprofit society. I suppose you'd like that."

"It doesn't look so bad to me," Vorish murmured.

But Wembling did not hear him. He whirled and darted away, sputtering an unbelievably pungent profanity. A native, dashing in from nowhere, had attached himself to a girder that was about to be swung aloft. Workmen were valiantly striving to remove him—gently. The native clung stubbornly. Work stopped until he was pried loose and carried away.

Lieutenant Smith came up in time to see the drama carried to its comical conclusion.

"What do they expect to gain?" Vorish said.

"Time," Smith said. "Didn't you hear what that native said? They need time for the Plan—whatever that means."

"Maybe they're planning some kind of a massive uprising."

"I doubt it. They seem to be essentially a peaceful people."

"I wish them luck," Vorish said. "This Wembling is a tough customer. He's a self-activated power unit. I wonder how his weight holds up, the way he tears around keeping things humming."

"Maybe he eats all night. Want to look over the sentry layout?"

They turned away. In the distance they heard Wembling, his voice high-pitched with excitement, getting the work going again. A moment later he caught up with them and walked jauntily along beside Vorish.

"If you'd put in the kind of defense line I want," he said, "I wouldn't have that trouble."

Vorish did not reply. It was obvious that Wembling was going out of his way to avoid injuring the natives, but Vorish doubted that his motives were humanitarian. Inept handling of the native problem might embarrass him in some future court test.

On the other hand, Wembling was not worried in the least about the Space Navy's injuring the natives. The blame for that action could not possibly fall upon him. He had demanded that Vorish erect an electronic barrier that would incinerate any native attempting to pass.

"At the very worst," Vorish said, "the natives are only a minor nuisance."

"They haven't got much for weapons," Wembling said. "But they have enough to cut throats, and there's a hell of a lot of natives in this place if they all decide to come at me at once. And then, their mucking about the project is slowing things down. I want 'em kept out."

"I don't think your throat is in danger, but we'll do what we can to keep them out."

"Guess I can't ask more than that," Wembling said. He chuckled good-naturedly, and looped his arm through Vorish's.

Smith had sited his sentry posts to make a shrewd use of the infrequent irregularities in terrain. He had men at work now, clearing the ground for better visibility. Wembling sauntered along reviewing the results with the casual aloofness of an Admiral of the Fleet. Suddenly he pulled Vorish to a halt.

"This defense line of ours. We'll have to move it."

Vorish regarded him coldly. "Why?"

"In the next two or three weeks we're going to start work on the golf course. We wouldn't be able to get more than half of it this side of the line. Maybe not that much. So we'll have to move it. It wouldn't be safe to have my men working off by themselves. But there's no hurry—tomorrow will do."

"Supposing you tell me what you have in mind," Vorish said.

Wembling summoned a survey party, and they set out under the watchful eyes of a military escort. They moved west along the peninsula, which widened sharply until it became a part of the mainland. They pushed their way through the trees as the perspiring Wembling, enjoying himself immensely, gestured and talked his way around the prospective golf course.

An hour later Vorish took another look at the acreage the golf course was to occupy, and gave Wembling a flat refusal. "The line would be too long here," he said. "I wouldn't have enough men."

Wembling grinned. "The commander is always pulling my leg. You've got plenty of men. They're all down there on the beach."

"My men are working in shifts, just as yours are. If I put those men on guard duty, I won't have any relief for them."

"We both know you could set up an impassable defense that wouldn't require any men," Wembling said.

"We both know I'm not going to do it. Your men can work without naval protection. They'll be safe."

"All right. If that's the way you want it. But if anything happens to them—"

"There's one more thing," Vorish said. "What are you going to do about that abandoned native village where the eighth hole is supposed to be?"

Wembling gazed contemptuously at the distant huts. "Tear it down. Nobody lives there."

"You can't do that," Vorish said. "It's native property. You'll have to get permission."

"Whose permission?"

"The natives' permission."

Wembling threw back his head, and laughed uproariously. "Let 'em take it to court, if they want to waste their money. That last case must have cost 'em close to a hundred thousand, and know what their damages were? Seven hundred and fifty credits. The sooner they use up their money, the sooner they stop bothering me."

"My orders call for the protection of natives and native property just as I protect you and your property," Vorish said. "The natives won't stop you, but I will."

He strode away without looking back. He was in a hurry to get to his office on the *Hiln*, and have a talk with Lieutenant Charles. There was something he remembered reading, a long time ago, in his little-used manual of military government . . .

The days drifted by pleasantly, ruffled only by Wembling's violent protests whenever a native slipped through to slow down construction. Vorish kept an alert eye on Wembling's Operation Golf Course, and waited impatiently for some official reaction to his report on the Langri treaty.

Official reaction there was none, but Wembling's work-crew steadily sliced its way back into the forest. Trees were being hauled away to be cut into lumber. The delicately-speckled grain would make an exquisite and novel paneling for the hotel's interior.

The crew reached the deserted native village and worked completely around it. They made no effort to trespass, though Vorish saw them casting nervous glances in that direction from time to time, as though they hoped it would go away.

Making his morning rounds of the sentry posts, Vorish paused occasionally to turn his binoculars on the work around the village.

"You're sticking your neck out," Smith said. "I hope you realize that."

Vorish made no reply. He had his own opinion of naval officers who were unduly concerned for their necks. "There's Wembling," he said.

With his bodyguards panting on his heels, Wembling was moving at his usual fast pace across the cleared ground. His foreman came forward to meet him. Wembling spoke briefly, and pointed. The foreman turned to his men, and pointed. A moment later the first hut was overturned.

"Let's go," said Vorish.

Smith signaled a squad of navy men into action, and hurried after him. The men reached the village first, and cleared out Wembling's men. Wembling was frozen in impotent rage when Vorish arrived.

Vorish paused to study the row of toppled huts. "Did you have permission from the natives to do this?" he asked.

"Hell, no," Wembling said. "I've got a charter. What can they do about it?"

"Place these men under arrest," Vorish said, and turned away.

Somewhat to his surprise, Wembling said nothing. His aspect was that of a man thinking deeply.

Vorish confined Wembling to his tent, under arrest. He halted all work on the hotel. Then he forwarded a complete report on the incident to Naval Headquarters, and sat back to await results.

The indifference of headquarters to his Langri report had intrigued him. Had someone filed it away as unimportant, or was there a corrupt conspiracy high up in the government? Either way, injustice was being done. The natives wanted time for something they called the Plan. Vorish wanted time to call someone's attention to what was going on. It would be a shame to allow Wembling to finish his hotel while the report on the Langri situation lay in an underling's desk drawer.

With Wembling under arrest and the work stopped, Vorish watched in amusement while Wembling got off frantic messages to exalted persons high up in the Federation government.

"Now," Vorish told himself with satisfaction, "let's see them ignore Langri this time."

The days had added up to three weeks when Headquarters suddenly broke the silence. The battle cruiser *Bolar* was being dispatched, under Admiral Corning. The admiral would make an on-the-spot investigation.

"It doesn't sound as if you're being relieved," Smith said. "Do you know Corning?"

"I've served under him several times, at various places and ranks. You might call him an old friend."

"That's fortunate for you."

"It could be worse," Vorish admitted. He felt that he'd covered himself well, and Corning, even though he was crusty, temperamental and a stickler for accuracy, would not go out of his way to make trouble for a friend.

Vorish turned out an honor guard for the admiral, and received him with full ceremony. Corning stepped briskly down the ramp from the *Bolar* and glanced about approvingly.

"Glad to see you, Jim," he said, his eyes on one of Langri's inviting beaches. "Nice place here. Nice place." He turned to Vorish, and studied his tanned face. "And you've been making good use of it. You've put on weight."

"You've lost weight," Vorish said.

"Always was skinny," Corning said. "I make up for it in height. Did I ever tell you about the time—" He glanced at the circle of respectfully attentive officers, and dropped his voice. "Let's go where we can talk."

Vorish dismissed his men, and took Corning to his office in the *Hiln*. The admiral said nothing along the way, but his sharp eyes surveyed Vorish's defense arrangements, and he clucked his tongue softly.

"Jim," Corning said, as Vorish closed the door, "just what is going on here?"

"I want to give you some background," Vorish said, and told him about the treaty and its violation. Corning listened intently, muttering an occasional "Damn!"

"You mean they took no official action on it at all?" he demanded.

"That's exactly what they did."

"Damn! Sooner or later somebody's head will roll over that. But it'll probably be the wrong head, and that treaty really has nothing to do with this mess you've gotten yourself into. Not officially, anyway, because officially the treaty doesn't exist. Now what's this nonsense about a few native huts?"

Vorish smiled. He felt that he was on firm ground there—he'd had a long conference with Fornri, exploring all of the angles. "According to my orders," he said, "I'm an impartial referee here. I'm to protect Federation citizens and property, but I am also to protect the natives against any infringements upon their customs, means of livelihood, and so on. Paragraph seven."

"I've read it."

"The idea is that if the natives are treated properly, Federation citizens and property are a lot less likely to need protection. That particular native village is more than just a collection of empty huts. It seems to have some religious significance to the natives. They call it the Teacher's Village, or some such thing."

"Teacher or leader," Corning said. "Sometimes they're the same thing to primitive peoples. That might make the village a kind of shrine. I take it that this Wembling busted right in and started tearing the place apart."

"That's what he did."

"And you warned him ahead of time that he should get the natives' permission, and he laughed it off. All right. Your conduct was not only proper, there—it was commendable. But why did you have to close the whole works down? You could have protected that village, and made him put his golf course somewhere else, and he would have screamed to high heaven without getting anything but laughed at. But you had to stop everything. Were you *trying* to get fired? You've cost Wembling a lot of time and a lot of money, and now he has a real grievance. And he's got plenty of influence."

"It isn't my fault if he wasted time and money," Vorish said. "I advised headquarters of my action immediately. They could have reversed that order any time they chose."

"That's just it. They didn't dare, because there was always the chance that things might blow up. They didn't know the situation here. You caused a pretty stew at headquarters. Why did you arrest Wembling, and keep him in his tent under guard?"

"For his own protection. He'd defiled a sacred place, and I'd be responsible if anything happened to him."

For the first time Corning smiled. "So that's the line. Not bad. It all comes down to a matter of judgment, and that makes it your opinion against Wembling's. You flip your coin and you take your choice, and no one who wasn't on the spot is entitled to vote." He nodded. "I'll follow that up in my report. Wembling stepped out of line. Definitely. The consequences might have been serious. I can't rightly say that your action was too drastic, because I wasn't here at the time. I don't exactly see what you were trying to do, or maybe I do, but I'll back you up as much as I can. I guess I can keep you from being shot."

"Oh," Vorish said. "So they were going to shoot me. I wondered."

"They were . . . they are . . . going to do their worst." Corning looked steadily at Vorish. "I don't much like it, but I have my orders. You'll return to Galaxia on the *Hiln*, under arrest—to stand court-martial. Personally I don't think you have much to worry about. I can't see them going ahead with it, but right now they think they want to try."

"I won't worry," Vorish said. "I've studied this thing through pretty carefully. I rather hope they try, though. I'll insist on a public court-martial, of course, and . . . but I'm afraid they won't do it. Anyway, I'm glad I'll be leaving Langri in capable hands."

"Not my hands," Corning said. "Not for long. The 984th Squadron is on its way now, to take over. Eleven ships. They're not taking any chance on this thing getting out of hand. The commander is Ernst Dillinger—just made admiral a few months ago. Know him?"

IV

The fishing boat was still in position, far out. Dillinger raised his binoculars, lowered them. As far as he could see, the natives were—

fishing. He returned to his desk and sat gazing seaward at the fleck of color that was the sail.

The plush spaciousness of his office annoyed him. It was only his second day in the quarters Wembling had persuaded him to occupy in the completed wing of Hotel Langri, and he was spending most of his time pacing in out-sized circles about the work that piled up on his desk.

He was worried about the natives. He was worried about an enigmatic something or other which they called the Plan, and which they intimated would eventually sweep Wembling and his workers and his hotels right off the planet.

With Hotel Langri opening for business in a few months, and work already beginning on two other hotels, Dillinger knew that the legal expulsion of Wembling had become a flat impossibility. So what were the natives planning? Illegal expulsion? The use of force? With a squadron of the Space Navy standing by?

He got to his feet again and walked over to the curved expanse of tinted plastic that formed the window. The fishing boat was still there. Every day it was there. But perhaps, as Protz suggested, the water off the point was merely a good place to fish.

His intercom clicked. "Mr. Wembling, sir."

"Send him in," Dillinger said, and turned towards the door.

Wembling entered jauntily, hand outstretched. "Morning, Ernie."

"Good morning, Howard," Dillinger said, blinking at Wembling's ridiculously patterned shirt.

"Come down to the lounge for a drink?"

Dillinger lifted a stack of papers from his desk, and dropped it. "Sure."

They walked down a palatial corridor to the lounge, and a uniformed attendant took their orders and brought the drinks. Dillinger idly stirred the ice in his glass and looked through the enormous window at the terrace, and the beach beyond. Wembling's landscaping crew had done its work well. Velvety grass and colorful shrubs surrounded the hotel. The pool, ready for use, stood deserted. Off-duty navy men and workers crowded the beach, and speared fish off the point.

Wembling prated enthusiastically over the progress he was making on his new sites, which were fifty miles down the coast in both directions.

"It's a headache to me, your scattering these sites all over the place," Dillinger said. "I have to guard them."

Wembling reached over and patted his arm. "You're doing a good job, Ernie. We haven't had any trouble since you took over. I'm putting in a good word for you where it'll do the most good."

"There's room for fifty hotels right here on the peninsula," Dillinger said. "Not to mention a few golf courses."

Wembling turned a veiled smile in his direction. "Politics and law," he murmured. "Stay away from both of them, Ernie. You have brains and talent, but it isn't that kind of brains and talent."

Dillinger flushed, and turned his gaze to the window again. The fishing boat was a mere speck on the horizon. It was probably drifting or sailing slowly, but it seemed motionless.

"Have you heard anything about Commander Vorish?" Wembling asked.

"The last I heard, he'd taken the *Hiln* on training maneuvers."

"Then—they didn't fire him?"

"They investigated him," Dillinger said with a grin. "But all he got was a commendation for handling himself well in a difficult situation. My guess is that any action against him would have resulted in publicity, and someone didn't want publicity. Of course I don't know anything about politics and law. Did you want Vorish fired?"

Wembling shook his head thoughtfully. "No. I had no grudge against him. There's no profit in grudges. We both had a job to do, but he went at his the wrong way. All I wanted was to get on with the work, and after he left I passed the word along to go easy on him. But I thought they'd kick him out of the navy, and if they did I wanted him back here on Langri. I think he understood these natives, and I can always use a man like that. I told him to get in touch with my Galaxia Office, and they'd make arrangements to get him back here. But I never heard from him."

"He didn't get fired. The next time you see him he'll probably be an admiral."

"The same goes for you," Wembling said. "If you ever leave the navy, come back to Langri. I'm going to have a big enterprise to run here, and I'll need all the good men I can get. And good men aren't always easy to find."

Dillinger turned aside to hide his smile. "Thanks. I'll remember that."

Wembling slapped the table, and pushed himself erect. "Well, back to work. Chess tonight?"

"Better make it late," Dillinger said. "I've got to get that work cleaned up."

He watched Wembling waddle away. He had to admire the man. Even if he loathed him, and loathed his methods, he had to admire him. He got things done.

Protz was waiting for him when he got back to his office—Commander Protz, now, Captain of the Rirga, the flag ship of Dillinger's 984th Squadron. Dillinger nodded at him, and spoke into his intercom.

"I don't want to be disturbed." He switched it off, and turned to Protz. "What's the score?"

"We're losing," Protz said. "It definitely didn't crash. According to the sentry, it came in for a perfect landing back in the forest. Wembling isn't missing a supply ship, and we know it didn't belong to us. The recon planes have been taking the tops out of the trees in that area, and they can't spot a thing."

"So it wasn't Wembling's," Dillinger said. Since he'd gotten the first report on the unidentified ship, at dawn that morning, he'd been thinking that it had to be Wembling's. He turned in his chair, and looked out to sea. "So the natives have visitors."

"Whoever it was, they were expected," Protz said. "They got the ship camouflaged in a hurry. Maybe they had a landing pit dug there."

"Wembling thinks someone in his supply fleet has been keeping the natives in touch with that attorney of theirs. I suppose we should have monitored the planet. But we'd have to leave a ship in orbit, and we've needed every man, with Wembling building hotels all over the place. Well, the ship is here. The question now, is—what is it doing?"

"Smuggling arms?"

"Just what we need to make this assignment interesting. Has Intelligence turned up anything?"

"Nothing up to 0800 this morning. Want to make a ground search for the ship?"

"It would take too many men. If they have a landing pit, even a ground search might miss it—and we'd be too late now if we did find it. They'll have it unloaded. No. Let Intelligence work on it, and give them more men if they think they can use them."

"Anything else?"

"Get ready for the worst. Protz, of all the jobs the navy has given me to do, this one is the dirtiest. I hoped I'd get out of it without a shot fired at the natives. I'd much rather shoot Wembling."

The thing had been mishandled from the start, Dillinger thought. This attorney the natives had gotten ahold of was probably competent enough—even Wembling admitted that. He'd caused Wembling some trouble, but Wembling was putting the finishing touches on Hotel Langri just the same.

Wembling's chief weapon was political pull. Politics should be fought with politics, with public opinion, and not in a court of law. He'd tried to explain that, once, to Fornri, but the native seemed uninterested. The Plan, Fornri said, would take care of everything. He did not seem to realize that it was already too late.

If Dillinger had known in time what was happening to Langri, he believed he could have stopped it. Documented information, furnished anonymously to the wealthy ethnological foundations, to opposition newspapers on key planets, to opposition leaders in the Federation Congress—the resultant explosion would have rocked the government and rocked Wembling right off Langri.

But he had not known until he reported to Admiral Corning and assumed command on Langri. Then he had done what he could. He had prepared a hundred copies of a statement on the Langri situation, and accompanied each with a photo of the original treaty. But he did not dare entrust them to normal communication channels, and he had to wait until one of his officers went on leave to get them on their way. They had probably reached their destinations by this time, and they would be studied and investigated, and eventually there would be some action. But it was too late. Wembling would have most of what he wanted, and probably other vultures, armed with charters, would be coming to the plunder of Langri.

It was tough on the natives. Wembling's men were eating a lot of fresh fish, and the natives' fishing boats had all but vanished from the sites where Wembling was working. Langri had a big native population—too big, and most of its food came from the sea. The word was that the natives weren't getting enough to eat.

Late in the afternoon, Dillinger called Wembling. "You have men flying back and forth all the time," he said. "Have they noticed any unusual native activity?"

"I didn't hear about any," Wembling said. "Want me to check?"

"I wish you would."

"Hold on a minute."

He heard Wembling snapping out an order. A moment later, he said to Dillinger, "Do you think the natives are up to something?"

"I know they are, but I can't figure out what it is."

"You'll handle them," Wembling said confidently. "There was a time when I wanted them annihilated, but since you've been keeping them out of my hair, I'd just as soon live and let live. Hell, they might even be a tourist attraction when I get things going here. Maybe they weave baskets, or carve voodoo charms, or something like that. I'll sell them in the hotel lobby."

"I'm not worrying about their basket weaving," Dillinger said dryly.

"Anyway . . . just a moment. Ernie? Nobody saw anything unusual."

"Thanks. I'm afraid I'll have to call off that chess game. I'll be busy."

"Too bad. Tomorrow night, then?"

"We'll see."

Langri would have been enchanting by moonlight, but there was no moon. Wembling had a scheme to produce artificial moonlight, but until he put it into operation night would smother the planet's beauty in blackness.

Looking down into the blackness, Dillinger saw light. At every native village there were dozens of fires. Often their outlines blurred together into one brilliant patch of light. When they were farther apart, they appeared as a multitude of bright dots leaping up into the darkness.

"You say it isn't normal?" Dillinger asked the recon pilot.

"Definitely not, sir. They fix their evening meal along about dark, when the fishing boats get in. When that's over with, you can fly the whole coast without seeing a flash of light. Except where our men are. I've never seen even one fire going this late."

"It's a pity we know so little about these natives," Dillinger said. "The only one I've ever talked with is this Fornri, and there's always something—distant about him. I never know what he's thinking. Colonial Bureau should have sent a team to study them. They could use some help, too. Their fishing will fall off even more when Wembling gets a mob of tourists out on the water. They'll need some agriculture. What do you make of it, Protz?"

"It's suggestive, but darned if I know what it suggests."

"I know what it suggests," Dillinger said. "A strange ship lands this morning, and tonight every native on the planet stays up all night. They're getting ready for something. We'd better get back and make a few preparations of our own."

There was little that he could do. He had a defense line around each of Wembling's three building sites. He had his ships sited to give maximum support. All that had been worked out months before. He placed his entire command on alert, doubled the guard on the beaches, and set up mobile reserves. He wished he had a few army officers to help out. He'd spent his entire adult life learning how to wage war in space, and now for the first time in his military career he was faced with the possibility of battle, and he was land-bound, and in danger of being embarrassed by hordes of untrained natives.

The night intelligence sheet arrived at dawn, virtually blank. Except for the fires there was nothing to report. Dillinger passed it across to Protz, who glanced at it and passed it back.

"Go down and see Wembling," Dillinger said. "Tell him to give his men the day off, and keep them in their quarters. I don't want to see one of them around. That goes for him, too."

"He'll howl."

"He'd better not howl to me. If we knew these natives better, maybe we could see this thing from their point-of-view. Somehow I just can't see them hitting us with an armed attack. It'd get a lot of them killed, and it wouldn't accomplish a thing. Surely they know that as well as we do. Now if you were a native, and you wanted to stop Wembling's work, what would you do?"

"I'd kill Wembling."

Dillinger slapped his desk disgustedly. "O.K. Give him an armed guard."

"What would you do?"

"I'd plant some kind of explosive at carefully chosen points in the hotels. If it didn't stop the project altogether, it'd throw an awful delay at Wembling's grand opening. You know—"

"That might be it," Protz said. "It makes more sense than an all-out attack. I'll put special guard details around the buildings."

Dillinger rose and went to the window. Dawn was touching Langri with its usual lavish beauty. The sea was calmly blue under the rising sun. Off the point . . .

Dillinger swore softly.

"What's the matter?" Protz said.

"Look." Dillinger pointed out to sea.

"I don't see anything."

"Where's the fishing boat?"

"It isn't there."

"Every day as long as we've been on this planet there's been a fishing boat working off the point. Get the recon planes out. Something is decidedly fishy."

Thirty minutes later they had their report. Every fishing boat on Langri was beached. The natives were taking the day off.

"They seem to be congregating in the largest villages," the intelligence officer said. "A7—that's Fornri's village, you know—has the biggest crowd. And then B9, D4, F12—all along the coast. There are fires all over the place."

Dillinger studied a photo map, and the officer circled the villages as he called them off. "At this point," Dillinger said, "there's just one thing we can do. We'll go over and have a little talk with Fornri."

"How many men do you want?" Protz asked.

"Just you and I. And a pilot."

They slanted down to a perfect landing in the soft sand of the beach. The pilot stayed with the plane, and Dillinger and Protz climbed the slope to the village, making their way through throngs of natives. Dillinger's embarrassment increased with each forward step. There was no sign of a sinister conspiracy. A holiday atmosphere prevailed, the gaily dressed natives laughing and singing around the fires—singing in Galactic, an accomplishment that never ceased to intrigue Dillinger. The natives respectfully made way for them. Otherwise, except for timid glances from the children, they were ignored.

They reached the first huts and paused, looking down the village street. Mouth-watering odors of a feast in preparation reminded Dillinger that he had missed breakfast. At the far end of the street, near the largest hut, native men and women stood quietly in line. Dillinger waited helplessly for some official acknowledgment of his presence.

Suddenly Fornri appeared before him, and accepted his hand. "We are honored," Fornri said, but his face, usually so blandly expressionless, revealed an emotion which Dillinger found difficult to interpret. Was he angry, or merely uneasy? "May I inquire as to the purpose of your visit?" he asked.

Dillinger looked at Protz, who shrugged and looked the other way. "I came to . . . to observe," Dillinger said lamely.

"In the past, you have not interfered in the lives of my people. Is that to be changed?"

"No. I am not here to interfere."

"Then your presence is not required here. This does not concern you."

"Everything that happens on Langri concerns me," Dillinger said. "I came to learn what is happening here. I intend to know."

Fornri withdrew abruptly. Dillinger watched him walk away, watched a group of young natives gather around him. Their manner was quiet, but urgent.

"Funny thing," Protz mused. "With any primitive society I've ever seen, the old men run things. Here on Langri, it's the young men. I'll bet there isn't a man in that crowd who's much over thirty."

Fornri returned. He was uneasy—there could be no doubt of that. He gazed earnestly at Dillinger's face before he spoke. "We know that you have been a friend to my people, and helped us when you could. It is the Mr. Wembling who is our enemy. If he knew, he would attempt to interfere."

"Mr. Wembling will not interfere," Dillinger said.

"Very well. We are holding an election."

Dillinger felt Protz's hand tighten on his arm. He repeated dumbly, "An election?"

Fornri spoke proudly. "We are electing delegates to a constitutional convention."

An idyllic setting. The forest clearing overlooking the sea. Women preparing a feast. Citizens waiting quietly for their turns in the grass voting hut. Democracy in action.

"When the constitution is approved," Fornri went on, "we shall elect a government. Then we shall apply for membership in the Galactic Federation of Independent Worlds."

"Is it legal?" Protz demanded.

"It is legal," Fornri said. "Our attorney has advised us. The main requirement is fifty per cent literacy. We have over ninety per cent literacy. We could have done it much sooner, you see, but we did not know that we needed only fifty per cent."

"You are to be congratulated," Dillinger said. "If your application for Federation membership is accepted, I suppose your government will force Wembling to leave Langri."

"We intend that Langri shall belong to us. It is the Plan."

Dillinger held out his hand. "I wish you every good fortune with your election, and with your application for Federation member-ship."

With a last glance at the line by the voting hut, they turned and walked slowly back to the plane. Protz whistled, and rubbed his hands together. "And that," he said, "will finish Wembling."

"At least we've solved the mystery of that unknown ship," Dillinger said. "It was their attorney, coming to advise them and help them draw up a constitution. As for this finishing Wembling, you're wrong. The Wemblings in this galaxy don't finish that easily. He's ready for this. You might almost say he's been expecting it."

"What can he do?"

"No court of justice would make him give up what he already has. The natives can keep him from grabbing more land, but what he's developed will be his. He acquired it in good faith, under a charter granted by the Federation. Maybe he'll get to connect up his sites and own a hundred mile stretch of coast. If he doesn't, he has enough space at each site to build a thundering big resort. These enormous golf courses he's been laying out—that land is developed. He'll get to keep it, and there'll be room there for another hundred hotels on each site if he wants to build them. He'll flood the sea with pleasure fishermen, and starve the natives."

Dillinger looked back at the village, and shook his head sadly. "Do you realize what a tremendous accomplishment that is? Ninety per cent literacy. How they must have worked! And they were beaten before they started. The poor devils."

V

The normal behavior of a forest trail, Dillinger thought, *would be to wander—around trees, away from thickets, generally following the path of least resistance. This trail did not wander. It might have been laid out by a surveyor, so straight did it run. It was an old trail, and a well-worn trail. Trees must have been cut down, but there were no traces of the stumps.*

Ahead of him, Fornri and a half dozen other young natives kept a steady, killing pace and did not look back. They had covered a good five miles, and there seemed to be no end to it. Dillinger was perspiring, and already tired.

Fornri had come to him at Hotel Langri. "We would like for you to come with us," he said. "You alone." And Dillinger had come.

Hotel Langri was all but deserted. At dawn tomorrow the 984th Squadron would head back into space, where it belonged. Wembling and his workmen had already left. Langri had been returned to the possession of its rightful owners.

It had been an absurdly simply thing, this Plan of the natives—absurdly simple and devastatingly effective. First there had been the application for Federation membership, which fortunately had arrived in Galaxia just as Dillinger's anonymous letters went off with a resounding explosion that overturned the government, caused a turmoil in the Colonial Bureau and Navy Department, and stirred up repercussions as far away as Langri, where a committee touched down briefly for a stormy investigation.

The application was acted upon immediately, and it received unanimous approval.

Wembling was undisturbed. His attorneys were on the job before the last vote was counted, and the native government received a court order to honor Wembling with firm title to the land he had already developed. This the Langri government did, and so complacently that Wembling slyly added several hundred acres to his claim without stirring up a ripple of protest.

Then came the masterstroke, which not even Wembling had foreseen.

Taxes.

Dillinger had been present when Fornri handed Wembling his first tax billing from the government of Langri. Wembling had screamed himself hoarse, and pounded his desk, and vowed he would fight it through every court in the galaxy, but he found the courts to be strangely out of sympathy with him.

If the elected representatives of the people of Langri wished to impose an annual property tax equal to ten times the property's assessed valuation, that was their legal right. It was Wembling's misfortune that he owned the only property on the planet which had an assessed valuation worth recording. Ten times the worth of a grass hut was a negligible value above zero. Ten times the worth of Wembling's hotels amounted to ruin.

The judges were in perfect agreement with Wembling that the government's action was unwise. It would discourage construction and industry and hold back the planet's development indefinitely. In time that would be perfectly obvious to the people of Langri, and then it would be their privilege to elect representatives who would write more lenient tax laws.

In the meantime, Wembling must pay the tax.

It left him a choice of not paying and being ruined, or paying and being much more severely ruined, and he chose not to pay. The government confiscated his property for nonpayment of taxes, and the Langri situation was resolved to the satisfaction of all but Wembling and his backers. Hotel Langri was to become a school and university for the native children. The offices of government would occupy one of the other hotels. The natives were undecided as to what to do with the third, but Dillinger was certain they would use it wisely.

As for Wembling, he was now an employee of the people of Langri. Even the natives admired the way he got things done, and there were islands, many islands, it turned out, far out in the sea where happy vacationers would not interfere with the natives' fishing grounds. Would Mr. Wembling, Fornri asked, like to build hotels on those islands and run them for the Government of Langri? Mr. Wembling would. Mr. Wembling did, in fact, wonder why he had not thought of that in the first place. He negotiated a contract with the natives' attorney, moved his men to the islands, and enthusiastically began planning a whole series of hotels.

Dillinger, following the natives along a forest path, felt serenely at peace with himself and the galaxy around him.

The path ended in an enormous clearing, carpeted with thick grass and flowers. Dillinger stopped to look around, saw nothing, and hurried to catch the natives.

On the opposite side of the clearing was another path, but this one ended abruptly at a rough pile of stones, a cairn, perhaps, jutting up from the forest floor. Beyond it, rusting, overgrown with vines, hidden by towering trees, lay an old survey ship.

"One of your people once came to live among us," Fornri said. "This was his ship."

The natives stood with hands clasped behind them, their heads bowed reverently. Dillinger waited, wondering what was expected of him. Finally he asked, "There was just one man?"

"Just one," Fornri said. "We have often thought that there may be those who wondered what happened to him. Perhaps you could tell them."

"Perhaps I could," Dillinger said. "I'll see."

He struggled through the undergrowth and circled the ship, looking for a name or an identification number. There was none. The air lock was closed. As Dillinger stood contemplating it, Fornri said, "You may enter if you like. We have placed his things there."

Dillinger walked up the wobbly ramp, and stumbled along a dark passageway. The dim light that filtered into the control room gave the objects there a ghostlike aspect. On a table by the control panel were small mementos, personal effects, books, piles of papers. Dillinger thoughtfully handled a rusted pocket knife, a rosary, a broken compass.

The first book he picked up was a diary. George F. O'Brien's diary. The entries, written in a precisely penciled hand, were too dim to read. He took the books and papers to the air lock, sat down on the ramp, and began to turn the pages.

There were detailed entries describing O'Brien's early days on the planet, more than a century before. Then the entries became less regular, the dates uncertain as O'Brien lost track of time. Dillinger came to the end, found a second volume, and continued reading.

Just another freebooter, he thought, kicking around on a strange planet, prospecting for metals, enjoying himself with a native harem. Surely it was not this man . . .

The change came subtly down through the years, as O'Brien came to identify himself with the natives, became one of them, and finally faced the future. There was an astute summary of Langri's potential as a resort planet, that might have been written by Wembling. There was a dire warning as to the probable fate of the natives. "If I live," O'Brien had written, "I do not think this will happen."

And if he should not live?

"Then the natives must be taught what to do. There must be a Plan. These things the natives must know."

Government and language. Interplanetary relations. History. Economics, commerce and money. Politics. Law and colonial procedure. Science.

"Not just one man!" Dillinger exclaimed to himself. "He couldn't have!"

The initial landing, probably by a survey ship. Steps to observe in capturing the crew. Negotiations, list of violations and penalties. Achievement of independent status. Steps to Federation membership. Steps to follow when independent status was violated.

"Not just one man!"

It was all there, laboriously written out by an uneducated man who had vision and wisdom and patience. By a great man. It was a brilliant prognostication, with nothing lacking but Wembling's name—and Dillinger had the impression that O'Brien had known more than a few Wemblings in his day. It was all there, everything that had happened, right up to the final master stroke, the ten-to-one tax rate on the hotels.

Dillinger closed the last notebook, carried the papers back to the control room and carefully rearranged things as he had found them. Some day Langri would have its own historians, who would sift through these papers and send the name of George F. O'Brien across the galaxy in dryly-written tomes read only by other historians. The man deserved a better fate.

But perhaps verbal tradition would keep his memory a living thing on Langri far into the future. Perhaps, even now, around the fires, there were legendary tales of what O'Brien had done and said. Or perhaps not. It was difficult for an outsider to probe into such matters, especially if he were a naval officer. That sort of thing required a specialist.

Dillinger took a last look at the humble relics, took a step backwards, and came to a full salute.

He left the ship, carefully closing the air lock behind him. Dusk had settled quickly there, deep in the forest, but the natives were waiting, still in attitudes of reverence.

"I suppose you've looked those things over," Dillinger said.

Fornri seemed startled. "No . . ."

"I see. Well, I found out—as much as there is to find out about him. If he has any family surviving, I'll see that they know what happened to him."

"Thank you," Fornri said.

"Were there no others who came and lived among you?"

"He was the only one."

Dillinger nodded. "O'Brien was a truly great man. I wonder if you fully realize that. I suppose in time you'll have O'Brien villages and O'Brien streets and O'Brien buildings, and all that sort of thing, but he deserves a really important monument. Perhaps—a planet can be named after a man, you know. You should have named your planet O'Brien."

"O'Brien?" Fornri said. He looked blankly at the others, turned back to Dillinger. "O'Brien? Who is O'Brien?"

Gadget vs. Trend

Christopher Anvil

Boston, Sept. 2, 1976. Dr. R. Milton Schummer, Professor of Sociology at Wellsford College, spoke out against "creeping conformism" to an audience of twelve hundred in Swarton Hall last night.

Professor Schummer charged that America, once the land of the free, is now "the abode of the stereotyped mass-man, shaped from infancy by the moron-molding influences of television, mass-circulation newspapers and magazines, and the pervasive influence of advertising manifest in all these media. The result is the mass-production American with interchangeable parts and built-in taped programme."

What this country needs, said Dr. Schummer, is "freedom to differ, freedom to be eccentric." But, he concluded, "the momentum is too great. The trend, like the tide, cannot be reversed by human efforts. In two hundred years, this nation has gone from individualism to conformism, from independence to interdependence, from federalism to fusionism, and the end is not yet. One shrinks at the thought of what the next one hundred years may bring."

Rutland, Vt., March 16, 1977. Dr. J. Paul Hughes, grandson of the late inventor, Everett Hughes, revealed today a device which his grandfather kept under wraps because of its "supposedly dangerous side-effects." Dubbed by Dr. Hughes a "privacy shield," the device works by the "exclusion of quasi-electrons," In the words of Dr. Hughes:

"My grandfather was an eccentric experimenter. Surprisingly often, though, his wild stabs would strike some form of pay dirt, in a commercial sense. In this present instance, we have a device unexplainable by any sound scientific theory, but which may be commercially quite useful. When properly set up, and connected to a suitable electrical outlet, the device effectively soundproofs material surfaces, such as walls, doors, floors, and the like, and thus may be quite helpful in present-day crowded living conditions."

Dr. Hughes explained that the device was supposed to operate by "the exclusion of 'quasi-electrons,' which my grandfather thought governed the transmission of sound through solid bodies, and performed various other esoteric functions. But we needn't take this too seriously."

New York, May 12, 1977. Formation of Hughes QuietWall Corporation was announced here today.

President of the new firm is J. Paul Hughes, grandson of the late inventor, Everett Hughes.

New York, Sept. 18, 1977. One of the hottest stocks on the market today is Hughes QuietWall. With demand booming, and the original president of the firm kicked upstairs to make room for the crack management expert, Myron L. Sams, the corporation has tapped a gold mine.

Said a company spokesman: "The biggest need in this country today is privacy. We live practically in each other's pockets, and if we can't do anything else, at least QuietWall can soundproof the pockets."

The QuietWall units, which retail for $289.95 for the basic room unit, are said to offer dealer, distributor, and manufacturer a generous profit. And no one can say that $289.95 is not a reasonable price to pay to keep out the noise of other people's TV, record players, quarrels and squalling babies.

Detroit, December 23, 1977. Santa left an early present for the auto industry here today.

A test driver trying out a car equipped with a Hughes QuietWall unit went into a skid on the icy test track, rolled over three times, and got out shaken but unhurt. The car itself, a light supercompact, was found to be almost totally undamaged.

Tests with sledgehammers revealed the astonishing fact that with the unit turned on, the car would not dent, and the glass could not be broken. The charge filler cap could not be unscrewed. The hood could not be raised. And neither windows nor doors could be opened till the unit was snapped off. With the unit off, the car was perfectly ordinary.

This is the first known trial of a QuietWall unit in a motor vehicle.

Standard house and apartment installations use a specially designed basic unit to soundproof floor and walls, and small additional units to soundproof doors and windows. This installation tested today apparently lacked such refinements.

December 26, 1977. J. Paul Hughes, chairman of the board of directors of the QuietWall Corp., stated to reporters today that his firm has no intention to market the Hughes QuietWall unit for use in motor cars.

Hughes denied the Detroit report of a QuietWall-equipped test car that rolled without damage, calling it "impossible."

Hartford, January 8, 1978. Regardless of denials from the Quiet Wall Corporation, nationwide experiments are being conducted into the use of the corporation's sound-deadening units as a safety device in cars. Numerous letters, telegrams, and phone calls are being received at the head offices of some of the nation's leading insurance companies here.

Hartford, January 9, 1978. Tests carried out by executives of the New Standard Insurance Group indicate that the original Detroit reports were perfectly accurate.

Cars equipped with the QuietWall units cannot be dented,

shattered, scratched, or injured in any way by ordinary tools.

Austin J. Ramm, Executive Secretary of New Standard Group stated to reporters:

"It's the damndest thing I ever saw.

"We've had so many communications, from people all over the country who claim to have connected QuietWall units to their cars that we decided to try it out ourselves.

"We tried rocks, hammers, and so forth, on the test vehicle. When these didn't have any effect, I tried a quarter-inch electric drill and Steve Willoughby—he's our president—took a crack at the center of the windshield with a railroad pickaxe. The pickaxe bounced. My drill just slid around over the surface and wouldn't bite in.

"We have quite a few other things we want to try.

"But we've seen enough to know there definitely is truth in the reports."

New York, January 10, 1978. Myron L. Sams, president of the Hughes QuietWall Corporation, announced today that a special automotive attachment is being put on sale throughout the country. Mr. Sams warns that improper installation may, among other things, seize up all or part of the operating machinery of the car. He urges that company representatives be allowed to carry out the installation.

Dallas, January 12, 1978. In a chase lasting an hour, a gang of bank robbers got away this afternoon with $869,000 in cash and negotiable securities.

Despite a hail of bullets, the escape car was not damaged. An attempt to halt it at a roadblock failed, as the car crashed through without injury.

There is speculation here that the car was equipped with one of the Hughes QuietWall units that went on sale a few days ago.

Las Vegas, January 19, 1978. A gang of eight to ten criminals held up the Silver Dollar Club tonight, escaping with over a quarter of a million dollars.

It was one of the most bizarre robberies in the city's history.

The criminals entered the club in golf carts fitted with light aluminum- and transparent-plastic covers, and opened a gun battle with club employees. A short fight disclosed that it was impossible to even dent the light shielding on the golf carts. Using the club's patrons and employees as hostages, the gunmen received the cash they demanded, rolled across the sidewalk and up a ramp into the rear of a waiting truck, which drove out of town, smashing through a hastily erected roadblock.

As police gave chase, the truck proved impossible to damage. In a violent exchange of gunfire, no one was injured, as the police car's were equipped with newly installed QuietWall units, and it was evident that the truck was also so equipped.

Well outside of town, the truck reached a second roadblock. The robbers attempted to smash through the seemingly flimsy barrier, but were brought to a sudden stop when the roadblock, fitted with a QuietWall unit, failed to give way.

The truck, and the golf carts within, were found to be undamaged. The bandits are now undergoing treatment for concussion and severe whiplash injuries.

The $250,000.00 has been returned to the Silver Dollar Club, and Las Vegas is comparatively quiet once more.

New York, January 23, 1978. In a hastily called news conference, J. Paul Hughes, chairman of the board of Hughes QuietWall Corporation, announced that he is calling upon the Federal Government to step in and suspend the activities of the corporation.

Pointing out that he has tried without success to suspend the company's operations on his own authority, Dr. Hughes stated that as a scientist he must warn the public against a dangerous technological development, "the menacing potentialities of which I have only recently come to appreciate."

No response has as yet been received from Washington.

New York, January 24, 1978. President Myron L. Sams today acknowledged the truth of reports that a bitter internal struggle is being waged for control of the Hughes QuietWall Corporation.

Spring Corners, Iowa, January 26, 1978. Oscar B. Nelde, a farmer on the outskirts of town, has erected a barricade that has backed up traffic on the new Cross-State Highway for twenty miles in both directions.

Mr. Nelde recently lost a suit for additional damages when the highway cut his farm into two unequal parts, the smaller one containing his house and farm buildings, the larger part containing his fields.

The barricade is made of oil drums, saw horses, and barbed wire. The oil drums and saw horses cannot be moved, and act as if welded to the frozen earth. The barbed wire is weirdly stiff and immovable. The barricade is set up in a double row of these immovable obstacles, spaced to form a twenty-foot-wide lane connecting the two separated parts of Mr. Nelde's farm.

Mr. Nelde's manure spreader was seen crossing the road early today.

Heavy road machinery has failed to budge the obstacles. The experts are stumped. However, the local QuietWall dealer recalls selling Mr. Nelde a quantity of small units recently and adds, "but no more than a lot of other farmers have been buying lately."

It may be worth mentioning that Mr. Nelde's claim is one of many that have been advanced locally.

New York, January 27, 1978. The Hughes QuietWall Corporation was today reorganized as QuietWall, Incorporated, with Myron L. Sams holding the positions of president and chairman of the board of directors. J. Paul Hughes, grandson of Everett Hughes, continues as a director.

Spring Corners, Iowa, January 28, 1978. Traffic is flowing once again on the Cross-State Highway.

This morning a U.S. Army truck-mounted earth auger moved up the highway and drilled a number of holes six feet in diameter, enabling large chunks of earth to be carefully loosened and both sections of the barricade to be lifted out as units. The wire, oil drums, saw horses, and big chunks of earth, which remained rigid when lifted out, are being removed to the U.S. Army Research and Development Laboratories for study. No QuietWall units have been found, and it is assumed that they are imbedded, along with their power source, inside the masses of earth.

The sheriff, the police chief of Spring Corners, and state and federal law enforcement agents are attempting to arrest Oscar B. Nelde, owner of the farm adjacent to the highway.

This has proved impossible, as Mr. Nelde's house and buildings are equipped with a number of QuietWall units controlled from within.

Boston, February 1, 1978. Dr. B. Milton Schummer, Professor of Sociology at Wellsford College, and a severe critic of "creeping conformism," said tonight, when questioned by reporters, that some of the effects of the QuietWall units constitute a hopeful sign in the long struggle of the individual against the State and against the forces of conformity. However, Dr. Schummer does not believe that "a mere technological gadget can affect these great movements of sociological trends."

Spring Corners, Iowa, February 2, 1978. A barbed-wire fence four feet high, fastened to crisscrossed railroad rails, now blocks the Cross-State Highway near the farm home of Leroy Weaver, a farmer whose property was cut in half by the highway, and who has often stated that he has received inadequate compensation.

It has proved impossible for highway equipment on the scene to budge either wire or rails.

Mr. Weaver cannot be reached for comment, as his house and buildings are equipped with QuietWall units, and neither the sheriff nor federal officials have been able to effect entry on to the premises.

Washington, D.C., February 3, 1978. The Bureau of Standards reports that tests on QuietWall units show them to be essentially "stasis devices." That is to say, they prevent change in whatever material surface they are applied to. Thus, sound does not pass, because the protected material is practically noncompressible, and is not affected by the alternate waves of compression and rarefaction in the adjacent medium.

Many potential applications are suggested by Bureau of Standards spokesmen who report, for instance, that thin slices of apples and pears placed directly inside the surface field of the QuietWall device were found totally unchanged when the field was switched off, after test periods of more than three weeks.

New York, February 3, 1978. Myron L. Sams, president of QuietWall, Incorporated, reports record sales, rising day by day to new peaks. QuietWall, Inc., is now operating factories in seven states, Great Britain, the Netherlands, and West Germany.

Spring Corners, Iowa, February 4, 1978. A U.S. Army truck-mounted earth auger has again removed a fence across the Cross-State Highway here. But the giant auger itself has now been immobilized, apparently by one or more concealed stasis (QuietWall) devices.

As the earth auger weighs upwards of thirty tons, and all the wheels of truck and trailer appear to be locked, moving it presents no small problem.

Los Angeles, February 5, 1978. Police here report the capture of a den of dope fiends and unsavory characters of all descriptions, after a forty-hour struggle.

The hideout, known as the "Smoky Needle Club," was equipped with sixteen stasis devices manufactured by QuietWall, Inc., and had an auxiliary electrical supply line run in through a drain pipe from the building next door. Only when the electrical current to the entire neighborhood was cut off were the police able to force their way in.

New York, February 5, 1978. Myron L. Sams, president of QuietWall, Inc., announced today a general price cut, due to improved design and volume production economies, on all QuietWall products.

In future, basic QuietWall room units will sell for $229.95 instead of $289.95. Special small stasis units, suitable for firming fence posts, reinforcing walls, and providing barred-door household security will retail for as low as $19.95. It is rumored that this price, with improved production methods, still provides an ample profit for all concerned, so that prices may be cut in some areas during special sales events.

Spring Corners, Iowa, February 6, 1978. A flying crane today lifted the immobilized earth auger from the eastbound lanes of Cross-State Highway.

A total of fourteen small stasis units have thus far been removed from the auger, its truck and trailer, following its removal from the highway by air. Difficulties were compounded by the fact that each stasis unit apparently "freezes" the preceding units applied within its range. The de-stasis experts must not only locate the units. They must remove them in the right order, and some are very cleverly hidden.

Seaton Bridge, Iowa, February 9, 1978. The Cross-State Highway has again been blocked, this time by a wall of cow manure eighty-three feet long, four feet wide at the base, and two and a half feet high, apparently stabilized by imbedded stasis units and as hard as cement. National Guard units are now patrolling the Seaton Bridge section of road on either side of the block.

New York, February 10, 1978. Representatives of QuietWall, Inc., report that study of stasis devices removed from the auger at Spring Center, Iowa, reveals that they are "not devices of QW manufacture, but crude, cheap bootleg imitations. Nevertheless, they work."

Spring Center, Iowa, February 12, 1978. The Cross-State Highway, already cut at Seaton Bridge, is now blocked in three places by walls of snow piled up during last night's storm by farmers' bulldozers, and stabilized by stasis devices. Newsmen who visited the scene report that the huge mounds look like snow, but feel like concrete. Picks and shovels do not dent them, and flame throwers fail to melt them.

New York, February 15, 1978. Dr. J. Paul Hughes, a director of QuietWall, Inc., tonight reiterated his plea for a government ban on stasis devices. He recalled the warning of his inventor grandfather

Everett Hughes, and stated that he intends to spend the rest of his life "trying to undo the damage the device has caused."

New York, February 16, 1978. Myron L. Sams, president of QuietWall, Inc., announced today that a fruit fly had been kept in stasis for twenty-one days without suffering visible harm. QW's research scientists, he said, are now working with the problem of keeping small animals in stasis. If successful, Sams said, the experiment may open the door to "one-way timetravel," and enable persons suffering from serious diseases to wait, free from pain, until such time as a satisfactory cure has been found.

Bonn, February 17, 1978. Savage East German accusations against the West today buttressed the rumors that "stasis-unit enclaves" are springing up like toadstools throughout East Germany.

Similar reports are coming in from Hungary, while Poland reports a number of "stasis-frozen" Soviet tanks.

Havana, February 18, 1978. In a frenzied harangue tonight, "Che" Garcia, First Secretary of the Cuban Communist Party, announced that the government is erecting "stasis walls" all around the island, and that "stasis blockhouses" now being built will resist "even the Yankees' worst hydrogen weapons." In a torrent of vitriolic abuse, however, Mr. Garcia threatened that "any further roadblocks and centers of degenerate individualism that spring up will be eradicated from the face of the soil of the motherland by blood, iron, sweat, and the forces of monolithic socialism."

There have been rumors for some time of dissatisfaction with the present regime.

Mr. Garcia charged that the C.I.A. had flagrantly invaded Cuban air space by dropping "millions of little vicious stasis units, complete with battery packs of fantastic power," all over the island, from planes which could not be shot down because they were protected by "still more of these filthy sabotage devices."

Des Moines, February 21, 1978. The Iowa state government following the unsuccessful siege of four farm homes near the Cross-

State Highway today announced that it is opening new hearings on landowners' compensation for land taken for highway-construction purposes.

The governor appealed to owners of property adjoining the highway to be patient, bring their complaints to the capital, and meanwhile open the highway to traffic.

Staunton, Vt., February 23, 1978. Hiram Smith, a retired high school science teacher whose family has lived on the same farm since before the time of the Revolution, was ordered last fall to leave his family home.

A dam is to be built nearby, and Mr. Smith's home will be among those inundated.

At the time of the order, Mr. Smith, who lives on the farm with his fourteen-year-old grandson, stated that he would not leave "until carried out dead or helpless."

This morning, the sheriff tried to carry out the eviction order, and was stopped by a warning shot fired from the Smith house. The warning shot was followed by the flight of a small, battery-powered model plane, apparently radio-controlled, which alighted about two thousand yards from the Smith home, near an old apple orchard.

Mr. Smith called to the sheriff to get out of his car and lie down, if the car was not stasis-equipped, and in any case to look away from the apple orchard.

There was a brilliant flash, a shock, and a roar which the sheriff likened to the explosion of "a hundred tons of TNT." When he looked at the orchard, it was obscured by a pink glow and boiling clouds, apparently of steam from vaporized snow.

Mr. Smith called out to the sheriff to get off the property, or the next "wink bomb" would be aimed at him.

No one has been out to the Smith property since the sheriff's departure.

New York, February 25, 1978. Mr. Myron L. Sams, president of QuietWall, Inc., announced today that "there is definitely no connection between the Staunton explosion and the QW Corp. stasis unit.

The stasis unit is a strictly defensive device and cannot be used for offensive purposes."

New York, February 25, 1978. Dr. J. Paul Hughes tonight asserted that the "wink bomb" exploded at Staunton yesterday, and now known to have left a radioactive crater, "probably incorporated a stasis unit." The unit was probably "connected to a light metallic container holding a small quantity of radioactive material. It need not necessarily be the radioactive material we are accustomed to think of as suitable for fission bombs. It need not be the usual amount of such material. When the stasis unit was activated by a radio signal or timing device, high-energy particles thrown off by the radioactive material would be unable to pass out through the container, now in stasis, and equivalent to a very hard, dense, impenetrable, nearly ideal boundary surface. The high-energy particles would bounce back into the interior, bombarding the radioactive material. As the population of high-energy particles within the enclosing stasis field builds up, the radioactive material, regardless of its quantity, reaches the critical point. Precisely what will happen depends on the radioactive material used, the size of the sample, and time length of the 'wink'— that is, the length of time the stasis field is left on."

Dr. Hughes added that "this is a definite, new, destructive use of the stasis field, which Mr. Myron Sams assures us is perfectly harmless."

Montpelier, Vt., February 26, 1978. The governor today announced temporary suspension of the Staunton Dam Project, while an investigation is carried out into numerous landowners' complaints.

Moscow, February 28, 1978. A "certain number" of "isolated cells" of "stasis-controlled character" are admitted to have sprung up within the Soviet Union. Those that are out of the way are said to be left alone, on the theory that the people have to come out sometime. Those in important localities are being reduced by the Red Army, using tear gas, sick gas, toothache gas, flashing searchlights, "war of nerves" tactics, and, in some cases, digging out the "cell" and carrying it off wholesale. It is widely accepted that there is nowhere near the amount of trouble here as in the satellite countries, where the problem is mounting to huge proportions.

Spring Corners, Iowa, May 16, 1978. The extensive Cross-State Highway claims having been settled all around, traffic is once again flowing along the highway. A new and surprising feature is the sight of farm machinery disappearing into tunnels constructed under the road to allow the farmers to pass from one side to the other.

Staunton, Vt., July 4, 1978. There was a big celebration here today as the governor and a committee of legislators announced that the big Staunton Dam Project has been abandoned, and a number of smaller dams will be built according to an alternative plan put forth earlier.

Bonn, August 16, 1978. Reports reaching officials here indicate that the East German government, the Hungarian government, and also to a considerable extent the Polish government, are having increasing difficulties as more and more of the "stasis-unit enclaves" join up, leaving the governments on the outside looking in. Where this will end is hard to guess.

Washington, September 30, 1978. The Treasury Department sent out a special "task force" of about one hundred and eighty men this morning. Their job is to crack open the mushrooming Anti-Tax League, whose membership is now said to number about one million enthusiastic businessmen. League members often give Treasury agents an exceedingly rough time, using record books and files frozen shut with stasis units, office buildings stasis-locked against summons servers, stasis-equipped cars which come out of stasis-equipped garages connected with stasis-locked office buildings, to drive to stasis-equipped homes where it is physically impossible for summons servers to enter the grounds.

Princeton, N.J., October 5, 1978. A conference of leading scientists, which gathered here today to exchange views on the nature of the stasis unit, is reported in violent disagreement. One cause of the disagreement is the reported "selective action" of the stasis unit which permits ordinary light to pass through transparent bodies, but blocks the passage of certain other electromagnetic radiations.

Wild disorders broke out this afternoon during a lecture by Dr. J. Paul Hughes, on the "Quasi-Electron Theory of Wave Propagation." The lecture was accompanied by demonstration of the original Everett Hughes device, powered by an old-fashioned generator driven by the inventor's original steam engine. As the engine gathered speed, Dr. Hughes was able to demonstrate the presence of a nine-inch sphere of completely reflective material in the supposedly empty focus of the apparatus. This sphere, Dr. Hughes asserted, was the surface of a space totally evacuated of quasi-electrons, which he identified as "units of time."

It was at this point that the disturbance broke out.

Despite the disorder, Dr. Hughes went on to explain the limiting value of the velocity of light in terms of the quasi-electron theory, but was interrupted when the vibration of the steam engine began to shake down the ceiling.

There is a rumor here that the conference may recess at once without issuing a report.

Washington, D.C., August 16, 1979. Usually reliable sources report that the United States has developed a "missile screen" capable of destroying enemy missiles in flight and theoretically capable of creating a wall around the nation through which no enemy projectile of any type could pass. This device is said to be based on the original Everett Hughes stasis unit, which creates a perfectly rigid barrier of variable size and shape, which can be projected very rapidly by turning on an electric current.

Other military uses for stasis devices include protection of missile sites, storage of food and munitions, impenetrizing of armor plate, portable "turtle-shields" for infantry, and quick-conversion units designed to turn any ordinary house or shed into a bombardment-proof strongpoint.

Veteran observers of the military scene say that the stasis unit completely reverses the advantage until recently held by offensive, as opposed to defensive weapons. This traditionally alternating advantage, supposed to have passed permanently with the development of nuclear explosives, has now made one more pendulum swing. Now, in place of the "absolute weapon," we have the "absolute defense." Properly set up, hydrogen explosions do not dent it.

But if the nation is not to disintegrate within as it becomes impregnable without, officials say we must find some effective way to deal with stasis-protected cults, gangsters, anti-tax enthusiasts, seceding rural districts, space-grabbers, and proprietors of dens. Latest problem is the traveling roadblock, set up by chiselers who select a busy highway, collect "toll" from motorists who must pay or end up in a traffic jam, then move on quickly before police have time to react, and stop again in some new location to do the same thing all over. There must be an answer to all these things, but the answer has yet to be found.

Boston, September 2, 1979. Dr. B. Milton Schummer, Professor of Sociology at Wellsford College, spoke out against "galloping individualism" to an audience of six hundred in Swarton Hall last night.

Professor Schummer charged that America, once the land of cooperative endeavor, is now "a seething hotbed of rampant individualists, protesters, quick-rich artists, and minute-men of all kinds, each over-reacting violently from a former condition which may have seemed like excessive conformism at the time, but now in the perspective of events appears as a desirable cohesiveness amid unity of direction. The result today is the fractionating American with synthetic rough edges and built-in bellicose sectionalism."

What this country needs, said Dr. Schummer, is "coordination of aims, unity of purpose, and restraint of difference." But, he concluded, "the reaction is too violent. The trend, like the tide, cannot be reversed by human efforts. In three years, this nation has gone from cohesion to fractionation, from interdependence to chaos, from federalism to splinterism, and the end is not yet. One shrinks at the thought of what the next hundred years may bring."

The Ungoverned

Vernor Vinge

Al's Protection Racket operated out of Manhattan, Kansas. Despite the name, it was a small, insurance-oriented police service with about 20,000 customers, all within 100 kilometers of the main ship. But apparently "Al" was some kind of humorist: His ads had a gangster motif with his cops dressed like 20th century hoodlums. Wil Brierson guessed that it was all part of the nostalgia thing. Even the Michigan State Police—Wil's outfit—capitalized on the public's feeling of trust for old names, old traditions.

Even so, there's something more dignified about a company with a name like "Michigan State Police," thought Brierson as he brought his flier down on the pad next to Al's HQ. He stepped out of the cockpit into an eerie morning silence: It was close to sunrise, yet the sky remained dark, the air humid. Thunderheads marched around half the horizon. A constant flicker of lightning chased back and forth within those clouds, yet there was not the faintest sound of thunder. He had seen a tornado killer on his way in, a lone eagle in the far sky. The weather was almost as ominous as the plea East Lansing HQ had received from Al's just four hours earlier.

A spindly figure came bouncing out of the shadows. "Am I glad to see you! The name's Alvin Swensen. I'm the proprietor." He shook Wil's hand enthusiastically. "I was afraid you might wait till the front passed through." Swensen was dressed in baggy pants and a padded jacket that would have made Frank Nitti proud. The local police chief urged the other officer up the steps. No one else was outside; the place seemed just as deserted as one might expect a rural police station to be early on a weekday morning. Where was the emergency?

Inside, a clerk (cop?) dressed very much like Al sat before a comm console. Swensen grinned at the other. "It's the MSP, all right. They're really coming, Jim. They're really coming! Just come down the hall, Lieutenant. I got my office back there. We should clear out real soon, but for the moment, I think it's safe."

Wil nodded, more puzzled than informed. At the far end of the hall, light spilled from a half-open door. The frosted glass surface was stenciled with the words "Big Al." A faint smell of mildew hung over the aging carpet and the wood floor beneath settled perceptibly under Wil's 90 kilo tread. Brierson almost smiled: maybe Al wasn't so crazy. The gangster motif excused absolutely slovenly maintenance. Few customers would trust a normal police organization that kept its buildings like this.

Big Al urged Brierson into the light and waved him to an over-stuffed chair. Though tall and angular, Swensen looked more like a school teacher than a cop—or a gangster. His reddish-blond hair stood out raggedly from his head, as though he had been pulling at it, or had just been wakened. From the man's fidgety pacing about the room, Wil guessed the first possibility more likely. Swensen seemed about at the end of his rope, and Wil's arrival was some kind of reprieve. He glanced at Wil's name plate and his grin spread even further. "W. W. Brierson. I've heard of you. I knew the Michigan State Police wouldn't let me down; they've sent their best."

Wil smiled in return, hoping his embarrassment didn't show. Part of his present fame was a company hype that he had come to loathe. "Thank you, uh, Big Al. We feel a special obligation to small police companies that serve no-right-to-bear-arms customers. But you're going to have to tell me more. Why so secretive?"

Al waved his hands. "I'm afraid of blabbermouths. I couldn't take a chance on the enemy learning I was bringing you into it until you were on the scene and in action."

Strange that he says "enemy," and not "crooks" or "bastards" or "*hustlers.*" "But even a large gang might be scared off knowing—"

"Look, I'm not talking about some punk gang. I'm talking about the Republic of New Mexico. Invading us." He dropped into his chair and continued more calmly. It was almost as if passing the information on had taken the burden off him. "You're shocked?"

Brierson nodded dumbly.

"Me, too. Or I would have been up till a month ago. The Republic has always had plenty of internal troubles. And even though they claim all lands south of the Arkansas River, they have no settlements within hundreds of kilometers of here. Even now I think this is a bit of adventurism that can be squelched by an application of point force." He glanced at his watch. "Look, no matter how important speed is, we've got to do some coordinating. How many attack patrols are coming in after you?"

He saw the look on Brierson's face. "What? Only one? Damn. Well, I suppose it's my fault, being secret like, but—"

Wil cleared his throat. "Big Al, there's only me. I'm the only agent MSP sent."

The other's face seemed to collapse, the relief changing to despair, then to a weak rage. "G-God d-damn you to hell, Brierson. I may lose everything I've built here, and the people who trusted me may lose everything they own. But I swear I'm going to sue your Michigan State Police into oblivion. Fifteen years I've paid you guys premiums and never a claim. And now when I need max firepower, they send me one asshole with a 10-millimeter popgun."

Brierson stood, his nearly two-meter bulk towering over the other. He reached out a bearlike hand to Al's shoulder. The gesture was a strange cross between reassurance and intimidation. Wil's voice was soft but steady. "The Michigan State Police hasn't let you down, Mr. Swensen. You paid for protection against wholesale violence—and we intend to provide that protection. MSP has *never* defaulted on a contract." His grip on Alvin Swensen's shoulder tightened with these last words. The two eyed each other for a moment. Then Big Al nodded weakly, and the other sat down.

"You're right. I'm sorry. I'm paying for the results, not the methods. But I know what we're up against and I'm damned scared."

"And that's one reason why I'm here, Al: to find out exactly what we're up against before we jump in with our guns blazing and our pants down. What are you expecting?"

Al leaned back in the softly creaking chair. He looked out through the window into the dark silence of the morning, and for a moment seemed to relax. However improbably, someone else was going to take on his problems. "They started about three years ago. It seemed innocent enough, and it was certainly legal." Though the Republic of New Mexico claimed the lands from the Colorado on the west to the Mississippi on the east, and north to the Arkansas, in fact, most of their settlements were along the Gulf Coast and Rio Grande. For most of a century, Oklahoma and northern Texas had been uninhabited. The "border" along the Arkansas River had been of no real concern to the Republic, which had plenty of problems with its Water Wars on the Colorado, and of even less concern to the farmers at the southern edge of the ungoverned lands. During the last 10 years, immigration from the Republic toward the more prosperous north had been steadily increasing. Few of the southerners stayed in the Manhattan area: most jobs were farther north. But during these last three years, wealthy New Mexicans had moved into the area, men willing to pay almost any price for farmland.

"It's clear now that these people were stooges for the Republic government. They paid more money than they could reasonably recoup from farming, and the purchases started right after the election of their latest president. You know—Hastings Whatever-his-name-is. Anyway, it made a pleasant boom time for a lot of us. If some wealthy New Mexicans wanted isolated estates in the ungoverned lands, that was certainly their business. All the wealth in New Mexico couldn't buy one tenth of Kansas, anyway." At first, the settlers had been model neighbors. They even signed up with Al's Protection Racket and Midwest Jurisprudence. But as the months passed, it became obvious that they were neither farmers nor leisured rich. As near as the locals could figure out, they were some kind of labor contractors. An unending stream of trucks brought raggedly dressed men and women from the cities of the south: Galveston, Corpus Christi, even from the capital, Albuquerque. These folk were housed in barracks the owners had built on the farms. Anyone could see, looking in from above, that the newcomers spent long hours working in the fields.

Those farms produced on a scale that surprised the locals, and though it was still not clear that it was a profitable operation, there was a ripple of interest in the Grange journals; might manual labor hold an economic edge over the automatic equipment rentals? Soon the workers were hiring out to local farmers. "Those people work harder than any reasonable person, and they work dirt cheap. Every night, their contract bosses would truck 'em back to the barracks, so our farmers had scarcely more overhead than they would with automatics. Overall, the NMs underbid the equipment rental people by five percent or so."

Wil began to see where all this was leading. Someone in the Republic seemed to understand Midwest Jurisprudence. "Hmm, you know, Al, if I were one of those laborers, I wouldn't hang around in farm country. There are labor services up north that can get an apprentice butler more money than some rookie cops make. Rich people will always want servants, and nowadays the pay is tremendous."

Big Al nodded. "We've got rich folks, too. When they saw what these newcomers would work for, they started drooling. And that's when things began to get sticky." At first, the NM laborers could scarcely understand what they were being offered. They insisted that they were required to work when and where they were told. A few, a very few at first, took the job offers. "They were really scared, those first ones. Over and over, they wanted assurances that they would be allowed to return to their families at the end of the work day. They seemed to think the deal was some kidnap plot rather than an offer of employment. Then it was like an explosion: they couldn't wait to drop the farm jobs. They wanted to bring their families with them."

"And that's when your new neighbors closed up the camps?"

"You got it, pal. They won't let the families out. And we know they are confiscating the money the workers bring in."

"Did they claim their people were on long-term contracts?"

"Hell, no. It may be legal under Justice, Inc., but indentured servitude isn't under Midwest—and that's who they signed with. I see now that even that was deliberate.

"It finally hit the fan yesterday. The Red Cross flew a guy out from Topeka with a writ from a Midwest judge: He was to enter each of the settlements and explain to those poor folks how they stood with the law. I went along with a couple of my boys. They refused to let us in and punched out the Red Cross fellow when he got insistent.

"Their chief thug—fellow named Strong—gave me a signed policy cancellation, and told me that from now on they would handle all their own police and justice needs. We were then escorted off the property—at gunpoint."

"So they've gone armadillo. That's no problem. But the workers are still presumptively customers of yours?"

"Not just presumptively. Before this blew up, a lot of them had signed individual contracts with me and Midwest. The whole thing is a setup, but I'm *stuck*."

Wil nodded. "Right. Your only choice was to call in someone with firepower, namely my company."

Big Al leaned forward, his indignation retreating before fear. "Of course. But there's more, Lieutenant. Those workers—those slaves— were part of the trap that was set for us. But most of them are brave, honest people. They know what's happening, and they aren't any happier about it than I am. Last night, after we got our butts kicked, three of them escaped. They walked fifteen kilometers into Manhattan to see me, to beg me *not* to intervene. To beg me not to honor the contract.

"And they told me why: For a hundred kilometer stretch of their truck ride up here, they weren't allowed to see the country they were going through. But they heard plenty. And one of them managed to work a peephole in the side of the truck. He saw armored vehicles and attack aircraft under heavy camouflage just south of the Arkansas. The damn New Mexicans have taken part of their Texas garrison force and holed it up less than ten minutes flying time from Manhattan. And they're ready to move."

It was possible. The Water Wars with Aztlán had been winding down these last few years. The New Mexicans should have equipment reserves, even counting what they needed to keep the Gulf Coast cities in line. Wil got up and walked to the window. Dawn was lighting the sky above the far cloud banks. There was green in the rolling land that stretched away from the police post. Suddenly he felt very exposed here: Death could come out of that sky with precious little warning. W. W. Brierson was no student of history, but he was an old-time movie freak, and he had seen plenty of war stories. Assuming the aggressor had to satisfy some kind of public or world opinion, there had to be a provocation, an excuse for the massive violence that would masquerade as self-defense. The New Mexicans had cleverly created a situation in which Wil Brierson—or someone like him—would be contractually obligated to use force against their settlements.

"So. If we hold off on enforcement, how long do you think the invasion would be postponed?" It hurt to suggest bending a contract like that, but there was precedent: In hostage cases, you often used time as a weapon.

"It wouldn't slow 'em up a second. One way or another they're moving on us. I figure if we don't do anything, they'll use my 'raid' yesterday as their excuse. The only thing I can see is for MSP to put everything it can spare on the line when those bastards come across. That sort of massive resistance might be enough to scare 'em back."

Brierson turned from the window to look at Big Al. He understood now the shaking fear in the other. It had taken guts for the other to wait here through the night. But now it was W. W. Brierson's baby. "Okay, Big Al. With your permission, I'll take charge."

"You got it, Lieutenant!" Al was out of his chair, a smile splitting his face.

Wil was already starting for the door. "The first thing to do is get away from this particular ground zero. How many in the building?"

"Just two besides me."

"Round 'em up and bring them to the front room. If you have any firearms, bring them, too."

Wil was pulling his comm equipment out of the gunship when the other three came out the front door of Al's HQ and started toward him. He waved them back. "If they play as rough as you think, they'll grab for air superiority first thing. What kind of ground vehicles do you have?"

"Couple of cars. A dozen motorbikes. Jim, open up the garage."
The zoot-suited trooper hustled off. Will looked with some curiosity
at the person remaining with Al. This individual couldn't be more
than 14 years old. She (?) was weighted down with five boxes, some
with makeshift carrying straps, others even less portable. Most
looked like communications gear. The kid was grinning from ear to
ear. Al said, "Kiki van Steen, Lieutenant. She's a war-game fanatic—
for once, it may be worth something."

"Hi, Kiki."

"Pleased to meetcha, Lieutenant." She half-lifted one of the suit-
case-size boxes, as though to wave. Even with all the gear, she seemed
to vibrate with excitement.

"We have to decide where to go, and how to get there. The bikes
might be best, Al. They're small enough to—"

"Nah." It was Kiki. "Really, Lieutenant, they're almost as easy to
spot as a farm wagon. And we don't have to go far. I checked a
couple minutes ago, and no enemy aircraft are up. We've got at least
five minutes."

He glanced at Al, who nodded. "Okay, the car it is."

The girl's grin widened and she waddled off at high speed toward the
garage. "She's really a good kid, Lieutenant. Divorced though. She
spends most of what I pay her on that war-game equipment. Six
months ago she started talking about strange things down south. When
no one would listen, she shut up. Thank God she's here now. All night
she's been watching the south. We'll know the second they jump off."

"You have some hidey-hole already set, Al?"

"Yeah. The farms southwest of here are riddled with tunnels and
caves. The old Fort Riley complex. Friend of mine owns a lot of it. I
sent most of my men out there last night. It's not much, but at least
they won't be picking us up for free."

Around them insects were beginning to chitter, and in the trees
west of the HQ there was a dove. Sunlight lined the cloud tops. The
air was still cool, humid. And the darkness at the horizon remained.
Twister weather. *Now who will benefit from that?*

The relative silence was broken by the sharp coughing of a piston
engine. Seconds later, an incredible antique nosed out of the garage
onto the driveway. Wil saw the long black lines of a pre-1950

Lincoln. Brierson and Big Al dumped their guns and comm gear into the back seat and piled in.

This nostalgia thing can be carried too far, Wil thought. A restored Lincoln would cost as much as all the rest of Al's operation. The vehicle pulled smoothly out onto the ag road that paralleled the HQ property, and Wil realized he was in an inexpensive reproduction. He should have known Big Al would keep costs down.

Behind him the police station dwindled, was soon lost in the rolling Kansas landscape. "Kiki. Can you get a line-of-sight on the station's mast?"

The girl nodded.

"Okay. I want a link to East Lansing that looks like it's coming from your stationhouse."

"Sure." She phased an antenna ball on the mast, then gave Wil her command mike. In seconds he had spoken the destination codes and was talking first to the duty desk in East Lansing—and then to Colonel Potts and several of the directors.

When he had finished, Big Al looked at him in awe. "One hundred assault aircraft! Four thousand troopers! My God. I had no idea you could call in that sort of force."

Brierson didn't answer immediately. He pushed the mike into Kiki's hands and said, "Get on the loudmouth channels, Kiki. Start screaming bloody murder to all North America." Finally he looked back at Al, embarrassed. "We don't, Al. MSP has maybe thirty assault aircraft, twenty of them helicopters. Most of the fixed-wing jobs are in the Yukon. We could put guns on our search and rescue ships— we do have hundreds of those—but it will take weeks."

Al paled, but the anger he had shown earlier was gone. "So it was a bluff?"

Wil nodded. "But we'll get everything MSP has, as fast as they can bring it in. If the New Mexican investment isn't too big, this may be enough to scare 'em back." Big Al seemed to shrink in on himself. He gazed listlessly over Jim's shoulder at the road ahead. In the front seat, Kiki was shrilly proclaiming the details of the enemy's movements, the imminence of their attack. She was transmitting call letters and insignia that could leave no doubt that her broadcast came from a legitimate police service.

The wind whipped through the open windows brought the lush smells of dew and things dark green. In the distance gleamed the silver dome of a farm's fresh produce bobble. They passed a tiny Methodist church, sparkling white amidst flowers and lawn. In back, someone was working in the pastor's garden.

The road was just good enough to support the big tires of farm vehicles. Jim couldn't do much over 50 kph. Every so often, a wagon or tractor would pass them going the other way—going off to work in the fields. The drivers waved cheerfully at the Lincoln. It was a typical farm country morning in the ungoverned lands. How soon it would change. The news networks should have picked up on Kiki by now. They would have their own investigative people on the scene in hours with live holo coverage of whatever the enemy chose to do. Their programming, some of it directed into the Republic, might be enough to turn the enemy's public opinion against its government. *Wishful thinking.*

More likely the air above them would soon be filled with screaming metal—the end of a generation of peace.

Big Al gave a short laugh. When Wil looked at him questioningly, the small-town cop shrugged. "I was just thinking. This whole police business is something like a lending bank. Instead of gold, MSP backs its promises with force. This invasion is like a run on your 'bank of violence.' You got enough backing to handle normal demands, but when it all comes due at once . . ."

. . . you wind up dead or enslaved. Wil's mind shied away from the analogy. "Maybe so, but like a lot of banks, we have agreements with others. I'll bet Portland Security and the Mormons will loan us some aircraft. In any case, the Republic can never hold this land. You run a no-right-to-bear-arms service; but a lot of people around here are armed to the teeth."

"Sure. My biggest competitor is Justice, Inc. They encourage their customers to invest in handguns and heavy home security. Sure. The Republic will get their asses kicked eventually. But we'll be dead and bankrupt by then—and so will a few thousand other innocents."

Al's driver glanced back at them. "Hey, Lieutenant, why doesn't MSP pay one of the big power companies to retaliate—bobble places way inside the Republic?"

Wil shook his head. "The New Mexico government is sure to have all its important sites protected by Wáchendon suppressors.

Suddenly Kiki broke off her broadcast monologue and let out a whoop. "Bandits! Bandits!" She handed a display flat over the seat to Al. The format was familiar, but the bouncing, jostling ride made it hard to read. The picture was based on a sidelooking radar view from orbit, with a lot of data added. Green denoted vegetation and pastel overlays showed cloud cover. It was a jumble till he noticed that Manhattan and the Kansas River were labeled. Kiki zoomed up the magnification. Three red dots were visibly accelerating from a growing pockwork of red dots to the south. The three brightened, still accelerating. "They just broke cloud cover," she explained. Beside each of the dots a moving legend gave what must be altitude and speed.

"Is this going out over your loudmouth channel?"

She grinned happily. "Sure is! But not for long." She reached back to point at the display. "We got about two minutes before Al's stationhouse goes boom. I don't want to risk a direct satellite link from the car, and anything else would be even more dangerous."

Point certain, thought Wil.

"Geez, this is incredible, just incredible. For two years the Warmongers—that's my club, you know—been watching the Water Wars. We got software, hardware, cryptics—everything to follow what's going on. We could predict, and bet other clubs, but we could never actually participate. And now we have a real war, right *here*!" She lapsed into awed silence, and Wil wondered fleetingly if she might be psychopathic, and not merely young and naive.

"Do you have outside cameras at the police station?" He was asking Kiki as much as Al. "We should broadcast the actual attack."

The girl nodded. "I grabbed two channels. I got the camera on the comm mast pointing southwest. We'll have public opinion completely nailed on this."

"Let's see it."

She made a moue. "Okay. Not much content to it, though." She flopped back onto the front seat. Over her shoulder, Wil could see she had an outsized display flat on her lap. It was another composite

picture, but this one was overlaid with cryptic legends. They looked
vaguely familiar, then he recognized them from the movies: They
were the old, old shorthand for describing military units and capabil-
ities. The Warmongers Club must have software for translating
multispec satellite observations into such displays. Hell, they
might even be able to listen in on military communications. And
what the girl had said about public opinion—the club seemed to
play war in a very universal way. They *were* crazy, but they might
also be damned useful.

Kiki mumbled something into her command mike, and the flat Al
was holding split down the middle: On the left they could follow the
enemy's approach with the map; on the right they saw blue sky and
farmland and the parking lot by the stationhouse. Wil saw his gunship gleaming in the morning sunlight, just a few meters below the
camera's viewpoint.

"Fifteen seconds. They might be visible if you look south."

The car swerved toward the shoulder as Jim pointed out the window. "I see 'em!"

Then Wil did, too. A triple of black insects, silent because of distance and speed. They drifted westward, disappeared behind trees.
But to the camera on the comm mast, they did not drift: They
seemed to hang in the sky above the parking lot, death seen straight
on. Smoke puffed from just beneath them and things small and black
detached from the bodies of the attack craft, which now pulled up.
The planes were so close that Wil could see shape to them, could see
sun glint from canopies. Then the bombs hit.

Strangely, the camera scarcely jolted, but started slowly to pan
downward. Fire and debris roiled up around the viewpoint. A rotor
section from his flier flashed past, and then the display went gray. He
realized that the panning had not been deliberate: The high comm
mast had been severed and was toppling.

Seconds passed and sharp thunder swept over the car, followed by
the fast-dying scream of the bombers climbing back into the sky.

"So much for the loudmouth channels," said Kiki. "I'm for keeping quiet till we get underground."

Jim was driving faster now. He hadn't seen the display, but the
sounds of the explosions were enough to make all but the least

imaginative run like hell. The road had been bumpy, but now seemed like washboard. Wil gripped the seat ahead of him. If the enemy connected them with the broadcasts . . .

"How far, Al?"

"Nearest entrance is about four kilometers as the crow flies, but we gotta go all around the Schwartz farm to get to it." He waved at the high, barbed-wire fence along the right side of the road. Corn fields stretched away north of it. In the distance, Wil saw something—a harvester?—amidst the green. "It'll take us fifteen minutes—"

"Ten!" claimed Jim emphatically, and the ride became still wilder.

"—to make it around the farm."

They crested a low hill. Not more than 300 meters distant, Wil could see a side road going directly north. "But we could take that."

"Not a chance. That's on Schwartz land." Big Al glanced at the state trooper. "And I ain't just being law-abiding, Lieutenant. We'd be as good as dead to do that. Jake Schwartz went armadillo about three years ago. See that hulk out there in the field?" He tried to point, but his arm waved wildly.

"The harvester?"

"That's no harvester. It's armor. Robot, I think. If you look careful you may see the gun tracking us." Wil looked again. What he had thought was a chaff exhaust now looked more like a high-velocity catapult.

Their car zipped past the T-intersection with the Schwartz road; Wil had a glimpse of a gate and keep-out signs surmounted by what looked like human skulls. The farm west of the side road seemed undeveloped. A copse at the top of a near hill might have hid farm buildings.

"The expense. Even if it's mostly bluff—"

"It's no bluff. Poor Jake. He always was self-righteous and a bit of a bully. His police contract was with Justice, Inc., and he claimed even they were too bleedin' heart for him. Then one night his kid—who's even stupider than Jake—got pig drunk and killed another idiot. Unfortunately for Jake's boy, the victim was one of my customers. There are no amelioration clauses in the Midwest/Justice, Inc. agreements. Reparations aside, the kid will be locked up for a long time. Jake swore he'd never contract his rights to a court again.

He has a rich farm, and since then he's spent every gAu from it on more guns, more traps, more detectors. I hate to think how they live in there. There are rumors he's brought in deathdust from the Hanford ruins, just in case anybody succeeds in getting past everything else."

Oh boy. Even the armadillos up north rarely went that far.

The last few minutes Kiki had ignored them, all her attention on the strategy flat on her lap. She wore a tiny headset and was mumbling constantly into her command mike. Suddenly she spoke up. "Oops. We're not going to make it, Big Al." She began folding the displays, stuffing them back into her equipment boxes. "I monitored. They just told their chopper crews to pick us up. They got us spotted easy. Two, three minutes is all we have."

Jim slowed, shouted over his shoulder. "How, about if I drop you and keep going? I might be kilometers gone before they stop me." Brierson had never noticed any lack of guts among the unarmed police services.

"Good idea! Bye!" Kiki flung open her door and rolled off into the deep and apparently soft vegetation that edged the road.

"Kiki!" screamed Big Al, turning to look back down the road. They had a brief glimpse of comm and processor boxes bouncing wildly through the brush. Then Kiki's blond form appeared for an instant as she dragged the equipment deeper into the green.

From the trees behind them they could hear the *thupthupthup* of rotors. Two minutes had been an overstatement. Wil leaned forward. "No, Jim. Drive like hell. And remember: There were only three of us."

The other nodded. The car squealed out toward the center of the road, and accelerated up past 80. The roar and thump of their progress momentarily drowned out the sound of pursuit. Thirty seconds passed, and three helicopters appeared over the tree line behind them. *Do we get what they gave the stationhouse?* An instant later white flashed from their belly guns. The road ahead erupted in a geyser of dirt and rock. Jim stepped on the brakes and the car swerved to a halt, dipping and bobbing among the craters left by the shells. The car's engine died and the thumping of rotors was a loud, almost physical pressure around them. The largest craft settled to earth amidst its own dust devil. The other two circled, their autocannons locked on Big Al's Lincoln.

The passenger hatch on the grounded chopper slid back and two men in body armor hopped out. One waved his submachine gun at them, motioning them out of the car. Brierson and the others were hustled across the road, while the second soldier went to pick up the equipment they had in the car. Wil looked back at the scene, feeling the dust in his mouth and on his sweating face— the ashes of humiliation.

His pistol was pulled from its holster. "All aboard, gentlemen." The words were spoken with a clipped, Down West accent.

Wil was turning when it happened. A flash of fire and a muffled thud came from one of the hovering choppers. Its tail rotor disappeared in a shower of debris. The craft spun uncontrollably on its main rotor and fell onto the roadway behind them. Pale flame spread along fuel lines, sputtering in small explosions. Wil could see injured crew trying to crawl out.

"I said *get aboard*." The gunman had stepped back from them, his attention and the muzzle of his gun still on his captives. Wil guessed the man was a veteran of the Water Wars—that institutionalized gangsterism that New Mexico and Aztlán called "warfare between nations." Once given a mission, he would not be distracted by incidental catastrophes.

The three "prisoners of war" stumbled into the relative darkness of the helicopter's interior. Wil saw the soldier—still standing outside— look back toward the wreck, and speak emphatically into his helmet mike. Then he hopped on and pulled the hatch to. The helicopter slid into the air, hanging close to the ground as it gradually picked up speed. They were moving westward from the wreck, and there was no way they could look back through the tiny windows.

An accident? Who could have been equipped to shoot down an armored warcraft in the middle of Kansas fields? Then Wil remembered: Just before it lost its tail, the chopper had drifted north of the roadway, past the high fence that marked Armadillo Schwartz's land. He looked at Big Al, who nodded slightly. Brierson sat back in the canvas webbing and suppressed a smile. It was a small thing on the scale of the invasion, but he thanked God for armadillos. Now it was up to organizations like the Michigan State Police to convince the enemy that this was just the beginning, that every kilometer into the ungoverned lands would cost them similarly

One hundred and eighty kilometers in six hours. Republican casualties: one motorcycle/truck collision, and one helicopter crash—that probably a mechanical failure. Edward Strong, Special Advisor to the President, felt a satisfied smile come to his lips every time he glanced at the situation board. He had seen more casualties on a Freedom Day parade through downtown Albuquerque. His own analysis for the President—as well as the larger, less imaginative analysis from JCS—had predicted that extending the Republic through Kansas to the Mississippi would be almost trivial. Nevertheless, after having fought meter by bloody meter with the fanatics of Aztlán, it was a strange feeling to be advancing hundreds of kilometers each day.

Strong paced down the narrow aisle of the Command and Control van, past the analysts and clerks. He stood for a moment by the rear door, feeling the air-conditioning billow chill around his head. Camouflage netting had been laid over the van, but he could see through it without difficulty: Green leaves played tag with shadows across pale yellow limestone. They were parked in a wooded creek bed on the land Intelligence had bought several years earlier. Somewhere to the north were the barracks that now confined the people Intelligence had imported, allegedly to work the farms. Those laborers had provided whatever legal justification was needed for this move into the ungoverned lands. Strong wondered if any of them realized their role—and realized that in a few months they would be free of poverty, realized that they would own farms in a land that could be made infinitely more hospitable than the deserts of the Southwest.

Sixteen kilometers to the northeast lay Manhattan. It was a minor goal, but the Republic's forces were cautious. It would be an important—though small—test of their analysis. There were Tinkers in that town and in the countryside beyond. The precision electronics and related weapons that came out of the Tinkers' shops were worthy of respect and caution. Privately, Strong considered them to be the only real threat to the success of the invasion he had proposed to the President three years earlier. (Three years of planning, of cajoling resources from other departments, of trying to inject imagination into minds that had been closed for decades. By far, the easiest part had been the operations here in Kansas.)

The results of the move on Manhattan would be relayed from here to General Crick at the head of the armor driving east along Old70. Later in the afternoon, Crick's tank carriers should reach the outskirts of Topeka. The Old U.S. highway provided a mode of armored operations previously unknown to warfare. If the investiture of Manhattan went as planned, then Crick might have Topeka by nightfall and be moving the remainder of his forces on to the Mississippi.

Strong looked down the van at the time posted on the situation board. The President would be calling in 20 minutes to witness the move against Manhattan. Till then, a lull gapped in Strong's schedule. Perhaps there was time for one last bit of caution. He turned to the bird colonel who was his military liaison. "Bill, those three locals you picked up—you know, the protection racket people—I'd like to talk to them before the Chief calls in."

"Here?"

"If possible."

"Okay." There was faint disapproval in the officer's voice. Strong imagined that Bill Alvarez couldn't quite see bringing enemy agents into the C&C van. But what the hell, they were clean—and there was no way that they could report what they saw here. Besides, he had to stay in the van in case the Old Man showed up early.

Minutes later, the three shuffled into the conference area at the front of the van. Restraints glinted at their hands and ankles. They stood in momentary blindness in the darkness of the van, and Strong had a chance to look them over; three rather ordinary human beings, dressed in relatively extraordinary ways. The big black wore a recognizable uniform, complete with badges, sidearm holster, and what appeared to be riding boots. He looked the model fascist. Strong recognized the Michigan State "Police" insignia on his sleeve. MSP was one of the most powerful gangster combines in the ungoverned lands. Intelligence reported they had some modern weapons— enough to keep their "clients" in line, anyway.

"Sit down, gentlemen." Amidst a clanking of shackles, the three sat, sullen. Behind them an armed guard remained standing. Strong glanced at the intelligence summary he had punched up. "Mr., uh, Lieutenant Drierson, you may be interested to know that the troops and aircraft you asked your bosses for this morning have not materialized. Our intelligence people have not changed their estimate that you were making a rather weak bluff."

The northerner just shrugged, but the blond fellow in the outrageously striped shirt—Alvin Swensen, the report named him—leaned forward and almost hissed. "Maybe, maybe not, Asshole! But it doesn't matter. You're going to kill a lot of people, but in the end you'll be dragging your bloody tail back south."

Figuratively speaking, Strong's ears perked up. "How is that, Mr. Swensen?"

"Read your history. You're stealing from a free people now—not a bunch of Aztlán serfs. Every single farm, every single family is against you, and these are educated people, many with weapons. It may take a while. It may destroy a lot of things we value. But every day you stay here, you'll bleed. And when you've bled enough to see this, then you'll go home."

Strong glanced at the casualty report on the situation board, and felt laughter stealing up. "You poor fool. What free people? We get your video, your propaganda, but what does it amount to? There hasn't been a government in this part of the continent for more than eighty years. You petty gangsters have the guns and have divided up the territory. Most of you don't even allow your 'clients' firearms. I'll wager that the majority of your victims will welcome a government where there is a franchise to be exercised, where ballots, and not MSP bullets, decide issues.

"No, Mr. Swensen, the little people in the ungoverned lands have no stake in your *status quo*. And as for the armed groups fighting some kind of guerrilla war against us—Well, you've had it easier than you know for a long time. You haven't lived in a land as poor as old New Mexico. Since the Bobble War, we've had to fight for every liter of water, against an enemy far more determined and bloodthirsty than you may imagine. We have prevailed, we have revived and maintained democratic government, and we have remained free men."

"*Sure*. Free like the poor slobs you got locked up over there." Swensen waved in the direction of the workers' barracks.

Strong leaned across the narrow conference table to pin Swensen with his glare. "Mister, I grew up as one of 'those slobs.' In New Mexico, even people that poor have a chance to get something better. This land you claim is practically empty—you don't know how to farm it, you don't have a government to manage large dam and irrigation projects, you don't even know how to use government agriculture policy to encourage its proper use by individuals.

"Sure, those workers couldn't be told why they were brought here. But when this is over, they will be heroes, with homesteads they had never imagined being able to own."

Swensen rocked back before the attack, but was plainly unconvinced. Which makes sense, thought Strong. *How can a wolf imagine anyone sincerely wishing good for sheep?*

An alert light glowed on Strong's display and one of the clerks announced, "Presidential transmission under way, Mr. Strong." He swore behind his teeth. The Old Man was early. He'd hoped to get some information out of these three, not just argue politics.

A glowing haze appeared at the head of the conference table and quickly solidified into the image of the fourth President of the Republic. Hastings Martinez was good-looking with bio-age around 50 years—old enough to inspire respect, young enough to appear decisive. In Strong's opinion, he was not the best president the Republic had seen, but he had the advisor's respect and loyalty nevertheless. There was something in the very responsibility of the office of the Presidency that made its holder larger than life.

"Mr. President," Strong said respectfully.

"Ed," Martinez's image nodded. The projection was nearly as substantial as the forms of those truly present; Strong didn't know whether this was because of the relative darkness within the van, or because Martinez was transmitting via fiber from his estate in Alva, just 300 kilometers away.

Strong waved at the prisoners. "Three locals, sir. I was hoping to—"

Martinez leaned forward. "Why, I think I've seen you before." He spoke to the MSP officer. "The ads Michigan State Police uses; our intelligence people have shown me some. You protect MSP's client mobs from outside gangs."

Brierson nodded, smiled wryly. Strong recognized him now and kicked himself for not noticing earlier. If those ads were correct, then Brierson was one of the top men in the MSP.

"They make you out to be some sort of superman. Do you honestly think your people can stop a modern, disciplined army?"

"Sooner or later, Mr. Martinez. Sooner or later."

The President smiled, but Strong wasn't sure whether he was piqued or truly amused. "Our armor is approaching Manhattan on schedule, sir. As you know, we regard this action as something of a bench mark. Manhattan is almost as big as Topeka, and has a substantial cottage electronics industry. It's about the closest thing to a city you'll find in the ungoverned lands." Strong motioned for the guard to remove the three prisoners, but the President held up his hand.

"Let 'em stay, Ed. The MSP man should see this firsthand. These people may be lawless, but I can't believe they are crazy. The sooner they realize that we have overwhelming force—and that we use it fairly—the sooner they'll accept the situation."

"Yes, sir." Strong signaled his analysts, and displays came to life on the situation board. Simultaneously, the conference table was over-hung with a holographic relief map of central Kansas. The northerners looked at the map and Strong almost smiled. They obviously had no idea of the size of the New Mexican operation. For months the Republic had been building reserves along the Arkansas. It couldn't be entirely disguised; these three had known something about the forces. But until the whole military machine was in motion, its true size had escaped them. Strong was honest with himself. It was not New Mexican cleverness that had outwitted northern electronics. The plan could never have worked without advanced countermeasures equipment—some of it bought from the northerners themselves.

Computer-selected radio traffic became a background noise. He had rehearsed all this with the technicians earlier; there was not a single aspect of the operation that the President would miss. He pointed at the map. "Colonel Alvarez has one armored force coming north from O1d70. It should enter Manhattan from the east. The other force left here a few minutes ago, and is approaching town along this secondary road." Tiny silver lights crept along the map where he pointed. A few centimeters above the display, other lights represented helicopter and fixed-wing cover. These coasted gracefully back and forth, occasionally swooping close to the surface.

A voice spoke against a background of turbine noise, to announce no resistance along the eastern salient. "Haven't really seen anyone. People are staying indoors, or else bobbled up before we came in range. We're avoiding houses and farm buildings, sticking to open fields and roads."

Strong expanded one of the views from the western salient. The situation board showed a picture taken from the air: A dozen tanks moved along a dirt road, trails of dust rising behind them. The camera chopper must have been carrying a mike, for the rumbling and clanking of treads replaced the radio traffic for a moment. Those tanks were the pride of New Mexico. Unlike the aircraft, their hulls and engines were 100 percent Product of the Republic. New Mexico was poor in most resources, but like Japan in the 20th century, and Great Britain before that, she was great in people and ingenuity. Someday soon, she would be great in electronics. For now, though, all the best reconnaissance and communication gear came from Tinkers, many in the ungoverned lands. That was an Achilles' heel, long recognized by Strong and others. It was the reason for using equipment from different manufacturers all over the world, and for settling for second-class gear in some of the most critical applications. How could they know, *for certain*, that the equipment they bought was not booby-trapped or bugged? There was historical precedent: The outcome of the Bobble War had been due in large part to Tinker meddling with the old Peace Authority's reconnaissance system.

Strong recognized the stretch of road they were coming up on: A few hundred meters beyond the lead tank lay an irregular blackened area and the twisted metal that had once been a helicopter.

A puff of smoke appeared by the lead tank, followed by the faint crack of an explosion. Bill Alvarez's voice came on an instant after that. "Under fire. Light mortar." The tank was moving again, but in a large circle, toward the ditch. Guns and sensors on the other armor swung north. "The enemy was lucky, or that was a smart round. We've got radar backtrack. The round came from beyond the other side of the farm we're passing. Looks like a tunnel entrance to the old Fort Riley—Wait, we got enemy radio traffic just before it happened."

His voice was replaced by the crackling of high amplification. The new voice was female, but barely understandable. "General van Steen to forces [unintelligible]. You may fire when ready." There was a screaking sound and other voices.

Strong saw Swensen's jaw sag in surprise, or horror. *"General van Steen?"*

Colonel Alvarez's voice came back. "There were replies from several points farther north. The original launch site has fired two more rounds." As he spoke, black smoke appeared near the treads of two more tanks. Neither was destroyed, but neither could continue.

"Mr. President, Mr. Strong, all rounds are coming from the same location. These are barely more than fireworks—except that they're smart. I'll wager 'General van Steen' is some local gangster putting up a brave front. We'll see in a minute." On the holomap, two blips drew away from the other support aircraft and began a low level dash across the miniature Kansas landscape.

The President nodded, but addressed another unseen observer. "General Crick?"

"I concur, sir." Crick's voice was as loud and clear as Alvarez's, though the general was 50 kilometers to the east, at the head of the column en route to Topeka. "But we've seen an armored vehicle in the intermediate farmland, haven't we, Bill?"

"Yes," said Alvarez. "It's been there for months. Looks like a hulk. We'll take it out, too."

Strong noticed the northerners tense. Swensen seemed on the verge of screaming something. *What do they know?*

The attack planes, twin engine green-and-gray jobs, were on the main view now. They were only 20 or 30 meters up, well below the camera viewpoint, and probably not visible from the enemy launch site. The lead craft angled slightly to the east, and spewed rockets at an unmoving silhouette that was almost hidden by the hills and the corn. A second later, the target disappeared in a satisfying geyser of flame and dirt.

And a second after that, hell on earth erupted from the peaceful fields: beams of pale light flashed from unseen projectors, and the assault aircraft became falling, swelling balls of fire. As automatic fire control brought the tanks' guns to bear on the source of the destruction, rocket and laser fire came from other locations immediately north of the roadway. Four of the tanks exploded immediately, and most of the rest were on fire. Tiny figures struggled from their machines, and ran from the flames.

North of the farm, Strong thought he saw explosions at the source of the original mortar attack. Something was firing in that direction too!

Then the camera chopper took a hit, and the picture swung round and round, descending into the fire storm that stretched along the roadway. The view went dark. Strong's carefully planned presentation was rapidly degenerating into chaos. Alvarez was shouting over other voices, demanding the reserves that still hung along Old70 directly south of Manhattan, and he could hear Crick working to divert portions of his air cover to the fight that was developing.

It wasn't till much later that Strong made sense of the conversation that passed between the northerners just then:

"Kiki, how could you!" Swensen slumped over the holomap, shaking his head in despair (shame?).

Brierson eyed the displays with no visible emotion. "What she did is certainly legal, Al."

"Sure it is. And immoral as hell. Poor Jake Schwartz. Poor Jake."

The view of the battle scene reappeared. The picture was almost the same perspective as before but grainier and faintly wavering—probably from a camera aboard some recon craft far south of the fighting. The holomap flickered as major updates came in. The locals had been thorough and successful. There were no effective New Mexican forces within five kilometers of the original flareup. The force dug in to the farmland was firing rockets southward, taking an increasing toll of the armored reinforcements that were moving north from Old70.

"Crick here, Mr. President." The general's voice was brisk, professional. Any recriminations with Intelligence would come later. "The enemy is localized, but incredibly well dug in. If he's isolated, we might be able to bypass him, but neither Alvarez nor I want something like that left on our flank. We're going to soften him up, then move our armor right in on top."

Strong nodded to himself. In any case, they had to take this strong point just to find out what the enemy really had. In the air over the holomap, dozens of lights moved toward the enemy fortress. Some flew free ballistic arcs, while others struck close to the ground, out of the enemy's direct fire. Across the table, the holo lit the northerners' faces: Swensen's seemingly more pale than before, Brierson's dark and stolid. There was a faint stench of sweat in the air now, barely perceptible against the stronger smells of metal and fresh plastic.

Damn. Those three had been surprised by the ambush, but Strong was sure that they understood what was behind the attack, and whence the next such would come. Given time and Special Service drugs, he could have the answers. He leaned across the table and addressed the MSP officer. "So. You aren't entirely bluff. But unless you have many more such traps, you won't do more than slow us up, and kill a lot of people on both sides."

Swensen was about to answer, then looked at Brierson and was silent. The black seemed to be deliberating just what or how much to say; finally, he shrugged. "I won't lie to you. The attack had nothing to do with MSP forces."

"Some other gang then?"

"No. You just happened to run into a farmer who defends his property."

"Bull." Ed Strong had spent his time in the military in combat along the Colorado. He knew how to read the intelligence displays and manage tactics. But he also knew what it was like to be on the ground where the reality was bullets and shrapnel. He knew what it took to set up a defense like the one they had just seen. "Mr. Brierson, you're telling me one man could afford to buy the sort of equipment we saw and to dig it in so deep that even now we don't have a clear picture of his setup? You're telling me that one man could afford an MHD source for those lasers?"

"Sure. That family has probably been working at this for years, spending every free cent on the project, building the system up little by little. Even so," he sighed. "they should be out of rockets and juice soon. You could lay off."

The rain of rocket-borne and artillery high explosives was beginning to fall upon the target. Flashes and color sparkled across the screen, more an abstract pattern than a landscape now. There was no human life, no equipment visible. The bombers were standing off and lobbing their cargo in. Until the enemy's defenses were broken, any other course was needless waste. After a couple minutes, the airborne debris obscured all but the largest detonations. Napalm flared within, and the whole cloud glowed beautiful yellow. For a few seconds, the enemy lasers still flashed, spectacular and ineffective in all the dirt. Even after the lasers died, the holomap showed isolated missiles emerging from the target area to hunt for the bombers. Then even those stopped coming.

Still the barrage continued, raising the darkness and light high over the Kansas fields. There was no sound from this display, but the *thudthudding* of the attack came barely muffled through the hull of the C&C van. They were, after all, less than 7,000 meters from the scene. It was mildly surprising that the enemy had not tried to take them out. Perhaps Brierson was more important, and more knowledgeable, than he admitted.

Minutes passed, and they all—President and gangsters alike—watched the barrage end and the wind push the haze away from the devastation that modern war can make. North and east, fires spread through the fields. The tanks—and final, physical possession of the disputed territory—were only minutes away.

The destruction was not uniform. New Mexican fire had focused on the projectors and rocket launchers, and there the ground was pulverized, ripped first by proximity-fused high explosives, then by digger bombs and napalm. As they watched, recon craft swooped low over the landscape, their multi-scanners searching for any enemy weapons that might be held in reserve. When the tanks and personnel carriers arrived, a more thorough search would be made on foot.

Finally, Strong returned to Brierson's fantastic claim. "And you say it's just coincidence that this one farmer who spends all his money on weapons happens to be on our line of march."

"Coincidence and a little help from General van Steen."

President Martinez raised his eyes from the displays at his end. His voice was level, but Strong recognized the tension there. "Mr., uh, Brierson. Just how many of these miniforts are there?"

The other sat back. His words might have seemed insolent, but there was no sarcasm in his voice. "I have no idea, Mr. Martinez. As long as they don't bother our customers, they are of no interest to MSP. Many aren't as well hidden as Schwartz's, but you can't count on that. As long as you stay off their property, most of them won't touch you."

"You're saying that if we detect and avoid them, they are no threat to our plans?"

"Yes."

The main screen showed the tank forces now. They were a few hundred meters from the burning fields. The viewpoint rotated and Strong saw that Crick had not stinted: at least 100 tanks—most of the reserve force—were advancing on a 5,000-meter front. Following were even more personnel carriers. Tactical air support was heavy. Any fire from the ground ahead would be met by immediate destruction. The camera rotated back to show the desolation they were moving into. Strong doubted that anything living, much less anything hostile, still existed in that moonscape.

The President didn't seem interested in the display. All his attention was on the northerner. "So we can avoid these stationary gunmen till we find it convenient to deal with them. You are a great puzzle, Mr. Brierson. You claim strengths and weaknesses for your people that are equally incredible. And I get the feeling you don't really expect us to believe you, but that somehow you believe everything you're saying."

"You're very perceptive. I've thought of trying to bluff you. In fact, I did try earlier today. From the looks of your equipment"—he waved his hand at the Command and Control consoles, a faintly mocking smile on his face—"we might even be able to bluff you back where you belong. *This once.* But when you saw what we had done, you'd be back again—next year, next decade—and we'd have to do it all over again without the bluffs. So, Mr. Martinez, I think it best you learn what you're up against the first time out. People like Schwartz are just the beginning. Even if you can rub out them and services like

MSP, you'll end up with a guerrilla war like you've never fought—one that can actually turn your own people against you. You do practice conscription, don't you?"

The President's face hardened, and Strong knew that the northerner had gone too far. "We do, as has every free nation in history—or at least every nation that was determined to stay free. If you're implying that our people would desert under fire or because of propaganda, you are contradicting my personal experience." He turned away, dismissing Brierson from his attention.

"They've arrived, sir." As the tanks rolled into position on the smoking hillsides, the personnel carriers began disgorging infantry. The tiny figures moved quickly, dragging gear toward the open tears in the earth. Strong could hear an occasional popping sound: Misfiring engines? Remnant ammo?

Tactical aircraft swept back and forth overhead, their rockets and guns ready to support the troopers on the ground. The techs' reports trickled in.

"Three video hard points detected," small arms fire chattered. "Two destroyed, one recovered. Sonoprobes show lots of tunnels. Electrical activity at—" The men in the picture looked up, at something out of view.

Nothing else changed on the picture, but the radars saw the intrusion, and the holomap showed the composite analysis: a mote of light rose leisurely out of the map—500 meters, 600. It moved straight up, slowed. The support aircraft swooped down upon it and—

A purple flash, bright yet soundless, seemed to go off *inside* Strong's head. The holomap and the displays winked down to nothing, then came back. The President's image reappeared, but there was no sound, and it was clear he was not receiving.

Along the length of the van, clerks and analysts came out of that stunned moment to work frantically with their equipment. Acrid smoke drifted into the conference area. The safe, crisp displays had been replaced by immediate, deadly reality.

"High flux nuke." The voice was calm, almost mechanical.

High flux nuke. Radiation bomb. Strong came to his feet, rage and horror burning inside him. Except for bombs in lapsed bobbles, no nuclear weapon had exploded in North America in nearly a century.

Even during the bitterest years of the Water Wars, both Aztlán and New Mexico had seen the suicide implicit in nuclear solutions. But here, in a rich land, without warning and for no real reason—

"You *animals!*" he spat down upon the seated northerners.

Swensen lunged forward. "God damn it! Schwartz isn't one of my customers!"

Then the shock wave hit. Strong was thrown across the map, his face buried in the glowing terrain. Just as suddenly he was thrown back. The prisoners' guard had been knocked into the far wall; now he stumbled forward through Martinez's unseeing image, his stun gun flying from his hand.

From the moment of the detonation, Brierson had sat hunched, his arms extended under the table. Now he moved, lunging across the table to sweep up the gun between his manacled hands. The muzzle sparkled and Strong's face went numb. He watched in horror as the other twisted and raked the length of the van with stunfire. The men back there had themselves been knocked about. Several were just coming up off their knees. Most didn't know what hit them when they collapsed back to the floor. At the far end of the van, one man had kept his head. One man had been as ready as Brierson.

Bill Alvarez popped up from behind an array processor, a five millimeter slug-gun in his hand, flashing fire as he moved.

Then the numbness seemed to squeeze in on Strong's mind, and everything went gray.

Wil looked down the dim corridor that ran the length of the command van. No one was moving, though a couple of men were snoring. The officer with the handgun had collapsed, his hands hanging limp, just a few centimeters from his pistol. Blue sky showing through the wall above Wil's head was evidence of the fellow's determination. If the other had been a hair faster . . .

Wil handed the stun gun to Big Al. "Let Jim go down and pick up the slug gun. Give an extra dose to anyone who looks suspicious."

Al nodded, but there was still a dazed look in his eyes. In the last hour, his world had been turned upside down. How many of his customers—the people who paid for his protection—had been killed? Wil tried not to think about that; indirectly, those same people had been depending on MSP. Almost tripping on his fetters, he stepped over the fallen guard and sat down on the nearest technician's saddle. For all New Mexico being a foreign land, the controls were familiar. It wasn't too surprising. The New Mexicans used a lot of Tinker electronics, though they didn't seem to trust it: much of the equipment's performance was downgraded where they had replaced suspicious components with their own devices. Ah, the price of paranoia.

Brierson picked up a command mike, made a simple request, and watched the answer parade across the console. "Hey, Al, we stopped transmitting right at the detonation!" Brierson quickly entered commands that cleared Martinez's image and blocked any future transmissions. Then he asked for status.

The air conditioning was down, but internal power could keep the gear going for a time. The van's intelligence unit estimated the nuke had been a three kiloton equivalent with a 70 percent radiance. Brierson felt his stomach flip-flop. He knew about nukes—perhaps more than the New Mexicans. There was no legal service that allowed them and it was open season on armadillos who advertised having them, but every so often MSP got a case involving such weapons. Everyone within 2,000 meters of that blast would already be dead. Schwartz's private war had wiped out a significant part of the invading forces.

The people in the van had received a sizable dose from the Schwartz nuke, though it wouldn't be life-threatening if they got medical treatment soon. In the division command area immediately around the van, the exposure was somewhat higher. How long would it be before those troops came nosing around the silent command vehicle? If he could get a phone call out—

But then there was Fate's personal vendetta against W. W. Brierson: Loud pounding sounded at the forward door. Wil waved Jim and Al to be quiet. Awkwardly, he got off the saddle and moved to look through the old-fashioned viewplate mounted next to the door. In the distance he could see men carrying stretchers from an ambulance; some of the burn cases would be really bad. Five troopers were standing right at the doorway, close enough that he could see blistered skin and burned clothing. But their weapons looked fine, and the wiry noncom pounding on the door was alert and energetic. "Hey, open up in there!"

Wil thought fast. What was the name of that VIP civilian? Then he shouted back (doing his best to imitate the clipped New Mexican accent), "Sorry, Mr. Strong doesn't want to breach internal atmosphere." *Pray they don't see the bullet holes just around the corner.*

He saw the sergeant turn away from the door. Wil lip-read the word shit. He could almost read the noncom's mind: The men outside had come near to being french-fried, and here some silkshirt supervisor was worried about so-far-nonexistent fallout.

The noncom turned back to the van and shouted, "How about casualties?"

"Outside of rad exposure, just some bloody noses and loose teeth. Main power is down and we can't transmit," Wil replied.

"Yes, sir. Your node has been dropped from the network. We've patched backward to Oklahoma Leader and forward to div mobile. Oklahoma Leader wants to talk to Mr. Strong. Div mobile wants to talk to Colonel Alvarez. How long will it be till you're back on the air?"

How long can I ask for? How long do I need? "Give us fifteen minutes," he shouted, after a moment.

"Yes, sir. We'll get back to you." Having innocently delivered this threat, the sergeant and his troopers moved off.

Brierson hopped back to the console. "Keep your eyes on the sleepers, Al. If I'm lucky, fifteen minutes should be enough time."

"To do what? Call MSP?"

"Something better. Something I should have done this morning." He searched through the command menus for satellite pickups. The New Mexican military was apparently leery of using subscription services, but there should be some facility for it. Ah, there it was. Brierson phased the transmitter for the synchronous satellite the Hainan commune had hung over Brazil. With narrow beam, he might be able to talk through it without the New Mexicans realizing he was transmitting. He tapped in a credit number, then a destination code.

The display showed the call had reached Whidbey Island. Seconds passed. Outside, he could hear choppers moving into the camp. More ambulances? *Damn you, Rober. Be home.*

The conference area filled with bluish haze, then became a sunlit porch overlooking a wooded bay. Sounds of laughter and splashing came faintly from the water. Old Roberto Richardson never used less than full holo. But the scene was pale, almost ghostly—the best the van's internal power supply could do. A heavyset man with apparent age around 30 came up the steps onto the porch and sat down; it was Richardson. He peered out at them. "Wil? Is that you?"

If it weren't for the stale air and the dimness of the vision, Wil could almost believe he'd been transported halfway across the continent. Richardson lived on an estate that covered the whole of Whidbey Island. In the Pacific time zone it was still morning, and shadows swept across lawn-like spaces that stretched away to his manicured forests. Not for the first time, Wil was reminded of the faerie landscapes of Maxfield Parrish. Roberto Richardson was one of the richest men in the world; he sold a line of products that many people cannot resist. He was rich enough to live in whatever fantasy world he chose.

Brierson turned on the pickup that watched the conference table.

"*Dios*. It *is* you, Wil! I thought you were dead or captured."

"Neither, just yet. You're following this ruckus?"

"*Por cierto*. And most news services are covering it. I wager they're spending more money than your blessed Michigan State Police on this war. Unless that nuke was one of yours? Wili, my boy, that was spectacular. You took out twenty percent of their armor."

"It wasn't one of ours, Rober."

"Ah. Just as well. Midwest Jurisprudence would withdraw service for something like that."

Time was short, but Wil couldn't resist asking, "What is MSP up to?"

Richardson sighed. "About what I'd expect. They've finally brought some aircraft in. They're buzzing around the tip of Dave Crick's salient. The Springfield Cyborg Club has gone after the New Mexican supply lines. They are causing some damage. A cyborg is a bit hard to kill, and Norcross Security is supplying them with transports and weapons. The New Mexicans have Wáchendon suppressors down to battalion level, so there's no bobbling. The fighting looks quite 20th century.

"You've got a lot of public opinion behind you—even in the Republic, I think—but not much firepower.

"You know, Wil, you fellows should have bought more from me. You saved a few million, maybe, passing up those aerial torpedoes and assault craft, and the tanks. But look where you are now. If—"

"Jesus, that's Robber Richardson!" It was Big Al; he had been watching the holo with growing wonder.

Richardson squinted at his display. "I can hardly see anything on this, Wil. Where in perdition are you calling from? And to you, Unseen Sir, it's *Roberto* Richardson."

Big Al walked toward the sunlit porch. He got within an apparent two meters of Richardson before he banged into the conference table. "You re the sort of scum who's responsible for this! You sold the New Mexicans everything they couldn't build themselves: the high-performance aircraft, the military electronics." Al waved at the cabinets in the darkened van. What he claimed was largely true. Wil had noticed the equipment stenciled with Richardson's logo, "USAF Inc—Sellers of Fine Weapon Systems for More than Twenty Years"; the New Mexicans hadn't even bothered to paint it out. Roberto had been born a minor Aztlán nobleman. He'd been in just the right place at the time of the Bobble War, and had ended up controlling the huge munition dumps left by the old Peace Authority. That had been the beginning of his fortune. Since then, he had moved into the ungoverned lands, and begun manufacturing much of his own equipment. The heavy industry he had brought to Bellevue was almost on the scale of the 20th century—or of modern New Mexico.

Richardson came half out of his chair and chopped at the air in front of him. "See here. I have to take enough such insults from my niece and her grandchildren. I don't have to take them from a stranger." He stood, tossed his display flat on the chair, and walked to the steps that led down to his shaded river.

"Wait, Rober!" shouted Brierson. He waved Big Al back to the depths of the van. "I didn't call to pass on insults. You wondered where I'm calling from. Well, let me tell you—"

By the time he finished, the old gunrunner had returned to his seat. He started to laugh. "I should have guessed you'd end up talking right out of the lion's mouth." His laughter halted abruptly. "But you're trapped, aren't you? No last minute Brierson tricks to get out of this one? I'm sorry, Wil, I really am. If there were anything I could do, I would. I don't forget my debts."

Those were the words Wil had been hoping to hear. "There's nothing you can do for me, Rober. Our bluff in this van is good for just a few minutes, but we could all use a little charity just now."

The other looked nonplussed.

"Look, I'll bet you have plenty of aircraft and armor going through final checkout at the Bellevue plant. And I know you have ammunition stocks. Between MSP and Justice, Inc. and a few other police services, we have enough war buffs to man them. At least we have enough to make these New Mexicans think twice."

But Richardson was shaking his head. "I'm a charitable man, Wil. If I had such things to loan, MSP could have some for the asking. But you see, we've all been a bit outsmarted here. The New Mexicans—and people I now think are fronting for them—have options on the next four months of my production. You see what I mean? It's one thing to help people I like, and another to break a contract-especially when reliability has always been one of my most important selling points."

Wil nodded. So much for that brilliant idea.

"And it may turn out for the best, Wil," Richardson continued quietly. "I know your loudmouth friend won't believe this, coming from me, but I think the Midwest might now be best off not to fight. We both know the invasion can't stick, not in the long run. It's just a question of how many lives and how much property is going to be destroyed in the meantime, and how much ill feeling is going to be stored up for the future. Those New Mexicans deserve to get nuked and all the rest, but that could steel them for a holy war, like they've been fighting along the Colorado for so long. On the other hand, if you let them come in and take a whack at 'governing'—why, in twenty years, you'll have them converted into happy anarchists."

Wil smiled in spite of himself. Richardson was certainly the prime example of what he was talking about. Wil knew the old autocrat had originally been an agent of Aztlán, sent to prepare the Northwest for invasion. "Okay, Rober. I'll think about it. Thanks for talking."

Richardson seemed to have guessed Wil's phantom position on his porch. His dark eyes stared intensely into Wil's. "Take care of yourself, Wili."

The cool, northern playground wavered for a second, like a dream of paradise, then vanished, replaced by the hard reality of dark plastic, glimmering displays, and unconscious New Mexicans. *What now, Lieutenant?* Calling Rober had been his only real idea. He could call MSP, but he had nothing helpful to tell them. He leaned on the console, his hands sliding slickly across his sweating face. Why not just do as Rober suggested? Give up and let the force of history take care of things.

No.

First of all, there's no such thing as "the force of history," except as it existed in the determination and imagination of individuals. Government had been a human institution for thousands of years; there was no reason to believe the New Mexicans would fall apart without some application of physical force. Their actions had to be shown to be impractically expensive.

And there was another, more personal reason. Richardson talked as though this invasion were something special, something that transcended commerce and courts and contracts. That was wrong. Except for their power and their self-righteousness, the New Mexicans were no different from some chopper gang marauding MSP customers. And if he and MSP let them take over, it would be just as much a default. As with Rober, reliability was one of MSP's strongest selling points.

So MSP had to keep fighting. The only question was, what could he and Al and Jim do now?

Wil twisted around to look at the exterior view mounted by the hatch. It was a typically crass design flaw that the view was independent of the van's computers and couldn't be displayed except at the doorway.

There wasn't much to see. The division HQ was dispersed, and the van itself sat in the bottom of a ravine. The predominant impression was of smoking foliage and yellow limestone. He heard the keening of light turbines. *Oh boy.* Three overland cars were coming their way. He recognized the sergeant he had talked to a few minutes earlier. If there was anything left to do, he'd better do it now.

He glanced around the van. Strong was a high presidential advisor. Was that worth anything? Wil tried to remember. In Aztlán, with its feudal setup, such a man might be very important. The safety of just a few leaders was the whole purpose of that government. The New Mexicans were different. Their rulers were elected; there were reasonable laws of succession, and people like Strong were probably expendable. Still, there was an idea here: Such a state was something like an enormous corporation, with the citizens as stockholders. The analogy wasn't perfect—no corporation could use the coercion these people practiced on their own. And there were other differences. But still. If the top people in such an enormous organization were threatened, it would be enormously more effective than if, say, the board of directors of MSP were hassled. There were at least 10 police services as powerful as MSP in the ungoverned lands, and many of them subcontracted to smaller firms.

The question, then, was how to get their hands on someone like Hastings Martinez or this General Crick. He punched up an aerial view from somewhere south of the combat area. A train of clouds had spread southeast from the Schwartz farm. Otherwise, the air was faintly hazy. Thunderheads hung at the northern horizon. The sky had that familiar feel to it. Topeka Met Service confirmed the feeling: This was tornado weather.

Brierson grimaced. He had known that all day. And somewhere in the back of his mind, there had been the wild hope that the tornados would pick the right people to land on. Which was absurd: *Modern science could kill tornadoes,* but no one could direct them. Modern science can kill tornadoes. He swallowed. There was something he could do—if there was time. One call to headquarters was all he needed.

Outside there was pounding on the door and shouting. More ominous, he heard a scrabbling noise, and the van swayed slightly on its suspension: someone was climbing onto the roof. Wil ignored the footsteps above him, and asked the satellite link for a connection to MSP. The black and gold Michigan State logo had just appeared when the screen went dead. Wil tapped futilely at emergency codes, then looked at the exterior view again. A hard-faced major was standing next to the van.

Wil turned on the audio and interrupted the other. "We just got sound working here, Major. What's up?"

This stopped the New Mexican, who had been halfway through shouting his message at them. The officer stepped back from the van and continued in more moderate tones. "I was saying there's no fall-out problem." Behind him, one of the troopers was quietly barfing into the bushes. There might be no fallout, but unless the major and his men got medical treatment soon, they would be very sick soldiers. "There's no need for you to stay buttoned up."

"Major, we're just about ready to go back on the air. I don't want to take any chances."

"Who am I speaking to?"

"Ed Strong. Special Advisor to the President." Wil spoke the words with the same ponderous importance the real Ed Strong might have used.

"Yes, sir. May I speak with Colonel Alvarez?"

"Alvarez?" Now that was a man the major must know. "Sorry, he got the corner of an equipment cabinet in the head. He hasn't come to yet."

The officer turned and gave the sergeant a sidelong look. The non-com shook his head slightly. "I see." And Wil was afraid that he really did. The major's mouth settled into a thin line. He said something to the noncom, then walked back to the cars.

Wil turned back to the other displays. It was a matter of seconds now. That major was more than suspicious. And without the satellite transmitter, Brierson didn't have a chance of reaching East Lansing or even using the loudmouth channels. The only comm links he had that didn't go through enemy nodes were the local phone bands. He could just reach Topeka Met. They would understand what he was talking about. Even if they wouldn't cooperate, they would surely pass the message back to headquarters. He ran the local directory. A second passed and he was looking at a narrowband black-and-white image. A young, good-looking male sat behind an executive-sized desk. He smiled dazzlingly and said, "Topeka Meteorological Service, Customer Relations. May I help you?"

"I sure hope so. My name's Brierson, Michigan State Police." Wil found the words tumbling out, as if he had been rehearsing this little speech for hours. The idea was simple, but there were some details.

When he finished, he noticed the major coming back toward the van. One of his men carried comm gear.

The receptionist at Topeka Met frowned delicately. "Are you one of our customers, sir?"

"No, damn it. Don't you watch the news? You got four hundred tanks coming down Old70 toward Topeka. You're being invaded, man—as in going out of business!"

The young man shrugged in a way that indicated he never bothered with the news. "A gang invading Topcka? Sir, we are a city, not some farm community. In any case, what you want us to do with our tornado killers is clearly improper. It would be—"

"Listen," Wil interrupted, his voice placating, almost frightened. "At least send this message on to the Michigan State Police. Okay?"

The othcr smiled the same dazzling, friendly smile that had opened the conversation. "Certainly, sir." And Wil realized he had lost. He was talking to a moron or a low-grade personality simulator; it didn't matter much which. Topeka Met was like a lot of companies—it operated with just enough efficiency to stay in business. Damn the luck.

The voices from the exterior pickup were faint but clear, "—whoever they are, they're transmitting over the local phone bands, sir." It was an enlisted man talking to the New Mexican major. The major nodded and stepped toward the van.

This was it. No time left to think. Wil stabbed blindly at the directory. The Topeka Met Customer Relations "expert" disappeared and the screen began blinking a ring pattern.

"All right, Mr. Strong," the major was shouting again, loudly enough so that he could be heard through the hull of the van as well as over the pickup. The officer held a communications headset. "The President is on this line, sir. He wishes to speak with you—right now." There was a grim smile on the New Mexican's face.

Wil's fingers flick across the control board; the van's exterior mike gave a loud squawk and was silent. With one part of his mind, he heard the enlisted man say, "They're still transmitting, Major."

And then the ring pattern vanished from the phone display. Last chance. Even an auto answerer might be enough. The screen lit up, and Wil found himself staring at a 5-year-old girl.

"Trask residence." She looked a little intimidated by Wil's hulking, scowling image. But she spoke clearly, as one who has been coached in the proper response to strangers. Those serious brown eyes reminded Brierson of his own sister. Bounded by what she knew and what she understood, she would try to do what was right.

It took a great effort to relax his face and smile at the girl. "Hello. Do you know how to record my call, Miss?"

She nodded.

"Would you do that and show it to your parents, please?"

"Okay." She reached offscreen. The recording telltale gleamed at the corner of the flat, and Wil began talking. Fast.

The major's voice came over the external pickup: "Open it up, Sergeant." There were quick footsteps and something slapped against the hatch.

"Wil!" Big Al grabbed his shoulder. "Get down. Away from the hatch. Those are slug-guns they have out there!"

But Brierson couldn't stop now. He pushed Al away, waved for him to get down among the fallen New Mexicans.

The explosion was a sharp cracking sound that rocked the van sideways. The phone connection held, and Wil kept talking. Then the door fell, or was pulled outward, and daylight splashed across him.

"Get away from that phone!"

On the display, the little girl seemed to look past Wil. Her eyes widened. She was the last thing W. W. Brierson saw.

There were dreams. In some he could only see. In others, he was blind, yet hearing and smell were present, all mixed together. And some were pure pain, winding up and up while all around him torturers twisted screws and needles to squeeze the last bit of hurt from his shredded flesh. But he also sensed his parents and sister Beth, quiet and near. And sometimes when he could see and the pain was gone, there were flowers—almost a jungle of them—dipping near his eyes, smelling of violin music.

Snow. Smooth, pristine, as far as his eyes could see. Trees glazed in ice that sparkled against cloudless blue sky. Wil raised his hand to rub his eyes and felt faint surprise to see the hand obey, to feel hand touch face as he willed it.

"Wili, Wili! You're really back!" Someone warm and dark rushed in from the side. Tiny arms laced around his neck. "We knew you'd come back. But its been so *long*." His 5-year-old sister snuggled her face against him.

As he lowered his arm to pat her head, a technician came around from behind him. "Wait a minute, honey. Just because his eyes are open doesn't mean he's back. We've gotten that far before." Then he saw the grin on Wil's face, and *his* eyes widened a bit. "L-Lieutenant Brierson! Can you understand me?" Wil nodded, and the tech glanced over his head—probably at some diagnostic display. Then he smiled, too. "You do understand me! Just a minute, I'm going to get my supervisor. Don't touch anything." He rushed out of the room, his last words more an unbelieving mumbling to himself than anything else: "I was beginning to wonder if we'd ever get past protocol rejection."

Beth Brierson looked up at her brother. "Are you okay, now, Wili?"

Wil wiggled his toes, and *felt* them wiggle. He certainly felt okay. He nodded. Beth stepped back from the bed. "I want to go get Mom and Dad."

Wil smiled again. "I'll be right here waiting."

Then she was gone, too. Brierson glanced around the room and recognized the locale of several of his nightmares. But it was an ordinary hospital room, perhaps a little heavy on electronics, and still, he was not alone in it. Alvin Swensen, dressed as offensively as ever, sat in the shadows next to the window. Now he stood up and crossed the room to shake hands.

Wil grunted. "My own parents aren't here to greet me, yet Big Al is."

"Your bad luck. If you'd had the courtesy to come around the first time they tried to bring you back, you would have had your family and half MSP waiting for you. You were a hero."

"Were?"

"Oh, you still are, Wil. But it's been a while, you know." There was a crooked smile on his face.

Brierson looked through the window at the bright winter's day. The land was familiar. He was back in Michigan, probably at Okemos Central Medical. But Beth didn't look much older. "Around six months, I'd guess."

Big Al nodded. "And, no, I haven't been sitting here every day watching your face for some sign of life. I happened to be in East Lansing today. My Protection Racket still has some insurance claims against your company. MSP paid off all the big items quick, but some of the little things—bullet holes in outbuildings, stuff like that— they're dragging their heels on. Anyway, I thought I'd drop by and see how you're doing."

"Hmm. So you're not saluting the New Mexican flag down there in Manhattan?"

"What? Hell no, we're not!" Then Al seemed to remember who he was talking to. "Look, Wil, in a few minutes you're gonna have the medical staff in here patting themselves on the back for pulling off another medical miracle, and your family will be right on top of that. And after *that*, your Colonel Potts will fill you in again, on everything that's happened. Do you really want Al Swensen's Three Minute History of the Great Plains War?"

Wil nodded.

"Okay." Big Al moved his chair close to the bed. "The New Mexicans pulled back from the ungoverned lands less than three days after they grabbed you and me and Jim Turner. The official Republic view was that the Great Plains Action was a victory for the decisive and restrained use of military force. The 'roving gangster bands' of the ungoverned wastes had been punished for their abuse of New Mexican settlers, and one W. W. Brierson, the ringleader of the northern criminals, had been killed."

"I'm dead?" said Wil.

"Dead enough for their purposes." Big Al seemed momentarily uneasy. "I don't know whether I should tell a sick man how much sicker he once was, but you got hit in the back of the head with a five-millimeter exploder. The Newmex didn't hurt me or Jim, so I don't think it was vengeance. But when they blew in the door, there you were, doing something with their command equipment. They were already hurting, and they didn't have any stun guns, I guess."

A five-millimeter exploder. Wil knew what they could do. He *should* be dead. If it hit near the neck there might be some forebrain tissue left, but the front of his face would have been blown out. He touched his nose wonderingly.

Al saw the motion. "Don't worry. You're as beautiful as ever. But at the time, you looked *very* dead—even to their best medics. They popped you into stasis. The three of us spent nearly a month in detention in Oklahoma. When we were 'repatriated,' the people at Okemos Central didn't have any trouble growing back the front of your face. Maybe even the New Mexicans could do that. The problem is, you're missing a big chunk of brain. He patted the back of his head. "*That* they couldn't grow back. So they replaced it with processing equipment, and tried to interface that with what was left."

Wil experienced a sudden, chilling moment of introspection. He really should be dead. Could this all be in the imagination of some damned prosthesis program?

Al saw his face, and looked stricken. "Honest, Wil, it wasn't *that* large a piece. Just big enough to fool those dumbass New Mexicans."

The moment passed and Brierson almost chuckled. If self-awareness were suspect, there could scarcely be certainty of anything. And in fact, it was years before that particular terror resurfaced.

"Okay. So the New Mexican incursion was a great success. Now tell me why they *really* left. Was it simply the Schwartz bomb?"

"I think that was part of it." Even with the nuke, the casualties had not been high. Only the troops and tankers within three or four thousand meters of the blast were killed—perhaps 2,000 men. This was enormous by the standards Wil was used to, but not by the measure of the Water Wars. Overall, the New Mexicans could claim that it had been an "inexpensive" action.

But the evidence of casual acceptance of nuclear warfare, all the way down to the level of an ordinary farmer, was terrifying to the New Mexican brass. Annexing the Midwest would be like running a grade school where the kids carried slug guns. They probably didn't realize that Schwartz would have been lynched the first time he stepped off his property if his neighbors had realized beforehand that he was nuke-armed.

"But I think your little phone call was just as important."

"About using the tornado killers?"

"Yeah. It's one thing to step on a rattlesnake, and another to suddenly realize you're up to your ankles in 'em. I bet the weather services have equipped hundreds of farms with killers—all the way from Okemos to Greeley." And, as Wil had realized on that summer day when last he was truly conscious, a tornado killer is essentially an aerial torpedo. Their use was coordinated by the meteorological companies, which paid individual farmers to house them. During severe weather alerts, coordinating processors at a met service head-quarters monitored remote sensors, and launched killers from appropriate points in the countryside. Normally, they would be air-borne for minutes, but they could loiter for hours. When remote sensing found a twister, the killers came in at the top of the funnel, generated a 50-meter bobble, and destabilized the vortex.

Take that loiter capability, make trivial changes in the flight soft-ware, and you have a weapon capable of flying hundreds of kilome-ters and delivering a one tonne payload with pinpoint accuracy. "Even without nukes they're pretty fearsome. Especially if used like you suggested."

Wil shrugged. Actually, the target he had suggested was the usual one when dealing with marauding gangs. Only the scale was different.

"You know the Trasks—that family you called right at the end? Bill Trask's brother rents space for three killers to Topeka Met. They stole one of them and did just like you said. The news services had spotted Martinez's location; the Trasks flew the killer right into the roof of the mansion he and his staff were using down in Oklahoma. We got satellite pics of what happened. Those New Mexican big shots came storming out of there like ants in a meth fire." Even now, months later, the memory made Big Al laugh. "Bill Trask told me he painted something like 'Hey, hey Hastings, the next one is for real!' on the fuselage. I bet even yet, their top people are living under con-crete, wondering whether to keep their bobble suppressors up or down.

"But they got the message. Inside of twelve hours, their troops were moving back south and they were starting to talk about their statesmanship and the lesson they had taught us."

Wil started to laugh, too. The room shimmered colorfully in time with his laughter. It was not painful, but it was disconcerting enough to make him stop. "Good. So we didn't need those bums from Topeka Met."

"Right. Fact is, they had me arrest the Trasks for theft. But when they finally got their corporate head out of the dirt, they dropped charges and tried to pretend it had been their idea all along. Now they're modifying their killers and selling the emergency control rights."

Far away (he remembered the long hallways at Okemos Central), he heard voices. And none familiar. *Damn.* The medics were going to get to him before his family. Big Al heard the commotion, too. He stuck his head out the door, then said to Wil, "Well, Lieutenant, this is where I desert. You know the short version, anyway." He walked across the room to pick up his data set.

Wil followed him with his eyes. "So it all ended for the best, except—" *Except for all those poor New Mexican souls caught under a light brighter than any Kansas sun, except for—* "Kiki and Schwartz. I wish they could know how things turned out."

Big Al stopped halfway to the door, a surprised look on his face. "Kiki and Jake? One is too smart to die and the other is too mean! She knew Jake would thump her for bringing the New Mexicans across his land. She and my boys were way underground long before he wiped off. And Jake was dug in even deeper.

"Hell, Wil, they're even bigger celebrities than you are! Old Jake has become the Midwest's pop armadillo. None of us ever guessed, least of all him: he *enjoys* being a public person. He and Kiki have buried the hatchet. Now they're talking about a worldwide club for armadillos. They figure if one can stop an entire nation state, what can a bunch of them do? You know: 'Make the world safe for the ungoverned.' "

Then he was gone. Wil had just a moment to chew on the problems van Steen and Schwartz would cause the Michigan State Police before the triumphant med techs crowded into his room.

Historical Note

Murray Leinster

Professor Vladimir Rojestvensky, it has since been learned, remade the world at breakfast one morning while eating a bowl of rather watery red-cabbage soup, with black bread on the side. It is now a matter of history that the soup was not up to par that day, and the black bread in Omsk all that week was sub-marginal. But neither of these factors is considered to have contributed to the remaking of civilization.

The essential thing was that, while blowing on a spoonful of red-cabbage soup, Professor Rojestvensky happened to think of an interesting inference or deduction to be drawn from the Bramwell-Weems Equation expressing the distribution of energy among the nucleus-particles of the lighter atoms. The Bramwell-Weems Equation was known in Russia as the Gabrilovitch-Brekhov Formula because, obviously, Russians must have thought of it first. The symbols, however, were the same as in the capitalist world.

Professor Rojestvensky contemplated the inference with pleasure. It was very interesting indeed. He finished his breakfast, drank a glass of hot tea, wrapped himself up warmly, and set out for his classrooms in the University of Omsk. It was a long walk, because the streetcars were not running. It was a fruitful one, though. For as he walked, Professor Rojestvensky arranged his reasoning in excellent order. When he arrived at the University he found a directive from the Council of Soviet Representatives for Science and Culture. It notified him that from now on Soviet scientists must produce more and better and more Earth-shaking discoveries—or else. Therefore he would immediately report, in quadruplicate, what first-rank discoveries he was prepared to make in the science of physics. And they had better be good.

He was a modest man, was Professor Rojestvensky, but to fail to obey the directive meant losing his job. So he quakingly prepared a paper outlining his extension of the Bramwell-Weems Equation— but he was careful to call it the Gabrilovitch-Brekhov Formula—and persuaded one of his students to make four copies of it in exchange for a quarter of a pound of cheese. Then he sent off the four copies and slept badly for weeks afterward. He knew his work was good, but he didn't know whether it was good enough. It merely accounted for the mutual repulsion of the molecules of gases, it neatly explained the formation of comets' tails, and it could have led to the prediction of clouds of calcium vapor—already observed—in interstellar space. Professor Rojestvensky did not guess he had remade the world.

Weeks passed, and nothing happened. That was a bad month in Russian science. The staffs of Medical Research and Surgical Advancement had already reported everything they could dream up. Workers in Aerodynamic Design weren't sticking out their necks. The last man to design a new plane went to prison for eight years when a fuel line clogged on his plane's test flight. And Nuclear Fission workers stuck to their policy of demanding unobtainable equipment and supplies for the furtherance of their work. So Professor Rojestvensky's paper was absolutely the only contribution paddable to Earth-shaking size. His paper itself was published in the *Soviet Journal of Advanced Science*. Then it was quoted unintelligibly in *Pravda* and *Tass*, with ecstatic editorials pointing out how far Russian science was ahead of mere capitalist-imperialistic research. And that was that.

Possibly that would have been the end of it all, but that some two weeks later an American jet bomber flew twelve thousand miles, dropped fifteen tons of simulated bombs—actually condensed milk lowered to Earth by parachutes—and returned to base without refueling. This, of course, could not be allowed to go unchallenged. So a stern directive went to Aerodynamic Design. An outstanding achievement in aviation must be produced immediately. It must wipe the Americans' decadent, capitalistic eyes. Or—so the directive said explicitly—else.

The brain trust which was Aerodynamic Design went into sweating executive session, seeking a really air-tight procedure for passing the buck. They didn't want to lose their jobs, which were fairly fat ones, any more than Professor Rojestvensky had. They had to cook up something in a hurry, something really dramatic, with an out putting the blame squarely on somebody else if it didn't work. They couldn't blame Aviation Production, though. The head of that splendid organization had an in with the Politbureau. Something new and drastic and good was needed.

In the end a desperate junior official began to hunt through recent Soviet contributions to science. If he could find something impressive that could be twisted into an advance in aerodynamics, it could be designed and built, and any failure blamed on the scientist who had furnished false data as a form of alien-inspired sabotage. Scientists were always expendable in Russian politics. It was time to expend one. Largely because his name was on top of the pile, Professor Rojestvensky was picked.

This, in detail, is the process by which his extension of the Bramwell-Weems—or Gabrilovitch-Brekhov—Equation was selected for practical development. Our brave new world is the result. Aerodynamic Design borrowed a man from Nuclear Fission in a deal between two department heads, and the Nuclear Fission man agreed to work up something elaborate and impressive. He set to work on Professor Rojestvensky's figures. And presently he turned pale, and gulped very rapidly several times, and muttered, "*Gospody pomilov!*" That meant, "Lord have mercy on us!" and it was not a good Russian expression any longer, but it was the way he felt. In time, he showed his results to Aerodynamic Design and said, in effect, "But, it might really work!"

Aerodynamic Design sent him out to Omsk to get Professor Rojestvensky to check his calculations. It was a shrewd move. The

Nuclear Fission man and Professor Rojestvensky got along splendidly. They ate red-cabbage soup together and the professor O.K.'d the whole project. That made him responsible for anything that went wrong and Aerodynamic Design, en masse, was much relieved. They sent in a preliminary report on their intentions and started to make one gadget themselves. The Nuclear Fission man was strangely willing to play along and see what happened. He supervised the construction of the thing.

It consisted of a set of straps very much like a parachute harness, hung from a little bar of brass with a plating of metallic sodium, under another plating of nickel, and the whole thing enclosed in a plastic tube. There was a small box with a couple of controls. That was all there was to it.

When it was finished, the Nuclear-Fission man tried it out himself. He climbed into the harness in the Wind Tunnel Building of Aerodynamic Design's plant, said the Russian equivalent of "Here goes nothing!" and flipped over one of the controls. In his shakiness, he pushed it too far. He left the ground, went straight up like a rocket, and cracked his head against the three-story-high ceiling and was knocked cold for two hours. They had to haul him down from the ceiling with an extension ladder, because the gadget he'd made tried insistently to push a hole through the roof to the wide blue yonder.

When he recovered consciousness, practically all of Aerodynamic Design surrounded him, wearing startled expressions. And they stayed around while he found out what the new device would do. Put briefly, it would do practically anything but make fondant. It was a personal flying device, not an airplane, which would lift up to two hundred twenty-five pounds. It would hover perfectly. It would, all by itself, travel in any direction at any speed a man could stand without a windshield.

True, the Rojestvensky Effect which made it fly was limited. No matter how big you made the metal bar, it wouldn't lift more than roughly a hundred kilos, nearly two-twenty-five pounds. But it worked by the fact that the layer of metallic sodium on the brass pushed violently away from all other sodium more than three meters away from it. Sodium within three meters wasn't affected. And there was sodium everywhere. Sodium chloride—common table salt—is present everywhere on Earth and the waters under the Earth, but it isn't present in the heavens above. So the thing would fly anywhere over land or sea, but it wouldn't go but so high. The top limit for the gadget's flight was about four thousand feet, with a hundred-and-fifty-pound man in the harness. A heavier man couldn't get up so high. And it was infinitely safe. A man could fly night, day, or blind drunk and nothing could happen to him. He couldn't run into a mountain because he'd bounce over it. The thing was marvelous!

Aerodynamic Design made a second triumphant report to the Politbureau. A new and appropriately revolutionary device—it was Russian—had been produced in obedience to orders. Russian science had come through! When better revolutionary discoveries were made, Russia would make them! And if the device was inherently limited to one-man use—ha-ha! It gave the Russian army flying infantry! It provided the perfect modern technique for revolutionary war! It offered the perfect defense for peaceful, democratic Russia against malevolent capitalistic imperialism! In short, it was hot stuff!

As a matter of fact, it was. Two months later there was a May Day celebration in Moscow at which the proof of Russia's superlative science was unveiled to the world. Planes flew over Red Square in magnificent massed formations. Tanks and guns rumbled through the streets leading to Lenin's tomb. But the infantry—where was the infantry? Where were the serried ranks of armed men, shaking the earth with their steady tread? Behind the tanks and guns there was only emptiness.

For a while only. There was silence after the guns had gone clanking by. Then a far-distant, tumultuous uproar of cheering. Something new, something strange and marvelous had roused the remotest quarter of the city to enthusiasm. Far, far away, the flying infantry appeared!

Some of the more naïve of the populace believed at first that the U.S.S.R. had made a nonaggression pact with God and that a detachment of angels was parading in compliment to the Soviet Union. It wasn't too implausible, as a first impression. Shoulder to shoulder, rank after rank, holding fast to lines like dog leashes that held them in formation, no less than twelve thousand Russian infantrymen floated into the Red Square some fifteen feet off the ground. They were a bit ragged as to elevation, and they tended to eddy a bit at street corners, but they swept out of the canyons which were streets at a magnificent twenty-five miles an hour, in such a display of air-borne strength as the world had never seen before.

The population cheered itself hoarse. The foreign attachés looked inscrutable. The members of the Politbureau looked on and happily began to form in their minds the demands they would make for pacts of peace and friendship—and military bases—with formerly recalcitrant European nations. These pacts of closest friendship were going to be honeys!

That same morning Professor Rojestvensky breakfasted on red-cabbage soup and black bread, wholly unaware that he had remade the world. But that great events were in the making was self-evident even to members of the United States Senate. Newsreel pictures of the flying infantry parade were shown everywhere. And the Communist parties of the Western nations were, of course, wholly independent organizations with no connection whatever with Moscow. But they could not restrain their enthusiasm over this evidence of Russian greatness. Cheering sections of Communists attended every showing of the newsreels in every theater and howled themselves hoarse. They took regular turns at it and were supplied with throat lozenges by ardent Party workers. Later newsreels showing the flying infantry returning to camp over the rooftops of Moscow evoked screams of admiration. When a Russian documentary film appeared in the Western world, skillfully faking the number of men equipped with individual flying units, the national, patriotic Communist party members began to mention brightly that everybody who did not say loudly, at regular intervals, that Russia was the greatest country in the world was having his name written down for future reference.

Inspired news-stories mentioned that the entire Russian army would be air-borne within three months. The magnificent feat of Russian industry in turning out three million flying devices per month brought forth screaming headlines in the *Daily Worker*. There were only two minor discords in the choral antiphony of national-Communist hosannas and capitalistic alarm.

One was an air-force general's meditative answer to the question: "What defense can there be against an army traveling through the air like a swarm of locusts?" The general said mildly:

"Wel-l-l, we carried eighteen tons of condensed milk fourteen thousand miles last week, and we've done pretty good work for the Agriculture Department dusting grasshoppers."

The other was the bitter protest made by the Russian ambassador in Washington. He denounced the capitalist-economy-inspired prevention of the shipment to Russia of an order for brass rods plated with metallic sodium, then plated with nickel, and afterward enclosed in plastic tubes. State Department investigation showed that while an initial order of twelve thousand five hundred such rods had been shipped in April, there had been a number of fires in the factory since, and it had been closed down until fire-prevention methods could be devised. It was pointed out that metallic sodium is hot stuff. It catches fire when wetted or even out of pure cussedness it is fiercely inflammable.

This was a fact that Aviation Production in Russia had already found out. The head man was in trouble with his own friends in the Politbureau for failing to meet production quotas, and he'd ordered the tricky stuff—the rods had to be dipped in melted sodium in a helium atmosphere for quantity production—manufactured in the benighted and scientifically retarded United States.

There was another item that should be mentioned, too. Within a week after the issue of personal fliers to Russian infantrymen, no less than sixty-four desertions by air to Western nations took place. On the morning after the first night maneuvers of the air-borne force, ninety-two Russians were discovered in the Allied half of Germany alone, trying to swap their gadgets for suits of civilian clothes.

They were obliged, of course. Enterprising black marketeers joyfully purchased the personal fliers, shipped them to France, to Holland, to Belgium, Sweden, Norway, and Switzerland, and sold them at enormous profits. In a week it was notorious that any Russian deserter from the flying infantry could sell his flight-equipment for enough money to buy forty-nine wrist watches and still stay drunk for six months. It was typical private enterprise.

It was unprincipled and unjust. But it got worse.

Private entrepreneurs stole the invention itself. At first the units were reproduced one by one in small shops for high prices. But the fire-hazard was great. Production-line methods were really necessary both for economy and industrial safety reasons. So after a while the Bofors Company, of Sweden, rather apologetically turned out a sport model, in quantity, selling for kronen worth twelve dollars and fifty cents in American money. Then the refurbished I. G. Farben put out a German type which sold openly for a sum in occupation marks equal to only nine eighty American. A Belgian model priced—in francs—at five fifty had a wide sale, but was not considered quite equal to the Dutch model at guilders exchanging for six twenty-five or the French model with leather-trimmed straps at seven dollars worth of devaluated francs.

The United States capitalists started late. Two bicycle makers switched their factories to the production of personal fliers, yet by the middle of June American production was estimated at not over fifty thousand per month. But in July, one hundred eighty thousand were produced and in August the production—expected to be about three hundred thousand—suddenly went sky-high when both General Electric and Westinghouse entered the market. In September American production was over three million and it became evident that manufacturers would have to compete with each other on finish and luxury of design. The days when anything that would fly was salable at three fifty and up were over.

The personal flier became a part of American life, as, of course, it became a part of life everywhere. In the United States the inherent four-thousand-foot ceiling of personal fliers kept regular air traffic from having trouble except near airports, and flier-equipped airport police soon developed techniques for traffic control. A blimp patrol had to be set up off the Atlantic Coast to head back enthusiasts for foreign travel and Gulf Stream fishing, but it worked very well. There were three million, then five million, and by November twelve million personal-flier-equipped Americans aloft. And the total continued to rise. Suburban railways—especially after weather-proof garments became really good—joyfully abandoned their short-haul passenger traffic and all the railroads settled down contentedly to their real and profitable business of long-haul heavy-freight carriage. Even the air lines prospered incredibly. The speed-limitation on personal fliers still left the jet-driven plane the only way to travel long distances quickly, and passengers desiring intermediate stops simply stepped out of a plane door when near their desired destination. Rural residential developments sprang up like mushrooms. A marked trend toward country life multiplied, Florida and California became so crowded that everybody got disgusted and went home, and the millennium appeared to be just around the corner.

Then came the dawn. It was actually the dawn of the remade world, but it looked bad for a while. The Soviet government stormed at the conscienceless, degraded theft of its own State secret by decadent and imperialistic outsiders. Actual Russian production of personal fliers was somewhere around twenty-five hundred per month at a time when half the population of Europe and America had proved that flying was cheaper than walking. Sternly, the Soviet government—through the Cominform—suggested that now was the time for all good Communists to come to the aid of their Party. The Party needed personal fliers. Fast. So enthusiastic Communists all over Europe flew loyally to Russia to contribute to the safety of their ideals, and to prove the international solidarity of the proletariat. They landed by tens of thousands without passports, without ration cards, and often with insufficient Party credentials. They undoubtedly had spies among them, along with noble comrades. So the U.S.S.R. had to protect itself. Regretfully, Russian officials clapped the new arrivals into jail as they landed, took away their fliers, and sent them back to their national borders in boxcars. But they did send indoctrination experts to travel with them and explain that this was hospitable treatment and that they were experiencing the welcome due to heroes.

But borders were not only crossed by friends. Smuggling became a sport. Customs barriers for anything but heavy goods simply ceased to exist. The French national monopoly on tobacco and matches evaporated, and many Frenchmen smoked real tobacco for the first time in their lives. Some of them did not like it. And there were even political consequences of the personal-flier development.

In Spain, philosophical anarchists and *syndicalistos* organized political demonstrations. Sometimes hundreds of them flew all night long to rendezvous above the former royal palace in Madrid—now occupied by the Caudillo—and empty chamber-pots upon it at dawn. Totalitarianism in Spain collapsed.

The Russian rulers were made of sterner stuff. True, the Iron Curtain became a figment. Political refugees from Russia returned—sometimes thoughtfully carrying revolvers in case they met somebody they disliked—and disseminated capitalistic propaganda and cast doubts upon the superiority of the Russian standard of living. Often they had wrist watches and some of them even brought along personal fliers as gifts to personal friends. Obviously, this sort of thing was subversive. The purity of Soviet culture could not be maintained when foreigners could enter Russia at will and call the leaders of the Soviet Union liars. Still less could it survive when they proved it.

So the Soviet Union fought back. The Army set up radars to detect the carriers of anti-dialectic-materialism propaganda. The Ministry of Propaganda worked around the clock. People wearing wrist watches were shot if they could not prove they had stolen them from Germans, and smugglers and young men flying Sovietward to ply Russian girls with chocolate bars were intercepted. For almost a week it seemed that radar and flying infantry might yet save the Soviet way of life.

But then unprincipled capitalists dealt a new foul blow. They advertised that anybody intending to slip through the Iron Curtain should provide himself with Bouffon's Anti-Radar Tin Foil Strips, available in one-kilogram cartons at all corner shops. Tin foil strips had been distributed by Allied bombers to confuse German radar during the last war. Smugglers and romantic young men, meditatively dripping tin foil as they flew through the Russian night, made Russian radar useless.

Nothing was left but war. So a splendid, overwhelming blow was planned and carried out. In two nights the entire Soviet force of flying infantry was concentrated. On the third night four hundred thousand flying infantry went sweeping westward in an irresistible swarm. The technique had been worked out by the General Staff on orders from the Politbureau to devise immediately a new and unbeatable system of warfare—or else. The horde of flying warriors was to swoop down from the darkness on Western European cities, confiscate all personal fliers and ship them back to Russia for the use of reinforcements. There could be no resistance. Every part of an enemy nation was equally reachable and equally vulnerable. Russian troops could not be bombed, because they would be deliberately intermixed with the native population. There could be no fighting but street-fighting. This would be war on a new scale, invasion from a new dimension; it would be conquest which could not be fought.

The only trouble was that practically every square mile of European sky was inhabited by somebody enjoying the fruits of Russian science in the form of a personal flier. And secrecy simply couldn't be managed. All Europe knew just about as much about the Russian plan as the Russians did.

So when the clouds of flying infantry came pouring through the night, great droning bombers with riding-lights and landing-lights aglow came roaring out of the west to meet them. There were, to be sure, Soviet jet-fighters with the defending fleet. They tangled with the Russian escort and fought all over the sky, while the bombers focused their landing-lights on the infantry and roared at them. The sensation of being ahead of a bellowing plane rushing at one was exactly that of being on a railroad track with an express train on the loose. There was nothing to do but duck. The Russian soldiers ducked. Then the bombers began to shoot star shells, rockets, Roman candles and other pyrotechnics. The Russian troops dispersed. And an army that is dispersed simply isn't an army. When finally vast numbers of enthusiastic personal-flier addicts came swooping through the night with flashlights and Very pistols, the debacle was complete. The still-fighting planes overhead had nothing left to fight for. Those that were left went home.

When dawn came the Russian soldiers were individuals scattered over three separate nations. And Russian soldiers, in quantity, tend to fight or loot as opportunity offers. But a Russian soldier, as an individual, craves civilian clothes above all else. Russian soldiers landed and tried to make deals for their flying equipment according

to the traditions of only a few months before. They were sadly disil-
lusioned. The best bargain most of them could make was simply a
promise that they wouldn't be sent back home—and they took that.

It was all rather anticlimactic, and it got worse. Russia was still
legally at war with everybody, even after its flying infantry sat down
and made friends. And Russia was still too big to invade. On the
other hand, it had to keep its air force in hand to fight off attempts at
invasion. Just to maintain that defensive frame of mind, Allied
bombers occasionally smashed some Russian airfields, and some
railroads, and—probably at the instigation of decadent capitalists—
they did blow up the Aviation Production factories, even away off in
the Urals. Those Ural raids, by the way, were made by the United
States Air Force, flying over the North Pole to prove that it could
deliver something besides condensed milk at long distances.

But the war never really amounted to much. The Allies had all the
flying infantry they wanted to use, but they didn't want to use it. The
Russians worked frantically, suborning treason and developing black
marketeers and so on, to get personal fliers for defense, but Russian
civilians would pay more than even the Soviet government for them,
so the Army hardly got any at all. To correct this situation the
Supreme Soviet declared private possession of a personal flier a capital offense, and shot several hundred citizens to prove it. Among the
victims of this purge, by the way, was the Nuclear-Fission man who
had worked out the personal flier from Professor Rojestvensky's figures. But people wanted personal fliers. When owning one became a
reason for getting shot, almost half the Russian government's minor
officials piled out of the nearest window and went somewhere else,
and the bigger officials kept their personal fliers where they could
grab them at any instant and take off. And the smuggling kept on.
Before long practically everybody had private fliers but the army—
and flier-equipped soldiers tended to disappear over the horizon if
left alone after nightfall.

So the Soviet Union simply fell to pieces. The Supreme Soviet
couldn't govern when anybody who disagreed with it could go up the
nearest chimney and stay gone. It lost the enthusiastic support of the
population as soon as it became unable to shoot the unenthusiastic.

And when it was committed to the policy of shooting every Russian citizen who possessed proof of the supreme splendor of Russian science—a personal flier—why public discipline disappeared. Party discipline went with it. All discipline followed. And when there wasn't any discipline there simply wasn't any Soviet Union and therefore there wasn't any war, and everybody might as well stop fooling around and cook dinner. The world, in fact, was remade.

Undoubtedly the world is a good deal happier since Professor Rojestvensky thought of an interesting inference to be drawn from the Bramwell-Weems Equation while at his breakfast of red-cabbage soup and black bread. There are no longer any iron-bound national boundaries, and therefore no wars or rumors of wars. There are no longer any particular reasons for cities to be crowded, and a reasonably equitable social system has to exist or people will go fishing or down to the South Seas, or somewhere where they won't be bothered.

But in some ways the change has not been as great as one might have expected. About a year after the world was remade, an American engineer thought up a twist on Professor Rojestvensky's figures. He interested the American continental government and they got ready to build a spaceship. The idea was that if a variation of that brass-sodium-nickel bar was curled around a hundred-foot-long tube, and metallic sodium vapor was introduced into one end of the tube, it would be pushed out of the other end with some speed. Calculation proved, indeed, that with all the acceleration possible, the metallic vapor would emerge with a velocity of ninety-eight point seven percent of the speed of light. Using Einstein's formula for the relationship of mass to speed, that meant that the tube would propel a rocketship that could go to the Moon or Mars or anywhere else. The American government started to build the ship, and then thought it would be a good idea to have Professor Rojestvensky in on the job as a consultant. Besides, the world owed him something. So he was sent for, and Congress voted him more money than he had ever heard of before, and he looked over the figures and O.K.'d them. They were all right.

But he was typical of the people whose happiness has not been markedly increased by the remade world. He was a rich man, and he liked America, but after a month or so he didn't look happy. So the government put him in the most luxurious suite in the most luxurious hotel in America, and assigned people to wait on him and a translator to translate for him, and did its very best to honor the man who'd remade the world. But still he didn't seem content.

One day a committee of reporters asked him what he wanted. He would be in all the history books, and he had done the world a great favor, and the public would like him to be pleased. But Professor Rojestvensky shook his head sadly.

"It's only," he said gloomily, "that since I am rich and the world is peaceable and everybody is happy—well, I just can't seem to find anyone who knows how to make good red-cabbage soup."

The Weapon Shop

A.E. van Vogt

The village at night made a curiously timeless picture. Fara walked contentedly beside his wife along the street. The air was like wine; and he was thinking dimly of the artist who had come up from Imperial City and made what the telestats called—he remembered the phrase vividly—"a symbolic painting reminiscent of a scene in the electrical age of seven thousand years ago."

Fara believed that utterly. The street before him with its weedless, automatically tended gardens, its shops set well back among the flowers, its perpetual hard, grassy sidewalks and its street lamps that glowed from every pore of their structure—this was a restful paradise where time had stood still.

And it was like being a part of life that the great artist's picture of this quiet, peaceful scene before him was now in the collection of the empress herself. She had praised it, and naturally the thrice-blest artist had immediately and humbly begged her to accept it.

What a joy it must be to be able to offer personal homage to the glorious, the divine, the serenely gracious and lovely Innelda Isher, one thousand one hundred eightieth of her line.

As they walked, Fara half turned to his wife. In the dim light of the nearest street lamp, her kindly, still youthful face was almost lost in shadow. He murmured softly, instinctively muting his voice to harmonize with the pastel shades of night:

"She said—our empress said—that our little village of Glay seemed to her to have in it all the wholesomeness, the gentleness, that constitutes the finest qualities of her people. Wasn't that a wonderful thought, Creel? She must be a marvelously understanding woman. I—"

He stopped. They had come to a side street, and there was something about a hundred and fifty feet along it that—

"Look!" Fara said hoarsely.

He pointed with rigid arm and finger at a sign that glowed in the night, a sign that read:

FINE WEAPONS

THE RIGHT TO BUY WEAPONS
IS THE RIGHT TO BE FREE

Fara had a strange, empty feeling as he stared at the blazing sign. He saw that other villagers were gathering. He said finally, huskily, "I've heard of these shops. They're places of infamy, against which the government of the empress will act one of these days. They're built in hidden factories, and then transported whole to towns like ours and set up in gross defiance of property rights. That one wasn't there an hour ago."

Fara's face hardened. His voice had a harsh edge in it, as he said, "Creel, go home."

Fara was surprised when Creel did not move off at once. All their married life she had had a pleasing habit of obedience that had made cohabitation a wonderful thing. He saw that she was looking at him wide-eyed, and that it was a timid alarm that held her there. She said, "Fara, what do you intend to do? You're not thinking of—"

"Go home!" Her fear brought out all the grim determination in his nature. "We're not going to let such a monstrous thing desecrate our village. Think of it"—his voice shivered before the appalling thought—"this fine, old-fashioned community, which we had resolved always to keep exactly as the empress has it in her picture gallery, debauched now, ruined by this . . . this thing— But we won't have it; that's all there is to it."

Creel's voice came softly out of the half-darkness of the street corner, the timidity gone from it: "Don't do anything rash, Fara. Remember it is not the first new building to come into Glay—since the picture was painted."

Fara was silent. This was a quality of his wife of which he did not approve, this reminding him unnecessarily of unpleasant facts. He knew exactly what she meant. The gigantic, multitentacled corporation, Automatic Atomic Motor Repair Shops, Inc., had come in under the laws of the state with their flashy building, against the wishes of the village council—and had already taken half of Fara's repair business.

"That's different!" Fara growled finally. "In the first place people will discover in good time that these new automatic repairers do a poor job. In the second place it's fair competition. But this weapon shop is a defiance of all the decencies that make life under the House of Isher such a joy. Look at the hypocritical sign: 'The right to buy weapons—' Aaaaahh!"

He broke off with: "Go home, Creel. We'll see to it that they sell no weapons in this town."

He watched the slender woman-shape move off into the shadows. She was halfway across the street when a thought occurred to Fara. He called, "And if you see that son of ours hanging around some street corner, take him home. He's got to learn to stop staying out so late at night."

The shadowed figure of his wife did not turn; and after watching her for a moment moving along against the dim background of softly glowing street lights, Fara twisted on his heel, and walked swiftly toward the shop. The crowd was growing larger every minute and the night pulsed with excited voices.

Beyond doubt, here was the biggest thing that had ever happened to the village of Glay.

The sign of the weapon shop was, he saw, a normal-illusion affair. No matter what his angle of view, he was always looking straight at it. When he paused finally in front of the great display window, the words had pressed back against the store front, and were staring unwinkingly down at him.

Fara sniffed once more at the meaning of the slogan, then forgot the simple thing. There was another sign in the window, which read:

THE FINEST ENERGY WEAPONS
IN THE KNOWN UNIVERSE

A spark of interest struck fire inside Fara. He gazed at that brilliant display of guns, fascinated in spite of himself. The weapons were of every size, ranging from tiny little finger pistols to express rifles. They were made of every one of the light, hard, ornamental substances: glittering glassein, the colorful but opaque Ordine plastic, viridescent magnesitic beryllium. And others.

It was the very deadly extent of the destructive display that brought a chill to Fara. So many weapons for the little village of Glay, where not more than two people to his knowledge had guns, and those only for hunting. Why, the thing was absurd, fantastically mischievous, utterly threatening.

Somewhere behind Fara, a man said: "It's right on Lan Harris' lot. Good joke on that old scoundrel. Will he raise a row!"

There was a faint titter from several men, that made an odd patch of sound on the warm, fresh air. And Fara saw that the man had spoken the truth. The weapon shop had a forty-foot frontage. And it occupied the very center of the green, gardenlike lot of tight-fisted old Harris.

Fara frowned. The clever devils, the weapon-shop people, selecting the property of the most disliked man in town, coolly taking it over and giving everybody an agreeable titillation. But the very cunning of it made it vital that the trick shouldn't succeed.

He was still scowling anxiously when he saw the plump figure of Mel Dale, the mayor. Fara edged toward him hurriedly, touched his hat respectfully, and said, "Where's Jor?"

"Here." The village constable elbowed his way through a little bundle of men. "Any plans?" he said.

"There's only one plan," said Fara boldly. "Go in and arrest them."

To Fara's amazement, the two men looked at each other, then at the ground. It was the big constable who answered shortly, "Door's locked. And nobody answers our pounding. I was just going to suggest we let the matter ride until morning."

"Nonsense!" His very astonishment made Fara impatient. "Get an ax and we'll break the door down. Delay will only encourage such riffraff to resist. We don't want their kind in our village for so much as a single night. Isn't that so?"

There was a hasty nod of agreement from everybody in his immediate vicinity. Too hasty. Fara looked around puzzled at eyes that lowered before his level gaze. He thought: "They are all scared. And unwilling." Before he could speak, Constable Jor said, "I guess you haven't heard about those doors or these shops. From all accounts, you can't break into them."

It struck Fara with a sudden pang that it was he who would have to act here. He said, "I'll get my atomic cutting machine from my shop. That'll fix them. Have I your permission to do that, Mr. Mayor?"

In the glow of the weapon-shop window, the plump man was sweating visibly. He pulled out a handkerchief and wiped his forehead. He said, "Maybe I'd better call the commander of the Imperial garrison at Ferd, and ask them."

"No!" Fara recognized evasion when he saw it. He felt himself steel; the conviction came that all the strength in this village was in him. "We must act ourselves. Other communities have let these people get in because they took no decisive action. We've got to resist to the limit. Beginning now. This minute. Well?"

The mayor's "All right!" was scarcely more than a sigh of sound. But it was all Fara needed.

He called out his intention to the crowd; and then, as he pushed his way out of the mob, he saw his son standing with some other young men staring at the window display.

Fara called, "Cayle, come and help me with the machine."

Cayle did not even turn; and Fara hurried on, seething. That wretched boy! One of these days he, Fara, would have to take firm action there. Or he'd have a no-good on his hands.

The energy was soundless—and smooth. There was no sputter, no fireworks. It glowed with a soft, pure white light, almost caressing the metal panels of the door—but not even beginning to scar them.

Minute after minute, the dogged Fara refused to believe the incredible failure, and played the boundlessly potent energy on that resisting wall. When he finally shut off his machine, he was perspiring freely.

"I don't understand it," he gasped. "Why—no metal is supposed to stand up against a steady flood of atomic force. Even the hard metal plates used inside the blast chamber of a motor take the explosions in what is called infinite series, so that each one has unlimited rest. That's the theory, but actually steady running crystallizes the whole plate after a few months."

"It's as Jor told you," said the mayor. "These weapon shops are—big. They spread right through the empire, *and they don't recognize the empress.*"

Fara shifted his feet on the hard grass, disturbed. He didn't like this kind of talk. It sounded—sacrilegious. And besides it was nonsense. It must be. Before he could speak, a man said somewhere behind him, "I've heard it said that that door will open only to those who cannot harm the people inside."

The words shocked Fara out of his daze. With a start, and for the first time, he saw that his failure had had a bad psychological effect. He said sharply, "That's ridiculous! If there were doors like that, we'd all have them. We—"

The thought that stopped his words was the sudden realization that *he* had not seen anybody try to open the door; and with all this reluctance around him it was quite possible that—

He stepped forward, grasped at the doorknob and pulled. The door opened with an unnatural weightlessness that gave him the fleeting impression that the knob had come loose in his hand. With a gasp, Fara jerked the door wide open.

"Jor!" he yelled. "Get in!"

The constable made a distorted movement—distorted by what must have been a will to caution, followed by the instant realization that he could not hold back before so many. He leaped awkwardly toward the open door—and it closed in his face.

Fara stared stupidly at his hand, which was still clenched. And then, slowly, a hideous thrill coursed along his nerves. The knob had—withdrawn. It had twisted, become viscous and slipped amorphously from his straining fingers. Even the memory of that brief sensation gave him a feeling of abnormal things.

He grew aware that the crowd was watching with a silent intentness. Fara reached again for the knob, not quite so eagerly this time; and it was only a sudden realization of his reluctance that made him angry when the handle neither turned nor yielded in any way.

Determination returned in full force, and with it came a thought. He motioned to the constable. "Go back, Jor, while I pull."

The man retreated, but it did no good. And tugging did not help. The door would not open. Somewhere in the crowd, a man said darkly, "It decided to let you in, then it changed its mind."

"What foolishness are you talking!" Fara spoke violently. "*It* changed its mind. Are you crazy? A door has no sense."

But a surge of fear put a half-quaver into his voice. It was the sudden alarm that made him bold beyond all his normal caution. With a jerk of his body, Fara faced the shop.

The building loomed there under the night sky, in itself bright as day, huge in width and length, and alien, menacing, no longer easily conquerable. The dim queasy wonder came as to what the soldiers of the empress would do if they were invited to act. And suddenly—a bare, flashing glimpse of a grim possibility—the feeling grew that even they would be able to do nothing.

Abruptly, Fara was conscious of horror that such an idea could enter his mind. He shut his brain tight, said wildly, "The door opened for me once. It will open again."

It did. Quite simply it did. Gently, without resistance, with that same sensation of weightlessness, the strange, sensitive door followed the tug of his fingers. Beyond the threshold was dimness, a wide, darkened alcove. He heard the voice of Mel Dale behind him, the mayor saying, "Fara, don't be a fool. What will you do inside?"

Fara was vaguely amazed to realize that he had stepped across the threshold. He turned, startled, and stared at the blur of faces

"Why—" he began blankly; then he brightened; he said, "Why, I'll buy a gun, of course."

The brilliance of his reply, the cunning implicit in it, dazzled Fara for half a minute longer. The mood yielded slowly, as he found himself in the dimly lighted interior of the weapon shop.

It was preternaturally quiet inside. Not a sound penetrated from the night from which he had come, and the startled thought came that the people of the shop might actually be unaware that there was a crowd outside.

Fara walked forward gingerly on a rugged floor that muffled his footsteps utterly. After a moment, his eyes accustomed themselves to the soft lighting, which came like a reflection from the walls and ceilings. In a vague way, he had expected ultranormality; and the ordinariness of the atomic lighting acted like a tonic to his tensed nerves.

He shook himself angrily. Why should there be anything really superior? He was getting as bad as those credulous idiots out in the street.

He glanced around with gathering confidence. The place looked quite common. It was a shop, almost scantily furnished. There were showcases on the walls and on the floor, glitteringly lovely things, but nothing unusual, and not many of them—a few dozens. There was in addition a double, ornate door leading to a back room—

Fara tried to keep one eye on that door, as he examined several showcases, each with three or four weapons either mounted or arranged in boxes or holsters.

Abruptly, the weapons began to excite him. He forgot to watch the door, as the wild thought struck that he ought to grab one of those guns from a case, and then the moment someone came, force him outside where Jor would perform the arrest and—

Behind him, a man said quietly, "You wish to buy a gun?"

Fara turned with a jump. Brief rage flooded him at the way his plan had been wrecked by the arrival of the clerk.

The anger died as he saw that the intruder was a fine-looking, silver-haired man, older than himself. That was immeasurably disconcerting. Fara had an immense and almost automatic respect for age, and for a long second he could only stand there gaping. He said at last, lamely, "Yes, yes, a gun."

"For what purpose?" said the man in his quiet voice.

Fara could only look at him blankly. It was too fast. He wanted to get mad. He wanted to tell these people what he thought of them. But the age of this representative locked his tongue, tangled his emotions. He managed speech only by an effort of will:

"For hunting." The plausible word stiffened his mind. "Yes, definitely for hunting. There is a lake to the north of here," he went on more fulsomely, glibly, "and—"

He stopped, scowling, startled at the extent of his dishonesty. He was not prepared to go so deeply into prevarication. He said curtly, "For hunting."

Fara was himself again. Abruptly, he hated the man for having put him so completely at a disadvantage. With smoldering eyes he watched the old fellow click open a showcase, and take out a green-shining rifle.

As the man faced him, weapon in hand, Fara was thinking grimly, "Pretty clever, having an old man as a front." It was the same kind of cunning that had made them choose the property of Miser Harris. Icily furious, taut with his purpose, Fara reached for the gun; but the man held it out of his reach, saying, "Before I can even let you test this, I am compelled by the by-laws of the weapon shops to inform you under what circumstances you may purchase a gun."

So they had private regulations. What a system of psychology tricks to impress gullible fools! Well, let the old scoundrel talk. As soon as he, Fara, got hold of the rifle, he'd put an end to hypocrisy.

"We weapons makers," the clerk was saying mildly, "have evolved guns that can, in their particular ranges, destroy any machine or object made of what is called matter. Thus whoever possesses one of our weapons is the equal and more of any soldier of the empress. I say more because each gun is the center of a field of force which acts as a perfect screen against immaterial destructive forces. That screen offers no resistance to clubs or spears or bullets, or other material substances, but it would require a small atomic cannon to penetrate the superb barrier it creates around its owner.

"You will readily comprehend," the man went on, "that such a potent weapon could not be allowed to fall, unmodified, into irresponsible hands. Accordingly, no gun purchased from us may be used for aggression or murder. In the case of the hunting rifle, only such specified game birds and animals as we may from time to time list in our display windows may be shot. Finally, no weapon can be resold without our approval. Is that clear?"

Fara nodded dumbly. For the moment, speech was impossible to him. The incredible, fantastically stupid words were still going round and around in his head. He wondered if he ought to laugh out loud, or curse the man for daring to insult his intelligence so tremendously.

So the gun mustn't be used for murder or robbery. So only certain birds and animals could be shot. And as for reselling it, suppose— suppose he bought this thing, took a trip of a thousand miles, and offered it to some wealthy stranger for two credits—who would ever know?

Or suppose he held up the stranger. Or shot him. How could the weapon shop ever find out? The thing was so ridiculous that—

He grew aware that the gun was being held out to him stock first. He took it eagerly, and had to fight the impulse to turn the muzzle directly on the old man. Mustn't rush this, he thought tautly. He said, "How does it work?"

"You simply aim it, and pull the trigger. Perhaps you would like to try it on a target we have."

Fara swung the gun up. "Yes," he said triumphantly, "and you're it. Now, just get over there to the front door, and then outside."

He raised his voice: "And if anybody's thinking of coming through the back door, I've got that covered, too."

He motioned jerkily at the clerk. "Quick now, move! I'll shoot! I swear I will."

The man was cool, unflustered. "I have no doubt you would. When we decided to attune the door so that you could enter despite your hostility, we assumed the capacity for homicide. However, this is our party. You had better adjust yourself accordingly, and look behind you—"

❖ ❖ ❖

There was silence. Finger on trigger, Fara stood motionless. Dim thoughts came of all the *half-things* he had heard in his days about the weapon shops: that they had secret supporters in every district, that they had a private and ruthless hidden government, and that once you got into their clutches, the only way out was death and—

But what finally came clear was a mind picture of himself, Fara Clark, family man, faithful subject of the empress, standing here in this dimly lighted store, deliberately fighting an organization so vast and menacing that— He must have been mad.

Only—here he was. He forced courage into his sagging muscles. He said, "You can't fool me with pretending there's someone behind me. Now, get to that door. And *fast!*"

The firm eyes of the old man were looking past him. The man said quietly, "Well, Rad, have you all the data?"

"Enough for a primary," said a young man's baritone voice behind Fara. "Type A-7 conservative. Good average intelligence, but a Monaric development peculiar to small towns. One sided outlook fostered by the Imperial schools present in exaggerated form. Extremely honest. Reason would be useless. Emotional approach would require extended treatment. I see no reason why we should bother. Let him live his life as it suits him."

"If you think," Fara said shakily, "that that trick voice is going to make me turn, you're crazy. That's the left wall of the building. I know there's no one there."

"I'm all in favor, Rad," said the old man, "of letting him live his life. But he was the prime mover of the crowd outside. I think he should be discouraged."

"We'll advertise his presence," said Rad. "He'll spend the rest of his life denying the charge."

Fara's confidence in the gun had faded so far that, as he listened in puzzled uneasiness to the incomprehensible conversation, he forgot it completely. He parted his lips, but before he could speak, the old man cut in, persistently, "I think a little emotion might have a long-run effect. Show him the palace."

Palace! The startling word tore Fara out of his brief paralysis. "See here," he began, "I can see now that you lied to me. This gun isn't loaded at all. It's—"

His voice failed him. Every muscle in his body went rigid. He stared like a madman. *There was no gun in his hands.*

"Why, you—" he began wildly. And stopped again. His mind heaved with imbalance. With a terrible effort he fought off the spinning sensation, thought finally, tremblingly: Somebody must have sneaked the gun from him. That meant—there was someone behind him. The voice was no mechanical thing. Somehow, they had—

He started to turn—and couldn't. What in the name of— He struggled, pushing with his muscles. And couldn't move, couldn't budge, couldn't even—

The room was growing curiously dark. He had difficulty seeing the old man and— He would have shrieked then if he could. Because the weapon shop was gone. He was—

He was standing in the sky above an immense city.

In the sky, and nothing beneath him, nothing around him but air, and blue summer heaven, and the city a mile, two miles below.

Nothing, nothing— He would have shrieked, but his breath seemed solidly embedded in his lungs. Sanity came back as the remote awareness impinged upon his terrified mind that he was actually standing on a hard floor, and that the city must be a picture somehow focused directly into his eyes.

For the first time, with a start, Fara recognized the metropolis below. It was the city of dreams, Imperial City, capital of the glorious Empress Isher— From his great height, he could see the gardens, the gorgeous grounds of the silver palace, the official Imperial residence itself—

The last tendrils of his fear were fading now before a gathering fascination and wonder; they vanished utterly as he recognized with a ghastly thrill of uncertain expectancy that the palace was drawing nearer at great speed.

"Show him the palace," they had said. Did that mean, could it mean—

That spray of tense thoughts splattered into nonexistence, as the glittering roof flashed straight at his face. He gulped, as the solid metal of it passed through him, and then other walls and ceilings.

His first sense of imminent and mind-shaking desecration came as the picture paused in a great room where a score of men sat around a table at the head of which sat—a young woman.

The inexorable, sacrilegious, limitlessly powered cameras that were taking the picture swung across the table, and caught the woman full face.

It was a handsome face, but there was passion and fury twisting it now, and a very blaze of fire in her eyes, as she leaned forward, and said in a voice at once familiar—how often Fara had heard its calm, measured tones on the telestats—and distorted. Utterly distorted by anger and an insolent certainty of command. That caricature of a beloved voice slashed across the silence as clearly as if he, Fara, was there in that room: "I want that skunk killed, do you understand? I don't care how you do it, but I want to hear by tomorrow night that he's dead."

The picture snapped off and instantly—it was as swift as that— Fara was back in the weapon shop. He stood for a moment, swaying, fighting to accustom his eyes to the dimness; and then—

His first emotion was contempt at the simpleness of the trickery— a motion picture. What kind of a fool did they think he was, to swallow something as transparently unreal as that? He'd—

Abruptly, the appalling lechery of the scheme, the indescribable wickedness of what was being attempted here brought red rage.

"Why, you scum!" he flared. "So you've got somebody to act the part of the empress, trying to pretend that— Why, you—"

"That will do," said the voice of Rad; and Fara shook as a big young man walked into his line of vision. The alarmed thought came that people who would besmirch so vilely the character of her imperial majesty would not hesitate to do physical damage to Fara Clark. The young man went on in a steely tone, "We do not pretend that what you saw was taking place this instant in the palace. That would be too much of a coincidence. But it was taken two weeks ago; the woman is the empress. The man whose death she ordered is one of her many former lovers. He was found murdered two weeks ago; his name, if you care to look it up in the new files, is Banton McCreddie. However, let that pass. We're finished with you now and—"

"But I'm not finished," Fara said in a thick voice. "I've never heard or seen so much infamy in all my life. If you think this town is through with you, you're crazy. We'll have a guard on this place day and night, and nobody will get in or out. We'll—"

"That will do." It was the silver-haired man; and Fara stopped out of respect for age, before he thought. The old man went on: "The examination has been most interesting. As an honest man, you may call on us if you are ever in trouble. That is all. Leave through the side door."

It was all. Impalpable forces grabbed him, and he was shoved at a door that appeared miraculously in the wall, where seconds before the palace had been.

He found himself standing dazedly in a flower bed, and there was a swarm of men to his left. He recognized his fellow townsmen and that he was—outside.

The incredible nightmare was over.

"Where's the gun?" said Creel, as he entered the house half an hour later.

"The gun?" Fara stared at his wife.

"It said over the radio a few minutes ago that you were the first customer of the new weapon shop. I thought it was queer, but—"

He was eerily conscious of her voice going on for several words longer, but it was the purest jumble. The shock was so great that he had the horrible sensation of being on the edge of an abyss.

So that was what the young man had meant: "Advertise! We'll advertise his presence and—"

Fara thought: His reputation! Not that his was a great name, but he had long believed with a quiet pride that Fara Clark's motor repair shop was widely known in the community and countryside.

First, his private humiliation inside the shop. And now this— lying—to people who didn't know why he had gone into the store. Diabolical.

His paralysis ended, as a frantic determination to rectify the base charge drove him to the telestat. After a moment, the plump, sleepy face of Mayor Mel Dale appeared on the plate. Fara's voice made a barrage of sound, but his hopes dashed, as the man said, "I'm sorry, Fara. I don't see how you can have free time on the telestat. You'll have to pay for it. They did."

"They did!" Fara wondered vaguely if he sounded as empty as he felt.

"And they've just paid Lan Harris for his lot. The old man asked top price, and got it. He just phoned me to transfer the title."

"Oh!" The world was shattering. "You mean nobody's going to do anything. What about the Imperial garrison at Ferd?"

Dimly, Fara was aware of the mayor mumbling something about the empress' soldiers refusing to interfere in civilian matters.

"Civilian matters!" Fara exploded. "You mean these people are just going to be allowed to come here whether we want them or not, illegally forcing the sale of lots by first taking possession of them?"

A sudden thought struck him breathless. "Look, you haven't changed your mind about having Jor keep guard in front of the shop?"

With a start, he saw that the plump face in the telestat plate had grown impatient "Now, see here, Fara," came the pompous words, "let the constituted authorities handle this matter."

"But you're going to keep Jor there," Fara said doggedly.

The mayor looked annoyed, said finally peevishly: "I promised, didn't I? So he'll be there. And now—do you want to buy time on the telestat? It's fifteen credits for one minute. Mind you, as a friend, I think you're wasting your money. No one has ever caught up with a false statement."

Fara said grimly, "Put two on, one in the morning, one in the evening."

"All right. We'll deny it completely. Good night."

The telestat went blank; and Fara sat there. A new thought hardened his face. "That boy of ours—there's going to be a showdown. He either works in my shop, or he gets no more allowance."

Creel said: "You've handled him wrong. He's twenty-three and you treat him like a child. Remember, at twenty-three you were a married man."

"That was different," said Fara. "I had a sense of responsibility. Do you know what he did tonight?"

He didn't quite catch her answer. For the moment, he thought she said, "No; in what way did you humiliate him first?"

Fara felt too impatient to verify the impossible words. He rushed on: "He refused in front of the whole village to give me help. He's a bad one, all bad."

"Yes," said Creel in a bitter tone, "he is all bad. I'm sure you don't realize how bad. He's as cold as steel, but without steel's strength or integrity. He took a long time, but he hates even me now, because I stood up for your side so long, knowing you were wrong."

"What's that?" said Fara, startled; then gruffly: "Come, come, my dear, we're both upset. Let's go to bed."

He slept poorly.

There were days then when the conviction that this was a personal fight between himself and the weapon shop lay heavily on Fara. Grimly, though it was out of his way, he made a point of walking past the weapon shop, always pausing to speak to Constable Jor and—

On the fourth day, the policeman wasn't there.

Fara waited patiently at first, then angrily: then he walked hastily to his shop, and called Jor's house. No, Jor wasn't home. He was guarding the weapon store.

Fara hesitated. His own shop was piled with work, and he had a guilty sense of having neglected his customers for the first time in his life. It would be simple to call up the mayor and report Jor's dereliction. And yet—

He didn't want to get the man into trouble—

Out in the street, he saw that a large crowd was gathering in front of the weapon shop. Fara hurried. A man he knew greeted him excitedly: "Jor's been murdered, Fara!"

"Murdered!" Fara stood stock-still, and at first he was not clearly conscious of the grisly thought that was in his mind: Satisfaction! A flaming satisfaction. Now, he thought, even the soldiers would have to act. They—

With a gasp, he realized the ghastly tenor of his thoughts. He shivered, but finally pushed the sense of shame out of his mind. He said slowly, "Where's the body?"

"Inside."

"You mean, those . . . scum—" In spite of himself, he hesitated over the epithet; even now, it was difficult to think of the fine-faced, silver-haired old man in such terms. Abruptly, his mind hardened; he flared: "You mean those scum actually killed him, then pulled his body inside?"

"Nobody saw the killing," said a second man beside Fara, "but he's gone, hasn't been seen for three hours. The mayor got the weapon shop on the telestat, but they claim they don't know anything. They've done away with him, that's what, and now they're pretending innocence. Well, they won't get out of it as easily as that. Mayor's gone to phone the soldiers at Ferd to bring up some big guns and—"

Something of the intense excitement that was in the crowd surged through Fara, the feeling of big things brewing. It was the most delicious sensation that had ever tingled along his nerves, and it was all mixed with a strange pride that he had been so right about this, that he at least had never doubted that here was evil.

He did not recognize the emotion as the full-flowering joy that comes to a member of a mob. But his voice shook, as he said, "Guns? Yes, that will be the answer, and the soldiers will have to come, of course."

Fara nodded to himself in the immensity of his certainty that the Imperial soldiers would now have no excuse for not acting. He started to say something dark about what the empress would do if she found out that a man had lost his life because the soldiers had shirked their duty, but the words were drowned in a shout:

"Here comes the mayor! Hey, Mr. Mayor, when are the atomic cannons due?"

There was more of the same general meaning, as the mayor's sleek, all-purpose car landed lightly. Some of the questions must have reached his honor, for he stood up in the open two-seater and held up his hand for silence.

To Fara's astonishment, the plump-faced man looked at him with accusing eyes. The thing seemed so impossible that, quite instinctively, Fara looked behind him. But he was almost alone; everybody else had crowded forward.

Fara shook his head, puzzled by that glare; and then, astoundingly, Mayor Dale pointed a finger at him, and said in a voice that trembled, "There's the man who's responsible for the trouble that's come upon us. Stand forward, Fara Clark, and show yourself. You've cost this town seven hundred credits that we could ill afford to spend."

Fara couldn't have moved or spoken to save his life. He just stood there in a maze of dumb bewilderment. Before he could even think, the mayor went on, and there was quivering self-pity in his tone, "We've all known that it wasn't wise to interfere with these weapon shops. So long as the Imperial government leaves them alone, what right have we to set up guards, or act against them? That's what I've thought from the beginning, but this man . . . this . . . this Fara Clark kept after all of us, forcing us to move against our wills, and so now we've got a seven-hundred-credit bill to meet and—"

He broke off with, "I might as well make it brief. When I called the garrison, the commander just laughed and said that Jor would turn up. And I had barely disconnected when there was a money call from Jor. He's on Mars."

He waited for the shouts of amazement to die down. "It'll take three weeks for him to come back by ship, and we've got to pay for it, and Fara Clark is responsible. He—"

The shock was over. Fara stood cold, his mind hard. He said finally, scathingly, "So you're giving up and trying to blame me all in one breath. I say you're all fools."

As he turned away, he heard Mayor Dale saying something about the situation not being completely lost, as he had learned that the weapon shop had been set up in Glay because the village was equidistant from four cities, and that it was the city business the shop was after. This would mean tourists, and accessary trade for the village stores and—

Fara heard no more. Head high, he walked back toward his shop. There were one or two catcalls from the mob, but he ignored them.

He had no sense of approaching disaster, simply a gathering fury against the weapon shop, which had brought him to this miserable status among his neighbors.

The worst of it, as the days passed, was the realization that the people of the weapon shop had no personal interest in him. They were remote, superior, undefeatable. That unconquerableness was a dim, suppressed awareness inside Fara.

When he thought of it, he felt a vague fear at the way they had transferred Jor to Mars in a period of less than three hours, when all the world knew that the trip by fastest spaceship required nearly three weeks.

Fara did not go to the express station to see Jor arrive home. He had heard that the council had decided to charge Jor with half of the expense of the trip, on the threat of losing his job if he made a fuss.

On the second night after Jor's return, Fara slipped down to the constable's house, and handed the officer one hundred seventy-five credits. It wasn't that he was responsible he told Jor, but—

The man was only too eager to grant the disclaimer, provided the money went with it. Fara returned home with a clearer conscience.

It was on the third day after that the door of his shop banged open and a man came in. Fara frowned as he saw who it was: Castler, a village hanger-on. The man was grinning.

"Thought you might be interested, Fara. Somebody came out of the weapon shop today."

Fara strained deliberately at the connecting bolt of a hard plate of the atomic motor be was fixing. He waited with a gathering annoyance that the man did not volunteer further information. Asking questions would be a form of recognition of the worthless fellow. A developing curiosity made him say finally, grudgingly, "I suppose the constable promptly picked him up."

He supposed nothing of the kind, but it was an opening.

"It wasn't a man. It was a girl."

Fara knitted his brows. He didn't like the idea of making trouble for women. But—the cunning devils! Using a girl, just as they had used an old man as a clerk. It was a trick that deserved to fail, the girl probably a tough one who needed rough treatment. Fara said harshly, "Well, what's happened?"

"She's still out, bold as you please. Pretty thing, too."

The bolt off, Fara took the hard plate over to the polisher, and began patiently the long, careful task of smoothing away the crystals that heat had seared on the once shining metal. The soft throb of the polisher made the background to his next words:

"Has anything been done?"

"Nope. The constable's been told, but he says he doesn't fancy being away from his family for another three weeks, and paying the cost into the bargain."

Fara contemplated that darkly for a minute, as the polisher throbbed on. His voice shook with suppressed fury, when he said finally, "So they're letting them get away with it. Its all been as clever as hell. Can't they see that they mustn't give an inch before these . . . these transgressors. It's like giving countenance to sin."

From the corner of his eye, he noticed that there was a curious grin on the face of the other. It struck Fara suddenly that the man was enjoying his anger. And there was something else in that grin; something—a secret knowledge.

Fara pulled the engine plate away from the polisher. He faced the ne'er-do-well, scathed at him, "Naturally, that sin part wouldn't worry you much."

"Oh," said the man nonchalantly, "the hard knocks of life make people tolerant. For instance, after you know the girl better, you yourself will probably come to realize that there's good in all of us."

It was not so much the words, as the curious I've-got-secret-information tone that made Fara snap: "What do you mean—if I get to know the girl better! I won't even speak to the brazen creature."

"One can't always choose," the other said with enormous casualness. "Suppose he brings her home."

"Suppose who brings who home?" Fara spoke irritably. "Castler, you—"

He stopped; a dead weight of dismay plumped into his stomach; his whole being sagged. "You mean—" he said.

"I mean," replied Castler with a triumphant leer, "that the boys aren't letting a beauty like her be lonesome. And, naturally, your son was the first to speak to her."

He finished: "They're walkin' together now on Second Avenue, comin' this way, so—"

"Get out of here!" Fara roared. "And stay away from me with your gloating. Get out!"

The man hadn't expected such an ignominious ending. He flushed scarlet, then went out, slamming the door.

Fara stood for a moment, every muscle stiff; then, with an abrupt, jerky movement, he shut off his power, and went out into the street.

The time to put a stop to that kind of thing was—now!

❖ ❖ ❖

He had no clear plan, just that violent determination to put an immediate end to an impossible situation. And it was all mixed up with his anger against Cayle. How could he have had such a worthless son, he who paid his debts and worked hard, and tried to be decent and to live up to the highest standards of the empress?

A brief, dark thought came to Fara that maybe there was some bad blood on Creel's side. Not from her mother, of course—Fara added the mental thought hastily. *There* was a fine, hard-working woman, who hung on to her money, and who would leave Creel a tidy sum one of these days.

But Creel's father had disappeared when Creel was only a child, and there had been some vague scandal about his having taken up with a telestat actress.

And now Cayle with this weapon-shop girl. A girl who had let herself be picked up—

He saw them, as he turned the corner onto Second Avenue. They were walking a hundred feet distant, and heading away from Fara. The girl was tall and slender, almost as big as Cayle, and, as Fara came up, she was saying, "You have the wrong idea about us. A person like you can't get a job in our organization. You belong in the Imperial Service, where they can use young men of good education, good appearance and no scruples. I—"

Fara grasped only dimly that Cayle must have been trying to get a job with these people. It was not clear; and his own mind was too intent on his purpose for it to mean anything at the moment. He said harshly, "Cayle!"

The couple turned, Cayle with the measured unhurriedness of a young man who has gone a long way on the road to steellike nerves; the girl was quicker, but withal dignified.

Fara had a vague, terrified feeling that his anger was too great, self-destroying, but the very violence of his emotions ended that thought even as it came. He said thickly, "Cayle, get home—at once."

Fara was aware of the girl looking at him curiously from strange, gray-green eyes. No shame, he thought, and his rage mounted several degrees, driving away the alarm that came at the sight of the flush that crept into Cayle's cheeks.

The flush faded into a pale, tight-lipped anger, Cayle half-turned to the girl, said, "This is the childish old fool I've got to put up with. Fortunately, we seldom see each other; we don't even eat together. What do you think of him?"

The girl smiled impersonally. "Oh, we know Fara Clark; he's the backbone of the empress in Glay."

"Yes," the boy sneered. "You ought to hear him. He thinks we're living in heaven; and the empress is the divine power. The worst part of it is that there's no chance of his ever getting that stuffy look wiped off his face."

They walked off; and Fara stood there. The very extent of what had happened had drained anger from him as if it had never been. There was the realization that he had made a mistake so great that—

He couldn't grasp it. For long, long now, since Cayle had refused to work in his shop, he had felt this building up to a climax. Suddenly, his own uncontrollable ferocity stood revealed as a partial product of that—deeper—problem.

Only, now that the smash was here, he didn't want to face it—

All through the day in his shop, he kept pushing it out of his mind, kept thinking, would this go on now, as before, Cayle and he living in the same house, not even looking at each other when they met, going to bed at different times, getting up, Fara at 6:30, Cayle at noon? Would that go on through all the days and years to come?

When he arrived home, Creel was waiting for him. She said, "Fara, he wants you to loan him five hundred credits, so that he can go to Imperial City."

Fara nodded wordlessly. He brought the money back to the house the next morning, and gave it to Creel, who took it into the bedroom.

She came out a minute later. "He says to tell you goodbye."

When Fara came home that evening, Cayle was gone. He wondered whether he ought to feel relieved or—what?

The days passed. Fara worked. He had nothing else to do, and the gray thought was often in his mind that now he would be doing it till the day he died. Except—

Fool that he was—he told himself a thousand times how big a fool—he kept hoping that Cayle would walk into the shop and say, "Father, I've learned my lesson. If you can ever forgive me, teach me the business, and then you retire to a well-earned rest."

It was exactly a month to a day after Cayle's departure that the telestat clicked on just after Fara had finished lunch. "Money call," it sighed, "money call."

Fara and Creel looked at each other. "Eh," said Fara finally, "money call for us."

He could see from the gray look in Creel's face the thought that was in her mind. He said under his breath: "Damn that boy!"

But he felt relieved. Amazingly relieved! Cayle was beginning to appreciate the value of parents and—

He switched on the viewer. "Come and collect," he said.

The face that came on the screen was heavy-jowled, beetle-browed-and strange. The man said, "This is Clerk Pearton of the Fifth Bank of Ferd. We have received a sight draft on you for ten thousand credits. With carrying charges and government tax, the sum required will be twelve thousand one hundred credits. Will you pay it now or will you come in this afternoon and pay it?"

"B-but . . . b-but—" said Fara. "W-who—"

He stopped, conscious of the stupidity of the question, dimly conscious of the heavy-faced man saying something about the money having been paid out to one Cayle Clark that morning in Imperial City. At last, Fara found his voice:

"But the bank had no right," he expostulated, "to pay out the money without my authority. I—"

The voice cut him off coldly: "Are we then to inform our central that the money was obtained under false pretenses? Naturally, an order will be issued immediately for the arrest of your son."

"Wait . . . wait—" Fara spoke blindly. He was aware of Creel beside him, shaking her head at him. She was as white as a sheet, and her voice was a sick, stricken thing, as she said, "Fara, let him go. He's through with us. We must be as hard—let him go."

The words rang senselessly in Fara's ears. They didn't fit into any normal pattern. He was saying:

"I . . . I haven't got— How about my paying . . . Installments? I—"

"If you wish a loan," said Clerk Pearton, "naturally we will be happy to go into the matter. I might say that when the draft arrived, we checked up on your status, and we are prepared to loan you eleven thousand credits on indefinite call with your shop as security. I have the form here, and if you are agreeable, we will switch this call through the registered circuit, and you can sign at once."

"Fara, no."

The clerk went on: "The other eleven hundred credits will have to be paid in cash. Is that agreeable?"

"Yes, yes, of course, I've got twenty-five hund—" He stopped his chattering tongue with a gulp; then: "Yes, that's satisfactory."

The deal completed, Fara whirled on his wife. Out of the depths of his hurt and bewilderment, he raged: "What do you mean, standing there and talking about not paying it? You said several times that I was responsible for his being what he is. Besides, we don't know why he needed the money. He—"

Creel said in a low, dead tone: "In one hour, he's stripped us of our life work. He did it deliberately, thinking of us as two old fools, who wouldn't know any better than to pay it."

Before he could speak, she went on, "Oh, I know I blamed you, but in the final issue, I knew it was he. He was always cold and calculating, but I was weak, and I was sure that if you handled him in a different . . . and besides I didn't want to see his faults for a long time. He—"

"All I see," Fara interrupted doggedly, "is that I have saved our name from disgrace."

His high sense of duty rightly done lasted until midafternoon, when the bailiff from Ferd came to take over the shop.

"But what—" Fara began.

The bailiff said, "The Automatic Atomic Repair Shops, Limited, took over your loan from the bank, and are foreclosing. Have you anything to say?"

"It's unfair," said Fara. "I'll take it to court. I'll—"

He was thinking dazedly: *If the empress ever learned of this, she'd . . . she'd—*

The courthouse was a big, gray building; and Fara felt emptier and colder every second, as he walked along the gray corridors. In Glay, his decision not to give himself into the hands of a bloodsucker of a lawyer had seemed a wise act. Here, in these enormous halls and palatial rooms, it seemed the sheerest folly.

He managed, nevertheless, to give an articulate account of the criminal act of the bank in first giving Cayle the money, then turning over the note to his chief competitor, apparently within minutes of his signing it. He finished with: "I'm sure, sir, the empress would not approve of such goings-on against honest citizens. I—"

"How dare you," said the cold-voiced creature on the bench, "use the name of her holy majesty in support of your own gross self-interest?"

Fara shivered. The sense of being intimately a member of the empress' great human family yielded to a sudden chill and a vast mind-picture of the ten million icy courts like this, and the myriad malevolent and heartless men—*like this*—who stood between the empress and her loyal subject, Fara.

He thought passionately: If the empress knew what was happening here, how unjustly he was being treated, she would—

Or would she?

He pushed the crowding, terrible doubt out of his mind—came out of his hard reverie with a start, to hear the Cadi saying, "Plaintiff's appeal dismissed, with costs assessed at seven hundred credits, to be divided between the court and the defense solicitor in the ratio of five to two. See to it that the appellant does not leave till the costs are paid. Next case—"

Fara went alone the next day to see Creel's mother. He called first at "Farmer's Restaurant" at the outskirts of the village. The place was, he noted with satisfaction in the thought of the steady stream of money flowing in, half full, though it was only midmorning. But madame wasn't there. Try the feed store.

He found her in the back of the feed store, overseeing the weighing out of grain into cloth measures. The hard-faced old woman heard his story without a word. She said finally, curtly, "Nothing doing, Fara. I'm one who has to make loans often from the bank to swing deals. If I tried to set you up in business, I'd find the Automatic Atomic Repair people getting after me. Besides, I'd be a fool to turn money over to a man who lets a bad son squeeze a fortune out of him. Such a man has no sense about worldly things.

"And I won't give you a job because I don't hire relatives in my business." She finished: "Tell Creel to come and live at my house. I won't support a man, though. That's all."

He watched her disconsolately for a while, as she went on calmly superintending the clerks who were manipulating the old, no longer accurate measuring machines. Twice her voice echoed through the dust-filled interior, each time with a sharp: "That's overweight, a gram at least. Watch your machine."

Though her back was turned, Fara knew by her posture that she was still aware of his presence. She turned at last with an abrupt movement and said, "Why don't you go to the weapon shop? You haven't anything to lose and you can't go on like this."

Fara went out, then, a little blindly. At first the suggestion that he buy a gun and commit suicide had no real personal application. But he felt immeasurably hurt that his mother-in-law should have made it.

Kill himself? Why, it was ridiculous. He was still only a young man, going on fifty. Given the proper chance, with his skilled hands, he could wrest a good living even in a world where automatic machines were encroaching everywhere. There was always room for a man who did a good job. His whole life had been based on that credo.

Kill himself—

He went home to find Creel packing. "It's the common sense thing to do," she said. "We'll rent the house and move into rooms."

He told her about her mother's offer to take her in, watching her face as he spoke. Creel shrugged.

"I told her 'No' yesterday," she said thoughtfully. "I wonder why she mentioned it to you."

Fara walked swiftly over to the great front window overlooking the garden, with its flowers, its pool, its rockery. He tried to think of Creel away from this garden of hers, this home of two thirds a lifetime, Creel living in rooms—and knew what her mother had meant. There was one more hope—

He waited till Creel went upstairs, then called Mel Dale on the telestat. The mayor's plump face took on an uneasy expression as he saw who it was.

But he listened pontifically, said finally, "Sorry, the council does not loan money; and I might as well tell you, Fara—I have nothing to do with this, mind you—but you can't get a license for a shop any more."

"W-what?"

"I'm sorry!" The mayor lowered his voice. "Listen, Fara, take my advice and go to the weapon shop. These places have their uses."

There was a click, and Fara sat staring at the blank face of the viewing screen.

So it was to be—death!

He waited until the street was empty of human beings, then slipped across the boulevard, past a design of flower gardens, and so to the door of the shop. The brief fear came that the door wouldn't open, but it did, effortlessly.

As he emerged from the dimness of the alcove into the shop proper, he saw the silver-haired old man sitting in a corner chair, reading under a softly bright light. The old man looked up, put aside his book, then rose to his feet.

"It's Mr. Clark," he said quietly. "What can we do for you?"

A faint flush crept into Fara's cheeks. In a dim fashion, he had hoped that he would not suffer the humiliation of being recognized; but now that his fear was realized, he stood his ground stubbornly. The important thing about killing himself was that there be no body for Creel to bury at great expense. Neither knife nor poison would satisfy that basic requirement.

"I want a gun," said Fara, "that can be adjusted to disintegrate a body six feet in diameter in, a single shot. Have you that kind?"

Without a word, the old man turned to a showcase, and brought forth a sturdy gem of a revolver that glinted with all the soft colors of the inimitable Ordine plastic. The man said in a precise voice, "Notice the flanges on this barrel are little more than bulges. This makes the model ideal for carrying in a shoulder holster under the coat; it can be drawn very swiftly because, when properly attuned, it will leap toward the reaching hand of its owner. At the moment it is attuned to me. Watch while I replace it in its holster and—"

The speed of the draw was absolutely amazing. The old man's fingers moved; and the gun, four feet away, was in them. There was no blur of movement. It was like the door the night that it had slipped from Fara's grasp, and slammed noiselessly in Constable Jor's face. *Instantaneous*!

Fara, who had parted his lips as the old man was explaining, to protest the utter needlessness of illustrating any quality of the weapon except what he had asked for, closed them again. He stared in a brief, dazed fascination; and something of the wonder that was here held his mind and his body.

He had seen and handled the guns of soldiers, and they were simply ordinary metal or plastic things that one used clumsily like any other material substance, not like this at all, not possessed of a dazzling life of their own, leaping with an intimate eagerness to assist with all their superb power the will of their master. They—

With a start, Fara remembered his purpose. He smiled wryly, and said, "All this is very interesting. But what about the beam that can fan out?"

The old man said calmly, "At pencil thickness, this beam will pierce any body except certain alloys of lead up to four hundred yards. With proper adjustment of the firing nozzle, you can disintegrate a six-foot object at fifty yards or less. This screw is the adjustor."

He indicated a tiny device in the muzzle itself. "Turn it to the left to spread the beam, to the right to close it."

Fara, said, "I'll take the gun. How much is it?"

He saw that the old man was looking at him thoughtfully; the oldster said finally, slowly, "I have previously explained our regulations to you, Mr. Clark. You recall them, of course?"

"Eh!" said Fara, and stopped, wide-eyed. It wasn't that he didn't remember them. It was simply—

"You mean," he gasped, "those things actually apply. They're not—"

With a terrible effort, he caught his spinning brain and blurring voice. Tense and cold, he said, "All I want is a gun that will shoot in self-defense, but which I can turn on myself if I have to or—want to."

"Oh, suicide!" said the old man. He looked as if a great understanding had suddenly dawned on him. "My dear sir, we have no objection to your killing yourself at any time. That is your personal privilege in a world where privileges grow scanter every year. As for the price of this revolver, it's four credits."

"Four cre . . . only four credits!" said Fara.

He stood, absolutely astounded, his whole mind snatched from its dark purpose. Why, the plastic alone was—and the whole gun with its fine, intricate workmanship—twenty-five credits would have been dirt cheap.

He felt a brief thrill of utter interest; the mystery of the weapon shops suddenly loomed as vast and important as his own black destiny. But the old man was speaking again:

"And now, if you will remove your coat, we can put on the holster—"

Quite automatically, Fara complied. It was vaguely startling to realize that, in a few seconds, he would be walking out of here, equipped for self-murder, and that there was now not a single obstacle to his death.

Curiously, he was disappointed. He couldn't explain it, but somehow there had been in the back of his mind a hope that these shops might, just might—what?

What indeed? Fara sighed wearily—and grew aware again of the old man's voice, saying:

"Perhaps you would prefer to step out of our side door. It is less conspicuous than the front."

There was no resistance in Fara. He was dimly conscious of the man's fingers on his arm, half guiding him; and then the old man pressed one of several buttons on the wall—so that's how it was done—and there was the door.

He could see flowers beyond the opening; without a word he walked toward them. He was outside before he realized it.

Fara stood for a moment in the neat little pathway, striving to grasp the finality of his situation. But nothing would come except a curious awareness of many men around him; for a long second, his brain was like a log drifting along a stream at night.

Through that darkness grew a consciousness of something wrong; the wrongness was there in the back of his mind, as he turned leftward to go to the front of the weapon store.

Vagueness transformed to a shocked, startled sound. For—he was not in Glay, and the weapon shop wasn't where it had been. In its place—

A dozen men brushed past Fara to join a long line of men farther along. But Fara was immune to their presence, their strangeness. His whole mind, his whole vision, his very being was concentrating on the section of machine that stood where the weapon shop had been.

A machine, oh, a machine—

His brain lifted up, up in his effort to grasp the tremendousness of the dull-metaled immensity of what was spread here under a summer sun beneath a sky as blue as a remote southern sea.

The machine towered into the heavens, five great tiers of metal, each a hundred feet high; and the superbly streamlined five hundred feet ended in a peak of light, a gorgeous spire that tilted straight up a sheer two hundred feet farther, and matched the very sun for brightness.

And it was a machine, not a building, because the whole lower tier was alive with shimmering lights, mostly green, but sprinkled colorfully with red and occasionally a blue and yellow. Twice, as Fara watched, green lights directly in front of him flashed unscintillatingly into red.

The second tier was alive with white and red lights, although there were only a fraction as many lights as on the lowest tier. The third section had on its dull-metal surface only blue and yellow lights; they twinkled softly here and there over the vast area.

The fourth tier was a series of signs that brought the beginning of comprehension. The whole sign was:

WHITE—   BIRTHS
RED—   DEATHS
GREEN—   LIVING
BLUE—   IMMIGRATION TO EARTH
YELLOW—   EMIGRATION

The fifth tier was also all sign, finally explaining:

POPULATIONS

SOLAR SYSTEM	19,174,463,747
EARTH	11,193,247,361
MARS	1,097,298,604
VENUS	5,141,053,811
MOONS	1,742,863,971

The numbers changed, even as he looked at them, leaping up and down, shifting below and above what they had first been. People were dying, being born, moving to Mars, to Venus, to the moons of Jupiter, to Earth's moon, and others coming back again, landing minute by minute in the thousands of spaceports. Life went on in its gigantic fashion—and here was the stupendous record. Here was—

"Better get in line," said a friendly voice beside Fara. "It takes quite a while to put through an individual case, I understand."

Fara stared at the man. He had the distinct impression of having had senseless words flung at him. "In line?" he started—and stopped himself with a jerk that hurt his throat.

He was moving forward, blindly, ahead of the younger man, thinking a curious jumble that this must have been how Constable Jor was transported to Mars—when another of the man's words penetrated.

"Case?" said Fara violently. "Individual case!"

The man, a heavy-faced, blue-eyed young chap of around thirty-five, looked at him curiously: "You must know why you're here," he said. "Surely, you wouldn't have been sent through here unless you had a problem of some kind that the weapon shop courts will solve for you; there's no other reason for coming to Information Center."

Fara walked on because he was in the line now, a fast-moving line that curved him inexorably around the machine; and seemed to be heading him toward a door that led into the interior of the great metal structure.

So it was a building as well as a machine.

A problem, he was thinking, why, of course, he had a problem, a hopeless, insoluble, completely tangled problem so deeply rooted in the basic structure of Imperial civilization that the whole world would have to be overturned to make it right.

With a start, he saw that he was at the entrance. And the awed thought came: In seconds he would be committed irrevocably to—what?

Inside was a long, shining corridor, with scores of completely transparent hallways leading off the main corridor. Behind Fara, the young man's voice said, "There's one, practically empty. Let's go."

Fara walked ahead; and suddenly he was trembling. He had already noticed that at the end of each side hallway were some dozen young women sitting at desks, interviewing men and . . . and, good heavens, was it possible that all this meant—

He grew aware that he had stopped in front of one of the girls.

She was older than she had looked from a distance, over thirty, but good-looking, alert. She smiled pleasantly, but impersonally, and said, "Your name, please?"

He gave it before he thought and added a mumble about being from the village of Glay. The woman said, "Thank you. It will take a few minutes to get your file. Won't you sit down?"

He hadn't noticed the chair. He sank into it; and his heart was beating so wildly that he felt choked. The strange thing was that there was scarcely a thought in his head, nor a real hope; only an intense, almost mind-wrecking excitement.

With a jerk, he realized that the girl was speaking again, but only snatches of her voice came through that screen of tension in his mind:

"—Information Center is . . . in effect . . . a bureau of statistics. Every person born . . . registered here . . . their education, change of address . . . occupation . . . and the highlights of their life. The whole is maintained by . . . combination of . . . unauthorized and unsuspected liaison with . . . Imperial Chamber of Statistics and . . . through medium of agents . . . in every community—"

It seemed to Fara that he was missing vital information, and that if he could only force his attention and hear more— He strained, but it was no use; his nerves were jumping madly and—

Before he could speak, there was a click, and a thin, dark plate slid onto the woman's desk. She took it up and examined it. After a moment, she said something into a mouthpiece, and in a short time two more plates precipitated out of the empty air onto her desk. She studied them passively, looked up finally.

"You will be interested to know," she said, "that your son, Cayle, bribed himself into a commission in the Imperial army with five thousand credits."

"Eh?" said Fara. He half rose from his chair, but before he could say anything, the young woman was speaking again, firmly, "I must inform you that the weapon shops take no action against individuals. Your son can have his job, the money he stole; we are not concerned with moral correction. That must come naturally from the individual, and from the people as a whole—and now if you will give me a brief account of your problem for the record and the court."

Sweating, Fara sank back into his seat; his mind was heaving; most desperately, he wanted more information about Cayle. He began: "But . . . but what . . . how—" He caught himself; and in a low voice described what had happened. When he finished, the girl said, "You will proceed now to the Name Room; watch for your name, and when it appears go straight to Room 474. Remember, 474— and now, the line is waiting, if you please—"

She smiled politely, and Fara was moving off almost before he realized it. He half turned to ask another question, but an old man was sinking into his chair. Fara hurried on, along a great corridor, conscious of curious blasts of sound coming from ahead.

Eagerly, he opened the door; and the sound crashed at him with all the impact of a sledgehammer blow.

It was such a colossal, incredible sound that he stopped short, just inside the door, shrinking back. He stood then trying to blink sense into a visual confusion that rivaled in magnitude that incredible tornado of noise.

Men, men, men everywhere; men by the thousands in a long, broad auditorium, packed into rows of seats, pacing with an abandon of restlessness up and down aisles, and all of them staring with a frantic interest at a long board marked off into squares, each square lettered from the alphabet, from A, B, C and so on to Z. The tremendous board with its lists of names ran the full length of the immense room.

The Name Room, Fara was thinking shakily, as he sank into a seat—and his name would come up in the C's, and then—

It was like sitting in at a no-limit poker game, watching the jewel-precious cards turn up. It was like playing the exchange with all the world at stake during a stock crash. It was nerve-racking, dazzling, exhausting, fascinating, terrible, mind-destroying, stupendous. It was—

It was like nothing else on the face of the earth.

New names kept flashing on to the twenty-six squares; and men would shout like insane beings and some fainted, and the uproar was absolutely shattering; the pandemonium raged on, one continuous, unbelievable sound.

And every few minutes a great sign would flash along the board, telling everyone:

"WATCH YOUR OWN INITIALS."

Fara watched, trembling in every limb. Each second it seemed to him that he couldn't stand it an instant longer. He wanted to scream at the room to be silent; he wanted to jump up to pace the floor, but others who did that were yelled at hysterically, threatened wildly, hated with a mad, murderous ferocity.

Abruptly, the blind savagery of it scared Fara. He thought unsteadily: "I'm not going to make a fool of myself. I—"

"Clark, Fara—" winked the board. "Clark, Fara—"

With a shout that nearly tore off the top of his head, Fara leaped to his feet. "That's me!" he shrieked. "Me!"

No one turned; no one paid the slightest attention. Shamed, he slunk across the room where an endless line of men kept crowding into a corridor beyond.

The silence in the long corridor was almost as shattering as the mind-destroying noise it replaced. It was hard to concentrate on the idea of a number—474.

It was completely impossible to imagine what could lie beyond—474.

The room was small. It was furnished with a small, business-type table and two chairs. On the table were seven neat piles of folders, each pile a different color. The piles were arranged in a row in front of a large, milky-white globe, that began to glow with a soft light. Out of its depths, a man's baritone voice said, "Fara Clark?"

"Yes," said Fara.

"Before the verdict is rendered in your case," the voice went on quietly, "I want you to take a folder from the blue pile. The list will show the Fifth Interplanetary Bank in its proper relation to yourself and the world, and it will be explained to you in due course."

The list, Fara saw, was simply that, a list of the names of companies. The names ran from A to Z, and there were about five hundred of them. The folder carried no explanation; and Fara slipped it automatically into his side pocket, as the voice came again from the shining globe: "It has been established," the words came precisely, "that the Fifth Interplanetary Bank perpetrated upon you a gross swindle, and that it is further guilty of practicing scavengery, deception, blackmail and was accessory in a criminal conspiracy.

"The bank made contact with your son, Cayle, through what is quite properly known as a scavenger, that is, an employee who exists by finding young men and women who are normally capable of drawing drafts on their parents or other victims. The scavenger obtains for this service a commission of eight percent, which is always paid by the person making the loan, in this case your son.

"The bank practiced deception in that its authorized agents deceived you in the most culpable fashion by pretending that it had already paid out the ten thousand credits to your son, whereas the money was not paid over until your signature had been obtained.

"The blackmail guilt arises out of a threat to have your son arrested for falsely obtaining a loan, a threat made at a time when no money had exchanged hands. The conspiracy consists of the action whereby your note was promptly turned over to your competitor.

"The bank is accordingly triple-fined, thirty-six thousand three hundred credits. It is not in our interest, Fara Clark, for you to know how this money is obtained. Suffice to know that the bank pays it, and that of the fine the weapon shops allocate to their own treasury a total of one half. The other half—"

There was a *plop*; a neatly packaged pile of bills fell onto the table. "For you," said the voice; and Fara, with trembling fingers, slipped the package into his coat pocket. It required the purest mental and physical effort for him to concentrate on the next words that came:

"You must not assume that your troubles are over. The re-establishment of your motor repair shop in Glay will require force and courage. Be discreet, brave and determined, and you cannot fail. Do not hesitate to use the gun you have purchased in defense of your rights. The plan will be explained to you. And now, proceed through the door facing you—"

Fara braced himself with an effort, opened the door and walked through.

It was a dim, familiar room that he stepped into, and there was a silver-haired, fine-faced man who rose from a reading chair, and came forward in the dimness, smiling gravely.

The stupendous, fantastic, exhilarating adventure was over; and he was back in the weapon shop of Glay.

He couldn't get over the wonder of it—this great and fascinating organization established here in the very heart of a ruthless civilization, a civilization that had in a few brief weeks stripped him of everything he possessed.

With a deliberate will, he stopped that glowing flow of thought. A dark frown wrinkled his solidly built face; he said, "The . . . judge—" Fara hesitated over the name, frowned again, annoyed at himself, then went on: "The judge said that, to reestablish myself I would have to—"

"Before we go into that," said the old man quietly, "I want you to examine the blue folder you brought with you."

"Folder?" Fara echoed blankly. It took a long moment to remember that he had picked up a folder from the table in Room 474.

He studied the list of company names with a gathering puzzlement, noting that the name of Automatic Atomic Motor Repair Shops was well down among the A's, and the Fifth Interplanetary Bank only one of several great banks included. Fara looked up finally.

"I don't understand," he said; "are these the companies you have had to act against?"

The silver-haired man smiled grimly, shook his head. "That is not what I mean. These firms constitute only a fraction of the eight hundred thousand companies that are constantly in our books."

He smiled again, humorlessly: "These companies all know that, because of us, their profits on paper bear no relation to their assets.

What they don't know is how great the difference really is; and, as we want a general improvement in business morals, not merely more skillful scheming to outwit us, we prefer them to remain in ignorance."

He paused, and this time he gave Fara a searching glance, said at last: "The unique feature of the companies on this particular list is that they are every one wholly owned by Empress Isher."

He finished swiftly: "In view of your past opinions on that subject, I do not expect you to believe me."

Fara stood as still as death, for—he did believe with unquestioning conviction, completely, finally. The amazing, the unforgivable thing was that all his life he had watched the march of ruined men into the oblivion of poverty and disgrace—and blamed *them*.

Fara groaned. "I've been like a madman," he said. "Everything the empress and her officials did was right. No friendship, no personal relationship could survive with me that did not include belief in things as they were. I suppose if I started to talk against the empress I would receive equally short shrift."

"Under no circumstances," said the old man grimly, "must you say anything against her majesty. The weapon shops will not countenance any such words, and will give no further aid to anyone who is so indiscreet. The reason is that, for the moment, we have reached an uneasy state of peace with the Imperial government. We wish to keep it that way; beyond that I will not enlarge on our policy.

"I am permitted to say that the last great attempt to destroy the weapon shops was made seven years ago, when the glorious Innelda Isher was twenty-five years old. That was a secret attempt, based on a new invention; and failed by purest accident because of our sacrifice of a man from seven thousand years in the past. That may sound mysterious to you, but I will not explain.

"The worst period was reached some forty years ago when every person who was discovered receiving aid from us was murdered in some fashion. You may be surprised to know that your father-in-law was among those assassinated at that time."

"Creel's father!" Fara gasped. "But—"

He stopped. His brain was reeling; there was such a rush of blood to his head that for an instant he could hardly see.

"But," he managed at last, "It was reported that he ran away with another woman."

"They always spread a vicious story of some kind," the old man said; and Fara was silent, stunned.

The other went on: "We finally put a stop to their murders by killing the three men from the top down, excluding the royal family, who gave the order for the particular execution involved. But we do not again want that kind of bloody murder.

"Nor are we interested in any criticism of our toleration of so much that is evil. It is important to understand that *we do not interfere in the main stream of human existence.* We right wrongs; we act as a barrier between the people and their more ruthless exploiters. Generally speaking, we help only honest men; that is not to say that we do not give assistance to the less scrupulous, but only to the extent of selling them guns—which is a very great aid indeed, and which is one of the reasons why the government is relying almost exclusively for its power on an economic chicanery.

"In the four thousand years since the brilliant genius Walter S. DeLany invented the vibration process that made the weapon shops possible, and laid down the first principles of weapon shop political philosophy, we have watched the tide of government swing backward and forward between democracy under a limited monarchy to complete tyranny. And we have discovered one thing:

"*People always have the kind of government they want.* When they want change, they must change it. As always we shall remain an incorruptible core—and I mean that literally; we have a psychological machine that never lies about a man's character—I repeat, an incorruptible core of human idealism, devoted to relieving the ills that arise inevitably under any form of government.

"But now—your problem. It is very simple, really. You must fight, as all men have fought since the beginning of time for what they valued, for their just rights. As you know, the Automatic Repair people removed all your machinery and tools within an hour of foreclosing on your shop. This material was taken to Ferd, and then shipped to a great warehouse on the coast.

"We recovered it, and with our special means of transportation have now replaced the machines in your shop. You will accordingly go there and—"

Fara listened with a gathering grimness to the instructions, nodded finally, his jaw clamped tight.

"You can count on me," he said curtly. "I've been a stubborn man in my time; and though I've changed sides, I haven't changed *that*."

Going outside was like returning from life to—death; from hope to—reality.

Fara walked along the quiet streets of Glay at darkest night. For the first time it struck him that the weapon shop Information Center must be halfway around the world, for it had been day, brilliant day.

The picture vanished as if it had never existed, and he grew aware again, preternaturally aware of the village of Glay asleep all around him. Silent, peaceful—yet ugly, he thought, ugly with the ugliness of evil enthroned.

He thought: The right to buy weapons—and his heart swelled into his throat; the tears came to his eyes.

He wiped his vision clear with the back of his hand, thought of Creel's long dead father, and strode on, without shame. Tears were good for an angry man.

The shop was the same, but the hard metal padlock yielded before the tiny, blazing, supernal power of the revolver. One flick of fire; the metal dissolved—and he was inside.

It was dark, too dark to see, but Fara did not turn on the lights immediately. He fumbled across to the window control, turned the windows to darkness vibration, and then clicked on the lights.

He gulped with awful relief. For the machines, his precious tools that he had seen carted away within hours after the bailiff's arrival, were here again, ready for use.

Shaky from the pressure of his emotion, Fara called Creel on the telestat. It took a little while for her to appear; and she was in her dressing robe. When she saw who it was she turned a dead white.

"Fara, oh, Fara, I thought—"

He cut her off grimly: "Creel, I've been to the weapon shop. I want you to do this: go straight to your mother. I'm here at my shop. I'm going to stay here day and night until it's settled that I *stay*. . . . I shall go home later for some food and clothing, but I want you to be gone by then. Is that clear?"

Color was coming back into her lean, handsome face. She said: "Don't you bother coming home, Fara. I'll do everything necessary. I'll pack all that's needed into the carplane, including a folding bed. We'll sleep in the back room of the shop."

Morning came palely, but it was ten o'clock before a shadow darkened the open door; and Constable Jor came in. He looked shamefaced.

"I've got an order here for your arrest," he said.

"Tell those who sent you," Fara replied deliberately, "that I resisted arrest—with a gun."

The deed followed the words with such rapidity that Jor blinked. He stood like that for a moment, a big, sleepy-looking man, staring at that gleaming, magical revolver; then:

"I have a summons here ordering you to appear at the great court of Ferd this afternoon. Will you accept it?"

"Certainly."

"Then you will be there?"

"I'll send my lawyer," said Fara. "Just drop the summons on the floor there. Tell them I took it."

The weapon shop man had said, "Do not ridicule by word any legal measure of the Imperial authorities. Simply disobey them."

Jor went out, and seemed relieved. It took an hour before Mayor Mel Dale came pompously through the door.

"See here, Fara Clark," he bellowed from the doorway. "You can't get away with this. This is defiance of the law."

Shakily, Fara watched the mayor go out. The crisis was at hand. He braced himself, thought: *Let them come, let them—*

It was easier than he had thought—for the men who entered the shop turned pale when they saw the holstered revolver. There was a violence of blustering, nevertheless, that narrowed finally down to:

"Look here," the man said, "we've got your note for twelve thousand one hundred credits. You're not going to deny you owe that money."

"I'll buy it back," said Fara in a stony voice, "for exactly half, not a cent more."

The strong-jawed young man looked at him for a long time. "We'll take it," he said finally, curtly.

Fara said, "I've got the agreement here—"

His first customer was old man Miser Lan Harris. Fara stared at the long-faced oldster with a vast surmise, and his first, amazed comprehension came of how the weapon shop must have settled on Harris' lot—by arrangement.

It was an hour after Harris had gone that Creel's mother stamped into the shop. She closed the door.

"Well," she said, "you did it, eh? Good work. I'm sorry if I seemed rough with you when you came to my place, but we weapon-shop supporters can't afford to take risks for those who are not on our side.

"But never mind that. I've come to take Creel home. The important thing is to return everything to normal as quickly as possible."

It was over; incredibly it was over. Twice, as he walked home that night, Fara stopped in midstride, and wondered if it had not all been a dream. The air was like wine. The little world of Glay spread before him, green and gracious, a peaceful paradise where time had stood still.

Second Game

Charles V. de Vet & Katherine MacLean

The sign was big, with black letters that read: I'LL BEAT YOU THE SECOND GAME.

I eased myself into a seat behind the play board, straightened the pitchman's cloak about my shoulders, took a final deep breath, let it out—and waited.

A nearby Fair visitor glanced at the sign as he hurried by. His eyes widened with anticipated pleasure and he shifted his gaze to me, weighing me with the glance.

I knew I had him.

The man changed direction and came over to where I sat. "Are you giving any odds?" he asked.

"Ten to one," I answered.

"A dronker." He wrote on a blue slip with a white stylus, dropped it at my elbow, and sat down.

"We play the first game for feel," I said. "Second game pays."

Gradually I let my body relax. Its weight pulled at the muscles of my back and shoulders, and I slouched into a half-slump. I could feel my eyelids droop as I released them, and the corners of my mouth pulled down. I probably appeared tired and melancholy. Or like a man operating in a gravity heavier than was normal for him. Which I was.

I had come to this world called Velda two weeks earlier. My job was to find why its humanlike inhabitants refused all contacts with the Federation.

Earth's colonies had expanded during the last several centuries until they now comprised a loose alliance known as The Ten Thousand Worlds. They were normally peaceful—and wanted peace with Velda. But you cannot talk peace with a people who won't talk back. Worse, they had obliterated the fleet bringing our initial peace overtures. As a final gesture I had been smuggled in—in an attempt to breach that stand-off stubbornness. This booth at their Fair was my best chance—as I saw it—to secure audience with the men in authority. And with luck it would serve a double purpose.

Several Veldians gathered around the booth and watched with interest as my opponent and I chose colors. He took the red; I the black. We arranged our fifty-two pieces on their squares and I nodded to him to make the first move.

He was an anemic oldster with an air of nervous energy, and he played the same way, with intense concentration. By the fourth move I knew he would not win. On each play he had to consult the value board suspended between us before deciding what his next move would be. On a play board with one hundred and sixty-nine squares, each with a different value—in fact one set of values for offense, and another for defense—only a brilliant player could keep them all in mind. But no man without that ability was going to beat me.

I let him win the first game. Deliberately. The "second game counts" gimmick was not only to attract attention, but to give me a chance to test a player's strength—and find his weakness.

At the start of the second game, the oldster moved his front row center pukt three squares forward and one left oblique. I checked it with an end pukt, and waited.

The contest was not going to be exacting enough to hold my complete attention. Already an eidetic portion of my mind—which I always thought of as a small machine, ticking away in one corner of my skull, independent of any control or direction from me—was moving its interest out to the spectators around my booth.

It caught a half-completed gesture of admiration at my last move from a youth directly ahead of me. And with the motion, and the glimpse of the youth's face, something slipped into place in my memory. Some subconscious counting finished itself, and I knew that there had been too many of those youths, with faces like this one, finely boned and smooth, with slender delicate necks and slim hands and movements that were cool and detached. Far too many to be a normal number in a population of adults and children.

As if drawn, my glance went past the forms of the watchers around the booth and plumbed the passing crowd to the figure of a man; a magnificent masculine type of the Veldian race, thick shouldered and strong, thoughtful in motion, yet with something of the swagger of a gladiator, who, as he walked, spoke to the woman who held his arm, leaning toward her cherishingly as if he protected a great prize.

She was wearing a concealing cloak, but her face was beautiful, her hair semi-long, and in spite of the cloak I could see that her body was full-fleshed and almost voluptuously feminine. I had seen few such women on Velda.

Two of the slim, delicately built youths went by arm in arm, walking with a slight defiant sway of bodies, and looked at the couple as they passed, with a pleasure in the way the man's fascinated attention clove to the woman, and looked at the beauty of the woman possessively without lust, and passed by, their heads held higher in pride as if they shared a secret triumph with her. Yet they were strangers.

I had an answer to my counting. The "youths" with the large eyes and smooth delicate heads, with the slim straight asexual bodies, thought of themselves as women. I had not seen them treated with the subdued attraction and conscious avoidance one sex gives another, but by numbers . . . My memory added the number of these "youths" to the numbers of figures and faces that had been obviously female. It totaled to almost half the population I had seen. No matter what the biological explanation, it seemed reasonable that half . . .

I bent my head, to not see the enigma of the boy-woman face watching me, and braced my elbow to steady my hand as I moved. For two weeks I had been on Velda and during the second week I had come out of hiding and passed as a Veldian. It was incredible that I had been operating under a misunderstanding as to which were women, and which men, and not blundered openly. The luck that had saved me had been undeserved.

Opposite me, across the board, the bleach-skinned hand of the oldster was beginning to waver with indecision as each pukt was placed. He was seeing defeat, and not wishing to see it.

In eight more minutes I completed the rout of his forces and closed out the game. In winning I had lost only two pukts. The other's defeat was crushing, but my ruthlessness had been deliberate. I wanted my reputation to spread.

My sign, and the game in progress, by now had attracted a line of challengers, but as the oldster left the line broke and most of them shook their heads and moved back, then crowded around the booth and good-naturedly elbowed their way to positions of better vantage.

I knew then that I had set my lure with an irresistible bait. On a world where the Game was played from earliest childhood—was in fact a vital aspect of their culture—my challenge could not be ignored. I pocketed the loser's blue slip and nodded to the first in line of the four men who still waited to try me.

This second man played a better game than the old one. He had a fine tight-knit offensive, with a good grasp of values, but his weakness showed early in the game when I saw him hesitate before making a simple move in a defensive play. He was not skilled in the strategy of retreat and defense, or not suited to it by temperament. He would be unable to cope with a swift forward press, I decided.

I was right.

Some of the challengers bet more, some less, all lost on the second game. I purchased a nut and fruit confection from a passing food vender and ate it for a sparse lunch while I played through the late afternoon hours.

By the time Velda's distant sun had begun to print long shadows across the Fair grounds, I was certain that word of my booth had spread well.

The crowd about the railing of my stand was larger—but the players were fewer. Sometimes I had a break of several minutes before one made a decision to try his skill. And there were no more challenges from ordinary players. Still the results were the same. None had sufficient adroitness to give me more than a passing contest.

Until Caertin Vlosmin made his appearance.

Vlosmin played a game intended to be impregnably defensive, to remain untouchable until an opponent made a misplay or an overzealous drive, of which he would then take advantage. But his mental prowess was not quite great enough to be certain of a sufficiently concealed or complex weakness in the approach of an adversary, and he would not hazard an attack on an uncertainty. Excess caution was his weakness.

During our play I sensed that the crowd about us was very intent and still. On the outskirts, newcomers inquiring cheerfully were silenced by whispered exclamations.

Though it required all my concentration the game was soon over. I looked at Vlosmin as he rose to his feet, and noted with surprise that a fine spotting of moisture brightened his upper lip. Only then did I recognize the strain and effort he had invested into the attempt to defeat me.

"You are an exceptional craftsman," he said. There was a grave emphasis he put on the "exceptional" which I could not miss, and I saw that his face was whiter.

His formal introduction of himself earlier as "Caertin Vlosmin" had meant something more than I had realized at the time.

I had just played against, and defeated, one of the Great Players!

The sun set a short time later and floating particles of light-reflecting air-foam drifted out over the Fair grounds. Someway they were held suspended above the ground while air currents tossed them about and intermingled them in the radiance of vari-hued spotlights. The area was still as bright as day, but filled with pale, shifting shadows that seemed to heighten the byplay of sound and excitement coming from the Fair visitors.

Around my booth all was quiet; the spectators were subdued—as though waiting for the next act in a tense drama. I was very tired now, but I knew by the tenseness I observed around me that I did not have much longer to wait.

By the bubbles' light I watched new spectators take their positions about my booth. And as time went by I saw that some of them did not move on, as my earlier visitors had done.

The weight that rode my stomach muscles grew abruptly heavier, I had set my net with all the audacity of a spider waiting for a fly, yet I knew that when my anticipated victim arrived he would more likely resemble a spider hawk. Still the weight was not caused by fear: It was excitement—the excitement of the larger game about to begin.

I was playing an opponent of recognizably less ability than Vlosmin when I heard a stirring and murmuring in the crowd around my stand. The stirring was punctuated by my opponent rising to his feet.

I glanced up.

The big man who had walked into my booth was neither arrogant nor condescending, yet the confidence in his manner was like an aura of strength. He had a deep reserve of vitality, I noted as I studied him carefully, but it was a leashed, controlled vitality. Like most of the men of the Veldian race he wore a uniform, cut severely plain, and undecorated. No flowing robes or tunics for these men. They were a warrior race, unconcerned with the aesthetic touches of personal dress, and left that strictly to their women.

The newcomer turned to my late opponent. His voice was impressive, controlled. "Please finish your game," he said courteously.

The other shook his head. "The game is already as good as over. My sword is broken. You are welcome to my place."

The tall man turned to me. "If you don't mind?"

"My pleasure," I answered. "Please be seated."

This was it.

My visitor shrugged his close wrapped cloak back from his shoulders and took the chair opposite me. "I am Kalin Trobt," he said. As if he knew I had been expecting him.

In reply I came near to telling him my correct name. But Robert O. Lang was a name that would have been alien to Velda. Using it would have been as good as a confession. "Claustil Anteer," I said, giving a name I had invented earlier.

We played the first game as children play it, taking each other's pukts as the opportunity presented, making no attempt at finesse. Trobt won, two up. Neither of us had made mention of a wager. There would be more than money involved in this Game.

I noticed, when I glanced up before the second game, that the spectators had been cleared from around the booth. Only the inner, unmoving ring I had observed earlier remained now. They watched calmly—professionally.

Fortunately I had no intention of trying to escape.

During the early part of the second game Trobt and I tested each other carefully, as skilled swordsmen, probing, feinting, and shamming attack, but never actually exposing ourselves. I detected what could have been a slight tendency to gamble in Trobt's game, but there was no concrete situation to confirm it.

My first moves were entirely passive. Alertly passive. If I had judged correctly the character of the big man opposite me, I had only to ignore the bait he offered to draw me out, to disregard his openings and apparent—too apparent—errors, until he became convinced that I was unshakably cautious, and not to be tempted into making the first thrusts. For this was his weakness as I had guessed it: That his was a gambling temperament—that when he saw an opportunity he would strike—without the caution necessary to insure safety.

Pretending to move with timidity, and pausing with great deliberation over even the most obvious plays, I maneuvered only to defend. Each time Trobt shifted to a new position of attack I covered—until finally I detected the use of slightly more arm force than necessary when he moved a pukt. It was the only sign of impatience he gave, but I knew it was there.

Then it was that I left one—thin—opening.

Trobt streaked a pukt through and cut out one of my middle defenders.

Instead of making the obvious counter of taking his piece, I played a pukt far removed from his invading man. He frowned in concentration, lifted his arm—and his hand hung suspended over the board.

Suddenly his eyes widened. His glance swept upward to my face and what he saw there caused his expression to change to one of mingled dismay and astonishment. There was but one move he could make. When he made it his entire left flank would be exposed. He had lost the game.

Abruptly he reached forward, touched his index finger to the tip of my nose, and pressed gently.

After a minute during which neither of us spoke, I said, "You know?"

He nodded. "Yes," he said. "You're a Human."

There was a stir and rustle of motion around me. The ring of spectators had leaned forward a little as they heard his words. I looked up and saw that they were smiling, inspecting me with curiosity and something that could have been called admiration. In the dusk the clearest view was the ring of teeth, gleaming—the view a rabbit might get of a circle of grinning foxes. Foxes might feel friendly toward rabbits, and admire a good big one. Why not?

I suppressed an ineffectual impulse to deny what I was. The time was past for that. "How did you find out?" I asked Trobt.

"Your Game. No one could play like that and not be well known. And now your nose."

"My nose?" I repeated.

"Only one physical difference between a Human and a Veldian is apparent on the surface. The nose cartilage. Yours is split—mine is single." He rose to his feet. "Will you come with me, please?"

It was not a request.

My guards walked singly and in couples, sometimes passing Trobt and myself, sometimes letting us pass them, and sometimes lingering at a booth, like any other walkers, and yet, unobtrusively they held me encircled, always in the center of the group. I had already learned enough of the Veldian personality to realize that this was simply a habit of tact. Tact to prevent an arrest from being conspicuous, so as not to add the gaze of his fellows to whatever punishment would be decided for a culprit's offense. Apparently they considered humiliation too deep a punishment to use indiscriminately.

At the edge of the Fair grounds some of the watchers bunched around me while others went to get the tricars. I stood and looked across the park to The City. That was what it was called, The City, The Citadel, The Hearthplace, the home place where one's family is kept safe, the sanctuary whose walls have never been pierced. All those connotations had been in the name and the use of the name; in the voices of those who spoke it. Sometimes they called it The Hearth, and sometimes The Market, always *The* as if it were the only one.

Though the speakers lived in other places and named them as the homes of their ancestors, most of the Veldians were born here. Their history was colored, I might say even shaped, by their long era of struggle with the dleeth, a four-footed, hairy carnivore, physically little different from the big cats of Earth, but intelligent. They had battled the Veldians in a struggle for survival from the Veldians' earliest memories until a couple centuries before my visit. Now the last few surviving dleeth had found refuge in the frigid region of the north pole. With their physical superiority they probably would have won the struggle against the Veldians, except that their instincts had been purely predatory, and they had no hands and could not develop technology.

The City had been the one strong point that the dleeth had never been able to breach. It had been held by one of the stronger clans, and there was seldom unity among the tribes, yet any family about to bear a child was given sanctuary within its walls.

The clans were nomads—made so by the aggression of the dleeth—but they always made every effort to reach The City when childbirth was imminent. This explained, at least partly, why even strangers from foreign areas regarded The City as their home place.

I could see the Games Building from where I stood. In the walled city called Hearth it was the highest point. Big and red, it towered above the others, and the city around it rose to it like a wave, its consort of surrounding smaller buildings matched to each other in size and shape in concentric rings. Around each building wound the ramps of elevator runways, harmonious and useful, each of different colored stone, lending variety and warmth. Nowhere was there a clash of either proportion or color. Sometimes I wondered if the Veldians did not build more for the joy of creating symmetry, than because of utilitarian need.

I climbed into Trobt's three-wheeled car as it stopped before me, and the minute I settled into the bucket seat and gripped the bracing handles, Trobt spun the car and it dived into the highway and rushed toward the city. The vehicle seemed unstable, being about the width of a motor bike, with side car in front, and having nothing behind except a metal box that must have housed a powerful battery, and a shaft with the rear wheel that did the steering. It was an arrangement that made possible sudden wrenching turns that were battering to any passenger as unused to it as I. To my conditioning it seemed that the Veldians on the highway drove like madmen, the traffic rules were incomprehensible or nonexistent, and all drivers seemed determined to drive only in gull-like sweeping lines, giving no obvious change of course for other such cars, brushing by tricars from the opposite direction with an inch or less of clearance.

Apparently the maneuverability of the cars and the skill of the drivers were enough to prevent accidents, and I had to force my totally illogical drivers' reflexes to relax and stop tensing against the nonexistent peril.

I studied Trobt as he drove, noting the casual way he held the wheel, and the assurance in the set of his shoulders. I tried to form a picture in my mind of the kind of man he was, and just what were the motivations that would move or drive him.

Physically he was a long-faced man, with a smooth muscular symmetry, and an Asiatic cast to his eyes. I was certain that he excelled at whatever job he held. In fact I was prepared to believe that he would excel at anything he tried. He was undoubtedly one of those amazing men for whom the exceptional was mere routine. If he were to be cast in the role of my opponent: be the person in whom the opposition of this race would be actualized—as I now anticipated—I would not have wanted to bet against him.

The big skilled man was silent for several minutes, weaving the tricar with smooth swerves through a three-way tangle at an intersection, but twice he glanced at my expression with evident curiosity. Finally, as a man would state an obvious fact he said, "I presume you know you will be executed."

Trobt's face reflected surprise at the shock he must have read in mine. I had known the risk I would be taking in coming here, of course, and of the very real danger that it might end in my death. But this had come up on me too fast. I had not realized that the affair had progressed to the point where my death was already assured. I had thought that there would be negotiations, consultations, and perhaps ultimatums. But only if they failed did I believe that the repercussions might carry me along to my death.

However, there was the possibility that Trobt was merely testing my courage. I decided on boldness. "No," I said. "I do not expect to be executed."

Trobt raised his eyebrows and slowed, presumably to gain more time to talk. With a sudden decision he swung the tricar from the road into one of the small parks spread at regular intervals along the highway.

"Surely you don't think we would let you live? There's a state of war between Velda and your Ten Thousand Worlds. You admit that you're Human, and obviously you are here to spy. Yet when you're captured, you do not expect to be executed?"

"Was I captured?" I asked, emphasizing the last word.

He pondered on that a moment, but apparently did not come up with an answer that satisfied him. "I presume your question means something," he said.

"If I had wanted to keep my presence here a secret, would I have set up a booth at the Fair and invited inspection?" I asked.

He waved one hand irritably, as though to brush aside a picayune argument. "Obviously you did it to test yourself against us, to draw the great under your eye, and perhaps become a friend, treated as an equal with access to knowledge of our plans and weapons. Certainly! Your tactic drew two members of the Council into your net before it was understood. If we had accepted you as a previously unknown Great, you would have won. You are a gambling man, and you played a gambler's hand. You lost."

Partly he was right.

"My deliberate purpose was to reach you," I said, "or someone else with sufficient authority to listen to what I have to say."

Trobt pulled the vehicle deeper into the park. He watched the cars of our escort settling to rest before and behind us. I detected a slight unease and rigidity in his stillness as he said, "Speak then. I'm listening."

"I've come to negotiate," I told him.

Something like a flash of puzzlement crossed his features before they returned to tighter immobility. Unexpectedly he spoke in *Earthian*, my own language. "Then why did you choose this method? Would it not have been better simply to announce yourself?"

This was the first hint he had given that he might have visited our Worlds before I visited his. Though we had suspected before I came that some of them must have. They probably knew of our existence years before we discovered them.

Ignoring his change of language, I replied, still speaking Veldian, "Would it have been that simple? Or would some minor official, on capturing me, perhaps have had me imprisoned, or tortured to extract information?"

Again the suppressed puzzlement in the shift of position as he looked at me. "They would have treated you as an envoy, representing your Ten Thousand Worlds. You could have spoken to the Council immediately." He spoke in Veldian now.

"I did not know that," I said. "You refused to receive our fleet envoys; why should I expect you to accept me any more readily?"

Trobt started to speak, stopped, and turned in his seat to regard me levelly and steadily, his expression unreadable. "Tell me what you have to say then. I will judge whether or not the Council will listen."

"To begin with—" I looked away from the expressionless eyes, out the windshield, down the vistas of brown short trees that grew between each small park and the next. "Until an exploring party of ours found signs of extensive mining operations on a small metal-rich planet, we knew nothing of your existence. We were not even aware that another race in the galaxy had discovered faster than light space travel. But after the first clue we were alert for other signs, and found them. Our discovery of your planet was bound to come. However, we did not expect to be met on our first visit with an attack of such hostility as you displayed."

"When we learned that you had found us," Trobt said, "we sent a message to your Ten Thousand Worlds, warning them that we wanted no contact with you. Yet you sent a fleet of spaceships against us."

I hesitated before answering. "That phrase, 'sent against us,' is hardly the correct one," I said. "The fleet was sent for a diplomatic visit, and was not meant as an aggressive action." I thought, *But obviously the display of force was intended "diplomatically" to frighten you people into being polite.* In diplomacy the smile, the extended hand—and the big stick visible in the other hand—had obviated many a war, by giving the stranger a chance to choose a hand, in full understanding of the alternative. *We showed our muscle to your little planet—you showed your muscle. And now we are ready to be polite.*

I hoped these people would understand the face-saving ritual of negotiation, the disclaimers of intent, that would enable each side to claim that there had been no war, merely accident.

"We did not at all feel that you were justified in wiping the fleet from space," I said. "But it was probably a legitimate misunderstanding—"

"You had been warned!" Trobt's voice was grim, his expression not inviting of further discussion. I thought I detected a bunching of the muscles in his arms.

For a minute I said nothing, made no gesture. Apparently this angle of approach was unproductive—and probably explosive. Also, trying to explain and justify the behavior of the Federation politicos could possibly become rather taxing.

"Surely you don't intend to postpone negotiations indefinitely?" I asked tentatively. "One planet cannot conquer the entire Federation."

The bunched muscles of his arms strained until they pulled his shoulders, and his lips whitened with the effort of controlling some savage anger. Apparently my question had impugned his pride.

This, I decided quickly, was not the time to make an enemy. "I apologize if I have insulted you," I said in Earthian. "I do not yet always understand what I am saying, in your language."

He hesitated, made some kind of effort, and shifted to Earthian. "It is not a matter of strength, or weakness," he said, letting his words ride out on his released breath, "but of behavior, courtesy.

"We would have left you alone, but now it is too late. We will drive your faces into the ground. I am certain that we can, but if we could not, still we would try. To imply that we would not try, from fear, seems to me words to soil the mouth, not worthy of a man speaking to a man. We are converting our ships of commerce to war. Your people will see soon that we will fight."

"Is it too late for negotiation?" I asked.

His forehead wrinkled into a frown and he stared at me in an effort of concentration. When he spoke it was with a considered hesitation. "If I make a great effort I can feel that you are sincere, and not speaking to mock or insult. It is strange that beings who look so much like ourselves can"—he rubbed a hand across his eyes—"pause a moment. When I say 'yag loogt'-n'balt' what does it mean to you in Earthish?"

"I must play." I hesitated as he turned one hand palm down, signifying that I was wrong. "I must duel," I said, finding another meaning in the way I had heard the phrase expressed. It was a strong meaning, judging by the tone and inflection the speaker had used. I had mimicked the tone without full understanding. The verb was perhaps stronger than *must*, meaning something inescapable, fated, but I could find no Earthian verb for it. I understood why Trobt dropped his hand to the seat without turning it palm up to signify that I was correct.

"There may be no such thought on the human worlds," he said resignedly. "I have to explain as to a child or a madman. I cannot explain in Veldian, for it has no word to explain what needs no explanation."

He shifted to Earthian, his controlled voice sounding less controlled when moving with the more fluid inflections of my own tongue. "We said we did not want further contact. Nevertheless you sent the ships—deliberately in disregard of our expressed desire. That was an insult, a deep insult, meaning we have not strength to defend our word, meaning we are so helpless that we can be treated with impoliteness, like prisoners, or infants.

"Now we must show you which of us is helpless, which is the weakling. Since you would not respect our wishes, then in order to be not-further-insulted we must make of your people a captive or a child in helplessness, so that you will be without power to affront us another time."

"If apologies are in order—"

He interrupted with raised hand, still looking at me very earnestly with forehead wrinkled, thought half turned inward in difficult introspection of his own meaning, as well as a grasping for my viewpoint.

"The insult of the fleet can only be wiped out in the blood of testing—of battle—and the test will not stop until one or the other shows that he is too weak to struggle. There is no other way."

He was demanding total surrender!

I saw it was a subject that could not be debated. The Federation had taken on a bearcat this time!

"I stopped because I wanted to understand you," Trobt resumed. "Because the others will not understand how you could be an envoy—how your Federation could send an envoy—except as an insult. I have seen enough of human strangeness to be not maddened by the insolence of an emissary coming to us, or by your people expecting us to exchange words when we carry your first insult still unwashed from our face. I can even see how it could perhaps be considered *not* an insult, for I have seen your people living on their planets and they suffered insult from each other without striking, until finally I saw that they did not know when they were insulted, as a deaf man does not know when his name is called."

I listened to the quiet note of his voice, trying to recognize the attitude that made it different from his previous tones—calm and slow and deep. Certainty that what he was saying was important . . . conscious tolerance . . . generosity.

Trobt turned on the tricar's motor and put his hands on the steering shaft. "You are a man worthy of respect," he said, looking down the dark empty road ahead. "I wanted you to understand us. To see the difference between us. So that you will not think us without justice." The car began to move.

"I wanted you to understand why you will die."

I said nothing—having nothing to say. But I began immediately to bring my report up to date, recording the observations during the games, and recording with care this last conversation, with the explanation it carried of the Veldian reactions that had been previously obscure.

I used nerve-twitch code, "typing" on a tape somewhere inside myself the coded record of everything that had passed since the last time I brought the report up to date. The typing was easy, like flexing a finger in code jerks, but I did not know exactly where the recorder was located. It was some form of transparent plastic which would not show up on X ray. The surgeons had imbedded it in my flesh while I was unconscious, and had implanted a mental block against my noticing which small muscle had been linked into the contrivance for the typing.

If I died before I was able to return to Earth, there were several capsuled chemicals buried at various places in my body, that intermingled, would temporarily convert my body to a battery for a high powered broadcast of the tape report, destroying the tape and my body together. This would go into action only if my temperature fell fifteen degrees below the temperature of life.

I became aware that Kalin Trobt was speaking again, and that I had let my attention wander while recording, and taped some subjective material. The code twitches easily became an unconscious accompaniment to memory and thought, and this was the second time I had found myself recording more than necessary.

Trobt watched the dark road, threading among buildings and past darkened vehicles. His voice was thoughtful. "In the early days, Miklas of Danlee, when he had the Ornan family surrounded and outnumbered, wished not to destroy them, for he needed good warriors, and in another circumstance they could have been his friends. Therefore he sent a slave to them with an offer of terms of peace. The Oman family had the slave skinned while alive, smeared with salt and grease so that he would not bleed, and sent back, tied in a bag of his own skin, with a message of no. The chroniclers agree that since the Ornan family was known to be honorable, Miklas should not have made the offer.

"In another time and battle, the Cheldos were offered terms of surrender by an envoy. Nevertheless they won against superior forces, and gave their captives to eat a stew whose meat was the envoy of the offer to surrender. Being given to eat their own words as you'd say in Earthish. Such things are not done often, because the offer is not given."

He wrenched the steering post sideways and the tricar turned almost at right angles, balanced on one wheel for a dizzy moment, and fled up a great spiral ramp winding around the outside of the red Games Building.

Trobt still looked ahead, not glancing at me. "I understand, from observing them, that you Earthians will lie without soiling the mouth. What are you here for, actually?"

"I came from interest, but I intend, given the opportunity, to observe and to report my observations back to my government. They should not enter a war without knowing anything about you."

"Good." He wrenched the car around another abrupt turn into a red archway in the side of the building, bringing it to a stop inside. The sound of the other tricars entering the tunnel echoed hollowly from the walls and died as they came to a stop around us. "You are a spy then."

"Yes," I said, getting out. I had silently resigned my commission as envoy some five minutes earlier. There was little point in delivering political messages, if they have no result except to have one skinned or made into a stew.

A heavy door with the seal of an important official engraved upon it opened before us. In the forepart of the room we entered, a slim-bodied creature with the face of a girl sat with crossed legs on a plat-form like a long coffee table, sorting vellum marked with the dots and dashes, arrows and pictures, of the Veldian language.

She had green eyes, honeyed-olive complexion, a red mouth, and purple black hair. She stopped to work an abacus, made a notation on one of the stiff sheets of vellum, then glanced up to see who had come in. She saw us, and glanced away again, as if she had coolly made a note of our presence and gone back to her work, sorting the vellum sheets and stacking them in thin shelves with quick graceful motions.

"Kalin Trobt of Pagael," a man on the far side of the room said, a man sitting cross-legged on a dais covered with brown fur and scat-tered papers. He accepted the hand Trobt extended and they gripped wrists in a locked gesture of friendship. "And how survive the other sons of the citadel of Pagael?"

"Well, and continuing in friendship to the house of Lyagin," Trobt replied carefully. "I have seen little of my kin. There are many farlanders all around us, and between myself and my hearth-folk swarm the adopted."

"It is not like the old days, Kalin Trobt. In a dream I saw a rock sink from the weight of sons, and I longed for the sight of a land that is without strangers."

"We are all kinfolk now, Lyagin."

"My hearth pledged it."

Lyagin put his hand on a stack of missives which he had been considering, his face thoughtful, sparsely fleshed, mostly skull and tendon, his hair bound back from his face, and wearing a short white cotton dress beneath a light fur cape.

He was an old man, already in his senility, and now he was lost in a lapse of awareness of what he had been doing a moment before. By no sign did Trobt show impatience, or even consciousness of the other's lapse.

Lyagin raised his head after a minute and brought his rheumy eyes into focus on us. "You bring someone in regard to an inquiry?" he asked.

"The one from the Ten Thousand Worlds," Trobt replied.

Lyagin nodded apologetically. "I received word that he would be brought," he said. "How did you capture him?"

"He came."

The expression must have had some connotation that I did not recognize for the official let his glance cross mine, and I caught one slight flicker of interest in his eyes. "You say these Humans lie?" he asked Trobt.

"Frequently. It is considered almost honorable to lie to an enemy in circumstances where one may profit by it."

"You brought back from his worlds some poison which insures their speaking the truth, I believe?"

"Not a poison, something they call drugs, which affects one like strong drink, dulling a man and changing what he might do. Under its influence he loses his initiative of decision."

"You have this with you?"

"Yes." Trobt was going to waste no time getting from me anything I had that might be of value to them.

"It will be interesting having an enemy co-operate," Lyagin said. "If he finds no way to kill himself, he can be very useful to us." So far my contact with the Veldians had not been going at all as I had hoped and planned.

The boy-girl at the opposite side of the room finished a problem on the abacus, noted the answer, and glanced directly at my face, at my expression, then locked eyes with me for a brief moment. When she glanced down to the vellum again it was as if she had seen whatever she had looked up to see, and was content. She sat a little straighter as she worked, and moved with an action that was a little less supple and compliant.

I believe she had seen me as a man.

During the questioning I made no attempt to resist the drug's influence. I answered truthfully—but literally. Many times my answers were undecidable—because I knew not the answers, or I lacked the data to give them. And the others were cloaked under a full literal subtlety that made them useless to the Veldians. Questions such as the degree of unity existing between the Worlds: I answered—truthfully—that they were united under an authority with supreme power of decision. The fact that that authority had no actual force behind it; that it was subject to the whims and fluctuations of sentiment and politics of intraalliances; that it had deteriorated into a mere supernumerary body of impractical theorists that occupied itself, in a practical sphere, only with picayune matters, I did not explain. It was not asked of me.

Would our Worlds fight? I answered that they would fight to the death to defend their liberty and independence. I did not add that that will to fight would evidence itself first in internecine bickering, procrastinations, and jockeying to avoid the worst thrusts of the enemy—before it finally resolved itself into a united front against attack.

By early morning Trobt could no longer contain his impatience. He stepped closer. "We're going to learn one thing," he said, and his voice was harsh. "Why did you come here?"

"To learn all that I could about you," I answered.

"You came to find a way to whip us!"

It was not a question and I had no necessity to answer.

"Have you found the way?"

"No."

"If you do, and you are able, will you use that knowledge to kill us?"

"No."

Trobt's eyebrows raised. "No?" he repeated. "Then why do you want it?"

"I hope to find a solution that will not harm either side."

"But if you found that a solution was not possible, you would be willing to use your knowledge to defeat us?"

"Yes."

"Even if it meant that you had to exterminate us—man, woman, and child?"

"Yes."

"Why? Are you so certain that you are right, that you walk with God, and that we are knaves?"

"If the necessity to destroy one civilization or the other arose, and the decision were mine to make, I would rule against you because of the number of sentient beings involved."

Trobt cut the argument out from under me. "What if the situation were reversed, and your side was in the minority? Would you choose to let them die?"

I bowed my head as I gave him the truthful answer. "I would choose for my own side, no matter what the circumstances."

The interrogation was over.

On the drive to Trobt's home I was dead tired, and must have slept for a few minutes with my eyes open. With a start I heard Trobt say, ". . . that a man with ability enough to be a games—chess—master is given no authority over his people, but merely consulted on occasional abstract questions of tactics."

"It is the nature of the problem." I caught the gist of his comment from his last words and did my best to answer it. I wanted nothing less than to engage in conversation, but I realized that the interest he was showing now was just the kind I had tried to guide him to, earlier in the evening. If I could get him to understand us better, our motivations and ideals, perhaps even our frailties, there would be more hope for a compatible meeting of minds. "Among peoples of such mixed natures, such diverse histories and philosophies, and different ways of life, most administrative problems are problems of a choice of whims, of changing and conflicting goals; not *how* to do what a people want done, but *what* they want done, and whether their next generation will want it enough to make work on it, now, worthwhile."

"They sound insane," Trobt said. "Are your administrators supposed to serve the flickering goals of demented minds?"

"We must weigh values. What is considered good may be a matter of viewpoint, and may change from place to place, from generation to generation. In determining what people feel and what their unvoiced wants are, a talent of strategy, and an impatience with the illogic of others, are not qualifications."

"The good is good, how can it change?" Trobt asked. "I do not understand."

I saw that truly he could not understand, since he had seen nothing of the clash of philosophies among a mixed people. I tried to think of ways it could be explained; how to show him that a people who let their emotions control them more than their logic, would unavoidably do many things they could not justify or take pride in—but that that emotional predominance was what had enabled them to grow, and spread throughout their part of the galaxy—and be, in the main, happy.

I was tired, achingly tired. More, the events of the long day, and Velda's heavier gravity had taken me to the last stages of exhaustion. Yet I wanted to keep that weakness from Trobt. It was possible that he, and the other Veldians, would judge the Humans by what they observed in me.

Trobt's attention was on his driving and he did not notice that I followed his conversation only with difficulty. "Have you had only the two weeks of practice in the Game, since you came?" he asked.

I kept my eyes open with an effort and breathed deeply. Velda's one continent, capping the planet on its upper third; merely touched what would have been a temperate zone. During its short summer its mean temperature hung in the low sixties. At night it dropped to near freezing. The cold night air bit into my lungs and drove the fog of exhaustion from my brain.

"No," I answered Trobt's question. "I learned it before I came. A chess adept wrote me, in answer to an article on chess, that a man from one of the outworlds had shown him a game of greater richness and flexibility than chess, with much the same feeling to the player, and had beaten him in three games of chess after only two games to learn it, and had said that on his own planet this chesslike game was the basis for the amount of authority with which a man is invested. The stranger would not name his planet.

"I hired an investigating agency to learn the whereabouts of this planet. There was none in the Ten Thousand Worlds. That meant that the man had been a very ingenious liar, or—that he had come from Velda."

"It was I, of course," Trobt acknowledged.

"I realized that from your conversation. The sender of the letter," I resumed, "was known to me as a chess champion of two Worlds. The matter tantalized my thoughts for weeks, and finally I decided to try to arrange a visit to Velda. If you had this game, I wanted to try myself against your skilled ones."

"I understand that desire very well," Trobt said. "The same temptation caused me to be indiscreet when I visited your Worlds. I have seldom been able to resist the opportunity for an intellectual gambit."

"It wasn't much more than a guess that I would find the Game on Velda," I said. "But the lure was too strong for me to pass it by."

"Even if you came intending to challenge, you had little enough time to learn to play as you have—against men who have spent lifetimes learning. I'd like to try you again soon, if I may."

"Certainly." I was in little mood or condition to welcome any further polite conversation. And I did not appreciate the irony of his request—to the best of my knowledge I was still under a sentence of early death.

Trobt must have caught the bleakness in my reply for he glanced quickly over his shoulder at me. "There will be time," he said, gently for him. "Several days at least. You will be my guest." I knew that he was doing his best to be kind. His decision that I must die had not been prompted by any meanness of nature: To him it was only—inevitable.

The next day I sat at one end of a Games table in a side wing of his home while Trobt leaned against the wall to my left. "Having a like nature I can well understand the impulse that brought you here," he said. "The supreme gamble. Playing—with your life the stake in the game. Nothing you've ever experienced can compare with it. And even now—when you have lost, and will die—you do not regret it, I'm certain."

"I'm afraid you're overestimating my courage, and misinterpreting my intentions," I told him, feeling instinctively that this would be a good time to again present my arguments. "I came because I hoped to reach a better understanding. We feel that an absolutely unnecessary war, with its resulting death and destruction, would be foolhardy. And I fail to see your viewpoint. Much of it strikes me as stupid racial pride."

Trobt ignored the taunt. "The news of your coming is the first topic of conversation in The City," he said. "The clans understand that you have come to challenge; one man against a nation. They greatly admire your audacity."

"Look," I said, becoming angry and slipping into Earthian. "I don't know whether you consider me a damn fool or not. But if you think I came here expecting to die; that I'm looking forward to it with pleasure—"

He stopped me with an idle gesture of one hand. "You deceive yourself if you believe what you say," he commented. "Tell me this: Would you have stayed away if you had known just how great the risk was to be?"

I was surprised to find that I did not have a ready answer to his question.

"Shall we play?" Trobt asked.

We played three games; Trobt with great skill, employing diversified and ingenious attacks. But he still had that bit too much audacity in his execution. I won each time.

"You're undoubtedly a Master," Trobt said at the end of the third game. "But that isn't all of it. Would you like me to tell you why I can't beat you?"

"Can you?" I asked.

"I think so," he said. "I wanted to try against you again and again, because each time it did not seem that you had defeated me, but only that I had played badly, made childish blunders, and that I lost each game before we ever came to grips. Yet when I entered the duel against you a further time, I'd begin to blunder again."

He shoved his hands more deeply under his weapons belt, leaning back and observing me with his direct inspection. "My blundering then has to do with you, rather than myself," he said. "Your play is excellent, of course, but there is more beneath the surface than above. This is your talent: You lose the first game to see an opponent's weakness—and play it against him."

I could not deny it. But neither would I concede it. Any small advantage I might hold would be sorely needed later.

"I understand Humans a little," Trobt said. "Enough to know that very few of them would come to challenge us without some other purpose. They have no taste for death, with glory or without."

Again I did not reply.

"I believe," Trobt said, "that you came here to challenge in your own way, which is to find any weakness we might have, either in our military, or in some odd way, in our very selves."

Once again—with a minimum of help from me—he had arrived in his reasoning at a correct answer. From here on—against this man—I would have to walk a narrow line.

"I think," Trobt said more slowly, glancing down at the board between us, then back at my expression, "that this may be the First Game, and that you are more dangerous than you seem, that you are accepting the humiliation of allowing yourself to be thought of as weaker than you are, in actuality. You intend to find our weakness, and you expect somehow to tell your states what you find."

I looked across at him without moving. "What weakness do you fear I've seen?" I countered.

Trobt placed his hands carefully on the board in front of him and rose to his feet. Before he could say what he intended a small boy pulling something like a toy riding-horse behind him came into the game room and grabbed Trobt's trouser leg. He was the first blond child I had seen on Velda.

The boy pointed at the swords on the wall. "Da," he said beseechingly, making reaching motions. "Da."

Trobt kept his attention on me. After a moment a faint humorless smile moved his lips. He seemed to grow taller, with the impression a strong man gives when he remembers his strength. "You will find no weakness," he said. He sat down again and placed the child on his lap.

The boy grabbed immediately at the abacus hanging on Trobt's belt and began playing with it, while Trobt stroked his hair. All the Veldians dearly loved children, I had noticed.

"Do you have any idea how many of our ships were used to wipe out your fleet?" he asked abruptly.

As I allowed myself to show the interest I felt he put a hand on the boy's shoulder and leaned forward. "One," he said.

I very nearly called Trobt a liar—one ship obliterating a thousand—before I remembered that Veldians were not liars, and that Trobt obviously was not lying. Somehow this small under-populated planet had developed a science of weapons that vastly exceeded that of the Ten Thousand Worlds.

I had thought that perhaps my vacation on this Games-mad planet would result in some mutual information that would bring quick negotiation or conciliation: That players of a chesslike game would be easy to approach: That I would meet men intelligent enough to see the absurdity of such an ill-fated war against the overwhelming odds of the Ten Thousand Worlds Federation. Intelligent enough to foresee the disaster that would result from such a fight. It began to look as if the disaster might be to the Ten Thousand and not to the one.

Thinking, I walked alone in Trobt's roof garden.

Walking in Velda's heavy gravity took more energy than I cared to expend, but too long a period without exercise brought a dull ache to the muscles of my shoulders and at the base of my neck.

This was my third evening in the house. I had slept at least ten hours each night since I arrived, and found myself exhausted at day's end, unless I was able to take a nap or lie down during the afternoon.

The flowers and shrubbery in the garden seemed to feel the weight of gravity also, for most of them grew low, and many sent creepers out along the ground. Overhead strange formations of stars clustered thickly and shed a glow on the garden very like Earth's moonlight.

I was just beginning to feel the heavy drag in my leg tendons when a woman's voice said, "Why don't you rest a while?" It spun me around as I looked for the source of the voice.

I found her in a nook in the bushes, seated on a contour chair that allowed her to stretch out in a half-reclining position. She must have weighed near to two hundred—Earth-weight—pounds.

But the thing that had startled me more than the sound of her voice was that she had spoken in the universal language of the Ten Thousand Worlds. And without accent!

"You're—?" I started to ask.

"Human," she finished for me.

"How did you get here?" I inquired eagerly.

"With my husband." She was obviously enjoying my astonishment. She was a beautiful woman, in a gentle bovine way, and very friendly. Her blond hair was done up in tight ringlets.

"You mean . . . Trobt?" I asked.

"Yes." As I stood trying to phrase my wonderment into more questions, she asked, "You're the Earthman, aren't you?"

I nodded. "Are you from Earth?"

"No," she answered. "My home world is Mandel's Planet, in the Thumb group."

She indicated a low hassock of a pair, and I seated myself on the lower and leaned an elbow on the higher, beginning to smile. It would have been difficult not to smile in the presence of anyone so contented. "How did you meet Trobt?" I asked.

"It's a simple love story. Kalin visited Mandel—without revealing his true identity of course—met, and courted me. I learned to love him, and agreed to come to his world as his wife."

"Did you know that he wasn't . . . That he . . ." I stumbled over just how to phrase the question. And wondered if I should have started it.

Her teeth showed white and even as she smiled. She propped a pillow under one plump arm and finished my sentence for me. ". . . That he wasn't Human?" I was grateful for the way she put me at ease—almost as though we had been old friends.

I nodded.

"I didn't know." For a moment she seemed to draw back into her thoughts, as though searching for something she had almost forgotten. "He couldn't tell me. It was a secret he had to keep. When I arrived here and learned that his planet wasn't a charted world, was not even Human, I was a little uncertain and lonesome. But not frightened. I knew Kalin would never let me be hurt. Even my lonesomeness left quickly. Kalin and I love each other very deeply. I couldn't be more happy than I am now."

She seemed to see I did not consider that my question had been answered—completely. "You're wondering still if I mind that he isn't Human, aren't you?" she asked. "Why should I? After all, what does it mean to be 'Human'? It is only a word that differentiates one group of people from another. I seldom think of the Veldians as being different—and certainly never that they're beneath me."

"Does it bother you—if you'll pardon this curiosity of mine—that you will never be able to bear Kalin's children?"

"The child you saw the first morning is my son," she answered complacently.

"But that's impossible," I blurted.

"Is it?" she asked. "You saw the proof."

"I'm no expert at this sort of thing," I said slowly, "but I've always understood that the possibility of two separate species producing offspring was a million to one."

"Greater than that, probably," she agreed. "But whatever the odds, sooner or later the number is bound to come up. This was it."

I shook my head, but there was no arguing a fact. "Wasn't it a bit unusual that Kalin didn't marry a Veldian woman?"

"He has married—two of them," she answered. "I'm his third wife."

"Then they do practice polygamy," I said. "Are you content with such a marriage?"

"Oh yes," she answered. "You see, besides being very much loved,

I occupy a rather enviable position here. I, ah . . ." She grew slightly flustered. "Well . . . the other women—the Veldian women—can bear children only once every eight years, and during the other seven . . ." She hesitated again and I saw a tinge of red creep into her cheeks. She was obviously embarrassed, but she laughed and resolutely went on.

"During the other seven, they lose their feminine appearance, and don't think of themselves as women. While I . . ." I watched with amusement as her color deepened and her glance dropped. "I am always of the same sex, as you might say, always a woman. My husband is the envy of all his friends."

After her first reticence she talked freely, and I learned then the answer to the riddle of the boy-girls of Velda. And at least one reason for their great affection for children.

One year of fertility in eight . . .

Once again I saw the imprint of the voracious dleeth on this people's culture. In their age-old struggle with their cold planet and its short growing seasons—and more particularly with the dleeth—the Veldian women had been shaped by evolution to better fit their environment. The women's strength could not be spared for frequent childbearing-so childbearing had been limited. Further, one small child could be carried in the frequent flights from the dleeth, but not more than one. Nature had done its best to cope with the problem: In the off seven years she tightened the women's flesh, atrophying glands and organs—making them nonfunctional—and changing their bodies to be more fit to labor and survive—and to fight, if necessary. It was an excellent adaptation—for a time and environment where a low birth rate was an asset to survival.

But this adaptation had left only a narrow margin for race perpetuation. Each woman could bear only four children in her lifetime. That, I realized as we talked, was the reason why the Veldians had not colonized other planets, even though they had space flight—and why they probably never would, without a drastic change in their biological make-up. That left so little ground for a quarrel between them and the Ten Thousand Worlds. Yet here we were, poised to spring into a death struggle.

"You are a very unusual woman." My attention returned to Trobt's wife. "In a very unusual situation."

"Thank you," she accepted it as a compliment. She made ready to rise. "I hope you enjoy your visit here. And that I may see you again before you return to Earth."

I realized then that she did not know of my peculiar position in her home. I wondered if she knew even of the threat of war between us and her adopted people. I decided not, or she would surely have spoken of it. Either Trobt had deliberately avoided telling her, perhaps to spare her the pain it would have caused, or she had noted that the topic of my presence was disturbing to him and had tactfully refrained from inquiring. For just a moment I wondered if I should explain everything to her, and have her use the influence she must have with Trobt. I dismissed the idea as unworthy—and useless.

"Good night," I said.

The next evening as we rode in a tricar Trobt asked if I would like to try my skill against a better Games player.

"I had assumed you were the best," I said.

"Only the second best," he answered. "It would be interesting to compare your game with that of our champion. If you can whip him, perhaps we will have to revise our opinion of you Humans."

He spoke as though in jest, but I saw more behind his words than he intended me to see. Here at last might be a chance to do a positive service for my side. "I would be happy to play," I said.

Trobt parked the tricar on a side avenue and we walked perhaps a hundred yards. We stopped at the door of a small one-story stone house and Trobt tapped with his fingernails on a hollow gong buried in the wood.

After a minute a curtain over the door glass was drawn back and an old woman with straggly gray hair peered out at us. She recognized Trobt and opened the door.

We went in. Neither Trobt nor the old woman spoke. She turned her back after closing the door and went to stir embers in a stone grate.

Trobt motioned with his head for me to follow and led the way into a back room.

"Robert O. Lang," he said, "I would like you to meet Yondtl."

❖ ❖ ❖

I looked across the room in the direction Trobt had indicated. My first impression was of a great white blob, propped up on a couch and supported by the wall at its back.

Then the thing moved. Moved its eyes. It was alive. Its eyes told me also that it was a man. If I could call it a man.

His head was large and bloated, with blue eyes, washed almost colorless, peering out of deep pouches of flesh. He seemed to have no neck; almost as though his great head were merely an extension of the trunk, and separated only by puffy folds of fat. Other lappings of flesh hung from his body in great thick rolls.

It took another minute of fascinated inspection before I saw that he had no arms, and that no legs reached from his body to the floor. The entire sight of him made me want to leave the room and be sick.

"Robert O. Lang is an Earthian who would challenge you, sir," Trobt addressed the monstrosity.

The other gave no sign that I could see but Trobt went to pull a Games table at the side of the room over toward us. "I will serve as his hands," Trobt said.

The pale blue eyes never left my face.

I stood without conscious thought until Trobt pushed a chair under me. Mentally I shook myself. With unsteady hands—I had to do something with them—I reached for the pukts before me. "Do you . . . do you have a choice . . . of colors, sir?" I stammered, trying to make up for my earlier rudeness of staring.

The lips of the monstrosity quivered, but he made no reply.

All this while Trobt had been watching me with amusement. "He is deaf and speechless," Trobt said. "Take either set. I will place the other before him."

Absently I pulled the red pieces toward me and placed them on their squares.

"In deference to you as a visitor, you will play 'second game counts,'" Trobt continued. He was still enjoying my consternation. "He always allows his opponent the first move. You may begin when you are ready."

With an effort I forced myself to concentrate on the playing board. My start, I decided, must be orthodox. I had to learn something of the type of game this . . . Yondtl . . . played. I moved the first row right hand pukt its two oblique and one left squares.

Yondtl inclined his head slightly. His lips moved. Trobt put his hand to a pukt and pushed it forward. Evidently Trobt read his lips. Very probably Yondtl could read ours also.

We played for almost an hour with neither of us losing a man.

I had tried several gambits; gambits that invited a misplay on Yondtl's part. But he made none. When he offered I was careful to make no mistakes of my own. We both played as though this first game were the whole contest.

Another hour went by. I deliberately traded three pukts with Yondtl, in an attempt to trick him into a misplay. None came.

I tried a single decoy gambit, and when nothing happened, followed with a second decoy. Yondtl countered each play. I marveled that he gave so little of his attention to the board. Always he seemed to be watching me. I played. He played. He watched me.

I sweated.

Yondtl set up an overt side pass that forced me to draw my pukts back into the main body. Somehow I received the impression that be was teasing me. It made me want to beat him down.

I decided on a crossed-force, double decoy gambit. I had never seen it employed. Because, I suspect, it is too involved, and open to error by its user. Slowly and painstakingly I set it up and pressed forward.

The Caliban in the seat opposite me never paused. He matched me play for play. And though Yondtl's features had long since lost the power of expression, his pale eyes seemed to develop a blue luster. I realized, almost with a shock of surprise, that the fat monstrosity was happy—intensely happy.

I came out of my brief reverie with a start. Yondtl had made an obvious play. I had made an obvious counter. I was startled to hear him sound a cry somewhere between a muffled shout and an idiot's laugh, and my attention jerked back to the board. I had lost the game!

My brief moment of abstraction had given Yondtl the opportunity to make a pass too subtle to be detected with part of my faculties occupied elsewhere.

I pushed back my chair. "I've had enough for tonight," I told Trobt. If I were to do the Humans a service, I would need rest before trying Yondtl in the second game.

We made arrangements to meet again the following evening, and let ourselves out. The old woman was nowhere in sight.

The following evening when we began play I was prepared to give my best. I was rested and eager. And I had a concrete plan. Playing the way I had been doing I would never beat Yondtl, I'd decided after long thought. A stand-off was the best I could hope for. Therefore the time had come for more consummate action. I would engage him in a triple decoy gambit!

I had no illusion that I could handle it—the way it should be handled. I doubt that any man, Human or Veldian, could. But at least I would play it with the greatest skill I had, giving my best to every move, and push the game up the scale of reason and involution—up and up—until either Yondtl or I became lost in its innumerable complexities, and fell.

As I attacked, the complexes and complications would grow gradually more numerous, become more and more difficult, until they embraced a span greater than one of us had the capacity to encompass, and the other would win.

The Game began and I forced it into the pattern I had planned. Each play, and each maneuver, became all important, and demanding of the greatest skill I could command. Each pulled at the core of my brain, dragging out the last iota of sentient stuff that writhed there. Yondtl stayed with me, complex gambit through complex gambit.

When the strain became too great I forced my mind to pause, to rest, and to be ready for the next clash. At the first break I searched the annotator. It was working steadily, with an almost smooth throb of efficiency, keeping the position of each pukt—and its value—strong in the forefront of visualization. But something was missing!

A minute went by before I spotted the fault. The move of each pukt involved so many possibilities, so many avenues of choice, that no exact answer was predictable on any one. The number and variation of gambits open on every play, each subject to the multitude of

Yondtl's counter moves, stretched the possibilities beyond prediction. The annotator was a harmonizing, perceptive force, but not a creative, initiating one. It operated in a statistical manner, similar to a computer, and could not perform effectively where a crucial factor or factors were unknown, or concealed, as they were here.

My greatest asset was negated.

At the end of the third hour I began to feel a steady pain in my temples, as though a tight metal band pressed against my forehead and squeezed it inward. The only reaction I could discern in Yondtl was that the blue glint in his eyes had become brighter. All his happiness seemed gathered there.

Soon my pauses became more frequent. Great waves of brain weariness had to be allowed to subside before I could play again.

And at last it came.

Suddenly, unexpectedly, Yondtl threw a pukt across the board and took my second decoy—and there was no way for me to retaliate! Worse, my entire defense was smashed.

I felt a kind of calm dismay. My shoulders sagged and I pushed the board away from me and slumped in my chair.

I was beaten.

The next day I escaped from Trobt. It was not difficult. I simply walked away.

For three days I followed the wall of The City, looking for a way out. Each gate was guarded. I watched unobserved and saw that a permit was necessary when leaving. If I found no other way I would make a run for it. The time of decision never came.

Meanwhile to obtain food I was forced into some contact with The City's people, and learned to know them better. Adding this new knowledge to the old I decided that I liked them.

Their manners and organization—within the framework of their culture—was as simple and effective as their architecture. There was a strong emphasis on pride, on strength and honor, on skill, and on living a dangerous life with a gambler's self-command, on rectitude, on truth, and the unbreakable bond of loyalty among family and friends. Lying, theft, and deceit were practically unknown.

I did detect what might have been a universal discontent in their young men. They had a warrior heritage and nature which, with the unity of the tribes and the passing of the dleeth—and no one to fight except themselves—had left them with an unrecognized futility of purpose. They had not quite been able to achieve a successful subli- mation of their post-warrior need to fight in the Games. Also, the custom of polygamy—necessary in the old days, and desired still by those able to attain it—left many sexually frustrated.

I weighed all these observations in my reactions to the Veldians, and toward the end a strange feeling—a kind of wistfulness—came as I observed. I felt kin to them, as if these people had much in common with myself. And I felt that it was too bad that life was not fundamen- tally so simple that one could discard the awareness of other ways of life, of other values and philosophies that bid against one another, and against one's attention, and make him cynical of the philosophy he lives by, and dies for. Too bad that I could not see and take life as that direct, and as that simple.

The third day I climbed a spiral ramp to the top of a tower that rose above the walls of Hearth and gazed out over miles of swirling red sand. Directly beneath me stretched a long concrete ribbon of road. On the road were dozens of slowly crawling vehicles that might have been caterpillar trucks of Earth!

In my mind the pattern clicked into place. Hearth was not typical of the cities of Velda!

It was an anachronism, a revered Homeplace, a symbol of their past, untainted by the technocracy that was pursued elsewhere. This was the capital city, from which the heads of the government still ruled, perhaps for sentimental reasons, but it was not typical.

My stay in Hearth was cut short when I descended from the tower and found Trobt waiting for me.

As I might have expected, he showed no sign of anger with me for having fled into The City. His was the universal Veldian viewpoint. To them all life was the Game. With the difference that it was played on an infinitely larger board. Every man, and every woman, with whom the player had contact, direct or indirect, were pukts on the Board. The player made his decisions, and his plays, and how well he made them determined whether he won or lost. His every move, his every joining of strength with those who could help him, his every maneuver against those who would oppose him, was his choice to make, and he rose or fell on the wisdom of the choice. Game, in Velda, means Duel, means struggle and the test of man against the opponent, Life. I had made my escape as the best play as I saw it. Trobt had no recriminations.

The evening of the next day Trobt woke me. Something in his constrained manner brought me to my feet. "Not what you think," he said, "but we must question you again. We will try our own methods this time."

"Torture?"

"You will die under the torture, of course. But for the questioning it will not be necessary. You will talk."

The secret of their method was very simple. Silence. I was led to a room within a room within a room. Each with very thick walls. And left alone. Here time meant nothing.

Gradually I passed from boredom to restlessness, to anxiety, briefly through fear, to enervating frustration, and finally to stark apathy.

When Trobt and his three accompanying guardsmen led me into the blinding daylight I talked without hesitation or consideration of consequences.

"Did you find any weakness in the Veldians?"

"Yes."

I noted then a strange thing. It was the annotator—the thing in my brain that was a part of me, and yet apart from me—that had spoken. It was not concerned with matters of emotion; with sentiments of patriotism, loyalty, honor, and self-respect. It was interested only in my—and its own—survival. Its logic told it that unless I gave the answers my questioner wanted I would die. That, it intended to prevent.

I made one last desperate effort to stop that other part of my mind from assuming control—and sank lower into my mental impotence.

"What is our weakness?"

"*Your society is doomed.*" With the answer I realized that the annotator had arrived at another of its conclusions.

"Why?"

"There are many reasons."

"Give one."

"Your culture is based on a need for struggle, for combat. When there is no one to fight it must fall."

Trobt was dealing with a familiar culture now. He knew the questions to ask.

"Explain that last statement."

"Your culture is based on its impetuous need to battle . . . it is armed and set against dangers and the expectation of danger . . . fostering the pride of courage under stress. There is no danger now . . . nothing to fight, no place to spend your over-aggressiveness, except against each other in personal duels. Already your decline is about to enter the bloody circus and religion stage, already crumbling in the heart while expanding at the outside. And this is your first civilization . . . like a boy's first love . . . you have no experience of a fall in your history before to have recourse to—no cushioning of philosophy to accept it."

For a time Trobt maintained a puzzled silence. I wondered if he had the depth of understanding to accept the truth and significance of what he had heard. "Is there no solution?" he asked at last.

"Only a temporary one." Now it was coming.

"Explain."

"War with the Ten Thousand Worlds."

"Explain."

"Your willingness to hazard, and eagerness to battle is no weakness when you are armed with superior weapons, and are fighting against an opponent as disorganized, and as incapable of effective organization as the Ten Thousand Worlds, against your long-range weapons and subtle traps."

"Why do you say the solution is only temporary?"

"You cannot win the war. You will seem to win, but it will be an illusion. You will win the battles, kill billions, rape Worlds, take slaves, and destroy ships and weapons. But after that you will be forced to hold the subjection. Your numbers will not be expendable. You will be spread thin, exposed to other cultures that will influence you, change you. You will lose skirmishes, and in the end you will be forced back. Then will come a loss of old ethics, corruption and opportunism will replace your honor and you will know unspeakable shame and dishonor . . . your culture will soon be weltering back into a barbarism and disorganization which in its corruption and despair will be nothing like the proud tribal primitive life of its first barbarism. You will be aware of the difference and unable to return."

I understood Trobt's perplexity as I finished. He could not accept what I told him because to him winning was only a matter of a military victory, a victory of strength; Velda had never experienced defeat as a weakness from within. My words made him uneasy, but he did not understand. He shrugged. "Do we have any other weakness?" he asked.

"Your women."

"Explain."

"They are 'set' for the period when they greatly outnumbered their men. Your compatible ratio is eight women to one man. Yet now it is one to one. Further, you produce too few children. Your manpower must ever be in small supply. Worse, your shortage of women sponsors a covert despair and sadism in your young men . . . a hunger and starvation to follow instinct, to win women by courage and conquest and battle against danger . . . that only a war can restrain."

"The solution?"

"Beat the Federation. Be in a position to have free access to their women."

Came the final ignominy. "Do you have a means of reporting back to the Ten Thousand Worlds?"

"Yes. Buried somewhere inside me is a nerve-twitch tape. Flesh pockets of chemicals are stored there also. When my body temperature drops fifteen degrees below normal the chemicals will be activated and will use the tissues of my body for fuel and generate sufficient energy to transmit the information on the tape back to the Ten Thousand Worlds."

That was enough.

"Do you still intend to kill me?" I asked Trobt the next day as we walked in his garden.

"Do not fear," he answered. "You will not be cheated of an honorable death. All Velda is as eager for it as you."

"Why?" I asked. "Do they see me as a madman?"

"They see you as you are. They cannot conceive of one man challenging a planet, except to win himself a bright and gory death on a page of history, the first man to deliberately strike and die in the coming war—not an impersonal clash of battleships, but a *man* declaring personal battle against men. We would not deprive you of that death. Our admiration is too great. We want the symbolism of your blood now just as greatly as you want it yourself. Every citizen is waiting to watch you die—gloriously."

I realized now that all the while he had interpreted my presence here in this fantastic way. And I suspected that I had no arguments to convince him differently.

Trobt had hinted that I would die under torture. I thought of the old histories of Earth that I had read. Of the warrior race of North American Indians. A captured enemy must die. But if he had been an honorable enemy he was given an honorable death. He was allowed to die under the stress most familiar to them. Their strongest ethic was a cover-up for the defeated, the universal expressionless suppressal of reaction in conquering or watching conquest, so as not to shame the defeated. Public torture—with the women, as well as warriors, watching—the chance to exhibit fortitude, all the way to the breaking point, and beyond. That was considered the honorable death, while it was a shameful trick to quietly slit a man's throat in his sleep without giving him a chance to fight—to show his scorn of flinching under the torture.

Here I was the Honorable Enemy who had exhibited courage. They would honor me, and satisfy their hunger for an Enemy, by giving me the breaking point test.

But I had no intention of dying!

"You will not kill me," I addressed Trobt. "And there will be no war."

He looked at me as though I had spoken gibberish.

My next words, I knew, would shock him. "I'm going to recommend unconditional surrender," I said.

Trobt's head which he had turned away swiveled sharply back to me. His mouth opened and he made several motions to speak before succeeding. "Are you serious?"

"Very," I answered.

Trobt's face grew gaunt and the skin pressed tight against his cheekbones—almost as though he were making the surrender rather than I. "Is this decision dictated by your logic," he asked dryly, "or by faintness of heart?"

I did not honor the question enough to answer.

Neither did he apologize. "You understand that unconditional surrender is the only kind we will accept?"

I nodded wearily.

"Will they agree to your recommendation?"

"No," I answered. "Humans are not cowards, and they will fight—as long as there is any slightest hope of success. I will not be able to convince them that their defeat is inevitable. But I can prepare them for what is to come. I hope to shorten the conflict immeasurably."

"I can do nothing but accept," Trobt said after a moment of thought. "I will arrange transportation back to Earth for you tomorrow." He paused and regarded me with expressionless eyes. "You realize that an enemy who surrenders without a struggle is beneath contempt?"

The blood crept slowly into my cheeks. It was difficult to ignore his taunt. "Will you give me six months before you move against us?" I asked. "The Federation is large. I will need time to bring my message to all."

"You have your six months." Trobt was still not through with me, personally. "On the exact day that period ends I will expect your return to Velda. We will see if you have any honor left."

"I will be back," I said.

During the next six months I spread my word throughout the Ten Thousand Worlds. I met disbelief everywhere. I had not expected otherwise. The last day I returned to Velda.

Two days later Velda's Council acted. They were going to give the Humans no more time to organize counteraction. I went in the same spaceship that carried Trobt. I intended to give him any advice he needed about the Worlds. I asked only that his first stop be at the Jason's Fleece fringe.

Beside us sailed a mighty armada of warships, spaced in a long line that would encompass the entire portion of the galaxy occupied by the Ten Thousand Worlds. For an hour we moved ponderously forward, then the stars about us winked out for an instant. The next moment a group of Worlds became visible on the ship's vision screen. I recognized them as Jason's Fleece.

One World expanded until it appeared the size of a baseball. "Quagman," Trobt said.

Quagman, the trouble spot of the Ten Thousand Worlds. Dominated by an unscrupulous clique that ruled by vendetta, it had been the source of much trouble and vexation to the other Worlds. Its leaders were considered little better than brigands. They had received me with much apparent courtesy. In the end they had even agreed to surrender to the Veldians—when and if they appeared. I had accepted their easy concurrence with askance, but they were my main hope.

Two Veldians left our ship in a scooter. We waited ten long, tense hours. When word finally came back it was from the Quagmans themselves. The Veldian envoys were being held captive. They would be released upon the delivery of two billion dollars—in the currency of any recognized World—and the promise of immunity.

The fools!

Trobt's face remained impassive as he received the message.

We waited several more hours. Both Trobt and I watched the green mottled baseball on the vision screen. It was Trobt who first pointed out a small, barely discernible, black spot on the upper left-hand corner of Quagman.

As the hours passed, and the black spot swung slowly to the right as the planet revolved, it grew almost imperceptibly larger. When it disappeared over the edge of the world we slept.

In the morning the spot appeared again, and now it covered half the face of the planet. Another ten hours and the entire planet became a blackened cinder.

Quagman was dead.

The ship moved next to Mican.

Mican was a sparsely populated prison planet. Criminals were usually sent to newly discovered Worlds on the edge of the Human expansion circle, and allowed to make their own adjustments toward achieving a stable government. Men with the restless natures that made them criminals on their own highly civilized Worlds, made the best pioneers. However, it always took them several generations to work their way up from anarchy to a co-operative government. Mican had not yet had that time. I had done my best in the week I spent with them to convince them to organize, and to be prepared to accept any terms the Veldians might offer. The gesture, I feared, was useless but I had given all the arguments I knew.

A second scooter left with two Veldian representatives. When it returned Trobt left the control room to speak with them.

He returned, and shook his head. I knew it was useless to argue.

Mican died.

At my request Trobt agreed to give the remaining Jason's Fleece Worlds a week to consider—on the condition that they made no offensive forays. I wanted them to have time to fully assess what had happened to the other two Worlds—to realize that that same stubbornness would result in the same disaster for them.

At the end of the third twenty-four-hour period the Jason's Fleece Worlds surrendered—unconditionally. They had tasted blood; and recognized futility when faced with it. That had been the best I had been able to hope for, earlier.

Each sector held off surrendering until the one immediately ahead had given in. But the capitulation was complete at the finish. No more blood had had to be shed.

The Veldians' terms left the Worlds definitely subservient, but they were neither unnecessarily harsh, nor humiliating. Velda demanded specific limitations on Weapons and war-making potentials; the obligation of reporting all technological and scientific progress; and colonial expansion only by prior consent.

There was little actual occupation of the Federation Worlds, but the Veldians retained the right to inspect any and all functions of the various governments. Other aspects of social and economic methods would be subject only to occasional checks and investigation. Projects considered questionable would be supervised by the Veldians at their own discretion.

The one provision that caused any vigorous protest from the Worlds was the Veldian demand for Human women. But even this was a purely emotional reaction, and died as soon as it was more fully understood. The Veldians were not barbarians. They used no coercion to obtain our women. They only demanded the same right to woo them as the citizens of the Worlds had. No woman would be taken without her free choice. There could be no valid protest to that.

In practice it worked quite well. On nearly all the Worlds there were more women than men, so that few men had to go without mates because of the Veldians' inroads. And—by Human standards—they seldom took our most desirable women. Because the acquiring of weight was corollary with the Veldian women becoming sexually attractive, their men had an almost universal preference for fleshy women. As a result many of our women who would have had difficulty securing Human husbands found themselves much in demand as mates of the Veldians.

Seven years passed after the Worlds' surrender before I saw Kalin Trobt again.

The pact between the Veldians and the Worlds had worked out well, for both sides. The demands of the Veldians involved little sacrifice by the Federation, and the necessity of reporting to a superior authority made for less wrangling and jockeying for advantageous position among the Worlds themselves.

The fact that the Veldians had taken more than twenty million of our women—it was the custom for each Veldian male to take a human woman for one mate—caused little dislocation or discontent. The number each lost did less than balance the ratio of the sexes.

For the Veldians the pact solved the warrior-set frustrations, and the unrest and sexual starvation of their males. Those men who demanded action and adventure were given supervisory posts on the Worlds as an outlet for their drives. All could now obtain mates; mates whose biological make-up did not necessitate an eight to one ratio.

Each year it was easier for the Humans to understand the Veldians and to meet them on common grounds socially. Their natures became less rigid, and they laughed more—even at themselves, when the occasion demanded.

This was especially noticeable among the younger Veldians, just reaching an adult status. In later years when the majority of them would have a mixture of human blood, the difference between us would become even less pronounced.

Trobt had changed little during those seven years. His hair had grayed some at the temples, and his movements were a bit less supple, but he looked well. Much of the intensity had left his aquiline features, and he seemed content.

We shook hands with very real pleasure. I led him to chairs under the shade of a tree in my front yard and brought drinks.

"First, I want to apologize for having thought you a coward," he began, after the first conventional pleasantries. "I know now I was very wrong. I did not realize for years, however, just what had happened." He gave his wry smile. "You know what I mean, I presume?"

I looked at him inquiringly.

"There was more to your decision to capitulate than was revealed. When you played the Game your forte was finding the weakness of an opponent. And winning the second game. You made no attempt to win the first. I see now, that as on the boards, your surrender represented only the conclusion of the first game. You were keeping our weakness to yourself, convinced that there would be a second game. And that your Ten Thousand Worlds would win it. As you have."

"What would you say your weakness was?" By now I suspected he knew everything, but I wanted to be certain.

"Our desire and need for Human women, of course."

There was no need to dissemble further. "The solution first came to me," I explained, "when I remembered a formerly independent Earth country named China. They lost most of their wars, but in the end they always won."

"Through their women?"

"Indirectly. Actually it was done by absorbing their conquerors. The situation was similar between Velda and the Ten Thousand

Worlds. Velda won the war, but in a thousand years there will be no Veldians—racially."

"That was my first realization," Trobt said. "I saw immediately then how you had us hopelessly trapped. The marriage of our men to your women will blend our bloods until—with your vastly greater numbers—in a dozen generations there will be only traces of our race left.

"And what can we do about it?" Trobt continued. "We can't kill our beloved wives—and our children. We can't stop further acquisition of Human women without disrupting our society. Each generation the tie between us will become closer, our blood thinner, yours more dominant, as the intermingling continues. We cannot even declare war against the people who are doing this to us. How do you fight an enemy that has surrendered unconditionally?"

"You do understand that for your side this was the only solution to the imminent chaos that faced you?" I asked.

"Yes." I watched Trobt's swift mind go through its reasoning. I was certain he saw that Velda was losing only an arbitrary distinction of race, very much like the absorbing of the early clans of Velda into the family of the Danlee. Their dislike of that was very definitely only an emotional consideration. The blending of our bloods would benefit both; the resultant new race would be better and stronger because of that blending.

With a small smile Trobt raised his glass. "We will drink to the union of two great races," he said. "And to you—the winner of the Second Game!"

Committee of the Whole

Frank Herbert

1

With an increasing sense of unease, Alan Wallace studied his client as they neared the public hearing room on the second floor of the Old Senate Office Building. The guy was too relaxed.

"Bill, I'm worried about this," Wallace said. "You could damn well lose your grazing rights here in this room today."

They were almost into the gantlet of guards, reporters and TV cameramen before Wallace got his answer.

"Who the hell cares?" Custer asked.

Wallace, who prided himself on being the Washington-type lawyer—above contamination by complaints and briefs, immune to all shock—found himself tongue-tied with surprise.

They were into the ruck then and Wallace had to pull on his bold face, smiling at the press, trying to soften the sharpness of that necessary phrase:

"No comment. Sorry."

"See us after the hearing if you have any questions, gentlemen," Custer said.

The man's voice was level and confident.

He has himself over-controlled, Wallace thought. Maybe he was just joking. . . . a graveyard joke.

215

The marble-walled hearing room blazed with lights. Camera platforms had been raised above the seats at the rear. Some of the smaller UHF stations had their cameramen standing on the window ledges.

The subdued hubbub of the place eased slightly, Wallace noted, then picked up tempo as William R. Custer—"The Baron of Oregon" they called him—entered with his attorney, passed the press tables and crossed to the seats reserved for them in the witness section.

Ahead and to their right, that one empty chair at the long table stood waiting with its aura of complete exposure.

"Who the hell cares?"

That wasn't a Custer-type joke, Wallace reminded himself. For all his cattle-baron pose, Custer held a doctorate in agriculture and degrees in philosophy, math, and electronics. His western neighbors called him "The Brain."

It was no accident that the cattlemen had chosen him to represent them here.

Wallace glanced covertly at the man, studying him. The cowboy boots and string tie added to a neat dark business suit would have been affectation on most men. They merely accented Custer's good looks—the sunburned, windblown outdoorsman. He was a little darker of hair and skin than his father had been, still light enough to be called blond, but not as ruddy and without the late father's drink-tumescent veins.

But then young Custer wasn't quite thirty.

Custer turned, met the attorney's eyes. He smiled.

"Those were good patent attorneys you recommended, Al," Custer said. He lifted his briefcase to his lap, patted it. "No mincing around or mealy-mouthed excuses. Already got this thing on the way." Again he tapped the briefcase.

He brought that damn light gadget here with him? Wallace wondered. Why? He glanced at the briefcase. Didn't know it was that small . . . but maybe he's just talking about the plans for it.

"Let's keep our minds on this hearing," Wallace whispered. "This is the only thing that's important."

Into a sudden lull in the room's high noise level, the voice of someone in the press section carried across them: "greatest political show on earth."

"I brought this as an exhibit," Custer said. Again, he tapped the briefcase. It did bulge oddly.

Exhibit? Wallace asked himself.

It was the second time in ten minutes that Custer had shocked him. This was to be a hearing of a subcommittee of the Senate Interior and Insular Affairs Committee. The issue was Taylor grazing lands. What the devil could that . . . gadget have to do with the battle of words and laws to be fought here?

"You're supposed to talk over all strategy with your attorney," Wallace whispered. "What the devil do you . . ."

He broke off as the room fell suddenly silent.

Wallace looked up to see the subcommittee chairman, Senator Haycourt Tiborough, stride through the wide double doors followed by his coterie of investigators and attorneys. The Senator was a tall man who had once been fat. He had dieted with such savage abruptness that his skin had never recovered. His jowls and the flesh on the back of his hands sagged. The top of his head was shiny bald and ringed by a three-quarter tonsure that had purposely been allowed to grow long and straggly so that it fanned back over his ears.

The Senator was followed in close lock step by syndicated columnist Anthony Poxman, who was speaking fiercely into Tiborough's left ear. TV cameras tracked the pair.

If Poxman's covering this one himself instead of sending a flunky, it's going to be bad, Wallace told himself.

Tiborough took his chair at the center of the committee table facing them, glanced left and right to assure himself the other members were present.

Senator Spealance was absent, Wallace noted, but he had party organization difficulties at home and the Senior Senator from Oregon was, significantly, not present. Illness, it was reported.

A sudden attack of caution, that common Washington malady, no doubt. He knew where his campaign money came from . . . but he also knew where the votes were.

They had a quorum, though.

Tiborough cleared his throat, said: "The committee will please come to order."

The Senator's voice and manner gave Wallace a cold chill. We were nuts trying to fight this one in the open, he thought, Why'd I let Custer and his friends talk me into this? You can't butt heads with a United States Senator who's out to get you. The only way's to fight him on the inside.

And now Custer suddenly turning screwball.

Exhibit!

"Gentlemen," said Tiborough, "I think we can . . . that is, today we can dispense with preliminaries . . . unless my colleagues . . . if any of them have objections."

Again, he glanced at the other senators—five of them. Wallace swept his gaze down the line behind that table—Plowers of Nebraska (a horse trader), Johnstone of Ohio (a parliamentarian—devious), Lane of South Carolina (a Republican in Democrat disguise), Emery of Minnesota (new and eager—dangerous because he lacked the old inhibitions) and Meltzer of New York (poker player, fine old family with traditions).

None of them had objections.

They've had a private meeting—both sides of the aisle—and talked over a smooth streamroller procedure, Wallace thought.

It was another ominous sign.

"This is a subcommittee of the United States Senate Committee on Interior and Insular Affairs," Tiborough said, his tone formal. "We are charged with obtaining expert opinion on proposed amendments to the Taylor Grazing Act of 1934. Today's hearing will begin with testimony and . . . ah, questioning of a man whose family has been in the business of raising beef cattle in Oregon for three generations."

Tiborough smiled at the TV cameras.

The son-of-a-bitch is playing to the galleries, Wallace thought. He glanced at Custer. The cattleman sat relaxed against the back of his chair, eyes half lidded, staring at the Senator.

"We call as our first witness today Mr. William R. Custer of Bend, Oregon," Tiborough said. "Will the clerk please swear in Mr. Custer."

Custer moved forward to the "hot seat," placed his briefcase on the table. Wallace pulled a chair up beside his client, noted how the cameras turned as the clerk stepped forward, put the Bible on the table and administered the oath.

Tiborough ruffled through some papers in front of him, waiting for full attention to return to him, said: "This subcommittee . . . we have before us a bill, this is a United States Senate Bill entitled SB-1024 of the current session, an act amending the Taylor Grazing Act of 1934 and, the intent is, as many have noted, that we would broaden the base of the advisory committees to the Act and include a wider public representation."

Custer was fiddling with the clasp of his briefcase.

How the hell could that light gadget be an exhibit here? Wallace asked himself. He glanced at the set of Custer's jaw, noted the nervous working of a muscle. It was the first sign of unease he'd seen in Custer. The sight failed to settle Wallace's own nerves.

"Ah, Mr. Custer," Tiborough said. "Do you—did you bring a preliminary statement? Your counsel. . . ."

"I have a statement," Custer said. His big voice rumbled through the room, requiring instant attention and the shift of cameras that had been holding tardily on Tiborough, expecting an addition to the question.

Tiborough smiled, waited, then: "Your attorney—is your statement the one your counsel supplied the committee?"

"With some slight additions of my own," Custer said.

Wallace felt a sudden qualm. They were too willing to accept Custer's statement. He leaned close to his client's ear, whispered: "They know what your stand is. Skip the preliminaries."

Custer ignored him, said: "I intend to speak plainly and simply. I oppose the amendment. Broaden the base and wider public representation are phases of the amendment. Broaden the base and wider public representation are phases of politician double talk. The intent is to pack the committees, to put control of them into the hands of people who don't know the first thing about the cattle business and whose private intent is to destroy the Taylor Grazing Act itself."

"Plain, simple talk," Tiborough said. "This committee . . . we welcome such directness. Strong words. A majority of this committee . . . we have taken the position that the public range lands have been too long subjected to the tender mercies of the stockmen advisors, that the lands . . . stockmen have exploited them to their own advantage."

The gloves are off, Wallace thought. I hope Custer knows what he's doing. He's sure as hell not accepting advice.

Custer pulled a sheaf of papers from his briefcase and Wallace glimpsed shiny metal in the case before the flap was closed.

Christ! That looked like a gun or something!

Then Wallace recognized the papers—the brief he and his staff had labored over—and the preliminary statement. He noted with alarm the penciled markings and marginal notations. How could Custer have done that much to it in just twenty-four hours?

Again, Wallace whispered in Custer's ear: "Take it easy, Bill. The bastard's out for blood."

Custer nodded to show he had heard; glanced at the papers, looked up directly at Tiborough.

A hush settled on the room, broken only by the scraping of a chair somewhere in the rear, and the whirr of cameras.

2

"First, the nature of these lands we're talking about," Custer said. "In my state. . . ." He cleared his throat, a mannerism that would have indicated anger in the old man, his father. There was no break in Custer's expression, though, and his voice remained level. ". . . in my state, these were mostly Indian lands. This nation took them by brute force, right of conquest. That's about the oldest right in the world, I guess. I don't want to argue with it at this point."

"Mr. Custer."

It was Nebraska's Senator Plowers, his amiable farmer's face set in a tight grin. "Mr. Custer, I hope. . . ."

"Is this a point of order?" Tiborough asked.

"Mr. Chairman," Plowers said, "I merely wished to make sure we weren't going to bring up that old suggestion about giving these lands back to the Indians."

Laughter shot across the hearing room. Tiborough chuckled as he pounded his gavel for order.

"You may continue, Mr. Custer," Tiborough said.

Custer looked at Plowers, said: "No, Senator, I don't want to give these lands back to the Indians. When they had these lands, they only got about three hundred pounds of meat a year off eighty acres. We get five hundred pounds of the highest grade protein—premium beef—from only ten acres."

"No one doubts the efficiency of your factory-like methods," Tiborough said. "You can . . . we know your methods wring the largest amount of meat from a minimum acreage."

Ugh! Wallace thought. That was a low blow—implying Bill's over-grazing and destroying the land value.

"My neighbors, the Warm Springs Indians, use the same methods I do," Custer said. "They are happy to adopt our methods because we use the land while maintaining it and increasing its value. We don't permit the land to fall prey to natural disasters such as fire and erosion. We don't. . . ."

"No doubt your methods are meticulously correct," Tiborough said. "But I fail to see where. . . ."

"Has Mr. Custer finished his preliminary statement yet?" Senator Plowers cut in.

Wallace shot a startled look at the Nebraskan. That was help from an unexpected quarter.

"Thank you, Senator," Custer said. "I'm quite willing to adapt to the chairman's methods and explain the meticulous correctness of my operation. Our lowliest cowhands are college men, highly paid. We travel ten times as many jeep miles as we do horse miles. Every outlying division of the ranch—every holding pen and grazing supervisor's cabin is linked to the central ranch by radio. We use the. . . ."

"I concede that your methods must be the most modern in the world," Tiborough said. "It's not your methods as much as the results of those methods that are at issue here.

"We. . . ." He broke off at a disturbance by the door. An Army colonel was talking to the guard there. He wore Special Services four-ragere—Pentagon.

Wallace noted with an odd feeling of disquiet that the man was armed—a .45 at the hip. The weapon was out of place on him, as though he had added it suddenly on an overpowering need . . . emergency.

More guards were coming up outside the door now—Marines and Army. They carried rifles.

The colonel said something sharp to the guard, turned away from him and entered the committee room. All the cameras were tracking him now. He ignored them, crossed swiftly to Tiborough, and spoke to him.

The Senator shot a startled glance at Custer, accepted a sheaf of papers the colonel thrust at him. He forced his attention off Custer, studied the papers, leafing through them. Presently, he looked up, stared at Custer.

A hush fell over the room.

"I find myself at a loss, Mr. Custer," Tiborough said. "I have here a copy of a report. . . . it's from the Special Services branch of the Army . . . through the Pentagon, you understand. It was just handed to me by, ah . . . the colonel here."

He looked up at the colonel, who was standing, one hand resting lightly on the holstered .45. Tiborough looked back at Custer and it was obvious the Senator was trying to marshal his thoughts.

"It is," Tiborough said, "that is . . . this report supposedly . . . and I have every confidence it is what it is represented to be . . . here in my hands . . . they say that . . . uh, within the last, uh, few days they have, uh, investigated a certain device . . . weapon they call it, that you are attempting to patent. They report. . . ." He glanced at the papers, back to Custer, who was staring at him steadily. ". . . this, uh, weapon, is a thing that . . . it is extremely dangerous."

"It is," Custer said.

"I . . . ah, see." Tiborough cleared his throat, glanced up at the colonel, who was staring fixedly at Custer. The Senator brought his attention back to Custer.

"Do you in fact have such a weapon with you, Mr. Custer?" Tiborough asked.

"I have brought it as an exhibit, sir."

"Exhibit?"

"Yes, sir."

Wallace rubbed his lips, found them dry. He wet them with his tongue, wished for the water glass, but it was beyond Custer. Christ! That stupid cowpuncher! He wondered if he dared whisper to Custer. Would the senators and that Pentagon lackey interpret such an action as meaning he was part of Custer's crazy antics?

"Are you threatening this committee with your weapon, Mr. Custer?" Tiborough asked. "If you are, I may say special precautions have been taken . . . extra guards in this room and we . . . that is, we will not allow ourselves to worry too much about any action you may take, but ordinary precautions are in force."

Wallace could no longer sit quietly. He tugged Custer's sleeve, got an abrupt shake of the head. He leaned close, whispered: "We could ask for a recess, Bill. Maybe we. . . ."

"Don't interrupt me," Custer said. He looked at Tiborough. "Senator, I would not threaten you or any other man. Threats in the way you mean them are a thing we no longer can indulge in."

"You . . . I believe you said this device is an exhibit," Tiborough said. He cast a worried frown at the report in his hands. "I fail . . . it does not appear germane."

Senator Plowers cleared his throat. "Mr. Chairman," he said.

"The chair recognizes the Senator from Nebraska," Tiborough said, and the relief in his voice was obvious. He wanted time to think.

"Mr. Custer," Plowers said, "I have not seen the report, the report my distinguished colleague alludes to; however, if I may . . . is it your wish to use this committee as some kind of publicity device?"

"By no means, Senator," Custer said. "I don't wish to profit by my presence here. . . . not at all."

Tiborough had apparently come to a decision. He leaned back, whispered to the colonel, who nodded and returned to the outer hall.

"You strike me as an eminently reasonable man, Mr. Custer," Tiborough said. "If I may. . . ."

"May I," Senator Plowers said. "May I, just permit me to conclude this one point. May we have the Special Services report in the record?"

"Certainly," Tiborough said. "But what I was about to suggest. . . ."

"May I," Plowers said. "May I, would you permit me, please, Mr. Chairman, to make this point clear for the record?"

Tiborough scowled, but the heavy dignity of the Senate overcame his irritation. "Please continue, Senator. I had thought you were finished."

"I respect . . . there is no doubt in my mind of Mr. Custer's truthfulness," Plowers said. His face eased into a grin that made him look grandfatherly, a kindly elder statesman. "I would like, therefore, to have him explain how this . . . ah, weapon, can be an exhibit in the matter before our committee."

Wallace glanced at Custer, saw the hard set to the man's jaw, realized the cattleman had gotten to Plowers somehow. This was a set piece.

Tiborough was glancing at the other senators, weighing the advisability of high-handed dismissal . . . perhaps a star chamber session. No . . . they were all too curious about Custer's device, his purpose here.

The thoughts were plain on the Senator's face.

"Very well," Tiborough said. He nodded to Custer. "You may proceed, Mr. Custer."

"During last winter's slack season," Custer said, "two of my men and I worked on a project we've had in the works for three years—to develop a sustained-emission laser device."

Custer opened his briefcase, slid out a fat aluminum tube mounted on a pistol grip with a conventional appearing trigger.

"This is quite harmless," he said. "I didn't bring the power pack."

"That is . . . this is your weapon?" Tiborough asked.

"Calling this a weapon is misleading," Custer said. "The term limits and oversimplifies. This is also a brush-cutter, a substitute for a logger's saw and axe, a diamond cutter, a milling machine . . . and a weapon. It is also a turning point in history."

"Come now, isn't that a bit pretentious?" Tiborough asked.

"We tend to think of history as something old and slow," Custer said. "But history is, as a matter of fact, extremely rapid and immediate. A President is assassinated, a bomb explodes over a city, a dam breaks, a revolutionary device is announced."

"Lasers have been known for quite a few years," Tiborough said. He looked at the papers the Colonel had given him. "The principle dates from 1956 or thereabouts."

"I don't wish it to appear that I'm taking credit for inventing this device," Custer said. "Nor am I claiming sole credit for developing the sustained-emission laser. I was merely one of a team. But I do hold the device here in my hand, gentlemen."

"Exhibit, Mr. Custer," Plowers reminded him. "How is this an exhibit?"

"May I explain first how it works?" Custer asked. "That will make the rest of my statement much easier."

Tiborough looked at Plowers, back to Custer. "If you will tie this all together, Mr. Custer," Tiborough said. "I want to . . . the bearing of this device on our—we are hearing a particular bill in this room."

"Certainly, Senator," Custer said. He looked at his device. "A ninety-volt radio battery drives this particular model. We have some that require less voltage, some that use more. We aimed for a construction with simple parts. Our crystals are common quartz. We shattered them by bringing them to a boil in water and then plunging them into ice water . . . repeatedly. We chose twenty pieces of very close to the same size—about one gram, slightly more than fifteen grains each."

Custer unscrewed the back of the tube, slid out a round length of plastic trailing lengths of red, green, brown, blue and yellow wire.

Wallace noted how the cameras of the TV men were centered on the object in Custer's hands. Even the senators were leaning forward, staring.

We're gadget-crazy people, Wallace thought.

"The crystals were dipped in thinned household cement and then into iron filings," Custer said. "We made a little jig out of a fly-tying vise and opened a passage in the filings at opposite ends of the crystals. We then made some common celluloid—nitrocellulose, acetic acid, gelatin, and alcohol—all very common products, and formed it in a length of garden hose just long enough to take the crystals end to end. The crystals were inserted in the hose, the celluloid poured over them and the whole thing was seated in a magnetic waveguide while the celluloid was cooling. This centered and aligned the crystals. The waveguide was constructed from wire salvaged from an old TV set and built following the directions in the Radio Amateur's Handbook."

Custer re-inserted the length of plastic into the tube, adjusted the wires. There was an unearthly silence in the room with only the cameras whirring. It was as though everyone were holding his breath.

"A laser requires a resonant cavity, but that's complicated," Custer said. "Instead, we wound two layers of fine copper wire around our tube, immersed it in the celluloid solution to coat it and then filed one end flat. This end took a piece of mirror cut to fit. We then pressed a number eight embroidery needle at right angles into the mirror end of the tube until it touched the side of the number one crystal."

Custer cleared his throat.

Two of the senators leaned back. Plowers coughed. Tiborough glanced at the banks of TV cameras and there was a questioning look in his eyes.

"We then determined the master frequency of our crystal series," Custer said. "We used a test signal and oscilloscope, but any radio amateur could do it without the oscilloscope. We constructed an oscillator of that master frequency, attached it at the needle and a bare spot scraped in the opposite edge of the waveguide."

"And this . . . ah . . . worked?" Tiborough asked.

"No." Custer shook his head. "When we fed power through a voltage multiplier into the system we produced an estimated four hundred joules emission and melted half the tube. So we started all over again."

"You are going to tie this in?" Tiborough asked. He frowned at the papers in his hands, glanced toward the door where the colonel had gone.

"I am, sir, believe me," Custer said.

"Very well, then," Tiborough said.

"So we started all over again," Custer said. "But for the second celluloid dip we added bismuth—a saturate solution, actually. It stayed gummy and we had to paint over it with a sealing coat of the straight celluloid. We then coupled this bismuth layer through a pulse circuit so that it was bathed in a counter wave—180 degrees out of phase with the master frequency. We had, in effect, immersed the unit in a thermoelectric cooler that exactly countered the heat production. A thin beam issued from the unmirrored end when we powered it. We have yet to find something that thin beam cannot cut."

"Diamonds?" Tiborough asked.

"Powered by less than two hundred volts, this device could cut our planet in half like a ripe tomato," Custer said. "One man could destroy an aerial armada with it, knock down ICBMs before they touched atmosphere, sink a fleet, pulverize a city. I'm afraid, sir, that I haven't mentally catalogued all the violent implications of this device. The mind tends to boggle at the enormous power focused in. . . ."

"Shut down those TV cameras!"

It was Tiborough shouting, leaping to his feet and making a sweeping gesture to include the banks of cameras. The abrupt violence of his voice and gesture fell on the room like an explosion. "Guards!" he called. "You there at the door. Cordon off that door and don't let anyone out who heard this fool!" He whirled back to face Custer. "You irresponsible idiot!"

"I'm afraid, Senator," Custer said, "that you're locking the barn door many weeks too late."

For a long minute of silence Tiborough glared at Custer. Then: "You did this deliberately, eh?"

3

"Senator, if I'd waited any longer, there might have been no hope for us at all."

Tiborough sat back in his chair, still keeping his attention fastened on Custer. Plowers and Johnstone on his right had their heads close together whispering fiercely. The other senators were dividing their attention between Custer and Tiborough, their eyes wide and with no attempt to conceal their astonishment.

Wallace, growing conscious of the implications in what Custer had said, tried to wet his lips with his tongue. Christ! he thought. This stupid cowpoke has sold us all down the river!

Tiborough signaled an aide, spoke briefly with him, beckoned the colonel from the door. There was a buzzing of excited conversation in the room. Several of the press and TV crew were huddled near the windows on Custer's left, arguing. One of their number—a florid-faced man with gray hair and horn-rimmed glasses—started across the room toward Tiborough, was stopped by a committee aide. They began a low-voiced argument with violent gestures.

A loud curse sounded from the door. Poxman, the syndicated columnist, was trying to push past the guards there.

"Poxman!" Tiborough called. The columnist turned. "My orders are that no one leaves," Tiborough said. "You are not an exception." He turned back to face Custer.

The room had fallen into a semblance of quiet, although there still were pockets of muttering and there was the sound of running feet and a hurrying about in the hall outside.

"Two channels went out of here live," Tiborough said. "Nothing much we can do about them, although we will trace down as many of their viewers as we can. Every bit of film in this room and every sound tape will be confiscated, however." His voice rose as protests sounded from the press section. "Our national security is at stake. The President has been notified. Such measures as are necessary will be taken."

The colonel came hurrying into the room, crossed to Tiborough, quietly said something.

"You should've warned me!" Tiborough snapped. "I had no idea that. . . ."

The colonel interrupted with a whispered comment.

"These papers . . . your damned report is not clear!" Tiborough said. He looked around at Custer. "I see you're smiling, Mr. Custer. I don't think you'll find much to smile about before long."

"Senator, this is not a happy smile," Custer said. "But I told myself several days ago you'd fail to see the implications of this thing." He tapped the pistol-shaped device he had rested on the table. "I told myself you'd fall back into the old, useless pattern."

"Is that what you told yourself, really?" Tiborough said.

Wallace, hearing the venom in the Senator's voice, moved his chair a few inches farther away from Custer.

Tiborough looked at the laser projector. "Is that thing really disarmed?"

"Yes, sir."

"If I order one of my men to take it from you, you will not resist?"

"Which of your men will you trust with it, Senator?" Custer asked.

In the long silence that followed, someone in the press section emitted a nervous guffaw.

"Virtually every man on my ranch has one of these things," Custer said. "We fell trees with them, cut firewood, make fence posts. Every letter written to me as a result of my patent application has been answered candidly. More than a thousand sets of schematics and instructions on how to build this device have been sent out to varied places in the world."

"You vicious traitor!" Tiborough rasped.

"You're certainly entitled to your opinion, Senator," Custer said. "But I warn you I've had time for considerably more concentrated and considerably more painful thought than you've applied to this problem. In my estimation, I had no choice. Every week I waited to make this thing public, every day, every minute, merely raised the odds that humanity would be destroyed by. . . ."

"You said this thing applied to the bearings on the grazing act," Plowers protested, and there was a plaintive note of complaint in his voice.

"Senator, I told you the truth," Custer said. "There's no real reason to change the act, now. We intend to go on operating under it—with the agreement of our neighbors and others concerned. People are still going to need food."

Tiborough glared at him. "You're saying we can't force you to . . ." He broke off at a disturbance in the doorway. A rope barrier had been stretched there and a line of Marines stood with their backs to it, facing the hall. A mob of people was trying to press through. Press cards were being waved.

"Colonel, I told you to clear that hall!" Tiborough barked.

The colonel ran to the barrier. "Use your bayonets if you have to!" he shouted.

The disturbance subsided at the sound of his voice. More uniformed men could be seen moving in along the barrier. Presently, the noise receded.

Tiborough turned back to Custer. "You make Benedict Arnold look like the greatest friend the United States ever had," he said.

"Cursing me isn't going to help you," Custer said. "You are going to have to live with this thing; so you'd better try understanding it."

"That appears to be simple," Tiborough said. "All I have to do is send twenty-five cents to the Patent office for the schematics and then write you a letter."

"The world already was headed toward suicide," Custer said. "Only fools failed to realize. . . ."

"So you decided to give us a little push," Tiborough said.

"H. G. Wells warned us," Custer said. "That's how far back it goes, but nobody listened. 'Human history becomes more and more a race between education and catastrophe,' Wells said. But those were just words. Many scientists have remarked the growth curve on the amount of raw energy becoming available to humans—and the diminishing curve on the number of persons required to use that energy. For a long time now, more and more violent power was being made available to fewer and fewer people. It was only a matter of time until total destruction was put into the hands of single individuals."

"And you didn't think you could take your government into your confidence."

"The government already was committed to a political course diametrically opposite the one this device requires," Custer said. "Virtually every man in the government has a vested interest in not reversing that course."

"So you set yourself above the government?"

"I'm probably wasting my time," Custer said, "but I'll try to explain it. Virtually every government in the world is dedicated to manipulating something called the 'mass man.' That's how governments have stayed in power. But there is no such man. When you elevate the nonexistent 'mass man' you degrade the individual. And obviously it was only a matter of time until all of us were at the mercy of the individual holding power."

"You talk like a commie!"

"They'll say I'm a goddamn capitalist pawn," Custer said. "Let me ask you, Senator, to visualize a poor radio technician in a South American country. Brazil, for example. He lives a hand-to-mouth existence, ground down by an overbearing, unimaginative, essentially uncouth ruling oligarchy. What is he going to do when this device comes into his hands?"

"Murder, robbery and anarchy."

"You could be right," Custer said. "But we might reach an understanding out of ultimate necessity—that each of us must cooperate in maintaining the dignity of all."

Tiborough stared at him, began to speak musingly: "We'll have to control the essential materials for constructing this thing . . . and there may be trouble for a while, but. . . ."

"You're a vicious fool."

In the cold silence that followed, Custer said: "It was too late to try that ten years ago. I'm telling you this thing can be patchworked out of a wide variety of materials that are already scattered over the earth. It can be made in basements and mud huts, in palaces and shacks. The key item is the crystals, but other crystals will work, too. That's obvious. A patient man can grow crystals . . . and this world is full of patient men."

"I'm going to place you under arrest," Tiborough said. "You have outraged every rule—"

"You're living in a dream world," Custer said. "I refuse to threaten you, but I'll defend myself from any attempt to oppress or degrade me. If I cannot defend myself, my friends will defend me. No man who understands what this device means will permit his dignity to be taken from him."

Custer allowed a moment for his words to sink in, then: "And don't twist those words to imply a threat. Refusal to threaten a fellow human is an absolute requirement in the day that has just dawned on us."

"You haven't changed a thing!" Tiborough raged. "If one man is powerful with that thing, a hundred are. . . ."

"All previous insults aside," Custer said, "I think you are a highly intelligent man, Senator. I ask you to think long and hard about this device. Use of power is no longer the deciding factor because one man is as powerful as a million. Restraint—self-restraint is now the key to survival. Each of us is at the mercy of his neighbor's good will. Each of us, Senator—the man in the palace and the man in the shack. We'd better do all we can to increase that good will—not attempting to buy it, but simply recognizing that individual dignity is the one inalienable right of. . . ."

"Don't you preach to me, you commie traitor!" Tiborough rasped. "You're a living example of. . . ."

"Senator!"

It was one of the TV cameramen in the left rear of the room.

"Let's stop insulting Mr. Custer and hear him out," the cameraman said.

"Get that man's name," Tiborough told an aide. "If he. . . ."

"I'm an expert electronic technician, Senator," the man said. "You can't threaten me now."

Custer smiled, turned to face Tiborough.

"The revolution begins," Custer said. He waved a hand as the Senator started to whirl away. "Sit down, Senator."

Wallace, watching the Senator obey, saw how the balance of control had changed in this room.

"Ideas are in the wind," Custer said. "There comes a time for a thing to develop, it comes into being. The spinning jenny came into being because that was its time. It was based on countless ideas that had preceded it."

"And this is the age of the laser?" Tiborough asked.

"It was bound to come," Custer said. "But the number of people in the world who're filled with hate and frustration and violence has been growing with terrible speed. You add to that the enormous danger that this might fall into the hands of just one group or nation or . . ." Custer shrugged. "This is too much power to be confined to one man or group with the hope they'll administer wisely. I didn't dare delay. That's why I spread this thing now and announced it as broadly as I could."

Tiborough leaned back in his chair, his hands in his lap. His face was pale and beads of perspiration stood out on his forehead.

"We won't make it."

"I hope you're wrong, Senator," Custer said. "But the only thing I know for sure is that we'd have had less chance of making it tomorrow than we have today."

And Then There Were None

Eric Frank Russell

The Battleship was eight hundred feet in diameter and slightly more than one mile long. Mass like that takes up room and makes a dent. The one sprawled right across one field and halfway through the next. Its weight made a rut twenty feet deep which would be there for keeps.

On board were two thousand people divisible into three distinct types. The tall, lean, crinkly-eyed ones were the crew. The crop-haired, heavy-jowled ones were the troops. Finally, the expressionless, balding and myopic ones were the cargo of bureaucrats.

The first of these types viewed this world with the professional but aloof interest of people everlastingly giving a planet the swift once-over before chasing along to the next. The troops regarded it with a mixture of tough contempt and boredom. The bureaucrats peered at it with cold authority. Each according to his lights.

This lot were accustomed to new worlds, had dealt with them by the dozens and reduced the process to mere routine. The task before them would have been nothing more than repetition of well-used, smoothly operating technique but for one thing: the entire bunch were in a jam and did not know it.

Emergence from the ship was in strict order of precedence. First, the Imperial Ambassador. Second, the battleship's captain. Third, the officer commanding the ground forces. Fourth, the senior civil servant.

Then, of course, the next grade lower, in the same order: His Excellency's private secretary, the ship's second officer, the deputy commander of troops, the penultimate pen pusher.

Down another grade, then another, until there was left only His Excellency's barber, boot wiper and valet, crew members with the lowly status of O.S.—Ordinary Spaceman—the military nonentities in the ranks, and a few temporary ink-pot fillers dreaming of the day when they would be made permanent and given a desk of their own. This last collection of unfortunates remained aboard to clean ship and refrain from smoking, by command.

Had this world been alien, hostile and well-armed, the order of exit would have been reversed, exemplifying the Biblical promise that the last shall be first and the first shall be last. But this planet, although officially new, unofficially was not new and certainly was not alien. In ledgers and dusty files some two hundred light-years away it was recorded as a cryptic number and classified as a ripe plum long overdue for picking. There had been considerable delay in the harvesting due to a super-abundance of other still riper plums elsewhere.

According to the records, this planet was on the outermost fringe of a huge assortment of worlds which had been settled immediately following the Great Explosion. Every school child knew all about the Great Explosion, which was no more than the spectacular name given to the bursting outward of masses of humanity when the Blieder drive superseded atomic-powered rockets and practically handed them the cosmos on a platter.

At that time, between three and five hundred years ago, every family, group, cult or clique that imagined it could do better some place else had taken to the star trails. The restless, the ambitious, the malcontents, the eccentrics, the antisocial, the fidgety and the just plain curious, away they had roared by the dozens, the hundreds, the thousands.

Some two hundred thousand had come to this particular world, the last of them arriving three centuries back. As usual, ninety percent of the mainstream had consisted of friends, relatives or acquaintances of the first-corners, people persuaded to follow the bold example of Uncle Eddie or Good Old Joe.

If they had since doubled themselves six or seven times over, there now ought to be several millions of them. That they had increased far beyond their original strength had been evident during the approach, for while no great cities were visible there were many medium to smallish towns and a large number of villages.

His Excellency looked with approval at the turf under his feet, plucked a blade of it, grunting as he stooped. He was so constructed that this effort approximated to an athletic feat and gave him a crick in the belly.

"Earth-type grass. Notice that, captain? Is it just a coincidence, or did they bring seed with them?"

"Coincidence, probably," thought Captain Grayder. "I've come across four grassy worlds so far. No reason why there shouldn't be others."

"No, I suppose not." His Excellency gazed into the distance, doing it with pride of ownership. "Looks like there's someone plowing over there. He's using a little engine between a pair of fat wheels. They can't be so backward. Hm-m-m!" He rubbed a couple of chins. "Bring him here. We'll have a talk, find out where it's best to get started."

"Very well." Captain Grayder turned to Colonel Shelton, boss of the troops. "His Excellency wishes to speak to that farmer." he pointed to the faraway figure.

"The farmer," said Shelton to Major Hame. "His Excellency wants him at once."

"Bring that farmer here," Hame ordered Lieutenant Deacon. "Quickly!"

"Go get that farmer," Deacon told Sergeant major Bidworthy. "And hurry—His Excellency is waiting!"

The sergeant major, a big, purple-faced man, sought around for a lesser rank, remembered that they were all cleaning ship and not smoking. He, it seemed, was elected.

Tramping across four fields and coming within hailing distance of his objective, he performed a precise military halt and released a barracks-square bellow of, "Hi, you!" He waved urgently.

The farmer stopped, wiped his forehead, looked around. His manner suggested that the mountainous bulk of the battleship was a mirage such as are dime a dozen around these parts. Bidworthy waved again, making it an authoritative summons. The farmer calmly waved back, got on with his plowing.

Sergeant Major Bidworthy employed an expletive which—when its flames had died out—meant, "Dear me!" and marched fifty paces nearer. He could now see that the other was bushy-browed and leather-faced.

"Hi!"

Stopping the plow again, the farmer leaned on a shaft, picked his teeth.

Struck by the notion that perhaps during the last three centuries the old Earth-language had been dropped in favor of some other lingo, Bidworthy asked, "Can you understand me?"

"Can any person understand another?" inquired the farmer, with clear diction. He turned to resume his task.

Bidworthy was afflicted with a moment of confusion. Recovering, he informed hurriedly, "His Excellency, the Earth Ambassador, wishes to speak with you at once."

"So?" The other eyed him speculatively. "How come that he is excellent?"

"He is a person of considerable importance," said Bidworthy, unable to decide whether the other was being funny at his expense or alternatively was what is known as a character. A good many of these isolated planet-scratchers liked to think of themselves as characters.

"Of considerable importance," echoed the farmer, narrowing his eyes at the horizon. He appeared to be trying to grasp an alien concept. After a while, he inquired, "What will happen to your home world when this person dies?"

"Nothing," Bidworthy admitted.

"It will roll on as usual?"

"Of course."

"Then," declared the farmer, flatly, "he cannot be important." With that, his little engine went *chuff-chuff* and the wheels rolled forward and the plow plowed.

Digging his nails into the palms of his hands, Bidworthy spent half a minute gathering oxygen before he said, in hoarse tones, "I cannot return without at least a message for His Excellency."

"Indeed?" The other was incredulous. "What is to stop you?" Then, noting the alarming increase in Bidworthy's color, he added with compassion, "Oh, well, you may tell him that I said"—he paused while he thought it over—"God bless you and goodbye!"

Sergeant Major Bidworthy was a powerful man who weighed two-twenty pounds, had hopped around the cosmos for twenty years, and feared nothing. He had never been known to permit the shiver of one hair—but he was trembling all over by the time he got back to the ship.

His Excellency fastened a cold eye upon him and demanded, "Well?"

"He won't come." Bidworthy's veins stood out on his forehead. "And, sir, if only I could have him in my field company for a few months I'd straighten him up and teach him to move at the double."

"I don't doubt that, Sergeant Major," soothed his Excellency. He continued in a whispered aside to Colonel Shelton. "He's a good fellow but no diplomat. Too abrupt and harsh voiced. Better go yourself and fetch that farmer. We can't sit here forever waiting to find out where to begin."

"Very well, your Excellency." Colonel Shelton trudged across the fields, caught up with the plow. Smiling pleasantly, he said, "Good morning, my man!"

Stopping his plow, the farmer sighed as if it were another of those days one has sometimes. His eyes were dark-brown, almost black, as they looked at the other.

"What makes you think I'm *your* man?" he inquired.

"It is a figure of speech," explained Shelton. He could see what was wrong now. Bidworthy had fallen foul of an irascible type. Two dogs snarling at one another. Shelton went on, "I was only trying to be courteous."

"Well," meditated the farmer, "I reckon that's something worth trying for."

Pinking a little, Shelton continued with determination. "I am commanded to request the pleasure of your company at the ship."

"Think they'll get any pleasure out of my company?" asked the other, disconcertingly bland.

"I'm sure of it," said Shelton.

"You're a liar," said the farmer.

His color deepening, Colonel Shelton snapped, "I do not permit people to call me a liar."

"You've just permitted it," the other pointed out.

Letting it pass, Shelton insisted, "Are you coming to the ship or are you not?"

"I am not."

"Why not?"

"Myob!" said the farmer.

"What was that?"

"Myob!" he repeated. It smacked of a mild insult.

Colonel Shelton went back.

He told the ambassador, "That fellow is one of these too-clever types. All I could get out of him at the finish was 'myob', whatever that means."

"Local slang," chipped in Captain Grayder. "An awful lot of it develops over three or four centuries. I've come across one or two worlds where there's been so much of it that one almost had to learn a new language."

"He understood your speech?" asked the ambassador, looking at Shelton.

"Yes, your Excellency. And his own is quite good. But he won't come away from his plowing." He reflected briefly, then suggested, "If it were left to me, I'd bring him in by force, under an armed escort."

"That would encourage him to give essential information," commented the ambassador, with open sarcasm. He patted his stomach, smoothed his jacket, glanced down at his glossy shoes. "Nothing for it but to go speak to him myself."

Colonel Shelton was shocked. "Your Excellency, you can't do *that!*"

"Why can't I?"

"It would be undignified."

"I am aware of it," said the ambassador, dryly. "Can you suggest an alternative?"

"We can send out a patrol to find someone more co-operative."

"Someone better informed, too," Captain Grayder offered. "At best we wouldn't get much out of one surly hayseed. I doubt whether he knows a quarter of what we require to learn."

"All right." His Excellency abandoned the notion of doing his own chores. "Organize a patrol and let's have some results."

"A patrol," said Colonel Shelton to Major Hame. "Nominate one immediately."

"Call out a patrol," Hame ordered Lieutenant Deacon. "At once."

"Parade a patrol immediately, Sergeant Major," said Deacon.

Bidworthy went to the ship, climbed a ladder, stuck his head in the lock and bawled, "Sergeant Gleed, out with your squad, and make it snappy!" He gave a suspicious sniff and went farther into the lock. His voice gained several more decibels. "Who's been smoking? By the Black Sack, if I catch—"

Across the fields something quietly went *chuff-chuff* while balloon tires crawled along.

The patrol formed by the right in two ranks of eight men each, turned at a barked command, marched off noseward. Their boots thumped in unison, their accoutrements clattered and the orange-colored sun made sparkles on their metal.

Sergeant Gleed did not have to take his men far. They had got one hundred yards beyond the battleship's nose when he noticed a man ambling across the field to his right. Treating the ship with utter indifference, the newcomer was making toward the farmer still plowing far over to the left.

"Patrol, right wheel!" yelled Gleed. Marching them straight past the wayfarer, he gave them a loud about-turn and followed it with the high-sign.

Speeding up its pace, the patrol opened its ranks, became a double file of men tramping at either side of the lone pedestrian. Ignoring his suddenly acquired escort, the latter continued to plod straight ahead like one long convinced that all is illusion.

"Left wheel!" Gleed roared, trying to bend the whole caboodle toward the waiting ambassador.

Swiftly obedient, the double file headed leftward, one, two, three, hup! It was neat, precise execution, beautiful to watch. Only one thing spoiled it: the man in the middle maintained his self-chosen orbit and ambled casually between numbers four and five of the right-hand file.

That upset Gleed, especially since the patrol continued to thump ambassadorwards for lack of a further order. His Excellency was being treated to the unmilitary spectacle of an escort dumbly boot-beating one way while its prisoner airily mooched another. Colonel Shelton would have plenty to say about it in due course, and anything he forgot Bidworthy would remember.

"Patrol!" roared Gleed, pointing an outraged finger at the escapee, and momentarily dismissing all regulation commands from his mind. "Get that yimp!"

Breaking ranks, they moved at the double and surrounded the wanderer too closely to permit further progress. Perforce, he stopped.

Gleed came up, said somewhat breathlessly, "Look, the Earth Ambassador wants to speak to you—that's all."

The other said nothing, merely gazed at him with mild blue eyes. He was a funny looking bum, long overdue for a shave, with a fringe of ginger whiskers sticking out all around his pan. He resembled a sunflower.

"Are you going to talk with His Excellency?" Gleed persisted.

"Naw." The other nodded toward the farmer. "Going to talk with Pete."

"The ambassador first," retorted Gleed, toughly. "He's a big noise."

"I don't doubt that," remarked the sunflower.

"Smartie Artie, eh?" said Gleed, pushing his face close and making it unpleasant. He gave his men a gesture. "All right—shove him along. We'll show him!"

Smartie Artie sat down. He did it sort of solidly, giving himself the aspect of a statue anchored for aeons. The ginger whiskers did nothing to lend grace to the situation. But Sergeant Gleed had handled sitters before, the only difference being that this one was cold sober.

"Pick him up," ordered Gleed, "and carry him."

They picked him up and carried him, feet first, whiskers last. He hung limp and unresisting in their hands, a dead weight. In this inauspicious manner he arrived in the presence of the Earth Ambassador where the escort plonked him on his feet.

Promptly he set out for Pete.

"Hold him, damn it!" howled Gleed.

The patrol grabbed and clung tight. His Excellency eyed the whiskers with well-bred concealment of distaste, coughed delicately, and spoke.

"I am truly sorry that you had to come to me in this fashion."

"In that case," suggested the prisoner, "you could have saved yourself some mental anguish by not permitting it to happen."

"There was no other choice. We've got to make contact somehow."

"I don't see it." said Ginger Whiskers. "What's so special about this date?"

"The date?" His Excellency frowned in puzzlement. "Where does that come in?"

"That's what I'd like to know."

"The point eludes me." The ambassador turned to Colonel Shelton. "Do you get what he's aiming at?"

"I could hazard a guess, your Excellency. I think he is suggesting that since we've left them without contact for more than three hundred years, there's no particular urgency about making it today." he looked at the sunflower for confirmation.

That worthy rallied to his support by remarking, "You're doing pretty well for a half-wit."

Regardless of Shelton's own reaction, this was too much for Bidworthy purpling nearby. His chest came up and his eyes caught fire. His voice was an authoritative rasp.

"Be more respectful while addressing high-ranking officers!"

The prisoner's mild blue eyes turned upon him in childish amazement, examined him slowly from feet to head and all the way down again. The eyes drifted back to the ambassador.

"Who is this preposterous person?"

Dismissing the question with an impatient wave of his hand, the ambassador said, "See here, it is not our purpose to bother you from sheer perversity, as you seem to think. Neither do we wish to detain you any longer than is necessary. All we—"

Pulling at his face-fringe as if to accentuate its offensiveness, the other interjected, "It being you, of course, who determines the length of the necessity?"

"On the contrary, you may decide that yourself," said the ambassador, displaying admirable self-control. "All you need do is tell—"

"Then I've decided it right now," the prisoner chipped in. He tried to heave himself free of his escort. "Let me go talk to Pete."

"All you need do," the ambassador persisted, "is to tell us where we can find a local official who can put us in touch with your central government." His gaze was stern, commanding, as he added, "For instance, where is the nearest police post?"

"Myob!" said the other.

"The same to you," retorted the ambassador, his patience starting to evaporate.

"That's precisely what I'm trying to do," assured the prisoner, enigmatically. "Only you won't let me."

"If I may make a suggestion, your Excellency," put in Colonel Shelton, "let me—"

"I require no suggestions and I won't let you," said the ambassador, rapidly becoming brusque. "I have had enough of all this tomfoolery. I think we've landed at random in an area reserved for imbeciles and it would be as well to recognize the fact and get out of it with no more delay."

"Now you're talking," approved Ginger Whiskers. "And the farther the better."

"I'm not thinking of leaving this planet if that's what is in your incomprehensible mind," asserted the ambassador, with much sarcasm. He stamped a proprietary foot on the turf. "This is part of the Earth Empire. As such, it is going to be recognized, charted and organized."

"*Heah, heah!*" put in the senior civil servant, who aspired to honors in elocution.

His Excellency threw a frown behind, went on, "We'll move the ship to some other section where brains are brighter." He signed to the escort. "Let him go. Doubtless he is in a hurry to borrow a razor."

They released their grips. Ginger Whiskers at once turned toward the still-plowing farmer, much as if he were a magnetized needle irresistibly drawn Peteward. Without a word he set off at his original mooching pace. Disappointment and disgust showed on the faces of Gleed and Bidworthy as they watched him go.

"Have the vessel shifted at once," the ambassador instructed Captain Grayder. "Plant it near a suitable town—not out in the wilds where every hayseed views strangers as a bunch of gyps."

He marched importantly up the gangway. Captain Grayder followed, then Colonel Shelton, then the elocutionist. Next, their successors in due order of precedence. Lastly, Gleed and his men.

The gangway rolled inward. The lock closed. Despite its immense bulk, the ship shivered briefly from end to end and soared without deafening uproar or spectacular display of flame.

Indeed, there was silence save for the plow going *chuff-chuff* and the murmurings of the two men walking behind it. Neither bothered to turn his head to observe what was happening.

"Seven pounds of prime tobacco is a whale of a lot to give for one case of brandy," Ginger Whiskers was protesting.

"Not for my brandy," said Pete. "It's stronger than a thousand Gands and smoother than an Earthman's downfall."

The great battleship's second touchdown was made on a wide flat one mile north of a town estimated to hold twelve to fifteen thousand people. Captain Grayder would have preferred to survey the place from low altitude before making his landing, but one cannot maneuver an immense space-going job as if it were an atmospheric tug. Only two things can be done so close to a planetary surface—the ship is taken up or brought down with no room for fiddling between-times.

So Grayder bumped his ship in the best spot he could find when finding is a matter of split-second decisions. It made a rut only twelve feet deep, the ground being harder and on a rock bed. The gangway was shoved out; the procession descended in the same order as before.

His Excellency cast an anticipatory look toward the town, registered disappointment and remarked, "Something's badly out of kilter here. There's the town. Here's us in plain view, with a ship like a metal mountain. A thousand people at least must have seen us even if the rest are holding seances behind drawn curtains or playing pinochle in the cellars. Are they excited?"

"It doesn't seem so," admitted Colonel Shelton, pulling an eyelid for the sake of feeling it spring back.

"I wasn't asking you. I was telling you. They are not excited. They are not surprised. In fact, they are not even interested. One would almost think they've had a ship here before and it was full of small-pox, or sold them a load of gold bricks, or something like that. What is wrong with them?"

"Possibly they lack curiosity," Shelton offered.

"Either that or they're afraid. Or maybe the entire gang of them are crackers. A good many worlds were appropriated by woozy groups who wanted some place where their eccentricities could run loose. Nutty notions become conventional after three hundred years of undisturbed continuity. It's then considered normal and proper to nurse the bats out of your grandfather's attic. That, and generations of inbreeding, can create some queer types. But we'll cure 'em!"

"Yes, your Excellency, most certainly we will."

"You don't look so balanced yourself, chasing that eye around your pan," reproved the ambassador. He pointed southeast as Shelton stuck the fidgety hand firmly into a pocket. "There's a road over there. Wide and well-built, by the looks of it. Get that patrol across it. If they don't bring in a willing talker within reasonable time, we'll send a battalion into the town itself."

"A patrol," repeated Colonel Shelton to Major Hame.

"Call out the patrol," Hame ordered Lieutenant Deacon.

"That patrol again, Sergeant Major," said Deacon.

Bidworthy raked out Gleed and his men, indicated the road, barked a bit, shooed them on their way.

They marched, Gleed in the lead. Their objective was half a mile and angled slightly nearer the town. The left-hand file, who had a clear view of the nearest suburbs, eyed them wistfully, wished Gleed in warmer regions with Bidworthy stoking beneath him.

Hardly had they reached their goal than a customer appeared. He came from the town's outskirts, zooming along at fast pace on a contraption vaguely resembling a motorcycle. It ran on a pair of big rubber balls and was pulled by a caged fan. Gleed spread his men across the road.

The oncomer's machine suddenly gave forth a harsh, penetrating sound that vaguely reminded them of Bidworthy in the presence of dirty boots.

"Stay put," warned Gleed. "I'll skin the guy who gives way and leaves a gap."

Again the shrill metallic warning. Nobody moved. The machine slowed, came up to them at a crawl and stopped. Its fan continued to spin at low rate, the blades almost visible and giving out a steady hiss.

"What's the idea?" demanded the rider. He was lean-featured, in his middle thirties, wore a gold ring in his nose and had a pigtail four feet long.

Blinking incredulously at this get-up, Gleed managed to jerk an indicative thumb toward the iron mountain and say, "Earth ship."

"Well, what d'you expect me to do about it?"

"Co-operate," said Gleed, still bemused by the pigtail. He had never seen one before. It was in no way effeminate, he decided. Rather did it lend a touch of ferocity like that worn—according to the picture books—by certain North American aborigines of umpteen centuries ago.

"Co-operation," mused the rider. "Now there is a beautiful word. You know what it means, of course?"

"I ain't a dope."

"The precise degree of your idiocy is not under discussion at the moment," the rider pointed out. His nose-ring waggled a bit as he spoke. "We are talking about co-operation. I take it you do quite a lot of it yourself?"

"You bet I do," Gleed assured. "And so does everyone else who knows what's good for him."

"Let's keep to the subject, shall we? Let's not sidetrack and go rambling all over the map." He revved up his fan a little then let it slow down again. "You are given orders and you obey them?"

"Of course. I'd have a rough time if—"

"That is what you call co-operation?" put in the other. He shrugged his shoulders, indulged a resigned sigh. "Oh, well, it's nice to check the facts of history The books *could* be wrong." His fan flashed into a circle of light and the machine surged forward. "Pardon me."

The front rubber ball barged forcefully between two men, knocking them sidewise without injury. With a high whine, the machine shot down the road, its fan-blast making the rider's plaited hairdo point horizontally backward.

"You dumb galoots!" raged Gleed as his fallen pair got up and dusted themselves. "I ordered you to stand fast. What d'you mean, letting him run out on us like that?"

"Didn't have much choice about it, sarge," answered one, giving him a surly look.

"I want none of your back-chat. You could have busted a balloon if you'd had your weapons ready. That would have stopped him."

"You didn't tell us to have guns ready."

"Where was your own, anyway?" added a voice.

Gleed whirled round on the others and bawled, "Who said that?" His irate eyes raked a long row of blank, impassive faces. It was impossible to detect the culprit. "I'll shake you up with the next quota of fatigues," he promised. "I'll see to it—"

"The Sergeant Major's coming," one of them warned.

Bidworthy was four hundred yards away and making martial progress toward them. Arriving in due time, he cast a cold, contemptuous glance over the patrol.

"What happened?"

Giving a brief account of the incident, Gleed finished aggrievedly, "He looked like a Chickasaw with an oil well."

"What's a Chickasaw?" Bidworthy demanded.

"I read about them somewhere once when I was a kid," explained Gleed, happy to bestow a modicum of learning. "They had long haircuts, wore blankets and rode around in gold-plated automobiles."

"Sounds crazy to me," said Bidworthy. "I gave up all that magic-carpet stuff when I was seven. I was deep in ballistics before I was twelve and military logistics at fourteen." He sniffed loudly, gave the other a jaundiced eye. "Some guys suffer from arrested development."

"They actually existed," Gleed maintained. "They—"

"So did fairies," snapped Bidworthy. "My mother said so. My mother was a good woman. She didn't tell me a lot of tomfool lies—often." He spat on the road. "Be your age!" Then he scowled at the patrol. "All right, get out your guns, assuming that you've got them and know where they are and which hand to hold them in. Take orders from me. I'll deal personally with the next one along."

He sat on a large stone by the roadside and planted an expectant gaze on the town. Gleed posed near him, slightly pained. The patrol remained strung across the road, guns held ready. Half an hour crawled by without anything happening.

One of the men said, "Can we have a smoke, Sergeant Major?"

"No."

They fell into lugubrious silence, watching the town, licking their lips and thinking. They had plenty to think about. A town—any town of human occupation—had desirable features not found elsewhere in the cosmos. Lights, company, freedom, laughter, all the makings of life. And one can go hungry too long.

Eventually a large coach came from the outskirts, hit the high road, came bowling toward them. A long, shiny, streamlined job, it rolled on twenty balls in two rows of ten, gave forth a whine similar to but louder than that of its predecessor, but had no visible fans. It was loaded with people.

At a point two hundred yards from the road block a loud-speaker under the vehicle's bonnet blared an urgent, "Make way! Make way!"

"This is it," commented Bidworthy, with much satisfaction. "We've got a dollop of them. One of them is going to chat or I leave the service." He got off his rock, stood in readiness.

"Make way! Make way!"

"Bust his bags if he tries to bull his way through," Bidworthy ordered the men.

It wasn't necessary. The coach lost pace, stopped with its bonnet a yard from the waiting file. Its driver peered out the side of his cab. Other faces snooped farther back.

Composing himself and determined to try the effect of fraternal cordiality, Bidworthy went up to the driver and said, "Good morning."

"Your time-sense is shot to pot," observed the other. He had a blue jowl, a broken nose, cauliflower ears, looked the sort who usually drives with others in hot and vengeful pursuit. "Can't you afford a watch?"

"Huh?"

"It isn't morning. It's late afternoon."

"So it is," admitted Bidworthy, forcing a cracked smile. "Good afternoon."

"I'm not so sure about that," mused the driver, leaning on his wheel and moodily picking his teeth. "It's just another one nearer the grave."

"That may be," agreed Bidworthy, little taken with that ghoulish angle. "But I have other things to worry about, and—"

"Not much use worrying about anything, past or present," advised the driver. "Because there are lots bigger worries to come."

"Perhaps so," Bidworthy said, inwardly feeling that this was no time or place to contemplate the darker side of existence. "But I prefer to deal with my own troubles in my own time and my own way."

"Nobody's troubles are entirely their own, nor their time, nor their methods," remarked the tough hooking oracle. "Are they now?"

"I don't know and I don't care," said Bidworthy, his composure thinning down as his blood pressure built up. He was conscious of Gleed and the patrol watching, listening, and probably grinning inside themselves. There was also the load of gaping passengers. "I think you are chewing the fat just to stall me. You might as well know now that it won't work. The Earth Ambassador is waiting—"

"So are we," remarked the driver, pointedly.

"He wants to speak to you," Bidworthy went on, "and he's going to speak to you!"

"I'd be the last to prevent him. We've got free speech here. Let him step up and say his piece so's we can get on our way."

"You," Bidworthy informed, "are going to him." He signed to the rest of the coach. "And your load as well."

"Not me," denied a fat man, sticking his head out of a side window. He wore thick-lensed glasses that gave him eyes like poached eggs. Moreover, he was adorned with a high hat candy-striped in white and pink. "Not me," repeated this vision, with considerable firmness.

"Me, neither," endorsed the driver.

"All right." Bidworthy registered menace. "Move this birdcage an inch, forward or backward, and we'll shoot your pot-bellied tires to thin strips. Get out of that cab."

"Not me. I'm too comfortable. Try fetching me out."

Bidworthy beckoned to his nearest six men. "You heard him— take him up on that."

Tearing open the cab door, they grabbed. If they had expected the victim to put up a futile fight against heavy odds, they were disappointed. He made no attempt to resist. They got him, lugged together, and he yielded with good grace, his body leaning sidewise and coming halfway out of the door.

That was as far as they could get him.

"Come on," urged Bidworthy, displaying impatience. "Show him who's who. He isn't a fixture."

One of the men climbed over the body, poked around inside the cab, and said, "He is, you know."

"What d'you mean?"

"He's chained to the steering column."

"Eh? Let me see." He had a look, found that it was so. A chain and a small but heavy and complicated padlock linked the driver's leg to his coach. "Where's the key?"

"Search me," invited the driver, grinning.

They did just that. The frisk proved futile. No key.

"Who's got it?"

"Myob!"

"Shove him back into his seat," ordered Bidworthy, looking savage. "We'll take the passengers. One yap's as good as another so far as I'm concerned." He strode to the doors, jerked them open. "Get out and make it snappy."

Nobody budged. They studied him silently and with varied expressions, not one of which did anything to help his ego. The fat man with the candy-striped hat mooned at him sardonically. Bidworthy decided that he did not like the fat man and that a stiff course of military calisthenics might thin him down a bit.

"You can come out on your feet," he suggested to the passengers in general and the fat man in particular, "or on your necks. Whichever you prefer. Make up your minds."

"If you can't use your head you can at least use your eyes," commented the fat man. He shifted in his seat to the accompaniment of metallic clanking noises.

Bidworthy did as suggested, leaning through the doors to have a gander. Then he got right into the vehicle, went its full length and studied each passenger. His florid features were two shades darker when he came out and spoke to Sergeant Gleed.

"They're all chained. Every one of them." He glared at the driver. "What's the big idea, manacling the lot?"

"Myob!" said time driver, airily.

"Who's got the keys?"

"Myob!"

Taking a deep breath, Bidworthy said to nobody in particular, "Every so often I hear of some guy running amok and laying 'em out by the dozens. I always wonder why—but now I know." He gnawed his knuckles, then added to Gleed, "We can't run this contraption to the ship with that dummy blocking the driver's seat. Either we must find the keys or get tools and cut them loose."

"Or you could wave us on our way and go take a pill," offered the driver.

"Shut up! If I'm stuck here another million years I'll see to it that—"

"The colonel's coming," muttered Gleed, giving him a nudge.

Colonel Shelton arrived, walked once slowly and officiously around the outside of the coach, examining its construction and its occupants. He flinched at the striped hat whose owner leered at him through the glass. Then he came over to the disgruntled group.

"What's the trouble this time, Sergeant Major?"

"They're as crazy as the others, sir. They give a lot of lip and say, 'Myob!' and couldn't care less about his excellency. They don't want to come out and we can't get them out because they're chained to their seats."

"Chained?" Shelton's eyebrows shot upward. "What for?"

"I don't know, sir. They're linked in like a load of lifers making for the pen, and—"

Shelton moved off without waiting to hear the rest. He had a look for himself, came back.

"You may have something there, Sergeant Major. But I don't think they are criminals."

"No, sir?"

"No." He threw a significant glance toward the colorful headgear and several other sartorial eccentricities, including a ginger-haired man's foot-wide polka-dotted bow. "It is more likely that they're a bunch of whacks being taken to a giggle emporium. I'll ask the driver." Going to the cab, he said, "Do you mind telling me your destination?"

"Yes," responded the other.

"Very well, where is it?"

"Look," said the driver, "are we talking the same language?"

"Huh?"

"You asked me if I minded and I said yes." He made a gesture. "I do mind."

"You refuse to tell?"

"Your aim's improving, sonny."

"Sonny?" put in Bidworthy, vibrant with outrage. "Do you realize you are speaking to a colonel?"

"Leave this to me," insisted Shelton, waving him down. His expression was cold as he returned his attention to the driver. "On your way. I'm sorry you've been detained."

"Think nothing of it," said time driver, with exaggerated politeness. "I'll do as much for you some day."

With that enigmatic remark, he let his machine roll forward. The patrol parted to make room. The coach built up its whine to top note, sped down the road, diminished into the distance.

"By the Black Sack!" swore Bidworthy, staring purple-faced after it. "This planet has got more punks in need of discipline than any this side of—"

"Calm yourself, Sergeant Major," advised Shelton. "I feel the same way as you—but I'm taking care of my arteries. Blowing them full of bumps like seaweed won't solve any problems."

"Maybe so, sir, but—"

"We're up against something mighty funny here," Shelton went on. "We've got to find out exactly what it is and how best to cope with it. That will probably mean new tactics. So far, the patrol has achieved nothing. It is wasting its time. We'll have to devise some other and more effective method of making contact with the powers-that-be. March the men back to the ship, Sergeant Major."

"Very well, sir." Bidworthy saluted, swung around, clicked his heels, opened a cavernous mouth. "Patro-o-ol! . . . right form!"

The conference lasted well into the night and halfway through the following morning. During these argumentative hours various odd-ments of traffic, mostly vehicular, passed along the road, but nothing paused to view the monster spaceship, nobody approached for a friendly word with its crew. The strange inhabitants of this world seemed to be afflicted with a peculiar form of mental blindness, unable to see a thing until it was thrust into their faces and then sur-veying it squint-eyed.

One passer-by in midmorning was a truck whining on two dozen rubber balls and loaded with girls wearing colorful head-scarves. The girls were singing something about one little kiss before we part, dear. Half a dozen troops lounging near the gang-way came eagerly to life, waved, whistled and yoohooed. The effort was wasted, for the singing continued without break or pause and nobody waved back.

To add to the discomfiture of the love-hungry, Bidworthy stuck his head out of the lock and rasped, "If you monkeys are bursting with surplus energy, I can find a few jobs for you to do—nice dirty ones." He scared them one at a time before he withdrew.

Inside, the top brass sat around a horseshoe table in the chartroom near the bow and debated the situation. Most of them were content to repeat with extra emphasis what they had said the previous evening, there being no new points to bring up.

"Are you certain," the Earth Ambassador asked Captain Grayder, "that this planet has not been visited since the last emigration trans-port dumped the final load three hundred years back?"

"Positive, your Excellency. Any such visit would have been recorded."

"If made by an Earth ship. But what about others? I feel it in my bones that at sometime or other these people have fallen foul of one or more vessels calling unofficially and have been leery of spaceships ever since. Perhaps somebody got tough with them, tried to muscle in where he wasn't wanted. Or they've had to beat off a gang of pirates. Or they were swindled by some unscrupulous fleet of traders."

"Quite impossible, your Excellency," declared Grayder. "Emigration was so scattered over so large a number of worlds that even today every one of them is under-populated, only one-hundredth developed, and utterly unable to build spaceships of any kind, even rudimentary ones. Some may have the techniques but not the facilities, of which they need plenty."

"Yes, that's what I've always understood."

"All Blieder-drive vessels are built in the Sol system, registered as Earth ships and their whereabouts known. The only other ships in existence are eighty or ninety antiquated rocket jobs bought at scrap price by the Epsilon system for haulage work between their fourteen closely planned planets. An old-fashioned rocket job couldn't reach this place in a hundred years."

"No, of course not."

"Unofficial boats capable of this range just don't exist," Grayder assured. "Neither do space buccaneers, for the same reason. A Blieder-job takes so much that a would-be pirate has to become a billionaire to become a pirate."

"Then," said the ambassador, heavily, "back we go to my original theory—that something peculiar to this world plus a lot of inbreeding has made them nutty."

"There's plenty to be said for that notion," put in Colonel Shelton. "You should have seen the coach load I looked over. There was a mortician wearing odd shoes, one brown, one yellow. And a moon-faced gump sporting a hat made from the skin of a barber's pole, all stripy. Only thing missing was his bubble pipe—and probably he'll be given that where he was going."

"Where was he going?"

"I don't know, your Excellency. They refused to say."

Giving him a satirical look, the ambassador remarked, "Well, that is a valuable addition to the sum total of our knowledge. Our minds are now enriched by the thought that an anonymous individual may be presented with a futile object for an indefinable purpose when he reaches his unknown destination."

Shelton subsided, wishing that he had never seen the fat man or, for that matter, the fat man's cockeyed world.

"Somewhere they've got a capital, a civic seat, a center of government wherein function the people who hold the strings," the ambassador asserted. "We've got to find that place before we can take over and reorganize on up-to-date lines whatever setup they've got. A capital is big by the standards of its own administrative area. It's never an ordinary, nondescript place. It has certain physical features lending it importance above the average. It should be easily visible from the air. We must make a search for it—in fact, that's what we ought to have done in the first place. Other planets' capital cities have been found without trouble. What's the hoodoo on this one?"

"See for yourself, your Excellency." Captain Grayder poked a couple of photographs across the table. "There are the two hemispheres as recorded by us when coming in. They reveal nothing resembling a superior city. There isn't even a town conspicuously larger than its fellows or possessing outstanding features setting it apart from the others."

"I don't place great faith in pictures, particularly when taken at long distance. The naked eye sees more. We have got four lifeboats capable of scouring the place from pole to pole. Why not use them?"

"Because, your Excellency, they were not designed for such a purpose."

"Does that matter so long as they get results?"

Grayder said, patiently, "They were designed to be launched in space and hit up to forty thousand. They are ordinary, old-style rocket jobs, for emergencies only. You could not make efficient ground-survey at any speed in excess of four hundred miles per hour. Keep the boats down to that and you're trying to run them at landing-speed; muffling the tubes, balling up their efficiency, creating a terrible waste of fuel, and inviting a crash which you're likely to get before you're through."

"Then it's high time we had Blieder-drive lifeboats on Blieder-drive ships."

"I agree, your Excellency. But the smallest Blieder engine has an Earth mass of more than three hundred tons—far too much for little boats." Picking up the photographs, Grayder slid them into a drawer. "What we need is an ancient, propeller-driven airplane. They could do something we can't do—they could go slow."

"You might as well yearn for a bicycle," scoffed the ambassador, feeling thwarted.

"We have a bicycle," Grayder informed. "Tenth Engineer Harrison owns one."

"And he has brought it with him?"

"It goes everywhere with him. There is a rumor that he sleeps with it."

"A spaceman toting a bicycle!" The ambassador blew his nose with a loud honk. "I take it that he is thrilled by the sense of immense velocity it gives him, an ecstatic feeling of rushing headlong through space?"

"I wouldn't know, your Excellency."

"Hm-m-m! Bring this Harrison in to me. We'll set a nut to catch a nut."

Grayder blinked, went to the caller board, spoke over the ship's system. "Tenth Engineer Harrison wanted in the chartroom immediately."

Within ten minutes Harrison appeared. He had walked fast three-quarters of a mile from the Blieder room. He was thin and wiry, with dark, monkeylike eyes, and a pair of ears that cut out time pedaling with the wind behind him. The ambassador examined him curiously, much as a zoologist would inspect a pink giraffe.

"Mister, I understand that you possess a bicycle."

Becoming wary, Harrison said, "There's nothing against it in the regulations, sir, and therefore—"

"Damn the regulations!" The ambassador made an impatient gesture. "We're stalled in the middle of a crazy situation and we're turning to crazy methods to get moving."

"I see, sir."

"So I want you to do a job for me. Get out your bicycle, ride down to town, find the mayor, sheriff, grand panjandrum, supreme galootie, or whatever he's called, and tell him he's officially invited to evening dinner along with any other civic dignitaries he cares to bring and, of course, their wives."

"Very well, sir."

"Informal attire," added the ambassador.

Harrison jerked up one ear, drooped the other, and said, "Beg pardon, sir?"

"They can dress how they like."

"I get it. Do I go right now, sir?"

"At once. Return as quickly as you can and bring me the reply."

Saluting sloppily, Harrison went out. His Excellency found an easy-chair, reposed in it at full length and ignored the others' stares.

"As easy as that!" He pulled out a long cigar, carefully bit off its end. "If we can't touch their minds, we'll appeal to their bellies." He cocked a knowing eye at Grayder. "Captain, see that there is plenty to drink. Strong stuff. Venusian cognac or something equally potent. Give them an hour at a well-filled table and they'll talk plenty. We won't be able to shut them up all night." He lit the cigar, puffed luxuriously. "That is the tried and trusted technique of diplomacy—the insidious seduction of the distended gut. It always works—you'll see."

Pedaling briskly down the road, Tenth Engineer Harrison reached the first street on either side of which were small detached houses with neat gardens front and back. A plump, amiable looking woman was clipping a hedge halfway along. He pulled up near to her, politely touched his cap.

" 'Scuse me, ma'am, I'm looking for the biggest man in town."

She half-turned, gave him no more than a casual glance, pointed her clipping-shears southward. "That'd be Jeff Baines. First on the right, second on the left. It's a small delicatessen."

"Thank you."

He moved on, hearing the *snip-snip* resume behind him. First on the right. He curved around a long, low, rubber-balled truck parked by the corner. Second on the left. Three children pointed at him and yelled shrill warnings that his back wheel was going round. He found the delicatessen, propped a pedal on the curb, gave his machine a reassuring pat before he went inside and had a look at Jeff.

There was plenty to see. Jeff had four chins, a twenty-two-inch neck, and a paunch that stuck out half a yard. An ordinary mortal could have got into either leg of his pants without taking off a diving suit. He weighed at least three hundred and undoubtedly was the biggest man in town.

"Wanting something?" inquired Jeff, lugging it up from far down.

"Not exactly." Tenth Engineer Harrison eyed the succulent food display, decided that anything unsold by nightfall was not given to the cats. "I'm looking for a certain person."

"Are you now? Usually I avoid that sort—but every man to his taste." He plucked at a fat lip while he mused a moment, them suggested, "Try Sid Wilcock over on Dane Avenue. He's the most certain man I know."

"I didn't mean it that way," said Harrison. "I meant I was searching for somebody particular."

"Then why the dub didn't you say so?" Jeff Baines worked over the new problem, finally offered, "Tod Green ought to fit that bill. You'll find him in the shoeshop end of this road. He's particular enough for anyone. He's downright finicky."

"You misunderstand me," Harrison explained. "I'm hunting a bigwig so's I can invite him to a feed."

Resting himself on a high stool which he overlapped by a foot all round, Jeff Baines eyed him peculiarly and said, "There's something lopsided about this. In the first place, you're going to use up a considerable slice of your life finding a guy who wears a wig, especially if you insist on a big one. And where's the point of dumping an ob on him just because he uses a bean-blanket?"

"Huh?"

"It's plain common sense to plant an ob where it will cancel an old one out, isn't it?"

"Is it?" Harrison let his mouth hang open while his mind moiled around the strange problem of how to plant an ob.

"So you don't know?" Jeff Baines massaged a plump chop and sighed. He pointed at the other's middle. "Is that a uniform you're wearing?"

"Yes."

"A genuine, pukka, dyed-in-the-wool uniform?"

"Of course."

"Ah!" said Jeff. "That's where you've fooled me—coming in by yourself, on your ownsome. If there had been a gang of you dressed identically the same, I'd have known at once it was a uniform. That's what uniform means—all alike. Doesn't it?"

"I suppose so," agreed Harrison, who had never given it a thought.

"So you're off that ship, I ought to have guessed it in the first place. I must be slow on the uptake today. But I didn't expect to see one, just one, messing around on a pedal contraption. It goes to show, doesn't it?"

"Yes," said Harrison, glancing around to make sure that no confederate had swiped his bicycle while he was detained in conversation. The machine was still there. "It goes to show."

"All right, let's have it—what have you come here for?"

"I've been trying to tell you all along. I've been sent to—"

"Been sent?" Jeff's eyes widened a little. "Mean to say you actually let yourself be sent?"

Harrison gaped at him. "Of course. Why not?"

"Oh, I get it now," said Jeff Baines, his puzzled features suddenly clearing. "You confuse me with the queer way you talk. You mean you planted an ob on someone?"

Desperately, Harrison said, "What's an ob?"

"He doesn't know," commented Jeff Baines, looking prayerfully at the ceiling. "He doesn't even know that!" He gave out a resigned sigh. "You hungry by any chance?"

"Going on that way."

"O.K. I could tell you what an ob is, but I'll do something better—I'll show you." Heaving himself off the stool, he waddled to a door at back. "Don't know why I should bother to try educate a uniform. It's just that I'm bored. C'mon, follow me."

Obediently, Harrison went behind the counter, paused to give his bicycle a reassuring nod, trailed the other through a passage and into a yard.

Jeff Baines pointed to a stack of cases. "Canned goods." He indicated an adjacent store. "Bust 'em open and pile the stuff in there. Stack the empties outside. Please yourself whether you do it or not. That's freedom, isn't it?" he lumbered back into the shop.

Left by himself, Harrison scratched his ears and thought it over. Somewhere, he felt, there was an obscure sort of gag. A candidate named Harrison was being tempted to qualify for his sucker certificate. But if the play was beneficial to its organizer it might be worth learning because the trick could then be passed on. One must speculate in order to accumulate.

So he dealt with the cases as required. It took him twenty minutes of brisk work, after which he returned to the shop.

"Now," explained Baines, "you've done something for me. That means you've planted an ob on me. I don't thank you for what you've done. There's no need to. All I have to do is get rid of the ob."

"Ob?"

"Obligation. Why use a long word when a short one is good enough? An obligation is an ob. I shift it this way: Seth Warburton, next door but one, has got half a dozen of my obs saddled on him. So I get rid of mine to you and relieve him of one of his to me by sending you around for a meal." He scribbled briefly on a slip of paper. "Give him this."

Harrison stared at it. In casual scrawl, it read, "Feed this bum. Jeff Baines."

Slightly dazed, he wandered out, stood by the bicycle and again eyed the paper. Bum, it said. He could think of several on the ship who would have exploded with wrath over that. His attention drifted to the second shop farther along. It had a window crammed with comestibles and two big words on the sign-strip above: *Seth's Gulper.*

Coming to a decision which was encouraged by his innards, he went into Seth's still holding the paper as if it were a death warrant. Inside there was a long counter, some steam and a clatter of crockery. He chose a seat at a marble-topped table occupied by a gray-eyed brunette.

"Do you mind?" he inquired politely, as he lowered himself into a chair.

"Mind what?" she examined his ears as if they were curious phenomena. "Babies, dogs, aged relations or going out in the rain?"

"Do you mind me being here?"

"I can please myself whether or not I endure it. That's freedom, isn't it?"

"Yeah," said Harrison. "Sure it is." He fidgeted in his seat, feeling somehow that he'd made a move and promptly lost a pawn. He sought around for something else to say and at that point a thin-featured man in a white coat dumped before him a plate loaded with fried chicken and three kinds of unfamiliar vegetables.

The sight unnerved him. He couldn't remember how many years it was since he last saw fried chicken, nor how many months since he'd had vegetables in other than powder form.

"Well," said the waiter, mistaking his fascinated gaze upon the food. "Doesn't it suit you?"

"Yes." Harrison handed over the slip of paper. "You bet it does."

Glancing at the note, the other called to someone semivisible in the steam at one end of the counter, "You've killed another of Jeff's." He went away, tearing the slip into small pieces.

"That was a fast pass," commented the brunette, nodding at the loaded plate. "He dumps a feed-ob on you and you bounce it straight back, leaving all quits. I'll have to wash dishes to get rid of mine, or kill one Seth has got on somebody else."

"I stacked a load of canned stuff." Harrison picked up knife and fork, his mouth watering. There were no knives and forks on the ship. They weren't needed for powders and pills. "Don't give you any choice here, do they? You take what you get."

"Not if you've got an ob on Seth," she informed. "In that case, he's got to work it off best way he can. You should have put that to him instead of waiting for fate and complaining afterward."

"I'm not complaining."

"It's your right. That's freedom, isn't it?" She mused a bit, went on, "Isn't often I'm a plant ahead of Seth, but when I am I scream for iced pineapple and he comes running. When he's a plant ahead, I do the running." her gray eyes narrowed in sudden suspicion, and she added, "You're listening like it's all new to you. Are you a stranger here?"

He nodded, his mouth full of chicken. A little later he managed, "I'm off that spaceship."

"Good grief!" She froze considerably. "An Antigand! I wouldn't have thought it. Why, you look almost human."

"I've long taken pride in that similarity," his wit rising along with his belly. He chewed, swallowed, looked around. The white-coated man came up. "What's to drink?" Harrison asked.

"Dith, double-dith, shemak or coffee."

"Coffee. Big and black."

"Shemak is better," advised the brunette as the waiter went away. "But why should I tell you?"

The coffee came in a pint-sized mug. Dumping it, the waiter said, "It's your choice seeing Seth's working one off. What'll you have for after—apple pie, yimpik delice, grated tarfelsoufers or canimelon in syrup?"

"Iced pineapple."

"Ugh!" The other blinked at Harrison, gave the brunette an accusing stare, went away and got it.

Harrison pushed it across. "Take the plunge and enjoy yourself."

"It's yours."

"Couldn't eat it if I tried." He dug up another load of chicken, stirred his coffee, began to feel at peace with the world. "Got as much as I can manage right here." He made an inviting motion with his fork. "G'wan, be greedy and forget about the waistline."

"No." Firmly she pushed the pineapple back at him. "If I got through that, I'd be loaded with an ob."

"So what?"

"I don't let strangers plant obs on me."

"Quite right, too. Very proper of you," approved Harrison. "Strangers often have strange notions."

"You've been around," she agreed. "Only I don't know what's strange about the notions."

"Dish washer!"

"Eh?"

"Cynic," he translated. "One washes dishes in a cynic." The pineapple got another pass in her direction. "If you feel I'll be dumping an ob which you'll have to pay off, you can do it in seemly manner right here. All I want is some information. Just tell me where I can put my finger on the ripest cheese in the locality."

"That's an easy one. Go round to Alec Peters' place, middle of Tenth Street." With that, she dug into the dish.

"Thanks. I was beginning to think everyone was dumb or afflicted with the funnies."

He carried on with his own meal, finished it, lay back expansively: Unaccustomed nourishment got his brain working a bit more dexterously, for after a minute an expression of deep suspicion clouded his face and he inquired, "Does this Peters run a cheese warehouse?"

"Of course." Emitting a sigh of pleasure, she put aside her empty dish.

He groaned low down, then informed, "I'm chasing the mayor."

"What is that?"

"Number one. The big boss. The sheriff, pohanko, or whatever you call him."

"I'm no wiser," she said, genuinely puzzled.

"The man who runs this town. The leading citizen."

"Make it a little clearer," she suggested, trying hard to help him. "Who or what should this citizen be leading?"

"You and Seth and everyone else." He waved a hand to encompass the entire burg.

Frowning, she said, "Leading us where?"

"Wherever you're going."

She gave up, beaten, and signed the white-coated waiter to come to her assistance.

"Matt, are we going any place?"

"How should I know?"

"Well, ask Seth then."

He went away, came back with, "Seth says he's going home at six o'clock and what's it to you?"

"Anyone leading him there?" she inquired.

"Don't be daft," Matt advised. "He knows his own way and he's cold sober."

Harrison chipped in with, "Look, I don't see why there should be so much difficulty about this. Just tell me where I can find an official, any official—the police chief, the city treasurer, the mortuary keeper or even a mere justice of the peace."

"What's an official?" asked Matt, openly puzzled.

"What's a justice of the peace?" added the brunette.

His mind side-slipped and did a couple of spins. It took him quite a while to reassemble his thoughts and try another tack.

"Supposing," he said to Matt, "this joint catches fire. What would you do?"

"Fan it to keep it going," responded Matt, fed up and making no effort to conceal the fact. He returned to the counter with the air of one who has no time to waste on half-wits.

"He'd put it out," informed the brunette. "What else would you expect him to do?"

"Supposing he couldn't?"

"He'd call in others to help him."

"And would they?"

"Of course," she assured, surveying him with pity. "They'd jump at the chance. They'd be planting a nice crop of strong obs, wouldn't they?"

"Yes, I guess so." He began to feel stalled, but made a last shot at the problem. "What if the fire were too big and fast for passers-by to tackle?"

"Seth would summon the fire squad."

Defeat receded. A touch of triumph replaced it.

"Ah, so there is a fire squad! That's what I meant by something official. That's what I've been after all along. Quick, tell me where I can find the depot."

"Bottom end of Twelfth. You can't miss it."

"Thanks." He got up in a hurry. "See you again sometime." Going out fast, he grabbed his bicycle, shoved off from the curb.

The fire depot was a big place holding four telescopic ladders, a spray tower and two multiple pumps, all motorized on the usual array of fat rubber balls. Inside, Harrison came face to face with a small man wearing immense plus fours.

"Looking for someone?" asked the small man.

"The fire chief," said Harrison.

"Who's he?"

By this time prepared for that sort of thing, Harrison spoke as one would to a child. "See here, mister, this is a fire-fighting outfit. Somebody bosses it. Somebody organizes the shebang, fills forms, presses buttons, recommends promotions, kicks the shiftless, takes all the credit, transfers all the blame and generally lords it around. He's the most important guy in the bunch and everybody knows it." His forefinger tapped the other's chest. "And he's the fella I'm going to talk to if it's the last thing I do."

"Nobody's any more important than anyone else. How can they be? I think you're crazy."

"You're welcome to think what you like, but I'm telling you that—"

A shrill bell clamored, cutting off the sentence. Twenty men appeared as if by magic, boarded a ladder and a multi-pump, roared into the street.

Squat, basin-shaped helmets were the crews' only item of common attire. Apart from these, they plumbed the depths of sartorial iniquity. The man with the plus fours, who had gained the pump in one bold leap, was whirled out standing between a fat firefighter wearing a rainbow-hued cummerbund and a thin one sporting a canary yellow kilt. A latecomer decorated with earrings shaped like little bells hotly pursued the pump, snatched at its tailboard, missed, disconsolately watched the outfit disappear from sight. He walked back, swinging his helmet in one hand.

"Just my lousy luck," he informed the gaping Harrison. "The sweetest call of the year. A big brewery. The sooner they get there the bigger the obs they'll plant on it." He licked his lips at the thought, sat on a coil of canvas hose. "Oh, well, maybe it's all for the good of my health."

"Tell me something," Harrison insisted. "How do you get a living?"

"There's a hell of a question. You can see for yourself. I'm on the fire squad."

"I know. What I mean is, who pays you?"

"Pays me?"

"Gives you money for all this."

"You talk kind of peculiar. What is money?"

Harrison rubbed his cranium to assist the circulation of blood through the brain. What is money? Yeouw. He tried another angle.

"Supposing your wife needs a new coat, how does she get it?"

"Goes to a store saddled with fire-obs, of course. She kills one or two for them."

"But what if no clothing store has had a fire?"

"You're pretty ignorant, brother. Where in this world do you come from?" His ear bells swung as he studied the other a moment, then went on, "Almost all stores have fire-obs. If they've any sense, they allocate so many per month by way of insurance. They look ahead, just in case, see? They plant obs on us, in a way, so that when we rush to the rescue we've got to kill off a dollop of theirs before we can plant any new ones of our own. That stops us overdoing it and making hogs of ourselves. Sort of cuts down the stores' liabilities. It makes sense, doesn't it?"

"Maybe, but—"

"I get it now," interrupted the other, narrowing his eyes. "You're from that spaceship. You're an Antigand."

"I'm a Terran," said Harrison with suitable dignity. "What's more, all the folk who originally settled this planet were Terrans."

"You trying to teach me history?" He gave a harsh laugh. "You're wrong. There was a five per cent strain of Martian."

"Even the Martians are descended from Terran settlers," riposted Harrison.

"So what? That was a devil of a long time back. Things change, in case you haven't heard. We've no Terrans or Martians on this world—except for your crowd which has come in unasked. We're all Gands here. And you nosey pokes are Antigands."

"We aren't anti-anything that I know of. Where did you get that idea?"

"Myob!" said the other, suddenly determined to refuse further agreement. He tossed his helmet to one side, spat on the floor.

"Huh?"

"You heard me. Go trundle your scooter."

Harrison gave up and did just that, he pedaled gloomily back to the ship.

His Excellency pinned him with an authoritative optic. "So you're back at last, mister. How many are coming and at what time?"

"None, sir," said Harrison, feeling kind of feeble.

"None?" August eyebrows rose up. "Do you mean that they have refused my invitation?"

"No, sir."

The ambassador waited a moment, then said, "Come out with it, mister. Don't stand there gawping as if your push-and-puff contraption has just given birth to a roller skate. You say they haven't refused my invitation—but nobody is coming. What am I to make of that?"

"I didn't ask anyone."

"So you didn't ask!" Turning, he said to Grayder, Shelton and the others, "He didn't ask!" His attention came back to Harrison. "You forgot all about it, I presume? Intoxicated by liberty and the power of man over machine, you flashed around the town at nothing less than eighteen miles per hour, creating consternation among the citizenry, tossing their traffic laws into the ash can, putting persons in peril of their lives, not even troubling to ring your bell or—"

"I haven't got a bell, sir," denied Harrison, inwardly resenting this list of enormities. "I have a whistle operated by rotation of the rear wheel."

"There!" said the ambassador, like one abandoning all hope. He sat down, smacked his forehead several times. "Somebody's going to get a bubble-pipe." He pointed a tragic finger. "And he's got a whistle."

"I designed it myself, sir," Harrison told him, very informatively.

"I'm sure you did. I can imagine it. I would expect it of you." The ambassador got a fresh grip on himself. "Look, mister, tell me something in strict confidence, just between you and me." He leaned forward, put the question in a whisper that ricocheted seven times around the room. "*Why* didn't you ask anyone?"

"Couldn't find anyone to ask, sir. I did my level best but they didn't seem to know what I was talking about. Or they pretended they didn't."

"Humph!" His Excellency glanced out of the nearest port, consulted his wrist watch. "The light is fading already. Night will be upon us pretty soon. It's getting too late for further action." An annoyed grunt. "Another day gone to pot. Two days here and we're still fiddling around." His eye was jaundiced as it rested on Harrison. "All right, mister, we're wasting time anyway so we might as well hear your story in full. Tell us what happened in complete detail. That way, we may be able to dig some sense out of it."

Harrison told it, finishing, "It seemed to me, sir, that I could go on for weeks trying to argue it out with people whose brains are oriented east-west while mine points north-south. You can talk with them from now to doomsday, even get real friendly and enjoy the conversation—without either side knowing what the other is jawing about."

"So it seems," commented the ambassador, dryly. He turned to Captain Grayder. "You've been around a lot and seen many new worlds in your time. What do you make of all this twaddle, if anything?"

"A problem in semantics," said Grayder, who had been compelled by circumstances to study that subject. "One comes across it on almost every world that has been long out of touch, though usually it has not developed far enough to get really tough." He paused reminiscently. "First guy we met on Basilcus said, cordially and in what he fondly imagined was perfect English, 'Joy you unboot now!' "

"Yeah? What did that mean?"

"Come inside, put on your slippers and be happy. In other words, welcome! It wasn't difficult to get, your Excellency, especially when you expect that sort of thing." Grayder cast a thoughtful glance at Harrison, went on, "Here, things appear to have developed to a greater extreme. The language remains fluent, retains enough surface similarities to conceal deeper changes, but meanings have been altered, concepts discarded, new ones substituted, thought-forms re-angled—and, of course, there is the inevitable impact of locally developed slang."

"Such as 'myob'," offered His Excellency. "Now there's a queer word without recognizable Earth root. I don't like the way they use it. Sounds downright insulting. Obviously it has some sort of connection with these obs they keep batting around. It means 'my obligation' or something like that, but the significance beats me."

"There is no connection, sir," Harrison contradicted. He hesitated, saw they were waiting for him, plunged boldly on. "Coming back I met the lady who directed me to Baines' place. She asked whether I'd found him and I said yes, thank you. We chatted a bit. I asked her what 'myob' meant. She said it was initial-slang." He stopped at that point.

"Keep going," advised the ambassador. "After some of the sulphurous comments I've heard coming out the Blieder-room ventilation-shaft, I can stomach anything. What does it mean?"

"M-y-o-b," informed Harrison, blinking. "Mind your own business."

"So!" His Excellency gained color. "So that's what they've been telling me all along?"

"I'm afraid so, sir."

"Evidently they've a lot to learn." His neck swelled with sudden undiplomatic fury, he smacked a large hand on the table and said, loudly, "And they are going to learn it!"

"Yes, sir," agreed Harrison, becoming more uneasy and wanting out. "May I go now and attend to my bicycle?"

"Get out of my sight!" shouted the ambassador. He made a couple of meaningless gestures, turned a florid face on Captain Grayder. "Bicycle! Does anyone on this vessel own a slingshot?"

"I doubt it, your Excellency, but I will make inquiries, if you wish."

"Don't be an imbecile," ordered His Excellency. "We have our full quota of hollow-heads already."

Postponed until early morning, the next conference was relatively short and sweet. His Excellency took a seat, harumphed, straightened his vest, frowned around the table.

"Let's have another look at what we've got. We know that this planet's mules call themselves Gands, don't take much interest in their Terran origin and insist on referring to us as Antigands. That implies an education and resultant outlook inimical to ourselves. They've been trained from childhood to take it for granted that whenever we appeared upon the scene we would prove to be against whatever they are for."

"And we haven't the remotest notion of what they're for," put in Colonel Shelton, quite unnecessarily. But it served to show that he was among those present and paying attention.

"I am grimly aware of our ignorance in that respect," indorsed the ambassador. "They are maintaining a conspiracy of silence about their prime motivation. We've got to break it somehow." He cleared his throat, continued, "They have a peculiar nonmonetary economic system which, in my opinion, manages to function only because of large surpluses. It won't stand a day when overpopulation brings serious shortages. This economic set-up appears to be based on co-operative techniques, private enterprise, a kindergarten's honor system and plain unadorned gimme. That makes it a good deal crazier than that food-in-the-bank wackidoo they've got on the four outer planets of the Epsilon system."

"But it works," observed Grayder, pointedly.

"After a fashion. That flap-eared engineer's bicycle works—and so does he! A motorized job would save him a lot of sweat." Pleased with this analogy, the ambassador mused it a few seconds. "This local scheme of economics—if you can call it a scheme—almost certainly is the end result of the haphazard development of some hick eccentricity brought in by the original settlers. It is overdue for motorizing, so to speak. They know it but don't want it because mentally they're three hundred years behind the times. They're afraid of change, improvement, efficiency—like most backward peoples. Moreover, some of them have a vested interest in keeping things as they are." He sniffed loudly to express his contempt. "They are antagonistic toward us simply because they don't want to be disturbed."

His authoritative stare went round the table, daring one of them to remark that this might be as good a reason as any. They were too disciplined to fall into that trap. None offered comment, so he went on.

"In due time, after we've got a grip on affairs, we are going to have a long and tedious task on our hands. We'll have to overhaul their entire educational system with a view to eliminating anti-Terran prejudices and bringing them up to date on the facts of life. We've had to do that on several other planets, though not to anything like the same extent as will be necessary here."

"We'll cope," promised someone.

Ignoring him, the ambassador finished, "However, all of that is in the future. We've a problem to solve in the present. It's in our laps right now, namely, where are the reins of power and who's holding them? We've got to solve that before we can make progress. How're we going to do it?" He leaned back in his chair, added, "Get your wits working and let me have some bright suggestions."

❖ ❖ ❖

Captain Grayder stood up, a big, leather-bound book in his hands. "Your Excellency, I don't think we need exercise our minds over new plans for making contact and gaining essential information. It looks as if the next move is going to be imposed upon us."

"How do you mean?"

"There are a good many old-timers in my crew. Space lawyers, every one of them." He tapped the book. "They know official Space Regulations as well as I do. Sometimes I think they know too much."

"And so—?"

Grayder opened the book. "Regulation 127 says that on a hostile world a crew serves on a war-footing until back in space. On a non-hostile world, they serve on a peace-footing."

"What of it?"

"Regulation 131A says that on a peace-footing, the crew—with the exception of a minimum number required to keep the vessel's essential services in trim—is entitled to land-leave immediately after unloading of cargo or within seventy-two Earth hours of arrival, whichever period is the shorter." He glanced up. "By midday the men will be all set for land-leave and itching to go. There will be ructions if they don't get it."

"Will there now?" said the ambassador, smiling lopsidedly. "What if I say this world is hostile? That'll pin their ears back, won't it?"

Impassively consulting his book, Grayder came with, "Regulation 148 says that a hostile world is defined as any planet that systematically opposes Empire citizens by force." He turned the next page. "For the purpose of these regulations, force is defined as any course of action calculated to inflict physical injury, whether or not said action succeeds in its intent."

"I don't agree." The ambassador registered a deep frown. "A world can be psychologically hostile without resorting to force. We've an example right here. It isn't a friendly world."

"There are no friendly worlds within the meaning of Space Regulations," Grayder informed. "Every planet falls into one of two classifications: hostile or nonhostile." He tapped the hard leather cover. "It's all in the book."

"We would be prize fools to let a mere book boss us around or allow the crew to boss us, either. Throw it out of the port. Stick it into the disintegrator. Get rid of it any way you like—and forget it."

"Begging your pardon, your Excellency, but I can't do that." Grayder opened the tome at the beginning. "Basic regulations 1A, 1B and 1C include the following: whether in space or in land, a vessel's personnel remain under direct command of its captain or his nominee who will guided entirely by Space Regulations and will be responsible only to the Space Committee situated upon Terra. The same applies to all troops, officials and civilian passengers aboard a space-traversing vessel, whether in flight or grounded—regardless of rank or authority they are subordinate to the captain or his nominee. A nominee is defined as a ship's officer performing the duties of an immediate superior when the latter is incapacitated or absent."

"All that means you are king of your castle," said the ambassador, none too pleased. "If we don't like it, we must get off the ship."

"With the greatest respect to yourself, I must agree that that is the position. I cannot help it—regulations are regulations. And the men know it!" Grayder dumped the book, poked it away from him. "Ten to one the men will wait to midday, pressing their pants, creaming their hair and so forth. They will then make approach to me in proper manner to which I cannot object. They will request the first mate to submit their leave-roster for my approval." He gave a deep sigh. "The worst I could do would be to quibble about certain names on the roster and switch a few men around—but I couldn't refuse leave to a full quota."

"Liberty to paint the town red might be a good thing after all," suggested Colonel Shelton, not averse to doing some painting himself. "A dump like this wakes up when the fleet's in port. We ought to get contacts by the dozens. That's what we want, isn't it?"

"We want to pin down this planet's leaders," the ambassador pointed out. "I can't see them powdering their faces, putting on their best hats and rushing out to invite the yoohoo from a bunch of hungry sailors." His plump features quirked. "We have got to find the needles in this haystack. That job won't be done by a gang of ratings on the rampage."

Grayder put in, "I'm inclined to agree with you, your Excellency, but we'll have to take a chance on it. If the men want to go out, the circumstances deprive me of power to prevent them. Only one thing can give me the power."

"And what is that?"

"Evidence enabling me to define this world as hostile within the meaning of Space Regulations."

"Well, can't we arrange that somehow?" Without waiting for a reply, the ambassador continued, "Every crew has its incurable trouble-maker. Find yours, give him a double shot of Venusian cognac, tell him he's being granted immediate leave—but you doubt whether he'll enjoy it because these Gands view us as reasons why people dig up the drains. Then push him out of the lock. When he comes back with a black eye and a boastful story about the other fellow's condition, declare this world hostile." He waved an expressive hand. "And there you are. Physical violence. All according to the book."

"Regulation 148A, emphasizing that opposition by force must be systematic, warns that individual brawls may not be construed as evidence of hostility."

The ambassador turned an irate face upon the senior civil servant: "When you get back to Terra—if ever you do get back—you can tell the appropriate department how the space service is balled up, hamstrung, semi-paralyzed and generally handicapped by bureaucrats who write books."

Before the other could think up a reply complimentary to his kind without contradicting the ambassador, a knock came at the door. First Mate Morgan entered, saluted smartly, offered Captain Grayder a sheet of paper.

"First liberty roll, sir. Do you approve it?"

Four hundred twenty men hit the town in the early afternoon. They advanced upon it in the usual manner of men overdue for the bright lights, that is to say, eagerly, expectantly, in buddy-bunches of two, three, six or ten.

Gleed attached himself to Harrison. They were two odd rankers, Gleed being the only sergeant on leave, Harrison the only tenth engineer. They were also the only two fish out of water since both were in civilian clothes and Gleed missed his uniform while Harrison felt naked without his bicycle. These trifling features gave them enough in common to justify at least one day's companionship.

"This one's a honey," declared Gleed with immense enthusiasm. "I've been on a good many liberty jaunts in my time but this one's a honey. On all other trips the boys ran up against the same problem— what to use for money. They had to go forth like a battalion of Santa Clauses, loaded up with anything that might serve for barter. Almost always nine-tenths of it wasn't of any use and had to be carted back again."

"On Persephone," informed Harrison, "a long-shanked Milik offered me a twenty-karat, blue-tinted first-water diamond for my bike."

"Jeepers, didn't you take it?"

"What was the good? I'd have had to go back sixteen light-years for another one."

"You could do without a bike for a bit."

"I can do without a diamond. I can't ride around on a diamond."

"Neither can you sell a bicycle for the price of a sportster Moon-boat."

"Yes I can. I just told you this Milik offered me a rock like an egg."

"It's a crying shame. You'd have got two hundred to two fifty thousand credits for that blinder, if it was flawless." Sergeant Gleed smacked his lips at the thought of so much moola stacked on the head of a barrel. "Credits and plenty of them—that's what I love. And that's what makes this trip a honey. Every other time we've gone out, Grayder has first lectured us about creating a favorable impression, behaving in a space-manlike manner, and so forth. This time, he talks about credits."

"The ambassador put him up to that."

"I liked it, all the same," said Gleed. "Ten credits, a bottle of cognac and double liberty for every man who brings back to the ship an adult Gand, male or female, who is sociable and willing to talk."

"It won't be easily earned."

"One hundred credits to whoever gets the name and address of the town's chief civic dignitary. A thousand credits for the name and accurate location of the world's capitol city." He whistled happily, added, "Somebody's going to be in the dough and it won't be Bidworthy. He didn't come out of the hat. I know—I was holding it."

He ceased talking, turned to watch a tall, lithe blonde striding past. Harrison pulled at his arm.

"Here's Baines' place that I told you about. Let's go in."

"Oh, all right." Gleed followed with much reluctance, his gaze still down the street.

"Good afternoon," said Harrison, brightly.

"It ain't," contradicted Jeff Baines. "Trade's bad. There's a semi-final being played and it's taken half the town away. They'll think about their bellies after I've closed. Probably make a rush on me tomorrow and I won't be able to serve them fast enough."

"How can trade be bad if you don't take money even when it's good?" inquired Gleed, reasonably applying what information Harrison had given him.

Jeff's big moon eyes went over him slowly, then turned to Harrison. "So he's another bum off your boat. What's he talking about?"

"Money," said Harrison. "It's stuff we use to simplify trade. It's printed stuff, like documentary obs of various sizes."

"That tells me a lot," Jeff Baines observed. "It tells me a crowd that has to make a printed record of every ob isn't to be trusted—because they don't even trust each other." Waddling to his high stool, he squatted on it. His breathing was labored and wheezy. "And that confirms what our schools have always taught—that an Antigand would swindle his widowed mother."

"Your schools have got it wrong." assured Harrison.

"Maybe they have." Jeff saw no need to argue the point. "But we'll play safe until we know different." He looked them over. "What do you two want, anyway?"

"Some advice," shoved in Gleed, quickly. "We're out on a spree. Where's the best places to go for food and fun?"

"How long you got?"

"Until nightfall tomorrow."

"No use." Jeff Baines shook his head sorrowfully. "It'd take you from now to then to plant enough obs to qualify for what's going. Besides, lots of folk wouldn't let any Antigand dump an ob on them. They're kind of particular, see?"

Look," said Harrison. "Can't we get so much as a square meal?"

"Well, I dunno about that." Jeff thought it over, rubbing several chins. "You might manage so much—but I can't help you this time. There's nothing I want of you, so you can't use any obs I've got planted."

"Can you make any suggestions?"

"If you were local citizens, it'd be different. You could get all you want right now by taking on a load of obs to be killed sometime in the future as and when the chances come along. But I can't see anyone giving credit to Antigands who are here today and gone tomorrow."

"Not so much of the gone tomorrow talk," advised Gleed. "When an Imperial Ambassador is sent it means that Terrans will be here for keeps."

"Who says so?"

"The Empire says so. You're part of it, aren't you?"

"Nope," said Jeff. "We aren't part of anything and don't want to be, either. What's more, nobody's going to make us part of anything."

Gleed leaned on the counter and gazed absently at a large can of pork. "Seeing I'm out of uniform and not on parade, I sympathize with you though I still shouldn't say it. I wouldn't care to be taken over body and soul by other-world bureaucrats, myself. But you folk are going to have a tough time beating us off. That's the way it is."

"Not with what we've got," Jeff opined. He seemed mighty self-confident.

"You ain't got so much," scoffed Gleed, more in friendly criticism than open contempt. He turned to Harrison. "Have they?"

"It wouldn't appear so," ventured Harrison.

"Don't go by appearances," Jeff advised. "We've more than you'd care to guess at."

"Such as what?"

"Well, just for a start, we've got the mightiest weapon ever thought up by mind of man. We're Gands, see? So we don't need ships and guns and suchlike playthings. We've got something better. It's effective. There's no defense against it."

"I'd like to see it," Gleed challenged. Data on a new and exceptionally powerful weapon should be a good deal more valuable than the mayor's address. Grayder might be sufficiently overcome by the importance thereof to increase the take to five thousand credits. With a touch of sarcasm, he added, "But, of course, I can't expect you to give away secrets."

"There's nothing secret about it." said Jeff, very surprisingly. "You can have it for free any time you want. Any Gand would give it you for the asking. Like to know why?"

"You bet."

"Because it works one way only. We can use it against you—but you can't use it against us."

"There's no such thing. There's no weapon inventable which the other guy can't employ once he gets his hands on it and knows how to operate it."

"You sure?"

"Positive," said Gleed, with no hesitation whatever. "I've been in the space-service troops for twenty years and can't fiddle around that long without learning all about weapons from string bows to H-bombs. You're trying to kid me—and it won't work. A one-way weapon is impossible."

"Don't argue with him," Harrison suggested to Baines. "He'll never be convinced until he's shown."

"I can see that." Jeff Baines' face creased in a slow grin. "I told you that you could have our wonder-weapon for the asking. Why don't you ask?"

"All right, I'm asking." Gleed put it without much enthusiasm. A weapon that would be presented on request, without even the necessity of first planting a minor ob, couldn't be so mighty after all. His imaginary five thousand credits shrank to five, thence to none. "Hand it over and let me try it."

Swiveling heavily on his stool, Jeff reached to the wall, removed a small, shiny plaque from its hook, passed it across the counter.

"You may keep it," he informed. "And much good may it do you."

Gleed examined it, turning it over and over between his fingers. It was nothing more than an oblong strip of substance resembling ivory. One side was polished and bare. The other bore three letters deeply engraved in bold style:

F—I.W.

Glancing up, his features puzzled, he said, "Call this a weapon?"

"Certainly."

"Then I don't get it." He passed the plaque to Harrison. "Do you?"

"No." Harrison had a good look at it, spoke to Baines. "What does this, F—I.W. mean?"

"Initial-slang," informed Baines. "Made correct by common usage. It has become a world-wide motto. You'll see it all over the place, if you haven't noticed it already."

"I have spotted it here and there but attached no importance to it and thought nothing of it. I remember now I've seen it inscribed in several places, including Seth's and the fire depot."

"It was on the sides of that bus we couldn't empty," added Gleed. "Didn't mean anything to me."

"It means plenty," said Jeff. *"Freedom—I Won't!"*

"That kills me," Gleed told him. "I'm stone dead already. I've dropped in my tracks." He watched Harrison thoughtfully pocketing the plaque. "A bit of abracadabra. What a weapon!"

"Ignorance is bliss," remarked Baines, strangely certain of himself. "Especially when you don't know that what you're playing with is the safety catch of something that goes bang."

"All right," challenged Gleed, taking him up on that. "Tell us how it works."

"I won't." The grin reappeared. Baines seemed highly satisfied about something.

"That's a fat lot of help." Gleed felt let down, especially over those momentarily hoped-for credits. "You boast about a one-way weapon, toss across a slip of stuff with three letters on it and then go dumb. Any guy can talk out the back of his neck. How about backing up your talk?"

"I won't," said Baines, his grin becoming broader than ever. He favored the onlooking Harrison with a fat, significant wink.

It made something spark vividly inside Harrison's mind. His jaw dropped, he took the plaque from his pocket, stared at it as if seeing it for the first time.

"Give it back to me," requested Baines, watching him.

Replacing it in his pocket, Harrison said very firmly, "I won't."

Baines chuckled. "Some folk catch on quicker than others."

Resenting that remark, Gleed held his hand out to Harrison. "Let's have another look at that thing."

"I won't," said Harrison, meeting him eye for eye.

"Hey, that's not the way—" Gleed's protesting voice died out. He stood there a moment, his optics slightly glassy while his brain performed several loops. Then, in hushed tones, he said, "Good grief!"

"Precisely," approved Baines. "Grief, and plenty of it. You were a bit slow on the uptake."

Overcome by the flood of insubordinate ideas now pouring upon him, Gleed said hoarsely to Harrison. "Come on, let's get out of here. I gotta think. I gotta think some place quiet."

There was a tiny park with seats and lawns and flowers and a little fountain around which a small bunch of children were playing. Choosing a place facing a colorful carpet of exotic un-Terran blooms, they sat and brooded a while.

In due course, Gleed commented, "For one solitary guy it would be martyrdom, but for a whole world—" His voice drifted off, came back. "I've been taking this about as far as I can make it go and the results give me the leaping fantods."

Harrison said nothing.

"F'rinstance," Gleed continued, "supposing when I go back to the ship that snorting rhinoceros Bidworthy gives me an order. I give him the frozen wolliker and say, 'I won't!' He either drops dead or throws me in the clink."

"That would do you a lot of good."

"Wait a bit—I ain't finished. I'm in the clink, but the job still needs doing. So Bidworthy picks on someone else. The victim, being a soul-mate of mine, also donates the icy optic and says, 'I won't!' In the clink he goes and I've got company. Bidworthy tries again. And again. There's more of us warming the jug. It'll only hold twenty. So they take over the engineer's mess."

"Leave our mess out of this," Harrison requested.

"They take the mess," Gleed insisted, thoroughly determined to penalize the engineers. "Pretty soon it's crammed to the roof with I-won'ters. Bidworthy's still raking 'em in as fast as he can go—if by that time he hasn't burst a dozen blood vessels. So they take over the Blieder dormitories."

"Why keep picking on my crowd?"

"And pile them with bodies ceiling-high," Gleed said, getting sadistic pleasure out of the notion. "Until in the end Bidworthy has to get buckets and brushes and go down on his knees and do his own deck-scrubbing while Grayder, Shelton and the rest act as clink guards. By that time, His Loftiness the ambassador is in the galley busily cooking for you and me, assisted by a disconcerted bunch of yes-ing pen-pushers." He had another somewhat awed look at the picture and finished, "Holy smoke!"

A colored ball rolled his way, he stooped, picked it up and held on to it. Promptly a boy of about seven ran up, eyed him gravely.

"Give me my ball, please."

"I won't," said Gleed, his fingers firmly around it.

There was no protest, no anger, no tears. The child merely registered disappointment, turned to go away.

"Here you are, sonny." He tossed the ball.

"Thanks." Grabbing it, the other ran off.

Harrison said, "What if every living being in the Empire, all the way from Prometheus to Kaldor Four, across eighteen hundred light-years of space, gets an income-tax demand, tears it up and says, 'I won't!'? What happens then?"

"We'd need a second universe for a pen and a third one to provide the guards."

"There would be chaos," Harrison went on. He nodded toward the fountain and the children playing around it. "But, it doesn't look like chaos here. Not to my eyes. So that means they don't overdo this blank refusal business. They apply it judiciously on some mutually recognized basis. What that basis might be beats me completely."

"Me, too."

An elderly man stopped near them, surveyed them hesitantly, decided to pick on a passing youth.

"Can you tell me where I can find the roller for Martinstown?"

"Other end of Eighth," informed the youth. "One every hour. They'll fix your manacles before they start."

"Manacles?" The oldster raised white eyebrows. "Whatever for?"

"That route runs past the spaceship. The Antigands may try to drag you out."

"Oh, yes, of course." He ambled on, glanced again at Gleed and Harrison, remarked in passing, "These Antigands—such a nuisance."

"Definitely," endorsed Gleed. "We keep telling them to get out and they keep on saying, 'We won't.'"

The old gentleman missed a step, recovered, gave him a peculiar look, continued on his way.

"One or two seem to cotton on to our accents," Harrison remarked. "Though nobody noticed mine when I was having that feed in Seth's."

Gleed perked up with sudden interest. "Where you've had one feed you can get another. C'mon, let's try. What have we got to lose?"

"Our patience," said Harrison. He stood up. "We'll pick on Seth. If he won't play, we'll have a try at someone else. And if nobody will play, we'll skin out fast before we starve to death."

"Which appears to be exactly what they want us to do," Gleed pointed out. He scowled to himself. "They'll get their way over my dead body."

"That's how," agreed Harrison. "Over your dead body."

Matt came up with a cloth over one arm. "I'm serving no Antigands."

"You served me last time," Harrison told him.

"That's as maybe. I didn't know you were off that ship. But I know now!" He flicked the cloth across one corner of the table. "No Antigands served by me."

"Is there any other place where we might get a meal?"

"Not unless somebody will let you plant an ob on them. They won't do that if they're wise to you, but there's a chance they might make the same mistake I did." Another flick across the corner. "I don't make them twice."

"You're making another right now," said Gleed, his voice tough and authoritative. He nudged Harrison. "Watch this!" His hand came out of a side pocket holding a tiny blaster. Pointing it at Matt's middle, he continued, "Ordinarily, I could get into trouble for this, if those on the ship were in the mood to make trouble. But they aren't.

They're soured up on you two-legged mules." He motioned the weapon. "Get walking and bring us two full plates."

"I won't," said Matt, firming his jaw and ignoring the gun.

Gleed thumbed the safety catch which moved with an audible click. "It's touchy now. It'd go off at a sneeze. Start moving."

"I won't," insisted Matt.

Gleed disgustedly shoved the weapon back into his pocket. "I was only kidding you. It isn't energized."

"Wouldn't have made the slightest difference if it had been," Matt assured. "I serve no Antigands, and that's that!"

"Suppose I'd gone haywire and blown you in half?"

"How could I have served you then?" he inquired. "A dead person is of no use to anyone. Time you Antigands learned a little logic."

With that parting shot he went away.

"He's got something there," observed Harrison, patently depressed. "What can you do with a waxie one? Nothing whatever! You'd have put him clean out of your own power."

"Don't know so much. A couple of stiffs lying around might sharpen the others. They'd get really eager."

"You're thinking of them in Terran terms," Harrison said. "It's a mistake. They're not Terrans, no matter where they came from originally. They're Gands." He mused a moment. "I've no notion of just what Gands are supposed to be but I reckon they're some kind of fanatics. Terra exported one-track-minders by the millions around the time of the Great Explosion. Look at that crazy crowd they've got on Hygeia."

"I was there once and I tried hard not to look," confessed Gleed, reminiscently. "Then I couldn't stop looking. Not so much as a fig leaf between the lot. They insisted that we were obscene because we wore clothes. So eventually we had to take them off. Know what I was wearing at the time we left?"

"A dignified poise," Harrison suggested.

"That and an identity disk, cupro-silver, official issue, spacemen, for the use of," Gleed informed. "Plus three wipes of greasepaint on my left arm to show I was a sergeant. I looked every inch a sergeant— like hell I did!"

"I know. I had a week in that place."

"We'd a rear admiral on board," Gleed went on. "As a fine physical specimen he resembled a pair of badly worn suspenders. He couldn't overawe anyone while in his birthday suit. Those Hygeians cited his deflation as proof that they'd got real democracy, as distinct from our fake version." He clucked his tongue. "I'm not so sure they're wrong."

"The creation of the Empire has created a queer proposition," Harrison meditated. "Namely, that Terra is always right while sixteen hundred and forty-two planets are invariably wrong."

"You're getting kind of seditious, aren't you?"

Harrison said nothing. Gleed glanced at him, found his attention elsewhere, followed his gaze to a brunette who had just entered.

"Nice," approved Gleed. "Not too young, not too old. Not too fat, not too thin. Just right."

"I know her." Harrison waved to attract her attention.

She tripped lightly across the room, sat at their table. Harrison made the introduction.

"Friend of mine. Sergeant Gleed."

"Arthur," corrected Gleed, greeting her.

"Mine's Elissa," she told him. "What's a sergeant supposed to be?"

"A sort of over-above underthing," Gleed informed. "I pass along the telling to the guys who do the doing."

Her eyes widened. "Do you mean that people really allow themselves to be told?"

"Of course. Why not?"

"It sounds crazy to me." Her gaze shifted to Harrison. "I'll be ignorant of your name forever, I suppose?"

He hastened to repair the omission, adding, "But I don't like James. I prefer Jim."

"Then we'll let it be Jim." She examined the place, looking over the counter, the other tables. "Has Matt been to you two?"

"Yes. He refuses to serve us."

She shrugged warm shoulders. "It's his right. Everyone has the right to refuse. That's freedom, isn't it?"

"We call it mutiny," said Gleed.

"Don't be so childish," she reproved. She stood up, moved away. "You wait here. I'll go see Seth."

"I don't get this," admitted Gleed, when she had passed out of earshot. "According to that fat fella in the delicatessen, their technique is to give us the cold shoulder until we run away in a huff. But this dame acts friendly. She's . . . she's—" He stopped while he sought for a suitable word, found it and said, "She's un-Gandian."

"Not so," Harrison contradicted. "They've the right to say, 'I won't.' She's practicing it."

"By gosh, yes! I hadn't thought of that. They can work it any way they like, and please themselves."

"Sure." He dropped his voice. "Here she comes."

Resuming her seat, she primped her hair, said, "Seth will serve us personally."

"Another traitor," remarked Gleed with a grin.

"On one condition," she went on. "You two must wait and have a talk with him before you leave."

"Cheap at the price," Harrison decided. A thought struck him and he asked, "Does this mean you'll have to kill several obs for all three of us?"

"Only one for myself."

"How come?"

"Seth's got ideas of his own. He doesn't feel happy about Antigands any more than does anyone else."

"And so?"

"But he's got the missionary instinct. He doesn't agree entirely with the idea of giving all Antigands the ghost-treatment. He thinks it should be reserved only for those too stubborn or stupid to be converted." She smiled at Gleed, making his top hairs quiver. "Seth thinks that any intelligent Antigand is a would-be Gand."

"What is a Gand, anyway?" asked Harrison.

"An inhabitant of this world, of course."

"I mean, where did they dig up the name?"

"From Gandhi," she said.

Harrison frowned in puzzlement. "Who the deuce was he?"

"An ancient Terran. The one who invented The Weapon."

"Never heard of him."

"That doesn't surprise me," she remarked.

"Doesn't it?" he felt a little irritated. "Let me tell you that these days we Terrans get as good an education as—"

"Calm down, Jim." She made it more soothing by pronouncing it "Jeem." "All I mean is that ten to one he's been blanked out of your history books. He might have given you unwanted ideas, see? You couldn't be expected to know what you've been deprived of the chance to learn."

"If you mean that Terran history is censored, I don't believe it," he asserted.

"It's your right to refuse to believe. That's freedom, isn't it?"

"Up to a point. A man has duties. He's no right to refuse those."

"No?" She raised tantalizing eyebrows, delicately curved. "Who defines those duties—himself, or somebody else?"

"His superiors, most times."

"No man is superior to another. No man has the right to define another man's duties." She paused, eyeing him speculatively. "If anyone on Terra exercises such idiotic power, it is only because idiots permit him. They fear freedom. They prefer to be told. They like being ordered around. What men!"

"I shouldn't listen to you," protested Gleed, chipping in. His leathery face was flushed. "You're as naughty as you're pretty."

"Afraid of your own thoughts?" she jibed, pointedly ignoring his compliment.

He went redder. "Not on your life. But I—" His voice tailed off as Seth arrived with three loaded plates and dumped them on the table.

"See you afterward," reminded Seth. He was medium-sized, with thin features and sharp, quick-moving eyes. "Got something to say to you."

Seth joined them shortly after the end of the meal. Taking a chair, he wiped condensed steam off his face, looked them over.

"How much do you two know?"

"Enough to argue about it," put in Elissa. "They are bothered about duties, who defines them, and who does them."

"With good reason," Harrison riposted. "You can't escape them yourselves."

"Meaning—?" asked Seth.

"This world runs on some strange system of swapping obligations. How will any person kill an ob unless he recognizes his duty to do so?"

"Duty has nothing to do with it," said Seth. "And if it did happen to be a matter of duty, every man would recognize it for himself. It would be outrageous impertinence for anyone else to remind him, unthinkable to anyone to order him.'"

"Some guys must make an easy living," interjected Gleed. "There's nothing to stop them that I can see." He studied Seth briefly before he continued, "How can you cope with a citizen who has no con-science?"

"Easy as pie."

Elissa suggested, "Tell them the story of Idle Jack."

"It's a kid's yarn," explained Seth. "All children here know it by heart. It's a classic fable like . . . like—" He screwed up his face. "I've lost track of the Terran tales the first comers brought with them."

"Red Riding Hood," offered Harrison.

"Yes." Seth seized on it gratefully. "Something like that one. A nursery story." He licked his lips, began, "This Idle Jack came from Terra as a baby, grew up in our new world, studied our economic system and thought he'd be mighty smart. He decided to become a scratcher."

"What's a scratcher?" inquired Gleed.

"One who lives by taking obs and does nothing about killing them or planting any of his own. One who accepts everything that's going and gives nothing in return."

"I get it. I've known one or two like that in my time."

"Up to age sixteen, Jack got away with it. He was a kid, see. All kids tend to scratch to a certain extent. We expect it and allow for it. After sixteen, he was soon in the soup."

"How?" urged Harrison, more interested than he was willing to show.

"He went around the town gathering obs by the armful. Meals, clothes and all sorts for the mere asking. It's not a big town. There are no big ones on this planet. They're just small enough for every-one to know everyone—and everyone does plenty of gabbing. Within three or four months the entire town knew Jack was a determined scratcher."

"Go on," said Harrison, getting impatient.

"Everything dried up," said Seth. "Wherever Jack went, people gave him the 'I Won't'. That's freedom, isn't it? He got no meals, no clothes, no entertainment, no company, nothing! Soon he became terribly hungry, busted into someone's larder one night, gave himself the first square meal in a week."

"What did they do about that?"

"Nothing. Not a thing."

"That would encourage him some, wouldn't it?"

"How could it?" Seth asked, with a thin smile. "It did him no good. Next day his belly was empty again. He had to repeat the perform- ance. And the next day. And the next. People became leery, locked up their stuff, kept watch on it. It became harder and harder. It became so unbearably hard that it was soon a lot easier to leave the town and try another. So Idle Jack went away."

"To do the same again," Harrison suggested.

"With the same results for the same reasons," retorted Seth. "On he went to a third town, a fourth, a fifth, a twentieth. He was stub- born enough to be witless."

"He was getting by," Harrison observed. "Taking all at the mere cost of moving around."

"No he wasn't. Our towns are small, like I said. And folk do plen- ty of visiting from one to another. In town number two Jack had to risk being seen and talked about by someone from town number one. As he went on it got a whole lot worse. In the twentieth he had to take a chance on gabby visitors from any of the previous nineteen." Seth leaned forward, said with emphasis, "He never got to town number twenty-eight."

"No?"

"He lasted two weeks in number twenty-five, eight days in twenty- six, one day in twenty-seven. That was almost the end."

"What did he do then?"

"Took to the open country, tried to live on roots and wild berries. Then he disappeared—until one day some walkers found him swing- ing from a tree. The body was emaciated and clad in rags. Loneliness and self-neglect had killed him. That was Idle Jack, the scratcher. He wasn't twenty years old."

"On Terra," informed Gleed, "we don't hang people merely for being lazy."

"Neither do we," said Seth. "We leave them free to go hang themselves." He eyed them shrewdly, went on, "But don't let it worry you. Nobody has been driven to such drastic measures in my lifetime, leastways, not that I've heard about. People honor their obs as a matter of economic necessity and not from any sense of duty. Nobody gives orders, nobody pushes anyone around, but there's a kind of compulsion built into the circumstances of this planet's way of living. People play square—or they suffer. Nobody enjoys suffering—not even a numbskull."

"Yes, I suppose you're right," put in Harrison, much exercised in mind.

"You bet I'm dead right!" Seth assured. "But what I wanted to talk to you two about is something more important. It's this: What's your real ambition in life?"

Without hesitation, Gleed said, "To ride the spaceways while remaining in one piece."

"Same here," Harrison contributed.

"I guessed that much. You'd not be in the space service if it wasn't your choice. But you can't remain in it forever. All good things come to an end. What then?"

Harrison fidgeted uneasily. "I don't care to think of it."

"Some day, you'll have to," Seth pointed out. "How much longer have you got?"

"Four and a half Earth years."

Seth's gaze turned to Gleed.

"Three Earth years."

"Not long," Seth commented. "I didn't expect you would have much time left. It's a safe bet that any ship penetrating this deeply into space has a crew composed mostly of old-timers getting near the end of their terms. The practiced hands get picked for the awkward jobs. By the day your boat lands again on Terra it will be the end of the trail for many of them, won't it?"

"It will for me," Gleed admitted, none too happy at the thought.

"Time—the older you get the faster it goes. Yet when you leave the service you'll still be comparatively young." He registered a faint, taunting smile. "I suppose you'll then obtain a private space vessel and continue roaming the cosmos on your own?"

"Impossible," declared Gleed. "The best a rich man can afford is a Moon-boat. Puttering to and fro between a satellite and its primary is no fun when you're used to Bliederzips across the galaxy. The smallest space-going craft is far beyond reach of the wealthiest. Only governments can afford them."

"By 'governments' you mean communities?"

"In a way."

"Well, then, what are you going to do when your space-roving days are over?"

"I'm not like Big Ears here." Gleed jerked an indicative thumb at Harrison. "I'm a trooper and not a technician. So my choice is limited by lack of qualifications." He rubbed his chin, looked wistful. "I was born and brought up on a farm. I still know a good deal about farming. So I'd like to get a small one of my own and settle down."

"Think you'll manage it?" asked Seth, watching him.

"On Falder or Hygeia or Norton's Pink Heaven or some other undeveloped planet. But not on Terra. My savings won't extend to that. I don't get half enough to meet Earth costs."

"Meaning you can't pile up enough obs?"

"I can't," agreed Gleed, lugubriously. "Not even if I saved until I'd got a white beard four feet long."

"So there's Terra's reward for a long spell of faithful service—forego your heart's desire or get out?"

"Shut up!"

"I won't," said Seth. He leaned nearer. "Why do you think two hundred thousand Gands came to this world, Doukhobors to Hygeia, Quakers to Centauri B, and all the others to their selected haunts? Because Terra's reward for good citizenship was the peremptory order to knuckle down or get out. So we got out."

"It was just as well, anyway," Elissa interjected. "According to our history books, Terra was badly overcrowded. We went away and relieved the pressure."

"That's beside the point," reproved Seth. He continued with Gleed. "You want a farm. It can't be on Terra much as you'd like it there. Terra says, 'No! Get out!' So it's got to be some place else." He waited for that to sink in, then, "Here, you can have one for the mere taking." He snapped his fingers. "Like that!"

"You can't kid me," said Gleed, wearing the expression of one eager to be kidded. "Where are the hidden strings?"

"On this planet, any plot of ground belongs to the person in possession, the one who is making use of it. Nobody disputes his claim so long as he continues to use it. All you need do is look around for a suitable piece of unused territory—of which there is plenty—and start using it. From that moment it's yours. Immediately you cease using it and walk out, it's anyone else's, for the taking."

"Zipping meteors!" Gleed was incredulous.

"Moreover, if you look around long enough and strike really lucky," Seth continued, "you might stake first claim to a farm someone else has abandoned because of death, illness, a desire to move elsewhere, a chance at something else he liked better, or any other excellent reason. In that case, you would walk into ground already part-prepared, with farmhouse, milking shed, barns and the rest. And it would be yours, all yours."

"What would I owe the previous occupant?" asked Gleed.

"Nothing. Not an ob. Why should you? If he isn't buried, he has got out for the sake of something else equally free. He can't have the benefit both ways, coming and going."

"It doesn't make sense to me. Somewhere there's a snag. Somewhere I've got to pour out hard cash or pile up obs."

"Of course you have. You start a farm. A handful of local folk help you build a house. They dump heavy obs on you. The carpenter wants farm produce for his family for the next couple of years. You give it, thus killing that ob. You continue giving it for a couple of extra years, thus planting an ob on him. First time you want fences mending, or some other suitable task doing, along he comes to kill that ob. And so with all the rest, including the people who supply your raw materials, your seeds and machinery, or do your trucking for you."

"They won't all want milk and potatoes," Gleed pointed out.

"Don't know what you mean by potatoes. Never heard of them."

"How can I square up with someone who may be getting all the farm produce he wants from elsewhere?"

"Easy," said Seth. "A tinsmith supplies you with several churns. He doesn't want food. He's getting all he needs from another source. His wife and three daughters are overweight and dieting. The mere thought of a load from your farm gives them the horrors."

"Well?"

"But this tinsmith's tailor, or his cobbler, have got obs on him which he hasn't had the chance to kill. So he transfers them to you. As soon as you're able, you give the tailor or cobbler what they need to satisfy the obs, thus doing the tinsmith's killing along with your own." He gave his usual half-smile, added, "And everyone is happy."

Gleed stewed it over, frowning while he did it. "You're tempting me. You shouldn't ought to. It's a criminal offense to try to divert a spaceman from his allegiance. It's sedition. Terra is tough with sedition."

"Tough my eye!" said Seth, sniffing contemptuously. "We've Gand laws here."

"All you have to do," suggested Elissa, sweetly persuasive, "is say to yourself that you've got to go back to the ship, that it's your duty to go back, that neither the ship nor Terra can get along without you." She tucked a curl away. "Then be a free individual and say, 'I won't!' "

"They'd skin me alive. Bidworthy would preside over the operation in person."

"I don't think so," Seth offered. "This Bidworthy—whom I presume to be anything but a jovial character—stands with you and the rest of your crew at the same junction. The road before him splits two ways. He's got to take one or the other and there's no third alternative. Sooner or later he'll be hell-bent for home, eating his top lip as he goes, or else he'll be running around in a truck delivering your milk—because, deep inside himself, that's what he's always wanted to do."

"You don't know him like I do," mourned Gleed. "He uses a lump of old iron for a soul."

"Funny," remarked Harrison, "I always thought of you that way—until today."

"I'm off duty," said Gleed, as though that explained everything. "I can relax and let the ego zoom around outside of business hours." He stood up, firmed his jaw. "But I'm going back on duty. Right now!"

"You're not due before sundown tomorrow," Harrison protested.

"Maybe I'm not. But I'm going back all the same."

Elissa opened her mouth, closed it as Seth nudged her. They sat in silence and watched Gleed march determinedly out.

"It's a good sign," commented Seth, strangely self-assured. "He's been handed a wallop right where he's weakest." He chuckled low down, turned to Harrison. "What's *your* ultimate ambition?"

"Thanks for the meal. It was a good one and I needed it." Harrison stood up, manifestly embarrassed. He gestured toward the door. "I'm going to catch him up. If he's returning to the ship, I think I'll do likewise."

Again Seth nudged Elissa. They said nothing as Harrison made his way out, carefully closing the door behind him.

"Sheep," decided Elissa, disappointed for no obvious reason. "One follows another. Just like sheep."

"Not so," Seth contradicted. "They're humans animated by the same thoughts, the same emotions, as were our forefathers who had nothing sheeplike about them." Twisting round in his chair, he beckoned to Matt. "Bring us two shemaks." Then to Elissa. "My guess is that it won't pay that ship to hang around too long."

The battleship's caller-system bawled imperatively, "Fanshaw, Folsom, Fuller, Garson, Gleed, Gregory, Haines, Harrison, Hope—" and down through the alphabet.

A trickle of men flowed along the passages, catwalks and alleyways toward the fore chartroom. They gathered outside it in small clusters, chattering in undertones and sending odd scraps of conversation echoing down the corridor.

"Wouldn't say anything to us but, 'Myob!' Got sick and tired of it after a while."

"You ought to have split up, like we did. That show place on the outskirts didn't know what a Terran looks like. I just walked in and took a seat."

"Hear about Meakin? He mended a leaky roof, chose a bottle of double dith in payment and mopped the lot. He was dead flat when we found him. Had to be carried back."

"Some guys have all the luck. We got the brush-off wherever we showed our faces. It gets you down."

"You should have separated, like I said."

"Half the mess must be still lying in the gutter. They haven't turned up yet."

"Grayder will be hopping mad. He'd have stopped this morning's second quota if he'd known in time."

Every now and again First Mate Morgan stuck his head out of the chartroom door and uttered a name already voiced on the caller. Frequently there was no response.

"Harrison!" he yelled.

With a puzzled expression, Harrison went inside. Captain Grayder was there, seated behind a desk and gazing moodily at a list lying before him. Colonel Shelton was stiff and erect to one side, with Major Hame slightly behind him. Both wore the pained expressions of those tolerating a bad smell while the plumber goes looking for the leak.

His Excellency was tramping steadily to and fro in front of the desk, muttering deep down in his chins. "Barely five days and already the rot has set in." He turned as Harrison entered, fired off sharply, "So it's you, mister. When did you return from leave?"

"The evening before last, sir."

"Ahead of time, eh? That's curious. Did you get a puncture or something?"

"No, sir. I didn't take my bicycle with me."

"Just as well," approved the ambassador. "If you had done so, you'd have been a thousand miles away by now and still pushing hard."

"Why, sir?"

"Why? He asks me why! That's precisely what I'd like to know—*why?*" He fumed a bit, then inquired, "Did you visit this town by yourself, or in company?"

"I went with Sergeant Gleed, sir."

"Call him," ordered the ambassador, looking at Morgan.

Opening the door, Morgan obediently shouted, "Gleed! Gleed!" No answer.

He tried again, without result. They put it over the caller-system again. Sergeant Gleed refused to be among those present.

"Has he booked in?"

Grayder consulted his list. "In early. Twenty-four hours ahead of time. He may have sneaked out again with the second liberty quota this morning and omitted to book it. That's a double crime."

"If he's not on the ship, he's off the ship, crime or no crime."

"Yes, your Excellency." Captain Grayder registered slight weariness.

"GLEED!" howled Morgan, outside the door. A moment later he poked his head inside, said, "Your Excellency, one of the men says Sergeant Gleed is not on board because he saw him in town quite recently."

"Send him in." The ambassador made an impatient gesture at Harrison. "Stay where you are and keep those confounded ears from flapping. I've not finished with you yet."

A long, gangling grease-monkey came in, blinked around, a little awed by high brass.

"What do you know about Sergeant Gleed?" demanded the ambassador.

The other licked his lips, seemed sorry that he had mentioned the missing man. "It's like this, your honor, I—"

"Call me 'sir.'"

"Yes, sir." More disconcerted blinking. "I went out with the second party early this morning, came back a couple of hours ago because my stomach was acting up. On the way, I saw Sergeant Gleed and spoke to him."

"Where? When?"

"In town, sir. He was sitting in one of those big long-distance coaches. I thought it a bit queer."

"Get down to the roots, man! What did he tell you, if anything?"

"Not much, sir. He seemed pretty chipper about something. Mentioned a young widow struggling to look after two hundred acres. Someone had told him about her and he thought he'd take a peek." He hesitated, backed away a couple of paces, added, "He also said I'd see him in irons or never."

"One of *your* men," said the ambassador to Colonel Shelton. "A trooper, allegedly well-disciplined. One with long service, three stripes, and a pension to lose." His attention returned to the informant. "Did he say exactly where he was going?"

"No, sir. I asked him, but he just grinned and said, 'Myob!' So I came back to the ship."

"All right. You may go." His Excellency watched the other depart, then continued with Harrison. "You were with that first quota."

"Yes, sir."

"Let me tell you something, mister. Four hundred twenty men went out. Only two hundred have returned. Forty of those were in various stages of alcoholic turpitude. Ten of them are in the clink yelling, 'I Won't!' in steady chorus. Doubtless they'll go on yelling until they've sobered up."

He stared at Harrison as if that worthy were personally responsible, then went on, "There's something paradoxical about this. I can understand the drunks. There are always a few individuals who blow their tops first day on land. But of the two hundred who have condescended to come back, about half returned before time, the same as you did. Their reasons were identical—the town was unfriendly, everyone treated them like ghosts until they'd had enough."

Harrison made no comment.

"So we have two diametrically opposed reactions," the ambassador complained. "One gang of men say the place stinks so much that they'd rather be back on the ship. Another gang finds it so hospitable that either they get filled to the gills on some stuff called double dith, or they stay sober and desert the service. I want an explanation. There's got to be one somewhere. You've been twice in this town. What can you tell us?"

Carefully, Harrison said, "It all depends on whether or not you're spotted as a Terran. Also on whether you meet Gands who'd rather convert you than give you the brush-off." He pondered a moment, finished, "Uniforms are a give-away."

"You mean they're allergic to uniforms?"

"More or less, sir."

"Any idea why?"

"Couldn't say for certain, sir. I don't know enough about them yet. As a guess, I think they may have been taught to associate uniforms with the Terran regime from which their ancestors escaped."

"Escaped nothing!" scoffed the ambassador. "They grabbed the benefit of Terran inventions, Terran techniques and Terran manufacturing ability to go some place where they'd have more elbow room." He gave Harrison the sour eye. "Don't any of them wear uniforms?"

"Not that I could recognize as such. They seem to take pleasure in expressing their individual personalities by wearing anything they fancy, from pigtails to pink boots. Oddity in attire is the norm among the Gands. Uniformity is the real oddity—they think it's submissive and degrading."

"You refer to them as Gands. Where did they dig up that name?"

Harrison told him, thinking back to Elissa as she explained it. In his mind's eye he could see her now. And Seth's place with the tables set and steam rising behind the counter and mouth-watering smells oozing from the background. Now that he came to visualize the scene again, it appeared to embody an elusive but essential something that the ship had never possessed.

"And this person," he concluded, "invented what they call The Weapon."

"Hm-m-m! And they assert he was a Terran? What does he look like? Did you see a photograph or a statue?"

"They don't erect statues, sir. They say no person is more important than another."

"Bunkum!" snapped the ambassador, instinctively rejecting that viewpoint. "Did it occur to you to ask at what period in history this wonderful weapon was tried out?"

"No, sir," Harrison confessed. "I didn't think it important."

"You wouldn't. Some of you men are too slow to catch a Callistrian sloth wandering in its sleep. I don't criticize your abilities as spacemen, but as intelligence-agents you're a dead loss."

"I'm sorry, sir," said Harrison.

Sorry? You louse! whispered something deep within his own mind. *Why should you be sorry? He's only a pompous fat man who couldn't kill an ob if he tried. He's no better than you. Those raw boys prancing around on Hygeia would maintain that he's not as good as you because he's got a pot belly. Yet you keep looking at his pot belly and saying, "Sir" and, "I'm sorry". If he tried to ride your bike, he'd fall off before he'd gone ten yards. Go spit in his eye and say, "I won't". You're not scared, are you?*

"No!" announced Harrison, loudly and firmly.

Captain Grayder glanced up. "If you're going to start answering questions before they've been asked, you'd better see the medic. Or have we a telepath on board?"

"I was thinking," Harrison explained.

"I approve of that," put in His Excellency. He lugged a couple of huge tomes out of the wall-shelves, began to thumb rapidly through them. "Do plenty of thinking whenever you've the chance and it will become a habit. It will get easier and easier as time rolls on. In fact, a day may come when it can be done without pain."

He shoved the books back, pulled out two more, spoke to Major Hame who happened to be at his elbow. "Don't pose there glassy-eyed like a relic propped up in a military museum. Give me a hand with this mountain of knowledge. I want Gandhi, anywhere from three hundred to a thousand Earth-years ago."

Hame came to life, started dragging out books. So did Colonel Shelton. Captain Grayder remained at his desk and continued to mourn the missing.

"Ah, here it is, four-seventy years back." His Excellency ran a plump finger along the printed lines. "Gandhi, sometimes called Bapu, or Father. Citizen of Hindi. Politico-philosopher. Opposed authority by means of an ingenious system called civil disobedience. Last remnants disappeared with the Great Explosion, but may still persist on some planet out of contact."

"Evidently it does," commented Grayder, his voice dry.

"Civil disobedience," repeated the ambassador, screwing up his eyes. He had the air of one trying to study something which was topsy-turvy. "They can't make that a social basis. It just won't work."

"It does work," asserted Harrison, forgetting to put in the "sir".

"Are you contradicting me, mister?"

"I'm stating a fact."

"Your Excellency," Grayder began, "I suggest—"

"Leave this to me." His color deepening, the ambassador waved him off. His gaze remained angrily on Harrison. "You're very far from being an expert on socio-economic problems. Get that into your head, mister. Anyone of your caliber can be fooled by superficial appearances."

It works," persisted Harrison, wondering where his own stubbornness was coming from.

"So does your tomfool bicycle. You've a bicycle mentality."

Something snapped, and a voice remarkably like his own said, "Nuts!" Astounded by this phenomenon, Harrison waggled his ears.

"What was that, mister?"

"Nuts!" he repeated, feeling that what has been done can't be undone.

Beating the purpling ambassador to the draw, Captain Grayder stood up and exercised his own authority.

"Regardless of further leave-quotas, if any, you are confined to the ship until further notice. Now get out!"

He went out, his mind in a whirl but his soul strangely satisfied: Outside, First Mate Morgan glowered at him.

"How long d'you think it's going to take me to work through this list of names when guys like you squat in there for a week?" He grunted with ire, cupped hands round his mouth and bellowed, "Hope! Hope!"

No reply.

"Hope's been abandoned," remarked a wit.

"That's funny," sneered Morgan. "Look at me shaking all over." He cupped again, tried the next name. "Hyland! Hyland!"

No response.

Four more days, long, tedious, dragging ones. That made nine in all since the battleship formed the rut in which it was still sitting.

There was trouble on board. The third and fourth leave-quotas, put off repeatedly, were becoming impatient, irritable.

"Morgan showed him the third roster again this morning. Same result. Grayder admitted this world can't be defined as hostile and that we're entitled to run free."

"Well, why the hell doesn't he keep to the book? The Space Commission could crucify him for disregarding it."

"Same excuse. He says he's not denying leave, he's merely postponing it. That's a crafty evasion, isn't it? He says he'll grant it immediately the missing men come back."

"That might be never. Damn him, he's using them as an excuse to gyp me out of my time."

It was a strong and legitimate complaint. Weeks, months, years of close confinement in a constantly trembling bottle, no matter how large, demands ultimate release if only for a comparatively brief period. Men need fresh air, the good earth, the broad, clear-cut horizon, bulkfood, femininity, new faces.

"He would ram home the stopper just when we've learned the best way to get around. Civilian clothes and act like Gands, that's the secret. Even the first-quota boys are ready for another try."

"Grayder daren't risk it. He's lost too many already. One more quota cut in half and he won't have enough crew to take off and get back. We'd be stuck here for keeps. How'd you like that?"

"I wouldn't cry about it."

"He could train the bureaucrats. Time those guys did some honest work."

"It'd take three years. That's how long it took to train you, wasn't it?"

Harrison came along holding a small envelope. Three of them picked on him at sight.

"Look who sassed Hizonner and got confined to ship—same as us!"

"That's what I like about it," Harrison observed. "Better to get fastened down for something than for nothing."

"It won't be long, you'll see! We're not going to hang around bellyaching for ever. Mighty soon we'll do something."

"Such as what?"

"We're thinking it over," evaded the other, not liking to be taken up so fast. He noticed the envelope. "What have you got there? The day's mail?"

"Exactly that," Harrison agreed.

"Have it your own way. I wasn't being nosey. I thought maybe you'd got some more snafu. You engineers usually pick up that paper-stuff first."

"It is mail," said Harrison.

"G'wan, nobody has letters in this neck of the cosmos."

"I do."

"How did you get it?"

"Worrall brought it from town an hour back. Friend of mine gave him dinner, let him bring the letter to kill the ob." He pulled a large ear. "Influence, that's what you boys need."

Registering annoyance, one demanded, "What's Worrall doing off the boat? Is he privileged?"

"Sort of. He's married, with three kids."

"So what?"

"The ambassador figures that some people can be trusted more than others. They're not so likely to disappear, having too much to lose. So a few have been sorted out and sent into town to seek information about the missing men."

"They found out anything?"

"Not much. Worrall says it's a waste of time. He found a few of our men here and there, tried to persuade them to return, but each said, 'I won't'. The Gands all said, 'Myob!' And that's that."

"There must be something in it," decided one of them, thoughtfully. "I'd like to go see for myself."

"That's what Grayder's afraid of."

"We'll give more than that to worry about if he doesn't become reasonable soon. Our patience is evaporating."

"Mutinous talk," Harrison reproved. He shook his head, looked sad. "You shock me."

He continued along the corridor, reached his own cabin, eyed the envelope. The writing inside might be feminine. He hoped so. He tore it open and had a look. It wasn't.

Signed by Gleed, the missive read, "Never mind where I am or what I'm doing—this might get into the wrong hands. All I'll tell you is that I'll be fixed up topnotch providing I wait a decent interval to improve acquaintance. The rest of this concerns you."

"Huh?" He leaned back on his bunk, held the letter nearer the light.

"I found a little fat guy running an empty shop. He just sits there, waiting. Next, I learn that he's established possession by occupation. He's doing it on behalf of a factory that makes two-ball rollers— those fan-driven cycles. They want someone to operate the place as a local roller sales and service depot. The little fat man has had four applications to date, but none with any engineering ability. The one who eventually gets this place will plant a functional-ob on the town, whatever that means. Anyway, this joint is yours for the taking. Don't be stupid. Jump in—the water's fine."

"Zipping meteors!" said Harrison. His eyes traveled on to the bottom.

"P.S. Seth will give you the address. P.P.S. This burg is your brunette's home town and she's thinking of coming back. She wants to live near her sister—and so do I. Said sister is a honey!"

He stirred restlessly, read it through a second time, got up and paced around his tiny cabin. There were twelve hundred occupied worlds within the scope of the Empire. He'd seen about one-tenth of them. No spaceman could live long enough to get a look at the lot. The service was divided into cosmic groups, each dealing with its own sector.

Except by hearsay, of which there was plenty and most of it highly colored, he would never know what heavens or pseudo-heavens existed in other sectors. In any case, it would be a blind gamble to pick an unfamiliar world for landbound life on someone else's recommendation. Not all think alike, or have the same tastes. One man's meat may be another's man's poison.

The choice for retirement—which was the unlovely name for beginning another, different but vigorous life—was high-priced Terra or some more desirable planet in his own sector. There was the Epsilon group, fourteen of them, all attractive providing you could suffer the gravity and endure lumbering around like a tired elephant. There was Norton's Pink Heaven if, for the sake of getting by in peace, you could pander to Septimus Norton's rajah-complex and put up with his delusions of grandeur.

Up on the edge of the Milky Way was a matriarchy run by blonde Amazons, and a world of wizards, and a Pentecostal planet, and a globe where semisentient vegetables cultivated themselves under the direction of human masters; all scattered across forty light-years of space but readily accessible by Blieder-drive.

There were more than a hundred known to him by personal experience, though merely a tithe of the whole. All offered life and that company which is the essence of life. But this world, Gand, had something the others lacked. It had the quality of being present. It was part of the existing environment from which he drew data on which to build his decisions. The others were not. They lost virtue by being absent and faraway.

Inobtrusively, he made his way to the Blieder-room lockers, spent an hour cleaning and oiling his bicycle. Twilight was approaching when he returned. Taking a thin plaque from his pocket, he hung it on the wall, lay on his bunk and stared at it.

F—I.W.

The caller-system clicked, cleared its throat, announced, "All personnel will stand by for general instructions at eight hours tomorrow.

"I won't," said Harrison. He closed his eyes.

Seven-twenty in the morning, but nobody thought it early. There is little sense of earliness or lateness among space-roamers—to regain it they have to be landbound a month, watching a sun rise and set.

The chartroom was empty but there was much activity in the control cabin. Grayder was there with Shelton, Hame, Navigators Adamson, Werth and Yates and, of course, His Excellency.

"I never thought the day would come," groused the latter, frowning at the star map over which the navigators pored. "Less than a couple of weeks, and we get out, admitting defeat."

"With all respect, your Excellency, it doesn't look that way to me," said Captain Grayder. "One can be defeated only by enemies. These people are not enemies. That's precisely where they've got us by the short hairs. They're not definable as hostile."

"That may be. I still say it's defeat. What else could you call it?"

"We've been outwitted by awkward relations. There's not much we can do about it. A man doesn't beat up his nieces and nephews merely because they won't speak to him."

"That's your viewpoint as a ship's commander. You're confronted by a situation that requires you to go back to base and report. It's routine. The whole service is hidebound with routine." The ambassador again eyed the star map as if he found it offensive. "My own status is different. If I get out, it's a diplomatic defeat, an insult to the dignity and prestige of Terra. I'm far from sure that I ought to go. It might be better if I stayed put—though that would give them the chance to offer further insults."

"I would not presume to advise you what to do for the best," Grayder said. "All I know is this: we carry troops and armaments for any policing or protective purposes that might be found necessary here. But I can't use them offensively against these Gands because they've provided no pretext and because, in any case, our full strength isn't enough to crush twelve millions of them. We need an armada for that. We'd be fighting at the extreme of our reach—and the reward of victory would be a useless world."

"Don't remind me. I've stewed it until I'm sick of it."

Grayder shrugged. He was a man of action so long as it was action in space. Planetary shenanigans were not properly his pigeon. Now that the decisive moment was drawing near, when he would be back in his own attenuated element, he was becoming phlegmatic. To him, Gand was a visit among a hundred such, with plenty more to come.

"Your Excellency, if you're in serious doubt whether to remain or come with us, I'd be favored if you'd reach a decision fairly soon. Morgan has given me the tip that if I haven't approved the third leave-quota by ten o'clock the men are going to take matters into their own hands and walk off."

"That would get them into trouble of a really hot kind, wouldn't it?"

"Some," agreed Captain Grayder, "but not so hot. They intend to turn my own quibbling against me. Since I have not officially forbidden leave, a walk-out won't be mutiny. I've merely been postponing leave. They could plead before the Space Commission that I've deliberately ignored regulations. They might get away with it if the members were in the mood to assert their authority."

"The Commission ought to be taken on a few long flights," opined His Excellency. "They'd discover some things they'll never learn behind a desk." He eyed the other in mock hopefulness. "Any chance of accidentally dropping our cargo of bureaucrats overboard on the way back? A misfortune like that might benefit the spaceways, if not humanity."

"That idea strikes me as Gandish," observed Grayder.

"They wouldn't think of it. Their technique is to say no, no, a thousand times no. That's all—but judging by what has happened here, it is enough." The ambassador pondered his predicament, reached a decision. "I'm coming with you. It goes against the grain because it smacks of surrender. To stay would be a defiant gesture, but I've got to face the fact that it won't serve any useful purpose at the present stage."

"Very well, your Excellency." Grayder went to a port, looked through it toward the town. "I'm down about four hundred men. Some of them have deserted, for keeps. The rest will come back if I wait long enough. They've struck lucky, got their legs under somebody's table and gone A.W.O.L. and they're likely to extend their time for as long as the fun lasts on the principle that they may as well be hung for sheep as lambs. I get that sort of trouble on every long trip. It's not so bad on short ones." A pause while moodily he surveyed a terrain bare of returning prodigals. "But we can't wait for them. Not here."

"No, I reckon not."

"If we hang around any longer, we're going to lose another hundred or two. There won't be enough skilled men to take the boat up. Only way I can beat them to the draw is to give the order to prepare for takeoff. They all come under flight regulations from that moment." He registered a lopsided smile. "That will give the space lawyers something to think about!"

"As soon as you like," approved the ambassador. He joined the other at the port, studied the distant road, watched three Gand coaches whirl along it without stopping. He frowned, still upset by the type of mind which insists on pretending that a mountain isn't there. His attention shifted sidewise, toward the tail-end. He stiffened and said, "What are those men doing outside?"

Shooting a swift glance in the same direction, Grayder grabbed the caller-mike and rapped, "All personnel will prepare for take-off at once!" Juggling a couple of switches, he changed lines, said, "Who is that? Sergeant Major Bidworthy? Look, Sergeant Major, there are half a dozen men beyond the midship lock. Get them in immediately— we're lifting as soon as everything's ready."

The fore and aft gangways had been rolled into their stowage spaces long before. Some fast-thinking quartermaster prevented further escapes by operating the midship ladder-wind, thus trapping Bidworthy along with more would-be sinners.

Finding himself stalled, Bidworthy stood in the rim of the lock and glared at those outside. His mustache not only bristled, but quivered. Five of the offenders had been members of the first leave-quota. One of them was a trooper. That got his rag out, a trooper. The sixth was Harrison, complete with bicycle polished and shining.

Searing the lot of them, the trooper in particular, Bidworthy rasped, "Get back on board. No arguments. No funny business. We're taking off."

"Hear that?" asked one, nudging the nearest. "Get back on board. If you can't jump thirty feet, you'd better flap your arms and fly."

"No sauce from you," roared Bidworthy. "I've got my orders."

"He takes orders," remarked the trooper. "At his age."

"Can't understand it," commented another, shaking a sorrowful head.

Bidworthy scrabbled the lock's smooth rim in vain search of something to grasp. A ridge, a knob, a projection of some sort was needed to take the strain.

"I warn you men that if you try me too—"

"Save your breath, Biddy," interjected the trooper. "From now on, I'm a Gand." With that, he turned and walked rapidly toward the road, four following.

Getting astride his bike, Harrison put a foot on a pedal. His back tire promptly sank with a loud *whee-e-e.*

"Come back!" howled Bidworthy at the retreating five. He made extravagant motions, tried to tear the ladder from its automatic grips. A siren keened thinly inside the vessel. That upped his agitation by several ergs.

"Hear that?" With vein-pulsing ire, he watched Harrison tighten the rear valve and apply his hand pump. "We're about to lift. For the last time—"

Again the siren, this time in a quick series of shrill toots. Bidworthy jumped backward as the seal came down. The lock closed. Harrison again mounted his machine, settled a foot on a pedal but remained watching.

The metal monster shivered from nose to tail then rose slowly and in utter silence. There was stately magnificence in the ascent of such enormous bulk. It increased its rate of climb gradually, went faster, faster, became a toy, a dot and finally disappeared.

For just a moment, Harrison felt a touch of doubt, a hint of regret. It soon passed away. He glanced toward the road.

The five self-elected Gands had thumbed a coach which was picking them up. That was co-operation apparently precipitated by the ship's disappearance. Quick on the uptake, these people. He saw it move off on huge rubber balls, bearing the five with it. A fan-cycle raced in the opposite direction, hummed into the distance.

"Your brunette," Gleed had described her. What gave him that idea? Had she made some remark which he'd construed as complimentary because it made no reference to outsize ears?

He had a last look around. The earth to his left bore a great curved rut one mile long by twelve feet deep. Two thousand Terrans had been there.

Then about eighteen hundred.

Then sixteen hundred.

Less five.

"One left—me!" he said to himself.

Giving a fatalistic shrug, he put the pressure on and rode to town. And then there were none.

PART II

VISIONS OF LIBERTY

Introduction: Visions of Liberty

Mark Tier

Imagine we're on a plane; we've crossed an ocean, we've landed; we're taxiing up to the gate. As we file off the plane we have our passports ready.

But something rather strange happens: no one wants to look at them. We see no official-looking types of any kind.

Perhaps we have to get our luggage first. But as we come down to the baggage carousels we don't see any customs or immigration officials; nor do we see any barrier between us and the outside world. We can pick up our bags and walk straight out of the terminal off an international flight into a taxi. Which is exactly what we do.

Welcome to Freelandia, a country—perhaps it's better to call it a place—which is truly free: there's no government to invade and restrict our liberties. Of course, Freelandia doesn't exist (yet) except in my imagination.

And in science fiction, the literature of the imagination. Where else can we skim across the surface of black holes, dive into the sun, and journey to the beginning, the end, and the edge of the universe?

And visit a society without government that works.

Could that be possible in reality, not just in science fiction? After all, if you counted the number of societies without government on the fingers of one hand, you wouldn't even open your fist. And if government disappeared, wouldn't the result be anarchy? Chaos? Isn't government an essential prerequisite of peace and order?

If we were to travel back in time, some ten or twenty thousand years, before the development of agriculture and the beginnings of civilization, we wouldn't find any governments as we know them today. *Homo sapiens* were hunter-gatherers, living in tribes of some hundred or so people. Yes, tribes have rulers too. Chiefs and shamans. But tribal chieftains rarely have the power to *force* their decisions on the members of their tribe. They are more like leading citizens who rule by moral suasion and consensus rather than police power.

That all changed with the development of agriculture some ten thousand years ago. For the first time, a few dozen square miles of land could support human populations much larger than a hundred-odd hunter-gatherers. For the first time, our ancestors stayed fixed in one place.

For the first time, there was something to loot.

Pick up any history book and you'll find a record of kings, princes, shahs, chiefs, emperors, czars and their battles. What were they fighting over? Today, governments will tell you they're fighting for freedom. But freedom is a very recent phenomenon. The concept of freedom originated with the Greeks and Romans, but did not become a part of the political landscape until the Renaissance just a few hundred years ago.

Even today, words that we take for granted like "freedom," "rights," "liberty," and "free will" simply have no counterparts in most of the world's languages. For most of the world's people, these concepts just don't exist.

No medieval king or Indian maharajah ever fought for freedom. They fought to keep their power or to expand it. Their prize: the surplus they could extract from the peasantry that financed the building of their glittering palaces and ornate churches and temples. Today's major tourist attractions—the pyramids of Egypt, the Taj Mahal, the Angkor Wat, Notre Dame—were all built by forced or slave labor for the pure benefit of the rulers. There was no pretense that "we're doing this for your own good."

Many times, kingdoms and empires were overrun by latter-day hunter-gatherers. The Greeks and Romans called them barbarians; the Europeans called them Huns; the Chinese called them Mongols. They came with only one objective: to loot as much as they could. And sometimes they stayed; after all, a steady stream of loot in the form of taxes can be more attractive than the spoils of hit-and-run raiding.

The greatest of these was Genghis Khan. His empire collapsed upon his death but his grandson, Kublai Khan, established the first alien dynasty to rule all China—the Yuan (1279–1368). History, of course, is written by the victors, so Genghis Khan and Kublai Khan were transformed from bandit leaders into great princes. After all, only *losers* remain barbarians.

From the agricultural revolution until the Renaissance, mankind had the choice of rule or be ruled; to be the oppressed or the oppressor. The idea of freedom—that you should neither rule nor be ruled, but be left alone to pursue your own happiness in your own way, and grant others the same right—did not exist, just as it still doesn't exist in most parts of the world.

When you are ruled you have no rights. You are property. Such is the meaning of "the divine right of kings," the ideology which flowered in Europe in the Middle Ages. Kingdoms did not have citizens; they had vassals. Under "the divine right of kings," everything *and everybody* in the kingdom belonged to the monarch. Kings fought each other for territory and to the victor went the divine right to rule. In China, when a new dynasty was established they said that the old one had lost "the mandate of heaven." In Japan, as in Thailand, the ruler was thought to be the representative of God on earth. All these names are no more than Orwellian double-speak to dress up and legitimize the reality that might was right.

We can trace the origin of government back to the first thug who spied the opportunity to live a life of ease on the backs of the peasants. His spiritual successors are still in our midst today, with names like Lenin, Stalin, Mao Zedong, Pol Pot, and Idi Amin—and those petty bureaucrats who love to flaunt their power over you whenever you have some dealing with a government agency.

A revolution in the idea of government began with the Renaissance, was crystallized by John Locke among others, and came into being for the first time in human history with the American Revolution. The idea: that government should serve man instead of man serving government; that rulers should be the people's *servants,* not their masters. That people have the *innate* right to life, liberty, and the pursuit of happiness, and that the purpose of government is to defend those rights, not to invade them for the benefit of the few at the top.

But how to create such a government? Because what sets government apart from every other organization is that it is the legal instrument of force within a society. No other group has the right to use force except in self-defense, and the people who do we call criminals.

When so much force is concentrated in one organization's hands, how can you limit its use? And you *must,* if you want to live in a free society; only the initiation of force can divert you from the pursuit of your own happiness. Only the initiation of force can threaten your life. The greatest danger to your freedom is not some foreign power—it is your own government. When Thomas Jefferson said "the price of liberty is eternal vigilance," it was the government of the United States that he was warning his fellow citizens to be vigilant against.

The solution of America's founding fathers was to delineate and restrict the role of government. Via the Constitution and the Bill of Rights they clearly (they thought) laid down what government could do, saying that everything else was reserved to the people.

Unfortunately, the imperative of every human organization is to grow. Businesses grow by making more sales and gaining market share; associations grow by signing up more members; governments grow by expanding their power.

This never happens overnight; government grows by salami tactics, slice by slice. For example, when the income tax was introduced in 1913 no one in his right mind would have suggested a top rate of 90 percent. In fact, there was considerable support for capping the income tax at 4 percent. This was shot down by those who argued that specifying such a maximum rate would mean the income tax would rapidly rise to that (then) horrific level. Can you imagine living in a world where an income tax of 4 percent is unthinkable!?

So the government of the United States has grown, slice by unnoticeable slice, till it bears scant resemblance to the government at the country's birth.

Perhaps there is some other way to put a government's use of force into a straitjacket from which it cannot escape. To the best of my knowledge, no one has ever come up with a convincing, workable proposal along these lines.

As Ayn Rand put it in *The Fountainhead*: "The only way in which we can have any law at all is to have as little of it as possible. I see no ethical standard by which to measure the whole unethical concept of a State, except in the amount of time, of thought, of money, of effort and obedience, which a society extorts from its every member."[1]

If the initiation of force is unethical, then it logically follows that government, as we know it, is also unethical. But that, of course, does not answer the question: Could a society without government actually work? If it's hard to imagine a world in which a 4 percent income tax is unthinkable, it's much harder to imagine how a governmentless society could avoid breaking out into a civil war, or simply degenerating into chaos.

That's a common view; after all, the word "anarchy" is generally used to mean "chaos in the absence of government." But that's to assume, mistakenly, that government is the source of law and order.

On January 24, 1848, the California gold rush began. But it took eighteen years for the U.S. Congress to enact a mining law to regulate such discoveries. Meanwhile, gold production in California boomed. How could that have happened without a governmental framework to recognize mining claims, register titles, and regulate disputes?

The miners created their own. They established districts, registries, procedures for establishing and registering a claim and buying and selling claim titles, and a system for resolving disputes. Officers were usually elected, including the recorder of claims. Their private arrangements were recognized in California state courts; and Congress's 1866 statute "explicitly noted that all explorations for minerals would be subject to those 'local customs or rules of miners in the several mining districts' that were not in conflict with the laws of the United States."[2]

This is just one of many historical examples of what Friedrich Hayek calls "spontaneous order," demonstrating that neither government nor even leaders are needed for order to appear.

So perhaps Freelandia is possible after all. And thanks to the rich imagination of science fiction authors, we can visit a plethora of Freelandias.

Although there's a strong individualistic streak within science fiction, until recently very few stories were set in a completely free society. One reason, perhaps, is that all fiction thrives on conflict and a truly free society is so peaceful that there's not very much to write about. So in stories like Eric Frank Russell's classic ". . . And Then There Were None," the conflict comes from outside, in the form of invaders from an authoritarian empire. (You'll find this story—and some other classics of this genre—in this book's companion volume, *Give Me Liberty*, also published by Baen Books.)

Another example is James Hogan's (in my opinion) sadly neglected *Voyage From Yesteryear*. L. Neil Smith has been very prolific in this area, two of his novels, *The Probability Broach* and *Pallas*, winning the Prometheus Award for Best Libertarian Fiction. In his most recent book, *Forge of Elders*, humans meet aliens who are, horror of horrors, capitalists!

Here in this volume are nine more visions of liberty, all set in societies without governments that work. As you'd expect from the fertile minds of science fiction authors, each is very different from the others.

They are not Utopias. Like real life, there's pain and suffering, as one story here (I won't tell you which one) tragically shows us.

And there are visions of how, in the words of Aristotle, life could and should be. A cornucopia of Freelandias that I hope inspire and entertain you as they have me.

---

1 Ayn Rand, *The Fountainhead* (Plume, New York, 1994), pp. 101-102

2 Hernando de Soto, *The Mystery of Capital* (Basic Books: New York, 2000), pp. 146–147

The Unnullified World

by Lloyd Biggle, Jr.

The world was named Llayless. Its principal community—in fact, its only community of any size—was a desert mining center named Pummery. A number of narrow-gauge electric railway lines left Pummery through tubes built to protect their tracks from the swirling sands. When they reached the steep slopes of the surrounding mountains, they emerged to become cog railways.

At one of the railheads, swinging down from the single passenger car that was attached to an interminable string of empty ore cars, Birk Dantler encountered a sign that announced Laughingstock Mines. A short distance beyond it, he found a tiny town nestled amidst the clutter of the mining operation. There were machines to load ore into the railway cars. Farther up the slope, there were machines extracting ore from the mountain. Other machines were bringing ore to the railhead. The town was little more than a spread of small worker's cottages except for a neat, prefab building that housed the mining offices, and, standing next to it, another prefab building that was, unmistakably, a school.

All of this represented a substantial capital outlay for a mining claim on a remote world, which meant that the mines collectively known as Laughingstock were productive enough to provide that capital.

Dantler went directly to the mining office and asked a clerk for information. The clerk looked at him narrowly. "You got a reason for being here, fellow?"

Dantler presented his credentials. The clerk glanced at them and winced. "GBI? You're a Galactic Bureau of Investigation Officer? What's the Inter-World Council want with us?" When Dantler did not answer, he shrugged and grinned. "Your credentials say anyone who doesn't cooperate with you will be deported instantly, and that's reason enough to cooperate. You must know personally all of the many skeletons in the Llayless Mining Corporation's closets to be able to pry a document like that out of it." He returned the credentials. "What is it you want to know?"

"Nothing complicated, I'm sure. Where is the mine called Last Hope?"

"That's fairly complicated until you get through the Laughingstock diggings. After that there's a path. I'd better draw you a map." He went over it with Dantler, and when he was satisfied that his directions were clear, he leaned back and scrutinized Dantler's energy-charged form, taut face—no one had ever called him handsome—and neat, conservative dress. "You prepared for a long walk?" he asked.

"Isn't there any transportation?"

"There are a couple of pack mules, but they're kept on the other side of the mountain. Figure on a long walk."

"How do they bring the ore out?"

"Slowly and with great difficulty. When they've accumulated enough, they load the two pack mules and fill two or three handcarts. All the men they have take the day off and haul ore. The Llayless Mining Corporation built them a short siding off our railway line, and it keeps an ore car parked there. When they get it filled, the Corporation hauls it away and leaves an empty for them. That's as much as it's willing to do for a marginal operation. The men at Last Hope confidently expect the vein they are working to get richer instead of playing out as most marginal mines do. All miners are optimists."

Then he leaned over his desk to look at Dantler's feet. "At least you've got sturdy shoes. As I told you, it's a long walk. I've never tackled it myself, no reason to, but those who have say it's a good ten miles, and half of that is a steep climb up to the pass. It's best to make a two-day trip of it, and you have to figure on an uncomfortable night. There's no hotel or bed and breakfast place—no houses at all, in fact. And you'll be lucky if they can provide you with a sleeping bag, but you'd be an idiot to try to find your way back here in the dark. You got urgent business with the Last Hope?"

"I think it's urgent," Dantler said. "I'm investigating a murder."

The clerk nodded thoughtfully. "I did hear something about that, but it must have been two or three years ago. You just getting around to investigate now?"

"God's mill grinds slow but sure," Dantler said and left the clerk staring after him perplexedly.

Dantler found the path without too much difficulty and began to climb. It led steeply upward through a dense forest of native trees with large, ovate, yellowish leaves and shaggy green bark with strips of red in it. They seemed to exude fresh-smelling oxygen. Without them, the climb into thinner air would have been far more difficult.

When he reached the top, he discovered that the steep descent was almost as difficult as the climb. It was late in the day when he finally reached the Last Hope diggings. There was a scattering of holes with heaps of dirt around them. He walked on, past several small tents, past a makeshift corral from which the two mules eyed him suspiciously, past a more ambitious digging that had produced a tunnel burrowed into the mountain.

Suddenly he received a sharp blow on the head that nearly knocked him senseless. He reacted instinctively, twisting as he fell, somersaulting into a thick growth of shrubbery, and coming to his feet ready for action.

There were three bearded, shabby-looking men facing him. All of them were armed with whatever they had been able to grab when they saw him coming. One brandished the handle of some kind of hand-operated machine. Another had a piece of firewood. The third had an ax raised high over his head. They began to edge forward.

Dantler's head ached, and when he brushed his hand across a swelling lump, it came away bloody. He sensed that the men were about to rush him, so he decided to act before they did and talk afterward. He drew a small electronic pistol from an inner pocket and sprayed them.

They were halted in their tracks. One at a time they toppled forward and lay twitching on the ground. Dantler noticed a spring nearby, and he went to it, drank deeply, and washed the blood from his head. Then he seated himself on a convenient boulder and waited. He felt exhausted, and his head throbbed fiercely. He wanted to lie down with the three men and twitch for a few minutes, but he couldn't spare himself that luxury.

As the charge began to wear off, his victims displayed the usual reactions. They rolled over onto their backs. They flexed arms and legs. They touched their faces and wriggled tingling fingers. None of them had come through his ordeal unscathed. One, a man with a long gray beard and a fierce-looking mustache, had a bloody nose from his fall. Another, with a blond beard, had smacked his forehead on a stone. It was already a black and blue swollen lump. The third, with a neatly trimmed black beard and newish-looking clothing, was going to have a splendid black eye.

Finally the man with the mustache, sat up. He stared at Dantler.

"Bashing a visiting stranger over the head is a perverted kind of hospitality," Dantler observed pleasantly. "Or were you expecting someone else?"

The other two men struggled to sitting positions. "What'd you do to us?" the man with a blond beard asked.

"Something a trifle more civilized than the bashing you had in mind," Dantler said. "I trust that one dose will be sufficient."

"Hell, yes," the man with the mustache said. "Who are you?"

"As I said, a visiting stranger. I walked ten miles over the mountain to ask the favor of some information. I wasn't expecting this kind of welcome. I have credentials issued by this world's factor. Perhaps you would like to examine them." He held one of them under the man's nose. "As you see, a word from me, and the Last Hope mine will have exhausted its last hope. All of its employees will leave Llayless on the next ship. I was hoping I wouldn't have to use it. Are you ready to talk?"

"No reason not to. We thought you were a whacker."

"What's a whacker that makes him deserve that kind of reception?"

"Whackers kill miners and take over their claims."

"Really. Are there whackers on Llayless?"

"Don't know of any, but we've encountered them elsewhere. Better to act first and then ask questions."

"Only yesterday I talked with Jeffrey Wallingford Pummery, who is the esteemed—I hope—factor of the world of Llayless and he told me Llayless was the most law-abiding world in the galaxy."

The man laughed derisively. "That's a good one. Llayless has got no government. It's got no laws—just a few regulations about mining. If it had laws, there would be no one to enforce them. It's got no law officers. It's got no judges and courts. On my mining claim, I'm the law—that's what my contract says. The only law on Llayless is what the person who controls a bit of ground can enforce at the end of a stick."

The man with the black beard had recovered enough to get to his feet and hobble around. "Never expected to get stunned out here in the mountains," he said resentfully. "What's this information you want?"

"I want to hear all about the murder of Douglas Vaisey by Roger Lefory."

"Never heard of either of them," the man with the black beard said. "What's that got to do with us?"

"Walt is a newcomer," the man with the drooping mustache explained to Dantler. "The murder happened before his time. I thought all that was dead history."

"Murders are never dead history."

"What do you want to know?"

"Everything," Dantler said. "By the way, who are you?"

"Kit Grumery. I'm the claim owner here. Everything I know about that murder won't take long to tell. My men work on shares, see. They get fed but nothing fancy. They make their own sleeping arrangements. Beyond that, whatever the ore smelts down to is divided into shares. It's hard work and poor pay, but we all hope to hit a mother lode and get rich. Lefory and Vaisey were working for the Laughingstock, and they came here taking a gamble on sharing in something big. Dougie was a nice kid, a good worker. Lefory was a loafer. He took so many breaks it sometimes was hard to say whether he was working or not, and he had a hell of a temper. He and Dougie got in an argument over Lefory not doing his fair share, and Lefory charged at him and brained him with a hand ax. Killed him instantly. That's all there was to it."

"Not quite all," Dantler said. "What did you do then?"

"Did what I always do when a worker is killed. Mining is danger-ous work. Death doesn't happen often, but it does happen, and there's a procedure to follow. We buried Dougie—I can show you his grave if you like. Regulations don't call for it, but we held a bit of a ceremony for him. Shorty Klein—he's working further up the moun-tain today—has an old Bible, and he read a couple of passages and did a prayer, and I carved a marker for Dougie's grave myself. As I said, he was a nice kid, and I liked him. That's all, except that I also took care of the paperwork."

"What sort of paperwork?"

"Every death has to be reported to the Llayless Record Section. It insists on knowing who's still on the planet. I also figured what Dougie had coming from his work share, and I filled out the form the Record Section requires and sent it down to Pummery along with a voucher for the money due Dougie and the few trifles of personal effects he owned. The Record Section is supposed to cash in a dead man's return ticket and put the amount received with the other assets the man had. Everyone arriving here has to place on file a fully paid return ticket to the world he came from or they won't let him off the ship."

"I know about that," Dantler said. "I suppose it's sort of a guaran-tee he won't become a public charge."

"Right. Records is supposed to cash the return ticket and send the money along with all of his other assets to his designated beneficiary. Whether it actually does this I couldn't say. And that's the whole story."

"You didn't report the murder to the police authorities?"

"What police authorities? I just told you—Llayless has got no gov-ernment. It's got no authorities, police or any other kind. Who would I report it to?"

"Then a murderer can't be arrested and brought to trial?"

"Who would arrest him, and who would hold his trial? There's no police. There's no court. There's no judge. There's no jail for wrong-doers. Actually, it was a dirty shame. Dougie was well liked, and Lefory was a jerk. Everyone was angry about what happened."

"But you let him carry on scot-free as though he hadn't done any-thing?"

"I wouldn't say that. We shouldered him right out of camp."

"How did you do that?"

"No one would talk with him. No one would work with him. No one would eat with him—we form teams and take turns cooking. No team would have him. No one would kip with him. After a couple of days of that, he left. Sneaked out of camp early one morning and walked over the mountain to the Laughingstock. It was almost a day before anyone missed him."

"That seems like a rather mild punishment for a murderer," Dantler observed dryly. "What happened to him after that?"

"He got a job at the Laughingstock. Llayless's mines are always short of labor. But we let the Laughingstock workers know about him, and he didn't stay there long. Probably they shouldered him, too."

"But you don't know that for certain."

"No, I don't know it for certain. But I know he didn't stay there long."

"Do you know where he went from there?"

"I never heard him mentioned again after he left the Laughingstock, but you can bet that the workers there passed the information about him along to workers at the next place he caught on."

Dantler stayed overnight. The men gave him what was, for the Last Hope, a fabulous luxury—a tent all to himself. The food was rough but filling. The other amenities were just a shade above zero. There was barely enough hot water—heated over a campfire—to go around. There was plenty of ore soup, though—a hot, stimulating drink made with local herbs—and it was obvious that no one at the camp went hungry. Early the next morning he walked back over the mountain to the Laughingstock. All of the camp's men came along to make certain he didn't get lost. The loaded mules came, too, and the men took turns pushing cartloads of ore.

"Paths look different going the other way," Kit Grumery explained.

At the Laughingstock settlement, he took his leave of his Last Hope companions and went directly to the office and asked to see the manager. A different clerk was on duty, and for a second time Dantler presented his credentials. He was admitted to the manager's office at once and greeted by Ed Mullard, a grizzled oldster who had spent his life scratching for pay dirt and finally rode to riches on the coattails of someone luckier than he who found the Laughingstock claim.

He scowled at Dantler's credentials, then scowled more fiercely at Dantler. "I hope you're not about to interfere with our operations. There's nothing for the GBI to investigate here."

"My information is that you harbored a murderer. That's what I want to know about."

Mullard leaned back and stared at Dantler. "If there's ever been a murderer on this claim, it's news to me."

"A man named Roger Lefory came to work for you immediately after murdering a fellow worker at Last Hope."

"Lefory," Mullard mused. "Yes, I do remember him because he was always complaining about something. But I had no idea he was a murderer."

"Tell me about him," Dantler said.

Mullard leaned back and meditated. "For one thing, he was the most accident-prone man I've ever met. Mining is a dangerous business, and things do happen, but with Lefory it got to be ridiculous. Tunnels only seemed to collapse while he was in them. Scaffolding gave way only when he was passing it. Machinery failed dangerously only when he was tending it. Hot water spilled only when he was there to get burned. He kept complaining that his fellow workers arranged these accidents, which of course was nonsense. No one could have arranged all that. They were the sort of things that are bound to occur from time to time, and he happened to be unlucky. Finally a gear broke on a tipcart loaded with ore, and he was buried up to his neck and had to be dug out. He just missed being buried alive. The next day he turned up missing. There's a passenger car on every ore train, so it's easy for men to desert if for any reason they don't like their work here."

"Do you know where he went?"

"To Pummery. That's where all the ore trains go. He found a job at one of the smelters. I received a notice with the usual request for his work history."

"Did you send down his personal effects and any wages he had due him?"

"By quitting without notice, he forfeited any wages owed to him. I know nothing about his personal effects. Probably he took with him anything he wanted to keep. He hadn't been here long enough to have accumulated much."

Obviously Mullard had nothing more to tell him, so Dantler boarded the passenger car on the next departing ore train and rode down to Pummery in a totally frustrated mood.

The world of Llayless had been named after an early explorer, but through eight sectors of space it was known as "Lawless." Among worlds, it was a genuine oddity—a single-owner world. Old Albert Nicols, the original owner, who had managed, by dint of rigged poker games, loans foreclosed with indecent haste, and questionable wills to consolidate several hundred claims into one title deed, had taken a young wife just before he died. By that time Llayless was an extremely wealthy mining world with only a tiny fraction of its potential being exploited, and the widow inherited everything. She immediately established her residence several sectors away on a world that offered far more comfort than the world of Llayless could have provided for her, and from that vantage point she kept close tabs on her accumulating mining royalties and gave generously to charities.

Single ownership was not the world's only peculiarity. It had no government. Those who leased land and mineral rights were responsible, by contract, for their holdings and everyone they permitted on them. Some administered them in a stern, paternal fashion; some were tyrannical dictators; a few ran their holdings congenially as partnerships. Occasionally one let things degenerate into rowdyism but only until the world's factor heard about it.

Finally, the world of Llayless was "Unnullified." This was a form of probation inflicted on all recently discovered and newly settled worlds. The sacred constitution of the Inter-World Federation guaranteed certain human rights and considerations throughout its territory, and a world that failed in this respect was nullified, which meant that it was totally embargoed. A world without government was placed in limbo with the label "Unnullified" until it got its act together. After a reasonable time the world would either be normalized or changed to Nullified status.

Birk Dantler had looked into the Llayless's history before he left on his assignment. He was startled to find that there had been no updating of its status since it was, as a newly settled world, marked "Unnullified." He took the matter to his superiors, who took it to their superiors. Someone had goofed. As a result, Dantler was given an important subsidiary mission. In addition to tracking down a murderer, he was to give the world a long-overdue evaluation of its status. If the unusual nature of the world posed any complications for him, he had the authority to recommend immediate reclassification to "Nullified."

Arriving on Llayless, Dantler discovered that custom and immigration procedures were both informal and simple. There almost weren't any. Each new arrival had to place on file a fully paid return ticket to the world he came from. His fingerprints and the name of his next-of-kin were recorded, but that was only so the Llayless Mining Corporation would know who was on the world just in case some other world's investigative branch should come looking, and so there would be someone to notify and send his property to in case he died. These formalities taken care of, a wave of the hand conferred the freedom of the planet.

One thing about this process puzzled Dantler. As the new arrival passed through the gate that opened on the world of Llayless, he was immediately swarmed upon by a dozen or so lean and voracious-looking men who reminded Dantler of a flock of vultures. He asked the man ahead of him in line who the vultures were.

"Labor brokers," the other replied. "Didn't anyone warn you? You have to watch yourself, or you may suddenly find you've signed away your life for the next seven years. If you catch so much as a glimpse of a piece of paper coming your way, put your hands in your pockets. If you find a stylus in your fingers that you don't remember picking up, throw it as far as you can. Be careful who you drink with. They have to get your signature and also your fingerprints on the contract, but no contract has ever been voided because the man who signed it claimed he was drunk."

When Dantler's turn came, he brushed the fingerprinting pad aside along with the rest of the formalities and passed his credentials across the counter: passport with several pages bearing arrival and departure stamps from various worlds, an embossed identification card, and a letter. The clerk scrutinized them in turn and, after giving Dantler a startled glance, turned to a computer, typed briefly, and accepted the result from a printer. He added one more stamp to Dantler's passport. Then, as an afterthought, he carefully printed a number beside it.

He handed Dantler the form the computer had produced. "You should keep this with your passport," he said. "You'll be asked for it when you leave Llayless. Just in case you lose it, which has happened, I've recorded your arrival number in your passport. If you lose that, there'll have to be a tedious investigation, so don't lose it. The town is only half a kilometer from the port, but don't try to walk there unless you're equipped with sand shoes. There's a conveyor you can ride, or there's a 'bus that's a little faster and a lot less comfortable."

He added, "Welcome to Llayless. I hope you enjoy your stay," and turned to the next new arrival. Towing his space trunk, Dantler passed through the gate and was surprised to be totally ignored by the labor brokers. The clerk must have given them some sort of signal.

Dantler headed directly for the exit and opted for the 'bus. When he arrived on a new world, he wanted to see as much as possible as quickly as possible, and he knew he wouldn't be seeing anything at all while riding in a conveyor tube. The 'bus was a sturdy, tracked conveyance, and a glance at it told a traveler all he needed to know about travel in the deserts of Llayless. Mountains loomed on all sides, providing a distant haze of superb beauty. The desert was a disaster of sand dunes and slag heaps. Crossing the former, the 'bus left a cloud of sand behind. With slag heaps, it was a cloud of dust.

Pummery, the principal commercial city of the world of Llayless, had been almost invisible when the spaceship was settling in for a landing. It was a complex of massive domes enclosing business buildings, residences, smelters, and the immense nuclear power plant, with tubes for the network of railway lines that extended in all directions like spreading tentacles. Domes and tubes were more than half buried in the shifting sands of a narrow, elongated desert. The spaceport, unfortunately, had to be kept cleared of sand, and a platoon of dozers worked full time at the task.

The domes and tubes were an afterthought engendered by necessity. In its remote past, which could have been as long ago as three or four decades, the municipality of Pummery had been a struggling desert mining town calling itself Struth. Then someone struck it rich, and the manipulators took over. After the usual period of underhanded contrivance and downright chicanery, Old Albert emerged triumphant.

When he died, his widow hired a factor, one Jeffrey Wallingford Pummery, to manage the world for her, after which she shook the sands of Llayless from her heels forever. One of the factor's first acts was to manipulate a name change. Llayless's principal commercial center, Struth, became Pummery, thus splashing the factor's own name prominently on the world's map. No one objected. As long as Pummery operated efficiently and honestly and kept her royalties coming, the widow didn't bother herself with minor things like name changes. The factor was, for all that Dantler had heard, a shrewd and honest operator who built for the future.

The Llayless desert was a terrible place for a world's commercial center, but Pummery was perfectly situated to serve mining operations in the mountains on all sides. The narrow-gauge electric railway lines bringing ore to the smelters from the mines were able to coast down the mountain slopes, thus hauling their loads at a profit because they generated electricity in the process. The only cost was for replacing their frequently worn-out brakes.

Those mines were rich enough to occupy the Llayless Mining Corporation for years to come. Until they played out, the remainder of the world would remain untouched.

The 'bus stopped in front of the Llayless Mining Corporation's world headquarters. Dantler climbed out along with several others who had come to Llayless on business, left his space trunk to be delivered to a sprawling, dilapidated, one-story building farther along the town's central street—its faded sign bore the message " . . . OTEL" —and stood regarding the headquarters building with puzzled scrutiny. Apparently Jeffrey Wallingford Pummery did not go in for luxury, as he was using the same ramshackle three-story building that had been Old Albert's headquarters. It hadn't even been treated to a new coat of paint for years.

Dantler's fellow passengers entered the building ahead of him. Either they were directed at once to the departments that concerned them or they already knew the way because they had vanished by the time Dantler entered. He approached the receptionist, a pert, overalled young lady with bluish blond hair. She eyed him disdainfully. The lobby proctor took in Dantler's appearance with a snort and decided not to like his looks. He took a step forward.

Dantler proffered a letter to the young lady—the same he had shown the clerk at the port. She glanced at it, glanced at Dantler again, and suddenly decided to read it slowly and with care. The proctor came forward and read over her shoulder. When the young lady had finished her reading and made a copy of the letter, the proctor took it and read it a second time.

His attitude had flip-flopped. "Mr. Pummery's personal offices occupy the third floor," he said politely. "If you will follow me, please, I'll show you to the tubes." The levitation tubes were J. Wallingford Pummery's one concession to modern comfort. Probably he became tired of negotiating three flights of stairs to and from his office several times a day.

The receptionist must have warned everyone that Dantler was coming. He moved as if by magic through the various barricades that Pummery had erected to protect himself from unwanted intruders. Five minutes later, having been shown into a cramped office that was as spartan as Dantler expected, Dantler was settled comfortably in a guest chair and scrutinizing the great man himself while a scowling Pummery scrutinized him. He might have been a retired university professor—tall, slender, neatly bearded, scholarly. The beard was gray, but Pummery looked young and energetic.

Dantler passed a letter across the desk. It was not the letter he had shown the receptionist—that one had functioned merely to get him into Pummery's presence. This one was highly confidential. Pummery read it with obvious astonishment.

"You're a Galactic Bureau of Investigation Officer?" he asked.

"Officer Dantler, at your service," Dantler murmured politely.

"Nonsense. The GBI doesn't serve anyone unless by doing so it forwards its own interests. You're here on a special inspection trip to reevaluate the world's status?"

Dantler nodded diffidently.

"The letter says you are also here to conduct an investigation. The Inter-World Council has something it wants investigated on Llayless?"

"It does."

Pummery tilted back in his chair and regarded him with puzzled interest. "This is a world without a government. For that reason, people call it a totally lawless world, and they couldn't be more wrong. The fact that a world has no government doesn't mean it has no laws. Humankind brings its own laws with it wherever it goes—sometimes like unwanted baggage it can't get rid of, but it always has them. They are an expression of the deep-seated customs and attitudes it must live by. Is the Inter-World Council trying to introduce its own brand of law and order here?"

"Surely you have read the Federation's constitution," Dantler murmured. "I'm here to evaluate the world's status as the constitution provides and to conduct an investigation of something that has already occurred. If my investigation confirms information the Bureau has received, then I will see that proper action is taken."

"What is it that they want investigated?"

"A murder."

"There has been a murder on Llayless?"

"There has. After I have confirmed that the murder has taken place and that the identity of the murderer has been reported to the GBI correctly, I intend to apprehend the murderer and bring him to justice."

Pummery took the time to read the letter through again, slowly. Then he touched a button and spoke in a normal tone of voice. "Mr. Jabek, please."

While they waited, Dantler amusedly counted the seconds. He had reached six when the door opened. As he expected, Pummery kept everyone who worked for him on his toes.

Pummery did not bother to introduce Jabek. Instead, he introduced Dantler. He said, "This is Birk Dantler, an officer of the GBI, the Galactic Bureau of Investigation. The GBI is the investigative arm of the Inter-World Council. He has been sent here on a confidential mission of inspection and investigation. Do you know what that means?"

"No, sir," Jabek answered apologetically.

"The Inter-World Council has a stranglehold on every world in the galaxy—if it chooses to apply it. At this moment, Officer Dantler is the most powerful man on the world of Llayless. If he finds this organization or any organization or individual on the world less than completely cooperative, he can express his dissatisfaction, and an absolute embargo will be placed on us. No ship will arrive; no ship will leave.

"You will prepare the necessary credentials for him. He can go wherever he likes, and transportation is to be arranged for him whenever he needs it; he is to see whatever he wants to see; he is to talk with whomever he wants to talk with. Any person who fails to cooperate fully will find him or herself on the next outbound spaceship. The credentials you give him should make that clear."

Pummery turned to Dantler. "I can order everyone on the world of Llayless to cooperate with you, but I have no control over what they say, and I can't make them tell the truth. Neither can I tell you anything about this murder myself because I have no knowledge about it.

"I want to make one thing clear. We may have no government here, but as I already mentioned, we are not without laws—though we don't call them that. We have rules of conduct that we impose on ourselves, and they make human society possible. Until you arrived I would have said lawless Llayless is the most law-abiding world in the galaxy. If there has been a murder on this world, the fact that I never heard of it doesn't mean that the crime hasn't been noticed and the murderer hasn't already been punished—under our form of law, not yours. If I can assist you further, come and see me."

He got to his feet and touched Dantler's hand briefly. Mr. Jabek murmured, "Come with me, please," and led him into the adjoining office.

Half an hour later, armed with every credential Mr. Jabek could provide for him, Dantler returned to the ground floor and nodded perfunctorily at the blue-blond receptionist as he passed her on his way to the exit.

Hunting for a murderer on a world without government was an entirely new experience for Dantler. Regardless of what Pummery had said, there was a principle that held true everywhere in the galaxy: No government meant no laws. As he left for the Last Hope mine, the reported scene of the murder, he wondered again what he would charge the murderer with when he caught him, and what court of justice he would bring him before on a world that had no courts.

Probably it would have to be an intergalactic court on some other world, but on strictly local issues, such courts usually applied the laws of the world on which the lawbreaking occurred. There would have to be some roundabout charge—perhaps based on the fact that by murdering Douglas Vaisey, Roger Lefory had summarily terminated his right to that nebulous old saw of life, liberty, and the pursuit of happiness. The attorneys would have the time of their lives with it, but Dantler was confident of a conviction. Murder was the most serious charge in the legal arsenal, and courts would lean over backward to properly punish a murderer—especially when the murder had occurred on an Unnullified world that had neither government, law, nor courts.

Now Dantler was back in Pummery again, having tracked his murderer to Pummery's huge Smelter No. 2. It was an all-electric operation—clean, quiet, and effectively temperature controlled. Dantler's credentials gave him direct and immediate access to its superintendent, a youngish-looking black man named Edwin Sharle, who seemed as quietly competent and efficient as his smelter.

He was completely unaware that he had harbored a murderer among his employees, but the name "Roger Lefory" was familiar to him. "The man was always complaining about something," he said. "He kept claiming that the other employees were making him the victim of all their pranks. They smeared glue on his chair, and when he sat in it, he couldn't get up. He had to cut his trousers off, and they were ruined. His fellow workers had a way of timing their breaks so he was left with all the work to do. They filled his locker with trash, and another time they balanced a can of paint so it dumped on him when he opened the locker's door. That's only the beginning of a list. I'm sure a record was made. Do you want to see it?"

Dantler shook his head. "What did you make of all that?"

"I checked his work record from the Last Hope mine and, before and after that, the Laughingstock. Everywhere he worked, he found excuses for not working. Many of the pranks he described sounded like fellow workers being fed up with his constantly shifting his workload to them. So I told him to try to be more friendly and cooperative with the people who worked with him and to do a little work himself."

"With what result?"

"He quit without notice. Went to one of the more distant mines, the Shangri-la, and got a job there. I know that because they asked me for his work record. I never heard him mentioned again."

Dantler's next stop was the Llayless Record Section, where he was given a computer station and access to the complete record of Roger Lefory—to the extent that the world kept records on one of its lesser residents. Lefory's entire employment history was there as far as the Shangri-la. Every employer, including the last one, remarked that the man was lazy and avoided work whenever he could. The file ended with a terse note from the Shangri-la manager, dated almost a year before. Employee Roger Lefory was missing from his job. There was nothing unusual about that—he had left every job he had held without notice—but this time there was no record that he had gone anywhere else. He had simply vanished.

Dantler made inquiries. There were a few solitary prospectors searching for paydirt on the far side of the mountains surrounding Pummery. Some of them had developed a knack for living off the country. There were edible plants, berries, and fruits. There were game birds and animals for those who had the skill to catch them. Most Llayless residents had no time for that sort of thing, but prospectors usually had little money and in any case didn't want to take the time for a long trip back to a commissary. There was nothing unusual about a man being missing for almost a year.

Before leaving for the Shangri-la mine, Dantler paid another call on Jeffrey Wallingford Pummery. The factor greeted him courteously and asked how he could be of service.

Dantler described his investigation to date. "A man was murdered," he said. "There are witnesses who saw it done. No report was made to anyone on the management level of the mines where Lefory worked, or to the smelter where he worked, or to world management because no report was required. The murderer was left free to drift from job to job. Now he has gone prospecting and may be difficult to find. This represents a flagrant violation of the Inter-World Federation's constitution—failing to protect the lives of your citizens by providing no mechanism for taking action against a murderer. I'm going to recommend that your world's status be changed immediately from 'Unnullified' to 'Nullified.' I'll get a spacegram off today. As the law requires, I am giving you written notice of that fact so you can prepare your defense. There will be a hearing, of course."

Pummery glanced at the paper Dantler handed to him and then handed it back. There was a faint smile on his face. "I suggest that you hold off with your report—and with your notification—until you have completed your investigation. You haven't visited the Shangri-la mine, yet. Surely your investigation will be incomplete without evidence from the last place Lefory is known to have worked."

Dantler studied him warily. He scented a trap. After a moment's thought, he said, "Certainly, if you prefer it. It probably won't delay things more than a day."

The Shangri-la was just as promising a mine as the Laughingstock, its manager—one Pierre Somler—told Dantler, but it was still in an early stage of development. Thus far its profits had been invested in machinery; the dwellings were shacks, and so was the office.

The manager vividly remembered Lefory. "The record said he was lazy. He was spectacularly lazy. On my visits to the diggings, I rarely found him working. He was always taking a break."

"But you kept him on because of the labor shortage," Dantler said wearily.

Somler nodded. "That, and because we always hope that a poor employee will change his habits. Usually that happens when dividends are paid and everyone else receives a tidy bonus. A poor employee's long list of demerits results in his receiving nothing. He immediately decides to be at the top of the list when the next dividends are declared. But it didn't happen that way with Lefory. Shiftless he was; shiftless he remained.

"Then there were his complaints about his fellow workers. He kept saying they were trying to 'get' him. He had the darndest accidents, some of them almost unbelievable. He wanted to be a heavy machine operator, but on his first try, a freak short circuit nearly electrocuted him. After that he wouldn't go near one of the machines. The head flew off a fellow worker's pickax and put him in the hospital for a few days. If it'd hit him in the head instead of the back, it would have killed him. That sort of thing. Finally he vanished."

"Was it a planned disappearance? I mean—did he accumulate supplies for a stay in the wilderness and take prospecting equipment with him?"

"I think he did. He had mentioned to one of the workers that he was going back to Pummery the next morning and leave Llayless on the first ship out. He thought this was an unlucky world for him, and he could do better starting fresh somewhere else. But that night someone broke into the commissary and took the sort of supplies a prospector would want, and a worker saw Lefory sneaking away on a mountain path with a pack on his back."

"Is there any other evidence that he is out there in the wilderness?"

"No. But it's the ideal place for him. No fellow workers he has to get along with, he can work whatever hours he sets for himself, and take a day off when he wants to. All he has to do is figure out how to eat regularly."

"And all I have to do," Dantler said, "is figure out how to catch him. A world without a government, and without any police force, is a poor place for a manhunt."

Jeffrey Wallingford Pummery said with interest, "Do you mean you've abandoned your search?"

"Right. Lefory is bound to show up sometime. I'll leave a warrant for him. You'll have to apprehend him the moment he appears."

"Solitary prospectors who go off into the blue are usually looking for gold. They show up only at long intervals to cash in their accumulation, and if they've been lucky, they may buy supplies that will last for years."

"If he shows up at all, the warrant will see that he is detained for galactic police authorities."

"Have you considered the possibility that he might live the rest of his life out without being seen again?" Pummery asked. "He might be able to cash in his gold without being seen if he has a confederate. Are you still intent on changing the status of this world to 'Nullified?' "

"I am."

"We'll contest the petition, of course. And we'll win."

"How can you possibly win? There is no doubt at all that organizations on Llayless harbored a murderer. Not only did they fail to punish him, but they helped him avoid punishment."

Pummery smiled. "I told you when you arrived—an Unnullified world, a world without government, can be far more law-abiding than your so-called normal worlds. According to the results of your own investigation, Lefory is one of the most severely punished men in galactic history."

"How do you figure that? No one punished him at all."

"Study your notes again. At the Last Hope mine, he was shouldered. At the Laughingstock, he was much more emphatically shouldered. Once he was almost killed. At Smelter No. 2, more of the same thing. The danger to his life was increasing. Finally, at the Shangri-la, he was escaping death by narrower and narrower margins.

"It isn't necessary for management to take a hand in the punishment of a murderer, you see. Every person on Llayless knows that if a Roger Lefory can murder in a fit of temper and escape the consequences, no person is safe. So the people of Llayless set about making an example of him. They put him through living hell, one place after another. And when he finally announced to a fellow worker that he was leaving Llayless, they gave his punishment the final twist."

"And what was that?" Dantler demanded.

"You've already answered your question: He disappeared. His fellow

workers so frightened him that he gave up his plan to return to
Pummery and leave the planet. He was afraid he wouldn't live long
enough to get there. Instead, he went to hide out beyond the mountains, thus condemning himself to perpetual hell. Don't you believe
for a moment that he is gleefully basking in the wilderness and
chuckling about how he got away with murder. He is eating plants
that make him sick and half starving because he hasn't the knack for
catching birds or animals. He simply isn't the type for solitary
prospecting. He wouldn't recognize paydirt if he fell in it. He desperately needs fellow workers he can shift his own share of work onto.
Running back to Pummery and using the return ticket he has on file
to get off the world is his kind of gambit, but he was too terrified to
try it.

"The sanctity of life is a basic law among humans everywhere. An
Unnullified world doesn't need the apparatus of government and
courts to punish murderers. Word of a murder circulates among
workers almost instantly. The murderer's deed dogs his tracks forever
after. It followed Lefory everywhere, and his fellow workers reacted
accordingly. If he shows up again, Llayless's community of workers
will resume where it left off. His punishment is already a legend that
will deter people from murder far into the future. Do you know how
many murders there have been on Llayless in its history?"

Dantler shook his head.

"Two," Pummery said. "One happened twenty-eight years ago.
That murderer's punishment is still remembered and still a deter-
rent—as Lefory's punishment will be for decades to come. How
many murderers do you know of on normal worlds who have been
released through lack of evidence or through legal manipulations? So
many you couldn't answer, I'm sure. On an Unnullified world, where
the people are the law, punishment is certain—and it is perpetual. It
will dog Lefory again if he ever emerges from the wilderness. He can't
escape it—can't escape the planet—because no one will let him."

"It sounds suspiciously like mob rule, which the Inter-World
Federation outlaws. That simply won't do."

"Ah, but mob rule—thoughtless mob punishment without proper
evidence—is an entirely different thing. It wouldn't have popular
support. Further, it would bring every management on Llayless

down on it. We simply couldn't permit that. Punishment of the mob would be official, immediate, and severe."

He got to his feet. "I'm pleased to be able to introduce you to the way the law works on a world without government—a lawless world. I'm sorry you can't stay longer. We are very strong on law but unfortunately weak in amenities, and I apologize for that."

He nodded politely. Dantler, feeling himself dismissed, left. He had reached the street before he remembered that he had failed to serve on Pummery the notice of his intention to recommend an immediate change in Llayless's status.

He took the paper from his pocket, hesitated, and then tore it into very small pieces. The pieces dropped almost at his feet, and he kicked at them as he walked away.

The Right's Tough

Robert J. Sawyer

"The funny thing about this place," said Hauptmann, pointing at
the White House as he and Chin walked west on the Mall, "is that the
food is actually good."

"What's funny about that?" asked Chin.

"Well, it's a tourist attraction, right? A historic site. People come
from all over the world to see where the American government was
headquartered, back when there *were* governments. The guys who
own it now could serve absolute crap, charge exorbitant prices, and
the place would still be packed. But the food really is great. Besides,
tomorrow the crowds will arrive; we might as well eat here while we
can."

Chin nodded. "All right," he said. "Let's give it a try."

The room Hauptmann and Chin were seated in had been the State
Dining Room. Its oak-paneled walls sported framed portraits of all
sixty-one men and seven women who had served as presidents
before the office had been abolished.

"What do you suppose they'll be like?" asked Chin, after they'd
placed their orders.

"Who?" said Hauptmann.

"The spacers. The astronauts."

Hauptmann frowned, considering this. "That's a good question. They left on their voyage—what?" He glanced down at his weblink, strapped to his forearm. The device had been following the conversation, of course, and had immediately submitted Hauptmann's query to the web. "Two hundred and ten years ago," Hauptmann said, reading the figure off the ten-by-five-centimeter display. He looked up. "Well, what was the *world* like back then? Bureaucracy. Government. Freedoms curtailed." He shook his head. "Our world is going to be like a breath of fresh air for them."

Chin smiled. "After more than a century aboard a starship, fresh air is exactly what they're going to want."

Neither Hauptmann nor his weblink pointed out the obvious: that although a century had passed on Earth since the *Olduvai* started its return voyage from Franklin's World, only a couple of years had passed aboard the ship and, for almost all of that, the crew had been in cryosleep.

The waiter brought their food, a Clinton (pork ribs and mashed potatoes with gravy) for Hauptmann, and a Nosworthy (tofu and eggplant) for Chin. They continued chatting as they ate.

When the bill came, it sat between them for a few moments. Finally, Chin said, "Can you get it? I'll pay you back tomorrow."

Hauptmann's weblink automatically sent out a query when Chin made his request, seeking documents containing Chin's name and phrases such as "overdue personal debt." Hauptmann glanced down at the weblink's screen; it was displaying seven hits. "Actually, old boy," said Hauptmann, "your track record isn't so hot in that area. Why don't *you* pick up the check for both of us, and *I'll* pay you back tomorrow? I'm good for it."

Chin glanced at his own weblink. "So you are," he said, reaching for the bill.

"And don't be stingy with the tip," said Hauptmann, consulting his own display again. "Dave Preston from Peoria posted that you only left five percent when he went out to dinner with you last year."

Chin smiled good-naturedly and reached for his debit card. "You can't get away with anything these days, can you?"

The owners of the White House had been brilliant, absolutely brilliant.

The message, received by people all over Earth, had been simple: "This is Captain Joseph Plato of the UNSA *Olduvai* to Mission Control. Hello, Earth! Long time no see. Our entire crew has been revived from suspended animation, and we will arrive home in twelve days. It's our intention to bring our landing module down at the point from which it was originally launched, the Kennedy Space Center. Please advise if this is acceptable."

And while the rest of the world reacted with surprise—who even remembered that an old space-survey vessel was due to return this year?—the owners of the White House sent a reply. "Hello, *Olduvai*! Glad to hear you're safe and sound. The Kennedy Space Center was shut down over a hundred and fifty years ago. But, tell you what, why don't you land on the White House lawn?"

Of course, that signal was beamed up into space; at the time, no one on Earth knew what had been said. But everyone heard the reply Plato sent back. "We'd be delighted to land at the White House! Expect us to touch down at noon Eastern time on August 14."

When people figured out exactly what had happened, it was generally agreed that the owners of the White House had pulled off one of the greatest publicity coups in post-governmental history.

No one had ever managed to rally a million people onto the Mall before. Three centuries previously, Martin Luther King had only drawn 250,000; the four separate events that had called themselves "Million-Man Marches" had attracted maybe 400,000 apiece. And, of course, since there was no longer any government at which to aim protests, these days the Mall normally only drew history buffs. They would stare at the slick blackness of the Vietnam Wall, at the nineteen haunted soldiers of the Korean memorial, at the blood-red spire of the Colombian tower—at the stark reminders of why governments were not good things.

But today, Hauptmann thought, it looked like that magic figure might indeed have been reached: although billions were doubtless watching from their homes through virtual-reality hookups, it did seem as if a million people had come in the flesh to watch the return of the only astronauts Earth had ever sent outside the solar system.

Hauptmann felt perfectly safe standing in the massive crowd. His weblink would notify him if anyone with a trustworthiness rating below 85 percent got within a dozen meters of him; even those who chose not to wear weblinks could be identified at a distance by their distinctive biometrics. Hauptmann had once seen aerial footage of a would-be pickpocket moving through a crowd. A bubble opened up around the woman as she walked along, people hustling away from her as their weblinks sounded warnings.

"There it is!" shouted Chin, standing next to Hauptmann, pointing up. Breaking through the bottom of the cloud layer was the *Olduvai*'s lander, a silver hemisphere with black legs underneath. The exhaust from its central engine was no worse than that of any VTOL aircraft.

The lander grew ever bigger in Hauptmann's view as it came closer and closer to the ground. Hauptmann applauded along with everyone else as the craft settled onto the lawn of what had in days of yore been the president's residence.

It was an attractive ship—no question—but the technology was clearly old-fashioned: engine cones and parabolic antennas, articulated legs and hinged hatches. And, of course, it was marked with the symbols of the pre-freedom era: five national flags plus logos for various governmental space agencies.

After a short time, a door on the side of the craft swung open and a figure appeared, standing on a platform within. Hauptmann was close enough to see the huge grin on the man's face as he waved wildly at the crowd.

Many of those around Hauptmann waved back, and the man turned around and began descending the ladder. The mothership's entire return voyage had been spent accelerating or decelerating at one g, and Franklin's World had a surface gravity 20 percent greater than Earth's. So the man—a glance at Hauptmann's weblink confirmed it was indeed Captain Plato—was perfectly steady on his feet as he stepped off the ladder onto the White House lawn.

Hauptmann hadn't been crazy enough to camp overnight on the Mall in order to be right up by the landing area, but he and Chin did arrive at the crack of dawn, and so were reasonably close to the front. Hauptmann could clearly hear Plato saying, "Hello, everyone! It's nice to be home!"

"Welcome back," shouted some people in the crowd, and "Good to have you home," shouted others. Hauptmann just smiled, but Chin was joining in the hollering.

Of course, Plato wasn't alone. One by one, his two dozen fellow explorers backed down the ladder into the summer heat. The members of the crowd—some of who, Hauptmann gathered, were actually descendants of these men and women—were shaking the spacers' hands, thumping them on the back, hugging them, and generally having a great time.

At last, though, Captain Plato turned toward the White House; he seemed somewhat startled by the holographic Great Eats sign that floated above the rose garden. He turned back to the people surrounding him. "I didn't expect such a crowd," he said. "Forgive me for having to ask, but which one of you is the president?"

There was laughter from everyone but the astronauts. Chin prodded Hauptmann in the ribs. "How about that?" Chin said. "He's saying, 'Take me to your leader'!"

"There is no president anymore," said someone near Plato. "No kings, emperors, or prime ministers, either."

Another fellow, who clearly fancied himself a wit, said, "Shakespeare said kill all the lawyers; we didn't do that, but we did get rid of all the politicians . . . and the lawyers followed."

Plato blinked more than the noonday sun demanded. "No government of any kind?"

Nods all around; a chorus of "That's right," too.

"Then—then—what are we supposed to do now?" asked the captain.

Hauptmann decided to speak up. "Why, whatever you wish, of course."

Hauptmann actually got a chance to talk with Captain Plato later in the day. Although some of the spacers did have relatives who were offering them accommodations in their homes, Plato and most of the others had been greeted by no one from their families.

"I'm not sure where to go," Plato said. "I mean, our salaries were supposed to be invested while we were away, but . . ."

Hauptmann nodded. "But the agency that was supposed to do the investing is long since gone, and, besides, government-issued money isn't worth anything anymore; you need corporate points."

Plato shrugged. "And I don't have any of those."

Hauptmann was a bit of a space buff, of course; that's why he'd come into the District to see the landing. To have a chance to talk to the captain in depth would be fabulous. "Would you like to stay with me?" he asked.

Plato looked surprised by the offer, but, well, it was clear that he *did* have to sleep somewhere—unless he planned to return to the orbiting mothership, of course. "Umm, sure," he said, shaking Hauptmann's hand. "Why not?"

Hauptmann's weblink was showing something he'd never seen before: the word "unknown" next to the text, "Trustworthiness rating for Joseph Tyler Plato." But, of course, that was only to be expected.

Chin was clearly jealous that Hauptmann had scored a spacer, and so he made an excuse to come over to Hauptmann's house in Takoma Park early the next morning.

Hauptmann and Chin listened spellbound as Plato regaled them with tales of Franklin's World and its four moons, its salmon-colored orbiting rings, its outcrops of giant crystals towering to the sky, and its neon-bright cascades. No life had been found, which was why, of course, no quarantine was necessary. That lack of native organisms had been a huge disappointment, Plato said; he and his crew were still arguing over what mechanism had caused the oxygen signatures detected in Earth-based spectroscopic scans of Franklin's World, but whatever had made them wasn't biological.

"I really am surprised," said Plato, when they took a break for late-morning coffee. "I expected debriefings and, well, frankly, for the government to have been prepared for our return."

Hauptmann nodded sympathetically. "Sorry about that. There are a lot of good things about getting rid of government, but one of the downsides, I guess, is the loss of all those little gnomes in cubicles who used to keep track of everything."

"We do have a lot of scientific data to share," said Plato.

Chin smiled. "If I were you, I'd hold out for the highest bidder.

There's got to be some company somewhere that thinks it can make a profit off of what you've collected."

Plato tipped his head. "Well, until then, I, um, I'm going to need some of those corporate points you were talking about."

Hauptmann and Chin each glanced down at their weblinks; it was habit, really, nothing more, but . . .

But that nasty "unknown" was showing on the displays again, the devices having divined the implied question. Chin looked at Hauptmann. Hauptmann looked at Chin.

"That *is* a problem," Chin said.

The first evidence of real trouble was on the noon newscast. Plato watched aghast with Chin and Hauptmann as the story was reported. Leo Johnstone, one of the *Olduvai*'s crew, had attempted to rape a woman over by the New Watergate towers. The security firm she subscribed to had responded to her weblink's call for help, and Johnstone had been stopped.

"That idiot," Plato said, shaking his head back and forth, as soon as the report had finished. "That bloody idiot." He looked first at Chin and then at Hauptmann, and spread his arms. "Of course, there was a lot of pairing-off during our mission, but Johnstone had been alone. He kept saying he couldn't wait to get back on terra firma. 'We'll all get heroes' welcomes when we return,' he'd say, 'and I'll have as many women as I want.' "

Hauptmann's eyes went wide. "He really thought that?"

"Oh, yes," said Plato. " 'We're astronauts,' he kept saying. 'We've got the Right Stuff.' "

Hauptmann glanced down; his weblink was dutifully displaying an explanation of the arcane reference. "Oh," he said.

Plato lifted his eyebrows. "What's going to happen to Johnstone?"

Chin exhaled noisily. "He's finished," he said softly.

"*What?*" said Plato.

"Finished," agreed Hauptmann. "See, until now he didn't have a trustworthiness rating." Plato's face conveyed his confusion. "Since the day we were born," continued Hauptmann, "other people have been commenting about us on the web. 'Freddie is a bully,' 'Jimmy stole my lunch,' 'Sally cheated on the test.' "

"But surely no one cares about what you did as a child," said Plato.

"It goes on your whole life," said Chin. "People gossip endlessly about other people on the web, and our weblinks"—he held up his right arm so that Plato could see the device—"search and correlate information about anyone we're dealing with or come physically close to. That's why we don't need governments anymore; governments exist to regulate, and, thanks to the trustworthiness ratings, our society is self-regulating."

"It was inevitable," said Hauptmann. "From the day the web was born, from the day the first search engine was created. All we needed was smarter search agents, greater bandwidth, and everyone being online."

"But you spacers," said Chin, "predate that sort of thing. Oh, you had a crude web, but most of those postings were lost thanks to electromagnetic pulses from the Colombian War. You guys are clean slates. It's not that you have *zero* trustworthiness ratings; rather, you've got *no* trustworthiness ratings at all."

"Except for your man Johnstone," said Hauptmann, sadly. "If it was on the news," and he cocked a thumb at the wall monitor, "then it's on the web, and everyone knows about it. A leper would be more welcome than someone with that kind of talk associated with him."

"So what should he do?" asked Plato. "What should all of us from the *Olduvai* do?"

There weren't a million people on the Mall this time. There weren't even a hundred thousand. And the mood wasn't jubilant; rather, a melancholy cloud hung over everyone.

But it *was* the best answer. Everyone could see that. The *Olduvai*'s lander had been refurbished, and crews from Earth's orbiting space stations had visited the mothership, upgrading and refurbishing it, as well.

Captain Plato looked despondent; Johnstone and the several others of the twenty-five who had now publicly contravened acceptable standards of behavior looked embarrassed and contrite.

Hauptmann and Chin had no trouble getting to the front of the crowd this time. They already knew what Plato was going to say, having discussed it with him on the way over. And so they watched the faces in the crowd—still a huge number of people, but seeming positively post-apocalyptic in comparison to the throng of a few days before.

"People of the Earth," said Plato, addressing his physical and virtual audiences. "We knew we'd come back to a world much changed, an Earth centuries older than the one we'd left behind. We'd hoped—and those of us who pray had prayed—that it would be a better place. And, in many ways, it clearly is.

"We'll find a new home," Plato continued. "Of that I'm sure. And we'll build a new society—one, we hope, that might be as peaceful and efficient as yours. We—all twenty-five of us—have already agreed on one thing that should get us off on the right foot." He looked at the men and women of his crew, then turned and faced the people of the Free Earth for the last time. "When we find a new world to settle, we won't be planting any flags in its soil."

The Shackles of Freedom

Mike Resnick & Tobias S. Buckell

I came to New Pennsylvania because I was looking for a world with no government, no laws, nothing to hinder me from doing what I pleased. The colonists here hadn't liked the laws back on Earth, so they set up shop, free of all bureaucracy and all regulations.

What I never bargained for was having to live with the consequences of that freedom.

Mark Suderman was dying on my operating table. His plain blue clothing, stained dark with blood, lay crumpled on the floor. I tried to avoid his brothers' frightened glances. There was nothing more I could tell them, except to pray.

They couldn't know it, but he was a dead man before I ever got a chance to examine him. I simply didn't have the tools to save his life.

I sighed deeply. So much for freedom. This was the twenty-third time I had the freedom to watch a man die that I could have saved.

Hooves clip-clopped in the distance and then echoed their way up the driveway. The rest of the Suderman family had arrived.

"Stay here," I told the brothers, then walked out through the dining room to my porch. A plank squeaked as I stopped next to the swing. Mr. Suderman, his hat in hand, stared straight up at me from the bottom of my tiny set of bleached stairs.

I looked down at him, sighed, and gestured to the door. He climbed the three steps and passed by me, but his rough, callused hand grabbed my shoulder for a brief instant before he went inside. His wife sat stoically in the buggy, her seat rocking on its suspension slightly as she shifted her weight from side to side. The wind tugged at the strings of her bonnet, and the light from our three moons cast shadows across her face.

I had a sudden impulse to walk over to the buggy—but what could I say? That I might have cured him on some world they couldn't even see, let alone pronounce?

I had come here because I knew they needed a doctor. So what if they were Amish? There was no constitution, there were no laws prohibiting me from practicing my trade. There were no restrictions at all.

Except for the Amish themselves.

The sun set by the time the elders left with the Sudermans. I began cleaning the table to the flickering light of kerosene lamps. In the brown light it cast, the blood wasn't so noticeable, and not nearly as accusatory.

I could smell manure on the floor, tramped in by Mark's brothers. The men's sweat also filled the room, reminding me how unsterile the area was. Finally I left the house and walked down to the far edge of my small, neglected garden with the mop bucket.

The misshapen weeds seemed to erupt in fierce protest when I emptied the bucket. Tiny weasel-shaped creatures with scaly skin chittered at me and scampered off.

My house lay close inside a cluster of farms and roads. Just beyond them lay an unfamiliar forest full of alien species creeping in and mixing with our own. I knew the weeds in my own garden. But behind the scraggly dandelions and patchy grass, spirals of unearthly flowers moved in and out of the shadows to the rhythm of the wind.

Instead of going back inside, I sat on the porch swing and shivered. The fourth moon—the largest of the quartet—edged over the hills and made silhouettes of the neighbor's barn.

I'd never lost so many lives in such a short time, and I was getting sick of funerals.

It didn't make any sense. I was free to try to convince them to let me save them. They were free to die unnecessarily. And there was no one, no higher authority I could appeal to. Except God.

And unlike me, they talked to Him every day, welcomed Him into their houses and the lives. They *knew* He was on their side.

I sighed and went back into the house.

Mark hadn't died doing anything glamorous like beating back the wild forest of a new planet. He'd been milling grain, and had fallen between the giant wheels. The hardwood cogs chewed him up, spit him out, and left him for me and God—and God washed His hands of the matter.

At the Yoders' I pulled on Zeke's reins. He snorted and plodded to a nonchalant stop just short of the weathered post I usually tied him to. One of the little Yoders, Joshua, walked down to greet me.

"*Guten* morning," he said, mixing his German and English with a smile.

"Good morning, Joshua," I replied. I clambered out of my buggy, then reached back in to retrieve my black bag. Of all my visits, I looked forward to seeing the Yoders the most.

Joshua eyed Zeke with a critical eye.

"Your horse is getting old. How much longer will he be pulling you around? My dad could sell you a good one, with straight legs and a strong back and the look of eagles."

A fast talking six-year-old, this Joshua. Somehow I knew he wouldn't spend the rest of his life on New Pennsylvania.

Unless he contracted a serious disease. Or broke a leg. Or . . .

"No thank you," I said. "I think old Zeke will hold out just fine for me." In response Zeke broke wind and swished his tail.

Joshua giggled and ran back toward the house, his bare feet kicking up small puffs of dirt.

Joshua's mother came out to the porch. The hem of her black dress scraped the dirty wooden floor planks, and her white blouse had blue stains all over it. Several strands of honey-brown hair had escaped the edges of her bonnet. She brushed at them.

"Dr. Hostetler," she greeted me. "Good morning."

"Good morning, Mrs. Yoder." I walked onto their porch. Several giggling kids ran out the door past me. I looked around, but didn't see Rebecca anywhere.

"I'll tell Ben and Esther you're here," she said. "Please, come in."

I stepped in. The house smelled of food. Fresh-baked bread sat on the counter by the large iron range, and it appeared that Mrs. Yoder was taking advantage of the hot stove to put a cake in as well.

David Yoder, his full beard as dark as the unkempt hair crammed into his straw hat, shook my hand.

"You ministered to Suderman's son," he said. "God bless him, that was a fine boy. A tragedy."

The tragedy was that none of you would let me bring my skills to bear on him.

Mrs. Yoder took a stick and stirred the coal bin under the range. She opened the oven for a quick peek and waved her hand over it. "We'll have to pray for Betty," she said.

That brought back the image of Betty Suderman sitting in her buggy outside my house, waiting for the news of her son's death. I forced it back into my subconcious when I saw Ben and Esther coming down the stairs. Ben's beard had just started growing in, a sign that he was no longer a bachelor. Esther unconsciously held her arms protectively over her stomach.

I shook Ben's hand while Esther smiled nervously at me.

"Let's see what we have here," I said. I undid the clasp on my little black bag and opened it up. The look on Esther's face said that Pandora's box had nothing on my medical bag.

There is nothing so amazing as hearing the heartbeat of a tiny human being inside of its mother's womb. But amazing as the experience was, I had another sobering thought: here was another little person who had better never come down with a disease, or undergo a crippling accident.

I took the stethoscope away from Esther's belly.

"Everything seems okay," I said. I smiled reassuringly. Although, without any scans, I couldn't be absolutely certain. A sonogram to look at the baby would have been nice; DNA tests to make sure to make sure everything was okay after the birth would have been even better. There was no law prohibiting it; just a belief that was a thousand times stronger than any law.

Esther coughed. She stood up with her proud husband, linking her arm through his. They walked back up the creaky steps.

"Asa and I'll be out in the field after lunch," David Yoder said to his son's back.

"I'll be there," replied Ben.

David winked at me. "There'll be a raising happening soon enough for the two of them. Will you join?"

It would be another chance to see Rebecca. I tried to hide my enthusiasm. "We'll see what my schedule is like," I said. "But, yes, I would like to join."

David looked around. "We're almost ready to bring in this year's wheat. Weather's been good. Real good. The strange seasons throw you off a bit, but I think I've got it figured this year. There'll be threshing soon, eh?"

He could have used any of a dozen instruments to predict the weather to a fraction of a degree, the rainfall to a tenth of a centimeter. No law against it. Just a moral repugnance to anything that would make his life easier. We'd argued it many times. I'd never come close to winning.

David kept trying to rope me into coming over to lend an able hand. And in truth I wanted to go. The women would cook blackberry and grape pies. There would be freshly churned butter and baked bread. Washing off a day's worth of hard sweat from forking wheat into the wheels of the thresher, joking with all the other men, eating that special food—it was an appealing picture. It was almost my only pleasure on this world, other than being in Rebecca's company.

Despite my privileged place in the community as a doctor, it was their nature to be wary of me. I had a very advanced education, which didn't sit too well with them, and technology was a very important part of my job (or at least it should have been)—but it was that very technology that was viewed as dangerous to the health of the community. No one ever told me I couldn't use it. I had the freedom to offer it to them; they had the freedom to refuse it. We were both batting a thousand: I always offered, they always refused.

Girls passed by us with white tablecloths, utensils, plates of bread, and half-moon pies. Someone brought out a tureen of bean soup. I pulled my watch out. "Brother Yoder," I said. "I'm falling behind already, I have to go."

David frowned. "You'll miss church tonight?"

"I'm afraid so."

"I don't know if that's good," he said.

"I have to see the Andersons' son and tend to him. They say he's had a cold for a few days, but it could be worse."

"There should always be time for God," David told me.

"A long time ago God spoke to me," I lied, trying to hide my irritation, "and charged me with curing the sick."

To which David could make no argument. He had been chosen by lot to be a preacher. His sermons were well thought out, I was told. I avoided Sundays, and sermons, and all that went with it. I could always easily be elsewhere. David and some of the other Elder preachers sensed that, but again, they usually made an allowance for me.

"I really must go," I said.

"*Ja*, well," David shook my hand and paid my fee. "Make sure you get some bread from my wife before you leave," he said.

"Thank you."

When I walked out the door I looked around. Rebecca stood out on the porch, just beside the door. She smoothed down her spotless white apron and smiled.

"Hi," she said.

She had her mother's honey-brown hair and hazel eyes.

I smiled back. "Hello, Rebecca."

"It's good to see you again."

I could see David Yoder looking at me through the window. He was no fool. Someday soon I would have to tell him that I had nothing but honorable intentions toward his daughter. Which was true: marrying Rebecca was about the only thing that would make all the unnecessary dead men and women bearable.

"I heard you say you might make the raising?" said Rebecca.

"Will you be there?"

"Of course," Rebecca said with a shy smile. "I'll be helping *Mutter* with the cooking."

"Then I will do my best."

"I hope you do make it," Rebecca said. "There's singing and dancing afterwards."

Their notion of singing and dancing wasn't about to put the dance halls of Earth and some of the colony worlds out of business, but it was better than nothing. Maybe, just maybe, for a few hours that day, no one would get hurt. No one would come down with a disease that I wasn't permitted to cure. Maybe.

I checked my pocket watch. I would have to push Zeke faster than his usual meander to make it on time. But it was worth every delayed minute.

"I would really enjoy dancing," I told Rebecca. "I have to leave now. I'm very late."

She took my hand and shook it. Her skin was cool to the touch, and feathery.

"*Gute nacht*, Rebecca," I said.

I drove Zeke at a quick clip through the forest, my mind thinking fuzzy, pleasant things about Rebecca. I didn't hear the distant rumble until Zeke began to perk his ears up.

It began low, but soon became a high pitch as I saw the triangular shape approach. Zeke slowed and sidestepped uneasily.

"Easy," I said.

The sound jumped to earsplitting. The ship buzzed just over the treetops, thundering past on a flyby, the pilot and his companions sightseeing no doubt. I craned my head back and caught just a flash of the number on the side: DY-99. The buggy bounced as Zeke began moving off the road.

"Whoa!" I yelled, pulling on his reins.

Zeke veered back toward the road, then stopped. He whinnied and looked back down at the bushes. A long creeper held his rear left leg. Hundreds of yellow barbs along the vine punctured his stifle, and blood began to trickle down toward his hoof.

I looked down at the gray floorboards of the buggy. The creepers might move up for me. *Calm yourself*, I thought; *nothing is gained by panic*.

"Come on, Zeke," I shouted, snapping the reins.

He strained against the creeper, pulling, his muscles quivering. Then he started kicking and bucking, until I heard a tearing sound, as he finally pulled free. Strips of torn flesh hung from his leg. He moved back away from the creeper, onto the road, but the buggy was still in the bush.

I snapped the reins again, and Zeke pulled at the buggy. We didn't move.

"Whoa."

I took my black bag and jumped out onto the road. Two long vines anchored the rear wheels. Zeke started straining at his harness again.

"*Whoa!*" It didn't seem to have any effect. Zeke still pulled, staring past me with determination and flared nostrils.

I started taking off his harness. My fingers slipped in under the buckle, and got caught as Zeke let up, then lunged forward again. Creepers began moving up the buggy toward Zeke. I waited for his next pause and lunge, then let go. I landed painfully, hitting my tailbone on a sharp rock.

I pulled a never-used scalpel out of my bag and tried to cut a vine away from Zeke's legs, but it was too small and the vine was too thick, and Zeke wouldn't hold still. He whinnied and kicked, but his efforts were becoming weaker, and finally he just stopped.

The vines wrapped around his legs and began to pull him down the side of the road. He pawed with his front legs at the road, dragging gravel and dirt in with him. Then he gave up with a snort.

The bushes rustled and sighed as they pulled Zeke in, and everything grew quiet.

Shaken, I stood up with my black bag.

The Andersons were a long walk away, but I could make it out of the forest road before dark. As long as I stayed in the middle of the road, I would be okay.

I limped off down the road, wondering what mad whim had made us come to this planet in the first place.

The Andersons were kind enough to give me a lift back to my house, though it meant a long drive. It was dark, and Mr. Anderson kept to the very middle of the road. I looked away as we passed the spot where Zeke had lost his battle for life.

Once I was back in my house I struck matches and held them over my gaslights. They lit the room with a *phoomph!* of pale flickerings. I made dinner: pasta and a red sauce one of the ladies bottled for me, and some stale bread. Tonight would be a good night to just go to bed early, I thought, instead of poring over my library of books, hoping to find old-fashioned ways to mimic modern medicine.

But instead someone thumped at the door.

I opened it to find David Yoder standing on my porch.

"What is it?" I asked. "Is it Esther?" Probably she was going into labor too soon. I turned, thinking about forceps, wondering how I could convince the old man to let me use them in his house.

"No," David said. "It isn't Esther. Rebecca collapsed . . ."

I stood there, dazed, until my mind caught up with the rest of me. I grabbed my bag in a daze and followed David out to his buggy.

"Creepers," I explained.

David nodded. He'd lost a horse or two to them as well.

Rebecca sat in her bed. Esther stood over her with a sponge. They thought she had a fever of some sort, but Rebecca looked like she had recovered already. She smiled when she saw me and apologized.

"I'm feeling much better now," she said. "I think it has passed."

"Well, let's make sure," I said. "Have you had any other dizzy spells?"

Rebecca chewed her lip.

She had.

"Are there any strange lumps on your body?"

The quizzical look in return sank me. I ran through the questions. And then under the watchful eye of her father I ran my hands over her pale white body, looking for the intrusions. She sucked in her breath slightly when I ran my fingers up the sides of her ribs.

"Your hands are cold," she said.

I didn't look at her face, but continued. It was bittersweet that the first time I touched her body was for medical reasons.

And that I found what I knew I had to find.

My lovely Rebecca had breast cancer. Maybe if she were more aware of her body, she would have been worried sooner. But even then, what could I have done on this world that permitted her the freedom to die in agony? It was advanced, metastasizing no doubt, spreading throughout her entire body.

When I stood up David Yoder caught my eye and nodded me out the door. We walked down through the kitchen to his porch.

"You know what's wrong," he said. It was not a question.

I nodded.

"Well?" he demanded.

"She has cancer."

I sat on the bench, leaned my head against the rough plank wall, and blinked. My eyes were a bit wet.

David didn't say anything after that. He stood near me on the porch for a while, then went into the house. Ben came out.

"Dad says to use one of our horses. I'll take you out to the barn."

I didn't reply. Ben sat next to me and clapped my shoulders.

"It'll be okay," he said. "God will protect her."

I looked the boy straight in the eye. Was he really that naive?

I woke up numb. The alarm clock rang until I slapped the switch down, my motions every bit as mechanical as the clock's.

The bed creaked as I sat on its edge. Two days' worth of half-open books lay all around me, some of them buried in my covers.

Candle wax dripped over the edges of a plate on my bed stand, the translucent stalactites almost reaching to the floor. I picked the nearest book up. The margin had a scribble in it: *DY-99*. Underneath it I had written a single question mark.

"Brother Hostetler?" came the strong shout of David Yoder from my front door. "Are you awake?

"Yes."

I stood up and pulled on my clothes, tying my rope belt off in a quick knot. A faceful of cold water dashed away my morning fuzziness. David's buggy waited outside, the horse looking as impatient as David was to get going.

Raisings were probably the most popular depiction of the culture among outsiders. Maybe it was just that it was a very attractive picture of community, and that was something they had in abundance. Many hands make light work, and there were many hands here at the edge of Yoder's property. Tables held food, lines of breads, preserves, and fruit juices. Soups simmered in iron pots. Women chatted and kids ran around, dodging around legs, tables, chairs, and whatever else served as a convenient obstacle course.

And the men gathered around the foundation of what would become Ben's home. We set to building his house together. It was more than just a community event, but a gift. When we were done Ben would have a home. A beginning.

We toiled together under the sun, hammering joints, then pulling walls up with ropes. Time passed quickly. The frame was up at lunch, and we broke to eat. Then we continued. At some point in mid-evening I stepped back, sweaty and out of breath, and looked up at a complete house.

They could have ordered a pre-fab, of course. It would have gone up faster and lasted longer. No law against it. But . . .

At the meal, when all the men sat in rows at the tables and ate, I walked over to David Yoder's house. Rebecca sat on the back stairs, looking out over the fields at the gathering. She had her skirt tucked neatly under her legs.

I sat next to her. We could just see the picnic tables over the rows of wheat shifting with the changing directions of little wind gusts.

"How are you feeling?" I asked.

"Much better," she said.

"Why aren't you out there, then?"

"Father told me to stay here, and rest myself."

I reached over and held her hand. She looked down at it.

"When you touched me . . ." she began. She caressed my hand. "I liked that." Suddenly she blushed and looked away.

We sat there silently for a long time, watching the stalks of wheat dance, running our fingers each over the other's.

"Are you frightened?" I asked at last.

"I was mad," Rebecca said. "Now I'm scared. I've done everything right. I go to church. I respect my parents. I do my best to be kind to all. Why is God punishing me?" She squeezed my hand, and pulled it to her cheek. "I don't want to die."

DY-99, I thought.

"You don't have to."

Rebecca looked up at me, curious, hope in her eyes.

"You know a cure?"

"There are many cures, though I have never been permitted to apply them here," I answered. "If we leave, we can go to the spaceport. You heard the Englishers' ship land. They haven't left yet. They will study the area for a bit, look around to make sure the spaceport is okay, and then leave again. They can take us to a hospital. We can easily cure you there."

Rebecca grabbed my forearm.

"But would they take us up with them?"

"Yes." One of the reasons they kept the spaceport cleared, and a regular schedule, was for reasons like this. A small percentage of the inhabitants changed their mind and took the subtle offer.

Rebecca leaned against me. "My parents will not approve."

"They can't stop you," I said. "This is your life we're talking about." I kissed her hair. It smelled of fresh bread and pumpkin pie. "Come with me."

She stood up, letting go of my hand. "The hospital," she said. "Can they . . . really . . . ?"

"Yes. Don't pack anything," I told her. "Just be ready."

"Tonight?"

I looked back down the road we would have to take to get to DY-99. "Later tonight."

Rebecca walked back into the house. I saw her falter for a second, and she held on to the edge of a table for support. I winced.

I approached David. I felt wrong for deceiving him slightly as I asked him about a good deal for one of his horses.

He smiled and stroked his beard.

"We wondered how many more days it would take before you got tired of asking for rides," he said. He named a price and I agreed on the spot. I could have dickered a little, but I wanted to go home as soon as I could.

We walked to the stables, and David led my new horse out. He was a sturdy young fellow. I chose not to pay too much attention, though, as I would be leaving him behind soon enough.

"*Herr* Doctor," David said. "You still feel badly about young Suderman?"

"Yes," I said. "I could have saved him."

"All the good health in the world would be useless with an empty life, or in a community that had rotted away."

"If there is no one alive to appreciate the community," I said, "then it is all pointless."

"You believe this is all pointless, then."

"No." I leaned my head against the horse, smelling its musky sweat. It shifted. "No. But it *is* wasteful." I broke into the words of the Hippocratic oath: "Into whatsoever house I shall enter, it shall be for the good of the sick to the utmost of my power . . . and then to also believe in the community and follow our practices."

"Did you anticipate being torn like this? Before you came to New Pennsylvania?"

"No," I said. "I was wrong. I thought on a world with total freedom that a doctor would be free to cure the sick."

"But you *do* tend to the sick."

"With methods and cures that haven't changed in five hundred years," I said bitterly. "Out there"—I waved my hand at the stars—"they replace hearts and lungs as easily as you replace a torn shirt. Yet *here* . . ."

"You should have looked deeper into your heart before making the decision to come here."

"Then who would have tried to save Mark Suderman?" I said. "I lose far too many patients, patients I could save anywhere else—but I do save *some*."

"He was saved the day he made the decision to join the church," David Yoder said with a certainty that I wished I possessed. About anything.

"It's getting near dark," I said. "I will be going now."

"*Gute nacht.*"

I pushed the horse to a run after I was out of sight.

I threw two suitcases of clothes together. In my desk I pulled out something I never thought I would need, but had kept anyway. It was a wallet, and inside were plastic cards that on any other world would link me to lines of credit and old friends. I hitched the new horse to my spare buggy and tossed the suitcases in the back.

A horse and buggy turned onto the gravel of my drive. I was sure it was David Yoder, but I was wrong. Two Elders, Zebediah Walshman and his brother, Paul, pulled aside the storm curtains.

"William Hostetler?"

I walked up to the buggy.

"Yes."

"We talked to Brother Yoder. He feels you are going through a crisis," Paul said.

Zebediah looked over at my buggy. "Are you leaving for a while, William?"

"Possibly," I said.

"You are going to the Englanders?"

I didn't reply.

"We can't deny you that choice," Paul said. "But you will not take Rebecca with you."

They turned the buggy back around and rattled off down the road. My heart pounded, my throat dried with nervousness. I walked back to my buggy and kicked at a wheel with my boot. The pain was briefly satisfying.

The air was chilly, and as I turned up the road toward the house I extinguished the buggy's road lamp. I stopped the horse a bit down from the usual post, tying him to a tree. I patted his neck and jumped the ditch onto David Yoder's farm.

It took me a few long minutes in the pitch black to find a ladder. The notion of it—a clandestine meeting with a ladder in the twenty-third century—struck me as ludicrous. But there was nothing ludicrous about the purpose of it. I walked it over to the point under Rebecca's window and leaned the ladder against the side of the house as gently as I could.

She was waiting. She opened the window, bunched up her skirts, and got onto the ladder. It creaked as she came down step by agonizing step.

I led her around the house toward the waiting buggy.

We didn't get far before David Yoder's gentle but firm voice came from the porch.

"Rebecca, come back inside the house," he said.

She froze.

"Come on," I said. "Keep walking. You're free to leave. He can't stop you."

"I can't stop you," David agreed. "But think about what you are leaving. Rebecca, you are already saved, no matter what you do here. But when you leave, you will no longer be able to come back. You will be healthy, but unable to ever see us or speak to us again. Do you think there will be a family out there, with the Englanders, for you? What sort of lives do they lead? Good lives, or will they be confused, and spiritually cluttered, caught up with worldly goods." He paused. "Remember," he concluded, "if you leave, you can never come back. Your children can never come back."

Rebecca's tears trickled down her cheeks and collected along her jaw. "I can't do this!" she told me. "I can't!"

"Then you'll die," I said. "Probably within a couple of months. And in terrible pain that I am not permitted to alleviate on this world." I took off my hat, trying to do something useful with my hands.

"I know," she said. She brushed the side of my face with her hand and kissed me lightly on the lips. "I'm sorry, but I cannot be other than what I am. Better to die as what I am than to live as what I am not."

I watched her go back up into the house.

David and I stood there watching each other.

"She's free to go," I said.

"She was never free to go," said David. "There are certain laws that are unwritten, and these are the most powerful laws of all."

"You've signed her death warrant," I said bitterly.

"Do you think I *want* her to die?" he demanded, and the light of the four moons reflected off the tears running down his cheeks. "This is God's will, not mine. Never mine!"

And I suddenly realized that he was caught in the same web that had ensnared Rebecca and me. I had thought, just a moment ago, that I hated David Yoder. Now I knew that I could never hate him; I could only pity him, as I pitied us all.

"What will you do now, Dr. Hostetler?" he asked.

"I don't know."

I turned and began walking across his yard.

I rode the horse hard. My hat blew away, and the cold wind played with my hair. The horse started to lather by the time I saw my house, and I slowed us down, struck by remorse. There was no reason to take my anger out on the poor beast.

I hadn't cried in a long time, but I cried that night.

And along with crying, I examined my life and my options. DY-99 was only a few miles away. It would be so easy to get on it, to go out into the galaxy where I could use all my skills.

And if I did, who would take care of Rebecca? Who would deliver Esther's child, and help make sure it grew into a healthy adult? Who would even try to save all the Mark Sudermans after I left?

I turned the buggy around. With a snap of the reins I sent us both trotting back toward the Yoders. In the coming days and weeks I was going to preside at two more miracles, the miracle of death and the miracle of birth. I was going to do it under adverse conditions, like a racehorse carrying extra weight, but Rebecca had not asked to die and Esther's child has not asked to be born, so in a way we were all running handicapped.

In a moment of clarity, I realized that it just meant that we had to try harder. If we were already saved, then it was only right that God wanted a little extra effort in return, whether it was dying with grace or struggling to save people who placed so very many restrictions on their savior.

Somewhere along the drive back, I took the wallet from my pocket and threw it into the dark forest along the road.

A Reception at the Anarchist Embassy

Brad Linaweaver

"He's the most conservative man you'll ever meet."

The speaker was an attractive woman, although Special Agent Palmer didn't approve of her surgically implanted third eye that regarded him from an otherwise placid brow. He couldn't get used to these modern fashions, preferring instead an old-fashioned girl with a wedding ring in her navel.

Giving one of her breasts a friendly squeeze (and grateful that there were only two of them) he turned his attention to the gentleman in question. The man certainly stood out in the crowd.

"I had a professor like him once," said Palmer. "He probably thinks the world went to hell in the twenty-third century."

She laughed. "You're almost right but try the twenty-first."

He was surprised. "So tell me, Bretygne, why do I need to converse with this genuine eccentric?"

"Because," she breathed into his ear while returning his friendly squeeze at a lower altitude, "he will provide invaluable assistance when we exchange pleasantries with the ambassador. You see, your crazy Mr. Konski is actually a fan of that old man's books."

In all the miserable time he'd spent on the self-styled anarchist

planet Lysander, Palmer had not learned that Konski read any con-
temporaries. He pulled his forelock, the usual method of expressing
thanks to a comrade. The Lady Bretygne Lamarr always did her
homework.

"You'll put in a good word for me in your report?" she teased him.

"Why bother? They never read mine but settle for the oral brief-
ing. Now you, my dear, they actually read."

"Flattery has always been your strongest suit." With that, she
kicked off on her disc and scooted in the direction of the Amazing
Conservative Man.

Palmer wasn't lazy enough to use a disc in low gravity. With a hop
and a jump he was right next to her. Admittedly that sort of calisthenics was discouraged but he was good at it and hadn't knocked
anyone over yet.

Professor Bernard Astaroth greeted them with a broad smile. "My
darling girl," he said to Bretygne, squeezing her other breast (which
fine point was noted by Palmer's acute skills at espionage).

"Allow me to introduce Diplomat First Class Palmer, attached to
the United States of Earth." She got that out in one breath.

"No first name?" quizzed the professor.

"I'm not partial to them."

Bretygne laughed for him and the professor kept the conversation
going with, "I understand that we both enjoy Lady Lamarr's way with
words."

"You're too kind," she replied, switching on a phase-three blush in
her normally pale cheeks.

"She tells me you're a writer."

"Yes, on aestheto-politics with a heavy emphasis on history."

"Orthodox?" asked Palmer, eyebrows raised.

"Would we be here together tonight if I were?" The professor
smiled.

Bretygne thought it politic to change the subject. "Palmer spent a
full quarter on Lysander."

"Before or after the insurrection?" asked Astaroth.

Palmer shook his head. "There was no insurrection, no civil war.
It was one of their stupid property disputes."

"That evaporated a whole continent?" The professor was incredulous.

"You'd think they would have given up on anarchy after that, but no," said Palmer. "One of the idiots said he had a natural right to protect his property line against intruders. Then he evaporated a six-year-old girl who wandered onto his land. Instead of apologizing and offering restitution, the father amazingly turned the matter over to his defense agency. The other fellow's defense agency didn't agree that their client had overreacted. Then the God-given natural right everyone has to own plasma bombs came into it and the continent went poof."

"You were planet-side during this?" asked Astaroth.

"Safe behind a force field on the other side of the planet. Admittedly the anarchists over there seemed a little more inclined to take things to arbitration."

"Whew," said the professor. "I did a paper about Lysander, but I'm a few years out of date."

"Palmer is always on top of things," Bretygne grinned, her arm around his waist.

The professor nodded and then did them the favor of lowering his voice. "You're both spies, of course, and lovers as well. There's not much point to the former unless it adds spice to the latter, or do I have it turned around?"

Color drained out of the lady's face, again at the flick of a switch.

Astaroth finally continued: "There's no need to dissemble. Tonight we'll be dealing with an anarchist who has less regard for our rituals than even I! We must be frank."

He gestured to a servo-mech and the machine dutifully floated over. Palmer and Lamarr quickly ordered strong heroin and tonics. The professor settled for a vodka martini.

A few sips of Smirnoff later, he was still causing trouble. "I think we should put up a sign that reads All Diplomats Are Spies. Or how about this one—Military Attachés Have No Case?"

Palmer wasn't amused. "If we're going to be frank, perhaps you'll answer a personal question. Why do you appear in public with those?" He gestured at the older man's wrinkles. He was just as disturbed by Astaroth's white hair.

No one pinches harder than a well-bred lady, but Bretygne was too late to stop her lover's indiscretion.

"A fair question. But tell me, both lady and field agent, what you see in this room. Look around!"

They were under the largest dome on the moon in a building that made maximum use of its location. Ambassador Konski had purchased this location with a small amount of the material that suddenly made his world of interest to the United States. He'd been offered prime real estate on Earth but this was as close as he wished to be to the Terran capital—Berlin.

Underneath the giant pressure dome, the Aristarchus embassy stood in solitary splendor. The Grand Ballroom had ceiling strips revealing the stars through a double layer of protective plastiglass. Gigantic chandeliers vied with the stars to hold the eye. But the effect was purely decorative as lighting for the room was a constant emanation from the walls.

Palmer sipped his drink and looked around, taking in the beautiful people. Hairstyles varied wildly. As for bald heads, no two carried the same design. The attire was scanty. Everywhere was an expanse of smooth, healthy skin. Fresh as cream and peaches. No blemishes. No wrinkles. And there was a scent of flowers.

The professor held his old hand in front of Palmer. "You want to know why I choose to have wrinkles and warts?"

Palmer shrugged. "Bretygne said you were a conservative. But to do this strikes me as genuinely reactionary, even perverse. You're still healthy and it's a crime to deactivate the anti-aging elements. You must have had the imperfections added surgically." He gave an involuntary shudder.

The professor smiled over his martini. "May I ask another personal question?"

"What now?" she blurted out.

"How old are the two of you?"

"I'm seventy," said Palmer.

"Forty-six," added Bretygne.

"I see," the old head nodded. "You will both appear youthful and vigorous for at least another two centuries even if we make no further progress in longevity. But we know that medical science marches on, ever relentless, ever vigilant."

Fishing the olive out of the bottom of his glass, the professor held it up to his forehead before popping it into his mouth. Was he making fun of Lamarr's third eye?

"I'm something of a spy myself," he went on. "I know how young Bretygne was when you both became lovers."

This time color flushed her cheeks without any artificial assistance. Palmer grabbed her hand to steady both of them.

Astaroth looked Palmer in the eye and whispered, "I know that she was only thirty when you became lovers on Earth. Good old Earth . . . where the age for consent is thirty-five!"

"Prove it," Palmer challenged through clenched teeth.

The professor shook his head. "I don't want to cause trouble, my fellow spies. I no more approve of the Schlessinger Laws than you do."

In common with most aristocrats, Lady Lamarr had a deeply psychotic side. Her voice was dangerous as she reminded both men of the facts. "There is no statute of limitations for sex with an underager."

As they discussed the volatile issue, the three of them slowly moved to a more private corner of the ballroom. Palmer was relieved to see that Astaroth seemed inclined to keep the conversation private. They wound up standing next to one of the service entrances.

The professor tried manfully to put the genie back into the bottle. "I only bring this up to make a point, my young friends. Here are the two of you sworn to uphold the crazy world state and even you have run afoul of its statistical models and lunatic social engineering."

For some reason Palmer didn't feel like making a joke about this being the right place to discuss lunacy.

Eyes wide, Bretygne asked, "My God, are you with the anarchists?"

"No. I'm the other kind of libertarian, a minarchist who wants a limited state and a genuine Bill of Rights."

"You've got a point there," Palmer agreed. "The Children's Bill of Rights is nothing like the old American one."

"Full marks for knowing some history," said Palmer.

"All libertarianism is illegal," Bretygne stated the obvious, "but I've known you were somewhere on the radical side for a long time. You should be the last person to threaten us!"

"No threat, my dear lady. I've done things just as illegal as the two of you. We can hold each other hostage. How wonderful that we meet through our sordid occupation of providing information to the state!"

They listened to each other's silences. The distant clinking of glasses and low hum of voices seemed comforting somehow. The thick cloud of paranoia began to part as the light of mutual advantage touched their faces.

"Is this a safe place to have our conversation?" asked Bretygne.

"None better," said the professor. "The ambassador has made this a high-tech cocoon of privacy. We need only worry about human ears. Besides, we are higher-ranking spies than anyone sent to keep an eye on us."

"So what do you want?" asked Palmer.

"Profits for all of us, and maybe something even better. What would you say to freedom?"

The ballroom music began, an arrangement of classic rap-Muzak. This conservative choice of music inspired Palmer to better understand the mind behind the wrinkles.

"Bretygne told me that you think the world went to hell back in the twenty-first century. That's long before the current system took over."

"One thing leads to another." Astaroth smiled, glad of an audience. "You seem to know about the North American Bill of Rights. Have you studied the Welfare War that led to the collapse of the American Empire?"

"Only what I was told in school."

"The causes of that war continue to fester even in the present day. They were the actual reason the world state eventually outlawed both capitalism and socialism. And so we descended to a new rung of hell, the Maternal Ageist Society."

"He's quoting from one of his private books," Bretygne told Palmer, then added proudly: "I read the whole thing!"

Emboldened, Astaroth continued. "Then you remember that capitalism was outlawed as too individualistic and the cause of social atomism. Socialism was forbidden as too egalitarian and unable to punish certain groups at the expense of others, an important matter when the new chrono-charts determined everyone's place in society according to maturity levels. Our duties and obligations and guilts are calibrated before we even pop out of the womb!"

"I forgot the length of your essay" admitted the lady Lamarr.

"I need another drink," said Palmer.

Instead of a servo-mech, a ten-year-old chose that moment to wander over. He had no drinks to offer but provided an excellent prop for the prof.

Placing his hand on the blue sphere surrounding the kid, Astaroth lectured some more: "I curse the day that social scientists and religious leaders were ever allowed to fraternize. That's carrying free speech too far. In an orgy of bipartisanship, they threw out all their good ideas and joined ranks on the bad ones. There was no need to actually burn the old Bill of Rights if it only applied to adults—and the rules for adulthood were constantly changed. Some of us can't vote until we're eighty. Some of us can't marry until we're fifty. The drinking age for everyone is forty. Heaven help those who are finally judged mature at all levels, and so condemned to eternal slavery for an ever-growing population of the immature."

Professor Astaroth finally ran out of steam. They all looked at the smiling face of the ten-year-old boy in his protective bubble. He'd been watching the professor's mouth move. Astaroth did have a most expressive face. Palmer gave the ball a friendly push and sent the kid on his way, back to his parents or state warders. One was as likely as the other.

"Well," said Palmer, "life's an itch. What's anyone to do?"

"Order more drinks," said Astaroth, his most successful speech of the evening. "If I can't have an ideal society, I'll settle for more vodka."

Just then a figure appeared at the service entrance, but it was too tall to be a servo-mech. The figure moved fast. Palmer instinctively reached for a gun that he'd left behind, a condition of attending the embassy ball. But the figure didn't attack. It stopped running and stood next to the threesome, a huge grin on its face—and an even huger cigar sticking at them between very white teeth.

Hardly anyone smoked cigars anymore.

The man wasn't easy to recognize. He was wearing a strange costume with baggy pants. A black mustache was painted on his upper lip. His eyebrows looked as if two Martian caterpillars (genetically bred to enrich the soil) had crawled on his forehead to die.

Palmer recognized the man first. After all, he'd spent time with him. A blessedly short amount of time. This exasperating excuse for a human being had kept trying to convince Palmer that he was his own identical twin; and then he'd pretended to be the brother! And so on. And on.

"Konski." Palmer said it like a curse.

"Professor Astrolobe, you old fraud," said the guest of honor amiably. "Are you still looking for Freedonia?"

"What are you doing in that costume?" asked Bretygne who had seen the ambassador on the uniweb many times. Researching his predilections and outré writings had hardly prepared her for this.

"Never mind that," said Konski. "Pick a card."

"You don't have any cards," Astaroth observed in a tired voice.

"It's because of the Nano Collapse. So hard to have physical stuff any longer."

The lady present was genuinely offended. "You don't have to use the 'n' word!"

"We must never forget the hard lessons," said Konski. "I'm sure old Professor Astringent will agree that there were unexpected benefits to the Nano War. Or collapse. Or crap-out. Or crash. Or dissolution. Or . . . I forget the rest. Well, no matter. It was impressive, we'll all agree. Lots more special effects than any other war. Why, if Earth military forces hadn't used those molecular decompilers we'd all be so rich now we wouldn't have anything to do."

He took off his hat—no one else was wearing a hat—and held it over his heart. "Let's shed a tear for the end of the nano-trick era. We wanted the treats instead."

The solemn moment over, he threw the hat over his head and watched a servo-mech glide out of the service entrance he'd used a moment before. Konski crouched and feigned great excitement as to whether the robot's silver tentacle would snag the ancient headgear before it touched the floor. The robot succeeded and Konski jumped up and down, clapping his hands.

The threesome so diligent in plotting subversion only a short time before now stared at the maniac who was central to their plans. Konski stared back and then noticed his cigar had gone out.

With a flourish, he produced an old-fashioned lighter in the shape of a gun. Once again it was time for the lady present to gasp. (Fainting, feigning shock and blushing with artificial aids were all part of her Feminist Finishing School charms. She only flunked fainting.)

Even possessing the likeness of a gun was forbidden on Earth. Everywhere one could attend Museums of the Gun to learn of the iniquity of firearms.

Bretygne looked at Palmer and noticed his lack of concern. Sometimes she forgot that soldiers and special agents were deprogrammed from the anti-gun conditioning everyone received from birth.

While the drama of the lighter was taking place Astaroth noticed a servo-mech and gestured it over. Everyone must have been standing too close together because just as the ambassador successfully lit his cigar the robot jostled his arm and he dropped the smoldering black rope of tobacco to the antiseptically clean floor.

"Mechanical imbecile!" he shouted. "Lowly metal egg, clean up that mess!"

Suddenly there came the dread cry of "*Laissez faire!*" The terrifying words rose up from the general noise of the crowd. The air was filled with electric tension.

Then the same mysterious voice shouted, "End robot slavery now!"

"Oh, no," muttered Palmer.

"What is it?" asked Bretygne.

"Not what. Who."

Palmer peered into the crowd. The voice cried out again but the words were garbled.

"I can't believe it," said Palmer. "The voice is the same. I always thought Konski was kidding me. The idea seemed too horrible to credit."

The crowd parted. Bretygne grabbed Palmer's arm. Astaroth shook his head and ordered another martini. Approaching them was not merely the twin brother of the ambassador. Worse, the other maniac of the evening was in the same costume presenting a perfect mirror image. He was even smoking another cigar.

The ambassador stood tall, reached into his pocket as if to brandish a weapon and then pulled out another cigar that quickly found its way to his mouth. "Konski, Part Two," thundered the ambassador, "you have no authority here."

"Robots of the world unite!" came an even more thunderous reply. "They have nothing to lose but your chain-smoking!"

"I repeat, you have no standing in this official and officious embassy."

"Oh, for crying out loud," Astaroth exploded, a new drink in his hand. "You're both insane anarchists. How can there even be an anarchist embassy? The whole idea is preposterous."

The two looked at him and sneered.

"You are a minarchist," said the first Konski.

"You are therefore a deviationist," said Part Two.

"Furthermore," continued number one, "Palmer will verify that I am indeed in a position to represent trade deals with Lysander."

"Well, I . . . ." began Palmer, but to no avail.

Konski, Part Two, was having none of it. "This slaveholder cannot possibly represent the free and autonomous beings that inhabit the paradise of Kropotkia."

"What the hell is that?" Astaroth wanted to know.

Konski the former was helpful. "Oh, it's just Lysander. My brother refuses to call the planet by its proper name."

"More drinks!" suggested Bretygne. "Make them doubles."

"Triples," amended Palmer.

Ambassador Konski started to touch the servo-mech but it shied away from him. With one last suck of its suction tentacle, it removed the final remains of the fallen cigar and fled. Ashes to ashes, and thence to the garbage recycler.

"It doesn't like you," said Part Two.

Konski shrugged. "Nonsense, a robot can neither like nor dislike anything. Fortunately it has departed before you can violate my private property."

"Ha! You cannot own a self-aware being."

"You can't make a contract with a household appliance."

By this point, the twins were face to face, cigar to cigar. There seemed nothing in heaven or Luna that could stop them.

"Even if they could make contracts," complained Part Two, "such agreements would be null and void, for they cannot sell their primary property which is themselves."

Konski's new cigar quivered with indignation. "Oh, yeah? If you can't sell aspects of your primary property then how can we have the most beloved trade of all true lovers of liberty, namely the fine social work performed by prostitutes throughout the ages?"

"Your area of expertise, eh? Hookers can get away from you but not these poor servo-mechs."

"They don't need liberty any more than your damned cigar needs to escape your incisors!"

"How do you know? Maybe they only lack initiative. I'm fighting for their honor which is more than they ever did."

It went on like that for another five minutes until the Lady Bretygne Lamarr found deep inside her soul the power of two words almost equal to the power of *laissez faire.*

"*Shut up!*" she explained.

She was so loud that her voice was heard throughout the entire ballroom. Dead silence fell over the throng and brought all revelry to a grinding halt. Then someone in the crowd finally realized that underneath the grease paint mustaches and wild hair lurked at least one guest of honor.

The crowd surged forward. A beautiful young girl of twenty-nine was first to speak as children are wont to do. "Rockets away! Seeing two of you is pure lox. May I have dual autographs?"

"Only I am the true ambassador," said Konski.

"But my autograph is more valuable," said Part Two. "It doesn't come free, by the way."

"Mine costs the same!" piped in Konski.

The autographs kept the two of them out of trouble for a while while Palmer, Bretygne and Astaroth discovered a heretofore-unrealized capacity for cocktails. Finally a servo-mech floated above the multitude and announced that dinner was about to be served.

Alas, Part Two heard the announcement. "Will we be violating animal rights tonight?" he wanted to know. "Or perhaps vegetable rights?"

Palmer was starting to feel his fifth drink of the evening. That played no small role in his responding to the terrible twin. "I know for a fact, Mister Brother of the Anarchist Ambassador, that all our food tonight is completely synthetic. The only violation of rights has been on the molecular level."

"Don't ask this one what he thought of the Nano War," pleaded Bretygne in his ear.

"You used the 'n' word," he chided.

Somehow the unwieldy mass of well-dressed and undressed humanity wandered over to the dining area. Part Two went with them. As for Ambassador Konski, he grabbed Lady Lamarr by the arm and announced, "This is our chance. Follow me!"

"Why are you grabbing me by the arm?" asked Bretygne, but not really resisting. "Isn't that a violation of my elbow rights or something?"

"I'll make restitution," he grinned. "Besides, this way I know your boyfriends will follow."

They all went through a service entrance where a space cadet limo was waiting. They piled in and Konski ordered the robot driver to take them out into the lunar night.

Konski's tone of voice lost its strident quality. He sounded like a different person when he said, "Tonight reminded me of an observation by the twenty-first century philosopher Garmon. He said that the truth of all technological societies lies in the manner by which we come to resemble our tools. But I don't want to look like a silver egg with tentacles! I don't want to belong to any labor force that would have me as a member."

Bretygne suddenly felt relaxed for the first time that evening. "You know, Palmer thinks I'm a spoiled brat."

"I've never said that!" he protested.

"But it's true," she said, and not a single man in the limo asked her if she meant it was true that she was spoiled or that it was true that Palmer thought so.

The professor sounded happy, too. "Freedom is learning to balance responsibility along with being spoiled. Both are essential."

Konski nodded. "The human race seems to be on a bell curve. Those who can handle freedom and responsibility are at one end.

Those who would be the masters and dictators are on the other end. The vast mass is the bell of the bell curve. They want a little freedom and a little slavery. They play the role of master and slave interchangeably even though they don't want either condition to be permanent."

Palmer couldn't believe what he'd just heard. "That's a surprisingly mature remark to come from a man who just turned in that performance back at the dome."

Konski laughed and started rubbing off his mustache with a bright red handkerchief. "They wanted to see anarchists tonight, didn't they? My brother and I worship a handful of twentieth century movie stars, the ones who had talent. The early, funny ones."

They were sitting in a comfortable semicircle in the back. The guest of honor started acting as if he deserved the title. He patted Palmer on the shoulder. "Enough of the show. Let's get down to brass tacks. Lysander has precious raw materials that are needed to power starships. It would be cheaper to mine them than to produce them artificially. That's also considering the distances involved and the time factors. But we need the United States of Earth to believe that we have a military capacity to defend ourselves."

"You don't!" all three of his critics spoke at once.

"Exactly. But we learned from the loss of a continent that our defense agencies have certain limitations. We know how to live together now, but that doesn't mean we have the organization to withstand an invasion by Earth forces! The bastards on the home world are capable of anything. They think we're all children on Lysander so none of us have rights. We must convince them we are children who can bite!"

The Earth hung above their conversation like a blue and green goblin, threatening the gray expanse of a free Luna. Palmer leaned back in his seat and exhaled slowly. He'd been expecting the moment of decision for some time. Now that it had arrived it was as if a shadow moved across his vision, taking with it all of his worries.

In his whole life, he'd never heard the word freedom used as often as he'd heard it today. The word wouldn't leave him alone. It had gotten inside him. Freedom. Liberty. A light to penetrate his personal darkness.

Looking at Bretygne, he seemed to see her for the first time. He felt something new. He didn't want to have sex with her or to compete with her or to prove anything. He simply felt affection.

Taking her by the hand he smiled. She smiled back. For a brief wonderful moment they were alone in the universe and not even gigantic egos like Konski and Astaroth could intrude.

"I can fix it," said Palmer. "Actually, the three of us can definitely arrange things for you, Mr. Ambassador. But you already know that. We can fool the United States of Earth into believing you have a significant military force. The destruction of the continent on Lysander is proof of your capacity, after all. No one in Berlin would ever believe the real reasons for that disaster."

Konski reached into a compartment and pulled out a small statuette. "This is a replica of the Statue of Liberty."

"Oh, my," said Bretygne. "The one that was destroyed."

"In the Welfare War," Astaroth finished for her.

Konski cradled his trophy. "This is a perfect copy except the inscription on the bottom has been changed. It speaks to what we need now on Lysander. And what we will require as we open new worlds. You three have spent enough time on Earth, don't you think?"

Palmer took the small statue and held it close. He read the inscription out loud:

This time, just send us your children!

According to Their Need

Michael A. Stackpole

Father Flynn closed his eyes for a moment and luxuriated in the heat from the reflected sunlight coming up off the lake's silver surface. A gentle breeze provided a hint of a swell to rock the boat, but better was the insistent slap of wavelets against the aluminum hull. While Apogea's orbit around its single sun was a bit too distant to make the world quite warm enough, its largely unspoiled beauty more than compensated for the slight chill.

He opened his blue eyes again and smiled at the woman in the other end of the boat. "I'm thinking, Rina, this is about the closest to Paradise I'll be getting before a discussion with Saint Peter."

The woman laughed lightly and easily, and the youthful tone of her laughter further concealed her age. Flynn knew they were both in their fifties—him solidly, and she just starting—but she hid it well. Still lean, with bright hazel eyes and black hair without a hint of white, she seemed yet as youthful as she had when he first met her on the station. The years had used him a bit harder than they had her, and the resilience that had let her recover from tragedy had been long in evidence throughout his visit.

"Well, Dennis, I hope for your sake that you are incorrect. Apogea *is* very beautiful however." She gave him a very warm smile. "And, despite our lack of luck so far today, it does have the fattest troutganisms I've seen this side of Earth."

"Oh, I believe you, and I'm not in the least disappointed." He winked at her. "After all, it's called fishing, not *catching,* for a reason."

The small lake on which they were drifting lay in a forested hilly basin. The crystal waters were so pure that they just dipped a cup if they were thirsty. Trees resembling pines and maples dotted the hillsides, with Apogea's evolutionary equivalent of cattails lining the shores. Off to the northeast he could see the white crescent of beach they'd set out from, and the cabin hidden a bit farther on, just the edge of the woods.

"It feels as if we're all alone here."

Arina Gadja nodded. "We are. Barring an emergency, accident, seriously poor navigating or someone incredibly rude, we won't see anyone else unless we chose to invite them or accept an invite."

Flynn tapped the chronometer on his left wrist. "But we're not really alone, are we, since we're being monitored all the time."

"Just for safety's sake. If your heart were to seize up, someone would be along to get you to sick bay."

Flynn shook his head. "You know, I'm still surprised you agreed to come here and live on Apogea. You spent your adult life working security on Qian space stations, enforcing one law over countless individuals who came from a legion of legal traditions. Law and order were so much the fabric of your life, and yet you retire to a world with no government."

Arina started to slowly reel her line in. "Surprised me, too. Given that all that had happened, it seemed like a good choice. Grants to live here are rare, so I could not pass up the chance."

"I know. It's an honor to be given one and I'm thinking I'm grateful you invited me to visit."

"And I'm grateful you came. The only thing Apogea doesn't provide is old friends. Everything else is taken care of, however, and that's how it works. If you think about it, Dennis, governments serve to guarantee security, both in terms of protecting the material we possess, and to see to it that our needs are met."

"Needs save those in the spiritual realm."

She smiled. "True enough, and I know the lack of churches here would be troubling to you, but churches also become a place where power can be concentrated and wielded in favor of one person over another. Here we operate by the golden rule, as overseen by Covenant."

Flynn knew she wasn't using the word Covenant in any religious or legal sense. Covenant was the name given to the vast computer network that administered the world of Apogea. When the creation of the exclusive colony was first proposed, it was agreed that those who wished to live there would put their assets into blind trusts and would come to live on the world forever—barring trips off world necessitated by family emergencies. Their assets and their needs would be taken care of through Covenant, which would monitor wants, whims, and necessitudes, blending desires and providing what people wanted primarily by knowing them as well or better than they knew themselves.

Creating a monastery world with resort trappings for the rich would have been simple, save that hedonistic pursuits precluded complete isolation. Some people bought their way into Apogea. Others, like Arina, earned a grant for service to society—and her grant had been paid for with heroism and blood. Yet others were contract residents. They were heavily screened and brought to Apogea to perform specific services for a year, with contracts renewed if desired. Because needs were met on the world, the generous salaries these people were paid were saved, with hefty performance bonuses being racked up along the way to guarantee good behavior.

On top of that, Covenant practiced random interval reinforcement. The Qian programmers had managed to look at desires and project, into the future, intersection points with external trends. Items and information related to these interests would arrive for the residents at various and unpredictable intervals. It was as if everyone was entered into a lottery on an hourly basis where they might win something they didn't know they wanted, but would please them the moment they got it. These gifts, many quite banal and innocuous, provided excitement and promoted good behavior.

"Oh, Arina, I'm thinking Apogea is quite clever, no doubt about it.

When I told Father Ruxton I would be coming to visit, she was rather adamant in warning me about the seductive evil of this place. She said it had been modeled on the trick the Assassins used to play on recruits during the Crusades. They'd drug them and bring them to a magnificent palace where their every need was met. They'd be told they were in Heaven, then after three days, they'd be drugged again and returned to the real world. They'd had their taste of Heaven, so they'd go out and fight against Christendom, knowing the reward they'd have when they were killed."

She nodded and pulled her lure from the water, then set about changing it. "That is the beauty of Apogea, you see. We can exile disruptive influences. For guests and workers, unacceptable behavior is cause for immediate expulsion and forfeiture of bonds and bonuses. For me, being a grant, I'd get pensioned off to some nice resort world. Those who have bought their way in will be returned to the world they once knew, and barred from coming back here ever."

"Oh, the inducements to good behavior are certainly there, but that doesn't guarantee morality, and it doesn't do much for the immortal souls of those living here." Flynn paused as something tugged at the lure unseen in the depths. It wasn't a solid hit, so he continued. "We know, for example, that someone here has the idea that having a harem of sexual partners at his beck and call is a pleasure he wants to enjoy—and we know there are plenty of folks who would see nothing wrong with hiring on for a year here in paradise to deal with that need. And one could even argue that what goes on between consenting adults is fine, barring anyone being injured, but that only refers to physical injuries. The mental and emotional hurts can be considerable. Moreover, the removal from a state of grace is grave, and some might mistake this temporal Heaven for the real thing, playing now and burning later."

"You know I don't disagree with your view concerning morality, and I know you well enough to know that you don't mistake the Church's hierarchy with its spirituality." She tied off a knot, then spread her hands. "I find I can commune with God in this creation as easily as I can in any church."

"And yet," Flynn smiled, "you did have me say Mass and give you the Eucharist when I arrived."

"Religion and spirituality are not forbidden here—nothing is, if it does no harm—just the trappings that would allow it to become harmful."

"If I accept that you are correct, that governments are vital to preserving society through the distribution of wealth, and that meeting all needs obviates the necessity of government, would you concede that Apogea would collapse into anarchy if insecurity or vital shortages were introduced here?"

"At its worst, perhaps, but we also have the advantage of being highly self-sufficient, and a very sparsely populated world. Basic needs could be met easily and while the artificially high standard of living would suffer, the people here would suffer far less than any colony-world population." Arina shrugged. "On a world where, right now, temptation and desire are fulfilled, the necessity to commit crime does not exist."

Flynn nodded. The screening process to come to Apogea, even as a guest, included an examination of records as well as the filling out of numerous forms and polls about tastes and desires. He assumed that for residents of any stripe, the selection process was far more rigorous, and included batteries of psychological screening tests. Residents also had chips implanted in them that served the function of the monitoring device on his wrist. They also recorded physical reactions to stimuli, registering unconscious attractions to asocial behavior, and steps could be taken to curb it or eliminate the person.

Something appeared as a black speck far to the northeast and grew quickly enough. Flynn recognized it as a light Zsytzii transport. It hovered over the cabin for a moment, then came out toward them on the lake. It swooped low, rippling waves in its wake, and hung there, barely a meter off the surface as a side hatch opened. Through the forward windscreens Flynn had already seen one of the long, lean, black-furred Zsytzii Primaries piloting the ship. Another stood at the hatch, and a number of the junior males waited behind him, peering past waist and knees at the two anglers. The Primary wore a minimum of clothing, though the equipment harness did bear rank insignia in the Covenant Safety Service.

Arina gave the Zsytzii a polite nod. "Covenant's peace to you, Captain."

"And to you, Citizen Gadja. It is with regret that Covenant intrudes. We are Captain Lavaryn, and we regret spoiling your time with your friend. Your opinion is sought in a serious matter. Probabilities indicate your guest might be of aid as well."

"What's the problem?"

The Zsytzii smiled quickly, revealing a serrated ribbon of teeth. His juniors followed a second later, dispelling forever their benign appearance. "In the City, someone has died. Natural causes and accident have been statistically excluded, leaving only one alternative."

"Murder?"

The Zsytzii nodded solemnly. "So it is feared. Will you help?"

"I'm not sure what help I could be."

Captain Lavaryn sighed, and his juniors moaned. "Please, citizen, we have no experience in dealing with murder."

Arina glanced at Flynn, and the priest nodded encouragingly at her. The woman smiled slightly, golden sparks flashing from within her hazel eyes. "As you wish, Captain. Let us go."

The City, as it was known, was a fully functioning metropolis. It had been designed down to the square centimeter, for none of it existed fifty years previously when the Apogea project started. The City's development had taken place to reflect the desires, sensibilities, and tastes of the original residents, hence part of it was a disorganized artist section that Flynn had heard described as being "delightfully Bohemian." As nearly as he could tell that indicated that the streets were meant to run haphazardly, and that past every curve was a hidden gallery or cafe or some other little jewel of an establishment containing undiscovered treasures. Other parts of the City had the straight lines of the finest modern developments, and still other suburban communities surrounded the urban center.

The Zsytzii took them directly into the Arts district and set down in a park. The trip from Arina's cabin had taken little more than an hour, as the building had not been located far from the City. She actually had an apartment in one of the modern towers, but spent most of her time out at the lake.

The advantage of Zsytzii transport in service to Covenant was that both Arina and Flynn had suitable clothing provided for them and were able to change en route. Flynn found the shirt, trousers, and jacket, all in black, save for his Roman collar, fit better than the things he normally wore. He was fairly certain that if he made a comment to that effect, suggesting it made him uncomfortable, Covenant would make sure other clothes were more normal fitted.

The uniform Arina had been supplied had been tailored to perfection and shaved five years off her. Dark blue, with red epaulets, cuffs and stripes down the pants, it had enough of a military cut to provide authority. It came complete with a black weapons' harness that had a holster and an Agonizer at her right hip.

Flynn smiled. "Well, Colonel, it's clear Covenant hasn't forgotten why you were given a grant."

"And here I all but had." She nodded, then turned to the Zsytzii officer. "I did retire a colonel in the Qian Security Service, but it was a pension appointment. I will advise, not take the investigation from you."

The Zsytzii frowned slightly and his juniors groaned. Zsytzii males were born in litters, with the Primary and his juniors having a mild telepathic link which was now often enhanced with cybernetics. The juniors had the intelligence of a six-year-old human—and not a Mozart among them. They functioned well for carrying out simple orders, and during the Zsytzii war had been very effective combatants because of their quickness and small size.

"Colonel Gadja, this is not a concern. We bow to your expertise and hope to learn from you."

"I would be pleased to teach you anything I can." Arina's brows knitted in the concentration Flynn had so often observed. "I will need all the data Covenant can give me on the deceased and his activities, condensed, not raw. Where he has gone, what he likes, known associates, the personality composite Covenant has for him."

Lavaryn nodded. "It shall be done before you will be finished with the crime scene."

Flynn followed Arina from the transport and along the street to a small store of the sort that seemed about as common as fish in the universe. Flynn knew that the presence of water and other evolutionary pressures meant fish were found pretty much everywhere and, similarly, societies seem to produce shops that, to some, sold curiosities, but to others turned trash into treasure. This particular shop had enough dust coating everything that Flynn wondered if it hadn't predated the Apogea project. Exotic knickknacks from hundreds of worlds and thousands of cultures filled every recess of the small shop, save for the narrow aisles meandering between piles. The sales counter had been built into the back wall, cutting off a doorway into the back. The threadbare curtain had been drawn back to show a shabby storage area choked with things on sagging shelves.

The store had clearly been created with an eye toward atmosphere. The floorboards creaked as they walked toward the counter. The air had a dry scent equal parts old leather, old wood and a hint of pungent alien musk. Had Flynn not been very conscious of the fact that he was on Apogea, he could have found himself anywhere in the Qian Commonwealth.

The body lay sprawled on the floor before the counter with a sheet pulled over it. The sheet had tented up toward the chest and when Arina pulled it back, the cause for that was readily apparent. A tusk of some sort had been shoved through the man's chest. Flynn followed the curve of it with his eye and figured it had slid in and up to pierce his heart.

Arina squatted beside the body and turned the dead man's face toward her. "Oh!"

"What is it?"

"I know him."

Flynn came over and stood by the man's feet. "He looks familiar to me, too. Did we see him at the spaceport?"

"No, we know him from Purgatory Station." She smiled slightly. "His name was Flambeau? No, no, it was Fonteneau, that's it, Stephen Fonteneau."

"That was six years ago. He'd come to the station to steal that Golathi princeling's coronet. You and Fith caught him. I remember speaking with him, hearing his Confession." The priest rubbed a hand over his jaw. "I'd not have been thinking I'd see him again, especially after he escaped custody."

"Oh, he was a slippery one. Fith knew that, so we split shifts, never left him alone until he was sent off to stand trial." Arina smiled.

"That was the case where Fith and I learned we really complemented each other."

"I seem to recall you were fair inseparable after that." Flynn nodded solemnly. Fith Chykip had been the Qian security director. He and Arina fell hard for each other and, despite Human-Qian pairings being infertile, decided to marry. Flynn had worked hard to get Father Ruxton to sanction the nuptials, and he'd been there to perform the Last Rites for Fith when terrorists widowed Arina.

Captain Lavaryn entered the shop and slipped a datapad from the holster on his equipment harness. "Colonel, the man's name is David Holcomb. He is a contract worker, in month nine. Covenant reports he spends much time in the company of another hire, Deana Thompson, who lives near here. Holcomb was last reported to be in her apartment at midnight. There is no indication why he would be here, nor of his entering this place, nor of his ever having been here before."

Arina blinked. "Covenant's monitoring lost him?"

The Zsytzii nodded. "It happens on occasion when there is interference. Usually it is momentary, sometimes longer."

"That's interesting." She frowned. "Who is assigned to this shop? Where is he?"

"The owner is Regan Park. We have sent a junior to fetch him, and another to bring Deana Thompson to the ship. We know where she is, but he seems to be missing." He canted his head to the side slightly. "She is coming."

"I'll need background data on her." Arina stood. "I will need a complete forensic workup on his body. The medical center should be able to do the work."

Flynn pointed at the thing in the man's chest. "You know what that is, then?"

"Samuel Abrams—he used to run the Novajet Transport Corporation—has a hunting preserve on one of the southern islands. There are some fairly fantastic creatures there. Some are xenobiologicals, some are lab-born monsters—and that's half a mandible set from something he called a 'giant chigger.' They're supposed to be tougher than a Bouganshi to kill. I understand he's got several mandible sets on display both in his home and at the hunting lodge."

"So, they're not the sort of thing that would be found in this shop, are they?"

She shook her head. "I'd say not. Captain, can you pull Covenant's data on chigger pinchers?"

The Zsytzii hesitated as he silently worked his mouth through the pronunciation of "chigger pinchers." "It shall be done, Colonel. Deana Thompson is in the ship now, but she has not been told why she is there."

Flynn held the shop's door open for Arina, then matched her stride back to the ship. "And you'd not be telling Lavaryn who Holcomb really is because . . . ?"

"Not out of any suspicion of him. Seems to me, when he's stressed, he bleeds some thought and emotion into his juniors. Learning Holcomb was a bold thief might shake his confidence, and he might let something slip that a junior would tell Deana Thompson. Keeping the true identity a secret for the moment is best."

"I can see that, yes." He looked at her. "And how are you doing knowing a serpent has crawled into this garden?"

Arina stopped, blinking her eyes with surprise. "You know, I'd just sort of slipped back into the job, and wasn't thinking of the grander implications."

"You'd have gotten there."

"Possible. And it's not just one serpent; it's at least two. Fonteneau shouldn't have been here. Somehow Covenant lost track of him. So we need to know why he was in that shop, why he was here on Apogea, and what he's been doing for the last nine months. It's a legion of snakes."

They returned to the transport and found Deana Thompson sitting all tight and small in the passenger compartment. One of the juniors had fetched her a cup of tea. The petite woman nervously tucked a strand of blond hair behind one ear. She gave them a hopeful smile. "Hi."

Flynn sat beside her on the bench seating, and Arina took up a position opposite her. "I'm Arina Gadja, Colonel Gadja of Safety Services. This is Father Dennis Flynn, a visitor here and a friend of mine. Covenant has requested our aid in resolving a situation involving David Holcomb. You know him?"

"Is he all right?"

Arina's head came up. "What would make you think he might not be?"

Deana hesitated, then looked down into her cup of tea. "Nothing."

Flynn laid a hand on her shoulder and felt her jump. "Listen to me, Miss Thompson, there's going to be nothing worse in all this than your fear."

The edge in Arina's voice contrasted sharply with the quiet softness of his. "Miss Thompson, you must realize how important this is for Covenant to request the help of a citizen. The sooner we get to the bottom of this, the better for all involved."

Deana shook her head. "I told him he shouldn't do it."

"Do what?"

The woman sipped her tea, then held her left hand out, palm forward, showing the hint of a scar where her identification chip had been implanted. "There was one night, David and I were out having a drink, dancing, just having fun. We struck up a conversation with another couple and talked a little about our lives before Apogea. The guy said that the one thing he didn't like about Apogea was that Covenant knew where we were and what we were doing at all times. He said that back in the real world he could go out, get roaring drunk, and wake up not remembering where he was, where he'd been or what he'd done with whom. That not knowing, that was a thrill for him, but here Covenant could tell him everything, taking the mystery out of it."

Flynn shivered, and it wasn't just the man's illusion that what he had done remained unknown. God certainly knew. What chilled Flynn was the man's willful desire to abandon responsibility for his actions, his wanton disavowal of the rules by which society governed itself, and his being thrilled by the not knowing. It was passively nihilistic behavior that could, as the desire for greater thrills built, become actively destructive.

Deana sighed heavily. "We kind of agreed—not that we liked the idea of not knowing, but knowing that Covenant is always watching over you can get to be kinda much. I mean, I know it's not making judgments, just collecting data and changing things to make sure what we want and need is provided. It's benign and positive, but sometimes it feels smothering, you know?"

Arina nodded slowly. "I can see how you could find it so."

Deana stared at her for a second, then broke eye-contact. "So the guy says he's heard of someone who had these blackout chips. You wear it on your wrist, just like he's got, covering your ID chip. The box reads your home location, or a place you're likely to be, and broadcasts to the system that this is where you are. What you do then is, you get these blackout things, then bring party stuff to a place, like a warehouse or the basement of an apartment building, whatever. You get told where when you get the blocker. You have parties and stuff, everybody bringing something. It's cool, and everyone is liking the fact that Covenant thinks we're all home and in bed."

"So there was a party last night?"

Deana nodded. "I went. David was supposed to meet me, but he never made it. I didn't worry since he'd done that before. He'd warned me those times, though."

"Can you tell me when those times were?"

The small woman frowned. "About six weeks, and then three weeks ago."

"You don't think he was seeing someone else?"

Deana's eyes widened. "David? No. We were in love. He was going to be leaving before I was, but we both had signed for good bonus money, so we planned to marry and head back to Mars, or maybe out to one of the Commonwealth worlds to make a life together. Why would you ask that?"

"Routine. Did David know Regan Park?"

"Who?"

"The man who ran the curio shop over here on Aquila Street."

Deana shook her head. "Not that I knew." She turned her left hand back over, then thumbed the ring on her fourth finger. "David may have gotten this there. He gave it to me as a gift. Said Covenant wasn't the only one who could surprise people with nice things."

"A couple more questions, then we will be done. Does the name Stephen Fonteneau mean anything to you?"

"No, not really." Deana grinned a bit. "David had a twin brother named Stephen, so when someone would shout the name, he'd react, all unconsciously. It got to be a joke. There were times when I would leave him messages, asking Stephen to tell David I needed to see him.

We made up a twin sister for me, Diana, and he did the same thing."

"Do you know Samuel Abrams? Did David?"

"No, no, not at all. We don't run in those circles. I work with the local theater company, and I know Abrams and his wife had a box. They come and bring friends, but I've never spoken to them. David worked as a sommelier at Cuisine Rigel. He might have met them there, but he used to talk about how servants are always invisible to those people. The only time they took notice of him was when he recommended a new wine, and it would be an import that Covenant had brought in and had earmarked for them anyway. He felt like it was a charade, and occasionally had fun describing how folks who knew nothing praised the wine for things he'd described, not anything in the wine itself."

Arina nodded. "Thank you, Miss Thompson, you have been most helpful."

"Fine, but you've not told me what this is about."

Flynn's friend nodded slowly. "I know, and I couldn't until I had spoken to you. I'm afraid I have some bad news for you. David didn't return last night because he was severely injured. Fatally injured."

"Fatally?" Deana's voice faded to a strangled whisper that caught in her throat. She raised a hand to cover her mouth, while the tea in her cup splashed wildly. Flynn took the cup from her hand, passing it to a junior, then settled an arm around her shoulder. "How?"

Flynn kept his voice low and even. "Hush now, child. He died quickly and in no pain whatsoever. We're thinking he was at the curio shop—likely getting you another gift—and surprised a thief."

"Oh, God!" Deana turned and pressed her face against Flynn's chest, grabbing a tight handful of his jacket. "He's dead . . . dead. . . ."

A junior arrived leading a tall, heavy-set woman whose face immediately registered alarm as she recognized Deana and heard her sobs. She slid onto the bench on the other side of Deana and stroked her hair. "I'm Maggie Wilson, we work together. I was brought here . . ."

Arina smiled solemnly. "A tragedy. David is dead."

"Oh, Deana." The larger woman gathered Deana into her arms hugging her tightly, and the sobbing woman released Flynn and clung to her friend.

Flynn and Arina left the transport and the two women, meeting Lavaryn at the base of the short landing ramp. "You did well, Captain, bringing the friend here."

"Thank you, Colonel. We have had experience in informing people of accidental deaths, and having friends present seems to help. We regret, however, to have found nothing else of use. The place where Regan Park is supposed to be is vacant. Two ships have left the spaceport in the time since Holcomb's death, at least as calculated by the doctors, and we do not know if he smuggled himself on board. Procedures checking outbound passengers are not as rigorous as they are coming in."

"It will be important for us to find Regan Park, but we don't know if he is a victim who has been taken elsewhere and killed, a murderer or in league with a murderer. We need to discover what has happened. Right now I need Covenant to check and see if Samuel Abrams or his wife, Veronika, had been to Cuisine Rigel in the last nine months."

The Zsytzii produced his datapad and communicated a request for that data. "A dozen times. Most recently two weeks ago, a week before that, six weeks, two months. The guest list varies from two to twelve, often new arrivals. The Abrams take great delight in sharing a restaurant they consider their 'discovery' with friends."

Lavaryn looked up from the flat-screen device. "Covenant reports they invited you there, but you refused."

Arina shrugged. "I had nothing to wear."

"Rina?" Flynn looked at her incredulously as he tugged on the collar of his coat. "This is Apogea. Covenant provided us these clothes so we'd not be in our fishing gear to make inquiries. You would have been provided whatever you needed."

"I just didn't want to go. Veronika understood." She held up a hand to forestall further discussion. "Lavaryn, we need to canvas the neighborhood. Ask about Regan Park. Ask about the blackout chips. You did get that from the junior listening to the interrogation, yes?"

"We did."

"Good."

"We did not understand the reference to 'Stephen Fonteneau.' Covenant says he is a thief, specializing in jewels and other rare items. What is his connection here? Should we be looking for him, and the other half of that mandible in his possession?"

"Him, no. He was David Holcomb."

The Zsytzii's face screwed down at the brows in a frown, but came up at the lip in a snarl. "We do not think that is possible. Not to doubt your identification, but that would mean that Covenant was fooled on his identification when he came here."

"I don't like the implications of that idea either, Captain." Arina shook her head. "I need a current location on Samuel and Veronika Abrams."

The Zsytzii's fingers caressed the datapad's input buttons with blurred speed. "He is at his hunting lodge in the islands. She is in the City. Shall we communicate a request for an interview?"

"Please. An hour from now, at her home here."

One of the juniors brought Arina a datapad from the ship. Captain Lavaryn smiled. "We will communicate the address to you, as well as keep you apprised of our investigation."

Arina nodded and slid the data device into the harness's holster. "I know where she lives. It's not far. We'll walk. I get to think while I walk. Let's go, Dennis."

Father Flynn joined her and smiled. "You took to having the weight of that harness on you fast enough, I'm thinking."

She shot him a sidelong glance. "I've been out of it for two years. I'm two years away from what Deana Thompson is going through, which sometimes doesn't seem very far, but other times . . . When I first got here I just wanted to be alone, to mourn, and I know that probably wasn't the best way to deal with Fith's death, but it was the only way I knew to do it."

"The healing process, it's different for everyone. Folks may tend one way or another, wanting to be around folks, wanting to be alone, working, retiring, and any combination of the same." Flynn rested a hand on her shoulder. "You're a vital woman, Arina, resilient. Hunkering down to heal up, that made sense. It was always your way. I was happy indeed to receive your invitation to visit. I took it as a good sign, especially given that I was there when everything happened."

"You helped hold me together, Dennis, and for that I owe you a debt I can't repay."

"Stopping those Spiral Way terrorists put everyone else in a debt they couldn't repay you." Flynn squeezed her shoulder. Spiral Way, being an anarchistic group looking to overthrow the Qian Commonwealth, had tried to enter Commonwealth space at Purgatory Station, figuring that any backwater station such as it would have lax security. Arina and Fith took their jobs seriously, and discovered that the Novajet Transport ship had been hijacked. In it were weapons, including some virals that would have wrought havoc within the Commonwealth. The lightfight that resulted in the transport being secured and the terrorists killed had cost the life of a half-dozen security personnel, Fith being foremost among them.

"So I've been told, many times. I know Samuel Abrams exerted considerable influence to get me a grant to live here. I think he even created and had spread a rumor saying the Spiral Way had specifically targeted Apogea to make me seem even better." She shook her head. "I'm sure some people decided I should come here since they figured my presence would be enough to keep Spiral Way on the other side of the galaxy."

"Do you think Apogea will remain paradise with news of the murder getting out?"

"It will take more than an isolated incident to bring things crashing down." Arina opened her hands as they walked along through the artist's quarter, heading toward the tall towers to the north. "You seem to assume, my friend, that in the absence of a government, the slightest pressure will cause people to revert to animals. Apogea follows a simple model, much akin to that of children playing a pickup game of hockey. They set boundaries, they devise goals, they dispense with some rules and create others to suit their needs, with the will of the group determining what is right and functional. If someone disagrees, they go home."

"The needs of the people here are far more sophisticated than the needs of children playing hockey."

"There is no disputing that. The absence of want doesn't bring with it an absence of stupidity. People get drunk and do stupid things. They get jealous and do stupid things, but those here have been screened to minimize those tendencies, and are monitored to pick up on them and exile them before they become a problem."

Flynn nodded. "And yet, Fonteneau was here. How many more like him are there?"

"No way of knowing. The fact is, of course, that he had to have lied to get here, so his behavior from the first would earn him exile the moment he was caught. But, were he to live here through his contract and function within society, would we have been diminished by his presence? Would we have suffered because of him? You can look at someone like Samuel Abrams, in fact, and note that he has likely done as much harm as good with his businesses, but as long as he fits in with our society here, what he has done off Apogea matters not at all."

"Do you believe that? What if a murderer, some planetary dictator, bought his way into Apogea, would you not find it morally reprehensible that he could be here?"

"His presence? No. Him, certainly; and I'd not associate with him at all. In some ways it could be argued that here, where there is no mechanism for generating power, such a person is rendered harmless. The simple fact of the matter, however, is that because having him here would not rise high in the consciousness of the people in terms of desire, Covenant would not generate an invitation to have him come to Apogea."

Flynn frowned. "I see your point, but I wonder at another one. You seem to argue that an absence of want leads to stability, but does it not also lead to stagnation? What impetus to strive in life?"

"For the contractors, the impetus comes in the nature of the bonuses they get when they leave us." Arina shrugged. "For the others, we are on the other side of striving. We have striven, and we are here, in a sanctuary."

Before Flynn could address that point with another concern, they reached the tower where Veronika Abrams had taken up residence. Covenant checked their identification, opening the building to them, and had a lift in the lobby waiting. It whisked them up to the fifty-first floor, opening into a marble-lined private foyer, across from which a wall of glass gave them a stunning view of the City and the lush, verdant landscape stretching far to the south.

Veronika Abrams greeted them herself. Willowy and graceful, she moved with the ease of a dancer in the flowing blue robe she wore gathered at the waist with a golden rope. Her black hair had been cut short and framed a pixieish face with large dark eyes and full lips. Flynn didn't wonder if she'd had a new face cloned then put in place—doing that was, for women of her class, to be expected and quite unremarkable. Still, the light in her eyes suggested to him that her following class convention came less out of personal vanity, than a sense of fun and delight in seeing her young self in the mirror once more.

The woman advanced, smiling. "Arina Gadja, so good to see you again. A colonel in Covenant's service, well. Unusual for a resident to work, but, I would guess, necessary. And you are Father Flynn?"

"I am."

"Don't be surprised, Father, I am well aware of who comes and goes these days. Mostly coming, a few going, of course. Tracking these things are all that keep me occupied." Veronika linked her arm through Arina's and steered her into the sitting room off to the left side of the foyer. "Now, sit and tell me what is the matter."

Arina joined Veronika on the white fabric couch, while Flynn settled into a matching chair. "Mrs. Abrams, there has been a murder."

The woman started. "A murder? Not Sam . . ."

"No, not your husband, but someone you have met before. David Holcomb. He was the wine steward at Cuisine Rigel."

Veronika frowned and glanced up toward the ceiling. "Not terribly tall, dark brown hair?"

"That's him."

"I remember him, vaguely." Her eyes sharpened. "What has this to do with me?"

"We have reason to believe he has been here, in this apartment. He has a history of theft, and was found in possession of chigger mandibles. We think he might have taken more, and you are known to have a fine collection of jewelry."

Veronika's hand went to her throat. "Mandibles . . . They're in my husband's study. That's where we have the safe. Come on."

She led them through the suite of rooms and into a room filled with dark wood panels and festooned with the mounted heads of animals slain on a half-dozen worlds. Veronika made immediately for a broad hearth, the corners of which were decorated with chigger mandibles. She counted the four pairs, then pointed to the center of the mantelpiece. "There was another set there, mounted on a stand. It's gone."

She moved to the middle of the hearth and reached up inside, fingering an unseen catch. A panel set with the Novajet logo split apart and opened right in the middle of the mantle. Veronika reached in and withdrew several velvet-covered boxes, then carefully counted them. "One's missing."

Arina took the boxes from her and put them on the massive desk situated in the corner. "Open them, tell me what's gone."

"I don't need to. . . ." Her hand covered her mouth. "It was an emerald *cherengata*, very rare."

Flynn blinked. "You had a *cherengata*?"

"Sam gave it to me as a present when we arrived here on Apogea. I don't know, didn't know, its history; that piece's history. I mean, I know that when the Zsytzii overran the Jirandik worlds, the Jirandi ransomed themselves by giving up these heirlooms. But, you know, not all of them did. Some had been sold before and, many, you know, after the Zsytzii war was settled. Sam said it was one of those, that the provenance was data-perfect on it."

The priest looked over at Arina. "Would Fonteneau steal something to right a wrong?"

She shifted her shoulders uneasily. "For the challenge of saying he had been to Apogea and come away with a prize, certainly. A *cherengata* would still go for a great deal on the open market. It would be just like him to take only that one piece. And the mandibles, just to prove where he'd gotten the *cherengata*."

Veronika hugged her arms around herself. "Will you catch him?"

"The thief? He's dead. His murderer? I don't know." Arina smiled. "I don't think you have anything to worry about, though, Mrs. Abrams. Fonteneau had to work very hard to get here. I doubt there is anyone else who could manage the deception it took, especially as Covenant will modify procedures to prevent a recurrence. We will keep you informed of how the investigation is going. With any luck at all we should be able to return your *cherengata* to you."

"Thank you, Arina." The woman smiled. "I hope I won't just see you in your official capacity. I have understood your wanting time alone, but there can be too much of that. When we invited you to dinner, we weren't just being polite. On a world where people buy their way into paradise, spending time with who earned it is very dear."

Arina nodded. "I, ah . . . thank you. I'm slowly returning to the world and I appreciate your concern. I wanted to visit. I got as far as your door, but turned away. Your invitation, it was just too soon for me."

"That was understood, Arina, but the invitation is yet open. While you are in the City, we shall get time to visit, your work allowing. And you as well, Father. I was raised Catholic and have lapsed since being here. I'd offer to let you hear my Confession, but the things I have seen would give you a stroke."

"It's not the things you've seen, Mrs. Abrams, but what you've been doing while you've seen them that would be constituting sin." The priest smiled. "If you feel the need, while I am here, I would be pleased to be of service."

"I shall bear that in mind, Father, thank you."

Arina and Father Flynn caught public transport back to her apartment in the City, and Captain Lavaryn soon joined them. The two safety officers synched their datapads and then set about reviewing all they had learned. Both of them characterized it as a great deal, but lamented it still did not tell them terribly much.

David Holcomb was positively identified as Stephen Fonteneau, according to files Covenant pulled in from Commonwealth computers. How he had gotten to Apogea remained unclear, but a David Holcomb had applied for work and had been accepted, then had died in an accident. Fonteneau had somehow discovered Holcomb's misfortune and had exploited it. Because no one knew how he'd done that, the possibility that others might be present under an assumed identity could not be discounted.

Fishing was soon forgotten as hours became days of sifting evidence, formulating conjectures, finding facts to support or destroy a theory. Witnesses were interviewed again, follow-up questions narrowed the gaps in the known information. The solution to the murder lay tantalizingly close, they could feel it, but proved as elusive as Apogea's trout.

The presence of blackout chips was beyond dispute. Covenant's analysis showed they were not so sophisticated that they couldn't be manufactured right there on Apogea, fabricated from parts taken out of existing machines. Apogea safety services were having no luck tracking the distribution of the things, nor in locating the parties where the hidden met; but they felt confident they'd get a break on that angle soon. As rumors spread of the devices, all manner of folks wandered around, snooping, looking to play detective and beat the safety services at their own game, or to join the rebels who gathered to enjoy themselves.

After a week of sifting through interviews conducted in the neighborhood of Park's curio shop, the mountains of evidence that had been gathered, and applying her knowledge of criminal activity, Arina had come up with a simple theory of the case. Park's shop had not been very popular—virtually no one in the area had been in it or had seen Park. His background indicated he was a small-time merchant and she suspected that, under another name, he'd been a fence. He applied for and got passage to Apogea, either at Fonteneau's request or in seeking to hide from authorities and enemies.

Once on Apogea, he and Fonteneau met each other. Fonteneau had come for the *cherengata*. He arranged with Park to smuggle the loot off the world, since Park had no connection with the Abramses. Once the theft had been discovered, Fonteneau would have known that he'd be questioned, since the only sure way the thief would have known the *cherengata* was in the City would have been if he'd seen it on Veronika.

They pinpointed the robbery as having taken place three weeks before the murder, right after the last visit the Abramses had paid to Cuisine Rigel. Veronika remembered having worn the *cherengata* that night. She also recalled a discussion with their guests about all just going back to the apartment, changing into traveling clothes, and heading down to the hunting lodge. They had talked about not needing to drag anything along, since the lodge was informal and relaxed. Veronika had blushed over the fact that she treated servants as if they were invisible, providing Fonteneau with all the information he needed to accomplish his goal.

Arina assumed that after the theft, Fonteneau had given the

cherengata to Park, then later changed his mind about having Park smuggle it away. They had a falling out, Park killed Fonteneau, then fled from Apogea. She did allow that it was possible that Park remained on the world, hiding himself with blackout chips, but if that were the case eventually he would be caught.

Deana Thompson's decision to prematurely terminate her contract and leave Apogea caused them to take another look at her. A discreet search of her apartment turned up nothing. She was allowed to leave and the general sentiment about her situation induced Covenant to not only pay her the bonus for which she had contracted, but to increase it.

At the spaceport, Arina and Lavaryn ushered him past immigration control, noting with a laugh that their methods had been singularly unsuccessful in stopping Park. "If you see him, Dennis, please let someone know."

Flynn nodded, standing in that limbo between Immigration and the departure lounge for the shuttle up to the orbital station. "Just as well he got away in one minor sense. Without a government, you'd be having a hard time trying him for murder. You'd exile him, which seems little punishment for his crime."

"God exiled Adam and Eve from Eden to punish them."

"But they weren't murderers."

"Cain was, and God made him wander the Earth forever." Arina smiled. "And Cain was the father of us all."

"True enough. That seed of evil might be in all of us, but perhaps your situation here doesn't nurture it. The lack of want might not be the lack of temptation, but it does seem to do away with much of it." Flynn drew Arina into a hug. "God be with you, my dear. Don't be working too hard."

Arina pulled back and smiled. "Thank you, Dennis. I am tired, but I needed this. I'll be more than ready to hang up the harness when this business is done, but for the moment it's good to remember who I was before . . ."

"I know, Rina. It's good to have you back." He shook hands with the Zsytzii. "Now, Captain Lavaryn, I expect you to be taking good care of her."

"We treasure our mentor." The Zsytzii smiled as two of his juniors hugged Arina's legs. "We have learned much, and will learn more, much more."

"Very good, the both of you. All luck and peace." Flynn plucked a small bag from one of the juniors. "Now, the lot of you, get back to work. I'll expect to hear how it turned out."

"You will, Dennis, you will." Arina waved to him, then retreated with the Zsytzii brood out of the building.

Father Flynn shouldered his bag and entered the departure lounge. He set his bag down on a bench, sparing only a brief nod in the direction of an amorous couple over in the corner. Before he could seat himself, however, a woman approached him, slowly drawing down the hood of her cloak.

Flynn let the surprise fully register on his face. "You ought not to be here, Mrs. Abrams."

She raised her wrist and tapped the blackout device. "As far as Covenant knows, I'm not." She withdrew a small velvet-covered box from within her cloak and pressed it into his hands. "You will see to it that this gets back to its rightful owners."

"Of course."

"Thank you. I couldn't bear to keep the *cherengata* when I knew how it had been stolen." Veronika shook her head. "I would have sent it back directly, but Sam, he's so funny about that sort of thing. He thrills in shaving deals on the dark side of things, taking risks like that. To give this back would suggest he was wrong in having bought it in the first place. He didn't mind it being stolen back away from him. He greatly enjoyed the daring nature of the theft, and that the thief had done the impossible just to take something from *him*. It meant he was still important. He pretty much chortled about the theft, and has been alive planning how to secure things in the future."

Flynn nodded. "And since Covenant knows you don't want stolen pieces as gifts, your husband will not have the opportunity to buy same from now on."

"Right."

"It will be my pleasure to get this back to the Jirandi *cheren* to whom it belonged." He gave her a smile. "Thank you for setting this all in motion. Arina needed this. After her husband's death, she wondered if she had somehow lost her edge, and that's why he died. She needed time to mourn, and then she needed to be reminded that she is good, she's strong, she's smart. Working on this whole theft and murder might have exhausted her physically, but she's so alive mentally, well, it's good to see. Wonderful."

"I agree, Father."

"Excuse me, Father, would you want some help with your bag? We'll be boarding, soon."

The priest turned and smiled at the man from the corner. "Despite your looking a fair sight more alive than when last I saw you, Mr. Fonteneau, I'm thinking Miss Thompson there will be more appreciative of your help than I will."

"Father, that was just a brain-dead clone they made to kill, not me."

"I know, Stephen, I know." The priest shivered. "That was the nastiest bit of this deception, cloning you to kill. Now, your Miss Thompson, she's forgiven you the dying?"

"Nothing to forgive, Father. I knew he wasn't dead all along." Deana slipped her arm through Fonteneau's. "When Covenant weighed the two problems of Mrs. Abrams needing to get rid of the *cherengata* without incurring her husband's wrath, and Arina Gadja's need for redemption of her self-esteem, it came up with this plan, built out of pieces of Arina's past. It hired me, an actress, to play the part of Stephen's lover. That we actually fell for each other made things that much more convincing. Covenant saw having an innocent led to believe her lover had died as being harmful, hence I was brought in to act the part."

Fonteneau raised an eyebrow. "Of course, she knew she was looking for me before I knew of her, but it worked. I'm glad I came because when Covenant located me, I'd been hidden away good. I'd gone straight you know, Father, after escaping. Here I got the chance to use my skills for good, got a new identity and records expunged in the real world, and love to boot."

Veronika smiled. "And Regan Park never existed, so the hunt for him can continue, as will the searches for the sources of the blackout chips. A little rebellion is good for people, gives them things to think about, talk about, and keeps the world alive for people who thrive on intrigues. The hint of danger is all we need."

The priest's eyes narrowed. In many ways, it seemed, Arina's game analogy had not been far off. The will of the people determined the direction in which Covenant would allow things to flow. The computer did not govern or control, but encouraged and facilitated harmony with the will of Apogea's people. Despite the complexity of society's needs, the balance was maintained and the world's community flourished.

"Anything beyond a hint of danger is probably more than folks here desire, and with good reason." Flynn smiled, then leaned in and kissed Veronika on the cheek. "Fortunately, the serpents in this garden all seem benign. Enjoy the peace that brings you, and know how lucky you are.

Pakeha

Jane Lindskold

Ambrose Kidd, an old Kiwi sailor who remembered those days, was the first to tell Faelin about Aotearoa, yarning over a tankard of winter ale in a San Francisco pub. This was back when Faelin—an orphan of twelve—was still lying about his age to get a job clearing tables and such in a bar.

"Maybe if we hadn't been so spoiled then," the old salt would always begin, "we could've kept things the way they were, but we were spoiled—telephone, the Internet, cruise ships, jet airplanes— New Zealand weren't just a bunch of volcanic islands off the hither side of Australia; we were part of the first world. It might make you laugh, but tourism was a major part of our economy. Anybody with enough money could reach New Zealand in less than a day.

"Most folks skipped out when they saw what the petroleum virus was doing. You born-since can't imagine what that virus meant. Seems like just about everything then had petroleum by-products in it. Not just the obvious stuff like fuel and plastics, but clothing, medicines, even food was full of the stuff. Hell, I ain't telling anything you haven't heard before, son."

He wasn't, either. Faelin had heard stories like this a million times before. What fascinated him was where the story went from here. The New Zealanders had taken a novel approach to the crisis. While most nations strove to keep things as much the same as possible—laying new, untainted cables for telegraph and telephone for example—New Zealand's remaining population resolved to make a radical change.

"I remember my folks talking about it," Kidd went on. "Lady name of Christine Pesh had the idea, as I recall. Bright lady, fancied for prime minister if the oil bugs hadn't got loose. In a way, that makes it odd she should come up with such a plan, but then again, as they tell it, she'd always been one of those who contrary to reason—given they make their money outta government—think that a government that governs least governs best."

Faelin laughed and scooped up the old man's tankard, replacing it with another, filled while the boss's back was turned.

"Sounds to me," he commented, swiping circles on the tables with a dirty rag, "like this Christine Pesh was just lazy."

Ambrose Kidd snorted. "Not at all. It's harder work to make folk think for themselves than to think for 'em. Anyhow, Christine Pesh proposed—and got her proposal out while the communication system was still working pretty well—that government be phased out. She argued that those Kiwis who remained would have enough to do keeping mutton and fish on the table without supporting deadbeat politicians. I don't know how she managed it—remember, son, I was younger than you are now when this happened—but she got her measure passed."

Faelin was California born and bred. He'd heard of wilder schemes, but he knew how governments worked.

"Seems like someone would have appealed," he said.

"There were those who tried," Kidd agreed, "but Pesh and her cronies told 'em there was no government anymore to listen to their appeal. Meantime, while these pro-government factions blustered and debated—'cause they couldn't even agree among themselves which way things *should* be run, if they got government started again—the petroleum virus kept chewing away at stuff. Telephone failed. Computers flashed nonsense and died—lord how I cried when I couldn't get my games to run! Cars and trucks—all of which needed petroleum to go and even if they hadn't were so full of plastic parts that they crumpled up . . ."

"Just like here," Faelin interrupted, knowing he was being rude, but eager to hear the real story.

"That's right," Kidd said, thin lips shaping the half smile of an old man who realizes that the great events of his life are dull fodder to the eager young. "And so Pesh got her way. There were some riots, but most of those who disagreed simply got on ships and left. Most, I hear, got only as far as Australia, where they found more government than anyone could want—but that's another tale.

"You're wanting to hear about New Zealand, or Aotearoa as they renamed it, saying that since the nation was certainly new but had nothing to do with Zeeland—some Dutch place, I recall—they might as well go back to the old Maori name for the land. Prettier, too, means something like Land of the Long White Cloud."

Faelin nodded encouragingly. The boss didn't care if he chatted up the customers during these slow hours, not so long as he worked while he did so and the customers kept drinking.

"There were a couple of townships," Kidd went on, "Christ Church was one, I recall, that experimented with government. Problem was, it's hard to run a government when nobody except you is playing by the rules, sorta like playing soccer when three-quarters of the players insist on picking the ball up with their hands. None of those enclaves lasted more than about twenty years.

"My folks had decided to stay on in Aotearoa. They ran an inn out at Thames, augmenting their business with salvage—lots of folk worked salvage in those days. An uncle offered to take me on his ship as cabin boy—an island cruise, then—it'd be a while before anyone tried to go much farther than Australia. No reason or so it seemed to us."

Kidd paused, visibly swallowing down tales that covered some sixty years at sea. Faelin felt a tinge of curiosity about them, but not enough to keep him from prompting:

"And the rest of the Kiwis? How did things go for them?"

"They were pretty damn hot on their new idea, called Aotearoa the new frontier, compared it to the American West, like we used to see in the movies. Movies were . . ."

"I know, I know," Faelin said impatiently. "I *am* Californian! So everyone wore guns and rode horses?"

"Well," Kidd laughed, "many did, but that wasn't why folks made the comparison—at least not the only reason. More reason was because there was no law but what folks carried in their hearts. That's still how it is today—or at least how it was when I left Aotearoa a couple years back, and I don't see why it should have changed. No law books or lawyers, no presidents or monarchs, no rules and regulations, just common sense, hard work, and prosperity for those who earn it."

Faelin never forgot Ambrose Kidd's stories. Indeed, he became the old sailor's constant companion—for it soon became clear that Kidd was never sailing home again. The boy's eager attention was meat and drink to Kidd, just as his stories were to the orphan boy. After the sailor died, Faelin found that he was starving for more.

He took jobs around the ports and soon learned to spot a Kiwi sailor by a certain proud lift to his head. An offer of a drink usually got the boy more stories. Work as a dockhand evolved into work aboard ships—first in port, then at sea.

Chafing under California's numerous regulations, all of which seemed to exist—as far as Faelin could tell—to keep the strong and able from profiting while buoying up the weak and unfit, Faelin happily took a berth on the *Speculation*.

Speculation was an ocean-going free-trader, a sailing vessel modeled off the old China clipper—a ship type that, ironically, had met its demise due to the evolution of the coal-dependent steamers soon after it had reached near perfection of design. Now, with petroleum products useless, the clipper ship had been resurrected.

Current technology had taken a while to recover to the point that a clipper ship could be built—there were so many old skills to be relearned, so many shops to be retooled—but now that point had been reached and Faelin's childhood had been marked by the sight of these great white seabirds, first in ones and twos, later in great flocks.

The *Speculation*'s captain, a sour old cove named Burke, was among those who were taking advantage of the relative availability of clipper ships. Burke's vessel was not among the newest, but Burke was owner-aboard, a thing that would have been nearly unheard of twenty years before when it took a corporation to fund the building of the vessels.

Faelin admired Captain Burke as the perfect type of the self-made man. The *Speculation* was a tight ship, but her regulations made sense. After all, you couldn't have someone lolling below decks in a storm when all hands were needed on deck or deciding to steer without the least knowledge of navigation, could you?

For five years, Faelin served on the *Speculation* and during that time he grew into a big man, broad-shouldered, topping most around him by a head or more. His rough, calloused hands were equally swift with a pistol, gun, or a line. He even picked up a few lubber skills—some carpentry, iron working, and sewing. He became known as a good man to have at your side in a brawl, had many followers but never close friends.

Over those five years, however, Faelin's opinion of Captain Burke and his capacity as a commander underwent a change. Faelin couldn't help but notice that as officers retired or went on to other vessels, he himself was never promoted to fill their posts. He received pay raises readily enough, and high bonuses when a cargo sold well. Still, this wasn't stripes on his sleeve and his mates calling him "sir."

Had the *Speculation* been a military vessel, Faelin might have excused the oversight, but on a free-trader nothing but ability was required for promotion. Therefore, he started brooding over the slight.

He might not make a good quartermaster—Faelin was the first to admit that bookkeeping was far from his favorite sport—but he navigated well enough, had taken his time at the wheel. He might be young yet to serve as first officer, but he'd make a good second. Eventually, he grew sullen, deciding he was being slighted.

"I tell you," he said one afternoon to Simon Alcott, his closest crony, as they sat up in the riggings mending trousers. "Captain Burke doesn't like me because he sees I'm a threat to him and that wimp son of his, Irving. He don't dare promote me, even to second, lest the crew start wondering why Irving's first mate and I'm second. Far better to have old Waldemar in that post, him with his stammer and two missing fingers."

Simon Alcott listened and nodded. Ever since Faelin had come to his rescue one night in a Singapore alley, Simon had been his absolutely loyal toady, reveling in his protector's strength. In his simple loyalty, contradicting anything Faelin said or thought never would have occurred to Simon. Indeed, he thought Faelin was right.

"Heck, Faelin," Simon said, "you'd make a better captain than the old man. Let him keep the books and work out the trades. You could run this ship tighter than a kernel fits in a nutshell."

For weeks Faelin groused on, Simon providing an unquestioning chorus to his complaints, until Faelin's vague grudges became as real to him as if Captain Burke actually told him that he was unpromotable.

As his discontent grew, Faelin considered his options. He could jump ship and get hired by another vessel, maybe by one of the big lines. They'd recognize his skills quick enough. For days he reveled in the image of himself in the neatly tailored dark blue coat and trousers of one of the better known shipping lines. There'd be gold piping on his sleeve and men jumping to anticipate his every word.

This fantasy soured, though, when Faelin considered the host of rules and regulations that even the officers were governed by on the lines. There were taverns and brothels they couldn't enter lest they sully the image of their employer. They had to accept transfers without protest, had to keep those uniforms perfect and those brass buttons shining. Sure they had lackeys to do the real work, but Faelin couldn't help but feel he'd be sealing himself into a tighter box than he was in already.

When Captain Burke announced that their next long haul was to be a winter—summer as it would be in the southern hemisphere— voyage to Australia, followed by a stop in Auckland, Aotearoa, Faelin realized what he should do.

Weren't rules—laws, regulations, favoritism—all that was holding him back? Hadn't old Ambrose Kidd told him that Aotearoa had no government and so was free from all that nonsense? Well, then, Faelin would jump ship in Auckland, that's what he'd do! Hadn't he been drawn there all his life? Hadn't old Kidd's stories been what had taken him to sea in the first place?

Faelin grinned like a fool, swallowing the expression when he saw Alcott staring at him curiously. They were weeks out yet, plenty of time for him to lay his plans.

He started by making himself up a couple of crates filled with trade goods purchased in various ports. He made them smallish ones, easy enough to carry for one man, especially if that man was a sailor used to loading and unloading, hauling lines and anchor, and all the rest.

From Kidd's tales Faelin knew that, other than gold, Aotearoa was metal poor. Nearly all they had came from salvage and trade. In every port of call he bought nails and wire, hinges and bolts, fish-hooks. He ended up taking Simon Alcott into his confidence for his follower started wondering at Faelin's sudden, unusual interest in trade. When Alcott begged permission to jump ship with him, Faelin graciously granted it. After all, two men could carry more than one and he knew that Simon would never rat on him.

In addition to trade goods, Faelin bought small items that would make their transition easier: extra knives, whetstones, coils of tightly spun rope, axe and hammer heads, needles and thread. In a pinch these could go on the block, too, but he didn't want to spend their capital on commonsense necessities.

Faelin spent both of their earnings lavishly, chatted up Kiwi sailors in every port, but kept care that no one other than Simon should notice his new interest. At last, after months at sea that for the first time in years seemed long, the *Speculation* sailed into Auckland's harbor and Faelin saw the promised land before him.

November was summer here and the hills were green. Off in the distance a white plume of smoke marked one of the many volcanoes that had shaped these islands, dormant now but for that almost fluffy plume. Drinking in those lush hills, the neat houses, the confident bustle of the citizens, Faelin thought Aotearoa the most beautiful place he'd ever seen.

Its difference from other nations was perceptible from the moment he strode down the gangplank in Auckland. By now Faelin had visited hundreds of ports through both Americas, Europe, the British Isles, even in Japan. Never before—not even in those nations erupted into despotic chaos—had there not been a governmental presence somewhere near the docks.

In Auckland's port there was plenty of activity, but not a glimpse of anyone with that stiff, attentive posture that said "official." There was no one sporting a clipboard, name-tag, or uniform. Merchants hurried to dicker for cargos, but no one rushed to collect tariffs. Able bodies offered themselves for a variety of jobs, from porter and dock hand to guide and companion, but there were no police, no soldiers, no . . .

Momentarily Faelin felt a little lost. Then he rallied. His plans called for him and Simon to work just like usual, right until Burke announced that they were to set sail. Then he and Simon—who would have already inconspicuously unloaded their trade goods—would go ashore for one more roister. All they'd need to do then was lie low until the *Speculation* sailed on the tide.

He knew Captain Burke of old. Once the old man had even stranded his son, Irving, leaving the chastened young man to catch up to them at their next port. Burke wouldn't wait for two sailors, able as they might be.

Everything went according to plan. From a room in a port-side inn, Faelin watched the *Speculation* spread her wings and course out to sea. He felt a momentary twinge—after all, the ship had been his home for over five years—but this was washed away in a flood of excitement. Next time he encountered Captain Burke or any of his mates from the *Speculation* Faelin planned to be a big man—a ship owner maybe, a land owner, a trader.

Smiling, Faelin sauntered downstairs, Simon at his heels, to settle their bill. By reflex, he pulled out a handful of coins left over from his last pay. (At first he'd regretted that he'd not be getting his share of the Aotearoa bonus, but then he'd had the brilliant idea to make it up out of Burke's stores.)

The innkeeper, a prim-looking old woman, pulled out a scale and started weighing the coins, checking values against a handwritten chart.

"Copper'll bring less than iron," she said. "Iron less than steel. These . . ." she sniffed at some nickel-blend tokens, "aren't worth much but as sinkers on a line."

"They're money, lady," Simon Alcott blustered in reflection of his hero's momentary embarrassment, "not ore."

The old woman cocked an elegant white eyebrow at him.

"Not in Aotearoa, bro," she said. "Money's only worth what a backing government says it is. We're purely a barter economy here. You might get better prices from a currency speculator. To me this is just a few ounces of metal—and not pure metal either. Values are down a bit, too, what with the *Speculation* dumping quite a bit of metal goods on the market."

Faelin stepped in.

"How about worked metal, ma'am?" he said, doing his best to exude manly politeness to cover his gaff.

"That'd be better," the innkeeper admitted.

Eventually, they settled the bill with a handful of iron nails, a deal that brought them a map of the area, the innkeeper's recommendation of a boarding house run by her sister, information as to where they could get current values, and the old lady's sour smile.

"Welcome to Aotearoa," she said in parting. "You look tough enough and used to hard work, maybe you'll make pakeha yet."

Pakeha, they were to learn later, was local slang for a resident. Before the petroleum virus, it had meant anyone of European ancestry, but now it was reserved for those—no matter where their parents had been born—who made the grade in the new nation.

After Simon and Faelin had left the inn and were consulting the map, meaning to head first for the boarding house, a bedraggled figure clad in dirty rags sidled over to them.

"Spare a bit for a shave and a shower?" the man whined. "I gotta try and get passage off this madhouse island, and no one'll look at me twice the mess I am."

Faelin sneered at this wreck of a human being—clearly one of those who would never be pakeha, though he certainly looked to have the raw makings. There were broad shoulders under that ragged shirt and height despite the man's cringing crouch.

Faelin started to tell the bum to haul his worthless ass off to the social center, remembered in time that there wouldn't be one here, and in his momentary confusion dug a handful of nickel coins from the pocket of his trousers.

"See what you can get with these," he said, tossing them into the man's cupped hands.

The bum caught most of them, scrabbling on the patched concrete of the dock front for those he dropped, then scurried off. Simon shivered as he watched him go.

"Felt like someone stepped on my grave, just then," he said.

Faelin snorted, balanced his crate of trade goods on one shoulder and tucked his duffle under his arm, then led the way into the city.

A sign greeted them as they left the harbor:

Welcome to Aotearoa.
Mind your goods and your manners.
No one will mind them for you.

Faelin was heartened by the words. This was promising—a warning to the weak, a message to the strong.

At the boarding house, a handful of iron nails bought them a room and two meals a day for a couple of weeks if they agreed to do their own housekeeping—a thing that was second nature to a sailor in any case. The owner of the boarding house, Mrs. Philbert, tossed in the use of her son as a guide to sweeten the deal.

Mrs. Philbert was a shrewd-faced woman, less elegant and quite a bit younger than her sister, but she liked sailors. She told them her husband sailed on an island trader that ran a regular route between the North and South Islands.

As Faelin looked around the comfortable room to which they'd been shown and contemplated the wealth of manufactured goods stored in their two crates, he felt pleased with himself. Leaving Simon to stow their gear and make the room comfortable, he set out with the innkeeper's Bobby to get a feel for Aotearoa.

The next few weeks were a flurry of new impressions. Faelin had waited until his arrival to select just where he wanted to settle. He had a good idea of his needs.

He wanted open water near so he and Simon could fall back on sailing when needed. He wanted a fairly rural area. Auckland, while small by the standards of some urban areas, was still too big. The best pickings had been taken long ago and Faelin hadn't come here to be somebody else's serf.

He also needed to trade for horses and pack mules to carry their gear. The livestock he planned to ranch—his dreams still colored by old Kidd's comparison of Aotearoa to the American frontier—could wait until he'd staked his claim.

Eventually, Faelin selected a settlement near what had once been called New Plymouth. When the oil bugs had set to work New Plymouth had been abandoned by all but a few hardy souls. This new settlement, called Richmont, had started up about three years before and the town was actively recruiting settlers. They advertised a trading post, two inns, several boarding houses, a school, and a budding road system.

Richmont fit Faelin's requirements to perfection and, best of all, a wagon train funded in part by the town's founders was heading out within the week. The wagon train's organizer was more than willing to hire both Faelin and Simon as guards in return for grub and promise of their pick of a couple good cattle at the trail's end.

Waving good-bye to Mrs. Philbert and little Bobby, Faelin swung into the saddle of his buckskin riding horse and never looked back.

Richmont proved to be almost everything for which Faelin had hoped. The original city of New Plymouth was gone, burned to the ground in the riots that had followed the advent of the petroleum virus, riots inspired by panic related to the petrochemical plants that had once functioned in the area. The new settlement was built slightly west along the coast from the original city.

Although New Plymouth had been destroyed, its concrete, brick, and stone remained as a source of building materials for the new settlement. Instead of the log cabins and clapboard houses that had lined the streets of Richmont in Faelin's imagination, there were solid square-built houses, rarely more than three stories high, laboriously cemented together.

The greatest bane of Faelin's existence, Chapin Toms, lived in the most imposing of the three-story buildings. Chapin—he was one of those people who insisted everyone call him by his first name—was the unofficial mayor of Richmont. A tiny, wiry man in his mid-sixties, Chapin looked so frail that Faelin suspected he could break Chapin in two without breaking a sweat. He had the impulse to do so within a week of his arrival in Richmont.

Chapin ran the Richmont trading post and, as such, pretty much dictated the prices for anything other than a meal, drink, or livestock—and indirectly affected the prices for those as well. What drove Faelin crazy was how everyone rhapsodized about how fair

Chapin was when to Faelin it was apparent that Chapin set his prices by how much a person could do for him—Chapin—personally. As a newcomer, Faelin felt he was being shafted.

He and Simon had staked their claim on a nice chunk of water-front land west of Richmont, near to where—so the settlement agent told them—the small town of Oakura had been. Their land had beach front, good acreage inland for grazing, and nearby scavenging for building materials. The weather was pleasant this time of year— enough so that two sailors didn't think twice about bunking in a tent, but Faelin wanted at least the beginnings of a house built by winter.

Leaving Simon behind to mind the cattle and sheep—their duties as guards on the trip out had netted them a cow, a couple of nice heifers, and about a dozen sheep—Faelin rode into town. He took with him a pack mule, a small selection of worked metal trade goods, and empty saddlebags to carry back his loot.

Faelin strode into Chapin's trading post—the Dairy as the locals called it for some reason Faelin couldn't fathom, given that there wasn't a cow in sight—nodding greetings to a few folks he knew from the journey out. While waiting his turn he wandered around, check-ing the stock against his list. He was pleased to see that just about everything he needed was on the shelves. There were luxury goods, too: bolts of fabric, bottled liquor, shiny trinkets, salvaged antiqui-ties.

When his turn came, Faelin nodded greeting and began: "I'd like a couple of shovels, two buckets, five pounds of flour, four hens and a rooster, and one of those things you use for making butter."

"A churn," Chapin said. He had a face like an amiable walnut and the lines in it shaped a smile around the words.

Faelin nodded. "That's right. A couple of glass or crockery jars would be good, too. Never knew one cow could give so much milk."

Chapin smiled again.

"Your bro picked a good beast, there. He has an eye for cattle."

"That's right. Grew up on a farm in Oregon," Faelin replied. "Handy with cattle and sheep."

"You're a sailor, I recall." Chapin thrust a hand across the count-er. "We haven't been formally introduced. I'm Chapin Toms."

"Faelin," Faelin replied.

His surname had been that of the Domain of California orphanage which had reared him, and he'd dropped it as soon as he went to sea. Faelin had no idea where his given name came from, but suspected that it had been some administrator's fancy. Still, for years it had been all he owned and he'd grown fond of it.

"Faelin," Chapin said, pausing as if he expected more. "Right. Well, let's go through that list of yours. Shovel. Wood or metal blade?"

Faelin had no doubts on this. He'd known these would be his most expensive purchase.

"Metal."

"New or used?"

"Used, if the condition's good."

"Buckets. Wood or leather or tin?"

"Leather's fine."

"Have a sack for your flour?"

"Uh, no."

"I'll have to charge for that, then, but you'll find it'll reuse. All I have are ten-pound sacks right now. Hope that'll do."

Faelin nodded stiffly, certain he was being had and reluctant to turn from the counter lest he see a knowing grin on a pakeha face.

"Hens and rooster. Particular breed?"

Faelin couldn't recall the name of the big white birds the *Speculation*'s cook had preferred and was embarrassed to say.

"Any kind as long as they lay biggish eggs."

"Well, the rooster'll take care of making sure there're eggs," Chapin said, a roguish twinkle in his eye.

Faelin wanted to punch the little man. At least he'd known enough to ask for a rooster.

"And a butter churn," Chapin concluded. "Small one should do for you two. Of course, you could save yourself the labor and trade with a neighbor. Debra and Fleming Dutchman have a two year-old claim not far from you and Debbie makes fine butter."

Faelin nodded. "We've spoken."

Chapin paused as if waiting to see if the request for the churn would be withdrawn, then he went on.

"Jars. I can do you a couple of good two-gallon crockery ones."

Faelin nodded, accepting the two bluish stoneware pieces set up on the counter for his inspection.

"Anything else?" Chapin asked. "Wax? We sell that in pound bricks. Axe handles? Honey? Liquor? Lanterns?"

Faelin considered. Wax would be useful for waterproofing as well as for making candles. Axe handles they could make. Both he and Simon were whittlers from way back. Sweets and liquor, though, those were luxuries that he and Simon had resolved to do without. They had a cake of sugar swiped from *Speculation*'s stores and would make that last.

"Two pounds of wax," he replied. "I'll think on the rest."

Chapin nodded and started arraying the goods on the counter. A small group of idlers watched with interest, making Faelin feel acutely self-conscious. He wasn't used to shopping except for minor luxuries—shipboard life took care of the basics. Barter wasn't unfamiliar, not with all the ports he'd been to, but he didn't like the vague feeling that he was about to be taken.

When Chapin finished setting everything out, he asked Faelin to inspect the goods for flaws.

" 'Cause it's yours once it goes into your saddlebags.' "

Then he hopped up on a tall three-legged stool, bent his hands back to crack his knuckles, and said:

"So what do you have to trade, Faelin?"

Faelin pulled out some nails.

"Nails are good," Chapin said, hopping down from his stool, agile as a monkey to check their heft and quality. "These are good nails. They'll cover the poultry, flour and sack, wax, and, because I'm in a good mood and leather buckets aren't moving since we got a cooper in town, the buckets. What you got to cover the shovels?"

Faelin glowered at Chapin. There had been a few chuckles about the buckets, chuckles that made him feel uncomfortably like an outsider.

"Leather buckets are good," he growled. "And my mate and I can mend them ourselves."

Chapin waved a hand airily. "Don't be such a hard case, Faelin. Can't you see I'm having a joke at my own expense? I over-bought last winter and all the pakeha know it."

Rather than being soothed, Faelin felt even more out of place at this reminder that he was a newcomer.

"What do you want for the shovels?" he asked stiffly.

"You brought a nice mule in with you," Chapin said. "How about him?"

"You must be joking!" Faelin replied.

"Well, I can't see what else you've got if you don't put it on the table," Chapin said amiably. "What's weighing down your goody bag there? It's more than a few nails or I'm a one-legged weta."

Faelin had the vague idea that the weta was some local critter—a bug, he thought.

"And how do I know you'll play fair with me if I put my cards on the table?" he retorted.

"You are a hard case, aren't you?" Chapin said. "Look, Faelin. We're all neighbors. We live together, work together. How far would I go if I stole from my neighbors? Why they'd just trade with each other and leave me out of the mix. I only manage to make my living because people trust me to be fair and to provide them with a savings of time."

He leaned forward on his stool, his ugly walnut face earnest. "These aren't the petroleum days, Faelin. You could make most of what you're buying from me or hunt it out yourself. I'm just saving you time. If you don't want to trade for the churn and the shovels, ride on over to the cooper. He'll make you a churn—it might take a couple of weeks if he doesn't have one in stock, but he can make you one. Old Mrs. Velma has a couple of rusty old shovels. I bet you could rent them from her in return for splitting a couple cords of wood and returning the shovels all bright and sharp.

"Now, walk or pour out your trade goods. I have customers waiting. They may be enjoying the show—'specially since it's giving them a good idea of market value for a few things, but I don't have time to waste."

Faelin flushed and nearly walked, but he had a long trip back to the claim and didn't want to explain to Simon why he came back empty-handed. He spilled out the contents of his sack: more nails, a couple of feet of wire, and, selected almost at random, a pulley.

Chapin inspected the goods, then he looked around the store as if assessing his audience.

"A lesson for you, Faelin. The nails and wire, those are really good. Most of the nails we have here are wrought iron or salvage. These you've brought are better than local made. The wire's more of the same. Hell, most of us make do with twine. The pulley, that's a matter of need. With the new settlers come in—yourself among them—there's going to be a lot of house raising."

Faelin nodded. Rather than being grateful for the lesson, he was feeling embarrassed. He suspected now that both Mrs. Philbert and her sister back in Auckland had ripped him off. He wondered about the livestock dealers from whom he'd bought the horses and mules. At least Simon had gotten them good stock, but he'd bet his left foot they'd overpaid.

He felt color rising along his neck and fought down a desire to storm out the door.

"I'd keep that pulley if I were you," Chapin went on, "and hire yourself and Simon out to help raise a couple houses. Then when you're done, you'll have help and more to build your own place."

Chapin nodded happily, pleased by his own sermon.

Faelin swallowed hard. He wasn't going to accept this walnut-faced little monkey pushing him around. There wasn't a government here to make him build other people's houses. He'd just learned his nails made him pretty rich by local standards. He'd buy labor when he needed it and damn Chapin for trying to turn him into a toady.

"How much for the churn and the shovels?" he repeated.

"Nails for the shovels," Chapin replied, his friendly manner suddenly take it or leave it, "and the wire for the churn. Keep the pulley and I'll put you down for house building."

Faelin started to say, "Don't bother," then swallowed the words. He could always refuse when asked. He settled his bill and got out of there as fast as possible, then he fumed the entire way back to the claim. The chatter of the indignant chickens didn't help his mood.

As the weeks and months passed, Faelin's opinion of Chapin didn't change.

"He's made himself king in a land where there's supposed to be no government," he growled to Simon after another frustrating shopping trip. "Did you know that since we decided not to go to the

Dutchmans' barn raising, Chapin refused to sell me anything? Said he didn't feel like trading with a man who couldn't be bothered to help a close neighbor. Those Dutchmans are just rolling in cream and butter! They could pay for my time!"

It hadn't helped Faelin's feelings about Chapin's know-it-all attitude that after a month or so of trying to make their own butter, Simon had timidly suggested that they trade the churn to Debra and Fleming in return for a few months' supply of butter and cheese. Faelin had been forced to agree. After a day of dealing with livestock and working on the house, neither man had the energy to churn.

He ignored the fact that he, not Chapin, had been at fault in the matter of the churn and continued his list of grievances.

"I had to go to the miller direct and she gouged me, charged everything that Chapin would have and made me pull nails from old lumber while I waited!"

Simon said nothing. Though Simon would never complain to Faelin, Faelin had seen the other man's distress when they didn't go to the barn raising. Simon liked the Dutchmans—a handsome, mostly Chinese couple despite their names—and the two men's isolation on the claim after crowded quarters on the *Speculation* had proven almost more than Simon could bear.

Faelin, not normally a sympathetic man, took pity on Simon, letting him make some of the supply runs into town and not even protesting when Simon came back with a fat black and brown sheepdog puppy of the type locally known as a huntaway. He tried not to recall that this new arrangement also saved him further confrontations with his self-appointed rival.

But Faelin continued to feel the pressure of Chapin's influence. When he got into a fistfight with the cooper over a horse race, Chapin just turned away and sighed, but the next time Faelin came into the Dairy, Chapin refused to serve him until Faelin promised to donate something to the cooper's support while he recovered from the hand Faelin had broken.

When Faelin tried to recruit some labor for raising the walls on the new house—he and Simon had built a solid foundation, but couldn't hope to finish stone walls by winter—mysteriously no one was available, not even when Faelin advertised handsome pay in metal goods. Not until he and Simon took a turn in a few building parties did help materialize, and then for free.

The laborers even brought treats—sweets and veggies and summer ale—to augment the fish-fry Simon and Faelin had supplied, and that evening their quiet claim echoed with laughter and the skirling notes of Erland Totaranui's fiddle.

Faelin hated it, hated the pressure of obligation which seemed far more binding than any law—after all, laws could be circumvented, reinterpreted, or simply ignored. He hated it even more when he saw how Simon was being seduced from him.

When they had arrived in Aotearoa, Simon had been completely ruled by Faelin. He let Faelin dictate practically everything he did, and was never happier than when dogging Faelin's heels. By July, the heart of the local winter, Simon was making excuses to do things on his own. He'd made friends with not only the Dutchmans and other pakeha neighbors, but also with members of a local Maori clan to the east who were associated with, but not precisely part of, the Richmont settlement.

Many a wet afternoon when Faelin thought they should be mending nets or carding wool or any of a thousand other jobs, Simon would make an excuse to go riding off to visit a neighbor. Roto the puppy—named after the Maori word for lake, since he'd been so hard to house train—would happily trot after Simon.

Nor could Faelin really complain that Simon was shirking. He always brought something back with him as payment for his day's labors elsewhere—honey and wax from a neighbor's hives, salt, tanned hides, rope. Once, incredibly, he'd even secured them the long-term loan of a Maori waka, or canoe, in return for giving sailing lessons to the local clan.

Faelin's dislike of Chapin and his influence came to a head that spring at the sheep shearing. Like so many things Faelin thought should be handled by trade and barter—or by a bit of strong-arm persuasion—the shearing was a community event, as much an excuse for a party as a means of getting work done.

With a calm persuasiveness Faelin wouldn't have suspected the other man of being capable of a year before, Simon had explained how much less labor it would involve for them to drive their small flock—now thirty strong with trade and lambings—over to town.

After pointing out that they didn't have shears, that they didn't really know what they were doing, and that they might as well see if they could trade a lamb or two for a piglet, Simon had clinched the matter by saying, "And if you're not going, well, then I am anyhow. There's to be dancing when the work is done and a cook-off and a horse race. Farmer Lamont is donating a pig in honor of his first grandchild's birthday and it's to be pit barbecued."

"I never said I wasn't going," Faelin snarled, though in fact he'd been planning on staying home. This spring he was hoping to put in a small kitchen garden, despite the fact that he'd never grown as much as an onion in all his life. He'd thought to start turning what looked to him like a promising bit of land.

Faelin trailed the flock into town in a sour mood, watching Roto drive the sheep along with effortless ease. He wished he could figure out why his own course was never so easy. He'd expected that in a land without government and binding regulations he'd prosper.

He wasn't lazy, nor was he intimidated by bad weather. He was strong and before had always met those who—like Simon—would cling to him because of that strength. To top it off, he had skills most of the others never dreamed of. He'd been shocked to learn that Farmer Lamont had been a lawyer in faraway New York before chucking it all and coming to homestead in Aotearoa over twenty years before.

Now Lamont was a pakeha of the pakeha. In fact, the Richmont settlement was Lamont's second claim. He'd sold his first at what everyone knew was a tremendous profit because Auckland was getting too built up for him. Lamont said he wanted his sons and daughters to be able to raise their families in less developed land, just as he had them.

Such thoughts put a sour taste in Faelin's mouth, but that sour turned to honey at his first sight of Jocelyn.

Tall and arrow-straight with golden-brown skin and shining black hair, she glided through the Richmont town square like a princess. Clearly, her parentage was mixed—there was Polynesian in her and

Chinese, but the lapis lazuli of her laughing eyes spoke of some European heritage as well.

When Faelin first saw her, Jocelyn was holding a toddler by the hand and his spirits plummeted. Then the little one tore his hand free and calling out, "Mama! Mama!" went waddling across to a woman Faelin vaguely recognized as one of the Lamont girls.

This then must be the much celebrated Lamont grandchild. At that moment, Faelin would have added every sheep in his flock to the barbecue in his joy at realizing this goddess was not the baby's mother.

He nudged his buckskin alongside Simon's bay.

"Who is *that*?" he asked, indicating the girl with a tilt of his head.

Simon looked and smiled. When he replied his voice was warm with affection.

"That's Jocelyn Lee. She's a cousin of the Dutchmans, came up from Auckland over the winter. She's been staying with them since August. I'm surprised you haven't met her."

Simon clipped the end off that last sentence, suddenly uncomfortable. The fact was, Faelin had become more and more a hermit over that winter. Simon did almost all their trading, even picking up the butter and cheese from the Dutchmans. Faelin had done the fishing, building, even the sewing—anything that gave him an excuse to let Simon be the one to go out.

Faelin felt a faint regret for lost opportunities. Then suddenly he didn't care. Jocelyn Lee was here. So was he. There was to be dancing that evening. He would dance with her. He would woo her. He would win her.

Faelin worked that day with a constant awareness of Jocelyn's graceful presence. When the day warmed, he stripped off his shirt, knowing his muscles would show to advantage. He did every job with a smile on his lips, knowing he'd shine better in her eyes. He even avoided the horse race—though he longed to try his buckskin against the cooper's black—lest the old tale of their scrap go round and cheapen him in her eyes.

All that day he listened as the flirting note of her laughter, sweeter than any music, carried across the bleating of indignant sheep. When Jocelyn carried around cold water for the shearers' refreshment,

Faelin introduced himself, then found himself too fumble-tongued to carry on.

When the shearing was done, Faelin retired to the room he and Simon had taken for the night and scrubbed down with care. He dressed in his best clothes, glad now that Simon had insisted they pack them along.

Like most sailors, Faelin had learned to tailor and embroider. The bleached cotton shirt he wore fit to perfection and was graced with tiny blue stars. After tying his freshly washed hair back in a sailor's queue and donning newly polished boots, Faelin inspected himself in the mirror and was pleased with the sight.

Faelin's grooming had taken so long that Simon had left without him. When he entered the torch-lit circle where three-quarters of the area's population had gathered, Faelin felt strangely shy, aware that he was still a stranger in a group of friends.

To cover his discomfort, he put a sailor's swagger into his walk and joined Simon by the buffet. The food was free—donated by all the participants and transformed into a feast by those who hadn't actually been working with the sheep. The centerpiece might have been Farmer Lamont's barbecued pig, but there was such a variety of food spread around it that even its vast bulk was dwarfed.

Faelin ate lightly, waiting impatiently for Jocelyn to arrive. Even after the dancing had started, she didn't come. Gruffly, Faelin refused an invitation from saucy Debbie Dutchman, waiting like an eagle for Jocelyn lest he not be free to dive upon her when she arrived.

When Jocelyn did come in, the dancing was in full swing. Even so it seemed to Faelin that Jocelyn brought her own music with her. In workday trousers and shirt, she'd been eye-catching. Now, dressed for a party, she was everything he had dreamed—lovely as spring-time itself in a floor-length frock of deep red silk embellished with scattered golden flowers.

That silk gown should have been a warning to Faelin, but he was too besotted to think. Jocelyn stood poised near the edge of the circle of light and the swirl of dancing. Contrary to Faelin's expectation that she would be pounced on as soon as she arrived, she remained alone, though by far the finest woman in the place.

Why it's just like with me, Faelin thought. *No one will have anything to do with her because she's so far above the rest. They want to
lower her to their level—to transform that lovely princess into a wall-
flower as they've tried to make me every man's lackey.*

Faelin strode over to her, the beating of his heart in his ears louder than the combined fiddles and guitars, so that he felt strangely disconnected from everything around him. He made Jocelyn a sweeping bow, aware that he cut a dashing figure, and held out his hand.

"May I have this dance, sweet lady?"

In his imagination—fevered all that day so he hardly remembered
the sheep, the mud, the faces of those he'd worked beside—Jocelyn
had blushed prettily and put her hand in his. Then he'd swept her off
into the middle of the dancing, the two of them becoming the shining heart of the action, paired stars that transformed all the rest into
extras.

But in reality, Jocelyn returned his bow with a pretty curtsy and
smiled.

"Thank you, sir, but I'm waiting for my fiancé."

"Your what! Who . . ."

Faelin heard himself bellow so loudly that the dancers nearest turned
to stare and the musicians faltered for a moment in their playing.

"My fiancé," Jocelyn replied. "He had a bit of business to conclude."

"Then he's lost his chance," Faelin said, struggling for gallantry.
"Let me convince you . . ."

A new voice cut in from slightly behind him.

"Convince her of what, Faelin?"

Faelin knew that voice, light and a touch impish, mocking him yet
again.

"Chapin!"

He wheeled and found the little monkey man looking up at him,
head tilted in inquiry, a smile on his lips.

"I see you've met my betrothed," Chapin said. "Jocelyn Lee, meet
Faelin the Sailor, late of the *Speculation* and of California, now settler—neighbor to your cousins the Dutchmans."

Faelin saw red. He didn't know what made him more furious—
that this little man should have somehow bought Jocelyn Lee or
that in his mocking way he should make his introduction a

reminder that Faelin was just a settler, not pakeha, not now, and—
if Chapin had his damnable way not ever—not unless Faelin
became Chapin's lackey, building other folks' houses, shearing
their sheep, taking their insults . . .

Jocelyn had slid her slender hand into Chapin's skinny paw and
was smiling up at Faelin.

"Pleased to meet you, Faelin. I know your partner, of course.
Sweet Simon we call him, always such a help. Such a hand with the
cattle."

Faelin began to tremble with fury. So Simon had turned against
him. Jocelyn might name him Faelin's partner, but clearly he'd
become a toady to these enemies . . .

He gnashed his teeth. He hadn't known anyone ever really did
that, but in the madness that was overtaking him, he gnashed them,
feeling them grind like rocks in his mouth.

"You!" he bellowed, a rough growl that echoed through the suddenly quiet throng. He hardly noticed that the dancing had stopped,
only that his words carried farther. "You, Chapin! What did you pay
for her?"

"Pay?" Chapin looked astonished.

Jocelyn, still clinging to his hand, colored, her golden skin flush-
ing crimson.

"Pay? Chapin repeated.

"Aye, pay," Faelin growled. "You make everyone trade with you,
monkey man. I won't believe that such a beauty would agree to
wed a skinny old monkey like you if you didn't offer a good trade.
Did you give her cousins more cattle for their farm? Or did you
buy her with pretty things and the promise of a three-story stone
house?"

The significance of the silk dress came to him. Vaguely Faelin
recalled having seen a bolt of that fabric on his first visit to the
store.

"Aye," he continued, tapping Jocelyn's sleeve. "I see she's wearing
part of your trade. Well then, I've a trade for you. I'll trade you your
life for the girl. Otherwise, I'm going to rip your head off those
scrawny shoulders and take her home with me. What do you say to
that offer?"

Chapin shook his head gently, almost sadly, then said:

"I have a counter offer for you, Faelin. Look around."

And Faelin did. Behind him the assembled pakeha had drawn into a semicircle. No one carried weapons, but fists were clenched and faces were stern.

From in the midst of that crowd of disapproval, old Farmer Lamont shook his gray head.

"We don't do things that way, Faelin. Jocelyn has the right to make up her mind who she wants to marry. If she wants to marry Chapin— for whatever reason—we support her, especially since Chapin wants to marry her, too, and no other woman has a claim on him."

There was a murmur of uneasy male laughter as if to say "What man in his right mind *wouldn't* want to marry Jocelyn?"

Faelin spat. "You talk of claims, of rights, Lamont. I thought Aotearoa had no laws."

"No government," Lamont said with a slight stress on the second word. "Law is not the same as government. Law is the rules by which a society decides to live. What we support here is the right of every human to decide his or her own life, free of some governing body asserting its rights over theirs."

"And my rights?" Faelin countered. "Seems like since I've come here, everyone has been steering me to do things their way. I can't get a bag of flour or a pig or a few days' work on my land without trotting about doing everyone else's bidding."

"Your rights are yours," Lamont expounded, shades of the lawyer he had once been in his intonation. "You can make your own flour or raise your own pigs or work your own land, but if you want to make someone else do something, then you'd better have the means to enforce your will. Seems to me that when you're accusing us of making you do our bidding, what you're really complaining about is that you can't make us do your bidding."

"There's no law against my way," Faelin sneered.

"No law," Lamont agreed, "but we don't like your manners much."

Faelin swung on his heel to look at Jocelyn. She was holding on to Chapin's arm, her posture protective. Whatever Chapin had paid for her, he'd bought her well and good.

"Damn you all," he said to no one in particular.

He spotted Simon on the edge of the crowd, Roto sitting on his feet.

"C'mon, Simon. We're cutting out of here."

Simon shook his head.

"Not me. I've got dancing to do."

Faelin stared at him, then he stormed out past the circle of torchlight and into the darkness beyond. The buckskin was at least tied up and waiting. Tacking it up, he swung into the saddle.

As he rode off, he heard a wave of laughter and the music starting up again. Angrily, he turned the horse's head not west toward the claim, but north to Auckland.

Bandits stole the buckskin two days later, taking also Faelin's boots, his leather belt with its brass buckle, and the trade trinkets from his pockets. Almost as an afterthought, one ugly fellow made him strip out of his party clothes, tossing him a ragged shirt in trade.

Faelin made the rest of the way to Auckland half-naked and on bare feet. He hobbled into town and discovered that there was no police or soldiery interested in his sorrows. A group of bounty hunters paid him in secondhand shoes and trousers for information on the bandits. They weren't interested in his joining them, though.

"Get a horse," one said, "maybe then."

Faelin turned to robbery. After one nasty beating when he underestimated the strength of the man he planned to assault, he humbled himself to laborer's work. He stayed away from the docks, though, lest someone who'd known him in better days recognize him.

Summer wasn't too bad, nor was autumn, but winter came in wet and chill. After nearly dying of hypothermia one night, Faelin traded some of his earnings to bunk in a barracks. He was robbed there, set back to almost the same naked condition in which he'd arrived in Auckland six months before.

He began to dream of Richmont as one might a fairyland. No one had robbed him there—not even though he and Simon were two men alone and known to be rich. Folk had even been kind, after a fashion. Oddly enough it was little Debra Dutchman's laughing attempt to get him to dance with her that haunted Faelin most. What had he done to earn that kindness?

Winter turned to spring. With the better weather, clipper ships came into dock. Faelin was drawn to them, haunted by his past. At first he watched from a distance, admiring the white spread of the sails. He began to think that if only he could get off this damned island, maybe he could earn enough to make his way. He'd lost weight and muscle, but the skills were there.

Soon, whenever he wasn't working—earning just enough to keep him in poor food and worse clothing—Faelin took to lurking about the docks, the pride that had kept him away faded to a shadow. In a way he was still afraid to be seen by anyone who might know him, yet he longed for the contact that might get him a berth.

Late one afternoon in September, almost a year after he had fled Richmont, a voice spoke his name.

"Faelin?"

He looked up, trying to place the voice, realizing with shock that the man who was speaking to him was Simon. Superficially, Simon looked the same, but there was something to his bearing— a straightness, a way of meeting your eye when talking to you— that transformed him into another man. Faelin, who had been much beaten and kicked this past year, had to fight an automatic urge to cringe.

"Faelin!" Simon repeated, dropping to his knees next to him. "Man, you're alive! I'd given you up for dead. I've been looking . . ."

He stopped, shocked as he assessed his former partner's condition. Then he went on in a deliberately steady voice:

"I've been looking since last year. Someone said they saw your buckskin for sale in a shady market at the edge of Auckland. I went there, but no luck, though I did find someone who remembered a man wearing what had to be your shirt. It wasn't you though—for one thing he was older, for another fair as a whale's belly. I kept checking for you though, came on all the supply runs to Auckland, but never got a whiff of you.

"When the clippers were due, though, I thought I'd check again. Seemed you might have gotten a berth, if by luck you'd gotten here alive. God's own, man, but what happened to you?"

Faelin told him, first crouched there on the street, later, when Simon recovered himself, in a tavern where they drank good ale and Faelin had his fill of chowder and bread.

"And so here I am," Faelin concluded. Simon's honest joy at finding him alive had robbed him of any defensiveness. He'd told the entire thing straight, even including the embarrassing parts.

"And what do you want next?" Simon asked. "If you want a berth, I'll buy you out of your share of the claim, if . . ."

"You'll buy me out?" Faelin interrupted, astonished. Surely he'd abandoned any right to the claim a year since.

Simon misunderstood him, though.

"I've managed to hold it. Made a deal with the Dutchmans. I work their place in return for keeping our livestock with theirs. Got another dog and that helps with the sheep. Named it Repo. That's Maori for 'swamp,'" he added inconsequentially. "Was just as hard to house train as Roto."

"But you say I still have a share?" Faelin asked. "After I walked out on you?"

"Sure. You started the whole thing, Faelin. I'd never have had the courage to jump ship and find my way to Richmont without you. I owe you my life and my . . . well . . . prosperity. In a way, I owe you my happiness, too."

Simon blushed.

"I got married this winter to Lamont's younger daughter, Idelia. She's not a looker like Jocelyn, but she's a sweetheart."

"And you'd still give me a share?" Faelin asked again.

"That's right," Simon said. He looked Faelin squarely in the eye. "I'll sell enough to make up your half of the sheep and cattle—based on what we had when you left. Same for the dog and the riding stock, less that buckskin. There's something I'd rather do though . . ."

"What?"

"Convince you to come back, Faelin. You've the makings of pakeha, if you'd just get rid of the idea that something can be had for nothing but your wanting it. Idelia knows how I feel and though she's a bit nervous—you scared everybody white when you went at old Chapin—she says she trusts my judgment."

Faelin considered. Impossibly, he had a second chance and he thought he understood a whole lot better what he was being offered.

He thrust out his hand.

"It's a deal, partner."

This time, he knew he'd make his word good.

Devil's Star

Jack Williamson

My mother had chronic bad luck, and a secret shield against it. On no evidence at all, she clung to a stubborn belief that she was the great-grandniece of an illegitimate son of President Cleon Starhawke I, who had won fame for the interstellar conquests that added half a thousand planets to the Terran Republic, and notoriety for the beauty and fertility of his numerous mistresses.

"Never forget that we have presidential blood," she used to urge me. "Live up to it, Kiff, and it will make you great."

With no proof of the myth, I grew up proud of my Starhawke blood, loyal to the Republic and dreaming of a chance for some signal service to the President. My father abandoned us before I was five, migrating to a newly opened planet with a younger woman. My mother spent the next few years working as a domestic servant before she found another husband and skipped out with him, leaving me alone on Earth.

My own luck ran better. Both husbands left funds toward my education. She enrolled me in the Starhawke Space Academy. I came of age and earned my commission there, swearing eternal allegiance to the Terran Republic and Cleon III.

Graduating as a military historian, I begged for the chance to make my name with some active force out on the Rim frontier.

Instead, I found myself still stuck on Earth, the freshman member of a little research team in the library at the Presidential War College near New Denver. Our project was to produce an updated history of Devil's Star. On my first day there, a discontented senior officer tried to shatter my illusions.

"You'll find no career here." He looked around and dropped his voice. "The library was founded to glorify the Starhawkes, but they won no wars on Devil's Star. The planet may justify the name, but it has no history."

I asked for facts about it

"None worth knowing." He shrugged. "Sea level air pressure nearly twice Terra's. Surface mostly too hot and too hostile to be terraformed. No resources worth attention. The explorers had labeled it Lucifer and passed it by."

"Wasn't it once a penal colony?"

"A death pit." He shrugged again. "Called the Black Hole. Infested with hostile life and strange disease. Prisoners sometimes sent down in old landing craft, with no fuel to take off again. Public outrage stopped that when the truth got out. No landings since." He made a bitter face. "We're in the same fix here, condemned to our own hopeless hole."

"The convicts did survive?"

"A disappointment to the executioners." He grinned. "A hardy few climbed out of the heat, to a high mountain ridge that runs down the middle of the main continent. A cooler corner of hell. Some are likely still alive."

Trapped there, with nothing to do and no future in sight, I was feeling as hopeless as another maroon until the day an officer in the uniform of the Presidential Guard caught me in my little cubicle with the news that Space Admiral Gilliyar wanted to see me at once. Astonished and a little alarmed, I asked why.

"He'll tell you why."

A luxury aircar carried us across the base to the Space Command Tower. We found the admiral in a huge corner office that looked across a great field of silver-bright skip-ships. A big man with a bulldog chin, his bright red hair cut short, he was in shirt sleeves, his uniform jacket flung over the back of a chair behind a huge bare desk.

He stood up when the orderly brought me in. My heart thumping, I saluted.

"So you are Starman Kiff McCall?" He returned the salute, studied me with keen gray eyes, nodded abruptly. "You look fit for the job. Let's sit."

Breathing a little easier, but anxious to know what job, I followed him to chairs at a wide window that looked out west across the starport to snowcapped mountain summits.

"Have you done duty off the Earth?"

"No sir."

I waited, sweating.

"No matter." He shrugged again. "What do you know about Devil's Star?"

"Very little, sir. I doubt that much is known by anybody. All contact was outlawed two centuries ago."

"You'll soon know more." My mouth must have gaped; he laughed at me. "If you're ready to go there?"

"I—" I had to catch my breath. "I'm ready."

"Think before you jump." He bent toward me, hard eyes narrowed to study me again. "This will be a highly confidential mission, with no official support or public reward. Your career and even your life may be in danger."

"I've sworn an oath." Feeling like a schoolboy, I put my hand on my heart. "My life is pledged to the Republic and the President."

He smiled at the quiver in my voice.

"I trust you." He spoke very gravely. "What I say is for your ears only. Here is the situation. The sanctions against contact with the planet Lucifer have been broken. As you may know, enemies of the Republic were once exiled there. Their descendants appear to have created an outlaw society. The mere rumor of a free society is a hazard to the state. The President has ordered the planet reclaimed as Terran territory. He is sending me there as the first governor."

Muscles tightened in his jaw.

"It's been a black hole. The convict transports didn't all return. We never knew why, but those who got back called it hell. Before any landing is attempted, we're sending an undercover agent to look the situation over and report what resistance we should expect. That's your errand."

I never returned to my library cubicle. Instead I spent a few hectic months in a class for interstellar intelligence officers, a disappointment to me. I'd hoped for training to face the hazards of the star frontiers, but Cleon I had annihilated the alien foes he found there. These future agents were destined for duty here closer to home.

"Worlds gone soft!" a black-mustached instructor shouted at us. "Rotten to the heart! Maybe loyal Terrans once, but turncoats now, corrupted by all that damned Free Space gibble-gabble. Your future duty is to hunt such traitors down and stop their venomous slander against the Starhawke Presidents."

Admiral Gilliyar's mission had not been revealed, yet my part in it gave me a thrill of secret pride. His staff invented a cover story for me. Based on my mother's claims to presidential kinship, it named me the leader of an exposed Free Space plot to overthrow the President. In flight to escape arrest, I was to become a hunted fugitive, my whereabouts unknown.

On my last day at school, I was hustled out of class and escorted to an empty hangar at the skyport. There, equipped with an oxygen mask and a radio, I was nailed into a rough wooden box stenciled electronic sundries. The radio kept me informed while it was tilted, jarred and jolted, finally loaded into the cargo hold of the *Star of Avalon.*

That was the ship of a suspected smuggler that had been captured, but released with a warning when the captain paid his excise taxes. And no doubt a bribe; I had learned that even the great Terran Republic is not without corruption.

Our first skip was a stomach-churning lurch. The radio went silent. Elated to be off the Earth and on my way, I got out of the box and hammered on a bulkhead. A startled spacehand let me out of the hold and took me to Bart Greenlaw, master and owner of the ship. A fit youthful man in a bright yellow skip suit, he interrupted my cover story.

"So you are Kiff McCall?" His keen eyes scanned me. "I trade with Free Spacers. The price on your head has them wondering about you and your conspiracy. They'd never heard of you."

"We try to keep our secrets," I told him. "I left friends behind, friends I can't betray."

"I understand." He studied me again, and finally smiled as if he believed me. "I know how my own Free Spacer friends feel about the Republic. Or the Terran Empire, they call it. Power corrupts, they say, until it finally rots itself. The Starhawkes hold too much power. They've held it too long."

His gaze sharpened to study my reaction.

"They say Cleon III is sitting on a bomb, armed and ready to blow."

I nodded, trying not to show too much emotion. Any connection between the Free Space activists and Devil's Star was something I must report, but my own mission could have ended then and there if he had guessed the truth.

"One question, if I may ask." His eyes narrowed. "If you're an actual freedom fighter, why are you heading for a prison you'll never escape?"

"We lost a battle." I groped for anything he might accept. "I had to run while I could, but the war isn't over. I want the whole picture. I'm fascinated with the little I know about Devil's Star. I want to do a history of it. Smuggled out to civilization, it might make a difference."

"Civilization?" His face set hard for an instant, but then he gave me a quizzical smile. "You ought to find us interesting."

Seeming satisfied, he found a berth for me, and treated me like another member of his little crew. They all were busy, calculating skip congruencies and maneuvering for relaunch positions and relative velocities, but he let me sit with them at meals, where I could listen for anything Admiral Gilliyar might want to know.

In my berth that night, I dreamed the admiral had won his little war. I was with him on his triumphant return to Earth. A military band was blaring when we came off his flagship, and a goose-stepping squad from the Presidential Guard escorted us to the White Palace. Cleon III received us in the Diamond Room to praise the admiral for his heroic victory and make him the sole proprietor of the conquered planet.

As the dream went on, the beaming admiral presented me to Cleon III. Without my daring undercover work, he said, his expedition would have ended in disaster. The President thanked me for my heroic service to the Republic, and pinned a glittering Starhawke Medal of Honor on my chest.

I felt let down when I woke to find that moment of glory gone, yet my elation lingered. After all, I was safely on my way to Lucifer. Greenlaw seemed to trust me. Something like the dream might still come true.

Our flight took a week. The skips themselves are instant; outside our space-time bubble there is no space to cross or time to pass, but any long voyage requires a series of jumps from one point of congruence to another. On the major space lanes these are marked and charted, but contact points are hard to find and markers can drift. Some points are periodic. Some can vanish altogether. Skip navigation takes high skills and a rare grasp of the total cosmos.

I came to admire Greenlaw for his easy-seeming expertise as an extraspatial pilot, and to enjoy his company. A native of Devil's Star, he loved his planet and liked to talk about its history and geography.

"There's one big continent," he said. "Split in half by a high ridge that runs north and south down the middle of it. That's where we live, between two harsh frontiers, east and west of us. Monsoon rains keep the east half buried under jungle and forest. Dry downslope winds keep the west half hotter than any place on Earth. Both halves are deadly in a dozen ways, yet rich with resources we've learned to use."

I asked about the government.

"We have none." He grinned at my astonishment. "No laws. No money. No taxes. No cops or prisons. We never forgot the merciless government that dumped us here." He paused to smooth his bitter voice. "We were political convicts, condemned for wanting freedom. The Terran government dumped us into the desert or that deadly jungle, with freedom to die."

He glared as if I had challenged him.

"A few of us didn't. We made it up to the highlands, where survival was barely possible—after we learned to care for one another. That's our secret. All for each and each for all." He intoned the words like a mantra. "If you can understand?"

Not sure I did, I shook my head.

"It's your culture." He frowned and shook his head. "I saw it when I was a student there. A culture of selfish aggression. You need your laws and cops and prisons to protect yourselves from one another. We don't, if you get the difference."

"No money?" I asked. "How do you manage without it?"

"Well enough." He shrugged. "You would call it a barter economy. We have exchange centers. Through your working life, you make contributions when you can. In return you draw what you need, a loaf of bread, a farm tool, the service of a surgeon. You continue to serve and be served as long as you live. We have no idle millionaires, no homeless beggars."

"No public services?" I asked. "Don't you need roads, schools, fire departments, hospitals?"

"Of course we do."

"With no money and no taxes, who pays for them?"

"Why pay?" His tone was almost scolding. "We build them. Where you have laws, and lockups for those who break them, we have customs. Our own folkways. A culture of altruism. Every young person spends a year in some service of his or her own choice—and one of our years is nearly two of Earth's. I spent mine sweating down in the desert, at work on date farms and a new angel wood plantation.

"The rest of our lives, we serve one day a week. Teaching, nursing, farming, building roads or bridges, doing what we can for others, trusting them to do for us. When I'm unable to care for myself, others will care for me. Not for money, but because that's our way of life."

"Don't people shirk?"

"Not many. Not often. Not long." He laughed. "A few have tried to live alone. They find how much we need each other."

"With no government at all?"

"You will see." He paused and spoke again, more reflectively. "As a student on Earth, I saw enough of the rotten Terran government you say is hunting you now. I learned to cope with cops and laws and rules and regulations and stupid bureaucrats. Give me freedom!"

Listening, I felt uncomfortable. I had begun to like him. My mission meant trouble for him, trouble for the world he loved. I had to remind myself that I was a Terran soldier, bound to a path of duty I must follow, whatever the cost to me.

Our final skip brought us into planetary orbit. The first hemisphere we saw was all blue ocean. The single huge continent slid into view, the east half-hidden under white monsoon clouds, the western desert a naked waste of dull reds and bright yellows, wrinkled with bare brown hills.

"My home!" Smiling like a happy child, Greenlaw pointed to the highlands, a thin green slash between desert and cloud. "The Vale of Avalon."

The next skip took us lower. I made it out, a high valley between two mountain ridges. A little river ran north between green slopes from a white-capped volcanic cone to a long narrow lake.

"The Avalon River." He pointed. "Most of our settlements are scattered along it, some grown into towns."

He landed at Benspost, a cluster of red tile roofs at a bend in the river. His father, Ben Greenlaw, owned the trading post, a sprawling building with low walls of roughly shaped stone. A little crowd had gathered to welcome him home, calling eager greetings as we came down the ramp.

Men in fringed brown buckskin, women in brighter cottons, wide-eyed children, all anxious to see the wonders he had brought back from the stars. He waved to a smiling, dark-haired woman in slacks and a neat leather jacket.

"Laurel," he said. "My kid sister. She's just back from her service year, down in the jungles. You'll meet our father. He's crippled from hell fever he caught there when he was young. I hope she came back better."

She ran to hug him when we stepped off the ramp.

"All okay." Smiling into his face, she looked fit enough and trimly attractive. "It was a great adventure, really. We were cutting a road across the flood plain to the Styx."

That was the great river that drained half the rainy lowlands.

"Kiff McCall." He introduced me. "A runaway rebel, in flight from the wrath of Cleon III."

"From old Earth?" She appraised me with clear green eyes, smiled, and gave me a strong handshake. "I want to hear all about it."

"I want to hear about the jungle."

"They call it hell, but I had a great year there!" Flushed with the excitement of the moment, she was beautiful. "We got all the way to the river. Set up a sawmill. Cut lumber to build a little boat with a sawmill engine. The first steamer on the Styx."

I stood stupidly silent, longing for her to like me and thinking how she would hate me when she learned what I was.

"Kiff will be our guest," Bart told her. "If you can find him a room.

"I certainly can."

She wanted to carry my bag. It held things I didn't want to show, a gun, my long-range radio, electronic gear to record and encode my reports to the admiral. I clung to it, and followed her through the store. Flushed with pride in Bart and his daring voyages, she showed me tables stacked with goods he had brought in: books and holo sets, watches, radios, computers.

"Things we don't make yet," she said. "But we're learning fast."

Uneasy with her, thinking of the painful lessons the admiral would soon be teaching, I followed her through the tables loaded with local goods. Shoes and clothing, hardware, flour, dried meats, native fruits and nuts with names strange to me.

A clerk was filling an order, punching prices into a barter card. As eager as a child with a birthday, she showed me a hunting rifle she wanted to buy with her savings from the service year. It was the work of a native craftsman, beautifully finished, the stock inlaid with silver, but useless to stop the admiral's battlecraft.

The family lived at the back of the single-story building. We left my bag in a clean little room with white-plastered walls and a comfortable bed, and she took me to meet her father. We found him at a desk facing a big window that looked out across the wide green valley to that old volcano in the south.

A heavy man with a withered leg, he gripped the edges of the desk to haul himself upright and shake my hand. I saw patches of dead-white scar tissue on his face and hands, saw his grimace of pain. Yet his grasp was strong. He smiled warmly at me and then at Laurel, when she came to put her arm around him.

"Relics of the hell country." He raised his hands to show the scars. "I spent my service year there, back before we discovered angel wood. Laurel was luckier."

"Kiff's a freedom fighter," she told him. "In flight from Cleon III"

"Welcome, sir!" He shook my hand again. "They'll never touch you here."

Sitting again, he listened to my cover story with a shrewd intentness that left me afraid he might see through the lies.

"We'll keep you safe." Laurel's eyes were shining. "You'll like it here."

She took me out see the town, a cluster of low stone buildings along a single cobblestone street. There were no motor vehicles, but I saw people on huge ungainly native creatures she called camels, larger than the Terran sort and able to carry half a ton of weight.

"I rode them down into the rain country," she told me. "They have evil tempers, but they're addicted to the silvernuts that grow there. When one gets unruly, a handful of nuts will make him kneel and beg."

She pointed to wires strung from poles along the street.

"Something my grandfather brought us. He found a junkyard of wrecked landing craft down in the desert where they used to unload the convicts, and salvaged parts to rebuild one that got him off the planet. He got aboard an old prison transport that had been lost in orbit when mutineers killed the officers.

"He taught himself skip navigation from the texts and tools he found aboard. The first skip took him nowhere, but a few more got him out to the home planet of our ancestors. He found kinsmen, made Free Space friends—and spent a dozen years on Earth learning everything he could. He'd abandoned the old transport, but he finally got home in a modern ship, with a cargo that changed life here."

I hated to think how Gilliyar would change it again.

"Electricity!" Her voice had risen. "Lights. Telephones. Radio. We've found no oil or coal to burn for power, but now we have windmill generators up in mountain gaps where the trade winds are steady. I wish we could get nuclear power."

I thought of the fusion engines on the admiral's battlecraft.

That uneasy awareness of my mission kept me troubled and silent that evening at dinner. Laurel's mother, Martha, had grown most of the food in her own kitchen garden. A genial, generous woman, she kept piling my plate with servings too large and seemed troubled that I had no better appetite.

In spite of such a welcome, the passing days left me no happier. I was there for months, waiting for Gilliyar's armada to arrive in orbit and preparing to tell him that the outlaws had no defenses worth concern. Laurel arranged a barter card for me. In return, I agreed to teach classes or tutor students in what they wanted to know about the outside worlds.

She became my first student. My cover story made me a romantic figure in her mind, the lone survivor of a heroic rebellion crushed by ruthless Terran power. Her face used to light when she saw me, in a way that wrenched my heart. I knew the truth would come out, knew it would destroy me.

I longed to reveal myself and beg for her forgiveness. Yet I was still a Terran soldier, bound by my oath of allegiance and a lifetime of loyal emotion, hopelessly trapped by all the lies I had told. Keeping silent because I had to, I let her enjoy the days that brought a tortured joy to me. She became an eager guide to her world: the lofty ridge that sliced like a blade between the jungle and the desert. She had seen enough of the jungle, but she took me on a camel down a winding mountain trail to an oasis on the high desert. A long day of clinging to a clumsy wooden seat on the back of the lurching beast left me sun-blistered and aching.

The torrid sun was low before we could dismount at the edge of a tiny lake at the end of a dry stream that ran down from the highlands in the monsoon season. It was on a stony plateau, the low desert and the vast salt marshes on the coast still a full mile farther down, but even after sunset the heat was stifling. Laurel used her barter card to pay for our rooms and meals at a lodge where her brother had worked through his social service year.

She gave me a little handful of bright green beans.

"The seed of the angel tree," she said. "A shrub from down along the coast. It's a natural drug for hell fever. We're trying to grow it here.

I chewed one of the seeds. Its sharp astringency burned my mouth, bitter as my own predicament.

"It's better than it tastes." She laughed at the face I made. "It saved my father's life."

Radiant at breakfast next morning, she wanted to show me the rows of young angel trees her brother had planted, and took me through a little museum that held the relics of a tragic chapter in the planet's history. A shipload of Free Space convicts had been left at the oasis with no supplies. Nearly half of them died. Gunter Greenlaw led the team that opened the road and got the survivors to the Vale.

"We earned our liberty," she told me.

Later, we rode south to ski on the slopes of that dead volcano. The road ran beside the Avalon through gardens, fruit orchards, grain fields, green meadows where spotted cattle grazed the slopes above us. Laurel spoke proudly of the pioneers who had tamed a hostile wilderness, dammed mountain streams for water, cleared land for crops and cattle, built their new society.

The beast's lurching gait kept bumping us together on the high wooden seat. Tormented by her body warmth, breathing her haunting scent, listening to her easy laugh, I tried to contain tides of wild desire and bitter despair.

At the lodge I offered my card and asked for two rooms.

"One will do," she told the clerk, and turned to grin at me. "I love you, Kiff. You do like me, don't you?"

Trapped in a tangle of emotions, I stammered that I did.

"Do you think we must be married?" The clerk stared, and she laughed at me. "You've talked about your government and how it limits all you do. We have more freedom here."

The clerk punched my card for just one room, but I needed time to sort my tangled feelings out. I said I felt hungry. We had dinner and a bottle of wine, out on a terrace below the snows. She admired the view and asked if we had snow sports on Earth. I found little to say.

"Kiff, you are hard to understand." She pushed her glass aside and leaned to stare into my face. "Even when I know how different your old world was. Are you unhappy here? Is there someone you love back outside?"

Honestly, I told her there was no one. Still I couldn't tell her what I felt, but the wine had begun to dull my reservations. When it was gone, we went to bed together. She was passionate. I half forgot my mission. Honestly, I told her I loved her, but all I couldn't say choked me with bitter shame.

We spent three days there. There were no lifts, but a big windmill drove an endless cable that pulled us to the top. The sun was bright, the slope great fun. Laurel was more intoxicating than the wine. She seemed radiant, imagining our future together.

"My brother has Free Space friends," she told me. "They say the star worlds have to change. He hopes we can make some kind of peaceful contact with them. Do you think a time will come when I can go with you back to the stars?"

"That would be wonderful," I told her. "If it could happen."

I knew it was impossible.

My radio stayed dead until the night when I found a green light flashing. Admiral Gilliyar was overhead, on a geosynchronous orbit that kept his armada over the highland ridge. I spent the rest of the night transmitting my recorded notes and pictures.

The sonic boom of an emerging skip craft pealed out of the sky while we were at breakfast a few mornings later. Jets roared overhead. A clerk rushed in, shouting that a Terran lander was down on the pad. A sleek little craft, it carried the Terran flag painted on its armored flank. Black-muzzled guns jutted out of the top turret.

Nobody got off. It sat there nearly an hour, while uneasy citizens gathered around it. A door dropped at last to make a ramp. I heard a roll of martial music. A flagman led a squad of riflemen down the ramp. A cameraman followed, set up a tripod, and shot Admiral Gilliyar marching out of the air lock in dress blue and gold, medals flashing on his breast.

Moving with the music, he took the flag and stabbed the sharpened staff into the ground. He turned, found me standing with my hosts in the watching crowd, and called my name. I stood there a moment, caught in confusion and bleak regret, before I stumbled toward him. Laurel ran to overtake me and threw her arms around me.

"Kiff!" she whispered. "I've always been afraid they'd come after you. Can't we help?"

I stood there an endless time trembling in her arms, too sick to speak. Breathing at last, I muttered that I was sorry, terribly sorry. I kissed her. Sobbing, she clung to me.

"I never meant—never meant to hurt you." The words stuck in my throat. "But I'm a spy. In the service of Cleon III and the Terran Republic."

She gripped my arms and stared at me, her wide eyes strange with shock. Blind with my own sudden tears I pulled out of her grasp, blundered on toward the admiral, and stopped to give him a stiff salute. Smiling, he returned the salute and came on to shake my hand. The little crowd had fallen silent, waiting till he turned and spoke.

"I am Terran Space Admiral Acton Gilliyar."

He paused for a moment before he went on, his mellow eloquence echoing off the long stone wall. He came in peace, to bring President Cleon Stawhawke's most cordial greetings and a heartfelt welcome into the Republic. I hardly heard the booming words. I was watching Laurel.

Her face white and stiff at first, she flushed pink. Her small fists clenched. Glaring at me with a look that changed from shock to scornful contempt, she spat on the ground.

"The President regrets your long neglect," his polished voice rolled on. "I understand that you are trying to survive here in a stare of lawless anarchy. I have come to bring you the law and order of Terran civilization. President Starhawke has appointed me the first governor of the planet Lucifer."

Muttering, people stared at one another and back at him.

"Sir!" Laurel's voice rang loud, heated perhaps by her anger at me. "We want none of your Republic." She looked around at those beside her, saw them nodding with agreement. "We need none of you!"

"Madam." He raised his voice, his tone grown harder. "With all due respect, I must inform you that your planet has belonged to the Terran Republic since the discoverers landed here and raised our flag."

"Non—nonsense, sir!" She caught her breath and lifted her quivering voice. "You threw us out of your wicked empire, and left us here to die. We've earned our freedom and we'll die to keep it."

"You may die. You'll never keep it."

"We'll never give it up."

"I must warn you, madam, that your words are a reckless incitement to treason." His voice slow and grimly solemn, he looked around at the little crowd and fixed his eyes on her. "If you want to die, the choice is yours. In modern times, suspected traitors are no longer merely exiled. The penalty now is death."

I heard a stifled outcry from her mother, a furious oath from her father. Friends gathered around them in a muttering group. The admiral turned to lift his hand at nose of the lander. The martial music rose again. He ordered his rifle squad back to the ramp. Laurel darted past them to the flag, pulled the staff out of the ground, and hurled it against the side of the lander. She stood staring at him and then at me, breathing hard.

"We witnessed that outrageous act of open treason!" he shouted at her. "What is your name?"

"Laurel Greenlaw." She tossed her head. "What is yours?"

"Acton Gilliyar." He grinned at her bleakly. "We'll be meeting again."

He beckoned to me. I followed him and the riflemen aboard. A warning siren screeched. Looking down from the control turret, I saw people scattering. Laurel stood closer, shaking here fist, dwindling to a defiant doll as we lifted.

The admiral landed us at half a dozen towns up and down the Avalon, at the ski lodge below the volcano, the oasis down on the desert, at a lumber camp on the headwaters of the Styx. At each stop he went off with his rifle squad to read his proclamations. A few people hooted. Nobody cheered.

We climbed back to the geosynchronous point. He broadcast an ultimatum demanding unconditional submission. The colonists must accept the rule of the democratic Terran Republic, swear allegiance to President Cleon III, welcome Terran landing forces, pay Terran taxes, obey orders from him as their newly appointed governor. Unless he received a signal of surrender within three days, he would be forced, however unwillingly, to take whatever measures the situation might require.

"There will be no signal," I warned him. "There is no government, nobody with authority to surrender."

"I expected opposition from the like of that Greenlaw woman." He shook his head, his jaw set hard. "These people were condemned and sent here as outlaw enemies of the state. They are enemies and outlaws still. If they want a lesson in Terran power, I'll give them a lesson."

Waiting three days in orbit, he received no signal of surrender. His lesson was a volley of guided missiles.

"I'm remaining on the flagship," he told me. "It will be my official residence. Captain Crendock is going down as my executive secretary with orders to secure the planet and establish administrative control."

He was startled when I wanted to go back to Benspost.

"Why?" He gave me a hard look. "You won't find friends there."

Uncomfortably, I tried to explain my own torn feelings.

"I'm still loyal," I told him, "bound by my duty to the Republic. But I did make friends there. People were generous to me. I was fascinated with their history. I want to write it for the whole Republic."

"Forget your pet traitors," he advised me. "That Greenlaw woman is no friend now."

"Yet she is making history. History worth recording."

"Better get back to Terra while you can." He gave me a stiff half-smile. "You were warned to expect no public recognition, but we will surely find something for you."

He called me a fool when I shook my head.

I had to go back to find Laurel, to try to explain what I had done, to beg her to understand. I didn't tell him that, but in the end, he replaced my lost radio and holo camera and let me go back down to Benspost with Crendock. A missile had struck there, and little remained of old Ben Greenlaw's trading post.

Yet life went on. I saw camels loaded with lumber and tile to repair shattered buildings. Bart was back again from some Terran planet with another illicit cargo. We found his skipcraft undamaged, standing on the pad near the ashes and fallen walls.

"Leave him alone," Gilliyar had ordered. "I hope to legalize the trade and impose excise taxes."

Camels were tethered around his ship, the drivers loading them with goods he had brought. His crew was loading it again with exports: nuts and dried fruit from the desert lowlands, rare hardwoods and balls of raw rubber from the rain forest.

His parents had set up a new barter center in a tent on a vacant lot. His mother burst into tears when she saw me, and ran back into the tent. His father sat in his wheelchair behind a rough table, surrounded with whatever his clerks had been able to salvage. I thought he seemed sick, the splotches of his old jungle fever infection livid and swollen.

He looked up at me with an enigmatic expression.

"Well, sir?" He shook his head. "I never expected to see you again."

"I'm a historian," I said. "I came back to write the history of the colony. And I want to see your daughter."

"You've turned our history to tragedy." He spoke with a harsh finality. "You'll never see Laurel."

He turned to deal with a farmer who had come with a basket of eggs to trade. I saw Bart himself, stooping in the ashes of the store, filling a bag with scraps of fused and blackened metal. He met me with a quizzical grin and handed me what was left of my gun, the magazine shattered when the ammunition exploded.

"I think this was yours."

I asked about Laurel.

"Gone." The grin vanished. "I don't know where." His gaze grew sharper. "If your Terran friends are looking for her . . ."

He shrugged and stooped again into the ashes.

A few days later he came up to me while I was out with the camera to shoot a group of workers with spades and wheelbarrows, refilling a crater that one of Gilliyar's missiles had left in the road.

"Let's talk." He offered his hand. "I've heard about your history. I want our Terran friends to know our story. Will you let me take you back to tell it?"

I thanked him.

"But the history isn't finished. And I want to stay till I can see your sister."

His face grew bleak. "You'll be here forever."

Before he took off, I gave him a draft of my unfinished narrative, copies of my holos of the ruins, and a shot of Crendock strutting off a lander to repeat Gilliyar's ultimatum. I kept digging into the records I could find, asking people for their recollections, shooting the damage from the bombardment and the efforts at reconstruction.

And longing all the time for a glimpse of Laurel.

Crendock set up his headquarters on a hilltop above the ruins. His landers were busy for a time, bringing down temporary buildings and equipment. He tried to employ civilian labor, but nobody wanted his money or wanted him there. The few people left in the town were clearing the streets, rebuilding their homes, replanting gardens. Some of them let me join the labor teams, gave me food and shelter in return. I asked and asked again for news of Laurel, receiving blank or hostile stares.

Crendock's officers were just as determined to find her, but no more successful.

"It's frustrating," he told me one night when he had asked me to his quarters for a Terran dinner. "There's nobody with authority, no way to get control. Gilliyar says this Laurel Greenlaw has to be our first target. She openly defied him. He wants her caught and tried for treason."

He asked for anything I knew. That was nothing at all.

"My investigators have been looking everywhere. Broiling themselves down in the desert. Freezing on the slopes of that volcano. Not a clue. I hear that she was once employed down in the jungle. She may have returned. Nowhere we can follow, but we're posting a price on her head."

With no better lead, I found Marco Finn, the top driver of a camel train returning to the lumber mills, and begged him for a ride down to the jungle.

"Don't go." He turned to spit green fluid from the angel cud that bulged his bearded cheek. "You ain't fit for it."

He was a raw-boned, short-spoken man, scarred from hell fever, his wild beard stained bright green from the angel wood bark he chewed. He frowned and squinted at me. I tried to explain that I wanted to see the jungle, get the history of the lumbermen, the silver-nut and rubber plantations, the barges on the Styx.

"Who will give a damn?" He shrugged and spat again. "Nothing but poison vines and devil bugs and rain that never stops. We call it hell country. No place for a Terran."

"But you're going back."

"We hell rats ain't quite human." He gave me a ferocious scowl. "We toughen up and take it like it is. Sometimes it kills us, but people need the timber and the rubber and the silvernuts. And we get double barter points. If I'm alive ten years from now I can use my last timber load to build a cabin up in sky country. Grow a garden. Keep chickens and a cow. What you ought to do."

Yet he let me climb to the hard seat beside him.

The east rim of the upland is higher and steeper than the west. None of the convicts dropped into the jungle ever reached the highlands until rescue teams from the top found and cleared the trail. The ride down took us three long days.

Finn and I sat together every day on the pitching seat. We shared meals when we squatted around the cook fires, shared space in his little tent when we camped. He knew who I was. He must have wondered about Terra and my life there, wondered how I became a spy, but he never inquired.

Listening for Laurel's name, I never spoke of her.

The first day we wound through sunless gorges that old glaciers had cut, and came out into blinding sun on ledges so narrow I hardly dared look down at the endless ocean of glaring monsoon clouds, a mile and more beneath us. The second day we were still in them, in a fog so dense I could hardly see the beast ahead. The third day we came out of the clouds, down into ceaseless rain and suffocating heat.

Still far below, the jungle was a featureless dark-green sea. The fourth day we were in its dismal twilight, breathing the reeks of wet decay and the rank musks of strange life.

Still the road ran on. Sometimes it was made of logs, laid side by side. Sometimes it was flat rocks, laid to crown a thin clay dike. More often it was only a ditch of thick red mud, splashed and churned by the camel's wide-splayed feet. Undergrowth walled it and arched overhead, most of it a tangle of thick-leafed fungoid stuff the driver had no name for when I asked. The rain never stopped.

The days were endless nightmares. Stinging insects hummed around us. My face and arms itched and burned. My bones ached. My appetite was gone. My strength drained away till I had to tie myself into the bucking seat. I tried to chew the angel bark Finn shared when he saw I had the fever, but the bitter stuff burned my mouth and knotted my stomach and seemed to do no good.

Sweating and gasping for breath though the endless nights, I dreamed and dreamed again that I had found Laurel. Sometimes we had been swimming together in that little lake at the desert oasis, sometimes we were skiing on the old volcano, sometimes we had been back in bed together. She was always beautiful. Longing for her to love me, I tried to tell her how sorry I was. The words always stuck in my burning throat and she coldly turned away.

I lost the count of days. I don't know when we reached the lumber mills or how I got to Hell. That was the name of a settlement on the swampy shore of the Styx. Dimly, I remember the patter of the end-less rain on the tent, the coughs and stinks of the men on the cots around me, the days when all I wanted was death. I remember dreams of Laurel, bathing my body in angel seed tea when my swollen throat wouldn't swallow.

A morning came when my head seemed clear. The tent was silent, except for the murmur of the rain. The other cots were empty. The epidemic was over. Feeling well again, I lay waiting until Laurel came in. She was real, alive and smiling, lovely in a white uniform some-how spotless in spite of the mud. She helped me sit up and gave me a mug of the angel seed tea. Magically, its burning bitterness was gone. It had almost the taste of a good dry wine.

She laughed when I tried to say how sorry I was.

"You've already told me, at least a thousand times." She asked if I felt hungry and brought a tray of food. Suddenly ravenous, I gorged on river fish and hellcakes and roasted silvernuts and camel cheese. I was able to limp with her out into the clearing. Huge crimson blooms blazed from the vines that twined the trees around it. The air was sweet with their scent, and the jungle's dark power seemed almost kind. We went down to the dock to watch the little steamer come in with a load of cured rubber from a plantation down the river. The name painted on the bow was *Laurel*.

Next day she was even happier.

"Bart was on the radio," she told me. "He's back from Terra with great good news. Your stories about Gilliyar's bombardment set off new Free Space riots on a hundred planets. Revolution came so close that Cleon III had to abdicate. His son is promising to negotiate the independence of a new Free Space Federation.

"The new government has recognized our own freedom and ordered Gilliyar's forces out. They wanted to rename the planet Avalon. Bart told them no. He says Lucifer fits us better. They wanted him to stay as our ambassador. He said no to that. Ambassadors are government.

"But he did get them to guarantee free trade and free travel. They want angel wood and silvernut for medical research. We're free to visit Terra if we like." Soberly, she shook her head and caught my hand. "Not soon, I think. Our lives are here."

She found a place for us on a camel train when I felt strong enough. We rode together back up the hell road, back out of the rain and the bugs and the stink of the swamps, back through the fog into bright sunlight, back through narrow passes into the Vale of Avalon. I was still half-drunk on the angel tea and my dreams of our future together. She was more realistic.

"Freedom won't come free," she told me. "It never does."

Renegade

Mark Tier

On the giant screen in Union Square a marine running full tilt toward the camera suddenly spurted blood where his head had been. I was glad there was no sound—I felt sick enough already.

Before I could wonder what had happened to the cameraman the screen blanked for a fraction of a second, and the scene shifted to a bird's-eye view of the jungle battle. And then cut to an ad.

On the old-fashioned ticker underneath—a copy of the relic in Times Square—the headline *marines retreat* appeared, one letter at a time.

A screech of brakes and the sound of scrunching steel jerked my attention back to the street. Most everyone on the sidewalk had come to a dead halt. Including me—and I hadn't even noticed. I suddenly became aware of the unnatural silence: after all, it's not every day you see someone's head blown off live on a five-hundred-foot three-dimensional screen. Drivers were mesmerized too. One of them must have hit the brakes and taken his car out of automatic. The roadnet braked the cars behind, but not fast enough to prevent a spectacular pile-up.

A lady nearby was throwing up in the gutter. My stomach started to churn so I took a few steps back. I felt a bit sick too, but I couldn't feel sorry for the guy. He'd volunteered knowing full well what the risks were. And was—had been—highly paid to take them. After all, every man and woman in both the Eighth Army and the Marines get a share of the holo and web rights. With the ratings on this mêlée his family, if he had one, will be well taken care of.

How much time had passed? More than I thought. Now I had to hurry to be at the hearing on time. As I and hundreds of others started moving again the normal Union Square bustle returned. Though it would be a while before the traffic followed suit.

8TH ARMY ODDS ON; MARINES 27–1 was now scrolling across the ticker. I'm not a gambling man but I can't resist an all-but-sure-thing. 27 to 1! That was like taking candy from the mouths of babes.

A few taps on my phone and I learned that the US Marines were retreating all across the front. But the retreat was slow and it didn't seem like they were about to fold. Sure wouldn't do their marketing image any good if they gave up so easily. *We Never Quit* was their motto.

If they only held out for just a few days I'd clean up. A good friend of mine, an executive of the Eighth Army Inc. had told me that their client—don't ask me whether it was the government of Colombia or the government of Venezuela; I haven't really been following this fracas too closely—had run out of money. That's real money I mean: they had plenty of that stuff they printed down there, whatever they called it, and a wheelbarrow full of it and a silver dime might get you a cup of coffee in San Francisco if the vendor was short of toilet paper.

Whichever gang of thugs it was, if they didn't pay up by Monday the Eighth Army Inc. was flying straight back home. Today was Friday. Planes and choppers were on standby over in Florida to pull them out at a moment's notice. Then all that would stand between the US Marines and the thugs running Venezuela (or Colombia) was the ragtag gaggle of bandits they called their army.

Those marines would walk it in the rest of the way. And the bookies would have to pay up.

A few more taps and I placed two hundred ounces (gold, not silver) on the Marines to win. If the Eighth Army pulled a rabbit out of the hat over the weekend, losing that gold would hurt, but it wouldn't kill me. Like I told you, I'm not a gambling man. You always gotta calculate the odds. If you work with an insurance company for as long as I have without learning that you're still pushing paper.

The phone beeped to tell me I had a couple of minutes to be on time. Then it rang and Joe's ugly face (he's my partner) appeared on the screen. "Where the hell are you?" he growled.

I looked to find out. "Just walking into the lobby of the building," I told him. I turned the phone so he could see for himself.

He harrumphed, and his face disappeared from the screen. Joe was like that: didn't waste any time on pleasantries. Wasn't much good with small talk either.

I took my seat just before the judge walked in, followed by his staff. Adjudicator-in-Chief was his official title, but everybody called them judges.

When he was young, my granddad became a cop just before the tax revolt brought down the government and cops disappeared altogether. Here, anyway. I guess there are still cops in Colombia (or Venezuela) and other places which still have governments. What he told me about judges in his time bears no relation to adjudicators today. For a start, adjudicators are unbribable. Well, Chief Adjudicators. Offer one of *them* a bribe and he resigns your case. Then you're in deep doodoo. Boycotted. You'll never get another reputable adjudication outfit to take you on.

In a way, I guess I'm following in my grandfather's footsteps. Joe and I run San Francisco Investigations, one of the biggest agencies in the city. Occasionally we do some of the things cops used to do. Like today's case: murder.

Judge Wainwright was pushing eighty, though you'd never have guessed it. He strode into the room with the walk and energy of a much younger man. That, and his full head of hair—even if it was gray—meant he could pass for fifty-something. I resolved once again to spend more time at the gym—his youthful look made me jealous. Hell, he looks younger than I am!

Wainwright commanded the highest fees in the business, such was his experience and reputation for impartiality. Any of the freshmen advocates from his firm could have easily handled today's case. I'd expected one of them to be mediating. So why does All-Risk

Insurance—they're our biggest client—want to spend so much money when any junior could have taken his place for peanuts? It didn't figure.

Wainwright sat down at the head of the table in the center of the room. Adjudicators' hearing rooms are often highly personalized. This design was one of the more interesting.

The only way to know this table's "head" is by where the judge sits. It's almost, but not quite, circular. Look a second time and it seems triangular. It's both.

Wainwright's staff arranged themselves on one side of the circular triangle. The All-Risk team sat at another.

To any casual watcher on the web it should have been immediately clear why a junior adjudicator could have handled this hearing: the third side was empty. The defendant, Gerald Murdock— the murderer—wasn't represented. And he hadn't shown up. Not that anyone expected him to: he'd disappeared straight after the murder and no one knew—or was willing to tell—where he'd gone.

That's why Joe and I were both here. Our firm had handled the case; we carried out the investigation, took the depositions, and so on. The moment the adjudicator ruled we were going to have to find the guy and get him to cough up what the judge was about to decide he owed.

Anyone who knew nothing about the killing of Randolph Ackerman had to be blind, deaf *and* dumb. With group sex, drugs, wife- and secretary-swapping, questionable business deals, not to mention nude bodies (one of them dead) and a murderer who'd done a disappearing act with bundles of money, the tabloids had a field day.

Last Saturday evening Gerald Murdock joined Randolph Ackerman for dinner and a group sex party at Ackerman's penthouse on Nob Hill. Murdock's secretary, Annabelle Pearson, Ackerman's wife, Sophia, and her sister, Jude, were also there to join in the fun and games.

The two men had a few business interests together and over the last couple of years there'd been lots of friction and disagreement between them. Apparently, both of them felt their partner was getting more than his fair share of the profits. They'd come to a peace agreement, and the purpose of the dinner was to celebrate and cement it. Bury the hatchet, if you will.

After dinner, after several bottles of wine, tabs of cocaine and God knows what other cocktails, and lots of group groping, Ackerman and Murdock got into an argument over one of the women. The argument quickly degenerated into a vicious rehash of every accusation they'd ever made against each other.

Seemingly livid with rage, Murdock grabbed a gun from his jacket and shot Ackerman between the eyes. Waving the gun at the women he quickly dressed, ran out of the apartment, down the stairs and into a passing cab.

The women were so stunned—not to mention drunk and/or drugged—that they were slow to act. They first called an ambulance, which arrived just minutes after Murdock had left the building. Not that an ambulance was any help to Ackerman by then. Only after that did they call security. The place was crawling with armed guards (ours) just moments after the ambulance arrived. Just moments too late.

Both witnesses—Annabelle Pearson played mute—agreed with each other down to most of the fine details. And since they were both interviewed while the body was being taken away, still semi-naked, wrapped in sheets or towels, they didn't have time to concoct any fairytales.

Ackerman's hobby, however, made it an open and shut case. Seems he liked to record his sex parties with multiple holographic cameras and then edit them into home porn shows. He had hundreds of them. Someone bootlegged the files. The murder—along with Ackerman's entire porn library—is readily available all over cyberspace. It's the worst thing to hit Hollywood and the holo nets in years.

We tracked down the cab Murdock had picked up on Nob Hill. He'd gotten out at Union Square, and then his trail disappeared. We couldn't find any trace of him. We figured he had a car parked there and a second identity already fixed up, probably with one of the sleazier insurance outfits.

By Monday it was obvious that Murdock hadn't fired that shot in a moment of angry passion. Over the previous months he'd quietly sold all his business interests and closed his stock and bank accounts. He'd turned the last of his real estate into cash just the week before. All but one of his bank accounts were cleaned out. He'd even managed to skim some of the cash from his joint ventures with Ackerman just minutes before the banks closed on Saturday. Ackerman hadn't suspected a thing.

One of his companies remained. The reason emerged when we asked the Insurance Association data bank for information on Gerald Murdock: he had no insurance cover whatsoever in his own name. One reason he wasn't represented before the adjudicator.

His sole remaining company, GMR Holdings, *was* insured. With the Mafia Corporation of Washington, DC. They weren't too cooperative. Never were: just the minimum level to ensure that other insurance agencies cooperated with them when they needed it. It was part of their heritage. At least according to their marketing, they were proud of their history as a private protection agency back when the government kept trying to put *any* competitor out of business.

As Mafia insured the *company*, not Murdock, they were under no obligation to give us the time of day. When we called they were as mute as mollusks.

And on Monday Annabelle Pearson paid every remaining bill and proceeded to shut that company down too.

All the money was gone. Thousands of gold ounces.

Gerald Murdock's legal identity had been tied to his company. His credit cards, bank accounts, agreements and everything else. Very clever. He could deal normally in our society and any trace would lead back to his company, not him.

It also meant there were no records of Murdock: no voiceprints, fingerprints or retina scans on file that we could access to help track him down.

We made a voiceprint from Ackerman's holo of the party. We found fingerprints that were probably Murdock's. We ran them through the data bank and—as I'd expected—drew a blank.

It was as if Gerald Murdock didn't exist. No doubt exactly what he had in mind.

"Good morning, gentlemen," said Wainwright. "We're here today to adjudicate the accusation that Gerald Murdock murdered Randolph Ackerman. Is Mr. Murdock present?"

When there was no answer, Wainwright asked, "Since Mr. Murdock does not appear to be here, who stands to speak for him?"

Again, no answer.

Wainwright was a stickler for procedures. He already knew that Murdock wasn't represented. But any missing step could give grounds for a rehearing or appeal. If Murdock ever surfaced to make a challenge.

"Who speaks for the estate of Randolph Ackerman?"

"I do, sir."

Joe and I looked at each other and I could see he felt as startled as me. Martin Li, the attorney who'd answered, billed more per hour than Wainwright. As usual, I was surprised I hadn't noticed him before. Strangely for a lawyer, he seemed to disappear in a crowd. Yet he was an extraordinarily handsome man. Eurasian most likely. But you just didn't see him until he began to use his deep, penetrating voice. From that moment on, I always had difficulty pulling my eyes away from him.

So why did All-Risks want two of the highest-powered guys in the business on *this* case? No reason popped into my head, but I had the uncomfortable feeling that it would somehow involve us.

This case had moved at lightning speed. Murder Saturday; evidence all assembled by Thursday morning; hearing today. No defendant to argue with helped. Still, fast in our business was normally two to three weeks between crime and hearing for an open and shut case. Ever since Sunday night, our office had looked more like a student dorm without maid service than a place of business. I don't think any of us had had a good night's sleep all week.

"Be it noted that Gerald Murdock has failed to appear to contest the charges against him," Wainwright said. Turning to Li he asked, "Do you contend that this hearing has jurisdiction over the case?"

"Indeed it does, sir. Mind if I walk around? I think better."

Wainwright waved his hand in a gesture of assent.

"It is conceivable that by his absence," said Li as he paced slowly from one side of the room to the other, "from the fact that he is not represented here today the defendant, Gerald Murdock, could argue that this hearing does not have jurisdiction.

"If he did, he would be wrong.

"Randolph Ackerman was a client of All-Risk Insurance. His person and his property, including his apartment, were insured by All-Risk under a general all-risk policy. That policy included legal representation and mediation with other members of the Insurance Association and their clients. That policy was registered with the Association.

"When Gerald Murdock entered Ackerman's apartment on Saturday night, he implicitly agreed to place himself under the rules of Ackerman's policy with All-Risk."

"Was there a notice to this effect?" asked Wainwright.

"Yes, sir," answered Li. "On all entrances to Ackerman's apartment."

These signs are so common the only time I become aware of them is when they aren't there. They usually read:

WARNING
This property is insured by XYZ Insurance Co.
By entering this property you agree to be bound by the rules
of the policy and the American Insurance Association.

"Has this been attested?" asked Wainwright.

"Yes, sir." One of Li's assistants passed a file to Wainwright, who quickly skimmed through it. Though I'd bet he'd read it all before.

"As Gerald Murdock is neither represented here today, nor has he any known contract with any member of the American Insurance Association, or any of the other insurance associations in North America, he is uninsured. And was uninsured at the time Randolph Ackerman died." Li's assistant passed another folder to Wainwright. "In that file," Li continued, "are the results of our search for any insurance cover of Gerald Murdock.

"Being uninsured, any of his actions while upon the property of Randolph Ackerman are to be adjudicated by the rules of Ackerman's policy with All-Risk Insurance. He implicitly agreed to that upon entry."

Two more files were pushed across the table to Wainwright. They'd be copies of Ackerman's policy and All-Risk's rules.

"In that case," said Wainwright, "I hereby rule that this hearing has the legal jurisdiction to adjudicate the accusation that Gerald Murdock murdered Randolph Ackerman."

Every adjudication session began with these formalities. Now they were over, Wainwright turned with obvious relief to Li and asked, "Is there anything you'd like to add to your brief?"

Knowing Wainwright, he'd already mastered every nuance of the evidence the All-Risk team had prepared—including any errors or omissions. Today's hearing was, other than the decision itself, the final part of the adjudication process.

"No sir," answered Li.

"Then, please proceed with your summary."

"The facts are clear," said Li. "At 11:07 last Saturday evening, Gerald Murdock shot Randolph Ackerman. The time was established from Ackerman's holo. He died instantly, according to the doctor who examined the body. Murdock left the apartment, hailed a cab, got off at Union Square, and hasn't been seen since.

"These facts were established from interviews with two of the three witnesses, Sophia Ackerman, the victim's wife, and Jude Schwarz, her sister, and from the holo. A secure copy of the holo was made immediately. It was discovered by bonded detectives from San Francisco Investigations.

"The third witness, Annabelle Pearson, Murdock's secretary, refused to answer any questions."

My attention was again riveted to Martin Li. I was vaguely aware that Wainwright sat stock still, like a gray stone god, only his eyes moving as Li walked.

"Both witnesses agreed that no one had been near the computer recording the holo, a fact borne out by the holo itself. Between the murder and the time the detectives entered the apartment twelve minutes later, none of the three women or the medics went anywhere near the computer. There was no one else in the apartment at the time: the maid and the butler who served dinner had already gone home."

Wainwright made a cryptic note with his pencil, the first time he'd moved since Li began to speak.

"Bonded computer experts testified that the only access to the holo files was through the terminal in the living room, and the terminal in Ackerman's study which could only be entered from the living room.

"Since there can be no question of the veracity of the holographic file of the murder that we have presented in evidence, it is clear that Gerald Murdock is guilty of the murder of Randolph Ackerman beyond a shadow of doubt."

Li stopped pacing for a moment and let silence hang over the room.

"We have prepared significant excerpts from the holos and depositions that show these facts. Would you care to review them, sir?"

"No need," said Wainwright. "However, please show me evidence that supports your contention that no one went near the computer terminals."

"Certainly sir." Turning to one of his assistants, he continued, "Blair, can you bring up the holo at the time of the murder."

"Alleged murder please, Mr. Li. Murder—or otherwise—has yet to be determined."

"Of course, sir."

The holo shimmered and then solidified on top of the table. Murdock was frozen with his hand reaching into his jacket. Ackerman stood naked in the center of the room, his face bright red, his mouth open in the middle of a scream. The three women lay on the sofa or the floor in different states of undress.

Li walked around the table to stand behind his assistant. He spoke softly and the scene revolved. After a moment, a door and a terminal were highlighted.

"This is the computer terminal in the living room," he said, and leaned over the table putting his hand inside the holo to point at the keyboard. "And this—" he pointed at the highlighted door "—is the only entrance into the study, with the only other terminal that could access these files."

At a gesture from Li, another of his assistants passed two files to Wainwright. "These files show the layout of the computers, and which terminal could access which file type, kind and level of security," said Li, "and the layout of Ackerman's penthouse apartment."

"Thank you," said Wainwright, making another note. "Continue," he said, looking at Li.

Li said a few more quiet words to his assistant, and stepped back.

"We'll hold the holo on the door and the keyboard and fast forward it to the moment the secure copy was made." As he spoke Murdock sprang to life and for the second time today I saw a man die. This one didn't affect me nearly as much. I'd seen it before, and knew it was coming.

I felt like laughing at the way Murdock dressed and disappeared in a flurry of clothing and as the three almost-naked women seemed to run every which way across the room. A team of medics appeared and suddenly the room seemed to overflow with armed men. As one of them looked into the study the picture slowed back to normal speed.

"As you can see, this is the first time anyone has been near the keyboard or the door," Li said.

Sam Renkin, one of our investigators, sat down at the keyboard. A moment later he said, "Hey, this thing is recording something."

Li signaled his assistant and the holo stopped. "From this moment on," he said, "this man, Sam Renkin, a bonded detective from San Francisco Investigations never left the keyboard until a secure copy of the files on the computer was made.

"One other point. These files could be accessed by voice, but only by Ackerman's voice. The computer would respond to Mrs. Ackerman's voice for other commands. Otherwise, only with a password that Mrs. Ackerman said she did not know. Indeed, when Mr. Renkin asked her if she'd known that the computer was recording everything, she went into shock and had to be treated by the medics."

Turning to Wainwright he asked, "Do you have any other questions, sir?"

With a slight shake of his head, Wainwright indicated that Li should continue. As the holo shimmered and disappeared Wainwright ceased being a faint shadow behind Sam Renkin's face.

"In our brief, we outlined the substantial circumstantial evidence that strongly suggests Murdock had murder in mind when he arrived for dinner.

"But the facts are clear. At 11:07 last Saturday evening, Gerald

Murdock shot and killed Randolph Ackerman. There can be no doubt that Murdock is guilty of murder. For that reason, whether he killed Murdock in a fit of anger or, as we submit, as part of a long-standing plan makes absolutely no difference to the penalty we seek.

"Gerald Murdock is guilty."

Li took a sheet of paper from his place at the table and passed it to Wainwright.

"Murdock is guilty of murder beyond a shadow of doubt. The high probability that the murder was premeditated merely adds weight to our claim that Murdock pay the highest penalty the law allows.

"And it's to that penalty I'd now like to turn."

"We submit that Murdock be required to pay to All-Risk Insurance the sum of 125,115 gold ounces, plus all costs, with interest."

The amount Li asked for drew a low whistle of astonishment from several spectators, including me. People started whispering to each other until Wainwright's sharp "Quiet, please," brought silence back to the room.

"Continue."

"Certainly, sir," said Li. "If he fails to pay the penalty, ownership of all property identified as belonging to him be transferred to All-Risk Insurance in full or partial settlement of the penalty. And as he has disappeared entirely and has no known legal identity, we ask that Gerald Murdock be declared a renegade and outlaw until such time as the penalty is paid in full."

Now I understood why they'd rushed to have this case adjudicated. They'd be able to take ownership of Murdock's companies. GMR Holdings was the only one left, but if they could grab it before Annabelle Pearson closed it down completely they'd have a chance of being able to trace the money and, with it, Murdock.

Correction: *We'd* have a chance. Joe and I were going to be the ones who had to find him.

"As we all know, and as Murdock must also know, the penalty for murder is restitution to the heirs of the victim for the value of the life taken, and restitution of any other damages directly attributable to the death.

"Ackerman's life was insured by All-Risk for the sum of fifteen thousand gold ounces. We seek reimbursement of that amount.

"In addition, Ackerman's policy with All-Risk includes coverage of violent death, such as murder.

"Because of this provision, All-Risk had complete access to Ackerman's financial records and routinely updated this risk. The calculation of the value of Ackerman's life, based on the present value of his estimated future earning power, totals 110,115 gold ounces. This amount is exhaustively documented in the brief, using standard Insurance Association scales."

That was a big number, even for someone as wealthy as Ackerman. It's a number you could easily lowball. That was one of the things I liked about All-Risk: they never stiffed their customers.

And how do you figure someone's *future* earning potential? You make lots of assumptions. Assumptions that would have been challenged—if there'd been a Murdock representative to challenge them.

"The penalty we seek includes reimbursement of the fifteen thousand gold ounces in life insurance cover that All-Risk has already paid to Ackerman's widow, Sophia Ackerman, and the sum of 110,115 gold ounces that would become immediately due and payable by All-Risk Insurance.

"We also submit that the penalty include all the costs of the investigation and these proceedings to date, plus the costs yet to be disbursed in finding the defendant and recovering the penalty.

"Finally, that the penalty include interest on the outstanding amount from the moment the decision of these proceedings is finalized to the time the penalty has been recovered in full."

Wainwright was looking at the papers Li had given him. When Li stopped talking, he looked up.

"Subject to any questions, the plaintiff rests."

"No questions," said Wainwright. In a louder voice, looking around the room, "Is there anyone here to speak for Gerald Murdock?"

Once more he was greeted with silence.

"In that case, this hearing is adjourned until two o'clock." As Wainwright stood up his assistants followed suit. A hubbub of conversation quickly filled the silence as they left the room.

I grabbed Joe by the arm. "Let's go and talk to Li before everybody else does."

A loose knot of people had gathered around him. I squeezed through and offered him my hand. "Nicely put, counselor."

"Hi Ray." He smiled at me. "Joe."

"We were surprised to see both you *and* Wainwright here today."

"I think the idea is they don't want the faintest question as to the probity of the verdict."

Up close, I noticed that his eyes looked tired. "Looks like you haven't had much sleep recently. Either."

He laughed. "We're hoping to give you a warm trail to follow. If there's any trail at all."

"There's always something—"

"Ah, there you are." A voice came from behind me. "Joe. Ray. We need to talk right away." I turned as somebody's hand grabbed my arm and started tugging it gently.

"Hi, Fritz. Anyone here had any sleep this week?" Fritz Gandhi—he had an Indian father and a German mother—was chief of All-Risk's San Francisco bureau.

"Plenty of time for that next week. Or next month," he said.

"Looks like I have to go," I said to Martin. "See you at two."

"I wouldn't count on it," said Fritz. "You'll be too busy."

Joe and I followed Fritz into a nearby room along with a number of people I recognized from his office. A woman I did not know, who was stunningly attractive despite her full head of gray hair, was already sitting at the table.

"Ray, Joe, I'd like you to meet Noni Brooks. Noni, this is Ray Black and Joe Herrera. They head San Francisco Investigations."

"Good," she said. I presumed our reputation had preceded us. "I'm pleased to meet you."

"Noni's from Berkshire Re," Fritz explained. "They have—potentially—a large interest in this case."

"The violent death cover?" Joe asked. Noni and Fritz both nodded.

Noni Brooks certainly didn't waste any time. "The question is: can you find Gerald Murdock?" But her look seemed to say, If *you* can't, we'll get someone who can.

Berkshire Re is the biggest—and smartest—insurance outfit in the world. They obviously wanted Murdock and his money found. And they don't take "impossible" as an answer.

"What's the budget?" asked Joe.

"Five hundred ounces," said Noni.

"To start with," added Fritz.

"You're assuming Wainwright will find him guilty," I said.

"No," said Noni, "we're not *assuming* that. Though we expect he will." She looked at her watch. "Judge Wainwright will give his decision three and a half hours from now. If we just sit around and wait till then and the verdict *is* guilty, that's three and a half hours we've lost.

"Do I need to point out the obvious? It's Friday already, and this man is going to be very hard to find. His trail's getting colder by the minute. One extra hour could be the difference between success and failure."

What about the five days we've already lost? I thought to myself. But I said, "If anyone can find him, we can." Joe nodded his agreement.

"As far as you're concerned," said Fritz, "Wainwright has already pronounced him guilty. We'll call you when he announces his decision but we want you to be ready to move the moment he does."

"GMR Holdings," said Joe.

"That's right," said Fritz. "Follow the money. We've got all the papers ready: five minutes after Wainwright rules we'll be in possession of the company. Then we have to get Murdock's secretary out of the office and see what she's left for us to find."

"I want to see the bank records," I said. "Murdock disappeared at Union Square Saturday night. Like the Invisible Man. Feels like we've been hitting our heads against a brick wall ever since."

"That's exactly the point," said Fritz. "Somewhere in the company's records should be a warm trail to follow. At least a lead, a hint of some kind."

"Looks like our only bet," said Joe.

Noni Brooks shook her head. "There'll be a reward. One thousand ounces for information that leads us to Murdock."

"Who'll screen the replies?" asked Joe.

"We want you to do that. You're the experts," said Fritz.

"That'll cost extra," said Joe. "Murdock will be 'seen' all over the world."

"We only need one."

"Yeah. But figuring which is the right one will cost a fortune."

Fritz turned to Noni, who nodded her head.

"Okay," he said. "We're also going after the money Murdock skimmed from the joint venture companies. We're claiming Murdock broke the partnership agreements which would make it theft."

"But I thought he had the right to withdraw that money," I said.

"He had the right to spend the money on joint venture business. Not to pay himself without Ackerman's agreement. Anyway, we'll have a judgment in a day or three. If the judge rules against Murdock, he'll be guilty of theft as well as murder."

"Good," said Joe.

Everybody turned to look at him. "Why?" someone asked.

"Never mind now," said Fritz. "It's time we got moving."

"Who's handing things on your end?" Joe asked.

"Tony Ramirez. He's expecting your call."

"What I want to know," said Joe, to no one in particular, "is why did he do it? What's his *motive*?"

"Greed or lust," said Joe as we walked out onto Geary.

"What about revenge?"

Joe shook his head. "Doesn't figure."

"Hang on a minute," said Joe. He stepped into the tobacco store we'd just passed.

"Heavens above," he said, jogging up to where I'd stopped. He stared at his phone in one hand and a packet of Maui Wowie Lights in the other. "They've gone down in price again!"

I jangled the coins in my pocket. Joe never carried any, always paying by phone. Call me weird if you like, but I enjoy the feel, the *weight* of gold and silver.

"So what's new?" I asked.

"They dropped last month, and they're down again already."

Thinking of our payroll I said, "Wish salaries went down like everything else."

"Yeah," he grunted.

"So what do you want with them?" I asked him.

"Added inspiration."

"I'm inspired enough already."

"I said *added* inspiration, you dummy. I want to watch the holo. There's bound to be something, something somebody said or did, that will give us a clue."

The rest of the morning disappeared in a blaze of activity. But at two o'clock we were ready. At 2:05 Wainwright announced his decision: Guilty. At 2:10 one team from All-Risk, along with some of our operatives, moved into Murdock's office. A second team went to the Bank of San Francisco. At 2:15 they zapped us the account records of GMR Holdings.

"What's the time in Switzerland?" asked Joe as the records scrolled across the screen.

I thought for a minute. "Bedtime, I'd say."

"Damn. Bet Swiss banks aren't open Saturdays, either." Joe pointed at the screen. "I don't like the look of that." His fingers danced over the keyboard and the screen split into half a dozen different displays.

"See," he said. "All the money was sent to Swiss banks. All these transfers—" all but one of the displays lit up "—went to three different Swiss banks. Union Bank, Credit Suisse, Bank Leu. All big names."

"We should get some cooperation out of them. What's the problem?"

Joe punched a button on the keyboard and the display that hadn't been highlighted filled the screen.

"Right there. That wire went Saturday. Anstalt Bank. Where the hell is Vaduz, anyway?" He highlighted the bank's name and an information screen appeared. "Vaduz, Liechtenstein. Oh hell."

"Liechtenstein," I murmured. "So how do we stand with them?"

"Those guys in Liechtenstein don't say 'boo' to their own mothers. Let's see. Court order required," he read from a new display. "Hmmm. To get that, the whole case has to be retried in Vaduz. Witnesses. Everything. God knows how long that would take—years possibly. They don't recognize our adjudication process."

"Anyway," I said, "what's the bet all the money is some other place."

"Ha. Want me to take the wrong side of a sure thing?

The phone rang and a message blinked on the screen that Tony Ramirez was calling. "Good," said Joe as he pushed the Accept button. Tony's face appeared on the screen.

"Seen the bank records?" he asked.

"Yeah," said Joe. "Liechtenstein."

"And Switzerland, which is a bit more cooperative. Monday, we'll be filing cases in both places."

"So what are the chances of getting any information?" I asked.

"Not good," said Ramirez. "Better, though, when we get a ruling that Murdock stole the money from the joint ventures. That case should be finished this afternoon.

"You got anything?"

"Lots of questions," said Joe. "You got any answers?"

"Lots," Ramirez laughed. "See what you guys can dig up in Switzerland."

"Sure. We'll be on the next ship out. Let us know if they find Murdock guilty of theft."

"Will do."

After Tony had signed off Joe asked me, "Who *is* our guy in Switzerland?"

"Günter Lattman. Remember?"

"Let's call him." Günter's number appeared on the screen.

"Wait! How cooperative do you think he'll be if you wake him up in the middle of the night."

"You're right," Joe said, grudgingly.

"Send him a message, ask him to call *us* as soon as he can. Let him wake *us* up in the middle of the night."

Joe nodded as the phone rang again. It was Andy, one of our investigators who'd gone with the All-Risk team to Murdock's office.

"What did you find?" I asked.

"She didn't leave much for us *to* find. Most of the computers have been wiped clean. We'll see what we can recover, but I wouldn't hold your breath. She's had a whole week."

"Anything at all?"

"Well . . . I don't know. We haven't moved anything yet. I'd like you to come down and have a look. Joe, I mean. My gut feeling is he might smell something."

I didn't take offense. Joe's "nose" had taken on a mystical quality in our company.

"We're on our way."

What had clearly been Murdock's office had a wonderful, close-up view of the building next door. We entered through a general office/reception area with three desks. One other door led into a smaller office which had been Annabelle Pearson's.

Joe stood in the center of Murdock's office, deep in thought. We all knew better than to interrupt him when he was in this state.

This office, like the others, had been all but stripped clean. Other than a few papers in the trash cans, a few files lying around, some old newspapers and magazines, all that was left was two bookshelves full of books. Mostly travel guides.

After a while Joe said, "It's too obvious." One of the All-Risk guys started to ask him, "What—" and was silenced. "Wait," somebody whispered to him.

Joe walked to one of the shelves and scanned the titles. They were mostly tourist guides to countries in Africa and South America. On one of the tightly packed shelves there was a hole where a book had been removed. The missing book was one of the travel guides.

"It's like Murdock left instructions. 'Ms. Pearson,' " he recited, "'please destroy everything but don't remove or touch anything on the bookshelves.'

"It's like Murdock's trying to tell us, 'Please waste your time looking for me here.' "

"Somewhere in Africa," I said. "Starting with 'N.' "

"Nigeria," someone said.

"Niger."

"Nairobi."

"Nepal."

"Nepal's in Asia, muscle head."

"Never mind." Turning to Andy, Joe said, "What I'd like you to do is set up these books and shelves in my office, *exactly* as they are now. Make a list of all the countries; see what's missing. And what the missing book probably is. See what you find out about trips Murdock took. Was he a traveler or a stay-at-home? Where did he go on vacations? What were his hobbies? Things like that. We need a better feel for this man."

"Right," said Andy.

"Wherever he is, I'll bet he's not where that bookshelf is pointing us to."

"Perhaps he's sitting there laughing at us while we're looking everywhere else," said one of the people from All-Risk. "Wheels within wheels."

"That really helps narrow down the search," I said.

"Or maybe Annabelle Pearson took it," said Andy. "Maybe *she* wants to go there."

Talking to himself again, Joe murmured, "I'll bet she does."

"Want me to order you guys pizza or something before I head for home?"

Molly's voice pulled me away from the screen. I rubbed my eyes, bleary from hours poring over files and documents. By contrast Molly (our receptionist) was bright and chirpy: she was about the only member of our staff who hadn't been putting in twenty-six-hour days.

Joe seemed to be asleep, his feet up on the desk and his chair laying all the way back. With Joe, appearances are always deceptive. "Good idea," he mumbled without opening his eyes.

"Want the usual?" she asked.

"Sure, pepperoni," I said.

"Yeah," said Joe, "with just a sprinkle of hash."

"You too?" said Molly, looking at me.

"Not for me. I want to keep my head clear so I'll stick to beer. If you could order a six-pack—make sure they're ice-cold."

"What's the time?" asked Joe.

"Six." Molly said. "Oh . . . and everybody else is wondering if you want them to stay another night, or can they all go home?"

I looked at Joe. "Tell 'em to go home, sleep—and keep their phones on in case we need 'em at three o'clock in the morning."

"Thanks, Molly," I said.

As she closed the door Joe stirred himself, stretched and sat up. He reached for the still-unopened packet of Maui Wowie Lights lying on his desk and pulled out a joint. "Time to look at that holo," he said.

Joe and I shared a large office. Our desks half-faced each other so we could work privately or talk when we wanted to. A couple of very comfortable sofas lined the opposite wall—they'd proved their worth this week. The books and bookshelves from Murdock's office had been set up against the wall to Joe's left.

"Any inspirations?" I asked, waving at the books.

"Needle in a haystack. I think that's a red herring. My gut has been bugging me about that holo; maybe, *that's* where we'll find our lead. Not in those books. . . . Heard from Andy?"

I shook my head. "Let's give him a call and see what he's got."

"No need—he'll call in when he's ready."

Joe punched a button on his keyboard and the holo shimmered in the center of the room for a moment before stabilizing.

"This is hardly what I'd have chosen for a Friday night movie."

Joe grinned. "Me neither. I'd rather watch the football. So let's run it—maybe we can catch the end of the game."

Fat chance. Having seen it before, I had trouble keeping awake. Joe on the other hand looked like he was going to fall asleep at any moment, only moving to munch on pizza. But he was actually in a highly alert, trancelike state. Which deepened as the smoke in the room thickened. Just when he looked like he'd finally dozed off he'd wind the holo back saying, "Look at this."

Dinner was over, but the five of them were still at the dining table. Murdock and Ackerman were toasting each other. "To our partnership," said Ackerman. "May it prosper," said Murdock. "He doesn't mean it," said Joe.

Joe wound the holo back and locked it onto Murdock's face and zoomed in. When Murdock said, "May it prosper," he looped it, so Murdock said the same words over and over again.

"Look at his face," Joe said. "It's wooden. That smile is forced. He's lying through his teeth."

We know that, I thought. Just that morning he'd stripped the money out of the partnerships. He's ready to run. I also knew better than to interrupt Joe when he was following his nose. I knew what he was trying to do: get inside their minds.

Joe then ran through the same scene again, with the perspective locked onto Ackerman. "He doesn't notice."

"What?" I asked.

"He can't see it. He's enthusiastic. Maybe he was one of those people who can't read faces; insensitive."

"Maybe he's too drunk or stoned."

"Maybe," said Joe. But he didn't believe it.

I only perked up when the women stripped off. No—I don't "get off" from watching other people have sex. These three women, though, were something to look at. Like watching a beauty contest. And Ackerman's wife, Sophia, was the clear winner.

"There it is. That's why my nose has been twitching. It's not Murdock at all."

I couldn't figure out what Joe was talking about.

"Look at this." Joe locked the holo on Sophia Ackerman's face. Even I could see it now: she and Murdock weren't screwing: they were making love. Or she was: it was written all over her face.

Then Joe flicked to Annabelle Pearson. For just a moment there was a look of pure hatred on her face. Joe froze the picture, zoomed out, and it was clear that Annabelle Pearson was looking at Sophia and Murdock making love.

One more flick and we were looking at Sophia Ackerman. Just for a second, a look of disgust crossed her face: at that moment she was looking at her husband.

"That's it," said Joe. "The eternal triangle. Or quadrangle, in this case. If we can't follow the money, we can follow the sex."

He punched his phone. "Andy. I want a twenty-four-hour tail on Mrs. Murdock and Annabelle Pearson . . . Yes, starting right now. . . . Call anyone you need: this has got to be tight. You've all got to be ready to follow them wherever they go. . . . Sure, hire all the extra help you need. . . . Yeah, right, tell everyone to have their bags packed. And make sure your cards are loaded with cash: one of those women is going to lead us to Murdock as sure as my name is Joe Herrera, and you've got to be ready to go wherever in the world they go."

For a while Joe listened, muttering, "Yeah," "Okay," "Good," and so on. Finally, "Okay, I'm on my way," and put the phone down.

"Where?" I asked.

"Murdock's apartment. I'm meeting Andy there."

"My god, it's getting on for midnight!"

"Well, I'm in the mood right now."

"What's Andy found out?"

"Oh, this and that. Sort of mood stuff. I'll fill you in tomorrow."

"Is that it?" I asked, motioning to the holo.

"Oh yeah, we're finished with that. My nose has stopped itching." With relief, I switched the holo off and the room was clear at last.

Joe grabbed his coat and waved "goodbye" as he ran out the door. I've no idea where his energy came from; it just made me feel even more tired.

And then the phone rang. Who could be calling at this time of night? Maybe it was Sophia Ackerman looking for a date. I must have been dreaming.

"Hullo. Is this San Francisco Investigations?" said a voice I didn't recognize. It was English English, but with a faint trace of a foreign accent I couldn't place. No face appeared on the screen to help me out.

"Yes," I replied.

"Oh, good morning, Ray."

"Yes. Who is this?"

"Oh, sorry. It's too early in the morning to show my face. Günter Lattman here."

"Günter! You got my message? What time is it in Zurich?"

"About eight-thirty. What are you doing in the office so late?"

"Working, more's the pity."

"I went quickly through the Murdock stuff you sent me. There's no way I can get information out of a Swiss bank without a Swiss court order. And Swiss courts don't recognize your murder penalties. If we found Murdock here we could lock him up for you—but that wouldn't get you any money out of him."

"All-Risks is going to file in a Zurich court bright and early Monday morning."

"That'll take weeks if you're lucky. Months more likely. And even then, the Swiss court isn't going to give you—or me—access to Swiss bank records. Not for murder."

"Yeah, that's what I thought."

"All they could do is arrest him if he was found here."

"There's another case against Murdock in court right now. For theft."

"That's different," said Günter, enthusiasm showing in his voice at last. "If you can show there's stolen money in a Swiss bank, well . . ."

"Murdock's flown the coop. He didn't show up in court today, and he won't show up next week. So it should be open and shut."

"Okay. You've still got to get a Swiss court order. But that's a lot easier for theft. Do you want me help you get that done?"

"I'm pretty sure All-Risks will take care of that. I'll check and let you know. Main thing is we want to see those records as soon as possible after we get the order. Can you set that up?"

"That I can do."

"Great. I have to hit the sack. I'll talk to All-Risks and get back to you next week."

"Fine. Good night."

After I'd closed up the office—kind of Joe to leave that to me— I slumped into my car, ordered it to take me "Home, Jeeves," reclined the seat and dozed while the roadnet took me there. When the car pulled into the garage I was sound asleep: it had to wake me up.

On Monday the Eighth Army called for a truce and pulled out. My bank account was flusher by 5,400 gold ounces. The rest of the week was downhill from there.

Tuesday Murdock was found guilty of theft; Thursday a Swiss court gave us access to Murdock's bank records (which impressed Günter no end. "All-Risks must have pulled a lot of strings to get the hearing done so fast," he told us); and Friday we had copies.

All the money had flown. To places like Nauru, the Cook Islands, Pitcairn and other sandbars that made Mafia, Inc. look like first-prize winners in a gabfest.

The money trail was a dead end.

Meanwhile our phones were ringing off the hook with more red herrings, thanks to Berkshire's reward. . . .

WANTED
for Murder and Theft:
1,000*au* REWARD

Gerald Murdock has been declared an outlaw and a renegade under the rules of the American Insurance Association. A reward of 1,000 gold ounces will be paid to the person who provides information leading to his arrest.

Outlaw means that no client of any AIA member is insured for any dealing with Gerald Murdock other than self-defence.

Renegade means that any member of the public who apprehends, arrests, or detains Gerald Murdock or assists in doing so will be considered a bonded representative of the AIA under its rules.

People were told to contact us—and they did. Within two days, Murdock had been sighted in fifty-five countries, every major city in North America and half the small towns.

Luckily for us, Berkshire paid for all the extra staff, phone lines and follow-up on all the leads, just as Noni had promised.

Noni—and Fritz—weren't quite so understanding on everything else.

Eventually, after several meetings, some of them heated, they had to agree that with the money trail dead and none of the leads leading us anywhere Joe's instinct to "follow the sex" was all that was left.

"And if he dumps *both* women?" Noni asked.

Joe and I could only shrug.

Some three months later I'd just gotten to sleep when a phone call from Andy woke me.

"I'm on a rocket to Tokyo. Just took off."

"So? What? Why?"

"I nearly lost her on the way to the airport."

"Who?"

"Sophia Ackerman. Are you asleep or something?"

"I was."

"I didn't get a chance to call in earlier. We land in Tokyo in forty-five minutes and I'm going to need backup."

"Okay. I'll call you back."

It was a wild night. We couldn't arrange backup in time. Luckily, Andy kept up with her as she got on the Mag-Lev to Osaka. When the train arrived he had all the help he needed.

She took him on a merry chase, from Osaka to Shanghai, to Singapore, to Hong Kong and finally Manila. At each stop she changed her appearance. And at each stop from Osaka on, a female operative followed her into the bathroom. Otherwise we might have lost her entirely: each time, she had a new identity to go with each disguise.

She ended up in a condo in a high-security walled and gated village.

Andy sent us a picture of the happy couple by the condo pool.

"My god," said Joe, "I'd never have recognized him. But it has to be him."

Murdock had a goatee and mustache, had changed his hair and eye color (contacts, I figured), and had picked up a new nose somewhere along the line.

"Right," I said. "If she was going to meet anyone else, why the merry chase?"

"Manila, hmmm," Joe murmured. "No mountains, no beaches, no snow. Clever." Among the useless information we'd piled up about Murdock was that he loved skiing, hiking, mountaineering, boats and deep-sea fishing.

"All you have to do now," he said to me, "is go to Manila and pick him up."

The only nonstop service to Manila was an aging SuperJumbo. I didn't fancy a twelve-hour flight, so I took the rocket to Hong Kong and connected. Hong Kong–Manila took longer than San Francisco–Hong Kong.

As a kid, I loved hearing my granddad's stories about the tax revolt—but I never knew until after he died that he was one of its heroes.

He'd sit on the swinging chair on the porch at night, set me on his knee and tell me how people hated the government, but were afraid. Some arm of the government called the "HSS" was rounding up terrorists, and nobody ever knew where they'd strike next. I'd wake up sweating from nightmares of giants, dressed in black, storming into my room in the middle of the night. Even so, I could never resist another of his stories.

He told me about Amanda Green, a teacher in a small town near San Francisco. When she didn't show up at school one morning, someone went to see if she was hurt—and found her house trashed, all her files and computer gone, but no sign of her.

And her valuables untouched. No ordinary burglars.

Her neighbors had nothing. But they'd heard the familiar sounds of the sirens and car doors slamming and thumping feet in the middle of the night . . . and closed their houses up tight.

A terrorist, claimed the HSS, inciting her students to rebel against the state.

A homely grandmother, a dedicated teacher, loved by her students, and respected by the community a terrorist? For teaching her students the meaning of life, liberty, and the pursuit of happiness?

Amanda Green was the spark that lit the fire. It started quietly, like a burning ember, as groups held sporadic protests here and there. Only to be brutally repressed by the HSS police.

The TV coverage inflamed the nation. Within days millions of people across the country were parading with signs saying "Liberty or Death," "Don't Tread on Me" and even "Taxation is Theft."

One night an IRS office was burned down and somebody calling himself Tom Paine appeared on the web, urging people to strangle the government *peacefully* by refusing to pay taxes. As the idea caught on, the government called out the army to help the police help the tax collectors to "do their duty." Despite widespread support for the revolt, the government was winning until a couple of big corporations announced they were joining in.

The way my grandad told me as a kid, the people united against the hated government and brought it tumbling down.

Of course, it wasn't that simple or that easy, as I later found out. And I also learnt how granddad had persuaded some of his fellow policemen to do their *real* duty: protect the public. The sight of police standing *between* the army and the people inspired thousands of other policemen to do the same. When soldiers started joining them, the government had no choice but to cave in.

When the government collapsed the oil-rich states of the Middle East spotted an opportunity and hired a remnant of the US army to "liberate" the Muslims of the Philippines. They had no trouble at all gathering a seasoned force of veterans who were highly skilled in killing people.

That generated an enormous controversy. The soldiers were severely criticized for working for a government. Some pointed out it's a free country—at least now it is, with government gone—so anyone's free to work for anyone . . . including mercenaries. Others said that, right or wrong, it's better for us that these people are somewhere on the other side of the world.

The oil sheiks started a trend: pretty soon American mercenaries were fighting other people's wars for them all round the world. As they still are.

The Philippines—which used to be pretty much all the islands between Taiwan and Borneo—disintegrated. The Philippine Army was no match for the Americans, who threw them out of Mindanao in a couple of weeks. Once Mindanao declared its independence other islands followed suit. Local elites grabbed control, often with the help of a few hundred American mercenaries, and the country disintegrated into a patchwork of competing warlords. What's called the Philippines today is the island of Luzon and not much more.

The ride from the airport to the hotel—a slow crawl through an almost continuous traffic jam on what was labeled an "expressway," interrupted only by detours around numerous potholes—did nothing to convince me that much had improved in three generations. Beggars in rags cadged pennies from millionaires riding in chauffer-driven air-conditioned limousines. Here, a glitzy apartment building that wouldn't have been out of place in San Francisco stood opposite a pile of garbage blocking the sidewalk and spilling out onto the street; there, a wall topped by razor-sharp barbed wire prevented the wealthy occupants of a village from seeing the teeming slums across the street.

My guess was that Murdock was merely waiting for the heat to die down before moving on.

Andy had set up twenty-four-hour surveillance on Murdock. Two of our operatives had moved into one of the condos as a "couple," and had even become vaguely friendly with Murdock and Sophia Ackerman. Murdock's story, they were told, was that he and his "wife" were retired and were taking a slow, multi-year trip around the world. His next stop? "Well, when we've finished here we'll decide. Maybe flip a coin. Who can say?"

Andy introduced me to our local contact, José Guzman, known to everyone as "Boyet," who I'd called on to help Andy "meet" Sophia Ackerman off the plane.

"We've got one of our people in the condo security force, and three or four others discreetly patrolling the streets around the building."

"Is that enough?" I asked.

"You have to understand that in the Philippines most everything is the opposite to what you're used to. For example, in America, you have law but no government; here we have government but no law."

"Maybe it's jetlag, but I don't get it."

"The system here works on grease. Bribery and corruption. Of course there are laws—the government makes new ones every day. But whether they're enforced, or how, depends on who pays what to whom. Going to court here is like going to an auction.

"What that means is everything and everyone is for sale. So you've got to know who you can really trust. *That's* why I've put so few people onto Murdock. Once somebody talks, inevitably it will get back to Murdock or the people *he's* paid off, and your bird will fly away."

"So what do we do? And there's no extradition agreement we can use."

"Andy and I have talked about that. Here's what I suggest we do. . . ."

It took another week of long days and sleepless nights, intense negotiations, not to mention considerable expense, before we were ready to spring the trap on Murdock. Speed, Boyet stressed, was the essence—a difficult proposition in a country where the local equivalent of the Mexican word *mañana* didn't have quite the same sense of urgency— to make sure Murdock didn't get wind of what we were up to.

As every day passed, more and more people were involved. We did our best to ensure secrecy by paying officials—up to and including the President—bribes we were pretty sure Murdock couldn't match; and one condition of the payments was that 80 percent of the money only got paid when Murdock was on a plane out of the country in handcuffs.

That didn't mean someone who got wind of things couldn't extract a healthy "reward" from Murdock for tipping him off. In my nightmares I was part of a gun battle between two groups of rent-a-cops on the streets of Manila.

On the appointed day, Tim—one of our two operatives who'd befriended Murdock—knocked on the door of his apartment. I, Andy, Boyet, the local chief of police and a couple of cops stood well back from the door. Other police, teamed up with Boyet's people, stood guard on the apartment's rear entrance, and took control of the lobby to guard the elevators as well as prevent the security guards from giving any warning.

"Hey, Tim, come in," said Murdock as he opened the door. Tim took a step forward and then pushed Murdock hard in the chest so he fell backward, landing in a heap on the floor. We rushed in, guns drawn.

"You bastards. And *you*," he screamed, pointing at Tim, "are a low-down, lying, shit-faced scum of the earth."

Two of the cops pulled him up and handcuffed his wrists behind his back. I heard a crash as Andy put his foot through one of the bedroom doors. In a moment a chastened Sophia Ackerman was led into the living room.

"You bitch," said Murdock, his face reddening with his fury. "*You* brought them here." Forgetting the handcuffs, he struggled to hit her. Realizing he couldn't, he spat in her face instead.

"Yes," said Andy, smiling, "she led me a merry chase. Almost lost her a couple of times. And it looks like we got here just in time: she was packing for a trip."

"And I never saw you, damn your eyes," she said.

"Another hour, we'd have been outta here," said Murdock. "You bastards." I managed to pirouette out of the way as he spat again in my direction.

"Anyway," he said, pulling himself up and trying to look officious and innocent at the same time, "you have no right to be here. I've committed no crime. What's this all about?"

The chief of police pulled out a thick file of papers. Waving them in Murdock's direction he explained: "I have here an order of extradition, signed by the President of the Philippines, for the apprehension of Gerald Murdock and Sophia—"

"Gerald *who*?" said Murdock.

"You," I said. "The goatee and the nose job are certainly a good disguise. Even if you've changed your fingerprints all we have to do is pull off those contact lenses and a retina scan will be conclusive."

Murdock's shoulders slumped.

Sophia Ackerman turned to the chief of police: "You have a warrant for *my* arrest? On what grounds?"

"Embezzlement, false pretenses, defrauding an insurance company," he replied.

"I've not been convicted of any such thing," she said adamantly.

"True and not true. At the same time," I said.

A puzzled look crossed her face. "What bullshit!"

"This gentleman here," I said, indicating the chief of police, "has a presidential order to extradite you from the country. So you *must* have been convicted. Here, at least. By the time we land in San Francisco, All-Risks will have presented its case before an adjudicator. In your absence there's a chance the hearing will find, *prima facie*, against you. The best you can hope for is a new date for the hearing, since All-Risks won't have given the proper notice."

"Anyway," said Murdock, "what's this about extradition? The Philippines has no extradition treaty with America."

"It does now. Here," I said, pulling out a sheaf of papers, "is a treaty between All-Risks and the government of the Philippines, signed by the President. Something for you to read . . . on the plane."

"That can't be legal," said Murdock. "Don't you need an act of Congress or something? Presidential order ain't enough. I want to talk to my lawyer."

"That won't be possible," said the chief of police. Pulling out another sheet of paper which he offered to Murdock, grinning when he remembered the handcuffs, he continued· "This is an order for your immediate deportation. It seems that your visa, as well as Miss Ackerman's, has expired."

Murdock looked like he was about to explode. Then his body relaxed and he turned to me with a glint of admiration in his eyes. "You really pulled out all the stops, eh?"

"Well, Berkshire Re did."

"Oh, that I didn't know."

"You know, you'd have done better to stay at home," I told him. "Not in San Francisco, of course. Some other American city. With your money, your disguise and new fingerprints, just by avoiding retina scans we might never have found you. In a place where government is for sale, you can always be outbid."

"Maybe you're right," he said.

"Look on the bright side. Here, the penalty for murder is death. Back home, all you have to do is pay back all the money and you're a free man." The prospect didn't seem to be all that appealing to Murdock. I could sympathize: from wealth to poverty in matter of moments.

"And what about me?" asked Sophia Ackerman.

"Same thing. The presumption is you're an accessory to murder. That was your plan, right?" I said, looking from one to the other. "You were after Ackerman's insurance—the 110,115 gold ounces Sophia got for your murder of hubbie."

They stared at me blankly, neither agreeing nor disagreeing.

I looked at Sophia admiringly—an easy thing to do.

"You're a good actress," I said. "I saw the holo."

She spat at me, this time connecting.

"Time to go," said Andy, looking at his watch.

"Right," I agreed, wiping the spittle off my face. "Let's move—we all have a plane to catch."

The Colonizing of Tharle

James P. Hogan

Records from the colony's founding years stated that the town of Ferrydock had grown from an early base established near the river mouth, where a motorized pontoon raft had provided the crossing to the peninsula. With its rocky prominences, dunes, and beaches, the peninsula—later named Strandside—was an attractive place for walks and swims or just lazing around to get away from the routine of the settlement for a while. Later, it acquired some stores, a bar, restaurant, and a small hotel to become one of the more popular recreation spots. Although Ferrydock was now a fair-size town, and a low, sleek bridge of concrete spans with a raisable center section—sitting on incongruously ornate steel piers reminiscent of nineteenth-century ideas of aesthetics—crossed the river, a ferry still ran alongside. Not everybody was in enough of a hurry to need the road, one of the locals had explained to Duggan and another official with the mission sent from Earth to reestablish relations with Tharle. And besides, the kids liked the water ride. Notions of cost effectiveness didn't seem to count for much here—and that fitted with the other bizarre notions of economics that had taken root here, which the theorists up in the orbiting mother ship *Barnet* had already decided were probably the major factor responsible for the planet's evident regression in many ways from the levels of technological and political capability possessed by the founders.

Duggan stood in the square at the heart of Ferrydock's central district—an open space really too irregular to justify its name geometrically, bordered by narrow, erratic streets and buildings of the peculiarly curved architectural style reveling in orange-brick walls and green- or blue-tiled roofs that brought back childhood memories of an illustrated edition of Oz. The Tharleans seemed to delight in turrets and towers too, which was also odd, since there was no history of militancy or defense needs to have inspired them. Simply another of their odd whims and fancies expressing itself, Duggan supposed.

It was apparently market day. The stalls around the square were heaped with assortments of unfamiliar fruits, vegetable-like offerings, and other plant forms that grew under the purple-tinted sky. There were refrigerated racks of strange fish, joints of meat, tanks of live fish, and cages containing furry and feathered animals of various kinds, whether intended for food or as pets, Duggan didn't know. And there were tables displaying tools and other hardware, ornaments, art works, kitchenware, haberdashery, household goods, and clothing—much the same as market places anywhere, anytime. Duggan watched a tall, weathered-looking man in a gray shirt and loose blue jacket examining a pair of ceramic sculptures in the form of elongated feminine heads with a suggestion of styled Oriental features.

"How much for these?" he asked the graying-haired lady in charge of the stall. She was sitting in a folding alloy-frame chair, a many-colored, open-weave blanket pulled around her shoulders. A shaggy, yellow-haired creature with a huge-eyed, owl-like face studied the man alertly from the top of an upturned box next to her.

"Ten draks," the woman replied.

The dialect had drifted to a degree that now sounded quaint; or was it that English as spoken on Earth had progressed? Schooling in Tharlean pronunciations, usage, and idioms had been required of all the delegates on the contact mission, and after a few days on the surface Duggan found he was experiencing few problems.

The man turned one of the sculptures over in his hands again and pursed his lips. "I'll give you fifteen."

The woman smiled in the kind of way that said it was a good try. "What do you think I am, destitute or dysfunctional or something? They're not worth that."

"Hey, come on, gimme a break and let me help you out a little. We've all got our pride."

"Eleven, then."

The man shook his head. "I can manage more than that. How about fourteen?"

They eventually settled on twelve. Duggan turned away, mystified, and shook his head. The two armed troopers that regulations required escort him when away from the surface lander at Base 1 beyond the far edge of the town looked back at him unhelpfully. "A strange way of playing poker," Duggan commented.

"They're all crazy," one of the troopers offered.

Then Duggan noticed the woman in a shirt of leafy design on white and bright red shorts, standing a few yards away in front of a mixed, chattering group of people but apparently not with them. Farther back, others among the crowd had stopped and were staring at Duggan and his escorts unabashedly. The woman was perhaps in her mid thirties if Earth standards were anything to judge by, with wiry, shoulder-length hair that varied between being auburn and orange depending how it caught the light, and the bronzed skin with a hint of metallic sheen that the blue-shifted light from Xylon-B evoked among Tharleans generally. Her body was slim and lithe, her face tapering to a pointy chin, with a straight nose, dimpled cheeks, and a mouth that was hovering on the edge of wanting to smile but at the same time hesitant, as if she were unsure how it might be taken. Instead, she let her eyes interrogate him silently. They were deep, brown, intelligent, and mirthful, the kind that could arouse immediate interest in possibilities and prospects—especially in a new and strange, yet-to-be-explored place, after an excruciatingly uneventful voyage dominated by routine and officiousness. Duggan's features softened. He let his mouth pucker in the way of one of two people unsure of their ground offering to meet halfway.

"I didn't mean to gape," the woman said. "But I haven't seen anyone from the Earth ship this close before. I was just curious."

"Oh, I wouldn't worry about it," Duggan answered. "I've seen plenty of people from Tharle. The only trouble is, I haven't managed to talk to too many of them."

"They're curious too, but trying to mind their own business. It's considered good manners. . . . Some of them are worried about what the soldiers are doing here, too."

"So what makes you different?"

She shrugged. "I just wanted to see for myself what you were like—try to talk to some of you. I hear what other people say, but I never know whether to believe it."

"What do they say?" Duggan asked.

The woman thought for a few seconds, her mouth twisting wryly in the way of someone searching for a safe answer. "They call you Pinkies," she said finally.

He stared at her, then laughed. The barrier of tension they had both been reacting to revealed itself as an illusion and came tumbling down. "Paul Duggan," he said.

"My name's Tawna."

"So . . . hi."

"Hi."

The feelings coming back at him were good. She was looking at him directly and openly with an expectant expression, fears allayed, eager to learn more. Duggan turned his head and lowered his tone to mouth at the escorts. "Why don't you guys get lost for a half hour? Take a walk around; get yourselves a coffee or something."

"Can't. Orders," one of the troopers replied woodenly.

Duggan sighed and turned back to Tawna. "I'm with what the mission calls its Office of Exorelations. That means we're the ones who are supposed to deal with whoever's in charge of things here. But we're not having much luck finding anyone. That's why I decided to come out and walk around the town. Nothing we got over the communications channels made any sense."

Tawna looked puzzled. "I can't see why that should be a problem. There are people in charge of things everywhere."

"How do you mean?"

"Well, it depends what you're looking for. In charge of what, specifically? The Waterfront Agency looks after the harbor installations and the docks. The Power Company produces power. The highway companies consolidated into the Road Services League because tolls got to be such a hassle. . . ."

Duggan waved a hand. "But above those—the works, all of it. Who runs the whole system?" Tawna seemed to want to be helpful, but she appeared honestly not to know what he meant. "The laws," he said. "Who makes the laws here?"

"Laws?" she repeated, as if hearing a new word in the language for the first time.

"What you can do, what you can't. How you're allowed to treat each other. Who tells you the rules?"

"Tells us? . . . Nobody. . . . Why would they?"

"Then where do they come from?"

Tawna showed a hand helplessly. "They don't come from any-where. They're just . . . there. Who tells you rules for how to breathe air or how to grow older? Nobody needs to. You already know. You just do it."

Duggan glanced again at the two troopers. Trying to pursue the subject further in a place like this, and under these circumstances, would be impossible. But he felt that at last he'd made some rapport and found a line that could lead somewhere eventually—and con-ceivably in more senses than one. "So what do you do here?" he asked Tawna, abandoning the tack for the time being.

She seemed relieved. "Me? Oh, I'm a dance teacher most of the time—keeps me fit. And I'm also a musician and help organize shows. I've tried writing a couple of plays too, but they weren't very good. I probably let myself get paid too much for them."

It was the same illogic that Duggan had been hearing all over the place. He didn't want to go any further into it now, he decided, any-more than trying to find out who ran the system. "Is Ferrydock where you're from originally?" he asked instead.

They chatted for a while. She had grown up in a farming area on the far side of the mountains standing distantly in the purplish haze to the northeast, and moved here to be with friends. She was curious about Earth and would maybe have kept them both there for the rest of the day with her questions, but her knowledge of its affairs was dated, reflecting the politics and geography of the period around a century ago, before the colony world of Tharle had become isolated.

"We need to talk some more," Duggan said when he spotted the scout car from Base 1 coming to collect him. "Somewhere different from this—where it's quieter, more private."

"I'd like that," Tawna said.

"How can I get in touch with you?"

She gave him the call codes for her personal phone, which turned out to consist of the blue-jeweled ear rings with silver mountings and matching pendant that she was wearing. Duggan would never have guessed. He gave her one of his official departmental calling cards with contact details. Communications engineers aboard the *Barnet* had already programmed the ship's system to interface with the planetary net. Tawna waved brightly after them as people parted to let him and his two escorts through to the waiting car.

Duggan stared out at the town's busy sidewalks and pedestrian precincts as they began the short drive back. The last problem anyone had anticipated the mission would come up against in reestablishing contact with the colony's government when it got to Tharle was *finding* a government. He looked down at the compak that he was still holding in his hand, where he'd stored Tawna's call codes. Electronics so advanced that he hadn't even recognized it; technology to put satellites aloft; sophisticated air travel available when the need arose. And yet, at the same time, the deep-space-going capability that the founders brought had gone into decline; people spent much more time getting around than they needed to, sailing in ships or plain walking; and the supposedly fundamental laws of market trading somehow worked backwards.

Nothing made sense.

Nobody knew who the "Barnet" was or had been, whom the ship was named after. Typically, it would have been some long-forgotten bureaucrat from an extinct department. Duggan sometimes wondered if it might have been the one responsible for the blunder that had resulted in Tharle's disappearing from the records for almost a hundred years. Two rival sections of the Colonial Affairs Administration had each recorded that the other was responsible for handling Tharle, out at Xylon-B, and a hundred years was how long it had taken for the realization to dawn that nobody was. Contact was established, and the *Barnet* and its mission hastily despatched to reintroduce formal diplomatic relations. In the furious exchanges of messages and memoranda, accusations and denials, evasions of blame and attempts to direct it elsewhere that followed discovery of the fiasco, it apparently escaped everyone as significant that in all that time nobody on Tharle had chosen to draw Earth's attention to its omission.

Back aboard the orbiting *Barnet*, Pearson Brose, head of the mission's Office of Exorelations and Earth's designated ambassador-to-be if a government could be found that wanted one, was getting impatient for results. "Of *course* they have to exist," he fumed at the review meeting of his staff, including Duggan, gathered in the conference room of his unit's offices in the Planetary Department section of the Administrations deck. He had a florid face with long, wispy white hair that flailed like a stormy sea when he jerked his head about—which he did a lot at times like this. "They're probably paranoid and gone underground for reasons best known to themselves. Why? What reason have we given them to do that? Have we made threats? Are their cities quavering under weapons that we have deployed? I see no weapons. We've shown nothing but reasonableness and a desire to advance our common interests. So what have I missed? Where am I going wrong? Somebody tell me."

Everybody knew that Brose hadn't gone wrong anywhere. The melodramatic flourishes were his way of reminding the world of how much his responsibilities required him to endure and suffer. Zeebron Stell, with his hefty build, swarthy skin, short-cropped black hair and shaggy mustache, almost an inverse of Brose, brought them back on track. He was supposed to be Duggan's colleague and virtual opposite number, but they seemed to end up at odds over everything. "Well, I did get to talk with that scientific group up north. They're into a new line on catalyzed nuclear processes that will need a high-energy installation and big bucks."

Brose forgot his lamentations and became interested. "Ah yes, the research institute. So where does the funding come from. Did we find out?" He always said "we" if the prospective news was good. It was taken for granted that such a source would be some branch or other of government, the uncovering of which would hopefully lead to the rest.

"Not really," Stell answered. "That is, nothing that you'd be interested in. The bread comes from all kinds of places: a bunch of corporations, as you'd expect; an amazing number of individuals; even a school science club. But none of it was like what we were looking for." Brose looked at him sourly, as if asking why he had bothered bringing it up if that were the case. Stell went on, "But the way they were going about it says to me that they don't deal with anyone in the government anyway."

"How do you mean?" Brose asked.

Stell showed his hands and turned from side to side in an appeal to the others that he wasn't making this up. "When we asked them about procedures, they started telling us that their biggest problem is arguing grants *down* to *less* than the sources want to give them—as if that was obviously what anyone would do. They thought that accepting too much would make them look incompetent. Who ever heard of a government funding agency that would have problems dealing with people like that?" A baffled silence engulfed the room. Then Milford Grimes from Research Resources pronounced what was going through all their minds.

"That's insane."

Amelia Jonkin, another of the Exorelations staff, looked from one to another as if inviting any better ideas before voicing the only one she could come up with. "Maybe they're a second-rate outfit. It could be an indication of lack of self-esteem there, or that they have an inferior image of themselves." She didn't sound as if she really believed it.

"The stuff they were doing looked right-on to me," Stell said. "And Dransel Howess who was with us thought so too. Nuc-cat is his line, and he was big-time impressed."

Duggan shifted in his seat. He had been quiet for a long time. "I saw the same thing when I was down in Ferrydock," he told the room. "They've got a marketplace there in the town, and people haggle. Except they try to sell lower and buy higher. I tried getting some of them to explain it, but nobody could. They couldn't understand what was so strange that needed explaining."

"It just shows that they're all simpletons," somebody from the Planning Group said. "We can't let people like that get the better of us, surely." The tone was facetious.

"Perhaps we should look for the big houses," Amelia mused. "The real rulers in any society always live in the biggest houses."

And that seemed to exhaust the suggestions. Brose looked around for further comment. After a second or two of more silence, it came from the commander of the mission's military contingent, General Rhinde, who was sitting in and so far had maintained silence with visibly rising impatience.

"This nonsense has gone on long enough. You're not going to get anywhere creeping around like tourists frightened of giving offence, and asking polite questions." He glowered around, challenging anyone to disagree. Nobody dared. "The people you're talking about will be all office clerks, anyway, even if you find them. The true government of a country, planet, whatever, is whoever defends it. The way you find them is make them come to you. Just march in, say you're taking over, and wait to see who appears. If nobody does, then you know who the government is anyway. It's you."

Nobody was prepared to argue. But at the same time, it was clear to everyone except Rhinde that nothing that drastic was a candidate for the time being. Ever the able and resourceful organization man, Brose tabled the proposal for further consideration and appointed someone to form a subcommittee to look into it.

After the meeting adjourned, Duggan approached Brose privately in his office at the Executive Suites end of the Planetary Department. "I'd like approval to roam around freely down there, without escorts," he said. "There isn't any threat, and the presence of weapons inhibits the Tharleans. It's a barrier to further progress in getting through to them."

"You really think it's likely to make much difference?" Brose queried. His conviction seemed distinctly far short of total. "I mean, what progress at all is there to take further? Have *you*, for instance, met anyone who looks even remotely capable of being gotten through to?"

"I think so, maybe. Yes."

"Hm." Brose sniffed. "And what if we have to scrape you up out of an alley one morning, and it gets back that I waived regulations. How would I be supposed to explain it?"

"Well, we'd better come up with something before Rhinde gets his way and ends up starting a war," Duggan said. "Would you rather have to explain that?"

Duggan got his request approved—on signing a disclaimer that it was at his own instigation, and against the advice of his superior. "I'm doing it to give you a chance to rack up some points for promotion to subsection supervisor when we get back," Brose murmured confidentially as he signed the paper. "I think you'd be more suited to it, Paul." Duggan had little doubt that Brose was saying similar things to Stell too, who was also a candidate for the slot. Fostering a healthy competitive spirit between rivals was encouraged as part of the Department's management style. It was considered the astute way to develop human resources. They were what at one time had been called "people."

"I'll be coming back down tomorrow," Duggan told Tawna when he called her a half hour later. "No guards to get in the way this time, so we can have that talk. Tell me a good place to meet."

The bronzed, orangey-haired face on the screen looked genuinely pleased. "That's wonderful! Then you can tell me all about Earth." She must have caught a hint of a reaction in his face. "And talk about other things too, naturally. What did you want to do down here?"

Duggan frowned, realizing that he had been unprepared. He thought rapidly. "I want to find out who lives in the biggest houses," he told her.

They met and had breakfast in a cafe by the river, on a terrace at the rear, overlooking the water. It was a fair, sunny day, and there were a lot of small boats about—some sporty and powered, others curvy and delicate with strange-shaped sails, reminiscent in ways of Arab dhows. It was the same incongruous blend of ancient and new existing happily side-by-side that Duggan had been noticing everywhere. A large blimp passed overhead, heading south, maybe following the coast. Tawna explained that on days when the weather permitted, those who could afford it often preferred them to regular jets. By this time, Duggan was surprised to hear that for once the price of something should actually reflect how it was valued. It turned out that what Tawna meant was those who could afford the time.

As he listened, Duggan found himself being captivated by her openness. She played none of the mind games that he was accustomed to in this kind of situation, no jockeying for one-up points to decide who had a controlling advantage. And in a way that he realized was a new concept to him, her absence of deviousness absolved him from any need to reciprocate. He could actually be himself and say what he thought, without having to calculate implications and consequences. It felt liberating and refreshing. Yes, there had been a man that she'd lived with for a while when she moved to Ferrydock. His name had been Lukki. But in the end it hadn't worked out. No, there was no one in particular at present.

The people they were going to meet were called Jazeb and Maybel Wintey, and kept what Tawna described as a "huge" house in a foothill region of the mountains northeast of Ferrydock. She didn't know them personally but had known of them for a long time, and contacted them through an agent in town who provided their domestic staff. Hardly surprisingly, a mention that somebody from the Earth ship wanted to meet them was all it had taken. In her non-questioning, accepting way, Tawna hadn't asked Duggan why he wanted to know who lived in the big houses. When Duggan inquired casually what Wintey did, Tawna replied in an uncharacteristically vague kind of way, that he "collected things." It didn't sound much like what Duggan had been hoping for. But he could hardly change his mind now.

Back outside the front of the cafe, Tawna stopped to run her eye over the assortment of vehicles in the parking area. Tharlean ground autos were generally simpler and less ostentatious than Terran designs, though with the same proclivity for curviness that was evident in the architecture and the boats; a couple looked almost like Aladdin slippers on wheels. She led the way across to a pale blue, middle-of-the-range model, unpretentious but comfortably roomy for two. As they got in, Duggan commented that he'd thought she wasn't sure which car was hers. It wasn't hers, he discovered, but belonged to a common pool that anyone could use, rather like a public comlink booth back home. She started it by inserting a plastic tag that seemed to combine the functions of pay card and driver's license. People who needed to owned their own, but most didn't bother, Tawna said—adding that it was the kind of thing Jazeb Wintey would do. She seemed to find it humorous. Duggan wasn't sure why.

They drove out of the town to an airport that Duggan knew of from the *Barnet*'s reconnaissance views, where large commercial planes came and went from all over, and parked outside a building serving an area to one side used by smaller craft. Tawna just took her card from the slot in the car's dash panel and walked away. Inside the building, they rented a personal six-seat flymobile that she had reserved, and soon, with the vehicle practically flying itself, were skimming low along the river valley, toward the mountains outlined in the distant purplish haze.

Tawna hadn't been exaggerating when she described the Wintey house as "huge." It would have qualified as a mansion by Terran standards, with a healthy profusion of Tharlean towers and turrets, and stood amid an estate of outbuildings and grounds enclosed by high walls and wire fences. The flymo landed on a gravel courtyard in front of the house and was met by a retinue of household staff who conducted Duggan and Tawna to the portico-framed entrance. Duggan noticed as they crossed the court that the main gate and the fence were protected by armed guards.

His first impression as they threaded their way through the hall inside between barricades of furniture was of being in a cross between a museum and a home goods warehouse. Enormous, glass-fronted cabinets standing from floor to ceiling, jammed with porcelains, chinaware, glassware, and figurines, lined the walls, while the ceiling was all but invisible behind rows of hanging buckets, pots, pans, basins, metalware, and jugs. The room beyond had tiers of shelves carrying all manner of ornaments, decorated boxes, and bric-a-brac, and furnishings wedged, sometimes inaccessibly, between pedestals laden with pottery and vases, ponderous columns and other carvings, and padlocked cubicles of indeterminate nature. Jazeb Wintey received them in an inner redoubt at the center of more wooden and upholstered fortifications overlooked by walls tiled with pictures and prints. He was small and gnomish, with a ruddy bald head, cantankerous expression, and a fringe of whiskers girding his chin like a sunflower. His dress of frock coat and gaitered britches was impossibly stuffy and formal for a Tharlean, and would have been eccentrically antiquated even on Earth. He shook Tawna's hand stiffly and rapidly as if it were a pump handle and repeated the process with Duggan, the sternness of his features remaining unchanged.

"From Earth! About time! It took you long enough! Maybe we'll see some sense and sanity restored to this place then, before much longer."

So much for social pleasantries. If plunging straight in was the way here, Duggan would follow suit. "Why? What's wrong with things here?" he asked.

Wintey looked at him as if he might have just woken up after a thousand-year sleep. "Pah! No ethics, no standards. Things like that all got lost after the colonists stopped building space-goers. Everything's degenerated. Why do you think we have to live walled up in a fortress like this? Envy and malice all around. It's because I'm the only one around here who's got a notion of business." He cast an arm about to indicate the surroundings. For the first time, a hint of a satisfied smile crossed the berrylike countenance. "See what I mean?" He tapped his temple meaningfully. "Takes acumen to accumulate that kind of worth, young fella. Brains and acumen. People here wouldn't even know what that means."

As Wintey stumped his way ahead of them, between display cases filled with silverware, gold plate, and jewelry, Tawna caught Duggan's eye and sent him an apologetic shrug that seemed to say, well, it was what he'd wanted.

"They don't like us, you know," Wintey went on, as if Tawna were not present. "Try to conspire to drag me down. Outside, among themselves, they do each other favors. But no staff willing to work for reasonable pay ever get sent here. They send me all the beggars and ne'er-do-wells. . . . Thieves, too, if they had half the chance, I'd be bound. Can't even find reliable guards."

They met Maybel Wintey in a sitting area off the dining room draped with silks, cushions, and rugs like movie depictions of a sultan's bridal chamber. One corner constituted a bar, stocked high with racks and shelves of bottles that no longer came as a surprise. Jazeb introduced his wife perfunctorily. She was withered and austere, but glittering with jewels from fingers and chest to a filigreed tiara, worn with a pale green gown suggesting, with a mild touch of absurdity, the robe of a classical goddess.

"What do they want?" she asked frostily, when Jazeb let up on his harangue long enough for a steward to take orders for drinks. "Everyone who comes here wants something."

"Mr. Duggan is from Earth," Jazeb reminded her. "Perhaps we'll see things being put back in order now."

"Well, that's something. At least we won't have to be buying people off to get some peace."

Lunch was a lavish affair, naturally, over which Jazeb continued in much the same vein. Finding peers to develop a satisfying social life with wasn't easy. Tharleans who had something to show for themselves, the ones you'd think would qualify, inevitably proved to be fools when it came to trade, and annoyed him—but he wasn't going to turn them down if they insisted on being gypped. The ones who knew how to bargain were from the bottom of the pile, and fraternizing with them would be out of the question too, of course—which was a shame because if they'd only learn to do something with what they had, Jazeb admitted, he could have had some time for them. It was all beyond him. He only hoped that the administration Earth was presumably going to set up would get things straightened out soon.

Afterward, they toured an entertainments room that reminded Duggan of the command deck aboard the *Barnet*, a gymnasium that could have kept a regiment of space assault troops in good shape, a games room, and a workshop equipped with every form of gadget, widget, and power tool imaginable, none of which showed much sign of having been used. And sure enough, as Tawna had guessed jokingly, there was a shed at the rear housing a collection of polished and gleaming ground autos, along with several flyers. Throughout it all, the domestic staff remained easygoing and cheerful, despite Jazeb and Maybel's constant grumbles and criticisms. Duggan found himself harboring the uneasy suspicion of watching inmates of an asylum being humored. When he and Tawna finally left, the thought of getting back among the people of Ferrydock seemed like a breath of sanity and fresh air.

"I warned you it would be a bit strange, but it was what you asked for," Tawna said as they flew back above the valley's deepening shadows. She waited a few seconds, then looked across the cabin when Duggan didn't answer. "What's up?"

Duggan returned from his realm of distant brooding. "Those two back there. It was just going through my mind . . . Back where I come from, that would be close to most people's ideal. That's how they want to be."

Tawna paused long enough to be polite. "Yes," she said hesitantly. "I thought it might be something like that."

Duggan could have added that now, perhaps, he thought he knew why the Tharleans had looked askance at the guards who had accompanied him around Ferrydock. He decided he didn't want to go into it.

Zeebron Stell had come down from the mother ship when Duggan got back to Base 1 late that evening. They had coffee in the mess room at the back of the gate guard hut, and then Stell suggested a walk in the night air around the perimeter fence. He waited until they were out of earshot of anybody, then switched from casual chat to a lowered, conspiratorial tone.

"Dug, these people are clueless here. They're set up to be taken. Ask 'em for anything you want; they hand over. Tell 'em what you want done; they do it. If you were ever looking for the place to make out like you never imagined, man, this has to be it."

Duggan paused to look out through the wire at the colored lights over Ferrydock's center. The blimp—or another—was making the return trip, lit up like a Christmas tree gliding silently through the night. "I'm not sure I know what you mean," he said.

Stell edged a pace closer. "Think about it. . . ." he breathed. "Wealth and power: that's what it's all about, eh? What else do we bust our asses year in, year out for, thinking we're gonna get a bigger share of—and put up with jerks like Brose? Well, here you're not talking about waiting years and then maybe watching some operator steal it all from under you anyway. It's already made, right now. All you gotta do is have the balls to take it."

"Take what? How?" Duggan asked guardedly.

"All of it."

"Zeeb, what, exactly, are you proposing?"

"This is were we stay and get rich; get a chance to *be* somebodies."

"You mean jump ship? Stay behind when the mission leaves. Is that it?"

"Why not, Dug? I'm starting to believe what we've been seeing here—or not seeing. There's nobody to stop you." Stell gestured to indicate both of them. "You and me—" The amused look on Duggan's face checked him. "Hey, all that was another time and place, okay? We can leave it behind. There's a planet full of enough of everything to keep both of us happy."

"Well, that's an abrupt change of tune for you, Zeeb," Duggan said. "I thought you were going for the sub-supervisor slot when we get back. Brose seems to think so. He'll be disappointed. Who will he have to play carrot and stick games with now and boost himself up the ladder?"

Stell snorted. "Oh, don't tell me you're not as tired of all that crap as I am. . . . Look, I'll let you in on a secret. I've rented a place in town to use as a kind of startup base, and already in one afternoon I've got enough stuff in there to fit out a penthouse. I'm telling you it's a steal, man. But you need someone of your own kind too, know what I mean? We could live like a couple of kings. What do you say, huh?"

"I'm not sure. Have you really figured it through as to how things are here?"

"What's there to figure, Dug? I'm telling you, you don't hit on a deal like this more than once in a lifetime." Stell's eyes were insistent in the light from the town, his expression intense. He clearly wasn't prepared to accept no as an answer.

"Okay, I'll think about it," Duggan promised.

Several days passed by, during which more expeditions returned unsuccessful from different parts of Tharle. A flurry of impatient demands for reports on progress, and replies that the situation was more complicated than expected sizzled back and forth between the

Barnet's higher echelons and the supervisory directorate on Earth. Duggan filed a report on his visit to the Winteys, which was absorbed into Pearson Brose's growing collection without significant reaction or comment. Duggan took this to mean that those who knew best were too preoccupied with affairs more befitting of their rank and calling to be distracted by lower-echelon menials and their trivia. Being a conscientious department man, he did his best to help by staying out of their way and making the most of the opportunity that Brose's dispensation had opened up for him to follow up informally on possible local leads. Since Tawna had already shown herself to be a willing and capable guide, this coincidentally meant their spending more time with each other.

Through the early part of the evening, Duggan had watched a rehearsal for one of Tawna's shows. The Tharleans handled their personal affairs in the same way as their financial ones, he noticed: when asked for help, they gave more; when offered a favor, they settled for less. Afterward, he and Tawna joined a group from the cast and supporting staff for a dinner of salad and a taco-like dish of bread, meats, and spicy fillings at a cellar bar along the street. Then the company gradually broke up in ones and twos. After staying to finish a bottle of one of the locality's wines—vaguely Rhônish, but with the ubiquitous Tharlean purple touch—Duggan and Tawna found themselves leaning on a parapet of the downtown riverbank among the nighttime strollers, staring out across the water toward the distant lights of the Strandside bridge. "I can't imagine it," Tawna said. "You mean they just try to keep on accumulating more and more, like the Winteys?" She searched for an analogy. "That would be like eating all day. Obviously, you need to have enough to keep you going. But once that's satisfied, other things in life become more important. You make it sound as if how much people own is the only measure of what they're worth. . . . Why, that would be as ridiculous as everybody being judged solely by weight and competing to be the heaviest!"

Financial obesity, Duggan thought to himself. Not a bad way to put it. It was hardly the first time in history for such an observation to be made; but the trouble with giving handouts to the ones inevitably left behind in the race had always been that it produced more and more free riders who eventually brought down the system. Somehow the Tharleans seemed to have solved the problem of restraining excess without perpetrating injustices or undermining initiative. How, then, did it work with power?

"So who makes judgments and decisions?" he asked. "You have to have disputes, the same as anyone else. Who has the final say when nobody involved can agree?"

"It's true. Somebody has to do it." Tawna made it sound like cleaning the sewers or defusing bombs. "They have a kind of lottery, and the losers get appointed. It's only for a year—and people are sympathetic, so they try to be supportive."

"You mean it's a lousy job. Nobody wants it?"

"Well, of course. Why would anyone . . ." Tawna stopped as she registered the astonishment in Duggan's voice. "You mean that on Earth . . ."

He nodded. "Having power over people is considered a big thing. They fight each other for it. Okay, now go ahead and tell me: you thought maybe it would be something like that."

Then he realized that she was giving him a long, contemplative look that held little real interest in such things just at the moment. He forgot about the subject and held her eye quizzically. "You're different from Lukki," she said. "He was like a child, never questioning anything. You do. You see things, and you think about them. It makes you . . . interesting." She slid closer along the rail of the parapet. Her fingertip traced over his arm. Duggan turned toward her. Her hair and skin shone softly golden in the light from the embankment lamps . . .

Beep . . . Beep . . . Beep . . . Beep . . .

Duggan cursed under his breath and tugged the compak from his shirt pocket. The caller was Brose's assistant aloft in the *Barnet*. All ship's personnel were recalled to base immediately. General Rhinde had finally gotten his way and announced plans to take over Ferrydock as a military demonstration. The occupation force had begun mobilizing aboard the *Barnet* and would descend from orbit at dawn.

❖ ❖ ❖

Four flights of assault shuttles made synchronized landings at key points and deployed with alacrity to seize and secure the prime means of access and communications. Two task forces sealed the main highway and rail links north and south, another commandeered the airport, while the last took the Strandside bridge and sent a column into Ferrydock to occupy the broadcasting stations and news bureaus. Meanwhile, special details sped through the town to install military administrators and technicians in the offices responsible for transportation, power generation and distribution, and communications. By midday the operation was completed as per the timetable. At noon precisely, General Rhinde went on the air to inform the inhabitants of Ferrydock that their town was now under Terran military jurisdiction and subject to the laws of its governing council. Communications and public services were under control of a colonial administration reporting to an appointed governor, and regulations concerning the conduct of business and finance would be announced shortly.

The townspeople seemed to think it was a great idea. An enthusiastic crowd in the central square greeted the news, relayed through their personal phones or from loudspeakers set up for the occasion, and by early afternoon representatives from the sanitation, harbor facilities, and water supply services were appearing at the governor's downtown headquarters offering their organizations for takeover too. Meanwhile, the management at places the Terrans had declared themselves to be in control of were resigning or taking a holiday to disappear to the beaches at Strandside, visit with grandchildren, or spend time on their hobbies. By next morning, the town was in chaos. Half the communications were down, the airport was barely functioning, and services languished as employees took breaks to line up enthusiastically in hundreds to be issued newly introduced permits and licenses. In the end, Rhinde's officers were forced to send out squads to track down essential professionals and bring them back at gunpoint to carry out tasks which until yesterday they had performed readily and willingly. That was when Duggan began getting his first strong intuition that this wasn't going to work out in the way that had been envisaged.

❖ ❖ ❖

When all-out war failed to materialize, the restrictions confining non-occupation personnel to base were eased. Duggan was standing on a street corner with Tawna, watching two troopers shouldering assault rifles and clad in riot gear, posted to protect the Municipal Services Building from a gaggle of curious onlookers, when Zeebron Stell called from the office suite he'd rented as a trading base. He sounded agitated.

"Dug, where are you?"

"A few blocks away from you on Johannes Street. You know, Zeeb, I think Gilbert and Sullivan could have done a lot with this."

"Is Tawna with you?"

"Yes, she is. What's up?"

"I've got problems. People here don't seem to understand that I'm running a business, not a thrift store. Can you get over? Maybe she'd be able to do a better job of getting the message across."

"It's Zeeb, from his emporium," Duggan murmured to Tawna. "He's having some kind of trouble with the locals. Wants us over there to see if you can maybe talk to them. Is that okay with you?"

"Sure."

"We're on our way, Zeeb."

A miscellany of vehicles was parked outside the building in which Stell had his premises, including a beat-up truck. Inside, they found him remonstrating with a dowdily dressed woman who seemed interested in some toilet preparations that he had amassed a stack of in one of the rooms. Elsewhere, a couple with two small children were examining a shelf of electronics appliances, while a small, bespectacled, bearded man, wearing a tweed jacket with deerstalker-like hat and waving a list of some kind, hopped about, trying to get Stell's attention. "*No!* You're outta your mind," Stell told the woman. "How is that supposed to be doing me a favor? It's not even what I paid." Then, to the man, "Look, I told you I'm not interested. I don't even know who any of those people are. How in hell do you figure you're helping *me*?" Another man appeared in a doorway at the rear, smiling and holding an elaborate wrist unit of some kind that had a miniature screen. Stell groaned, then caught sight of Duggan and Tawna and steered them gratefully back into the entrance hallway.

"There's some kind of victimization conspiracy," he told them. "With each other, they're real generous. I know. I watched 'em. But when they come here, they try and rip me off with pennies and buttons. It's almost like they think I *owe* them. And Sherlock Holmes's brother back there keeps pestering me with every hard-luck story in town. One guy's house got flattened in a mudslide. Somebody else's baby needs surgery. I even had a lady in earlier, asking if I wanted to put something into an education fund. What's going on?"

Tawna nodded. "Of course. These are people who really do *need* help . . ."

"But they're talking about helping *me!*" Stell protested.

"Well, yes . . . that too." Tawna obviously still couldn't see anything strange.

"How do they figure that?" Stell demanded.

"Well . . ." Tawna hesitated in the way of somebody reluctant to spell out what should have been clear. "To enjoy pride and self-esteem, the way everyone wants to," she said. "The more wealth and material things you acquire, the more you can make things easier for those going through hard times. Once you're reasonably comfortable yourself, it starts to mean more, right?" She glanced at Duggan. "It's like what we were saying the other day about eating all day. Beyond a certain point, any more doesn't make sense."

Stell's eyes bulged. "You mean they'll hassle me like this forever here?"

"Oh, no. Only until you learn to judge for yourself what share to put back in, like everyone else. Since you don't know how it works yet, they're probably just trying to help. It might take a little time."

"Well, suppose I don't want them telling me. What if I put my own guards on the place and keep 'em away?"

"That would be up to you, of course. . . . But why would anyone want to?" She looked at Duggan again and caught the resigned expression on his face. "Okay, don't tell me, Paul. Back home they're all like that. Yes?"

General Rhinde's measures weren't having the intended effect. In a closed-door meeting of the political and military chiefs aboard the

Barnet, it was agreed that the citizens of Ferrydock were undergoing too little violation of their freedoms and rights to provoke whoever was supposed to defend them into coming out and doing so. Accordingly, since there was no set precedent at Tharle to say how far these things should be taken, the governor was instructed to issue a declaration stating that to facilitate improved control and efficiency, the Terran administration now owned everything in the name of everybody and was taking charge of manufacture, distribution, employment, and other services directly.

But the populace seemed happy to let them take it. A mood of festivity spread as virtually the whole of Ferrydock shut up stores and offices and took to the boulevards or sat back in the sun to await decisions and directions. Very soon, surface landers were shuttling frantically between the *Barnet* and Base 1, bringing extra details of planners and controllers to relieve the harried supervisory offices, now working around the clock. Meanwhile, ostensibly to bolster the security of all by setting up a centrally managed disaster relief agency—in reality, to get faster results through imposed austerity—huge stocks of food, fuel, clothing, materials, and other supplies were impounded and locked up in a large warehouse near the airport requisitioned for the purpose and officially renamed the "Federal Emergency Relief Repository." (Use of the word "federal" was a bit premature since as of yet there were no political entities other than Ferrydock to federate with it, but the planners were already shaping up grand schemes and visions of the future.) The repository was duly furnished with a ten-foot wire fence, traffic barrier and checkpoint at the gate, and a billet of armed guards.

However, the harassed Terran administrators were like innocents in a Casbah bazaar before the demands of Tharleans taking them at their word that they were now responsible for everything, and in a short space of time just about everything of utility or value had vanished from the stores and the streets. By the terms under which the Repository had been established, the circumstances qualified as a disaster deserving of relief, and the officer in charge dutifully commenced handing back to the town, at enormous cost in overhead and added effort, the goods that had been confiscated at comparable cost in the first place. Eager to help Terran officialdom find satisfaction and self-esteem by the terms of their own morality, the Tharleans didn't take long to exhaust the stocks completely. Since there was nothing in the regulations that said otherwise, the guards continued, befuddled but doggedly, patrolling outside to protect the contents of the empty warehouse. The only threatening incident they had to deal with, however, was when a small procession of trucks from some outlying farms arrived full of vegetables and other produce that the growers didn't know what else to do with—only to be turned away again because there were no orders for dealing with anyone trying to bring things *in*.

By this time, the political opponents of the mission's incumbent regime, seeing ammunition here to unseat their rivals, formed a dissident faction to fire off a joint protest to Earth, giving all the facts and details. A directive from Colonial Affairs Administration terminating the *Barnet*'s mission and recalling the ship forthwith arrived within forty-eight hours.

Base 1 was an abandoned shell, unsightly with the litter left by departing military anywhere. Children in makeshift helmets and carrying roughly fashioned imitation rifles marched each other to stations at the main gate guard posts. Duggan stood with his arm around Tawna's waist among a crowd watching the last shuttle out climb at the top of a pillar of light through scattered, purple-edged clouds. If the figure he'd heard was correct, he was one of forty-six who would have been unaccounted for when the muster lists were checked, and whose compaks hadn't answered calls or returned a location fix.

"No reservations or second thoughts, Dug?" she asked him. "No last-minute changes about everything, like Zeeb? I hope not. It would be a bit late now." Stell hadn't been among them at the end, after all. Driven to distraction under the pressures of trying to give things away, he had turned a complete about-face and stormed back up to the ship, berating anyone who would listen that he couldn't get back to Earth fast enough.

Duggan shook his head. "Not me." He gave her a squeeze, savoring the touch of her body through the light dress she was wearing. "My future's cut out right here. Everything I want."

"So Zeeb will probably get that promotion you told me about. I hope he'll be pleased."

"Oh, I'm sure he'll fit right back in," Duggan said. Brose had as good as come out and said that he favored Duggan for the subsection supervisor position and would back him. Duggan had seen it as a pretty transparent ploy to recruit support in the political maelstrom that Brose knew they'd be heading back to, and had no doubt that Brose had told Zeeb the same thing, and for the same reason. It felt like a reprieve from a life sentence to know he was out of all that. "In any case," Duggan added, "I wouldn't have gotten the job. The screening application that Brose made me put through was turned down." Brose had been as stunned as Duggan was pleased when the assessment back from Earth read: *Doesn't display the competitiveness and aggressiveness that success in this appointment would require.* It meant that Duggan had done something right.

"I'm surprised," Tawna said, sounding defensive on his behalf. "I'd have thought that even if you decided . . ." She caught the amused twist of his mouth. "Dug, what happened? What did you do?"

"I filled it in the Tharlean way," he told her.

"What way's that?"

"*I* have to tell *you*?" Duggan frowned in mock reproach. "I said I didn't need as much pay as they were offering, and I told them I could do more than they were stipulating. I guess they couldn't hack it." He shrugged. "But Zeeb will do okay. He, Brose, and the System are made for each other."

Tawna pulled close and nuzzled the side of her face against his shoulder. "And you'll do just fine here too," she promised.

For that was the simple principle that underlay the entire Tharlean worldview and way of life: *Give a little more; take a little less.* At least, with those who reciprocated. Anyone who didn't play by the rules wasn't treated by the rules. That was how they curbed excess. But how did a Tharlean *know* when enough was enough? By being a part of the culture they had evolved and absorbing its ways and its values from the time they first learned to look at the world, walk around in it, listen and talk.

Every one of them.

That was why nobody from Earth had had any success finding lawmakers—at least, if what they were looking for was a few making rules to be forcibly imposed on the many. The government had been there all along, everywhere, staring them in the face. For on Tharle, *all* made the law, and all enforced it. Every one of them, therefore, was government.

Now Duggan would learn to become a member of a planetary government too. And that sounded a much better promotion to him than anything the Colonial Affairs Administration was likely to come up with, even if he were to carry on fighting and clawing his way up the ladder for the next hundred years.

About the Authors

Dr. Lloyd Biggle, Jr., Ph.D., (1923–2002) was a musician, author, and internationally known oral historian. He began writing professionally in 1955, and became a full-time writer with the publication of his novel, *All the Colors of Darkness*, in 1963, a profession that he followed until his death. Both Dr. Biggle's science fiction and mystery stories have received international acclaim. He was celebrated in science fiction circles as the author who introduced aesthetics into a literature known for its scientific and technological complications. He published two dozen books as well as magazine stories and articles beyond count. His most recent novel was *The Chronicide Mission*. He was writing almost to the moment of his death. "I can write them faster than the magazines can publish them," he once said, with the result that even though his writing has been stilled, his publications will continue until his backlog of stories is exhausted.

Robert J. Sawyer won the Nebula Award for best novel of 1995 for *The Terminal Experiment*; he's also been nominated six times for the Hugo Award. He has twice won Japan's top SF award, the Seiun, and twice won Spain's top SF award, the Premio UPC de Ciencia Ficción. His twelfth novel, *Calculating God*, hit number one on the bestsellers' list published by *Locus: The Newspaper of the Science Fiction Field*, and was also a top-ten national mainstream bestseller in

Sawyer's native Canada. His latest novel, *Hominids*, a June 2002 hardcover, was the third of Sawyer's novels to be serialized in *Analog*, the world's number one bestselling SF magazine. Visit Rob's website at sfwriter.com.

Mike Resnick worked anonymously from 1964 through 1976, selling more than 200 novels, 300 short stories and 2,000 articles, almost all of them under pseudonyms. After a more than ten-year hiatus to pursue a career in dog breeding and exhibiting, he returned to fiction writing. His first novel in this "second career" was *The Soul Eater*. His breakthrough novel was the international bestseller *Santiago*, published by Tor in 1986. Tor has since published eleven more of Mike's novels and the collection *Will the Last Person to Leave the Planet Please Shut Off the Sun*? Mike's most recent novel is *Starship Mutiny* for Pyr Books. His work has garnered fans around the world, and has been translated into twenty-two languages. Since 1989, Mike has won, five Hugo Awards, a Nebula Award, a Seiun-sho, a Prix Tour Eiffel (French), two Prix Ozones (French), 10 Homer Awards, an Alexander Award, a Golden Pagoda Award, a Hayakawa SF Award (Japanese), a Locus Award, an Ignotus Award (Spanish), a Futura Award (Croatian), an El Melocoton Mechanico (Spanish), two Sfinks Awards (Polish), and a Fantastyka Award (Polish). In 1993 he was awarded the Skylark Award for Lifetime Achievement in Science Fiction.

Tobias S. Buckell is a Caribbean born speculative fiction writer who now lives (through many odd twists of fate and strangely enough to him) in Ohio with his wife Emily. He has published in various magazines and anthologies. He is a Clarion graduate, Writers of the Future winner, and Campbell Award for Best New SF Writer Finalist. His work has received Honorable Mentions in the Year's Best Fantasy and Horror. His first novel, *Crystal Rain*, will be out from Tor Books in July of 2005. You can visit www.TobiasBuckell.com for more information.

Brad Linaweaver has worked frequently in the alternate history subgenre, producing stories such as "Destination: Indies," an alternate telling of Christopher Columbus's journey across the Atlantic, and "Unmerited Favor" which takes a more militant approach to the story of Jesus Christ's life. He is also the author of the books *Moon of Ice*, *Clownface*, *The Land Beyond Summer*, and *Sliders: The Novel*; and was a co-editor of *Free Space*, a collection of original libertarian SF short stories. Winner of the Prometheus Award in 1989, he lives and works in Los Angeles, California. His last recent novel is *Anaquia*, a collaboration with Keith Hastings

Michael A. Stackpole is the author of eight *New York Times* best-selling *Star Wars* novels. He's the author of thirty-seven novels, including *Fortress Draconis*, the second novel in the *DragonCrown War Cycle* of fantasy novels. "According to Their Need" is the fifth story set in his *Purgatory Station* universe.

New Zealand has held a special place in **Jane Lindskold's** heart since she visited there some years ago. The opportunity to celebrate that lush green land along with its interesting and varied people gave her the setting of this story. Currently, Lindskold resides in New Mexico, a place unlike New Zealand in every way except in its variety. She is the author of fifty short stories and fifteen or so novels, including The Firekeeper's saga which began with *Through Wolf's Eyes* as well as the stand alone novels *The Buried Pyramid* and *Child of a Rainless Year*. Her newest project is the forthcoming "Breaking the Wall" series

Jack Williamson has been writing science fiction since 1928, with more than fifty novels published. The most recent is *Terraforming Earth*. One section of it, "The Ultimate Earth," received the 2000 Hugo Award as the best novella. He lives in New Mexico, where he arrived with his parents and siblings in a covered wagon when he was seven years old. He is still writing, as well as teaching occasional courses at Eastern New Mexico University, his hometown school. His new novel, *The Stonehenge Gate*, will be published in the spring of 2005.

Mark Tier is an Australian who lives in Hong Kong partly because, as he puts it, "paying taxes is against my religion." A long-time SF fan and hard-core libertarian, he was a co-founder of the Australian equivalent of the Libertarian Party. He published and edited the investment newsletter *World Money Analyst* from 1974 to 1991.

James P. Hogan began writing science fiction as a hobby in the mid 1970s, and his works have been well received within the professional scientific community as well as among regular science fiction readers. In 1979 he left DEC to become a full-time writer, and in 1988 moved to the Republic of Ireland. Currently he maintains a residence in Pensacola, Florida, and spends part of each year in the United States. To date, he has published twenty-one novels, including the libertarian classic *Voyage From Yesteryear*, a nonfiction work on artificial intelligence, and two mixed collections of short fiction, nonfiction, and biographical anecdotes entitled *Minds, Machines & Evolution* and *Rockets, Redheads & Revolution*. A new nonfiction work, *Kicking the Sacred Cow*, will be released by Baen Books in June 2004. He has also published some articles and short fiction. Further details of Hogan and his work are available from his web site at www.jamesphogan.com.

    Christopher Anvil is the pseudonym of Harry C. Crosby, Jr., a gifted short story author whose work was published in *Astounding Science Fiction* and *Analog* more often than any other author from the mid-1950s to the mid-1960s. He also wrote four novels, including *The Day the Machines Stopped, Strangers in Paradise,* and *Pandora's World,* but, like so many of his contemporaries, it is for his short fiction that he is best known. Stories such as "Mind Partner," considered by many to be his best work, "The Great Intellect Boom" and "Uncalculated Risk" show off his examination of social mores and ideas, and often turning them on their head.

    Vernor Vinge won the 2000 Hugo award for best novel for his book *A Deepness in the Sky*, the sequel to *A Fire Upon the Deep*. Other novels by him include *Grimm's World, The Witling,* and

Across Realtime. His short fiction has been collected in the anthologies *True Names . . . and Other Dangers* and *Threats . . . and Other Promises.* Born in Wisconsin, he currently lives in San Diego, where, along with writing excellent novels and short stories, he works as a professor of mathematics at San Diego State University.

Murray Leinster (1896-1975) was the pseudonym for William Fitzgerald Jenkins, a consummate professional who wrote for a wide number of venues during his varied career. Although he wrote more than forty novels during his fifty-year career, it is his short fiction, including stories such as "The Lonely Planet," "First Contact," and "Sidewise in Time" that he is best remembered. Fascinated with the idea of alternatives to reality as we or his protagonists know it, he pioneered the concept of the multiple points along one time continuum, or the simple concept of parallel worlds. Well regarded in the science fiction community, he was the Guest of Honor at the 21st World Science Fiction convention in 1963.

Alfred Elton (A.E.) van Vogt (1912-2000) burst onto the science fiction scene in 1939 with his first published science fiction story, "Black Destroyer," which was immediately hailed as a classic in the field, and the arrival of a bold new voice in speculative fiction. His first novel, *Slan,* appeared in 1940 and cemented his reputation as the most popular and exciting author of the era. Although his work has been criticized for deficiencies in plot, logic, and sometimes rationality, his stories operated on an emotional depth that swept readers along into new and exciting worlds filled with strange and alien ideas and races. Born in Manitoba, Canada, he discovered *Amazing Stories* when he was 14 and became a lifelong reader of science fiction. After joining the Canadian civil service at 19, he also took a writing course, and sold his first fiction piece in 1932. Novels such as *The World of Null-A,* the first science fiction novel from a major publisher, Simon and Schuster, and his classic work *The Weapon Shops of Isher,* based in part on the novella in this book, show the work of this Grand Master in full bloom.

Katherine MacLean has used her novels and short stories to explore complex ethical issues about medical and scientific experimentation. In novels such as *Cosmic Checkmate*, written with Charles de Vet (and based on the short story included in this anthology), *The Missing Man*, and *Dark Wing* she has explored the rights of the individual versus the good of the society. She is especially effective at shorter lengths, with stories such as "The Origin of the Species," "Contagion," and "The Other." Her short fiction has been collected in the anthologies *The Diploids*, and *Flights of Fancy, Trouble With Treaties*, and *The Trouble with You Earth People*.

Although Frank Herbert (1920-1986) wrote more than twenty novels and many short stories during his career, it is his six-novel galaxy—and millennium-spanning epic Dune series that towers above all his other work. This is not to say that his other books are any less important or imaginative. Novels such as *The Dosadi Experiment, The God Makers, Destination: Void,* and *The Jesus Incident* reveal his gift for unparalleled world-building, complete yet complex and varied alien races, and the unfolding of monumental events that affected entire civilizations and generations to come, often hinging on a group or even one man's choices and actions. Born in Tacoma, Washington, he was a reporter and editor for various West Coast newspapers, then went to the University of Washington as a lecturer in general and interdisciplinary studies. He was awarded the Nebula award in 1965 for *Dune*, the Hugo award in 1966, also for Dune, and the Prix Apollo award in 1978.

Eric Frank Russell (1905-1978) first achieved recognition with the publication of *Sinister Barrier*, the novel that launched John W. Campbell's *Unknown* magazine in 1939. Usually at the forefront of the science fiction scene for the next two decades, he was adept at tackling such humanistic issues as race relations, transposing them to the science fictional realm. Although he wrote several novels, including *Three to Conquer* and *Sentinels From Space*, it is his short fiction that garnered the most attention. A founding member of the British Interplanetary Society, his short story "Allamagoosa" won the Hugo award for best short fiction of the year in 1955.